FALL FROM GRACE

By the same author
(with Dominique Lapierre)

O Jerusalem!
Freedom at Midnight
Or I'll Dress you in Mourning
Is Paris Burning?
The Fifth Horseman

FALL FROM GRACE

Larry Collins

GRANADA
London Toronto Sydney New York

Granada Publishing Limited
8 Grafton Street, London W1X 3LA

Published by Granada Publishing 1985

British Library Cataloguing in Publication Data

Collins, Larry
Fall from grace.
I. Title
813'.54[F]   PS3553.04748/

ISBN 0-246-11894-6

Typeset by V & M Graphics Ltd, Aylesbury, Bucks
Printed in Great by
Mackays of Chatham Limited

TO NADIA

TOP SECRET

B68932
Copy No. *10*

CCS 459/3
3 December 1946
    Combined Chiefs of Staff: Cover and Deception-Classification
    Refs: a) CCS 2 81/5
        b) CCS 2 81/4
Information on all aspects of strategic cover and deception is hereby classified 'TOP SECRET' on a permanent basis. The existence, organization, responsibility, functions and techniques of all cover and deception agencies and staffs of the United States and its allies, employed in or directly responsible for, at any time in the past, present or future, the planning and implementation of strategic cover and deception shall fall under the jurisdiction of this order.

In particular, everything to do with 'special means', controlled enemy agents in communication with the enemy who have his confidence but are operated under our control, ... employment of deliberate leakages through diplomatic channels or friendly agents in contact with the enemy in the implementation of a strategic cover and deception plan is hereby assigned a permanent security classification of 'TOP SECRET'.

PROLOGUE

JUNE 17, 1973

Two small details, to the trained eye, gave the black Opel away. First were the letters on the licence plate: BG, for Bad Godesberg, the Bonn suburb where most Western intelligence agencies had their German headquarters. Second was the unusual thickness of what appeared to be the car's radio antenna rising from its left fender. It was linked, in fact, to its scrambler-equipped radiotelephone transmitter/receiver. The car's other features, such as its bulletproof windows and door panels, would have been quite impossible to detect without a thorough examination. The Bonn station chief had graciously made it available to T.F. O'Neill, the CIA's retiring Director of Operations, Eastern Europe, despite the fact that O'Neill was in Germany on personal rather than Agency business.

The driver, who had come with the car, gestured with his head towards a grey gravel footpath bisecting a series of metal fences, each of which set off a small private garden the size of a tennis court.'He's got the fourth one on the left, number 63,' he said.

'Okay. Drive a hundred yards or so up here and park. Has he had it long?'

'Since the Brits put him out to pasture when they were finished with him. He married an old girlfriend and they set him up here under her name. Gave him the usual new suit of clothes, so to speak. Spread word he was a retired businessman from Düsseldorf. Tiles, I think it was.'

The young Agency driver parked the car and switched off the engine. His eyes caught O'Neill fingering the Bonn station's target file he held in his lap. It was one of the old ones, the kind that came typed up on assessment sheets in a manila folder, the ones they'd used before computers came in. 'Head of the Gestapo for all of France,' the driver mused. 'Must have been some kind of big deal, this guy.'

'He was.'

'And he walked away without a scratch. Not bad when you figure he should have been wearing a rope around his neck in 1945.'

O'Neill did not reply. His fingers and his mind were wandering through the file. The driver studied him. O'Neill was something of a legend to agents of his generation, a controversial legend but a legend

3

nonetheless. He was of the old school, the Agency's founding fathers, the guys who had come out of the OSS after the war to start up the CIA with Allen Dulles and Walter Bedell Smith.

'Know something?' the driver asked. A superior's silence didn't necessarily inspire a respectful silence in return among the men and women of his generation. 'Our Nazi Documentation Center in Berlin still carries this guy as a wanted war criminal. The Interior Ministry in Lower Saxony even has a warrant out on him. Not that you'd get very far trying to serve it.'

'No,' T.F. agreed, 'I shouldn't have thought you would.' He had sensed a certain undercurrent of disapproval in the young agent's tone. One of the newer, more moralistic breed the Agency was recruiting these days. 'But I wouldn't be too harsh on British Intelligence. They made the usual trade-off: tell us all you know and we won't inquire into your past sins. It's a game we were all playing in those years right after the war: we, the British, the Russians, even the French when they got the chance. Everybody wanted a few inhouse Gestapo experts to help read the tea leaves in the other guy's cup.'

And have them we did, T.F. thought: Otto John, Reinhard Gehlen, Klaus Barbie. It was a time when kidnappings, discreet murders and dirty tricks were the standard tools of the espionage trade, not satellites and IBM 360 computers. It had been a period when ideals and illusions disappeared faster than snowflakes on a warm pavement. Just as Ridley had warned him they would.

He thought of old Henry Ridley dying of lung cancer at seventy-seven a couple of months back. Do you regret all those Players you chain-smoked during the war? he asked him.

Not one, Ridley had growled, not a single bloody one. But then, the old bastard had never been much of a one for regrets, had he? Ah, Ridley, T.F. thought, how right you English were! How naïve we Americans were when they sent us over in '43 and '44. Convent girls running loose and innocent through the whorehouse of life. Well, we lost our innocence soon enough. He looked at his driver, so eager, so anxious to please, so ready to do the right thing. Stay in this business a little longer, my friend, he thought, and so will you.

He gave a last glance at the Bonn file. He'd have to keep the kid gloves on during their chat. The gentleman was, after all, the private property of Her Majesty's Intelligence Service. One didn't go barging in on friendlies like Torquemada. 'I won't be long,' he said, getting out of the car.

The young agent gave him a querying look. 'Don't worry,' T.F. assured him. 'No problems here. Just a meeting of old friends.'

The driver watched him go. Sixty years old and he still walked like a thirty-year-old striding off to a squash game. They ran to a pattern, those old Agency guys did. They all spoke with that nasal twang that seemed to cross Maine lobstermen and Boston stockbrokers. 'Grotonese', they called it. And they all dressed the same. Just look at him, he thought following O'Neill's departing figure. He was wearing a Brooks Brothers grey flannel suit cut as if it had been made to fit an avocado, probably ten years old, and a yellow bow tie with black polka dots. A yellow bow tie, for Christ's sake! How many of those were you going to see in Germany in 1973?

All politeness and quiet chitchat – 'Wife's well, is she?' – those guys were, and steel underneath. Order some poor bastard killed, then go off for two martinis before dinner. How much blood does he have on those hairy hands of his? the driver wondered. Running Eastern European Operations for ten years, you'd want to figure he has been responsible for his share of the gore.

The object of the driver's curiosity strolled nonchalantly down the gravel path they had spotted earlier. *Kleingärten* Bonn had said they were called – little gardens – a particularly Germanic institution. Apartment dwellers in the thickly populated Ruhr, where the backyards of one town ran into the frontyards of another, rented or bought them to have a piece of greenery they could call their own. How neat, how precisely groomed and tended they were, he observed. Each had a little garden house, and most had the black, red and gold flag of the Federal Republic flying from a flagstaff in their little green lawns.

He paused at the gate of number 63. It too had a garden house with a TV aerial. The verdant lawn was mown to a precise three-quarters of an inch. Rows of marigolds, patches of azaleas, dark stains of violets were set around the property with the precision of figures in a mechanical drawing. The master of the property was pruning a wall of rambler roses. He was wearing, T.F. noted, a yellow oilcloth apron on which was printed a fist from which sprouted an enormous green thumb. A series of six-inch high statuettes of Snow White and the Seven Dwarfs had been set into the lawn with the same sense of random precision that seemed to characterize everything else he'd seen in the *Kleingärten*. How jolly, T.F. thought; how perfectly fucking jolly.

He opened the gate and approached the man, who looked up, surprised.

'Herr Hans-Dieter Strömelburg?'

The surprise turned to utter shock as the former head of the Gestapo for France heard himself addressed by his real name for the first time in thirteen years. The hands on the pruning shears began to tremble; the face whitened. For a second, T.F. thought the man was going to have a stroke or cardiac seizure right there in front of him. Quickly he introduced himself, displaying his ID as he did. 'It's a purely personal

5

visit,' he assured Strömelburg. 'Nothing of any consequence at all.'

'*Ach so, ach so*,' Strömelburg repeated, too stunned to say anything more. Finally, he gestured towards his garden house. 'Come,' he said. He paused an instant on the sun porch, then continued in. No reason to let the neighbours eavesdrop on this particular conversation.

He swept the crumbs of a sandwich from the table with an embarrassed gesture, then motioned to T.F. to sit down on the couch. He took a bottle of Riesling from the refrigerator and set it on the table with a pair of thimble glasses. T.F. studied him as he did so. Age had stooped his shoulders and thickened his waist. The blond hair was white now, but it was all there, meticulously combed straight back from his high forehead. Thinking of his wartime photographs, T.F. was prepared to wager the hairline had not retreated a quarter of an inch in almost thirty years. His face was ruddy; probably a touch of high blood pressure there. The eyes were blue and clearly at ease with the world; it was not a face you'd say had been marked by great suffering. Life, T.F. thought, has been kind to Hans-Dieter Strömelburg – a good deal kinder than it was to most of those who had crossed his path.

Strömelburg poured the wine into the glasses, offered T.F. one then raised his own. '*Prost*,' he said, his dour regard giving the lie to his salutation.

T.F. acknowledged his gesture with a nod. 'I've come to see you, Herr Strömelburg, because you and I were rivals, in a sense, many years ago.'

The former SS man leaned forward, trying to appear eager to listen, which he most emphatically was not. The past was not a subject onetime Gestapo officers discussed with enthusiasm.

'Just before the invasion, the organization I was working with in London landed a young lady in France. She was someone I felt very close to although I'd known her only briefly. She disappeared during the war. I've made it a little project of mine lately to try to find out what happened to her. You know, one tends to reach a point in life when one feels like tidying up the loose ends. Perhaps you've had the feeling?'

Strömelburg, who hadn't, wasn't sure whether he should nod his head in agreement or not. Judiciously, he chose to do nothing and let the American go on.

The American drew a black-and-white photograph from the leather folder in which he carried his CIA identity papers. It was an old wartime ID photo, the kind of flat, lifeless image that had once graced millions of identification cards around the world. He passed it over the oilcloth on the table to the German.

Strömelburg took the photograph and studied it intently, as though somehow sheer willpower might clear the cobwebs of the years from his mind. He, of course, recognized her instantly. What man could ever

6

forget so beautiful a woman? He could see her as though she were sitting there before him, her rich blond hair cascading down to her shoulders in elegant rolls, those dark green eyes of hers, eyes the colour of an Alpine meadow in the summer sunshine, fixing him with silent defiance. So composed, so proud. She had always been a proud one. He laid the photo on the table.

'No,' he said, sadly. 'I'm afraid I don't recognize her at all. What was her name?'

'Pradier. Catherine Pradier.'

'Her real name or her code name? I assume she was an agent of some sort.'

'Her real name. Her code name was Denise.'

Strömelburg picked up the photograph and studied it again as though the sound of her name on his ears might have aroused a memory his eyes had failed to awaken. Yes, it was all as clear as if it were yesterday. 'Why would I recognize her?'

'I have reason to believe she was taken to your Gestapo headquarters on Avenue Foch in June 1944.'

Strömelburg shook his head in dismay. 'So much was happening in those days. Your invasion. The Resistance everywhere. It was a madhouse. Do you know where she was arrested?'

'Somewhere in the North, I believe.'

'Ah!' The German's voice took on the reassuring tone of a doctor who's just uncovered the key to his diagnosis. 'She wouldn't have fallen under my jurisdiction at all. The North came under the Gestapo in Brussels. She would have gone to Brussels. You know how we Germans are. We always do everything according to regulations. I can assure you I never saw her in Paris.'

He eased himself back into his chair convinced his explanation, couched as it was in a stereotyped portrayal of the German character, would be enough to satisfy his American visitor.

The cast of the American's blue eyes told him it was not; but for whatever reason, he chose to go on. 'We also believe she wound up at Ravensbrück. I understand you were assigned to Ravensbrück at the end of the war.'

'Ja,' Strömelburg agreed, trying to convey with his tone an expression of intense sympathy for the American and his quest. 'But Ravensbrück was a madhouse, you know. Twelve thousand women! They died by the dozens every day. No one ever kept records. There was not time.' He made a helpless gesture and grimaced as though he were trying to expunge a particularly evil and painful memory from his mind.

In fact, he was contemplating another and rather precise memory, the memory of that afternoon in April 1945 when he'd called Catherine

7

Pradier to his office in the camp's administration building on the *Lagerstrasse*. Already the rolling thunder of Red Army cannon was rising up from the eastern horizon. She had survived Ravensbrück's horror – she had always been a survivor. And survival was exactly what he had to offer that afternoon, wasn't it? He laid Catherine Pradier's photograph on the table again, something in his gesture indicating that this time he would not pick it up for another look.

'There was so much chaos, so much confusion at the end. Our only thought was of escape, not of the inmates.'

T.F. studied him coolly. But his mind was a quarter of a century back with Catherine Pradier on their final ride to the airfield, seeing her climb into that tiny plane off to – ? God knows. Had she died at Ravensbrück in some last outburst of SS savagery? Had the Russians taken her? Had she managed to flee and then, in the confusion of the Liberation, decided to fade off into obscurity, to try to put the pieces of her shattered life back together by herself, in some private world where no one could remind her of the past? After all, she had had a lot to forget – and forgive. While you, he mused, appraising the German, you managed to cut your deal with British Intelligence, and now here you sit in tranquil retirement, pruning your goddamned roses under the protective gaze of MI6, beyond my reach or anyone else's.

Strömelburg offered the CIA man just the faintest suggestion of a smile. 'Her face just means nothing to me. I'm sorry. And she looks as though she wasn't the kind of woman a man would be apt to forget, doesn't she? You haven't.'

T.F. sipped his wine. 'That's why I'm here.'

'Why is she so important to you? Was it something she did?'

'I'm about to retire, Herr Strömelburg. Before I do, my employers have asked me to prepare an official history of the operation in which you and I were rivals in the springtime of 1944. It was called *Fortitude*.'

'*Fortitude*?'

T.F. offered the German a quiet smile. 'It was an extremely secret operation designed to cover the Normandy invasion. It still remains highly secret. Without it, I feel quite certain the invasion could never have succeeded.'

Strömelburg fought to conceal his mounting excitement. After all these years: the pieces falling into place, the proof he'd always sought suddenly before him. 'And she, this woman was involved in that?'

'She was *vital*. Without her the invasion might have failed.'

The German slumped in his chair. So, he thought, it was just as he had suspected when it was too late. How clever the English were! How completely they deceived us! And all because we were so naïve we could not believe they would do such a thing! What was that old saying? – 'The

German has a cruel hand and a soft heart; the Englishman a soft hand and a cruel heart.' He cleared his throat. 'If the invasion had failed, Mr ...'

'O'Neill.'

'O'Neill.' A bitterness long suppressed but never forgotten underlay the German's voice. 'You might very well not have won the war.'

'The Russians would have had something to say about that.'

'The Russians? They would have had forty of the finest divisions of the Wehrmacht arriving in the East in July, if we'd defeated the invasion!' Strömelburg gave a sigh. 'Yes,' he said, 'had the invasion failed, Mr O'Neill, the world we are living in today would be a very different place.'

'I agree. That's why I'm so concerned to find out exactly what happened to her.'

Strömelburg stared at his American visitor, his features as blank as the pages of an empty note pad. Well, my friend, he thought, that is *one* final victory you shall not have! Besides, imagine what your French allies would think, if this story ever got out? Some stories, my friend, are better left untold ... 'I really wish I could help you,' he murmured, accompanying his words with a slight, helpless heave of his shoulders. 'But I can't remember a thing. It was all so long ago, wasn't it? So very long ago ... '

PART ONE

November 2, 1943

Catherine Pradier watched in amused fascination as the doorman of the Savoy Hotel descended on her taxicab. The man's Dickensian presence opening her taxi door with his majestic sweep both enthralled and reassured the English half of Catherine's being. With his silver-trimmed green greatcoat and his stovepipe hat, he was a reminder of a world that should have disappeared forever in the Blitz.

"'alf a crown, miss,' the cabby announced to her. As she fumbled through her purse for two shillings and a sixpence, then tried to calculate how much more she should give the cabby as a tip, the idiosyncrasies of the English currency system vexed, as they always did, the other dominant side of Catherine's being, her French side. Finally, thrusting an extra shilling into the cabby's welcoming palm, she stepped from the cab.

She felt wonderful. For the first time since September 1939 she was wearing an evening gown. It was a clinging black silk sheath she had bought at Chanel as part of her trousseau. The dress was a fragile, gossamer thing, and it had been the one touch of elegance she had taken with her in her hasty and tragic flight from Paris in June 1940. For more than three years it had hung unworn in her London closet, a ghost of revelries past. Now, feeling its satiny caress on her skin, sensing the swish of its folds as she moved, she felt as she had as a little girl when, dressed up for a costume party, she'd been ushered before the adults for their applause and admiration.

A pair of American pilots, wearing the floppy caps of the US Eighth Air Force, pushed their way out through the hotel's swinging doors. Seeing her, they stood aside. One let out a low whistle of awe as she passed by. The other whipped off his cap, made a half-bow and murmured, 'Can I have the next dance, angel?'

Catherine gave a toss to the long blond hair that fell in shimmering waves to her shoulders and offered the aviators a silent smile as she passed into the Savoy lobby. Well aware of the eyes following her, she walked through the lobby to the salon, its easy chairs filled with men in uniform, with the tweedy members of the county aristocracy, up from the country for a few days, eyeing the passing parade. At the end of the salon she turned left towards the bar of the Grill. She stood poised an instant at the door. From his stool, Rear Admiral Sir Llewellyn Crane saw her and hurried forward. He was in his late fifties, grey hair glistening at his temples, his face burnished by the Mediterranean sun.

'Catherine!' he exclaimed. 'How simply smashing you look! I'll be the most envied man in the Grill tonight.' He took her by the arm and guided her to a corner table, beckoning to a waiter as he did.

'What would you like?' he asked.

'I think I'll try a dry martini,' Catherine said.

'One very dry martini,' Crane instructed the waiter, 'and would you be so kind as to bring me my Pimm's from the bar. My goodness,' he exclaimed, turning back to Catherine, 'how long it's been! We've got a lot of catching up to do. What luck that I learned you were in London. Tell me, have you had any news of your father?'

'Not since Singapore fell,' Catherine replied. 'The International Red Cross told me in March 1942 that he was in a Japanese prisoner-of-war camp near Penang. Since then I've heard nothing, not a word. I send him parcels through the Red Cross once a month.' Catherine gave a resigned movement to her shoulders. 'God knows if they ever get to him.'

'Don't you worry about him, my dear,' the admiral said, placing a reassuring hand on her knee. 'He'll come through all right. He's as tough as they come, your father is. After all, I should know.' In 1917, when Catherine was born, her father and Crane had been young officers serving together on HMS *Coventry*. Indeed, they'd been close friends since their days at the Dartmouth Naval College. They'd been midshipmen when the Royal Navy's Pacific Squadron had called at Shanghai in 1913 and Catherine's father had met her mother, the daughter of the director for China of France's Banque de l'Indochine et de l'Orient. What was more natural than that her father ask his fellow officer to be her godfather when the news of Catherine's birth reached the *Coventry's* wardroom? And looking at the still trimly handsome man before her, Catherine reflected that 'Tuffy' Crane, as she had called him since childhood, had been a remarkably thoughtful and loyal godfather.

Her parents' marriage had been brief and unhappy, born of romantic illusions and destroyed in banal realities. Her mother had hated the inevitable long separations and constant relocations that befell the wife of an officer in the Royal Navy, nor had the rain-drenched English countryside held any charm for her. When her own father died and she came into her inheritance, she left Catherine's father to settle in the sunshine of Biarritz, there to raise her daughter as she felt a proper French girl should be raised. The French, she had repeatedly remarked to Catherine, in explanation of her divorce, 'travel well and export badly.'

'Oh, Tuffy, I do hope you're right,' Catherine sighed. 'I worry so about him. One hears awful things about those camps.'

14

'Of course. But he'll handle it, you'll see. And your mother? Is she here with you? Is she still in France?'

Catherine paled. 'You haven't heard?'

'Heard what?'

'She's dead.'

'My God!' Crane stuttered. 'I can't believe it! What happened to her, poor thing?'

She took a deep breath and a sip of her martini, as though its astringent taste would discipline her to continue. Her mother's death was constantly with Catherine, kept alive by the bright flame of her own bitter memories of it. 'It happened during the exodus,' she told Crane. 'Mother came up from Biarritz to stay with me for a while in May 1940, just before the Germans attacked. I'd taken a flat on the Rue Pergolèse and I was working for Coco Chanel.'

'You were still modelling?'

'No, no' – the words came as a protest. 'I had given that up a year earlier. It was such a boring, utterly worthless thing to do. I was helping Mademoiselle run the salon, looking after the foreign buyers – not that we had many of those after the war began. Anyway, when the attack started, we didn't want to leave. I simply could not believe the German army could defeat us.'

'Who could?'

'Then, as they got closer, I became so furious I wanted to go out and fight them on the barricades. Except, of course, we didn't put up any barricades.'

'Catherine, surely you weren't serious?'

'Of course I was, Tuffy. Don't forget, Papa took me to Scotland every August to shoot grouse. I got a matched pair of Purdeys for my eighteenth birthday. I could shoot almost as well as he could, and a lot better than most of the men who shot with us. I was quite ready to take those Purdeys out and defend a barricade – had there been a barricade to defend.'

The admiral smiled gently and again gave an affectionate pat to her knee. 'Of course; I'd forgotten there was a streak of the tomboy in you – although looking at you today, it's rather hard to believe.'

'So, finally, we decided to try to get to Biarritz. Mother had driven up in her Citroën, and just as a precaution we'd kept it filled with petrol. We left on June 10.' Catherine closed her eyes a second and saw herself again on the highway of the exodus. 'You can't imagine how terrible it was. Cars, bicycles, horse carts, people walking with packs on their backs, everyone screaming, fighting each other, ready to kill to pass a stalled car. They say a crisis brings out the best in people. Well, not in the French. It brings out our worst traits, believe me. You've never seen such

15

selfishness, such a lack of compassion for others, such a "save yourself and the others be damned" attitude. It took us a day and a night to get past Orléans.'

Catherine paused. She was back on the National Highway south of Orléans, crawling slowly south in the fresh June dawn. 'That was when the planes came. First there were the Stukas, with that terrifying whine. They bombed ahead of us. You could hear the kind of "whoosh" of the bombs and then see a cloud of black smoke billowing up into the sky. Then the fighters came at us from behind.' She shuddered. She could see the plane careening towards them, so close she could make out the pilot's face at the same instant she could hear his machine gun's bullets shredding the roof of their car and almost tearing her mother's head from her shoulders.

'It was horrible. I held her in my arms for a moment or two while she died. When the planes left, I begged someone to help me bury her. No one came. I was screaming for someone to help me bury my mother and everyone was screaming at me to start my car and get moving or stop blocking the road.' She took another sip of her martini and struggled to stop the tears that threatened to inundate her eyes. 'Finally, a couple of deserters came along. They agreed to help me bury her if I'd take them south in the car. So we dug a hole by the side of the road, buried her and started off again.'

'You poor girl,' Crane said, 'how absolutely ghastly! Where did you go?'

'Bordeaux. I decided all I wanted to do was get to Papa. I talked my way onto a Royal Navy minesweeper with my British passport and the fact I was the daughter of a navy officer. Of course, once I got there there was no way in the world I could get a priority space on a plane to the Far East; so I've spent an utterly useless war working as a typist at the Munitions Board.'

They finished their drinks; then Crane escorted her to a table in the Grill. The sight of the candlelit tables, the heavy linen, the crystal and silver of the place settings, the sounds of the orchestra playing for dancing in the background restored Catherine's spirits. So too did her anticipation of the delights of the potted shrimp and Dover sole Crane ordered for their dinner. 'Where have you been, Tuffy?' she asked as the waiter disappeared with their order. 'I looked for you as soon as I arrived, but no luck. Were you at sea?'

'No,' the admiral replied, wincing. 'I regret to say I haven't walked a bridge since December 1940. Someone saw fit to assign me to Middle East Command in Cairo. I spent almost three years out there in a lovely villa on the road to the Pyramids exposed to no danger greater than Gyppo Tummy.'

16

'Well, you should be thankful for that. What were you doing?'

'Oh, this and that. Not the sort of thing one talks about, really. When the Americans came in, they moved me over to Algiers.'

'To another lovely villa?' Catherine laughed

'To an even lovelier hotel, the Saint-Georges, overlooking the Bay of Algiers. I'm still there. They just sent me up here on an errand for a few days.'

The waiter poured their wine, and Crane somewhat absentmindedly tasted it. He did not want to remind his lovely goddaughter of her mother's death or her father's precarious circumstances. Finally, he turned to the least difficult subject of conversation. 'My war's uninteresting. Tell me what you've been doing. I don't think I've seen you since your wedding. Or to be more precise, your non-wedding.'

Catherine gave a quick tinkling laugh. 'Have you forgiven me for that?'

'I had nothing to forgive,' Crane laughed in reply. 'In fact, I had a marvellous time.'

'I can just imagine the reaction of most of the others.'

'Oh, indeed. Everyone was very quick to put it down to another capricious gesture by my rebellious, strong-willed goddaughter.'

'I'm sure. But it really wasn't that, you know.' Catherine sipped her wine. 'This is delicious. What is it?'

'A 1934 Chablis, from a favourite bottler of mine in Beaune, Joseph Drouhin. But tell me, my dear' – Crane was chuckling– 'whatever led you to do such a thing?'

'Ah, Tuffy, dear.' Catherine sighed and put down her glass. 'What they were trying to get us into wasn't a marriage, it was an alliance. Jean-Jacques's family is immensely wealthy.'

'So I had heard.'

'When Mummy saw his interest, she did everything to encourage it. So did his parents. And I liked Jean-Jacques. In fact, I adored him – as a friend. But as a husband? Honestly, I'm afraid I would have cuckolded him in no time at all. I would have given him horns so high he would have had to stoop down to get through our bedroom door.'

An ungodfatherly gleam appeared in the admiral's eyes. 'Then why did you let things go so far?'

'I didn't want to. Neither did Jean-Jacques, really. But we kept having these overpowering family conferences. The war is coming. The security of the family. Perhaps a wife and child to prevent Jean-Jacques being called up. I suppose at one of them, after too much champagne, I said, "Well, yes, it might be a good idea." Then two days later, I woke up and there it was in black-and-white in *Le Figaro*, the announcement of our engagement! I was livid.'

'That's when you should have stopped it.'

17

'Of course it was, Tuffy. But you have no idea what it is like to be swept up in something like that. You're caught on the flood tide. I was twenty-two, remember? All of a sudden it was a round of receptions, trips to Paris for the trousseau, wedding gifts arriving from all over the world. I was trapped.'

'Well, I must say, it certainly was going to be the wedding of the season.'

'Oh, God!' Catherine gave a deep laugh in which all the tension of that distant June day seemed released again. 'Can you imagine, two hundred people down from Paris in a special train just for the wedding? I still blush when I think about it.'

'I still don't understand how you did it. To say the very least, it was breathtakingly nervy of you.'

'I'll tell you, I sat there all morning in my room staring at my wedding dress. Not crying. I didn't shed a tear during the whole business. I had this most awful sinking feeling in my stomach, the utter certainty I was about to make a terrible, irreparable mistake. Then Mother came in. She said, "Darling, if you don't start getting into your dress this very minute, you're going to be late for your own wedding." At the instant she said that, I *knew*. It was wrong – wrong for me, wrong for Jean-Jacques, wrong for the children we might have. However much I was going to hurt Jean-Jacques, the hurt was going to be nothing compared with the hurt he would have suffered in a bad marriage.'

Catherine looked at her godfather, her green eyes flashing an echo of the defiance they'd shown five years before. 'I said, "I'm not going to have a wedding, Mother. I'm going to Paris."'

'My God!' The admiral gasped, imagining the incident. 'Your poor mother must have fainted dead away.'

'She went into hysterics. "What about the four hundred people we've invited to the British Club for the reception? What about the two hundred people that are starting to arrive at the town hall right now? What about Jean-Jacques?"

'"Mother," I said, "it's my life, not theirs. They're going to have a lovely party – but without me." And I walked out to the car. Just like that.' Catherine laughed gaily as she recalled the moment. 'I must tell you, getting into the car, I had an overwhelming feeling of relief. I knew that I'd had the courage to make the right decision.'

'Well,' Crane said with grudging admiration, 'you certainly caused a stir. It's not every Saturday a young lady invites four hundred members of French society to a wedding that isn't going to take place.'

'It must have been ghastly.'

'Jean-Jacques arrived all puffed up like a peacock. You would have thought he'd just won first prize in the school poetry contest – which in a sense, I suppose, he thought he had. Poor chap. You could see the air running out of him as the minutes went by. When you've been kept waiting in front of the mayor for your bride to show up for forty-five minutes, you begin to have your doubts. Mind you, I never much cared for the young man. Someone finally spirited him into another room while the mayor came out to inform us there'd been a slight change in plans.'

'You must have thought I'd taken leave of my senses. I can hear you all saying it now: "Crazy Catherine!" '

'Not really.' Crane chuckled in recollection of the moment. 'On the way to the reception, some of the sportier members of the party stopped by Sonny's Bar for a drink to talk things over as we eyed the *cocottes* – while you, I suppose, were racing up the road to Paris and freedom.'

The waiter interrupted their joint laughter by placing a bowl of potted shrimp before each of them. As he drew away, the orchestra struck up 'The Lady Is a Tramp.' Crane pushed back his chair. 'These won't get cold,' he said. 'Shall we dance?'

Returning to the table a few minutes later, Catherine reflected that the admiral's strong grip on the dance floor, the gleam in his eye bespoke an affection of a different order from that normally associated with godparents. 'Tuffy,' she said as they began their shrimp, 'I've something to ask you.'

'By all means.'

'I may very well come out of this war an orphan. And what have I done during it? Nothing, absolutely nothing except push papers around the Munitions Board. If I were a man, I would have fought. Isn't there something worthwhile I can do, even if I'm a woman? Can't you find something for me? Can't you take me to Algiers with you? There must be something really involved in the war I could do there?'

'Well,' Crane declared, 'that's a rather large order.'

'I know,' she persisted, 'but how can I live with myself after this if I haven't done anything? I've tried everywhere, and it's always the motor pool, typing or nursing.'

'And very worthwhile – and necessary.' Crane noted.

'I want something more.'

Crane appraised her a moment, then turned to his shrimp. He seemed to be savouring each tiny creature as it passed into his mouth. 'Delicious, these,' he remarked. 'Tell me, my dear, do you talk in your sleep?'

Catherine was aghast. What an absurd question to ask, she thought. 'Sometimes'.

'In French or in English?'

She blushed. 'Always in French – or so I've been told.'

Her godfather returned to his shrimp and remained silent for a moment or two. 'You might be surprised,' he observed, breaking his silence, ' how difficult it is to find an Englishman or woman who speaks absolutely flawless French. Urdu, Telegu, Hindi, Arabic, Swahili – ah yes, all of those. But French?'

He wants me to be someone's interpreter, Catherine thought. Will that be more worthwhile than the Munitions Board?

'His Majesty does continue to recognize you as one of his own, doesn't he, even if you're French to the core?'

'Of course,' Catherine replied. 'I always kept my British Nationality.'

Her godfather set down his fish knife and fork and fell silent for a long time. 'I do know of something,' he said, finally, 'in which you might be able to render great service.'

'That's all I ask for.'

'Well,' Crane said, 'let me make a phone call or two.'

LONDON
March 19, 1944

The man stood silently by his open window pondering the darkness of the great city. From Orchard Street, three storeys below, the sound of hurrying footsteps drifted up to his ears: Londoners rushing off to the air-raid shelters in Bond Street and Marble Arch tube stations. Major Frederick Cavendish glanced upwards. Almost every night for two weeks now, German bombers had been rolling up the Thames to London. 'The Little Blitz,' Londoners called it, and once again they were going out to dinner or cocktails with their steel helmets cradled under their arms.

Cavendish took a deep breath of the damp night air, redolent, it seemed, with the promise of change. The crocuses in Portman Square, he had noticed that morning, were ready to bloom on the first warm day. The daffodils would be early too. Spring was coming – perhaps the last spring of this wretched war.

Cavendish lit a French Gauloise cigarette from the package in his khaki uniform blouse and blew two long streams of smoke from his flaring nostrils. Almost every waking hour of his life for the past four years had been devoted to preparing the way for the invasion that was coming with the spring as surely as the flowers of Portman Square. This discreetly luxurious apartment, hidden behind the neo-Georgian façade of Orchard Court, was a subheadquarters for an organization as secret as any in wartime Britain. At his orders, more than two hundred agents had gone out of its panelled door marked only by a number, 6, to be

20

infiltrated into Occupied France by parachute, by aircraft, by sea. Peers and pederasts, safecrackers and scientists, students, businessmen, clerics, lawyers, indolent scions of the well-to-do or street-toughened products of London's East End, theirs had been the task to help organize the armies of the night, to sabotage Occupied France's German-run arms industries and, above all, to prepare to disrupt the German rear during the critical days when the success of the invasion would hang in the balance.

Two hundred men and women. Barely half of them, Cavendish knew, were still alive. The rest were dead or, perhaps worse, in Gestapo prisons in France and Germany.

The discreet murmur of the doorbell interrupted Cavendish's thoughts. He glanced at his watch. It was 7 o'clock. She was on time. That was a good sign. Punctuality was not usually the hallmark of attractive women. For his agents, however, it could provide the margin between life and death. Clearly, she had learned her lessons well.

His ears followed the footsteps of Park, the butler, advancing to the door, then the sound of her high heels clicking along the marble floor to the room she had been assigned. These would be difficult hours for her. The fears and the doubts would be creeping up on her now, the terror of the unknown, of what the next hours might bring.

Cavendish returned to her personal file in its manila folder stamped 'Top Secret' on his desk. He had liked Catherine Pradier from the moment they'd first brought her to him. Her background was perfect. She carried the blue-and-gold passport of His Majesty, but everything else about her was French.

Cavendish nervously cracked the knuckles of his left hand. These were trying hours for him too. It was now that the nagging doubts, the suppressed worries always made their way to the surface. Pinpointing in a man or woman those ill-defined qualities that would allow him or her to function effectively as a secret agent was a very imprecise science indeed. How could you predict which individual would be able to manoeuvre alone, without help or guidance, in a hostile world; who, despite unbearable strain and fatigue, would stay alert for the tiny error, the discordant gesture that might mean arrest or betrayal? How could you foresee who would remain silent under the tortures of the Gestapo; who would crack, and reveal the names of his comrades or their hiding places?   It came down, finally, to your own instincts. You looked for certain things. A kind of inner calm. What you wanted in the end was a man or woman whose character contained hidden reservoirs of patience and determination but whose appearance was so nondescript you could pass him or her on the street without a second glance.

Deciding whether a prospective agent had those qualities was particularly difficult when the candidate was a woman. The very fact they even employed women for those dangerous and dirty tasks was one of the more closely held secrets of his organization. It did not require much imagination to conjure up the roar of outrage from the press and public if it got out that young women were being dropped behind the German lines, certain to be tortured and shot if they were caught. There was no precedent for it in the annals of warfare. His superiors had constructed a nice rationalization to justify it: 'Women are as entitled to join in the defence of our common beliefs as are men. This war is total, not restricted to men alone.'

In fact, the decision to employ women agents was rooted in a consideration a good deal more calculating than that. Women could move around Occupied France more easily than men. They were less suspect at roadblocks and security checks. A woman couldn't be swept off the street or subway and shipped to Germany as a forced labourer as a man could. And there was still another, more cynical reason.

Cavendish shuddered. The balance in these decisions was always so fine, the calculations so precise. You could never forget how terrible the consequences of an error in judgement could be, or how high might be the price of your mistake for the agent or those working with him. Catherine Pradier's background was right; she was determined; her training reports were good. And he desperately needed wireless operators in the field. There was one difficulty with this girl, however, that troubled him greatly. It contradicted one of his cardinal rules. Nobody but a blind man was ever going to pass Catherine Pradier in the street without looking at her.

Two doors down from Cavendish's office, the object of his concern looked at herself in the mirror with ill-concealed disdain. Catherine Pradier was wearing the khaki blouse, skirt and beret of the FANYS, the Female Auxiliary Nurses and Yeomanry Service, and it was a sight she had always found particularly disagreeable. It might have been the uniform of His Majesty's Forces, but to her finely attuned Gallic eyes it was an ill-fitting, ill-cut demi-sack, just the kind of thing she would have expected a group of sexless middle-aged English ladies tramping about the countryside in their sensible tweeds to choose for a uniform.

They had made her wear it because she had had to have a military 'cover' during her training. Almost gleefully she began to take it off. Everything went – her underclothes, her hairpins, even the gold signet ring an admiring RAF flight lieutenant had bought for her one Saturday morning at the antique-jewellery market on Portobello Road. Standing in the middle of the bedroom stark naked, Catherine shivered.

It was not from the cold. In that simple act of undressing, she had become aware totally, finally, of what she was about to do. As tough and realistic as her training had been, nothing had quite prepared her for the reality of this moment. It was as though in stripping off her uniform, she had shed her real being along with her clothes; as though somehow her real self were now to be stored away in a London clothes closet along with the uniform and her sensible brown English shoes.

Carefully laid out on the bed before her were the belongings of the new and strange person she was about to become – the 'going-away' clothes that would convert her into Alexandra Boyneau, a twenty-six-year-old divorcée from Calais, born in Oran, a North African city Catherine had never even visited, of second-generation French settlers. Her father had been a French naval officer – at least, she thought, his occupation was right, even if it was the wrong navy.

Each item of her new wardrobe had been assembled with precise and loving care by Maurice Weingarten, a Jewish tailor from Vienna. Under Cavendish's orders, he operated a secret clothing factory on Margaret Street near Oxford Circus. No one followed the fashions of Occupied France more zealously. His cluttered shop was awash in Parisian magazines and newspapers brought from Madrid, Lisbon, Stockholm. Every Friday night, Weingarten prowled the synagogues of London looking for newly arrived refugees from the Continent whose wardrobes might be for sale or from whose clothes he could snip the label of a French designer or manufacturer.

For Catherine, he had assembled a slightly mannish suit of dark grey with white pinstripes. Every stitch had been sewn by Weingarten's tailors in the Continental manner so nothing would betray their origin to a skilled German eye. Then they had even been laundered and ironed a dozen times to hide their newness.

Her long blond hair, washed several times with ill-smelling French Occupation shampoo, was now partially swept up into the bouffant style Frenchwomen were wearing that spring. From a table, Catherine took a bottle of auburn liquid labelled 'Creation Bien Aimée, Paris' and patiently painted it onto her long, well-muscled legs. Brought back to London by one of Cavendish's returning agents, the liquid was the chic Frenchwoman's answer to the wartime shortage of silk stockings. Feeling its cool stickiness on her calves, she laughed. Here, at last, was a stocking that wouldn't run.

She dressed quickly, then hung her bag over her shoulder. Cavendish's service had thoughtfully stocked it with used *métro* tickets, French matches, an old compact, a half-empty *flacon* of perfume – appropriately enough, Je Reviens – a couple of frayed calling cards, a clipping from the March 3 issue of the collaborationist newspaper *Je Suis Partout* describing the spring collection of the Parisian dress designer Paquin.

23

Her little dressing ceremony over, Catherine returned to the mirror in which a few minutes earlier she had studied herself in her FANYS uniform. She smiled. The vision of herself as a chic Frenchwoman was infinitely more satisfying than the earlier image had been.

'Set Europe ablaze!' With that ringing phrase, uttered on July 16, 1940, Winston Churchill had heralded the addition of a new arm to England's depleted arsenal. It was called the SOE – the Special Operations Executive – and its orders were to 'promote terror, foster resistance, sow alarm, despondency and destruction behind the German lines.'

Still, the fires of hell would not have sufficed in July 1940 to ignite the occupied countries of western Europe; and on the summer day he blurted out his defiant words, Winston Churchill barely possessed a damp match. Promoting terror was the monopoly of the Gestapo, destruction the province of the Luftwaffe. As for the idea of rising against their Nazi conquerors, the notion was unthinkable to the vast majority of people in Occupied Europe.

Not to Churchill. He would not let the German rest easy in his newly conquered territories; if he did not possess the conventional arms to disturb his sleep, he knew other ways to trouble his nights. He had learned them fighting Britain's enemies on the edges of the empire. He had ridden against the Boers on the South African veld, chased the elusive Pathan on the Northwest Frontier, studied the tactics used by the gunmen of the IRA to mobilize Dublin's slums. The war they fought was one without principles, without rules, without ethics, as distant from the Anglo-Saxon virtues of fair play as the torture cellars of the Gestapo's Prinz-Albrecht-Strasse headquarters were from London's Old Bailey. But as he himself had seen, it was a deadly effective war, one that would render helpless large bodies of troops.

So he created the SOE. Its role models were the IRA, the guerrillas of Mao Tse-tung, even the Fifth Column of the Nazi enemy. The men and women of the SOE who would go off to fight on the dark and lonely outer marches of the war would do so knowing that their lives must be considered forfeit from the moment they stepped into their rubber dinghies or slipped through the parachute hole of a Halifax bomber; that their actions were apt to be disavowed by the nation they served. No official Order Paper would ever reveal the existence of their organization to the elected representatives of the British people in the House of Commons. History might never know what they did, or why.

By the March evening when Catherine Pradier's turn had come to take her place in Occupied France, the SOE had gone far towards the fulfilment of Churchill's dream. A return of the Allied armies to the

Continent, so unthinkable when Churchill had created the SOE, was now imminent. And when that day came, the Germans would indeed find their rear aflame in blazes kindled by the men and women of the SOE.

The leaders of the SOE, however, were the pariahs of the espionage establishment. None of them sat on the secret committees at which the clandestine war policies were decided. None of them had access to the material generated by the greatest secret of the war, the *Ultra* programme, which enabled the Allies to read Germany's wartime codes. For General Sir Stewart Menzies, 'C', the Chief of the Secret Intelligence Service, SIS, the SOE had been an unwarranted and unwelcome intrusion into a world he and his acolytes had been accustomed to running by themselves. The SIS had penetrated the SOE with a zeal comparable to that employed in penetrating the ranks of its German rivals, the Abwehr. For two years, the SIS had even handled all the SOE's secret radio communications and codes – all to ensure its control over its wartime rival.

Furthermore, the SOE had acquired a reputation as fatally unsecure. At White's Club and in the gathering places around St James's Park where the real heads of Britain's secret intelligence lived and worked, the word was passed: 'Never trust a secret to the SOE.' That should have crippled Churchill's brainchild. It had not, however, for in the war of the shadows, one secret organization's failing could become another's redeeming strength.

Cavendish stood up as soon as Catherine Pradier entered his office. Smiling broadly, he walked around his desk to greet her. 'Marvellous!' he exclaimed. 'I'd say you'd stepped right off the Champs-Elysées.'

Despite her nervousness, Catherine returned his smile and performed a mock curtsy. Gallant remarks, she had noticed, fell uneasily from the poor major's lips. He looked more like an Anglican churchman than a warrior. A very obtrusive Adam's apple rode up and down a long thin neck that would have appeared more suited for a clerical collar than a battle blouse. His face was elongated and angular: a jutting chin, a sharp nose, a high sloping forehead on which half a dozen strands of hair rested in dishevelled solitude. He was a tall man, well over six foot and, like many tall men, he tended to stoop, as though bending down to catch the words of those mortals whom God had placed closer to the earth.

Cavendish studied her carefully. Despite his entreaties, she had refused to cut the blond hair that fell alluringly down her shoulders. Weingarten's suit clung with uncharacteristic tightness to the lithe figure she could not or would not render inconspicuous. I'll just wager, he thought, she skipped off to his shop against orders to get him to take in the odd nip and tuck where it mattered most. I suppose, he told himself, we're just going to have to learn to live with her appearance – as she'll have to learn to survive with it. 'Now, my dear,' Cavendish announced as he settled comfortably into his chair, 'shall we review your orders?'

Catherine had been handed her final instructions on a mimeographed piece of paper a few hours before. She had memorized them, then returned them to her Escort Officer. 'My name in the field will be Denise. I am to leave this country by aircraft during the March moon – tonight if the weather holds. I will be landed somewhere southwest of Paris in the Loire Valley, where I will be taken in charge by the organization's Air Operations Officer. He will help me get to Paris by train, if all goes well, tomorrow.'

Hearing herself repeat those words, Catherine could hardly believe them. It seemed too crazy to be true. Can I really be sitting here tonight, safe and secure, in this comfortable flat and tomorrow be heading towards Paris, surrounded by German soldiers? 'I will break contact with the Air Operations Officer in Paris and continue on my own to Calais via Lille by train. On arrival in Calais, I will employ the apartment on the second floor left, 17 Rue des Soupirants, for which I have the key, until I have made contact with my network. Each morning at eleven o'clock I will go to the Café des Trois Suisses, where I will look for a man standing on the street corner in front of the café wearing blue denims and carrying a green metal toolbox. I will ask him if he's the plumber I've called to repair my blocked drain. He will ask me if I am Madame Dumesnil of the Rue Descartes. If those passwords have been satisfactorily exchanged, then I will know contact has been established. He will take me to Aristide, the chief of the network to which I will be attached. I will function as Aristide's radio operator and courier. I will make my first transmission at 2100 GMT the day following my initial contact with Aristide. Thereafter I will transmit according to my Sked.'

'Fine, Catherine. I think that covers it all. Now let me give you your going-away presents.' Cavendish turned to a table adjacent to his desk and opened a battered leather suitcase. He pushed aside several worn women's blouses, rayon stockings and pieces of soiled underwear to uncover a second smaller case, this one the size of an overnight bag. He snapped open its lid.

Fitted into it with remarkable compactness was a radio transmitter. Cavendish's fingers indicated the green coils of the antenna, the key with which Catherine would tap out her messages. He lifted the flap of a small compartment. 'Your extra quartzes are in here.' The quartzes were black plastic squares the size of a matchbox. By plugging a new quartz into the transmitter, the operator automatically changed the frequency on which he or she was broadcasting. That made the efforts of the German radio detection service to locate the clandestine transmitter much more difficult.

'Let me warn you again. Never transmit for more than twelve minutes without changing your quartz. And never, Catherine, under any circumstance, transmit for more than forty minutes. The German radio detection services are devastatingly effective. And Pas-de-Calais simply crawls with detection trucks.'

Cavendish snapped the smaller case shut. 'Remember – however precious this transmitter is, you're more precious. If you see you're about to tumble into a security check, try to ditch it. When you're on the train, put it in a luggage rack, then go and sit two or three carriages away. If the Germans spring one of their surprise luggage checks, the poor damn fool sitting underneath it is going to have to answer some very awkward questions indeed, but you, at least, will be safe.'

Cavendish scattered the old blouses and dirty underwear over the transmitter's case. 'Unfortunately, if you're caught with it, you're caught with it. That's the long and short of it, really. Rather difficult to convince anyone it's anything other than what it is.'

Cavendish picked a tube of French Cadum toothpaste from the suitcase. 'Your silk and your onetime pad are in the bottom of the tube rolled up in cellophane. No need to take it out until you get to Calais.' Each was a square piece of tissue which, unfolded, was slightly smaller than a woman's handkerchief. Printed on them were the keys to the code Catherine would use to encipher her messages. The FANY at Sevenoaks in Kent who would receive her broadcasts had an identical set of keys. The system, if properly used, was absolutely unbreakable.

Cavendish fondled a box of wooden French matches in his hand. 'This is rather important.' From his desk, he took a wooden match and struck it against the matchbox. Nothing happened. 'Don't assume your French friends have forgotten how to make matches.' He laughed. 'Here, have a look at this.'

Catherine studied the match carefully. It seemed to be an ordinary wooden match. Cavendish took it back, then indicated the phosphorus head. A chip, like an inverted 'U', was cut into one side of it.

'That's so you'll recognize this particular match – which is not in fact a match at all. It's a hollow wooden tube which contains a microfilm with new orders for Aristide. We wouldn't want you sending poor Aristide's orders up in a puff of smoke by mistake. Please see that he gets it as soon as you establish contact.' Cavendish took another match, this time from the box, and struck it. It flared into flames. He blew it out and with the air of a child delighted by a new toy put the loaded match into the box. 'Clever, those laboratory chaps.'

Cavendish went back to his deskside table. Curiously nothing in his background had prepared him for the extraordinarily complex and difficult role he had been called on to play in the underground war. His real qualification stemmed from the simple fact that he was an Old Etonian. Quite unknown to Cavendish, he'd been designated for his job by other, older and far more worldly-wise Etonians. That he was a rank amateur in their cynical world had suited their ends quite admirably. He worked incredibly hard. He was absolutely devoted to the men and women he sent off on their dangerous and, so often, fatal missions. Others referred to his organization as 'The Firm.' Cavendish preferred to think of it as a family, and in many ways it was just that for him. To its members he gave unstintingly of his self and skills – he gave them everything, in fact, except that one vital ingredient in a spymaster's character he could never give because he did not possess it: deviousness.

He picked up Catherine's ration card and her *carte d'identité*. Like her clothes, they had been printed up in another of Cavendish's secret workshops, this one run by a convicted forger, paroled from prison to His Majesty's Armed Forces. Meticulously, he studied them hunting any flaw, however small, that would betray Catherine to the Gestapo.

'We try to keep these things up to date, with all the changes they make over there,' he said, setting them before Catherine. 'I think these are perfect. Fortunately, as you very well know, swift compliance with the letter of the law is not something for which our French friends are widely known. If a *gendarme* should find something out of date on one of these, don't panic. You'll probably be the fifth person he's stopped since lunch with the same problem.'

He pointed to the ration card. 'You'll see we've pulled a few of the coupons, to show you've been using the card regularly.

'This' – he indicated a card stamped with the eagle and swastika of the *Standartkommandantur* in Calais – 'is your pass for the *Zone Interdite* along the French seacoast, and here's your *carte d'identité.*'

Catherine picked up the yellowish-brown folded document. The cardboard that composed it was carefully frayed and worn, as though it had already been thumbed by dozens of *gendarmes* at dozens of security checks in France. A grey lifeless picture, so typical of the portraits that seemed to grace every ID card ever printed, stared back at her from one of its pages. She shuddered. Each detail of her new identity was there: the names of her parents, her divorced husband's name, her birthplace, her birth date – each a hallmark of the stranger whose existence she would now have to wear as naturally as she wore Weingarten's suit.

'You'll want to sign here,' Cavendish said, indicating the square

28

marked '*Signature du Titulaire*.' When she had finished, he took her to a pad of purple ink and carefully rolled her fingerprints into the space provided for them on the card. After blowing on it to dry the ink, he folded it carefully.

'*Voilà*. Catherine Pradier, for the time being, no longer exists. Remember,' Cavendish cautioned, passing the card to her, 'this is not a charade we're asking you to play. Believe in those parents we've given you, love them, cherish them. Assume your new identity so completely, so totally that all the vestiges of your real self are forgotten.'

The phone interrupted him. He picked it up, nodded, then looked at Catherine. 'It looks as if the weather's holding. You're on for tonight.'

The time had come now for the final, and for Cavendish the most painful, phase of this carefully prepared departure ritual. 'Catherine.' His voice was soft, tender almost. 'You've known since you joined us that everyone in our organization is a volunteer. There is no compulsion here; no one is ever asked to do something they feel they cannot do. Let me now be terribly candid with you. As a wireless operator, you've got the most dangerous job we have. I've got to tell you in all honesty, your chances of a safe return are little better than fifty/fifty. If you're caught, there is virtually nothing we can do to help you. If you're wounded, as you know, your comrades have orders to leave you and save themselves.'

Cavendish took a long, contemplative drag on his Gauloise. He was perched on the corner of his desk, one long leg jack-knifed over the opposite knee, the cigarette dangling from his lips. 'The decision to go or not must be yours, Catherine, and yours alone. I want you to be able to make it fully aware of all the consequences. And aware that there is absolutely no stigma whatsoever attached to your saying no.' He turned away from Catherine and, very deliberately, very slowly tapped the ash of his cigarette into an ashtray, allowing her a few seconds to ponder the implications of his words without his eyes resting upon her.

When he turned back to her, his blue eyes seemed to radiate a special quality of concern and sympathy. He framed the ritual question he addressed to each of his agents leaving for the field: 'Catherine, do you wish to continue?'

For several seconds there was not a sound in the room. Somehow Catherine's tongue seemed incapable of articulating the word her mind commanded it to pronounce. When it finally came, it came in French, as though in unconscious response to the impulsion driving her forward.

'*Oui*,' she said.

Wordlessly, Cavendish walked to the little liquor cabinet he kept in his closet. He took out two glasses and a bottle of 1927 Crockford port. 'To your success, Catherine,' he said, raising his glass to hers. He was the cheerful *paterfamilias* once again. 'I'm sure you're going to do well.

29

Everything in your background, your training, your instructors' reports, your attitude tells us that.'

After both had sipped their port, he reached into his jacket and pulled out an object wrapped in tissue paper which he handed to Catherine. It was a 1939 Cartier gold compact, one of the limited series the jeweller had produced to commemorate the New York World's Fair. 'It's something from all of us here,' Cavendish told her. 'If ever you're lonely and a little worried over there, think of us when you powder that lovely nose of yours. We're behind you as totally as we can be. We believe in you. We trust you. Above all, we want you back.' Cavendish chuckled. 'And if you should ever have to cut and run without a sou in your purse, you can always pop it at a pawnbroker's.'

There was a knock on the door. Catherine's Escort Officer leaned in. 'Station-wagon's here, sir.'

Cavendish finished his port. 'Well,' he announced. 'I suppose we'd better be going.'

The two of them walked down the marble-floored hallway to the door of the apartment, where Park, the butler, waited. He gave a slight bow to Catherine. 'Merde, mademoiselle. Good luck,' he intoned as he opened the door and escorted them to the waiting elevator.

Silently, Cavendish and Catherine rode down to the ground floor, then marched under the building's crystal chandelier, past a huge bouquet of artificial flowers to the porte cochere where the Ford was waiting. The agent going out with Catherine was already sitting in the front seat with the WAAF driver in her blue uniform. As regulations stipulated, he and Catherine barely exchanged glances.

Cavendish leaned down and kissed her gently, French fashion, on both cheeks. Drawing up, he gave her a warm smile. 'Merde, my dear,' he murmured.

Catherine got in, and the driver eased the station-wagon up the drive to the arch cut into the middle of Orchard Court's façade, leading towards Portman Square and the blacked-out streets of London beyond. Catherine turned and glanced through her open window. There beside the driveway stood Cavendish, slightly stooped, his uniformed figure frozen in the tribute of a final salute to their departing vehicle. Slowly, she rolled up the window. As she did, she could just make out, faint yet reassuring, the distant echo of Big Ben's chimes.

Three hundred and fifty yards away, at the very heart of London the sound of those same resonant chimes echoed back across St James's Park, the Admiralty and Horse Guards' Parade to the ground-floor office suite in the massive building situated at the intersection of Great George Street and Storey's Gate. The office and the austere living

30

quarters that adjoined it were known to the senior officers and employees of His Majesty's Government as the 'annexe,' for they were close to Number 10 Downing Street, a five-minute walk away.

Downing Street's two-hundred-year-old, unsupported timbers had been considered far too dangerous as a wartime residence for His Majesty's first minister, and it was in these simple precincts that Winston Churchill and his wife had lived for most of the last four years. Directly below them was a maze of offices known as the Underground War Rooms. Held to be absolutely bombproof, they housed those organizations on which Churchill most often called, Britain's senior planning staffs and a handful of her most vital and secret agencies. The underground construction had been ordered, prophetically enough, on the spring day in 1938 when Neville Chamberlain had returned from Munich with the promise of 'peace in our time.'

His half-moon reading glasses well down his nose, Churchill sat at a small desk in the office adjoining his bedroom busily annotating some of the contents of his Black Box, which sat opened at his side. At the centre of the room, arranged around a mahogany table, the participants in the meeting about to begin awaited the Prime Minister in respectful silence.

Present were General Sir Alan Brooke, Chief of the Imperial General Staff; Air Chief Marshal Sir Arthur Tedder, deputy commander of SHAEF; Major Desmond Morton, Churchill's personal assistant and his liaison officer to the clandestine services; Captain Henry Pim of the Royal Navy, who maintained the maps, and a slightly intimidated brigadier of the Plans Section, who was to conduct the briefing.

In front of each man was a cardboard folder. Each was stamped with the word 'BIGOT' and the flaming-sword shield of Supreme Headquarters, Allied Expeditionary Force. They contained the detailed plans for *Overlord*, the forthcoming assault on Hitler's Fortress Europe. Beside each folder was a second, much smaller sheaf of papers stamped 'Top Secret' and headlined 'Weekly Review of the European Situation, March 18,1944, Joint Intelligence Committee.'

The last man to arrive, General Sir Hastings Ismay, Churchill's personal Chief of Staff, appeared in the doorway. Seeing him, the Prime Minister waved towards the liquor cabinet in a corner of the room. 'Make yourself a brandy-and-soda, Pug,' he ordered. He scrawled a few more notes on his paper, then snapped the self-locking dispatch box shut.

With his ambling, slouching walk, the PM crossed the room to take his place at the head of the table. With the exception of the brigadier, the men in the room were all Churchill's intimates; yet none of them was indifferent to or unaffected by that special sense Britain's leader emanated. Carefully, he relit his Romeo & Julieta cigar, puffed it twice to

31

set the tip aglow, then waved aside the smoke and peered down the table to the nervous brigadier. 'Pray proceed,' he commanded.

'Sir,' the man replied, getting to his feet, 'we have been asked for our current appraisal of the prospects of success in the coming invasion based upon our most recent intelligence estimates.' He picked up the smaller of the two folders. 'These indicate that there are at present fifty-two German divisions in France and the Low Countries.'

There was a rustle of paper as the men at the table followed his example and picked up their folders. 'We estimate that on D-Day there will be sixty: ten Panzer, two para, seventeen mobile first-class infantry divisions and thirty-one ordinary divisions, disposed as we show on this map.'

Captain Pim, in time to the brigadier's words, drew the curtains to an easel at the end of the room. 'The bulk of their strength is concentrated here in the Fifteenth Army, which covers the area from the Somme to the Dutch lowlands. A second army, the Seventh, covers Brittany and Normandy, our landing area, with about half the strength of the Fifteenth. The remaining units are scattered between their First Army down near Bordeaux and their Ninth on the Mediterranean Coast.

'We currently have thirty-two American, British and Canadian divisions here in the United Kingdom. By D-Day we will have thirty-seven, of which fifteen will be armoured and four para.'

'In other words, just over half the forces available to Hitler?' The speaker was General Brooke.

'Yes, sir.'

'And ours here on this island, separated from the battlefield by some one hundred miles of open water?'

'Yes, sir.'

The brigadier turned to his easel, a collapsible pointer in his hand. 'Hitler, however, is obliged at the moment to disperse his forces all along this long coastline.' The pointer swept the Atlantic from the Bay of Biscay to the Hook of Holland. 'We will be able to concentrate ours at the point of assault. In addition, we expect to have complete tactical air control of the landing area. And our naval bombardment. The success or failure of the invasion, sir, comes down, finally, to the one fairly simple equation which governs all seaborne assaults: can we build up our forces in the bridgehead by sea faster than the Germans can bring up reinforcements by land? If we can, we succeed. If we can't, we fail.'

'This supposes, of course, our initial landing succeeds,' Churchill observed.

'Winston.' It was Brooke again, the only man in the room privileged to address the Prime Minister by his first name. 'The troops will get ashore.'

'Despite the obstacles Rommel is planting up and down the French seacoast?'

'They may hinder the landing. They won't stop it.'

'Despite his evident determination to stop us on the beaches?'

'Rommel, Prime Minister, is a fine divisional commander, but he possesses no strategic grasp whatsoever. That is not the problem. It never has been. Our troops will get ashore. There is nothing Rommel can do to prevent that.'

There was a trace of barely suppressed petulance in Brooke's reply. Churchill's stubborn belief in his own military genius was a cross Brooke had borne through four years of war. It was a gift the British leader was firmly convinced had been bequeathed him by his illustrious forebear, the Duke of Marlborough, and like Hitler, he enjoyed nothing more than meddling in his generals' affairs. 'The problem, Prime Minister, is not "Can we *get* ashore?" It's "Will we be able to *stay* ashore once we're there?" '

Brooke sighed and waved the folder containing the Joint Intelligence Committee's most recent estimate to underscore his concern. 'One need only look at the numbers. The balance of forces available to the Germans as opposed to the number of divisions we can land in the first fortnight makes it clear what a damnably difficult proposition that's going to be. Unfortunately, Winston, whether this invasion succeeds or not doesn't depend on us. It's one of the factors which make the landing so unpalatable. It will all depend on whether or not Hitler and his generals make the right decisions at the right time. The critical moment for us will come between D plus 3 and, I should say, D plus 7. For Hitler, slightly earlier.' Brooke held his breath for a moment, closing his eyes and holding two fingers to his lip as though he were conjuring up an image of those invasion beaches cluttered with their men and machines, half paralysed by the chaos and confusion that always attended such undertakings. 'In my view,' he continued, 'the critical moment for Hitler is going to come on the evening of D plus 2. Not sooner. Not later. That is when he must take the decision to go the whole hog and risk everything on throwing us out of Normandy. Before that, he won't be sure Normandy is our main effort. If he waits too long after that, it'll be too late.

'Yes.' Brooke tapped the folder containing the Overlord plans with his forefinger to underscore his point. 'He's got to have the guts to sell out everything else and throw the lot against us. If he does, then the majority of his Panzer divisions should be assembling in Normandy by D plus 4. From D plus 5 onward we can expect a full-blooded counterattack by eight to ten Panzer divisions, plus another five mechanized-infantry divisions, plus the eleven divisions they already have in the invasion area.'

'Can't the French Resistance impede their arrival?'

'Winston, the resistance movement that can stop ten Panzer divisions has yet to be created.'

'Even with our air force interdicting them, destroying the bridges they'll have to use to reach the battlefield?'

Brooke glanced at Tedder, the senior airman present, as though soliciting his support for what he was about to say. 'We'll slow them. We won't stop them. The major obstacle is the Somme, and they'll cross that by night with the bridging equipment they've stored there for just that purpose. Those Panzer divisions are the best divisions in the Wehrmacht, Winston. They're well equipped, well trained, rested. If Hitler orders them to Normandy, they'll get there.'

Churchill scowled as he contemplated the Chief of Staff's sombre words. 'And how many divisions will we have ashore by then?'

'If all has gone according to schedule, thirteen.'

'Thirteen? Roughly half of what they'll have?'

Brooke nodded.

There was an uneasy silence while the soldiers in the room waited for Churchill to absorb the shock of those figures. Finally, he mumbled, 'It is a horrifying prospect.'

'It is the prospect, Prime Minister, that makes this the most hazardous operation of the whole war.'

Churchill stood and, hands knotted behind his back, stomped down the room to the easel. For a few seconds he paused, glowering at it. 'Isn't there some other place we can come ashore? Why – just why – do we have to land in Normandy?'

There was no question which the brigadier was better prepared to answer. For two and a half years, from the moment planning for an eventual invasion had begun, he had been assigned to that task. Sometimes it seemed to him there was no cove, no inlet, no strip of beach from Brittany to Dunkirk that he did not know as well as the byways of the Surrey village in which he had been born.

'Sir,' he began, 'we must use one of two ways to build up the beachhead with men and supplies. Either we do it through a captured deepwater port or we do it over the beaches.'

Churchill stood still, his hands behind his back, his cigar tip glowing. He nodded.

'Dieppe taught us one critical lesson. And, if I may say so, sir, a lesson so valuable that it was worth the life of every one of the Canadians who died there.'

'Poor devils.' The heavy loss of life in the raid and the humiliation the captured Canadians had been made to endure was still a sore point for Churchill.

'Thanks to Dieppe, Prime Minister, we know that we cannot capture a defended French deepwater port and get it working fast enough to sustain the buildup the invasion demands. That fact, sir, condemns us to the only alternative: the beaches. And there are no beaches that can sustain an invasion in Pas-de-Calais.'

'Winston.' The Prime Minister had been about to speak, but Brooke, pretending not to realize it, interrupted. Churchill was forever running after the odd thought at such gatherings, and Brooke felt it his special obligation to keep the PM's concentration on the essentials. 'The Joint Planners have been over this a thousand times. The fact is, if we are going to make this landing, we must make it in Normandy. There is no alternative. We know that. Hitler, thank God, does not.'

For a moment, Churchill said nothing, weighing Brooke's words. Then he began to pace the room. 'And what, pray,' he asked in a hoarse whisper, 'are your current estimates for the landing's success?'

The brigadier glanced about the room, hoping, perhaps, that one of his superiors might reply. None did. 'Sir, General Eisenhower's Chief of Staff evaluates them at fifty/fifty.'

The figure seemed to stun Churchill. To some in the room it appeared that he tottered backwards an instant on hearing it, as though it had struck him with some paraphysical force. 'So all our precious fortunes, all our hopes, are to be recklessly cast on just one turn of the wheel, are they?'

For several minutes he paced the room, shoulders slumped forward, hands clasped behind his back, his jutting cigar pointing the way like a kind of bowsprit through the troubled seas of his spirit. Many of his American allies accused Churchill of being fainthearted in his support of the invasion. They were wrong. Churchill had begun to dream of a return to the Continent almost before the last British soldier had left the beaches of Dunkirk. On June 3, 1940, only twenty-four hours after France had signed an armistice with Hitler, Churchill had ordered a one-hundred-and-twenty-man commando force in five private yachts to stage a hit-and-run raid on the Boulogne seacoast, a token pledge to Hitler and the French that one day the British would return. A month later, while England braced to repel an invasion herself, Churchill created Combined Operations Command to develop the tactics and techniques of a full-scale landing on the Continent.

As much as anyone in Washington, Churchill longed for a return to the Continent – but not at any price. His whole strategic thought came down to one principle: defeat the enemy by weakening and harassing his flanks, not by striking where he was strongest; win with guile, not a reckless squandering of men and machines.

He stopped and turned to the men at the table. 'The hazards of the coming battle are very great indeed. I have a recurring nightmare that

35

haunts my sleep. I see three hundred thousand dead, the flower of British and American youth, choking the beaches of Normandy. I see the Norman tides running red with their blood. I see a grey and silent beach wrapped in the dismal shroud of a defeat far worse than Dunkirk.' He shook his head as though to rid his spirit of such images. 'When those ghastly spectres arise to haunt my sleep, I have my doubts. Oh, God, I have my doubts.'

The troubled Prime Minister began to pace the room again. 'Another generation of Englishmen butchered by the folly of generals as ours was at the Somme! I swore upon the altar of the gods of war that I would never preside over such a slaughter. Now the Americans insist on throwing our forces against the steel doors of Europe. Why not the Balkans? Why not the Mediterranean?'

Churchill returned to his seat and slumped a moment in his chair, his chin pressed against the knot of his bow tie. 'They are an unblooded people. How can they understand our anguish? Their Somme is a century behind them, at Bull Run and Gettysburg.'

Again he fell silent, his spirit yielding slowly, reluctantly to the inevitable. 'Well,' he growled, 'we shall have to go. There is no doubt of that. And we shan't surprise them. The German is guided by the precept of Frederick the Great: "It is pardonable to be defeated but never to be surprised." '

Churchill took a long, meditative draw on his cigar. 'So finally, it all comes down to one thing, doesn't it? We're approaching the most critical battle in our nation's history and victory depends not on our force but on a Trojan Horse. Everything rests on whether or not a little band of amateur Machiavellis we've installed downstairs can make Hitler buy a pig in a poke. They are the ones who must stay his hand and keep his armour away from our bridgehead, aren't they?' A melancholy cast glazed his famous features. 'And suppose Hitler doesn't fall for their skein of deceit and falsehood? Suppose he divines our real intentions and resolves to hurl those Panzer divisions against us: what then?'

An awkward silence followed his words. It was a question no one in the room was eager to answer. Finally Tedder, the man closest to the invasion preparations, spoke up:

'If those Panzers of his come over the horizon in the first five days, Prime Miniser – we don't stand a chance in hell.'

BERCHTESGADEN

At about the same time, halfway across the vast spaces of Hitler's *Festung*

36

Europa from London, an open Horch touring car drove through stands of fir and spruce that soared above its route like vaulting arches towering over the nave of a Gothic cathedral. A chill fog rising off the valley floor covered the landscape in a grey shroud, giving it an air of gloom and foreboding worthy of a set for Wagner's *Die Götterdämmerung*. The two-and-a-half-mile ride from Berchtesgaden to Hitler's Berghof might have inspired a sense of melancholy in the most cheerful of human beings that night; and radiant good humour was something for which the figure sitting erect in the Horch had never been noted. Field Marshal Gerd von Rundstedt was the archetypical Prussian Imperial officer: austere, distant, uncompromising.

As a passion for the Church seemed to run in certain French families, so a passion for war seemed to run in the blood of the Von Rundstedts. For generations the family had provided warlords to Prussia. With his haughty demeanour, his duelling scars and monocle, the last of their line appeared the very embodiment of the German soldier.

Dubbed by his admiring staff 'the last Teutonic Knight,' he was a collection of contradictions. He was considered an armoured genius, but he had never been inside a tank. He could not abide the dirt, the grease, the noise. For all his austere bearing, he had a passion for good food and fine wine – a passion which his position as Germany's Commander in Chief in the West had allowed him to indulge almost daily at the Coq Hardi, a citadel of French culinary splendour. Von Rundstedt received his first daily report at the unsoldierly hour of 10 A.M. Not for the field marshal the concept of the officer leading his men at the front. He despised the idea of going out to inspect his forces, visit their messes, boost their morale. In his two and a half years as Commander in Chief in the West, he had visited Hitler's much-vaunted Atlantic Wall only twice – and both times reluctantly.

Von Rundstedt preferred to preside over Germany's military might in the West from his headquarters in the elegant pavilion of Saint-Germain-en-Laye, where Louis XIV had been born. There, he commanded as he believed a great captain should, surrounded by his maps and his staff, above the chaos of the battlefield, his mind free to ponder the grand sweep of strategy.

But of all his many contradictions, none was more striking, more ironic, than the fact that he despised Germany's Führer and the regime he had created, yet had served both without hesitation or reservation. And how well he had served them! It was on Von Rundstedt's escutcheon that the names of the most important victories of Hitler's Third Reich were emblazoned. He had driven his Southern Army Group across the Polish plain to Warsaw in thirty days, adding a new word to the lexicon of war: *Blitzkrieg*. His Army Group 'A' had humbled the invincible French army in May 1940 and destroyed Stalin's finest divisions in the summer of 1941. He could scorn Hitler as a 'Bohemian lance corporal' and his followers as a 'herd of hoodlums'; Hitler had given Von Rundstedt's army the steel and gold it needed to become a force worthy of his Prussian dreams, and Von Rundstedt, in return, had given the Third Reich half the civilized world.

Now the responsibility for defending the most vital part of those conquests was about to fall upon this bored, cynical sixty-eight-year-old field marshal. Hitler had summoned Von Rundstedt and his fellow marshals to Berchtesgaden for a conference to review Germany's strategy for the coming showdown in the West. Sometime in the next weeks, months perhaps, the Allies would attempt to land on the shores of the European continent. With that action would begin the climactic battle of the Second World War – the battle on which the destiny of Germany and all of Occupied Europe would depend. And it was Germany's last Teutonic Knight who would have the task of repulsing them for the Führer he so despised.

How often had he pondered the outlines it would take as he strolled the balcony of his palace, staring towards the distant rooftops of Paris. Like most battles, it would be decided by the unknowns; but as he awaited the showdown, Von Rundstedt knew at least one thing: he had the men and arms to hurl back the Allied assault. Everything would depend on his making the correct decisions, the correct judgements in the first days of the struggle. Get those right, prevent Eisenhower from splitting up his forces with feints and deception – and nothing on earth, he knew, could stop him from handing the Allies a defeat as devastating as those he had inflicted on the Poles, the French and the Russians.

LONDON

An almost eerie silence filled Catherine Pradier's station-wagon. In the front seat, her fellow passenger was hunched over a book cradled between his knees, the pages illuminated by the flashlight he held in his hand. She had assumed, quite wrongly, that he was studying some last-minute orders from Cavendish. In fact, she was touched to discover, he was reading a Penguin paperback edition of Shelley's poems, his lips moving silently as he recited each line to himself. Despite her orders, she hadn't been able to resist the temptation to study him. He had curly blond hair and smooth, slightly puffed cheeks that seemed to glow with adolescent fat. He reminded her of the famous soap ad that had graced the billboards of prewar France: Baby – Bébé – Cadum. It was as if they were sending Baby Cadum off to war reading Shelley.

Her own preoccupation was more prosaic. She was studying postcards of Calais: the statue of the Six Bourgeois, the quay of the Bassin du Paradis, the Grande Place and the *Hôtel de Ville,* where two bronze statues baptized Martin and Martine struck the hours in the belfry. It was a technique Cavendish had developed to enable an agent to recognize landmarks in an unfamiliar city and be able to get around its streets without having to ask directions. Ask directions, and you gave yourself away as a stranger – and there were no strangers allowed now inside the forbidden zone along France's Channel coast where she was going.

Bored, she turned away from her postcards and stared out at the streets of suburban London rolling past the station-wagon's window in their unending sameness. One after another for miles on end, those grim brick Victorian row houses, each with its window boxes, its little lawn and latched gate, slipped past. Normally she would have found them unspeakably dreary; tonight they seemed enchanted. Despite herself, she couldn't help thinking, Will I ever see them again? She shook her head and turned her eyes away; better to go back to her postcards.

Gradually, the London suburbs gave way to the narrow hedge-lined lanes of Surrey, then the low and open hills of Sussex. They stopped at a roadblock, where an RAF sergeant asked for their identification. Seconds later, the WAAF driver turned into a driveway opposite the main gate of the Royal Air Force's Tangmere Station. There, hidden behind the sentinel hedge of boxwood trees, was a rambling cottage, all peeling whitewash, ivy and sagging shutters – exactly the kind of retreat a London stockbroker might have chosen for his country weekends before the war. A stout RAF flight sergeant, rubbing his hands on an apron at the kitchen door, attested to the nature of its present occupants. Half cook, half guard, he waved them through his kitchen down a smoke-filled corridor towards an open door from which came the babble of male voices.

'Welcome to Tangmere,' a voice called out from inside. It came from a lean young man in khaki coveralls and a navy blue turtleneck who detached himself from the group lounging around the coal fire blazing in the grate. He extended his hand and offered them an engaging smile. 'I'll be running you in tonight. Come and have a whisky with my nondriving friends here.'

While their pilot mixed them drinks, the other officers of the 161st Special Duties Squadron swallowed them up in jovial conversation. One played tour guide for Catherine, pointing out the Roman numerals cut into the whitewashed walls which indicated that in Tudor days the mess had been a clandestine Catholic chapel; another got her fellow passenger

39

talking about England's chances in Saturday's rugby match with Scotland.

After a few minutes of animated conversation, the pilot asked, 'Care to have a look at our route in tonight?'

He took them across the hall to the squadron's Operations Room. A huge map of France was tacked to one wall. 'We'll be coming out over Bognor Regis,' he said, pointing to his map. 'Twenty minutes or so overwater and we should make the French coast here, a bit west of Bayeux.'

Catherine's eyes focused on a chain of reddish stains running along the map from Caen to Le Havre. 'What do the marks indicate?' she inquired.

'Flak. We'll want to give that a wide berth. Then from Bayeux we fly a single heading all the way down here to Angers, where we pick up the Loire River. That's the tricky part. After that, it's quite simple, really. Follow the Loire up to Tours, then pick up the Cher and run on in to our field, east of the city on the north bank of the river. It's a good field, by the way. We've used it before. All we ask you to do is sit back, make yourself as comfortable as you can and enjoy the ride. And keep an eye out for the odd German night fighter that may be prowling about.'

Catherine laughed. 'Well,' she said. 'I must say you make it all sound as jolly as a trip down to Brighton for a day by the sea.'

The trip the young pilot had just described to Catherine so casually in fact represented one of the most extraordinary aerial operations of the war. Alone, absolutely unarmed, with only a compass and a set of Michelin road maps to navigate by, the pilots of the 161st Special Duties Squadron flew regularly past the flak and night fighters of the Luftwaffe searching, somewhere in the blacked-out immensity of Occupied Europe, for some distant farmer's field, it's outlines marked by nothing more precise than three flashlights stuck into the turf a couple of hundred yards apart. The plane they flew, the Westland Lysander, was so slow and so ponderous that they joked the Germans could shoot it down with a slingshot. Indeed, other RAF pilots had categorically refused to fly it on the reconnaissance missions for which it had been built. Its one redeeming virtue was the fact that it was, in RAF parlance, 'a sturdy little bugger that could land and take off on five hundred yards of corrugated cow shit.'

Assigned to the SOE and 161st Squadron, the Lysander had been stripped of its guns to increase its range, which meant only God or a cloud could save the plane if it was sighted by a German night fighter. Yet every night when the moon was full those pilots went off in search of their remote cow pastures, picking their way through the seams in the German radar, dipping through clouds in search of a river bend, a railway line, a road junction that might give them the bearing they

40

needed to find their path over Europe's blacked-out landmass. It was a feat comparable to sending a fly off to find a postage stamp hidden in a football field – at night.

Before Catherine could make any further comments on their coming trip, her young pilot had slipped an arm over her shoulder. 'Come along now,' he said. 'Sergeant Booker should have supper ready, and we'll see if we can find a nice claret to send you on your way.'

BERCHTESGADEN

Six hundred and seventy-five miles from Tangmere, in the splendour of his home the Berghof, the master of the Third Reich was absorbed in a task that bore not the remotest connection to his meeting with his field marshal or the coming struggle for Western Europe. He was writing a note to accompany the champagne and flowers he was about to send his favourite secretary for her birthday. She was ill with bronchitis, and the man in whose name millions were being herded into the gas chambers of the Final Solution was urging her to give up smoking because it was bad for her health.

He signed the letter, 'Affectionately yours, Adolf Hitler,' sealed the envelope and addressed it himself. Then he rose and walked to his window. That view of the snow-covered Alps, eternal and enduring, never failed to solace Hitler. There was no place where he felt or worked better than here in the mountaintop retreat he had first purchased in 1928 with the royalties he'd earned from sales of *Mein Kampf*. Staring out at the majestic mountains, their snowy peaks glistening in the moonlight, he turned his mind at last to his conference, and his reasons for calling it. He did not fear the coming invasion. Quite the contrary: he awaited it eagerly. He was a gambler and knew that for Germany and the Allies the coming invasion would be the greatest gamble of the war, the one fateful toss of the dice on which everything else depended.

A knock on his door interrupted his thoughts.

'The field marshals are here,' announced General Rudolf Schmundt, his Wehrmacht adjutant.

'I'll be with them in a minute,' Hitler replied. The minute, of course, would escalate to ten. A brief wait would remind them all where the ultimate authority of the Third Reich lay. Finally, deciding enough time had elapsed, he put on his grey double-breasted uniform jacket decorated with the Iron Cross Second Class he'd won at Ypres in World War I and went downstairs to greet his field marshals.

For those, like Rommel, for whom he had a certain affection, there

41

was a warm word of welcome. For others, there was merely a cold nod. When he'd finished, he stepped aside and waved them into the Berghof dining room. As Von Rundstedt passed before him the Führer murmured, 'Enjoy your dinner, *Herr General Feldmarschall.*'

Hitler was absolutely indifferent to food, and his mess was justly notorious for the banality of its cuisine. The menu for the evening consisted of pork chops, red cabbage and gravy.

Hitler, of course, had his own vegetarian menu. Watching him noisily consuming his green pea soup, Von Rundstedt struggled to suppress a shudder of disgust. He said nothing; he never spoke his mind at Hitler's dinner table. Meals with the Führer were usually lugubrious affairs, dominated by a Hitlerian monologue on whatever subject crossed the dictator's mind. Even field marshals tended to be timid and diffident in his presence, rarely venturing an idea or comment.

The exception was Rommel. He frequently uttered his own, generally complimentary, observations on Hitler's theories. At one of his obsequious comments, Von Rundstedt glanced across the table at Field Marshal Fritz Erich Manstein. Rommel was the only member of their little band who did not spring from the Prussian military caste or some wealthy family with a long tradition of military service. He was a schoolteacher's son, barely a scion of the middle classes. What was far worse, he was the only marshal who was a member of the Nazi Party. He was also a cross Von Rundstedt now had to bear. Rommel had recently been placed under him as commander of the two German armies along the French seacoast. 'The clown who commands the circus,' Von Rundstedt whispered across the table to Von Manstein.

He sat back to allow a steward to place ostentatiously before him the dessert Hitler's mess had provided for his epicurean appetite this evening: one shiny red apple. Another steward followed with what was regarded as the high point of dinner at the Berghof, a cup of the Führer's coffee. It was brewed from a special Yemeni coffee bean forwarded once a year to the German consulate in Istanbul. There, secretly and at night, it was loaded into a U-boat for the dangerous run through the Mediterranean to Kiel. The whole operation was timed so that the coffee reached Berchtesgaden each year just before Christmas.

Hitler, of course, never touched it. He drank only tea. On rare and festive occasions he would lace that tea with a few drops of cognac. The sight of his mess steward setting a tiny burlap-shrouded bottle by his teacup was a reminder to his guests that this was not such an occasion. It contained Elixier Magenbitter, a vile-tasting concoction used by his countrymen to ease the distress of a hangover or the pains of an upset stomach.

While his guests husbanded their coffee, perfectly aware that even field marshals got only one cup, Hitler abruptly shifted the conversation to the real concern before them all. 'Gentlemen,' he announced as though he were a preacher speaking out from his pulpit. 'The coming invasion in the West will be the decisive event not only of this year, but of the entire war.' A mess steward had quietly placed a map on an easel behind him, and he turned to it. 'In fact, it will decide the outcome of the war.'

He paused to allow his words to register. 'If the landing succeeds, the war is lost. I have no illusions about this. In the East, the very vastness of space allows us to give up territory, even on a major scale, without a mortal blow being inflicted on Germany's chance for survival. Not so in the West! If the enemy succeeds there, consequences of staggering proportions will follow in a very short time. But they are not going to succeed. We have the forces to defeat them. And once defeated, the enemy will never again try to invade.'

His enthusiasm for his subject began to bring back to his eyes some of that hypnotic quality for which they were so famous. 'And once we've hurled them back, we'll throw everything into the war in the East. We can transfer forty-five divisions to the East. Forty-five divisions will revolutionize the war there.'

'But, gentlemen, defeating this invasion will give Germany the most precious gift of all: time! It will give our industry a full year. With that year we will win this war.'

Hitler's words were designed to fill his marshals with zeal for the coming conflict, but they were not an idle boast. Hitler had ten million men under arms, more than the Americans, British and Canadians combined. Despite Allied air attacks, despite shortages of manpower and materials, the factories of the Reich had produced 11,897 tanks in 1943, almost ten times their 1940 output; 22,050 warplanes, three times as many as in 1940; five times as many artillery pieces; three times as much ammunition.

Above all, Hitler had his secret weapons: the V-1 and V-2 missiles beginning to roll off his assembly lines in quantity; his new Type 19 and Type 21 U-boats, which would be able to stalk the Atlantic seaways immune to the probes of Allied sonar; his Me-262 jet fighter, far in advance of anything the Allies had. Give Hitler a year to build these planes and his Luftwaffe might once again rule the skies of Europe.

Hitler sighed and turned his eyes back to the map of France, to those long and distant seacoasts where so much was soon to be decided. 'The moment it starts will be a great relief. But where, where will they come? Almost any place along the coast is possible.'

His last words were a question directed at his Commander in Chief in the West. Von Rundstedt was ready for it.

'*Mein Führer*,' he said, the authority of his years giving weight to his words. 'They will land between Dunkirk and the Somme.' Von Rundstedt rose, went to the map and traced with his finger a little arc from Calais around the knob of Cap Gris-Nez south towards Le Touquet-Plage. 'But most probably they will make their landing right here, between Calais and Boulogne.'

The field marshal cast a reassuring glance at the map. He knew that all the imperatives of history underlay his choice. From the moment France had begun to emerge as a nation, those polderlands of Flanders opposite Dover's chalk cliffs, the low hills of Artois and Picardy, had been the gateway to the Continent. There, at places, barely 20 miles of open water separated England from the French seacoasts. Philip the Fair of France, England's Henry V, the Counts of Flanders and the Dukes of Burgundy had stormed over its terrain, bequeathing the centuries the names of the crossroads villages like Crécy and Agincourt where their arms had clashed. Von Rundstedt himself had planned to use the region as Germany's springboard to London in Operation *Sea Lion*, Germany's projected invasion of England in 1940.

'Every imperative of strategic design dictates a landing here,' Von Rundstedt continued. 'Here they will be able to deliver men and *matériel* to a bridgehead here four times faster than they could in Normandy, six times faster than in Brittany. The greatest asset the Allies will have in this assault is their airpower. Where can that airpower be employed best? Right here! Their fighters in southeastern England will be only minutes away. They will blanket the beaches with aircraft. We learned from the Allies' attack on Dieppe in August 1942 that their first aim is going to be to seize and open a major seaport to bring in their heavy equipment. Otherwise, their invasion fails. Here' – the field marshal was back at his map – 'they have three: Dunkirk, Calais, Boulogne. Any one of them could sustain their assault. The enemy knows that landing here they will encounter our greatest defensive strength. To land in Normandy or Brittany would be easier for them, but it would leave them isolated from the main battleground.'

Von Rundstedt turned to his audience. 'A successful landing in Pas-de-Calais will achieve the greatest strategic prize.' The old field marshal's fingers danced over the areas where so many lives had been expended in World War I. 'The land is flat, open, ideal for Patton's tanks. Once they've established themselves here they'll be a four-day march from the Rhine. They will be poised to thrust a dagger into the Ruhr and destroy our industrial capacity to make war.

'If they come ashore in Normandy or Brittany, they risk being bottled up there, useless for months. If they succeed in landing in Pas-de-Calais, however, *mein Führer* – the war will be over by Christmas.'

Hitler paled with anger. Only Von Rundstedt would have dared utter so defeatist a phrase in his presence. He gave him a perfunctory nod of thanks and shifted his attention to Rommel.

'I agree with the field marshal's conclusion,' declared the younger man – it was, in fact, one of the few points on which the two men agreed – 'although I believe they will come ashore slightly farther to the south, by the mouth of the Somme, so they can use the riverbank to protect their flank.'

For several seconds Hitler sat uncharacteristically silent, digesting their words. Then be began again.

'Well, gentlemen,' he announced. 'Both of you are wrong. They are not going to land in the Pas-de-Calais. They are going to land in Normandy.

'The Allies do not like the head-on approach. Thus far, at every landing, in North Africa, Sicily, in Italy, they have always chosen the indirect approach. In this landing, which is crucial, they are certainly not going to hit us where we are strongest.'

His own fingers went to the map, running along the beaches of Normandy from Arromanches west past Sainte-Mère-Eglise up the Cotentin Peninsula. 'This is where they will land. They will drive across the base of the Norman peninsula and isolate Cherbourg. Then they will build up their strength and break out across France.'

Quietly, as if speaking to himself, he said, 'It will be Normandy. That is where they will come, all right – Normandy.'

To Catherine, dinner had seemed so carefree, she might have been dining with friends at the White Tower or La Coquille in London. In fact, she'd almost forgotten where she was and why she was there when suddenly, like Banquo's ghost, her Escort Officer appeared behind her chair. 'Our BBC message has come through,' he announced. 'Perhaps we'd better be getting along.'

For the first time since stepping into the cottage, Catherine felt a tremor of nervous tension tightening her stomach. She rose and followed her escort from the mess.

He took her to a bedroom upstairs. Arranged on a bedside table were the final items she'd be taking with her. First came her money belt. It contained the two million francs she was to give to Aristide – more money than Catherine had ever handled in her life. What was more, it was authentic French currency. Some farsighted Frenchman had smuggled a set of currency plates out of France in the midst of the *débâcle* in 1940. Since then, every secret organization in England had been printing the currency it needed to finance its clandestine operations in France from those plates.

'Here's your knife,' the officer said, showing Catherine how to spring its blade. 'Here's your pistol. Magazine's loaded. There's the safety catch, see? It's a Mauser .32. They've taught you how to fire it, haven't they?'

'I don't want a pistol.'

'What?' The officer was astonished. 'You don't want a pistol?'

'No. It's of no interest to me at all. All it will do is tell the Germans if I'm caught with it that I'm some kind of spy. What I would like is a small flask of cognac.'

'Right.' He picked up a small container. 'Here it is. Filled with rum, actually.'

Next he reached for a tiny cellophane packet containing a dozen round green pills. 'Benzedrine, if you simply must keep going. Never more than one every twelve hours – otherwise you may never get to sleep again.'

Finally, his hand went to a piece of tissue paper, the last item on the bedside table. He opened it and picked out a square white pill which he displayed to her in the palm of his hand.

'You've been told about this, I know. It's an 'L' pill. They make them in this square shape so you can never mistake them for anything else, even in the dark. It's pure, quick-dissolving. Thirty seconds and it's over. I'm told it's not painful.'

Catherine stared with utter revulsion at the little square in his hand. It was pure cyanide, life or death pressed into the form of a tablet even smaller than an aspirin. Her escort gave an embarrassed cough. 'I don't know your religious convictions, if any. I'm authorized, however, to tell you that the Archbishop of Westminster has issued a dispensation to Roman Catholic agents who feel obliged to take this to avoid talking under torture. Their death will not be considered a suicide by the Church, so no mortal sin is attached to it.'

Catherine shuddered and made an involuntary sign of the Cross.

'If you'd give me your right shoe,' the officer continued, 'I'll show you the place our friend Weingarten has designed to hide the pill.'

While Catherine looked on fascinated, horrified, he pointed to the head of the decorative black tassel on the shoe. 'This unscrews left to right – contrary to the usual practice.' He twisted it open, revealing a tiny socket into which he placed the pill. 'Very little chance anyone will ever find it there.'

As Catherine slipped her foot back into the shoe, she heard the slow crunch of automobile tyres rolling over the gravelled driveway in the courtyard outside.

'They're here,' her escort said.

Outside, the light of the full moon painted the world pale grey. Catherine slipped into the back seat of the station-wagon beside the fellow agent she'd now baptized Baby Cadum. One salient feature distinguished this station-wagon from the one that had delivered them to Tangmere. All its windows except the driver's windshield were painted black. Neither Catherine nor Baby Cadum could furnish the Germans with any detailed description of Tangmere's installation if they were ever caught.

The pilot was in front beside the driver, all business now. An enlisted man came out of the cottage and leaned into the car. 'No sign of German fighter activity along your route on the radar, sir. The latest weather report gives scattered cloud cover over your target area. Otherwise, you should have a clear trip in and out. You'll find a fifteen-knot tail wind going in above six thousand feet.'

The pilot nodded, then turned to his passengers. 'Well,' he said, 'a good moon and a fair wind for France. What more could we ask?'

LONDON

'Any fool can tell the truth; only a clever man can tell a lie.'

Hand-lettered in India ink on a slip of white parchment, then fitted into the frame of a triangular paperweight, that maxim had been the departing gift of Colonel Sir Henry Evelyn Ridley's predecessor on the day Ridley had first taken up his assignment in Winston Churchill's Underground War Rooms at Storey's Gate in the heart of London. It was a particularly fitting *leitmotiv* for the organization Ridley commanded in that subterranean labyrinth. Ridley was the head of the 'little band of amateur Machiavellis' on whom Churchill had said so much depended in his earlier conference. His task was one of the most critical of the war, yet his organization was so secret that barely three hundred people even knew it existed. To Ridley and the dozen men around him had fallen the task of making Adolf Hitler and his General Staff swallow the greatest lie ever told. It was the lie on which the outcome of the Second World War might very well depend, a *ruse de guerre* of such dimension that the Trojan Horse would seem, in comparison, a child's hoax.

No one might appear less likely to conceive and tell that lie than Ridley. He was the very incarnation of those virtues of rectitude and fair play which an admirer would assign to Britain's ruling classes, that self-perpetuating little coterie of men who had governed the British Empire for four hundred years. He was, by taste and tradition, a lawyer. Indeed, Ridley's family and British law were so intertwined that one of his forebears had been among the barons who had forced the Magna Carta on King John. An oil painting of that historic June morning at

47

Runnymede had been passed from generation to generation in the Ridley chambers at Lincoln's Inn, a seal of the special bond which joined the Ridleys to the brotherhood of the wig and the writ.

Ridley was, on this March evening, the senior partner, on wartime leave, of the firm founded by his great-grandfather; a legal adviser to the Crown; a Privy Councillor as his father and grandfather had been; a director of Coutts Bank. Everything from the moment of his birth had prepared him for the exercise of the power that was now his. From the hands of his father's tutors, he'd gone off to Eton, 'the blessed college,' when it stood at the very apogee of its power in the decades before the First World War. His years at Eton had marked him for life. Breeding, he'd learned, was more important than brains; loyalty to one's friends and one's class the one indispensable ingredient of a gentleman; devotion to King and Country the one true faith. As good Etonians were urged to do, he went against the grain of Pope's dictum and plunged into learning a little about everything. Specialization was not for his class; rulers, after all, could always hire specialists to do their bidding.

His world had been shattered in the trenches of the Western Front. By 1917, Ridley had earned a captaincy in the Coldstream Guards, a Military Cross and three wound stripes. With his final wound, he was transferred to the staff of Field Marshal Lord Haig, Britain's Commander in Chief in France, as an intelligence officer.

It was an ironic appointment, for Ridley had come to loathe Haig and the bloody-minded generals around him with an unremitting passion. Never would he forgive them for sending so many of his kind to death in their war of attrition, to throw away their young lives for a few puddles of Flanders mud. Yet he demonstrated such uncanny skill in preparing intelligence estimates for Haig that he acquired a wizard's reputation in the British military establishment. Among those aware of his accomplishments was a young Cabinet minister, Winston Churchill. When, in the spring of 1942, Churchill wanted a fresh, innovative spirit to take over the most esoteric of his clandestine organizations, he summoned Ridley to London from the counterespionage posting he had held in Northern Ireland since the outbreak of the war and appointed him 'Controlling Officer for Deception.' What that meant was summed up in the directive, COSC(42) 180(0), that assigned him his task on June 21, 1942. 'You are to prepare deception plans on a worldwide basis with the object of causing the enemy to waste his military resources,' it read. 'Your work is not limited to strategic deception alone. It is to include any matter calculated to mislead or mystify the enemy wherever military advantage may be gained' – or, as Churchill put it to him orally and succinctly, he was to use 'every stratagem, every dirty trick of murder and mayhem imaginable to bugger the bloody Hun.'

His organization was called, in a bureaucratese designed to stifle unwelcome curiosity, the London Controlling Section. Ridley reported directly to Churchill through General Ismay. From his underground labyrinth in Storey's Gate, he had links to all Britain's secret organizations charged with the implementation of his devious schemes; to the code busters at Bletchley Park; to MI5, to 'C,' Sir Stewart Menzies, his close friend and fellow Etonian who ran MI-6, the Secret Intelligence Service. A silent and discreet man, Ridley was almost unknown outside the world in which he moved. But inside it, at White's and Brooks, in the anonymously labelled intelligence offices of St James's and in the Queen Anne houses around St James's Park, the men who did know of him knew that Sir Henry Evelyn Ridley was 'a very senior boy indeed.'

The art of military deception which he'd been called on to practice went back to the fourth century B.C. and the Chinese warlord Sun Tzu. 'Undermine the enemy,' he wrote; 'subvert him, attack his morale, corrupt him, sow internal discord among his leaders, destroy him without fighting him.' The Greeks at Troy; Hannibal; Belisarius, commander of the armies of the Emperor Justinian, were just a few of the historical forebears of Ridley.

In World War II, Britain's outnumbered and outgunned army had had to rely on guile and deceit not to win but to survive. Indeed, the organization over which Ridley presided had been born in a whorehouse behind Groppi's restaurant in Cairo during the struggle with Rommel's Afrika Korps for the Western Desert. In pursuit of its schemes, it had employed magicians, counterfeiters, murderers, safecrackers, soothsayers and, in 1943, a corpse floated ashore on the Spanish seacoast. Now it was Ridley's charge to put across the most challenging, the most critical and the most important deception scheme of all time. General Brooke had handed it to him with the admonition 'It won't work. But it bloody well has to.'

It was called *Fortitude*. Like all great ideas, it was beguiling in its simplicity. The Allies, *Fortitude* maintained, were not going to launch one invasion of Hitler's Fortress Europe. They were going to launch two. The first and lesser assault would fall on Normandy. Its aim would be to draw to the Cotentin Peninsula the crack Panzer divisions of Germany's Fifteenth Army. Once Hitler had hurled those élite units against the Norman bridgehead, then the second – and real – invasion would strike across the narrow Dover Strait at Pas-de-Calais. If Sir Henry and his London Controlling Section could lead Hitler and his generals to believe *Fortitude*'s lies, they would then immobilize the finest troops in the German army in Pas-de-Calais, their cannon unfired, their troops unblooded, waiting for an invasion that was never going to take place. If they failed, however, if the German dictator threw those Panzer divisions of his against Normandy rapidly and decisively, then the invasion would surely collapse, and with it, all the desperate hopes of Occupied Europe.

To put the lie of *Fortitude* across, Ridley first had to create an army of ghosts. On this March evening while he laboured in his underground office, the Allies had just over thirty divisions – Americans, English and Canadians – in all of the United Kingdom. That was barely enough troops to mount one invasion, to say nothing of two. Yet Hitler and his generals would never believe the lie of *Fortitude* if they did not first believe the Allies had enough troops in England to stage two major invasions. Most important, Ridley had to convince the Germans his second invasion would strike at precisely the right interval after the Normandy landings, at that critical moment two to three days after D-Day when Hitler would have to make up his mind to commit his Panzer divisions to Normandy.

It was a deadly game. A failure by Ridley could trigger disaster, since falsehood, in military deception, points the way to truth. If the Germans detected Ridley's game, they would have only to hold up a mirror to his lies to determine what the Allies' real intentions were. Then their Panzers would be ready and waiting to slaughter Eisenhower's invaders.

Putting across the lie of *Fortitude* was a slow, painstaking process. Ridley couldn't hand his lies to the enemy in a blue ribbon. Intelligence easily obtained was swiftly discarded. Ridley had to make the Germans work to uncover the ingredients of his lie, to ferret them out bit by bit, with much labour and at much cost, until the lie, born of much Teutonic effort, finally emerged with convincing clarity.

Ridley's aim was to enmesh the German in an invisible spider's web of deceit. The idea was to uncover all the sources of intelligence employed by the Germans, then to slowly and subtly poison the wellsprings of each with misinformation. If Ridley could succeed in that, he would be able to insert the fragments of his lie into Germany's intelligence machinery, there to rise slowly to the ultimate target of his scheme, the mind of Adolf Hitler himself.

It was an appallingly difficult job, and it was little wonder that its accomplishment kept Ridley at his desk late, as it had this March evening. The unexpected ring of his red secret telephone interrupted his study of the document before him.

'Ah, Squiff, they said I'd catch you working late.' 'Squiff' had been Ridley's obligatory Etonian nickname. 'I've just had some tidings I feel I ought to share with you.'

Ridley recognized immediately the grating voice of his Etonian classmate Sir Stewart Menzies, the head of MI6, the Secret Intelligence Service.

'Glad ones I hope. I rather need them these days.'

'No, the other kind, I'm afraid. Perhaps you'd like to join me for a brandy-and-soda at the club in, say, half an hour?'

Faithful almost to the second, Ridley stepped into the entry of White's Club. Seeing him, the porter slipped from the little cage in which he maintained a discreet but vigilant eye on anyone attempting to enter premises as tightly restricted as Buckingham Palace.

'Sir Henry, Sir Stewart is waiting in the smoking room,' he whispered, taking Ridley's coat, the confidentiality of his tone indicating that if the porters of White's were not privy to the secrets of the gods, they were at least aware of their movements. Ridley nodded, glanced at the Reuters ticker tape and started to the lounge through a portrait gallery of White's Old Boys in their braided uniforms, muttonchops, wigs and gowns. One was of one of his own forebears, a lawyer who'd tried with conspicuous lack of success to keep Charles I from Cromwell's executioners. He was, Ridley liked to note, a reminder of the constancy of the Ridleys' allegiance to the Crown, if not the brilliance of their advocacy.

He found Sir Stewart settled in a dimly lit corner of the smoking room. An elderly waiter, silver tray in hand, appeared as he sat down.

'Brandy-and-soda,' he ordered, sinking into an armchair and savouring the reassuring richness of the room's air, redolent of old leather, old port and centuries of good Havana cigar smoke. The two men chatted aimlessly about birds and dogs until Ridley's drink had been served and the waiter had disappeared in the shadows. Then Sir Stewart began. 'Had a rather distressing ISOS earlier this evening,' he said.

There was an imperceptible but real shift in Ridley's level of attentiveness. 'ISOS' stood for 'Intelligence Service Oliver Strachey,' and it was the code name for the most secret of the intercepts of Germany's radio transmission made by England's *Ultra* code breakers. They were the intercepts of the Abwehr – German Intelligence – and Himmler's RSHA – the *Reichssicherheitshauptamt*, main office for national security. 'Old Canaris, it seems, has been given the sack. Put under some form of house arrest, actually.'

As they often were, Ridley's eyes were half closed, eyelids drooping like half-moons over his eyeballs. Most people mistook his look for drowsiness – which suited Ridley perfectly. It was at such moments that he was most intensely concentrated, and he was now concentrated on the face of his old friend.

'Himmler has taken over all his external operations and assigned them to Schellenberg.'

'I say!' Ridley's eyes had popped open in surprise. 'That is bad news. About the worst, I should have said, you could have given me.'

'Mmm,' his friend murmured, sipping at his brandy-and-soda, 'I'm afraid it is.'

Ridley leaned back in his leather armchair, thinking. His three most vital channels for passing the fragments of his *Fortitude* scheme to the Germans were a Pole, a Spaniard and a Yugoslav. All three were trusted agents of the Abwehr. All three were in reality double agents, operating under British control.

'I suppose the first thing Schellenberg will do is go over every single operation the Abwehr is running, looking for funnies.'

'I should have thought so,' Sir Stewart answered. 'He's a clever sod, and an ambitious bastard into the bargain. No doubt he's behind this. I'm sure he'd love to spot a few rotten apples and serve them up to Himmler on a silver platter, to justify what they've done.'

'You realize, of course, if they spot ours, *Fortitude* is blown, with all that implies.'

'I do indeed. You do, however, have some things working for you. Schellenberg is going to have to have some sources he can count on to form his estimates. It's rather late in the day, isn't it, for him to bring new assets into play? So most likely he'll have to decide to go with some of Canaris' assets. Let's hope that the ones he picks are yours.' Sir Stewart swirled his brandy-and-soda thoughtfully. 'At least you can feel certain those Abwehr controllers in Hamburg will do everything in their power to persuade Schellenberg your chaps are sound. If they don't, it's the first train east for them.'

'God,' Ridley sighed, 'this really is appalling.' He fell silent a moment, oppressed by his worries. 'You're right, of course. Our chaps may survive. The problem is I can't count on it, can I?' The lack of a reply confirmed Ridley's thought. 'You mentioned the fact it's a bit late in the day for them to bring a new asset into play.'

'I don't really see how, with the time left, they can.'

'Suppose we provide the asset for them? Open up a new channel, so to speak, one Himmler's new boys can proudly call their own?'

Menzies quietly mulled over the idea. 'That could be a good move. Provided, of course, you had the right asset.'

'You wouldn't have any buried treasures we might call on, by any chance? After all, there's rather a lot at stake here.'

The head of the Intelligence Service fell silent for a long interval, listlessly swirling the remains of his brandy-and-soda while his mind tripped through whatever inventory it was he was taking. Finally, he stirred in his armchair like one of White's elderly members coming out of an after-lunch siesta.

'Yes,' he said. 'Yes, I think I just might. Let me talk it over with my people and come back to you.'

'Handyman Three Four Oh-er. How now, please?'

Crammed into the folding wooden seat behind the pilot's cockpit, her precious and dangerous suitcase clutched between her knees, Catherine followed the pilot's conversation over her intercom. 'Steer three port' came the reply from the last British radar station following their flight, giving the pilot his final course correction before they disappeared over the landmass of Occupied France.

Peering out of her window, Catherine followed the grey of the Channel as it gradually yielded to the darker coastline of France. I'm coming home, she thought. I'm coming home at last. Baby Cadum poked her shoulder and pointed to the horizon far to the north. A shower of golden-yellow balls like a fireworks display on Bastille Day etched delicate patterns across the sky. 'Flak,' the pilot announced. 'Bomber Command must be off to visit their friends in the Ruhr.'

Catherine returned to her contemplation of the ground. It rolled past in a blue-grey mass, not so much as a single glimmer of light betraying the existence of the thousands of people who were living down there. Occasionally she could pick out the darker mass formed by a clump of woods from the countryside surrounding it. Her eyes saw the tree-lined traces of a *Route Nationale* bisecting the land with its geometric pattern, caught the occasional glint of a river's water reflecting the moonlight. She could pick out the intersections of sleeping towns. Once she spotted a train lumbering through the night, the pale plume of its smoke twisting behind it like a snake. To her amazement, she could even make out the orange glow of the engine's open boiler. She dozed, then suddenly felt the plane descending in a steep dive. Below her in the grey moonlight she recognized the seventeen round towers of Saint Louis's *château* of Angers.

'Right on time,' the pilot announced. 'We'll be picking up the Loire on the port side in a minute or two.'

She sat back, eyes closed, trying not to think. Beside her, Baby Cadum was sound asleep. For him, she thought, it must be like a bus ride. It was, she had learned, his third trip to Occupied France.

One hundred and sixty miles northeast of Catherine's Lysander, another plane droned steadily through the night towards another rendezvous, this one not far from the Norman city of Rouen. It was a Halifax bomber, and inside its cold, noisy fuselage Alex Wild felt the friendly hand of his RAF dispatcher on his shoulder.

'How about a nice warm cup of tea?' he asked. Gratefully, Wild took the chipped mug from the flight sergeant's hands and sipped the warm liquid. Like Catherine, Wild was an SOE radio operator. Like her, he had received his final instructions from Cavendish at Orchard Court a few hours before. Their paths had not crossed. Park, Cavendish's security-conscious butler, had seen to that. He was being 'inserted,' in SOE terminology, into Occupied France by a more conventional tactic, a parachute drop to a waiting Resistance reception committee. Lined up in the rear of the plane were the five chutes that would be going down after him, each one hooked to a six-foot-long metal tube packed with Sten guns, ammunition and plastic explosives for the Norman Resistance.

Flight Sergeant Cranston, the dispatcher, unbolted the metal cover of the bunghole in the bottom of the fuselage. Wild edged over and hung his feet into the hole. The green light over the pilot's door switched to red. 'Coming up shortly now,' Cranston announced. He took the ripcord of Wild's chute and hooked it to the static line overhead, then gave a sharp tug to the line so that Wild could see it was firmly secured.

Wild smiled. Flight Sergeant Cranston and that gesture of his were both fixtures in SOE legend. SOE Security, the legend went, had detected a German agent infiltrated into the organization's training schools in 1943. He was a Frenchman sent to England on the Gestapo's orders to penetrate the SOE. Rather than reveal their hand by arresting him, SOE Security had allowed him to complete his training and return to Occupied France – except that on the night of his drop, Flight Sergeant Cranston had conveniently neglected to hook his ripcord to the static line, and he had been returned to the soil of the nation he'd meant to betray in a 100-mile-an-hour free fall performed without the benefit of a parachute. Since that night, Cranston had reassured his departing agents with a visible demonstration of the solidity of the ties binding their parachute to the static line.

Wild watched the darkened earth rushing past below his feet. Suddenly, the red light over the pilot's door switched back to green. Cranston's arm dropped. 'Go!' he said, shouting to make himself heard over the roar of the aircraft's engines. His mind focused on what he'd been taught to do, Wild clamped his feet firmly together and pushed forward so that he dropped straight through the bunghole, bracing as he did to prevent himself from tumbling heels over head when he hit the slipstream.

It was over in seconds. The SOE dropped its agents at 500 feet; at that altitude it took barely twenty seconds to reach the ground. Wild rolled forward to cushion the jolt of landing and started to collapse his chute. He could hear the hoarse whispers of the members of his reception committee running towards him; then a pair of friendly hands were helping him to haul in the chute. A second Resistant a few feet away was already beginning to dig a hole in the pasture in which to bury Wild's coveralls and chute. Off in the distance, he could see shadowy figures racing through the night after the five arms containers.

They didn't exchange a word until Wild's equipment was safely buried. Then, panting slightly, the man who'd 'received' him pulled a flask from his pocket. 'Cognac?' he asked. 'Better than that piss they give you at Tempsford.' Wild smiled at the mention of the RAF base from which the Halifaxes flew and took a grateful belt of liquor. The second Resistant was already starting off across the pasture. 'We're going first class tonight,' the leader told Wild. 'We've got a car.'

'Christ, how did you manage that?'

'Old Bernard there' – the leader nodded towards the second Resistant – 'does the odd bit of black market as a cover. He talked the Germans into giving him an after-curfew *Ausweis*. You know how the Boche react – if you've got the right papers, you've got to be all right.' The car was in a glade, partially covered by the branches the two Resistants had chopped down to conceal it. 'Good run in?' the leader asked as they threw aside their improvised camouflage.

'Better than last time. I was dropped blind twenty miles off target.'

'You've been in before?'

'Yeah, I was down in Troyes last time.'

'Troyes? Were you with Hector?'

Wild nodded. 'I was his radio.'

'You're lucky to be alive,' the Resistance chief said, opening the back door of the car.

'I sure am. I left two days before they jumped him.'

The two men settled into the back seat while Bernard took the wheel. 'Get some sleep,' the leader said. 'You'll need it later. I'll wake you up when we get in.' Wild nodded, leaned against the panel of the rear door and quickly fell asleep.

'Tours coming up,' the pilot announced. 'We'll be landing shortly.'

Catherine tensed at his words and sat upright. Outside Tours, the pilot dropped down to 1,000 feet, running along the Cher River's southeasterly course, keeping well south of the riverbank to confuse any German patrols on the ground that might have picked up the sound of his engine. Just east of Azay-sur-Cher he spotted the vital landmark he was looking for, a six-stanchion bridge. To the northeast, an immense black mass, the Forest of Amboise, confirmed that he was right on target. Barely a minute later he overflew a second bridge, 5 kilometres upstream at Saint-Martin-le-Beau. He put the plane into a lazy, leftward bank, crossed the river, then turned back upstream. Ahead, Catherine could make out three lights shining upwards in the form of an L. It was the Lysander's clandestine landing pattern, a design first laid out on the tablecloth of a Soho spaghetti palace in 1942. Since then, that L-shaped lighting pattern had guided dozens of Lysander pilots to safe landings. A fourth flashlight blinked out the letter M in Morse code – the prearranged signal that the field was safe.

The pilot throttled back to 70 mph and the plane began to sink. It barely cleared a stand of poplar trees, then, with a crash and a jolt, hit the ground, bounced upwards and settled to earth. The flashlights rushed past in a blur. Catherine could feel the shudder of the brakes as the plane pivoted around in a semicircle and came to a halt. 'Out, quick,' the pilot ordered, sliding back the canopy.

Four figures were already running towards the plane. The first climbed up and pressed a bottle into the pilot's hand. ' 'Twenty-nine Lafite,' he said. 'For the boys in the mess.' He jumped down and then Baby Cadum climbed out. 'Goodbye and good luck,' the pilot said, helping Catherine through the hatch. 'Save me a dance the next time you're at the Four Hundred. You'll be in good hands with old Paul there,' he said, pointing to the Air Operations Officer who'd just passed him his 1929 Bordeaux. 'He was flying before he could walk.'

'Wait over there,' Paul ordered, pointing towards the clump of trees while he turned back to the plane. The two outgoing passengers climbed in, the pilot shut the canopy, Paul sprinted away from the fuselage and waved the pilot forward. The plane had been on the ground barely three minutes. In a roar of clanging metal and barking exhaust Catherine felt sure the Germans could hear all the way to Paris, it skidded away down the pasture, fighting to lift off the damp earth. Already, Baby Cadum and the second man were disappearing into the darkness. How strange, Catherine thought: we've lived this extraordinary adventure together, exchanged barely two words in six hours, and now there he goes off into the night.

Paul was running through the field turning off the flashlights and collecting the stakes that had marked the flare path. Catherine stood still, her eyes following the hum of the Lysander heading back to England and safety, clinging to its fading drone until gradually it became lost in the calls of the night birds, the soughing of the breeze and the distant bark of a farmer's dog.

Never in her life had Catherine felt so totally, utterly alone. To the left she could see the ground mist floating up from the Cher in silvered twists. The field was in the river's floodplain. Its annual winter flood made the plain an uninhabitable pasture; there was not a single building along the riverbank from Azay-sur-Cher to Saint-Martin. It also made it a perfect clandestine landing strip. Ahead of her was a grove of poplar trees, bare branches silhouetted in the moonlight. Dark rolls of *gui* – mistletoe – nestled eerily in the forks of those branches: *gui*, the sacred plant of the ancient Druids, cut once a year by the high priest to bring good fortune to his people. An omen? she wondered.

Paul, stakes in hand, came back, puffing slightly from exertion. He was a tall man, in his middle thirties probably, wearing an old tweed jacket and slacks. On his feet he had a pair of floppy rubber boots. 'Stay here,' he ordered. 'I'll be right back.' He picked up her suitcase and walked off into the darkness. Not much given to small talk, are you, Paul? Catherine thought, watching him go.

The heavy fall of his boots announced Paul's return. Wordlessly, he stalked over to where Catherine was standing, scooped her up in his arms and started to lug her like some helpless cripple across the field. 'What in hell are you doing?' she shrilled, kicking and squirming to protest his actions.

'Shut up. Voices carry at night,' was the only answer she got.

Fuming in silent rage, Catherine allowed him to carry her across the spongy pasture and over a wooden-plank footbridge spanning a drainage ditch to a dirt road, where he set her down. A pair of bicycles were waiting for them. Her suitcase was already strapped to the luggage rack of one of them.

'You ride?'

Catherine nodded.

'Some of them don't. Now listen: we have five kilometres to do. Into Saint-Martin, then out the D-38 to our safe house on the edge of the forest. Stick right behind me and do exactly as I do. We hear a car, we hide. It will be either a German or a black-marketeer. No one else is out after curfew.' Then he took off his rubber boots and put them under the footbridge. He opened the basket fixed to the handlebars of his bike and pulled out a dead rabbit, fresh blood and entrails oozing from its carcass. While Catherine watched in growing revulsion, he tied it to the top of her suitcase. 'Dinner. We were out poaching,' he said, flinging a leg over his bicycle seat.

The first thing that struck Catherine was how perfectly oiled Paul's bikes were. She could barely make out the whir of their wheels as they pedalled east along the dirt track. The only sound she could hear, somewhere far off in the darkness, was the reassuring tinkle of a cowbell. Overhead, drifting clouds sliced across the full moon that had brought her home, scattering their irregular patterns over the ground around her. She breathed deeply of the moist night air impregnated with the faintly rancid odour left behind by the winter floods. For one strange moment, she had a crazy desire to stop, to kneel and kiss that soil of her native land passing beneath the wheels of her bike. She thought of the newsreels she'd seen of the Spanish Republicans at the end of the Civil War marching off to exile in France with a clump of the lost soil of Spain in their fists. How ridiculous that gesture had seemed to her then; how natural it seemed now. Suddenly, the absurdity of what was happening to her struck home. She didn't know where she was. She didn't know where she was going. She didn't even know whom she was with. All she knew was that her life was now entirely committed to the hands of this surly stranger pedalling along in front of her on a darkened road in a corner of France as unfamiliar to her as the surface of the moon.

They approached a railroad crossing. Beyond it lay the asphalt of the highway. Paul got off his bike and poised tensely, listening to the noises of the night. With a sweep of his arm he pointed to a clump of trees just off the road. Crouched in their shadows, Catherine strained to hear the sound that had alerted him. Her ears didn't pick it up until the car was in front of them, a black Citroën, lights out, engine muffled, gliding slowly along the road like a cat stalking some unsuspecting prey.

'Bastards!' Paul whispered as it disappeared. 'They must have heard the plane. We're going to have to sit here and try to wait them out.'

In Paris, Avenue Foch lay muzzled in the silence of the night. Not a single vehicle rolled along the splendid boulevard that linked the Arc de Triomphe to the green maw of the Bois de Boulogne. Not a single passerby, however furtive, stole down the sidewalks of its celebrated contre-allée, the inner road separated from the boulevard it paralleled by a broad and verdant swath of lawn. Without exception, the imposing stone residences that lined the contre-allée, secure and stolid manifestations of France's bourgeoisie, were lifeless shadows.

Towards the foot of the Avenue, near the point where it joined the Porte Dauphine, the two buildings that gave it a contemporary notoriety were as quiet and as dark as the rest. It was not always so. Those two buildings, at numbers 82 and 84, housed the principal Paris headquarters of the Gestapo. They accounted for the Avenue's new nickname 'Avenue Boche' and the fact that their good bourgeois neighbours seldom slept easily. The Gestapo preferred to perform its savagery by night, as though somehow night's concealing shades might add a dimension of their own to the horror it sought to impose on its victims. Besides, a practical concern underlay the Gestapo's predilection for the evening hours: its victims' screams tended to disturb the buildings' secretaries when it tortured its prisoners by day. Better, the Gestapo's chieftains reasoned, to disturb their neighbours' sleep than their secretaries' labours.

In any event, the torture cells on the fifth floor of number 84 were empty on this March night. The only sound emanating from either building came from the steady, muffled footfalls of a pair of crocodile shoes marching over a purplish carpet in a fourth-floor office at number 84. SS *Obersturmbannführer* Hans-Dieter Strömelburg, the chief for France of Section IV, Counterespionage, of the *Sicherheitsdienst*, the

German security service, was a tense and excited man. He always was on nights such as this. Although he would never admit it, Strömelburg was a sadist. Not a crude sadist like some of his subordinates – Klaus Barbie in Lyon, for example, who took physical pleasure in helping the interrogators beat his prisoners, or vicious sadists like Otto Langenbach, of his Paris office, who seemed to enjoy forcing prisoners to death's threshold in the *baignoire*, the bathtub torture, or a perverted sexual sadist like the former French pimp Strömelburg employed to pull out women's fingernails or assault their nipples and genitalia with lighted cigarettes. No, Strömelburg was an intellectual sadist. He loved to dominate his prisoners intellectually, to sense the fear oozing from them as he hinted at the excruciating ordeals that awaited them. He particularly relished occasions like the one ahead – the first horrified moments when an agent realized he or she was in the hands of the Gestapo.

It was not that Strömelburg scrupled at the use of torture. He was a thoroughly practical, efficient man, and he had no hesitation in employing whatever means were required to achieve his ends. It was simply that like his ultimate employer, Heinrich Himmler, he detested the sight of blood. He preferred to hand his prisoners over to the thugs he kept for that purpose and return when they'd finished their work, ready to play the role of the saddened counsellor, chagrined by what had taken place, anxious to intervene on the prisoner's behalf the moment he indicated the slightest willingness to cooperate. It was a role he played with devastating effectiveness.

He rehearsed it now in the inner chambers of his mind as he paced his tastefully furnished office, its premises almost garishly lit by the huge crystal chandelier that dominated the room. There were, of course, the requisite photos of the Führer above the mantelpiece, the signed photographs of Himmler and Strömelburg's immediate superior in Berlin, *Obergruppenführer* Ernst Kaltenbrunner. They were no reflection, however, of the personality of the officer pacing his purple rug.

Those reflections were to be found in the objects Strömelburg himself had brought to this room: the pair of matched eighteenth-century Sèvres porcelain vases on the mantelpiece; three original pages of the manuscript of Bach's *Toccata in C Major*, Number 17, for organ; an early Juan Gris Cubist painting and, over his desk, a Chagall oil of the Russian countryside. The fact that Strömelburg dared to display so blatantly in his office the work of a Jewish artist was a measure of both his independent nature and his stature inside the hierarchy of the SS.

In an organization whose ranks swelled with petty hoodlums, barnyard bullies, bright but underprivileged and undereducated workers' sons, Strömelburg was an anomaly. He came from an upper-

59

middle-class family of intellectuals in Magdeburg, just outside Berlin, where his father was the principal of a *Gymnasium* – a German high school. His mother was a distinguished organist who had once longed to see her son follow in her footsteps.

In 1922, at the age of twenty-three, young Strömelburg had taken a doctorate in Romance languages at the University of Freiburg – an achievement that should have destined him for a brilliant academic career. Instead, in the turbulent Germany of the twenties, it destined him for hunger, unemployment and bitterness. The bitterness was directed at the Communists running rampant throughout southern Germany, for whom Strömelburg was symbolic of the class and values they were determined to destroy. In his rage and frustration, he turned to a new prophet emerging in Munich who laid Germany's ills at the doorstep of the Jews and the Communists, and promised a national redemption through work and discipline. Strömelburg became Nazi Party member number 207,341 and in 1925, through the agency of a fellow Nazi, was recruited into the Bavarian State Police as a criminal inspector, there to keep watch on the Party's foes and incidentally pursue the odd criminal.

It was an unlikely vocation for a young man who had seemed promised for a professor's chair at a distinguished university; yet Strömelburg thrived on it. Pursuing criminals became a kind of game of chess for him, an intellectual wrestling match in which his skill almost invariably allowed him to draw the truants he sought into his trap. His rise was rapid, paralleled by his equally rapid ascent in the hierarchy of the Nazi Party. He joined the SS in 1932, his file noting him as a solid Aryan type with some Slavic traits. He was described as 'extremely intelligent, energetic and remarkably industrious in the pursuit of an objective; a fanatic National Socialist endowed with a special loathing of the Communists; strong-willed and unrelenting in his specialized field of activity; a good comrade and a good leader with the potential of exercising high SS rank.' He was, in short, the ideal SS recruit.

His unusual background brought Strömelburg to the attention of Reinhard Heydrich, Himmler's ambitious, volatile deputy. Heydrich's mother, like Strömelburg's, had been a musician, in his case an opera singer. In a company of men whose musical tastes were largely limited to Bavarian beer-cellar ballads or a thumping rendition of the Horst Wessel song, their family backgrounds provided the two with a special link. Heydrich recruited Strömelburg for the *Sicherheitsdienst* – the SD – the élite security service at the core of the SS. He assigned him first to Amt VI, the SD's espionage branch, sending him to the Paris embassy as a police attaché. Ostensibly, he was to coordinate Franco-German police activities in the pursuit of international criminals. In fact, his assignment was to establish a network of secret agents Germany could activate when war came.

He performed his task brilliantly – too brilliantly in fact. In April 1938 his activities were discovered by the French and he was unceremoniously thrown out of the country by the secretary-general of the Ministry of the Interior. Just over two years later he got his revenge when, bearing Himmler's mandate to establish the Reich's security services in Occupied France, he'd marched into the Rue de Saussaies office of the man who'd expelled him and placed him under arrest. He'd been in Paris ever since, presiding over 2,400 Gestapo officers, an army of informers and an irregular police force made up in almost equal number of former cops and criminals he'd sprung from France's jails. He even kept a small team of Corsican gunmen in an apartment not far from Avenue Foch to handle murders that might be too embarrassing or troublesome for the Gestapo.

Technically, Strömelburg was, on this March evening, the third-ranking SS official in France, after *Brigadeführer* Karl Oberg, a bullet-headed bureaucrat scorned by Berlin as an inept paper pusher, and Dr Helmut Knochen, the Gestapo's token sophisticate, sent to Paris to give the SS a kind of social *cachet* – as though such a thing were possible. In fact, as everyone knew, Strömelburg was Himmler's French representative, a man whose orders could be questioned only by officers as senior as Rommel and Von Rundstedt.

Just how vital he was in the SS hierarchy had been demonstrated only forty-eight hours earlier, when he'd been summoned to Prinz-Albrecht-Strasse for a meeting with Himmler. 'The discovery of the precise date and place of the Allied landing has become the overriding objective of the German Secret Services working in the West,' the SS *Reichsführer* had informed him.

There was a compelling urgency in Himmler's tone. For years Himmler had been scheming to grasp control of the Reich's foreign intelligence services from Admiral Wilhelm Canaris' Abwehr – Military Intelligence; to make himself the undisputed ruler of all of Germany's security services. His own vaulting ambition was behind that obsession, of course; but it was also buttressed by the growing conviction that the Abwehr had been penetrated by the Allies and was fomenting anti-Nazi resistance inside Germany.

To advance his cause, Himmler had regularly and personally laid before Hitler juicy tidbits of SD intelligence, some of it strategic, much of it salacious: photos of Berlin orgies of anti-Nazi aristocrats, accounts of the compromising sexual peccadillos of neutral diplomats. During the past six months, the ineptitude of the Abwehr in Italy had finally won the day for Himmler. The *Reichsführer*, however, was highly sceptical of the

61

value of the network of spies he'd inherited from Canaris. His real hopes of piercing the greatest secret of the war lay, he was sure, inside Section IV, Counterespionage, of his own organization and most particularly in Strömelburg's organization in the country where the Allies were certain to land – France.

His confidence had not been misplaced. Locked into the safe of the man pacing his office on Avenue Foch was a folder so secret only four men – Strömelburg; Kaltenbrunner; his deputy, Horst Kopkow, and Himmler were aware of its contents. It bore the few details Strömelburg had been prepared to commit to paper about the most valued secret agent in his employ. The agent's code name was 'Gilbert.' Strömelburg's contacts with him went all the way back to the summer of 1938, when the German had sent him to France to build a network of agents for the Reich. The destinies of war and his own adventuresome schemings had brought Gilbert to a position of critical importance inside one of the Allies' most secret agencies. He served as a kind of human roundhouse through which its most vital movements flowed. For almost a year, Strömelburg had stood guard over Gilbert's activities, making certain no untimely arrest could betray his real function to the Allies, patiently nurturing them against the supreme moment when Gilbert's operation would almost certainly reveal the location and the date of the Allied landing.

Gilbert had also been the source of a regular and critical flow into Strömelburg's hands of intelligence thanks to which – and quite unknown to Gilbert – Strömelburg had been able to set into motion a trap into which the Allies were tumbling with accelerating speed. It was an intelligence scheme of such diabolical cleverness that its harvest might ultimately prove of even greater value than that promised by Gilbert's operation.

There was a knock on the door. *Rottenführer* Müller entered with a silver pot of coffee. Strömelburg wanted the office permeated with its rich, reassuring aroma when his 'guest' arrived. He glanced at his watch. They should be here at any moment. He settled into his desk chair, an immensely contented man. He had prepared for the coming encounter, as he usually did, by following a well-established ritual guaranteed to put him in the best of moods.

First had been a visit to Saint-Sulpice to hear Marcel Dupré play vespers on the church's magnificent eighteenth-century organ. Strömelburg thrilled at the genius in Dupré's fingers. He loved to sit there in Saint-Sulpice, transported by the thundering, vaulting cadences of the great organ to a world less troubled than the one he inhabited. His next stop, at an apartment on Avenue Marceau, was designed to provide exaltation of a substantially different nature.

Among Strömelburg's hirelings was a Montmartre pimp named Pierre Villon whose task it had been to groom the best of his girls for service with certain German staff officers reputed to have too loose a tongue in pre- and postcoital conversation. The result of their efforts had been to provide Germany's Eastern Front armies with a steady stream of officer recruits. Occasionally, Strömelburg himself, acting *ex officio*, employed the services of Villon's ladies. He was, at forty-two, still a bachelor – a fact that could easily be misconstrued in an organization in which homosexuality was a rampant, if carefully concealed, practice. In fact, Strömelburg simply disdained women. The overriding trait of his character was vanity; it led him to regard women as slightly inferior, if desirable, beings whose primary function was as vessels for his pleasure.

This evening's vessel had been a sloe-eyed girl nicknamed Dodo. She had an unruly swarm of bright red hair, a tall, lean body and an air of repressed savagery which greatly appealed to Strömelburg. After a glass of champagne and a chat she'd retired to her bedroom, where, in response to the German's fancies, she'd changed into black silk lingerie: bra, panties, garter belt, long black hose. Strömelburg had quite literally pounced on her, ripped away the silk lingerie and taken her from behind with a frantic, frenzied fury. Immensely satisfied, he'd gone on to dine at his favourite black-market restaurant before taking up his vigil on Avenue Foch.

He sat up. He'd just heard the car glide down the driveway into the interior courtyard. A few minutes later he heard the courtyard gate snap shut, then the sound of footsteps advancing up his darkened staircase. There was a soft rap on the door.

'Come in,' he commanded.

Alex Wind staggered in utter disbelief as he stepped into the glare of Strömelburg's office. For a second, the man who just an hour earlier had dropped out of a Halifax bomber seemed about to faint from shock. Strömelburg got up and graciously waved him to the chair in front of his desk. Wild looked uncomprehendingly at the two Resistance fighters who had received him. They were both Alsatians, members of one of Strömelburg's commandos, and each now had a Walther pistol trained on Wild's rib cage.

Reeling, Wild plunged to the chair and, his head in his hands, collapsed in grief and shock. Strömelburg came around from behind his desk. 'It's true,' he murmured. 'You're in the hands of the Gestapo, Avenue Foch. I'm sorry.' He made it sound as if he meant it.

'You played a game,' he said, snapping open a silver cigarette case and extending it to his prisoner who accepted a cigarette with a trembling hand. 'A good game, but unfortunately one you lost.' Strömelburg noticed one of the Alsatians beckoning to him. He snapped his fingers at

Müller. 'Offer the gentleman a cup of coffee,' he ordered, and walked out of earshot with the Alsatian.

'He's a radio operator,' the Alsatian whispered. 'He was working for Hector in Troyes until two months ago.'

Strömelburg clasped the Alsatian's shoulders. He could not believe his good fortune. 'He's just what I want,' he whispered. 'Go get the Doctor as fast as you can.'

They had been hiding in the shadows for almost an hour before Paul finally signalled Catherine to get on her bike and follow him down the highway. Ahead, the village of Saint-Martin-le-Beau was sound asleep. Not even a candle's glow lit its primeval darkness. Catherine wanted to laugh. If you had any doubt you were in France, Saint-Martin-le-Beau would reassure you. This was the eternal France of a thousand lost villages, impervious to the tides of change and the centuries – and Germanic invaders.

Its main street ran straight to its square and the resolutely Gothic outlines of the village church. The houses seemed to grow straight out of the sidewalk, tilting ever so gently over the road like the sloping walls of a tunnel. Most were built of mud mortar over stone. Time and tempest had gnawed away the mud until now in the pale moonlight uncovered ribs of stone pushed through the dark façades as if they were the bones of a half-exposed skeleton. Every window, every door along the street was tightly shuttered, wooden barriers firmly set against the regard of the world and the miseries of Catherine's occupied homeland. Ahead of her, Paul turned right in the middle of the village. Half lost in her thoughts, Catherine followed.

That was when she saw they had been caught. A Wehrmacht truck blocked their way forward. Half a dozen soldiers, weapons drawn, stood around in the shadows. One already had a flashlight's beam focused on Paul's face, a machine pistol on his stomach. Catherine felt the blood rush from her head. For an instant, she thought fright was about to tumble her from her bike. Then a second German waved her to a stop beside Paul.

Paul was already talking intensely, boisterously almost, to the German in front of him. He jerked his head towards her. The German's flashlight followed his gesture. Catherine blinked in its bright glare. Beyond its glow she could see the German peering curiously at her, his stolid face framed by the terrifyingly familiar outlines of his Wehrmacht helmet. An incongruous thought struck her: he was the first German soldier she had ever seen, the first enemy she had looked in the eyes. He made a sound that seemed half laugh, half grunt and turned his flashlight's beam back to Paul's papers in his hand. He passed them to Paul and turned to her.

'*Papier.*'

Catherine fumbled in her sack for the ID card Cavendish had pressed on her barely six hours before. Her mouth was warm with fear as she pulled out the cardboard folder and tendered it to the German.

The German hardly looked at the card. He glanced at her photo, then up at her face. Leering slightly, he returned the card. '*Sehr gut,*' he said standing aside. '*In Ordnung!*'

It was at that instant that Catherine heard the car door slam. She turned. There, immediately behind them, was the black Citroën. Two civilians in leather overcoats that fell below their knees were walking towards them. '*Ein Moment,*' one said. They advanced with a pace so slow, so deliberate Catherine began to tremble. The first one took the flashlight from the soldier's hand and shined it on Paul's feet.

'Your shoes,' he commanded.

Catherine glanced at Paul. The bantering cockiness with which he'd treated the soldier was gone. His attitude identified their new inquisitors for her as surely as if she had seen a sign around their necks reading 'Gestapo.' Obediently, Paul took off his shoes and passed them to the German. Slowly, calmly, the German scrutinized them, turning them from side to side in the light as though he were a factory inspector hunting some defect in a worker's craftsmanship. Wordlessly he returned them to Paul. His light fell on Catherine's feet.

'Madame.'

She bent down, undid her shoes and handed them over. The German subjected them to the same searching examination he'd given Paul's. 'Your papers, please,' he said, returning her shoes.

For the second time, Catherine reached into her bag for Cavendish's counterfeit ID card. This German studied it with the care of a diamond merchant appraising a rare stone. He held it up to his light, twisted it upside down, right and left. He studied her photograph, then fixed her in the beam of his flashlight as though trying to engrave the image of her face on his memory. 'Now, madame' – his voice was soft with understated menace – 'perhaps you'll be good enough to explain to me just what it is you're doing wandering around the countryside of Saint-Martin-le-Beau at two o'clock in the morning when your ID card says you live in Calais?'

Catherine's mind had seized up with fear. She felt a bead of sweat dribbling down her backbone. Instinctively, spontaneously, in response probably to the hysteria gripping her, she began to laugh. Her laughter was deep and husky and in the circumstances, surprisingly sensual. Struggling to stop, she noticed the eyes of the German staring at her from under the brim of his hat. They were dull, penetrating and, it seemed to

Catherine, slightly perplexed by her outburst. They also offered the only escape she could think of.

'Monsieur,' she said, her laughter subsiding to a giggle, 'surely you understand there is only one thing in the world that could get a woman like me to this ghastly, godforsaken place.' Her gaze went to Paul. She offered him what she hoped was the warmest, most passionate smile a woman had ever bestowed on a man. 'It's utterly, entirely his fault. And it's also his fault if he has to sneak me around this horrible village like a criminal after curfew so all the gossiping old crones who live here won't tell his wife what's going on.' Catherine gave a barely perceptible toss of her head, her gesture calculated to send a ripple through her blond hair. She tendered the German a conspiratorial smile. 'Couldn't you help me get him to Calais? To work on your famous Atlantic Wall? I promise you I'll see that he gets to work on time. And stays home at night, too.'

'I'm sure you would, madame.' To Catherine's amazement, the German was actually smiling. He looked back at her ID card.

'You're from Oran, I see.'

'Yes.'

'I knew North Africa before the war. I lived in Algiers, selling radios for Siemens. What a lovely city Oran was. I used to love the café – what was it? – the Foch, I think – on the Place de la République where everyone used to go for an *apéritif* in the evening. Do you know it? Is it still there?'

'Ah, I left Oran when I was five. My father was in the navy. He was transferred to Indochina.'

'The navy? Where is he now?'

'He's dead. He was killed at Mers el-Kébir.'

At the mention of Mers el-Kébir a distinct change came over the German. 'British swine,' he said. 'What a terrible thing they did.' He passed her back her ID card and started to step back to wave them ahead. As he did, his flashlight beam fell on her suitcase with its transmitter hidden inside, strapped to the rear of the bike. He took half a step forward, then froze, a suggestion of disgust on his face as he eyed the mangled carcass of the rabbit. A jerk of his flashlight waved them on.

Behind them, the Gestapo agent watched quizzically as they rode off. 'Beautiful thing, isn't she?' he mumbled to his aide. 'I've never been near Oran in my life. Have you?'

PARIS

'Just look at this weapon!' Hans-Dieter Strömelburg exulted. He was waving one of the Sten guns that had come tumbling to earth into his trap

66

along with Alex Wild. 'It's the best machine gun we've ever seen. So primitive, so unpolished – even welded in places! What German workman could ever make something so crude as this? And yet' – the Gestapo chieftain began to swing the gun towards Wild as though mowing down an advancing mob – 'this ugly little thing will fire and fire and fire long after those refined and polished guns of ours have jammed.'

He placed the Sten on the table. 'Two regiments,' he declared. 'Two entire regiments of the Wehrmacht I have equipped with this gun thanks to your dear Major Cavendish.' He picked up a loaf of plastic explosive and tossed it in the air. 'And this. Marvellous stuff! Our troops mix it with a sticky tar and use it against tanks.' He laughed. 'If your Russian allies ever discover how many T-34 tanks they've lost to Major Cavendish's plastic, they'll want to march on London, not Berlin.'

His humour was wasted on Wild. The British agent was slumped in his chair struggling against the grip of depression that had overcome him the instant he'd heard the word 'Gestapo' and seen the portrait of Adolf Hitler on the wall. Obviously he'd been betrayed. But how? By whom?

The German sensed his hopelessness. This one, Strömelburg gloated silently, wasn't going to be hard. He was leaning against the edge of his desk, his six-foot frame towering over the wiry radio operator. 'You may not believe me, but it makes me furious too the way they drop you into a trap like that.' He offered Wild another cigarette and lit it with an elegant flick of his gold Dunhill lighter, like the Sten a product of British workmanship he much admired.

'You're a British officer, I know that. All Cavendish's agents are. I'm a German officer, so there is a bond between us. But I must speak to you very, very frankly. Cavendish has sent you here in violation of all the rules of the war. In civilian clothes. As a spy. To stir terrorism behind our lines. I don't have to tell you what the accepted penalty for that is, do I?'

Wild gave a little shrug of his head as though to indicate to his captor how total was his despair. In fact, he was barely listening to Strömelburg's words. He didn't have to; the German's speech was almost a word-for-word rendition of the one he had been trained to recognize in the event of such an unhappy occasion in the SOE's security school.

'You know as fellow soldiers we have to admire a man who gives his life on the battlefield, for his fatherland, for a cause. But to give away your life' – the German hesitated, searching for the tone that would convey the utter absurdity of it all – 'for some stupid, desk-bound fool in London who drops you into a trap?'

He circled around his desk and opened his centre drawer. 'They think at Orchard Court we're such bungling, heavy-handed oafs, all brutality and no brains. Have a look at this.' He pushed a chart across his desktop towards Wild. It was an organizational chart of SOE's London headquarters. This time the expression of horror and disbelief on the Englishman's face was genuine. The chart had been assembled with stunning accuracy, right down to the position of Park, the butler. 'Makes one think doesn't it?'

Wild looked at Strömelburg. 'It rather inclines me to vomit. Obviously we've got a traitor in our midst.'

A smile of coolest satisfaction lightened Strömelburg's dour regard. 'Obviously. My friend,' he continued, his voice as gently caressing as a woman's touch, 'on Avenue Foch, I cannot promise heaven. You know what happens here. I'm sure our reputation reached down to Troyes. I can promise you only one thing: your life. Our camps in Germany are not health spas, but they are not firing ranges either. You will survive. Then, at least, when this war is over, you may be able to find out who did this to you. And why.'

A knock on the door interrupted him. 'The Doctor's here,' Müller announced.

Strömelburg hesitated. Perhaps it would be just as well to let this one marinate a bit, stew in the juices of his own despair while he consulted with the Doctor.

'Think about it for a while. Some perfectly frightful things happen in this building. We don't want to have to get into that, you and I. Müller,' he ordered, 'get Mr Wild some more coffee and see if he'd like something to eat, while I talk with the Doctor.'

In the hallway, Strömelburg turned to an SS guard. 'Turn on the heater,' he ordered.

The 'heater' was a record, made, for the sake of dramatic realism, during a brutal torture session on the fifth floor. Strömelburg had discovered that heard from a distance in circumstances such as Wild's, it had a particularly salutary effect on a prisoner's disposition. And he thought, entering an office on the next floor, the record would spare Müller a trip to the kitchen. Listening to it was certainly going to ruin the Englishman's appetite.

The 'Doctor' was waiting for him standing by his desk. He was ten years Strömelburg's junior and, like Strömelburg, had taken a doctorate in Romance languages before the war. That accounted for both his nickname and his function on Avenue Foch.

'We have a file on him,' the man announced proudly. 'Everything we need is at the Boulevard Suchet. They've even broken his code.'

'Bravo!' Strömelburg murmured. He took the green file card from the Doctor's hand and glanced over the information it contained. Its gleanings represented just a slender share of the harvest Strömelburg had reaped from the trap he'd erected thanks to Gilbert. The trap was in fact a kind of game, a deadly little game called a *Funklspiel* – a radio game. Its object was to seize control of the one critical channel of communication SOE in London had to have to run its agents in the field, a clandestine radio transmitter. Ideally, while the radio's operator lay in a grave or languished in a cell in Fresnes Prison, Strömelburg and the Doctor performed his functions for him from this office on Avenue Foch. They made up his messages; wrote his reports; selected targets for his network's sabotage actions – even, on occasion, carried them out; chose the remote farmers' fields on which his imaginary agents could receive parachute drops of arms and ammunition.

When London swallowed the bait, believing that the operator running the set really was the SOE agent Cavendish had sent into the field, the harvest for the Gestapo was prodigious. Each radio successfully played back became a mirror into the heart of SOE operations, revealing to Strömelburg Cavendish's strategy, his tactics, his organization's objectives. The messages that flowed back from a trusting London led the Gestapo to new, undetected SOE agents, to networks of whose existence they had been unaware, to safe houses and letterboxes London assumed were secure.

Above all, the game had opened up to the Gestapo an unbelievable cornucopia of arms, ammunition and money. Since January, a veritable rainstorm of weaponry had come pouring out of the night-time skies of France straight into the arms of the Gestapo's Alsatian commandos manning the fields indicated to London by Avenue Foch. Strömelburg had indeed sent whole trainloads of Cavendish's captured SOE arms off to Berlin and the Eastern Front. His exchequer had received twenty-three million francs in the last three months – more than enough to underwrite the entire operating budget of Avenue Foch, to pay the salaries of every French traitor and collaborator Strömelburg employed to pursue the French Resistance. SOE London had even on one recent occasion messaged Strömelburg the licence-plate numbers of the vans employed by his radio detection service in Paris. A grateful Strömelburg had promptly changed them all.

All that had grown from an ordinary Michelin road map of the Sarthe which Gilbert had delivered to Strömelburg one day. Holding it up to the light, he'd discovered a pinprick whose coordinates corresponded to those in a message also supplied by Gilbert. Strömelburg had placed the field indicated by the pinprick under surveillance. Five weeks later, his patience was rewarded when a pair of SOE agents dropped onto the field. Trailed to Paris, they were arrested just as one of them had finished transmitting to London the original, clear text of the coded message still resting by his transmitter.

This auspicious beginning Strömelburg and the Doctor had nurtured with care. How well they had succeeded was summed up in one set of figures. The SOE that March evening was running just under fifty clandestine radio transmitters on French soil. Six of them, representing fifteen fictitious or decapitated Resistance networks, were in fact in the hands of the Gestapo.

Strömelburg digested the information on the Doctor's green card in seconds. He acknowledged it with the smile he bestowed on his young assistant. 'I think we'd better get over to the Boulevard Suchet right away. I want to see everything we have on him.'

The two Germans ran down the stairs to Strömelburg's car, a pre-war Skoda sports car appropriated from a family of Czech Jews and kept in perfect condition by his driver, a former racer with the Mercedes-Benz team. As they slipped through the dark, empty streets, Strömelburg leaned back in the front seat, smoking nervously, contemplating all the ramifications of the arrest in his office of the radio operator.

'What has happened tonight, Doctor,' he declared, letting two pale ribbons of smoke twist from his nostrils, 'is the most important thing that has happened to us since we started this game. Do you know why?'

The Doctor obediently shook his head. His employer, he realized, was not even vaguely interested in any reply he might make.

'Because tonight, for the first time, we are certain – one hundred per cent certain – that we have fooled them.

'There is one thing I'm absolutely sure of. Neither Cavendish nor the British would ever knowingly drop an agent – and particularly a British agent – into a German trap. To do something like that would be against everything we know of the British character. Arms, perhaps. Money, certainly. But an English agent? Never. Therefore we now know that the radio we used to set up his drop tonight is one hundred per cent sure.'

Strömelburg took a long, thoughtful draw on his cigarette. 'Did you study Kipling at Tübingen, Doctor?'

'Yes,' the Doctor replied. 'But I preferred E.M. Forster. I always thought –'

Strömelburg cut him off with a wave of his hand. 'I am not interested in discussing Anglo-Indian literature. I'm interested in winning the war. Do you remember how the British used to hunt tigers in India?'

'They would tether a goat to a stake at night near the tiger's water hole. Then they'd sit up in their hunting blinds waiting for him to take the bait.'

'Exactly. Those radios are going to be our tethered goats, Doctor. We are going to use them to draw the British out of the forests of the night.' Strömelburg, pleased with how apt his metaphor appeared, gave an exuberant wave of his hand. 'Why do you suppose Cavendish and the

SOE have been showering arms on us for the past three months? Not to ambush five Wehrmacht trucks in the Dordogne. Every time they make a drop they tell us to hide the arms and wait for orders, don't they? It's because they're preparing for the invasion. Those networks we're operating are all relatively close to the coastline, aren't they?'

'There's one in Brest and five in the north. The rest are around Rouen, Le Mans, Chartres.'

'Close enough. They'll want to use them to disrupt our communications, to try to keep us from getting reinforcements to the beaches when they land. But first they've got to assign each group its target. And then they've got to find a way to tell each group when to strike. And it's got to be a very precise, very swift, absolutely infallible technique. It's got to be one they can use at the very last moment, when their invasion fleet's already sailed. Now, how did London arrange this parachute drop with us tonight? We picked a field and radioed its location to them, didn't we? The RAF checked it out and they radioed back that the field was acceptable. We asked for a drop; we gave them the letter our team on the ground would flash to tell them the field was clear. Then they gave us that BBC message "The lights are on in Piccadilly." Listen every night, they said, and when you hear the message, your plane is on the way. At nine o'clock tonight, they broadcast the message. Three hours later, their Halifax is over our field dropping us arms.'

Strömelburg was as excited now as he had been hours before listening to the vaulting echoes of the organ shaking the tenebrous precincts of Saint-Sulpice. 'That, my dear Doctor, is exactly what they will do for the invasion. The tiger is going to walk right up and whisper his secret into the ear of our tethered goats. The British themselves are going to tell us when they're coming – and they're going to do it over the BBC.'

By the time they reached the Boulevard Suchet, Strömelburg was so excited he leaped from the Skoda before it had stopped and started across its inner courtyard at a trot. The courtyard was crowded with a bizarre assortment of trucks: dairy trucks, wine tankers, moving vans, delivery trucks, painted in the colours of Paris' great department stores the Bazar de l'Hôtel de Ville and Au Printemps. Most had torpedolike tubes fixed to their roofs or strapped with metal braces to their rear ends, indicating they ran on gases generated by burning wood or charcoal rather than gasoline, now almost unobtainable in Paris. Each, however, had a disclike ring affixed to some part of its roof. They were the nemesis of every clandestine radio operator in France, the Gestapo's terrifyingly effective radio detection vans. Strömelburg burst past a startled Wehrmacht guard into a brightly lit room from which the vans were controlled. Two dozen Wehrmacht signalmen, headsets clamped to their ears, lined both sides of the room, each prowling an assigned set of radio

71

frequencies in search of clandestine transmissions. Strömelburg marched by them into the office of the *Hauptsturmführer* who served as the intercept station's night-time duty officer.

'*Herr Hauptsturmführer*,' he ordered, 'I want you to bring me everything you've got on AKD right away.' The officer turned to a huge mahogany cabinet behind his desk. Those three critical letters, AKD, had been the call sign, the identity card of Wild's radio set in Troyes. Every radio London sent into the field had one. London used it to call up an operator's broadcasts, or to inform him the message about to be aired was his. For the operator, it was the tag which opened all his messages, the handle which allowed the SOE's receiving station to pluck his transmission from the garbage of military communications littering Europe's wartime ether. And in order to avoid any possibility of an error, the call sign was always the one part of a message that was broadcast in the clear, the constant and continuing hallmark of a clandestine transmitter.

It was an admirable and efficient system; but if it served the SOE well, their German foes had equal cause to be satisfied with it. Those same letters allowed the Boulevard Suchet to hang an ID tag of its own onto every clandestine transmission it was able to pick out of the airwaves.

The *Hauptsturmführer* took a bound folder from his cabinet, unwrapped the ribbon enclosing it and arranged its contents with Teutonic precision on his desk. 'He operated around Troyes,' he began.'Our first identified intercept was at 2313, August 27,1943. The last we show was 1907, January 23 this year. Our detection vans pinned him down to the triangle Maison Neuve–Brienne-le-Château–Dhuys. He seemed to employ several locations inside that area, probably isolated farmhouses. We tried to narrow the area with power cuts, but failed – undoubtedly because he was using a battery instead of the current, which is very irregular in those rural areas anyway. His set transmitted on 6693, 7587, 8237, 8377 and 8510 kilocycles. He transmitted every third day, coming on the air four hours after the conclusion of his last broadcast. We intercepted a total of forty-three broadcasts during the time we had him on the air.' The *Hauptsturmführer* glanced up at Strömelburg, just a suggestion of smugness creasing his pudgy face as he paused for breath.

'His first fifteen transmissions and all subsequent transmissions were forwarded to the Cryptographic Department of the Radio Intelligence Section in Berlin on October 3 last. They broke his code on November 16.' The *Hauptsturmführer* picked up a sheaf of papers among those he'd neatly arranged. 'All the decrypts are here. We have a trained stand-in. That's about all. Oh yes. His code phrase was apparently ' "O Captain! my Captain! our fearful trip is done." '

The *Hauptsturmführer* set down the papers from which he'd been reading and slumped back into his high armchair, anticipating a commendation for a job whose thoroughness should have impressed even a Gestapo officer. He got a grunt and a question instead: 'Where's the stand-in?'

The *Hauptsturmführer* consulted a roster. 'He's on duty out in the hall.'

'Go get him.'

The *Hauptsturmführer* returned trailing a middle-aged, bespectacled corporal, ashen with concern at being summoned into the presence of a senior Gestapo officer. 'How well can you imitate AKD?' Strömelburg demanded.

His question went to the heart of one of the Boulevard Suchet's most secret functions, an aspect of its work SOE London didn't even begin to suspect. Every radio operator had his own way of tapping out his messages on his sending key. It was called his 'fist,' a relatively unique signature whose continuing presence was an assurance to the SOE that the operator transmitting over a given radio was really its agent. From the moment he'd first envisaged setting a radio game into play, Strömelburg had ruled out forcing captured agents to transmit for him. The risk that one would slip in a give-away sign in the midst of a transmission was too great. His answer was here. Every clandestine broadcast intercepted by the Boulevard Suchet was recorded. As each radio was identified by its call sign, it was assigned a German radio operator. The German spent hours detecting and learning to imitate each idiosyncrasy of that unknown operator's 'fist' so that if the operator was arrested he could instantly step in and take his place without London's realizing what had happened. Alex Wild's German counterpart, considerably more intimidated by Strömelburg than the original, assured him that until he'd stopped imitating Wild in favour of an active operator, he had achieved a fair mastery of the Englishman's fist.

'Start practising again,' Strömelburg ordered. 'You may be going on the air soon. Pick that stuff up,' he ordered the Doctor, indicating Wild's file. 'It's time for a little talk with our Englishman.'

Strömelburg's headlong rush up the stairway of Avenue Foch towards his office was halted by an aide beckoning frantically to him from a door at the third-floor landing. Inside, ranged on a series of tables, were the contents of Wild's suitcase, each item meticulously ripped apart. Among his possessions was a tube of toothpaste, its contents squeezed out, its butt end sliced open with a razor. The aide reached for two squares of silk similar to those Cavendish had given Catherine in Orchard Court. 'We found this in there.'

Strömelburg picked them up. The first consisted of six columns of blocks of letters, five letters in each block. Along its base were the words 'Out Station to Home Station.' The print was so small that even squinting, he could barely make it out. There must have been at least five hundred blocks on the cloth. The second was headed by a row of the letters of the alphabet. Under each letter was another letter, these an apparently random list. He handed the cloths to the Doctor.

'What do you make of this?'

The Doctor squinted at the first cloth. 'They always use five-letter blocks in their messages. It must be some kind of new coding device they're using.'.

'You must be right.' Strömelburg agreed. 'But how the hell do they use it?'

'They begin with those blocks, obviously,' the Doctor said. 'And look here.' He pointed to the second cloth, across which ran the alphabet printed horizontally. 'Somehow they must use that alphabet as a key.'

'Well,' Strömelburg replied, carefully folding the swatch of silk into his pocket, 'I know who's going to explain the puzzle to us.'

A good interrogator, Strömelburg had learned during his police days, was a man of many parts. For the moment, the part he chose to play with Wild remained that of the reluctant captor, solicitous of his prisoner's well-being, just a touch embarrassed by the ease with which he'd fallen into their trap. Wild, however, was not totally deceived by his dissembling; he had experienced a queasy twinge on seeing two hulks in civilian clothes slip into the room behind Strömelburg. Were they, he wondered, the torturers who had been driving some poor prisoner mad upstairs?

Strömelburg carefully arranged some papers on his desk, punctuating his actions with a few offhand remarks to Wild and snatches of a Schubert *Lied* he hummed to himself.

'Well,' he finally announced with the air of an Oxford don about to review a term paper, 'just a few questions and then we can all get off to sleep. You were in Troyes, yes?'

Wild nodded.

'With Hector, poor chap.'

Again the Englishman nodded.

'Now, what was the code phrase you employed for your transmissions while you were there?'

' "One wise man's verdict outweighs all the fools",' Wild, an early admirer of Robert Browning, answered. Later, in his cell, trying to reconstruct the scene, Wild would try, unsuccessfully, to remember the gesture or sign from Strömelburg that had started it. Silently and without his noticing it, the two hulks had moved up behind his chair. The first blow smashed the left side of his head under the ear, driving his neck against the chair and sending a searing pain through his skull. The second shattered his nose, unleashing a fine spray of blood into the air. It seemed to hang there, for just an instant, like a red cloud before his eyes. Then the third and worst blow struck, across the ridge of his mouth, just below his nostrils, splitting his lip apart and snapping one of his front teeth from the hinge of its roots. Wild shrieked as an agony so intense it transpierced his being overwhelmed him. It came from the tooth's severed nerve. Strömelburg was towering over him, his face contorted in rage.

'Fool!' he shouted. 'Stupid English fool! How dare you lie to me? How dare you? You know what your code phrase was? I'll tell you: "O Captain! my Captain! our fearful trip is done".'

The German wheeled and grabbed a sheaf of papers from his desk. 'Look, look at these,' he shouted shoving the papers into Wild's bloody face. 'Every damn message you ever sent, we have. Every one. You don't believe me? December 13.' Strömelburg's fingers ripped through the papers. 'You want to know what you told London December 13? I'll tell you.'

Through the red filter of pain filling his being, Wild heard the German read out word for word the text of a transmission he recognized instantly as one of his own. Desperately he tried to prevent himself from slipping towards the despair to which his feeling of helplessness was thrusting him.

'Are you going to use the same phrase in Lille?'

Wild gasped. He was of course unaware of the fact that London had inadvertently given Strömelburg his destination over the Doctor's turned radio on which the Germans had arranged his drop. 'Yes,' he mumbled. 'Yes.'

The blows started again, this time to his body, culminating in one final, terrible truncheon blow to his groin.

'You damned idiot! Don't you ever learn?'

Through his filming vision of tears and pain Wild saw the German reach out into his pocket and whip out a piece of cloth. They'd found his coding silks and onetime pad. 'This is your code,' he hissed. 'You're using Cavendish's new system in Lille.'

His two torturers had pulled his arms down behind him so that he was pinned immobile to his chair, and the German's face was so close to Wild's a spray of spittle covered his bruises. 'Why are you dicking around with me?' Strömelburg screeched. 'I know more about the SOE than you do. I know Cavendish authorizes you to give up your code. Are you going to give it to me now or after I've let these two turn you into hamburger?'

Wild gave a kind of half-whimper. Far more than the pain, it was this German's knowledge that overwhelmed him. He was right. They were authorized to give up their code under torture. Had he suffered enough of a martyrdom? 'All right, all right,' he murmured.

Strömelburg gestured to the men to release him. Wild reached for the silks with an aching arm. 'It's simple. This one' – he indicated the silk covered with five blocks – 'is your pad. You write your message out in clear in five-letter blocks as always. Then you set the first message block under the first five-letter block on the pad, starting with the first one in the upper left-hand corner. If your message block is NOWIS, you pick out the letter right above the N. Say it's X. Then you go to the coding silk with the alphabet running along the top.'

Strömelburg took back the silk and studied it.

'The first letter of your real message is N.'

Strömelburg nodded.

'You find the N. Under it you've got two parallel lines of letters. Go down the first one until you find the letter in your code block, the X.'

'I have.'

'Now, opposite it, there's another letter.'

'It's an S.'

'That's the letter you transmit. That's how it works – just like that.'

'But how does London read it?'

'They have an exact replica of the silk. All they do is work backwards. You destroy each line of letter blocks on the silk after you've used them. The idea is never use them twice.'

Strömelburg looked at the thin swatch of material crumpled in his hand. He was hardly an expert on coding, but it was clear to him that the English had come up with a system all the cryptographers assembled in Berlin would never break. Trying to conceal his amazement, he looked back at Wild. 'When were you supposed to broadcast first?'

'At one today.'

The German exulted inwardly. He was on the verge of adding another priceless radio to his game. He had a stand-in for Wild, he had his code, the time he was first due to come up. He needed just one more thing – one last, precious key – and he could turn Wild's set against London. He looked at the Englishman slumped in his chair. The most difficult revelation for a prisoner to make was always the first one. He had started Mr Wild on the way.

'Look,' he said as nonchalantly as he could. 'I want one last thing and then you can go. I promise you. What,' he asked, 'is your security check?'

The 'security check' was the SOE's ultimate proof of a transmission's authenticity, a secret covenant between London and an operator in the field which guaranteed that the transmission was not being made under German control.

Wild groaned and slumped into his chair visibly wrestling with the ultimate dilemma of a captured agent, tottering on the terrible knife-edge between pain and revelation. The two torturers moved towards him, but Strömelburg knew better. He waved them off and gave Wild's battered head a gentle caress. 'Look,' he sighed, 'let's not get into this again.'

'Thirty-six,' Wild whimpered. 'It's a thirty-six between the third and fourth letter blocks.'

Strömelburg shot the Doctor, standing in a corner of the room, a triumphant glare. 'All right,' he said to the two men. 'Take him upstairs.'

Catherine Pradier's eyes feasted on the countryside rolling slowly past the windows of her train: so green, so rich, so miraculously untouched, it seemed, by five years of war. She almost wanted to sing out, 'France! France!' as the familiar yet half-forgotten sights swept past: a group of schoolchildren in their grey smocks, briefcases full of books hitched to their shoulders, waiting at the barriers of a grade crossing; the *chefs de gare*, swelling with self-importance in their ridiculous caps, whistling their train on its way. Are you still cuckolded, *Monsieur le Chef de Gare*, she thought half-laughing, as you were in the song we used to sing? She saw the wizened old men of France slouching off to work in their faded blue denims, the peasant couples side by side in their fields, hacking their living from their sacred earth. After England, in which every turn in the road brought its reminder of the war, France seemed so eerily at peace. A curious thought struck her: But the cows? Where were the cows? She realized she'd been looking out at the countryside for half an hour and hadn't seen a single cow. Of course: they must have been slaughtered, all of them, on German orders to nourish the insatiable appetites of the Wehrmacht.

Catherine returned her gaze to her jammed compartment. If the countryside was at peace, the war was in here, writ upon the dour, depressed faces of her fellow passengers. How drab, how shabby they were, all bundled up in layers of sweaters and coats. No French chic here. Above all, it was the total lack of animation in their faces that struck her. Gone was their boisterous, argumentative, vivacious Gallic spirit. Imagine, she thought. I've been in this compartment for over two hours and no one has said a single word. Can I really be in France?

She sighed and took a deep breath. The compartment's stale air reeked of sweat, onions, old wine and, above all, the pungent odour of garlic. No, she reassured herself as she smelled it, there's been no mistake. I'm in the right country, all right. She glanced into the corridor beyond her compartment. It was jammed with weary passengers clinging to the bar that ran along the windows. Stacks of luggage at their feet littered the passageway.

She gave a quick, reassuring glance to the cluttered luggage rack above her head. There, in bold defiance of Cavendish's orders, was her battered suitcase with her transmitter hidden inside. It had been a deliberate decision on her part. My whole reason for being here is inside that suitcase, she'd told herself. Without it, I'm useless.

At that instant, Paul's familiar figure picked its way past the passengers in the corridor, a rolled-up newspaper clutched in his left hand. She waited three or four minutes, then beckoned to a young woman, a whimpering young child entwined in her legs.

'Would you like to use my seat for a while?'

'Oh, yes!' replied the grateful girl, almost collapsing into her place while Catherine set off in pursuit of Paul.

He was in the dining car, reading his paper. The place opposite him was empty. 'Mademoiselle,' he said, 'may I offer you a seat?'

'Why, thank you,' Catherine replied, demurely slipping into the chair. She glanced around the car and trembled slightly. At least half the diners were in German uniform. She leaned towards Paul. 'How did you do it?'

Paul rubbed his thumb against his forefinger. 'Some things don't change.'

Catherine studied him carefully. You may be a surly chap when you're going about your business, Paul, she thought, but you are a rather attractive man. He was tall for a Frenchman, and rather broad as well. Good bloodlines, Catherine thought. Although, she noticed, his hands would argue against that. They were short and stubby, hands made to plunge into dirt or grease, not to grace a salon. He had thick auburn hair and a mischievous half-smile that for some reason he couldn't keep off his face. Everything about him seemed to radiate an air of poise, of self-assurance. Everything, that was, except his eyes. They were soft and brown, russet almost, sunken into sockets set with unusual depth into his skull. A kind of quiet sadness seemed to emanate from them, the melancholy air of a man who has looked out upon more misery and suffering than he might care to acknowledge.

He was notably well dressed. His tweed sports jacket must have come from the Faubourg Saint-Honoré before the war. He had a patterned foulard, English probably, around his neck and was wearing an off-white shirt and grey flannel slacks. A provincial landowner's son, she told herself, or some minor noble whose ancestors had managed to escape the guillotine.

'You're very elegant,' she said admiringly.

'For a reason. The better dressed you are, the more prosperous you look, the more likely it is' – he made an almost imperceptible motion of his head – 'you'll be taken for one of them. A collaborator or a black-marketeer.' He tapped the newspaper he'd been reading. It was the notorious collaborationist weekly *Je Suis Partout* – 'I Am Everywhere.' 'I always carry one of these to read. It reassures those bastards of the *milice* when they're running an identity check.'

The waiter set a plate of boiled lentils in front of each of them. He leaned towards Paul, whom he evidently knew. 'I've got a little rabbit pâté I can give you,' he whispered.

Paul nodded his approval. As the waiter left, he bent towards Catherine. 'Let me tell you again how good you were last night. You not only saved your neck, you saved mine too.'

She smiled. 'It worked – there's that to be grateful for. Although somehow, Paul, I don't see you pushing around a wheelbarrow full of cement up in Calais.'

'Better there than Dachau.'

As the waiter returned with their pâté, the train wheezed to a stop in open country. Paul looked up at him. 'What's going on? It's the third time we've stopped in an hour.' The waiter leaned down so the Germans across the aisle couldn't hear him. 'The RAF plastered the shit out of the marshalling yards in Amiens last night. Nothing's going north out of Paris, and the way in is all jammed up.'

'Nothing up to Lille or Calais?'

'Nothing.' The waiter could barely conceal his delight. 'Anybody who wants to get up there for the next two or three days better enjoy walking.'

'You have a problem,' said Paul as the waiter strolled away. 'Did they give you a safe house in Paris?'

She shook her head.

'Of course not. They wouldn't think of that.' He chewed his pâté silently for a minute. 'You understand we're supposed to have nothing to do with each other. You're supposed to know nothing about me and I'm supposed to know nothing about you. And I wouldn't even know where you're going if it hadn't been for that roadblock last night.'

Catherine nodded. 'We went to the same schools, remember?'

'Have you got anywhere safe to hide out in Paris?'

'None I can think of.'

'Do you know the city?'

'Yes.'

'At least there's that.' Paul sighed in evident distaste. 'Okay. Exactly two hours to the minute after we pass through the ticket barrier at the Gare Montparnasse, meet me on the terrace of the Brasserie Lorraine in the Place des Ternes. I'll be reading a copy of *Je Suis Partout* as a sign everything's okay. If I'm not reading it or if I'm not there, you're on your own. Avoid hotels. Your best bet is to try to bribe your way into a *maison de passe*. Have you got enough money?'

Catherine indicated she had. Paul leaned forward. 'The tricky moment is when we arrive. The Gestapo meets these trains the way the hotel hustlers used to meet them before the war. You'll be behind me. Try to see if I'm being followed. Look out for males, kind of sharply dressed, without baggage. Watch out for anybody who rides a train these days without baggage. If you see anybody like that tailing me, don't go near the brasserie.' The train lurched forward again as the waiter delivered their bill. Paul pushed his newspaper across the table to her. 'Take this. A little light reading may take your mind off your troubles.'

The composition of her compartment, Catherine noted, had changed. The place of the elderly couple opposite her had been taken by a pair of uniformed Germans. One of them, an uncharacteristically dark man, smiled at her as she sat down. Remembering Paul's words, she gave him just a suggestion of a smile in return, then plunged into her newspaper. It certainly justified Paul's parting comment. The front page was covered with an article on contemporary French justice. Her compatriots, she was pleased to note, were killing one another much less frequently these days for reasons of the heart. Of course, she thought, they've found better reasons to kill one another.

Catherine had drifted off to sleep when they finally reached the Gare Montparnasse. As she stretched towards her suitcase, she felt a presence behind her. 'Mademoiselle?' It was the dark German. 'May I?' He took her suitcase and lifted it out of the rack with a grunt. '*Mein Gott*, that's heavy. You must have a machine gun in there.'

'Not one,' Catherine replied with a laugh – 'three of them!'

A cloud sped across the German's face. The nuances of French humour were not to his taste; but his gallantry was equal to the occasion. 'May I carry them for you?'

She hesitated just an instant. 'That would be very kind of you.'

Starting down the crowded platform, she placed herself between the two Germans. Far ahead she could see Paul's tall figure easing through the crowd. No one seemed to be following him. From the corner of her eye she appraised the uniforms of her escorts. The one with the bag was an officer. They both wore standard Wehrmacht grey-green, but their uniforms were trimmed in gold rather than the usual silver. An artillery shell between a pair of golden wings was woven into their shoulder flashes. It was not, Catherine was sure, a flash she'd studied in her courses in England. At the ticket barrier, she started to reach into her bag for her ticket. 'She's with us,' the German with her suitcase curtly informed the frail ticket collector. The Frenchman bestowed a look of purest hatred on Catherine, then waved them ahead.

'Where are you going?' the German asked.

'I'm taking the *métro*,' Catherine answered, hoping he wasn't.

80

The German carried her suitcase to the *métro* entrance. 'Perhaps we could meet for a drink tonight?' he asked.

'Oh, thank you, I'm just passing through on my way up to Calais. I have to spend the evening with relatives.'

'Calais?' The German brightened at the word. 'We're stationed just outside Sangatte. Can't we meet up there? Where do you live?'

Catherine wanted to shriek out in fury. The name Sangatte meant nothing to her, but obviously it was near Calais. Why, for Christ's sake, didn't I say Reims or Lille? Flustered, she was starting to stammer until her well-memorized orders, the only association she had with Calais, emerged from her unconscious. 'My home, it's difficult . . . But often in the evening I go to the Café des Trois Suisses for an *apéritif*. Perhaps we'll see each other there one night?'

The German clicked his heels lightly, bowed and touched his fingers to his uniform cap. 'Les Trois Suisses. I know it well. I hope so, mademoiselle.'

Catherine picked up her suitcase and hurried down the steps to the *métro*. With each stride she cursed her stupidity and fought back the tears of anger and frustration watering her eyes. Ahead, the heavy green *métro* gate was starting to close. She squeezed through it onto the waiting train. Bitterly, she watched the station disappear, thinking, as she did: my first test – and I've failed.

Jackie Moore sat down before her receiving set at the SOE's secret radio station just outside the crossroads village of Sevenoaks in Kent and fixed a set of earphones to her head. It was exactly 12:30 A.M. Like most of the other girls manning radio sets in the receiving room, Jackie was a FANY – a volunteer – and a young lady of impeccable breeding. She was also, in SOE parlance, the 'godmother' of Alex Wild, the girl assigned to monitor his transmissions since his first drop into Occupied France. Neither flu, nor fever, nor the importuning of any number of beaux had kept Jackie from being present at Sevenoaks on every occasion during the past two years when Wild was scheduled to transmit. She had never met Wild: to have done so would have been against SOE's stringent security regulations. Yet she bore him an affection as tender, as deep in its way as the affection she felt for the young lieutenant in the Guards Armoured Brigade with whom she'd danced until dawn in London's 400 Club.

She adjusted her radio to the wavelength, 8350, on which Wild was due to transmit, oscillating its dial on either side of the band in case his call should come slightly off beam. At one o'clock, as faithful as the chimes of Big Ben, the familiar letters AKD came flashing across the airwaves to tell her he was there somewhere in Occupied France about to transmit. As her fingers began their ritual dance across the pages of her note pad recording his bursts of Morse code, a special sense of relief filled the young girl. Her ward, she knew, had just been parachuted back into Occupied France; clearly he'd arrived safely at whatever destination was his. His message finished, Jackie started to convert her Morse jottings into their coded text. The code, of course, meant nothing to her. Her tie to the faceless ward with whom she felt such a bond was in the idiosyncrasies of his transmitting fist, a Morse voiceprint as familiar to her as her father's stern voice.

Suddenly, Jackie froze. Wild, she knew, had been sent into the field with a new kind of security check. Aware that the Gestapo had discovered the workings of the security-check system, the SOE had evolved a new, more subtle system. It involved a double check. Agents were now sent out with not one, but two checks. Under torture, they were instructed to reveal to the Gestapo the security check the Germans demanded. Its presence in a message without the confirming second check would tell London a set was being operated under German control. Wild's first check, a 36 between his third and fourth letter blocks, was present. The second confirming check, an 18 between the fourth and fifth blocks, was missing.

For a moment, Jackie wanted to weep. Had Wild been caught? There had been absolutely nothing in his transmission, no unfamiliar note, to indicate that the man at the receiver was anybody but Wild. Perhaps, she assured herself, it was just an error. Wild, excited by his successful return to the field, had simply forgotten the second check. This was, after all, the first time he'd used the new and unfamiliar system. In any case, that judgement was not hers to make. She noted both the absence of the second check and the fact that in all other aspects the transmission was normal on her receiving sheet. Then she hand-carried it to the Decoding Officer. He in turn passed the decoded text to a London-bound despatch rider. Written in large red letters on its envelope was a three-word warning. It destined the text inside not to Cavendish but to SOE Security, a coterie of high-ranking intelligence officers whose task was to safeguard the security of all SOE operations from Warsaw to Athens.

'Security check missing,' it read.

Paul was there, just as he said he would be, apparently engrossed in his *Je Suis Partout*. He stood as she drew up and, to her surprise, swept her into his arms. He held her body tightly against his for a moment, then kissed her warmly.

'My angel,' he exclaimed loudly enough for all around to hear. 'It's been so long!'

'Much too long, *chéri*,' Catherine answered. Her voice dropped to a soft giggle reserved for Paul's ears. 'All of two hours, wasn't it?' She paused, then added, 'There was no one following you that I could see.'

Paul helped her into a chair and snuggled close to her, playfully nudging her cheek with his nose. He looped his arm around her back, drawing her head into the cradle of his shoulders.

'What did you do?' he whispered.

'Rode the *métro*.'

'With that?' Paul glanced at the suitcase at her feet. 'I hope there's nothing in it that can compromise you. Didn't they tell you in London never to ride the *métro* if you're hot? The Germans love to run their spot checks in those long corridors. They've got you trapped. If you try to turn around and get out it's a dead giveaway. Never, never take the *métro* if you've got something to hide.'

He beckoned to the waiter. 'Two Banyuls,' he ordered, 'My God, I'd almost forgotten how beautiful you are!' he exclaimed loudly again as he turned back to her. He leaned forward and gave her another long, sensual kiss. As he drew back, a mischievous smile was spread wide across his face. You may be acting out a little charade, Paul, Catherine thought, but you seem to be enjoying every minute of it. He leaned close to her again, letting his fingertips dance along the nape of her neck just below her earlobes. And so am I, she told herself.

'I've got two safe apartments, but unfortunately they're full,' he whispered.

'It doesn't matter. I can sleep on a chair or the floor.'

'That's not the problem. It's security. You shouldn't meet the people in them and they shouldn't meet you. Hotels are out; there's a Gestapo team at the Prefecture of Police that studies hotel registration cards every night. London thinks they're so clever with those North African birthplaces. They don't want to understand that the Gestapo tumbled on to that one eighteen months ago. When they see an Oran birthplace and a Calais residence, they may get curious. Anything that touches Calais gets them stirred up. If you were a man, we could let His Majesty's Government treat you to a couple of days rutting around the whorehouses. They're as safe as any place can be these days.' He shrugged his shoulders. As he was saying all this he had been looking into her eyes, a shy smile on his lips – for anyone troubling to watch them, a man very much in love with a lovely blonde girl. 'Our best bet is an *hôtel de passe*. I know one down in Saint-Germain. The woman who runs it never bothers with ID. She has ties to the underworld. Trades the cops a bit of information every now and then for peace and quiet.'

He's so intense, the people at the next table must think he's quoting Baudelaire or proposing marriage to me, Catherine thought.

'If a place like that gets raided it'll almost certainly be by the vice squad, ordinary *flics* with the frying-pan hats. No trouble from those guys.'

Paul settled back and sipped his drink, obviously pleased with his scheme. Catherine disentangled herself from his embrace and gave the relative stranger with whom she was evidently going to be spending a night or two an appraising stare. Well, *ma fille*, she told herself, it could be worse; it could be a great deal worse.

'We'll slip her a few francs. Let on we're off on a little tear while the wife's away.'

'How nice.' Catherine smiled.

Paul laughed and reached for her suitcase. He had set down change for their drinks, Catherine had noticed, as soon as the waiter placed them on their table. That precaution she recognized from her own training in England. Always pay as soon as you're served so you can leave in an instant if you have to without attracting attention.

Paul beckoned to a bicycle taxi from the line waiting in the square. The cyclist, some poor Parisian struggling to keep a family alive, had to strain like a Chinese coolie to get them up Avenue de Wagram to the Etoile.

Then they rounded the Etoile and started to roll down the Champs-Elysées. Catherine gasped. With the exception of a couple of German staff cars, the great avenue was empty. How wide, how handsome it seemed. And how unbelievably silent. A warm spring sun burnished the scene; the leaves of the chestnut trees were already out. Studying them, Catherine noticed how green, how soft they were, so unlike the greyish prewar leaves she remembered, withering almost as quickly as they unfolded under the impact of the exhaust fumes rising off the boulevard. 'It's unbelievable, Paul,' she whispered. 'Paris has never, never been so beautiful.'

'If you can pretend all those uniforms on the sidewalk aren't really there, yes it is.'

Catherine pondered the swarm of German soldiers strolling up the beloved avenue. It felt so wonderful to be back in Paris in this soft, silent spring. Nobody, not even those hordes, could take that away from her. 'All right' – she smiled – 'let's pretend.'

At Berchtesgaden the field marshals, the conference completed, had returned to their commands. Their place at the centre of the Führer's attention had been taken by Lieutenant General Hiroshi Baron Oshima, Japan's ambassador to Germany.

The incongruous character of the Japanese ambassador was a source of unending amusement to Hitler's entourage. He was an ardent Nazi who, out of a sense of admiration for his Prussian hosts, affected a monocle, a studied scowl and what he hoped was a rigorous martial bearing. None of these affectations came easily to the poor fellow. He resembled nothing quite so much as a dog-eared old Teddy bear left to moulder in a closet by an owner emerging from puberty. His uniforms usually looked as though he'd been sleeping in them for a week, and he had all the martial bearing of a melting ice cream cone. Oshima was in fact anything but the opaque, inscrutable Oriental of popular mythology. He was charming and outgoing – something which in itself set him apart from the vast majority of his countrymen. A jovial, boisterous man, he liked nothing better than staying up all night with Hitler's aides, gulping down shot after shot of Alsatian *eau de vie* and roaring out student *Lieder* to which he knew all the words. The sight of the rumpled little baron belting out 'Am Brunnen von dem Tore' in his lisping Japanese accent never failed to delight the Führer's staff.

For all that, he was a shrewd military observer who enjoyed Hitler's full confidence. Oshima was the only Japanese who never told the Führer anything besides banalities, and Hitler reciprocated by being particularly candid with him in their frequent conversations. He had toured the Western Front from the Skagerrak to the Spanish frontier, studied the Atlantic Wall in detail and depth and summarized everything he'd learned for Tokyo in voluminous reports. With his knack for sensing when conversations of importance were taking place, he'd arrived in Berchtesgaden in the field marshals' wake. His visit was brief and businesslike: a night drinking with Hitler's aides, a chat with the Führer, then back to Berlin by plane. As soon as he returned, he sat down to prepare a detailed account of what had been said at the field marshals' dinner. Oshima was as verbose on paper as he was in conversation; the report ran to two thousand words.

When he'd finished, he took it to the air-raid shelter under the ruins of his embassy. There he kept the two most precious possessions left to his embassy. The first was the imperial portrait of the Emperor, an oil painting which, in view of the Emperor's quasi-divine status, had the aura of a sacred icon. The second was a black machine bearing a vague resemblance to a typewriter. It was the Japanese Foreign Ministry's Type 97 coding machine, the most modern and impenetrable device of its kind in the world. Oshima adjusted the machine's complex settings and began to convert his message into coded blocks of five letters each. Since the Japanese language with its five thousand scroll characters was ill adapted to modern cryptography, the machine used Latin characters that represented Japanese words phonetically.

When Oshima had finished, he gave his text to a messenger, who delivered it to the offices of the Telefunken Cable Company. Like Japanese diplomats around the world, Oshima employed the regular commercial cable facilities of his host country to send his coded dispatches to Tokyo. From Berlin, Oshima's dispatch would be sent by landline to Königswusterhausen, where the Telefunken transmitters, capable of thrusting out one of the strongest directional signal beams in the world, were installed. By the time the ambassador was ready to sit down for his first drink of the evening in the Adlon Bar, the first words of his report would already be booming out into the ether en route to Tokyo via Istanbul and Bandung.

PARIS

The hotel was in a narrow alley called Rue de l'Echaudé, just a few steps from the Boulevard Saint-Germain. A shiny black plaque bearing the words 'Hôtel-Pension' marked the door. Its proprietress was ensconced in a cagelike room, strategically placed to guard the passage from the front door to the stairs. As they entered, Catherine noticed her swiftly – and silently – hang up the switchboard telephone to which she'd been listening with rapt attention. Eavesdropping on a client's call; out of boredom, I hope, Catherine thought.

'Monsieur, madame?' The proprietress' brown eyes appraised them coolly, calculating, no doubt, how much she could charge for a room from the elegance of their dress and seeking to detect how intense was their desire to get upstairs and into their coupling.

'We'd like a room.' Paul declared.

'Of course, mes chéris. Your name?'

'Dupont.'

Catherine looked down, marvelling at the seriousness with which the woman recorded the name in the register on her desk. She was a wonderfully blowsy creature, great, sloping breasts straining against her orchid satin blouse, the twisting tufts of her yellow-grey hair whitened with an occasional splash of peroxide. Two perfectly circular stains of rouge marked her cheeks, and glistening gashes of lipstick outlined her mouth in what could at best be described as a highly approximative manner.

'What time will you be leaving?' she asked, studying the keys that

86

dangled from the pigeonholes lining one wall of her office as though somehow the dimensions of their accommodation would be dependent on the staying power of their ardour.

Paul leaned forward, a wad of franc notes in his hand. 'We'd like to stay a while. My wife just left for the country for a couple of days. It's our first chance to spend some time –'

'But of course, *mes enfants*,' she interrupted, the enthusiasm in her voice reflecting the high esteem in which, with good reason, she held the practice of adultery. 'Young people like you, these terrible times. One must live while one can, *n'est–ce pas?*' The francs, meanwhile, had disappeared with a flash into the ample canyon of her bosom. 'Let's see if I can find a nice room for you.'

She contemplated the key rack with all the seriousness the occasion seemed to merit. Picked out a key and, a tiny poodle yapping at her heels, set off up the staircase. 'Napoléon, shut up,' she growled at the dog while she clomped up the stairs with the determined stride of an Alpine guide.

The stairwell reeked of old wax. Generations of illicit lovers' furtive steps had worn an indentation into each of the staircase's wooden steps, Catherine noted, and the metal railing swayed to the slightest touch. At the first floor, the proprietress unlocked a door and threw it open with the prideful sweep of an assistant manager of the Ritz showing a young couple into the hotel's bridal suite. The room contained a double bed, its mattress sagging on springs shattered from overuse, and a chair. In one corner, a faded cloth dangling from a brass rail waited to screen a washbasin and a portable bidet on a wooden stand. Well, Catherine thought, it's functional. '*Chéri*,' she exclaimed, squeezing Paul's hand, 'how lovely!'

The proprietress beamed and gestured to the window with its uninterrupted view onto the alley just below. 'You'll be nice and quiet here.' she said, bestowing on them a smile of infinite understanding. She started for the door. As she did, Catherine heard a shrill feminine voice ringing out in the room next door. 'Are you crazy?' it shrieked. 'You think I'm going to take off all my clothes for fifty francs?' The proprietress, untroubled, paused. 'You know,' she said, 'I have just the thing for you two downstairs. Some champagne, Veuve Cliquot 1934. From my late husband's own cellar.' She made a hasty sign of the Cross in memory of the Dear Departed.

'How nice,' Paul said. 'I'm sure we'd love a bottle.'

She closed the door and waddled off to get it. Catherine sat down on the bed and started to laugh.

'At least, Paul, we're with family here.'

He looked at her quizzically.

'Everyone else who's signed into the register's a Dupont too.'

Three thousand miles from the bomb-battered Nazi capital of Berlin, on a barren, windswept ridge 8,000 feet above the Red Sea in the former Italian colony of Eritrea, an alarm bell went off with a resounding screech. That bell was hooked up to an SCR–44 radio receiver. The receiver's antennae was in turn locked onto the frequency employed by Telefunken's Berlin transmitter. Every time the German transmitter went on the air, that alarm rang.

Hearing it, a technical sergeant of Charlie Company, Second Signal Service Battalion, US Army Signal Corps hit a switch that activated a large reel of paper tape which, like the alarm, was hooked to a radio receiver fixed to Berlin's frequency. Its dancing needle began to transcribe the flow of Morse code dots and dashes pouring out of Berlin much as an electrocardiograph records the impulses of a beating heart. The sergeant fixed a set of earphones to his head so he could monitor the machine's output, scanning as he did the addresses of the stream of messages heading to the Far East from Berlin. For the sergeant and his fellows, 99 per cent of the traffic they copied was garbage: orders for bank transfers, reports of a fishery's haul or the hallmarks of life's passage – a birth in Hanover, a death under Allied bombs in Berlin. Suddenly, he tensed. The dots and dashes streaming across the paper tape were beginning to take on the familiar configuration of the one part of Oshima's cables that was always transmitted in the clear: the address *Gaimu Dai Jim* – Foreign Office Big Man.

'We've got him!' he shouted. 'He's coming on line.'

Those words galvanized the tiny intercept station into action. It was solely to perform the vital task of intercepting Oshima's communications with Tokyo that the sergeant and his 250 fellow GIs had been stationed in the monsoon-battered heights of Asmara since the summer of 1943. The cliff on which Asmara perched rose with such sudden swiftness from the seafloor behind the port of Massawa, 8,000 feet below, that it was a natural antenna ideally situated to intercept Berlin's signal as it rolled into and out of its Istanbul relay station. The city itself was a godforsaken place where women paraded about with horse-tail flyswatters to drive off the swarms of insects clotting the air with the density of grit in a sandstorm. Laughing hyenas prowled outside the signal company's barracks by night; by day barefoot Eritrean nomads scrounged the dusty hills for a few scraps of firewood. Yet inside, in an installation so secret its address was 'somewhere in Africa,' a handful of American technicians performed one of the most vital intelligence tasks of the war. The harvest of their intercept station had been prodigious, and never had it been so critical to the Allied war effort as it was in this springtime of 1944.

At the sergeant's shout, three more tape machines were set to record the flow of Oshima's report, two catching it coming onto the Istanbul relay, two more picking it up again as it came back out of Istanbul en route to Bandung. The station's cigar-chewing commander, Colonel Charlie Cotter, a Bell Telephone executive in Michigan before the war, oversaw the operation. Noting the unusual length of the ambassador's transmission, he told his executive officer, 'We'll red-ball this one.'

The intercepts of Oshima's text would be on their way to Washington before their author had finished his first drink in the Adlon Bar.

PARIS

Paul couldn't take his eyes off her; nor, he noticed, could anyone else in the crowded room. A few tables away, a Luftwaffe colonel was almost toppling from his chair so impatient was he to get a better view of her passing figure. Her movements conveyed a sense of grace, of concealed strength – the result, no doubt, of all those morning runs through the Scottish moors, the hours of calisthenics performed under the barked imprecations of Cavendish's PT instructors. Her blond hair had been carefully combed out in the ladies' room so that now it tumbled to her shoulders in a golden spray. She'd slept in a hayloft in that dark suit of hers, travelled halfway across France in a packed train, yet to Paul she seemed as striking, as poised as a model showing off Maggy Rouff's clothes at Longchamps on a Sunday afternoon. She could also, as Paul well knew from his own training in the SOE's special schools, kill any man in the room with her bare hands if she had to.

'You know, you really are breathtaking,' he murmured as she eased herself back into her chair with lithe grace. 'Whatever got into old Cavendish? He has a reputation for avoiding beautiful women.'

'What got into old Cavendish' – Catherine hesitated just a moment – 'was an imperious need for piano players.'

Ah, thought Paul, registering the expression, that's why her suitcase was so heavy. They're sending Aristide a second radio. Why, he wondered, would they do that? Something to do with the invasion probably.

'How are things at Orchard Court? Everybody got invasion fever?'

'Racked with it. Worrying about where, when, will it work?'

Paul's becomingly evil smile flashed across his face like a streak of summer lightning. 'Not half as much as most of our fellow diners

89

tonight, I'll bet.' His eyes pointed Catherine to a round table in the corner to their right. A florid man, heavy face glistening with sweat, presided over a group of younger men in unfamiliar uniforms. 'Philippe Henri Pacquet. He's been telling us what a great chap Hitler is over Radio Paris for the last three years.'

'What are those uniforms?'

'LVF – Légion des Volontaires Français: the ones who were going to march off to Smolensk to save us all from Bolshevism – remember? One would have thought their digestion was a little troubled these days. A few nagging doubts that maybe, just maybe, they chose the wrong side back where our German friends were marching down the Champs-Elysées singing to us about how they were going to sail to England.'

Paul turned his attention to a more engaging sight, the tiny menu card the waiter had just placed on his plate. Catherine, too, picked up hers and studied it with ill-concealed wonder. Some of those cows so conspicuously missing from the French countryside had evidently been diverted into the refrigerator of this little black-market restaurant on their journey to Berlin and the Eastern Front. She leaned towards Paul. 'Do you realize' – there was just a touch of the disapproving schoolmistress in her tone – 'you couldn't eat a dinner like this anywhere in all of London tonight?'

'Tonight?' Clearly the notion of an association between the English capital and good food in even the best of circumstances was wholly foreign to Paul. 'You never could.'

'Paul, tell me something.' Their swift and seemingly effortless passage through the drab dining room of the Chapon Rouge into this secluded back room still puzzled Catherine. 'How do you get into a place like this?'

'Getting into a black-market restaurant is never a problem,' Paul said, laughing. 'The problem is having enough money to eat out. I have a simple philosophy about these things. If I'm going to wind up in front of a German firing squad on Mont Valérien, I'd rather not do it on an empty stomach.'

The owner, in shirt sleeves and a white apron, walked up to their table. He urged them to have baby spring lamb roasted in rosemary and thyme, with a cheese soufflé to start. Paul nodded in appreciative understanding of his counsel. 'That Vosne-Romanée 1934,' he inquired – 'do you still have a bottle in the *cave*?' As the owner left in search of it, he turned back to Catherine. 'It's a bit like travelling first class on the trains. The Germans tolerate places like this. Look around. Half the customers are Germans. So the Gestapo tends to let them alone. They've got their eyes on the workers' canteens down at the Place de la République.'

Catherine appraised the occupants of the back room's dozen tables. If it was the working class the Germans were after, the Chapon Rouge did not, it was true, hold out many prospects for them. Apart from the waiters – sallow-faced, resentful little creatures obviously not being fed from the back-room kitchens – and the women – give them credit, she thought, for being here in working hours – there was not a French person in the place she could imagine working up a sweat from anything besides fear or indigestion.

The owner returned with their Vosne-Romanée. Paul swirled it carefully in his glass, allowing it just the proper amount of air before tentatively inhaling its bouquet, then bestowing an approving nod at the bottle the owner had thrust before him. Paul raised his glass. 'What shall we drink to, Madame Dupont? Good health? Absent friends? Your success?'

Catherine touched the balloon of her glass to his. 'How about the lead bombardier in the RAF raid on Amiens last night?'

Her words were jarred by a sudden commotion. They both turned to see one of the LVF volunteers toppling to the floor in a drunken stupor. His efforts to clamber back onto his feet had a pathetic, Chaplinesque quality to them due, in part, to the alcohol befuddling his mind but also to something neither Catherine nor Paul had noticed in his precipitous plunge to the floor; the right sleeve of his uniform jacket was empty. A single rose ribbon was stitched to the front of his tunic, a German recompense, no doubt, for the arm he had left on some Soviet steppe.

'Poor thing,' Catherine whispered. 'Such a baby. I'll bet he's not even twenty.'

Paul appraised the boy with disdain. 'Some dumb cowherd from the Lozère. Got fed up pulling on a cow's tits twice a day, so he decided to run off to the war.' He sipped his wine. 'A simpleminded bastard who got the simpleminded war he deserved. March to the sound of the cannon. Except in his case, they turned out to be the wrong cannon.'

Catherine took an instant dislike to his harsh, despising tone. She was about to question it, but Paul continued rambling on. 'Here in the shadows where they've stuck us, nothing is clear, is it? No captains to point us to the sound of the cannon, are there? No clear-cut blacks and whites for us, just shades of grey. And as you're going to find out one day, my dear, sometimes it's very hard to tell one shade of grey from another.'

Field fever, Catherine thought: was Paul's sudden moroseness a first symptom of that malady they'd warned her about in London – was he beginning to succumb to the chill paranoia of an agent's clandestine life? The waiter set their cheese soufflé before them. The sight of its golden-brown dome undulating from the pressures bubbling beneath it banished the momentary melancholy that had gripped Paul. To

Catherine's relief, his roguish grin returned, and he remained enchanting and attentive for the rest of their meal.

It was, indeed, superb, far better than anything London could have offered. Only the watery *ersatz* coffee served as a reminder of the privations besetting millions of hungry Parisians in the city beyond the front doors of the Chapon Rouge. Paul finished his cup and looked at his watch. 'We've got to go. We don't want to get caught out after curfew. Our German friends have a charming habit of using curfew breakers as hostages, to feed to their firing squads if one of their soldiers gets killed during the night.'

At his sign, the waiter delivered their bill. To Catherine's amusement, it came in the form of a telephone number, Maillot 1207. As Paul started to pull bits and pieces of currency from his pockets, she stood up. 'I'm just going back to the Ladies' for a minute. It comes equipped with something our landlady overlooked – soap.'

Once again Paul followed her return, hungrily contemplating each suggestion of the muscular, slender thighs as they brushed the folds of her skirt, devouring the outlines of her pert, erect breasts moulded against the fabric of her jacket. Suddenly he froze. The Luftwaffe colonel who'd eyed her so avidly two hours before was on his feet. He lurched towards her, circling her waist with a heavy hand that came swiftly and surely to rest on her buttocks. Roughly, he jerked her to him. '*Hei, Fräulein*,' he gurgled. 'Come join my friends and me for a little nightcap. Then we'll all go to the Lido.'

His hands, no longer inert, slid clumsily towards the gap between her legs, where his probing fingers started poking into the lining of her skirt. Paul hurled his napkin on to the table and, ashen with anger, stood up. The German turned to him with a sneer. 'Go home, you black-market swine. The little lady's with us now.' The German's hand bit into Catherine's backside. 'Aren't you, *Schatz*?'

Catherine tried to draw away, but the German only tightened his grip. For a moment she thought of using one of the moves Sergeant Barker had taught her at Beaulieu, but she hesitated. Such knowledge could be dangerously revealing. She saw Paul striding across the room towards her, his features alive with ill-controlled fury. He was about to do something as gallant as it would be stupid and imperil them both. 'Paul,' she whispered forcefully, 'let me handle this!'

Suddenly, a German civilian was at her side. He flung a string of incomprehensible German phrases at the colonel. The man's arm dropped from her buttocks and fell to his side as though his shoulder joint had been severed by an axe. The civilian turned to Catherine. 'Please forgive him, madame,' he said in accentless French. 'Unfortunately, we are all of us under great stress these days; but some of us' – he

92

turned his icy blue eyes to the trembling colonel – 'do not seem able to control ourselves in a manner becoming the German Reich.'

A relieved and flustered Catherine mumbled her thanks to her German saviour. Paul's arm was already in hers. He too gave a perfunctory nod of gratitude towards the man, then started her towards the door. Their rescuer watched them go. As they disappeared through the doors of the Chapon Rouge into the Porte Maillot beyond, he made a mock formal bow to their fleeing figures, then, smiling, returned to his dinner.

The destination of the intercepts of Baron Oshima's report to Tokyo on his visit to Berchtesgaden was a former girls' school called Arlington Hall, set at the end of a corridor of stately oak trees in the heart of Washington, DC. Those trees and a handful of watchful sentries outside screened what was, along with the project to construct a nuclear bomb, the most secret activity of the United States at war. It was there that a small band of cryptographers broke down and read what the Japanese Foreign Ministry believed to be the impenetrable code of its Type 97 coding machine.

The harvest of their extraordinary achievement had already had an enormous impact on the course of the Pacific War. Now, against all expectations, it had become a precious source of intelligence on Nazi Germany. The British had broken the secret of Germany's codes with their *Ultra* programme in 1941, and the result of the prodigious feat had been invaluable to the Allied cause. For the coming invasion, the battle on which victory or defeat might depend, however, *Ultra* was of very limited value. The reason was simple. The German High Command relied almost exclusively on landlines, not the radio, to communicate with its subordinate commands in Western Europe. Those landlines were immune to Allied eavesdropping. The detail-filled dispatches of Japan's ambassador to Berlin had become virtually the sole device the Allies had to peer into the minds of Hitler and his entourage. As a result, they were treated at Arlington Hall with the veneration a cleric might have reserved for scraps of the first Bible.

The text of the Berchtesgaden dispatch was first broken out of Morse code by a navy signalman, who delivered it to an intelligence officer on the first floor of one of the wartime wings flaring out from the old school building. Employing a machine that was virtually a replica of the one Oshima had used to code his message in his Berlin air-raid shelter, the intelligence officer busted the text into phonetic Japanese almost exactly identical to Oshima's original. Then he in turn took the text across the hall to a former Harvard Oriental-languages scholar, who translated it into English. Minutes after he'd completed his task, the result was delivered in a locked leather pouch to Section C of the Special Distribution Branch of the US Army's Deputy Chief of Staff, Intelligence, at the recently completed Pentagon Building. From that office, twice a day, the intercepted Japanese traffic, assigned the code name *Magic*, was sent in locked dispatch boxes by officer courier to the two dozen people, beginning with the President, who were authorized to receive it.

By the time the Oshima report reached the Pentagon, the day's second delivery had already left the Section C office. As he read it, the magnitude of what he held in his hand became instantly apparent to the Section's duty officer, a major in the Intelligence Corps. He called for a staff car and shortly after 7:30 P.M. drove up in front of a brick Colonial residence on the 'Avenue of the Stars' at Fort Meyers, Virginia. A black orderly ushered him into a study. There, a few minutes later, he was joined by General George C. Marshall, Chief of Staff of the United States Army. Wordlessly, Marshall unlocked the pouch, signed a receipt for the report and began to read it. The stoicism, the icy calm of Marshall was a legend in Washington. Yet when he'd finished the text, he glanced up at the major standing beside his desk. An expression as close to panic as any that would ever cross those stern features lay upon Marshall's face.

'My God!' he mumbled. 'This is an unmitigated catastrophe!'

PARIS

'Napoléon, shut up!'

The proprietress of their *hôtel-pension* aimed a mock kick at her yapping poodle as she plucked Paul and Catherine's key from its rack. 'Almost caught out after curfew, weren't you?' she sniffled, tightening the folds of her flannel bathrobe across the imposing girth of her bosom. Clearly it was an unfathomable mystery to her why anyone would prefer wandering the streets of Paris to putting her accommodations to the purpose for which they were intended.

'Visiting old friends,' Paul assured her, guiding Catherine up the darkened staircase – darkened because the hotel's electric current had been cut off by the proprietress at sunset. Her ostensible reason was her high sense of civic responsibility: without the current, none of her clients could violate blackout regulations. In fact, she cut it off out of a fine Gallic meanness of mind and the conviction that electricity was neither a necessary nor a desirable asset in her establishment.

Catherine walked across the darkened room and glanced into the

94

silent, empty alley below. Not a single human being moved, not a bicycle or car passed on the Boulevard Saint-Germain. The *quartier* which, before the war, had been the heart and soul of Paris' Left Bank was dead. She stood there a moment in the shafts of moonlight falling through the windows, her figure enveloped by their pale grey shroud. Her thoughts were not on Paris' empty pavements but on the man behind her: her surly, calculating cavalier of the night before, carrying her protesting figure across the pasture to be sure there would be no mud on her shoes; her charming actor playing his role with such relish on the terrace of the Brasserie Lorraine; her impulsive escort making his ill-considered rush to her side at the black-market restaurant. You had only to look into those mischievous eyes of his, follow the malicious meanderings of his smile to know that he was a rogue. Oh, God, she wondered, why must I always fall for the rogues? Why can't I just once fall for the lawyer or doctor who goes to church on Sunday and dotes on his mother?

From the darkness behind, Paul studied her, watching the silver moonlight lace her blond hair, illuminate her high cheekbones, suggest each indentation of her slender figure.

'Denise ...'

Before he could finish, Catherine swung around to him, placing her fingers against his lips as she did. Giving a quick, almost imperceptible toss to her hair, she let her head arch backwards so that her proud blond mane hung down from her shoulders. She slid her hands around his neck. With deliberate, tantalizing slowness, she pressed her body into his, her pelvis thrust hard and demanding against his groin, her lean and muscled thighs driven taut against his own rigid limbs. For a moment they stood clinging to each other like that, bodies pressed together in the first glorious intimations of their passion.

Her mouth reached up for his, her long sensual lips enfolding his in their cool vice. They stayed that way for what seemed like ages, seeking each other in each undulation of their lips, in each sensuous twist of their interlocked bodies. Catherine leaned back as Paul's fingers began to comb through her hair. He lowered his head, pressed his lips onto the skin at the base of her throat, his arms around her waist drawing her tight against the urgent hardness of his erection. Gently at first, then with an almost savage frenzy, his lips and tongue nibbled the skin of her neck, her earlobes, her shoulders.

He drew back, holding her head inches from his, his eyes locking hers in hungry communion. Hips and legs pressed together as though in unconscious effort not to jar the magnetic field binding them together, they turned and plunged across the room to the bed. His hands opened her blouse and cupped over the tremulous breasts he had coveted for hours, caressing them, lightly twisting their nipples.

95

Catherine ripped open his shirt. Her fingernails ran with chill swiftness along his flat, broad chest down to his belt. She opened his trousers, and for an instant her long fingernails dallied provocatively over the skin of his inner thighs. Then her slender fingers slid with possessive hunger onto the prize they sought, grasping Paul with a strength that made him gasp in pain and pleasure. She managed him until, in a mutual frenzy, they both began to tear off their remaining bits of clothing.

She lay back down on the bed, her hair spilled in a golden halo over the pillow. Paul knelt above her, studying in hungry rapture her breasts, her lean stomach, the arching of her long legs. His lips bent to her navel, but her hands caught the side of his head.

'Now, Paul,' she commanded. 'Now!' He bent his knees and thrust his almost painfully rigid erection towards the opening of her thighs. Catherine gave a low moan of anticipation and rolled her hips up to meet him. With a deft move, she drew him down towards the chambers of her body. Tantalizingly slowly, Paul slid into her, then, with each forward thrust, pulled back, pausing for an excruciating second as though he might deny her forever the culmination she demanded before thrusting forward again, harder and deeper.

She writhed and struggled at each diabolical thrust until finally she let out a sharp cry. She threw her arms around his hips and with one snapping thrust pulled him full into her, driving her own pelvis up against him with all her force as she did. Her body arched against his, locking them in a curving of purest pleasure. They held together there in rigid ecstasy for the longest and shortest second mortals live. Finally, fluttering with spent sensuality, her hips sank back to the bed, drawing him down with her in his descent. For minutes they lay there like that, forcing a few last spasms of pleasure from each other, Paul staying inside her as long as he could as if by doing so he might somehow preserve the spell that had just united them.

Finally, Paul rolled over and reached for a cigarette in his trousers on the floor. For a long while, Catherine lay there beside him studying the swirls of his cigarette smoke disappearing into the darkness, thinking about this man with whom she'd just made love so spontaneously, so passionately. Virtually all she knew about him personally had been contained in that line of the Lysander pilot who had deposited her in France – his joke that Paul had learned to fly before he'd learned to walk. 'You flew before the war, Paul?' she asked.

She felt him nodding beside her, but he said nothing. 'How did you get into that? It certainly wasn't your regular, everyday line of work, was it?'

'Do you really want to know? The whole story?'

'Every bit of it. I detest making love to perfect strangers.'

Paul laughed. 'I was born up in the North, near Compiègne. I was a crazy kid. I always had to do what the other kids didn't dare do. Ride my bike faster around a curve or down a hill than they could, climb a higher tree, jump off a higher fence. I don't know why. I just loved knowing I could do things the others couldn't.' He took a long, deep breath of his cigarette. It was, Catherine noted, American.

'How did you get that?' she asked.

'Easy. The black market. Anyway, one Sunday – it was in June 1924; you know how there are certain days in your life you can never forget – this old Farmian biplane came over and landed in a pasture near our property. The whole village – the priest, the postman, everybody – came rushing out to see it. The pilot was selling aerial baptisms for thirty francs a ride. Nobody wanted to go. They were all afraid. So I begged my father for the thirty francs and off I went.'

Even lying there in their rumpled bed, he could still recall every detail of that five-minute flight: the smell of the seat and frayed leather in the front cockpit, the sensation of the pilot's strapping him into his seat, the sound of the motor as they accelerated down the field, the vibrating hum of the wind rushing through the wings' struts. He would always remember the way the flesh of his cheeks was thrust back from his mouth by the accelerating speed as the pilot pushed the plane into a dive, how the green horizon spun on itself as he banked the plane, how distant, how remote, how unintimidating the earth appeared from that altitude. Above all, what he would never forget was the eyes of the villagers gathered in the cow pasture when he returned to earth. There, reflected in their awe and admiration, he found what he'd been looking for. From that moment on, Henri Lemaire – 'Paul' to the SOE – knew it was up there, in those beckoning blue skies, that he would find one day the fulfilment for which his boyish heart so desperately yearned.

'And so another Saint-Exupéry was born,' Catherine said as he finished his account.

'Not quite. Deciding to become a pilot was one thing. Becoming one was another.'

'How did you learn to fly?'

'Well, there was an *aéro-club* in Compiègne. It consisted of an old hay barn and a cow pasture. The owner was a World War veteran who was getting by on wine, memories and a few aerial baptisms on Sunday afternoons. He taught me. I kept the place clean, fixed the planes, covered for him when he was drunk, and he gave me flying lessons. I soloed when I was eighteen.'

Catherine could sense the pride in the man beside her as he spoke those words. It was obvious flying was a very special part of his being. How galling it must be for him, she thought, to be directing the flights of others now rather than flying himself. 'Did you go to work for Air France?'

'Air France?' Paul laughed. 'They wouldn't have let an eighteen-year-old kid sweep out their hangars in those days. I had a friend named Clément. He had an old Blériot. We made a living organizing aerial circuses around Paris.'

He closed his eyes and saw himself again in those episodic and uncertain days. Their routine was simple. On Monday, they'd persuade some farmer to lend them his pasture Saturday or Sunday afternoon in return for a quick spin in Clément's Blériot. Then they'd paper the surrounding villages with hand-lettered posters announcing the coming of the Age of the Airplane in the form of their Aerial Circus and hope for the best on the weekend. The best, of course, was clear skies and a good crowd. Henri would collect a couple of francs' admission at the pasture gate while Clément stirred enthusiasm by noisily warming up his plane. Clément, the more experienced pilot, would go up first, run a few loops and spins, a couple of close flyovers, an upside-down pass over the crowd while Henri and his megaphone underlined for the gawking spectators the terrible danger of the stunts they were witnessing. Then, always the adventurer, Henri provided the crowd with the *pièce de résistance*, a wing walk and a parachute jump. After that, the two friends settled down to the meat and potatoes of the afternoon, luring as many of the spectators as they could into Clément's plane for a thirty-franc ride.

It was a precarious existence, but it was flying, and Henri Lemaire was at last the man in the leather jacket and white scarf he'd always wanted to be. For two seasons, the pair worked the countryside within a hundred miles of Paris until they'd run out of fields and cooperative farmers.

Catherine followed his account with rapt attention. 'Well, Paul dear,' she said when he'd finished, 'I must admit one thing. You certainly don't conform to the average French mother's prescription of the ideal mate for her daughter, do you? You don't sound much like the serious, hardworking family man, off to the office at nine and back faithfully at six.' She caressed one of his nipples with her fingernail. 'Maybe that's why I found you so attractive.'

'French girls don't pay much attention to their mothers' advice, you know.'

'Oh, yes, they do. At least in picking the ideal husband. Believe me, I did.'

'Are you married?' There was a swift rush of poignancy to his voice that Catherine found touching.

'I had a narrow escape. All because I listened too closely to my mother.' She rolled her still-warm body closer to his. 'When it comes to lovers, though,' she murmured, 'I operate more independently.'

'Well, if it's any consolation, I have held down a few regular jobs in my life, although the hours were never nine to six.'

'Flying?'

Paul exhaled. 'With Air Bleu – the old aerial postal service. I was one of the first pilots they signed on when they started up in '36.'

Catherine could hear the pride in his voice again. 'I was right, then. You are another Saint-Exupéry.'

Her lover grunted. 'It was tough flying. Not many instruments. Navigation was pretty much a question of getting down through the clouds to pick up a landmark so you could figure out where you were going – a canal, a river, a railroad line. Which is a fine way to navigate as long as there's a hole in the clouds. It's when there isn't that you earn your pay.' His thoughts wandered back again. They had flown out of Le Bourget each afternoon, to Lille, Le Havre, Rouen, Strasbourg, spent the night and flown back the next morning. He'd loved it. In Paris, his Air Bleu uniform had allowed him into the Le Bourget pilots' lounge, where he could drink with the men who'd become his gods, the international pilots of Air France, Imperial Airways, Lufthansa. He sighed. 'I'll tell you one thing: it was a great way to get to know the country.'

'Were you still flying for them when the war began?'

'Oh, Christ, no. I was let out in the spring of 1937. Air Bleu went broke. I got a job at Coulommiers, outside Paris, teaching aerobatics to fighter pilots for the Spanish Republic.' He laughed. 'Imagine! I'd never been in a fighter plane in my life and I was teaching those poor bastards aerobatics! Then one day the civilian who ran the field drove me back to Paris and asked me up for a drink in his apartment on the Boulevard Pasteur. He told me he was a colonel in the Spanish Air Force on a secret mission. They were buying every plane in sight and they needed pilots to fly them to Barcelona. No instruments, no radio, only a compass and a map to navigate by. Not even weather reports, because they didn't want to alert the weather bureau to what was going on by asking too many questions.'

Catherine was thrilled. The mention of the Spanish Civil War brought back so many turbulent memories. Marching through Biarritz denouncing Franco's rebellion with her Basque friends, defying her mother to collect money for the Republic, hiding Republican sympathizers going into and out of Spain in the family garage. It was then that her own rebellious spirit had been born. She snuggled closer to Paul. 'So your heart was in the right place from the beginning.'

'Oh, hell!' Paul snorted. 'I didn't give a damn for the Republicans. I was in it for the money. We got five thousand francs cash in an envelope from the colonel in his apartment before each trip. I was making more money in two months ferrying planes to Barcelona than I would have made at Air Bleu in a year. I loved it. We flew everything – Vultees, Northrups, Dragonflies, Blériots. Half the time the cockpits were open.' She could feel the pride rising again in his voice. 'We couldn't fly over the Pyrenees. We had to find a way to fly through them. I loved it.'

'Oh, dear Barcelona!' Catherine lamented. 'The shining city on the hill! And to think you saw it as an adventurer, not an idealist. Maybe I should have listened to my mother after all.'

'It was a great place, I'll admit that. We stayed at the Oriente Palace Hotel just above the Ramblas. I loved to wander up and down the Ramblas listening to people arguing at every newspaper stand.'

'And keeping out of the *flamenco* cabarets?'

'Sometimes.'

'Mmmm,' Catherine murmured. 'Probably spent half your time playing the guitar under some *señorita*'s window.'

'Not me. I've never been one for playing guitars under a young lady's window. I'd much rather head up to the bedroom and do my singing there.'

'Yes,' Catherine giggled. 'I'd noticed that.' She lapsed into a drowsy silence for a few moments. 'Wouldn't you rather be flying now?' she asked.

'This is what they told me to do.'

'How did you get into it?'

'That's one of the questions we don't ask each other, remember?'

'You're right,' she sighed. Then she gave a low, throaty laugh. 'We really are strangers in the night, aren't we? We're thrown together because of an air raid somewhere up north. We don't even know each other's real names because we're not allowed to know.'

Paul, half asleep now, turned in the bed and embraced her tenderly. 'I know all I need to know. You're the loveliest woman I've ever seen.'

Their bodies lay interlaced on the bed, a moth-eaten woollen blanket tossed over their nudity for whatever meagre warmth it could provide. Paul's head rested trustingly in the curve of Catherine's shoulder; he was sound asleep. She was awake, silently contemplating the shifting patterns of moonlight that dappled the floor, casting a grey afterglow upon their figures. She had just closed her eyes in quest of sleep when she heard the terrifying screech of tyres, then the roar of an automobile engine reverberating through the alleyway below their window. Her body tensed. There was a sudden fracas of squealing brakes, the metallic crack of car doors, the sound of running feet, a voice shouting, '*Deutsche Polizei! Aufmachen!*' and the pounding of fists on a wooden door.

Paul sat bolt upright. Catherine had been about to scream, but had stifled the cry in her throat. She grabbed Paul.

100

'What is it?'

'Gestapo.'

He leaped to his feet and ran to the window.

His naked body as taut as a stretched wire, he peered into the alleyway below. Catherine looked wildly about the room, groping on the floor for her clothes, wondering how they could possibly escape from the hotel. He beckoned to her. She rushed to his side and looked out.

The raid was on the building across the street.

Her trembling hands clutching the skirt she'd swept off the floor, Catherine slumped into Paul's arms in relief. There were two black Citroëns, motors running, doors open, in the alley right below their window. Half a dozen men in long leather overcoats milled around them. A shaft of light poured from the open door of a building on the other side of the alley just to their left. From inside they could hear distinctly the sound of furniture splintering, men shouting, feet thudding down a wooden staircase.

Catherine peered towards the façade of the building immediately across from theirs. At half a dozen of its windows she could see shadowy figures watching in silent terror the scene in the alley, Goyaesque faces distorted by fear and the uneven moonlight. The remaining windows were shuttered against the night, yet she sensed the shadowy figures behind them too – linked to her, to Paul, to their unseen and unknown neighbours by their shared fright at their helplessness. Suddenly a man clad only in a pyjama top, wrists handcuffed behind his back, was half-pushed, half-thrown out of the illuminated doorway into the night. One of the leather-coated figures stepped forward. He sent a vicious kick into the naked man's genitals. His scream was so shrill, so piercing it seemed to Catherine to set the panes of their window vibrating.

'*Wir haben Sie* ...' a guttural voice triumphed. Catherine and Paul both strained unsuccessfully to catch the prisoner's name as he was jammed head first into the back seat of the lead car.

'Poor bastard,' Paul whispered softly. 'If he knew what they have in store for him ...' He trembled slightly, and Catherine's arm tightened around his waist. 'I've got to get you out of here tomorrow. They may be coming around asking questions, trying to find out if he was working with anyone in the neighbourhood.'

Still shaking slightly, Catherine and Paul padded back to bed. There they clutched each other like frightened children in a storm, trembling bodies intertwined in an effort to draw the warmth and assurance each so desperately needed. They stayed that way for almost an hour, neither sleeping nor talking. Then, as the first muted grey of dawn eased the darkness, they made love again, this time in a deep communion quite unlike anything either of them had ever known.

101

On the other side of the Atlantic Ocean, Major Thomas Francis O'Neill III, T. F. to his friends, was, that same March morning, preparing to go to war. He was the youngest major in the youngest branch of the United States Army, the Office of Strategic Services. Nothing in the manner of his going, however, suggested in even the remotest way T.F.'s affiliation with either the US Army or its newly created secret intelligence service. As he had been doing for mornings as far back as his thirty-one-year-old mind could remember, T.F. was breakfasting in the mahogany-panelled gloom of the main dining room of his grandfather's Prospect Avenue mansion. His and his grandfather's places were laid, as they always were, at opposite ends of the long table, each setting gleaming with its Waterford crystal and Georgian silver. A bouquet of yellow roses freshly plucked from the family greenhouse graced the centre of the table, and a copy of *The Hartford Courant*, folded open to the New York Stock Exchange's closing quotations, rested on the reading rack before his grandfather's coffee cup.

Everything, indeed, was exactly as it should have been, right down to the fact that his grandfather was late, as usual. There was no question of T.F.'s beginning without him. He might be heading off to the war after breakfast; he wouldn't have dreamed of sitting down and starting in on his scrambled eggs until the patriarch who'd raised him from birth had taken his place at the head of the table.

'Off to England is it, now?' mused Clancy, his grandfather's valet, from his sentry's position at the sideboard where he stood guard over trays of scrambled eggs, sausages, a huge pitcher of freshly squeezed orange juice and a bubbling percolator of coffee. 'Sure, you'll want to watch out for that lot.'

Like most of his grandfather's servants, Clancy sprang from a seemingly endless reservoir of cousins, nephews and nieces living in the miserable village of Carrick-on-Shannon from which Grandfather O'Neill had immigrated to the United States in 1885 and to which he periodically sent off a summons for a fresh dispatch of cooks, maids, gardeners or drivers. Clancy, whose impoverished boyhood had been peopled with the legends of the bold Fenian men, had never been one to look upon the English with fondness.

T.F. laughed. He could remember so well the long childhood hours he'd spent at Clancy's feet, listening to him croon out 'Kevin Barry,' 'Who Dares to Speak of Easter Week?' 'The West's Awake' while the valet polished his grandfather's silver. 'Well, now, Clancy, the English aren't quite so bad as you make them out to be. I've been working with quite a few of them in Washington lately.'

102

'Sure, you're right, Tommy,' Clancy growled sourly. 'They're worse.'
'What a sight!'

It was his grandfather, striding into the room with all the aplomb of an Irish politician arriving at a wake. He marched down the table, clasped his grandson by the shoulders and tilted up on the balls of his feet so he could look proudly at his face. 'Sure, he'll do us all proud, won't he, Clancy?' He gave T.F.'s cheek an affectionate pinch and without pausing for a reply to his question, which like most of his queries was rhetorical, commanded, 'Easy on the eggs this morning. A touch of the indigestion last night.'

With the same purposeful stride with which he'd entered the room, he marched back to his place, whipped out his glasses and turned to his newspaper. The youth he loved more than anyone else in the world might be going off to war in a few hours; that was not going to delay Tom O'Neill's ritual contemplation of the stock tables in which his immense fortune had been made and was now being steadily augmented.

'Aircraft's up a point,' he noted approvingly. With characteristic prescience, the old man had seen war coming in 1937 and bought up thousands of shares of Pratt & Whitney at close to their Depression low. The financial acumen that decision represented was a legend in Hartford, Connecticut. Old Tom O'Neill was the acknowledged patriarch of the Irish of Hartford, a city to which fate had consigned him when the pittance he'd brought to the New World ran out in Hartford halfway between New York, where he'd landed, and Boston, his destination.

The key to his success in the New World lay in his education, or rather his almost total lack of it, in his parish church of Carrick-on-Shannon. His tutor had been a well-meaning but little-lettered priest who had taught Tom the one thing he knew: how to write. Somewhere in the mists of the priest's ancestry there must have lain one of those ancient monks who'd illumined the golden pages of the Book of Kells, for he had taught Tom to write with a script that simply flowed across the page. It was a precious gift for a fourteen-year-old boy in Hartford when it was beginning to emerge as the insurance capital of the world. All insurance policies at the time had to be written by hand, and Tom's penmanship got him the job of personal scribe to Morgan B. Bulkeley, the bearded Yankee patriarch who was president of the Aetna Life Insurance Company. Tom was assigned a corner of Bulkeley's office, where he awaited the regular verbal thunderbolts summoning him to set down the terms of a major company policy. He also kept his boyish ears alertly trained on his employer's discussions of his prospective stock-market manipulations. With every penny he could save or borrow, Tom went into the market in pursuit of his employer's unintentional tips. By the time he was thirty-five, he was the largest single shareholder in Aetna

103

Life, with a stake surpassing Bulkeley's. He quit to devote the rest of his life to the steady enhancement of his fortune.

As his grandfather set aside *The Hartford Courant* with a decisive snap of his wrist, T.F. was surprised to hear him utter a hoarse cough. That cough heralded a ritual rarely performed in old Tom's dining room: the saying of Grace.

'O Lord Jesus Christ,' he now began. 'We beseech today Thy special blessing upon Thy devoted servant Thomas Francis O'Neill the Third.' The old man intoned the name as though each reverently pronounced syllable were meant to underscore the distance he himself had travelled from his mud-floored cottage in Carrick-on-Shannon. 'Keep him from harm's way in the dangerous ways that attend him. Help him to serve his nation with courage and honour. Aid him to do right always as Thou wilt help him to see that right. And return him, we beseech Thee, through the intervention of Thy divine grace, to the bosom of his family when the blessings of Thy peace have been restored to earth. Amen.'

The old man made a hasty sign of the Cross, tucked his white linen napkin between two of the buttons of his waistcoat and beamed down on his scrambled eggs with the slightly bemused air of a man asking himself if his eloquence would be sufficient to prompt the Almighty to forget for a moment his other transgressions.

'Well, Tommy, will you still not tell me just what it is you're going to be doing over there?'

'Granddad,' T.F. replied, churning his way through his breakfast with the gusto of a man who knew he wouldn't be looking on such a feast for months to come, 'I know very little about it, and even the little I know I'm not really allowed to talk about. All I can say is I'm going to serve as the American liaison officer to an English organization attached to Churchill's office.'

'Something to do with this invasion business, I'll bet.'

'Very likely.'

'For the love of God, don't go getting yourself involved in that.' The old man sighed. 'Are you still going to be working for that lace-curtain lawyer from Buffalo?'

That 'lace-curtain lawyer' was Wild Bill Donovan, the founder of the OSS. In fact, Old Tom knew and liked Donovan, even if he represented what was to him the perfect anomaly, an Irish Republican.

'Only very indirectly. My real superiors now are going to be in the Combined Chiefs down in Washington.'

His words brought a gleam of pride to Old Tom's face. He had only the vaguest notion of what the Combined Chiefs might be, but the very words seemed to ring with importance. Whatever it was his grandson was going to do, it was somehow tied to the direction of the war, to its highest echelon of command, and the thought made the old man swell with pride. He studied the figure that had sat there at the other end of his breakfast table for more than three decades now. His own son – Tom, Jr – had drowned on the Connecticut shore in the summer of 1913 just five months after T.F.'s birth. His death had burdened Tom with that curse which, along with alcohol, was the affliction of the Irish, guilt. In this case it was an overwhelming sense of guilt for having neglected his son in his headlong pursuit of wealth. He'd moved the grandson and his mother into his Prospect Avenue mansion determined to lavish on the grandson the attention he'd denied his son. From that day forward he had overseen every aspect of T.F.'s upbringing with the same zeal he devoted to his manipulations in the stock market. When the time had come to choose a college for T.F., no less a personage than the Cardinal Archbishop himself had motored down from Boston in his new Packard to extol the virtues of Holy Cross and Boston College – envisioning, perhaps, the Thomas F. O'Neill Library or Gymnasium that might eventually grace one of those campuses if his advocacy was successful.

It was not. Old Tom was sending T.F. downstate to Yale, to become, if he had anything to do with it, a perfect replica of the New England Yankees, like Bulkeley, he so publicly hated and so secretly admired. Just how well he had succeeded might be measured in the near perfection of the appearance of his beloved grandson. The once unruly thickets of T.F.'s ash-blond hair were disciplined into the tight trim that was *de rigueur* on the Eastern Seaboard from Bar Harbor to Bryn Mawr. No wonder. In a decade, no barber outside the Yale Club in New York had laid a pair of scissors on it. He had the pale blue O'Neill eyes, tinted, according to legend, the colour of the waters of Donegal Bay on a summer morn. Only a crooked nose, the souvenir left by the stub of a Dartmouth hockey player's stick, gave a touch of character to what might otherwise have been too blandly regular a face.

'Well,' the old man said, pushing aside his half-finished breakfast and emitting a catarrh-rattling cough, 'I still say it's a terrible thing. Never mind. You won't tell me what you're off to do. I'll give you a few kind words for your parting anyway. Never do that, do I?'

'Oh, never,' replied a smiling T.F. thinking of the endless chain of sermons he'd received at this table to mark each of his life's turning points – one to send him off to Yale, another on his departure for Harvard Law School, yet another outpouring when he went to Washington to work in the Reconstruction Finance Corporation post his grandfather's New Deal connections had found for him.

'Just remember one thing, young fellow. No matter where you go, no matter how exalted the company you're keeping, don't ever forget who you are or where you come from.' A telephone rang in the hallway. 'I probably sheltered you too much from the rough-and-tumble of life while I was bringing you up. Well, you'll just have to learn to deal with it yourself when the rough times come. Just remember what's right and wrong isn't always what they wrote in the catechism or what you read in those books you studied up there at Harvard Law. What's right or wrong, Tommy, is what's written on your heart. Read that, follow it and you'll be all right.'

Bridget, the maid, interrupted the sermon. 'Sorry, sir, – it's for Mister Tommy.'

When T.F. returned, he was wearing a perplexed expression. 'It was Washington. They cancelled my flight from Bradley.' Bradley Field, a few miles from Hartford in Windsor Locks, was one of the jump-off points for the Army Air Forces' ferry-command flights to Europe. 'I've got to report back to the Pentagon. They're sending me out from Andrews tonight.' T.F. glanced at his watch. 'If Clancy can take me to the station, I can just catch the eight-twelve to the city.'

His grandfather got up, strode over to him and, clutching T.F. tightly, kissed his cheek. As the old man pulled away, T.F. saw glistening in his blue O'Neill eyes something he'd never seen there before – not at his grandmother's death in 1936; not at his own mother's death of flu so many years before: tears.

'Come back, laddie,' his grandfather whispered. 'Come back home to me.' The old man straightened up and gave a last squeeze to T.F.'s elbow. 'Be gone with you now.'

'That's him, over there. The one talking to the old woman in the newspaper kiosk.' Paul's glance indicated a squat man in blue denim working clothes whose truck had just pulled up to the curb of Avenue Jean Jaurés. 'He goes back and forth all the time and never gets bothered.' Catherine saw the words 'Pêcherie Delpienne, Boulogne' on the panel of his van. 'The Germans let them run a little fishing fleet up there – half the catch for us, half for them. He's going to drop you off near the train station so you can catch a train to Calais. He's waiting for you, so just slide into the cab as if you belong there.'

A soft rain as fine, almost, as fog sifted out of the grey March sky. The industrial backwater stretching away from the Porte de Pantin was a dreary, depressing spectacle; as depressing, almost, as the melancholia gripping Catherine.

'If you ever have to cut and run, you know how to contact me,' Paul whispered.

Catherine nodded.

'I'll get you on a plane back to England.'

Catherine clasped his hand in hers and held it tightly for a long

106

moment. Finally she released it and gathered up her handbag. 'I'd better go now.'

They stood up. Paul, as usual, had already paid for their *ersatz* coffees. He looked down at her, an immense, almost palpable longing in his unhappy eyes. 'I love you, Denise. I really do.'

Catherine placed her hands on the lapels of his raincoat. 'I know,' she whispered.

'Will there be a time for us?'

She made that little shaking gesture of her hair which so delighted him. 'I hope so. When ...' She hesitated. 'Perhaps when all this is over. Who knows?'

'Sure,' Paul sighed. 'If ...' He stopped the words and instead drew her to him in a sad final embrace. Finally, a glistening in her eyes, she pulled away. She bent down and picked up her suitcase. '*Au revoir*,' she whispered.

She turned and started her march across the empty boulevard towards the waiting van. Paul watched her go, her blue raincoat wrapped close around the body he'd loved with such passionate intensity only a few hours before. She opened the door of the truck and slid gracefully into the seat beside the driver. She did not look back.

Forty-five minutes after leaving Catherine, Paul was sitting at a table in another café, this one on Rue de Buci in the Latin Quarter, engrossed, as usual, in his study of *Je Suis Partout*. He gave no indication that he noticed the passage of a middle-aged woman in a blue turban carrying a string shopping bag; nor did he appear to notice her return fifteen minutes later.

He got up and wandered along Rue de Buci, past the open-air vendors hawking their pathetic collection of lentils and rutabagas, then strolled along Rue Saint-André-des-Arts to Rue des Grands Augustins. There he entered the dimly lit corner bar. There wasn't another customer in the place. Its two occupants were a sullen bartender and an equally sullen whore buffing her nails on a stool by the bar. Paul settled on a nearby stool and beckoned to the bartender.

'Cinzano,' he ordered. He turned to the whore. 'How's business?' he inquired.

'Stinks.'

'What's the problem? Our German friends running out of enthusiasm for *l'amour à l'aise*?'

She shrugged in indifferent silence.

'Well, never mind. One of these days you'll have the Americans to cheer you up.'

'What do I care?' she grunted. 'One prick's the same as another to me.

Look, mister, if it's talk you want, talk to him.' She pointed her nail buffer at the barman. 'You want to screw, it's fifty francs, a hundred if I take off all my clothes.'

'Well,' said Paul, 'another time.' He looked down at the newspaper on the bar between them.

'Mind if I read your paper?'

'Go ahead.'

Paul sipped his drink in leisurely fashion, glancing from time to time at the paper's headline. Then he got up, nodded to them both and left. As he walked up Rue Saint-André-des-Arts he clutched the whore's newspaper in his hands. Deftly his fingers searched its folds, looking for the envelope he knew would be there. Finding it, he turned into Rue Mazarin and quickened his pace towards the Odéon *métro* station.

Wordlessly the Doctor, the master of Hans-Dieter Strömelburg's radio game, walked across the office and laid the message he was carrying in front of the *Obersturmbannführer*. Strömelburg read it once, then twice. He looked up at his subordinate, his pleasant features clouded with the all-too-familiar signs of an internal rage.

'Can you imagine?' he asked, his incredulous tone providing its own answer to his query. 'The bastard tried to cheat on us.' He punched a buzzer on the phone beside his desk.

'Take the Englishman in Cell Five to the *baignoire*,' he ordered the two men in civilian clothes who answered his summons. 'Put him on the hoist and work him over until I come upstairs.'

The senior of the two gave Strömelburg a deferential half-bow. 'What should we ask him, sir?'

'Nothing. Just make him hurt. I'll do the talking when I get up there.'

For twenty minutes Strömelburg read his latest cable traffic from Berlin, listening in silent satisfaction as he did to the muffled screams of Wild's agony from the floor above. The last cable finished, he beckoned to the Doctor and headed upstairs. Wild had been stripped naked, handcuffed and hooked by the links of his handcuffs to a hoist suspended from the ceiling so that his feet did not quite reach the floor. As he dangled there, helpless as a side of beef, the two Gestapo men had pummelled him with their black rubber truncheons. His back, his chest, his groin, his thighs were a mass of red and bleeding welts left by their blows. His left shoulder had been yanked from its socket, sending a pain as excruciating as any a human being can be made to endure through his body.

Strömelburg gestured to his torturers to stop. For some time he stood in the doorway contemplating the Englishman dangling from the hoist, sobbing out his frightful agony. Then he walked slowly forward. 'You 'bastard,' he said, his voice as cold as the stare in his eyes. 'You thought you could cheat me, didn't you?'

The uncomprehending Wild half-gagged on the blood welling up from his internal injuries.

'Wanted to trick me, didn't you?'

Bewildered, Wild could only utter a half-human groan, like the frightened whimper of an injured animal.

'Cheating bastard!' Strömelburg's disdainful calm had turned to a furious roar. 'Read this!' He thrust the message the Doctor had handed him twenty minutes earlier at Wild so that its text rested only inches from his eyes. 'Read it!' he commanded.

'Your 9175 acknowledged,' the message said. 'You forgot your double security check. Next time be more careful.'

Wild had just time to gasp at the unutterable stupidity of his superiors before he passed out in pain and despair.

'Let him down,' Strömelburg ordered, his voice rich again with the resonance of command and self-assurance. 'I think we'll find him more cooperative from now on.' He turned to one of his torturers. 'Put that shoulder back into place before he comes to, won't you?'

As Strömelburg left the torture chamber, his acolyte following faithfully in his footsteps, he glanced at his watch. 'I've got to get to a meeting,' he informed the Doctor. 'Send Berlin a teletype, will you? I think we can assure Kaltenbrunner we're about to add another radio to our little orchestra.'

As he always did on such occasions, Paul carefully inserted himself into a knot of passengers debarking from his *métro* in the cavernous underground station of the Etoile. Sheltering in its anonymous flow, he moved up the staircase and out into the majestic heart of his nation's capital. The newspaper he'd picked up on the Rue Saint-André-des-Arts was riding off to Neuilly on an empty *métro* seat; the envelope it had contained was now tucked inside his coat pocket.

He circled the great esplanade, bridling as he always did at the blood-red flag waving from the symbol of France's distant triumphs over the very people represented by the Nazi banner. Then, turning down Avenue Mac-Mahon, he began a fastidious, time-consuming routine designed to reveal whether or not he was being followed.

It was a technique Paul had evolved himself, a refinement of the practices he'd been taught in England at the SOE's security school. The English approach was a classic, straightforward application of the double-back system. Stop and stare curiously into a shop window, then turn and swiftly retrace your earlier footsteps; pause at a newspaper kiosk to buy a paper, then do the same thing. Systematically applied by a

109

trained agent, it was a reasonably infallible system. Except, as Paul had realized on his return to Occupied France, it had one grave built-in disadvantage. If it allowed you to detect the presence of a tail dogging your footsteps, it also alerted the tail to the fact that you were looking for him. And in Paul's clandestine world, a suspicious man was a guilty man. Use the SOE technique, he'd concluded, and you'd signal anyone who was following you that his reason for doing so was well founded.

Moving at a pace so leisurely, so apparently unconcerned as to make a tail's task childishly simple, Paul set off down Avenue Mac-Mahon. At Rue de Brey, he stopped and entered a bookshop at the corner. Positioning himself so that he could glance on occasion through the shop's plate-glass window, he began a purposeful survey of the books on display. Finally, dissatisfied, he went to the bookseller and asked for an edition of Henri de Montherlant he knew perfectly well was out of print. A few seconds later he was outside, looking slightly baffled, glancing up and down the avenue in search of the easiest route to the nearby bookstore whose address the first bookseller had kindly furnished him. After repeating the tactic through three bookstores, Paul could feel reasonably certain he was not being followed. If he sensed someone on his path, he bought a book – and, of course, missed the rendezvous.

It was a boring, elaborate pantomime, but one to which Paul clung religiously. Satisfied he was unaccompanied this afternoon, he turned down Avenue des Ternes towards his real destination. Striding across the almost empty pavements of the Place des Ternes, Paul was struck by the abundance in the flower vendors' stalls, a dazzling palette of reds, golds, lavenders, oranges. It was almost as though those fragile coloured stalks represented a last reminder of peacetime Paris, the only commodities in France so perishable her German conquerors could not strip them from the countryside for dispatch to the factories and cities of the Reich. They were also, for Paul, a poignant reminder of something else, of the sharp yet delicious sadness which had overwhelmed him since he'd watched Catherine climb into the van at the Porte de Pantin. Almost unconsciously, he swept his nostrils with his fingertips, hoping some trace of her perfume, some last, slowly fading light might remain there on the skin that had caressed hers.

There was none. Sadly, Paul turned up his coat collar as a precaution against a concierge's curious glance and ducked into the doorway of a building abutting the square. Scorning the elevator, he walked up the stairs to the third floor, rapped quickly on one of the two doors at the landing and stepped inside. The apartment was ill lit and sparsely furnished. At the end of the living room, a Leica was fixed to a tripod under a single brilliant bulb whose cone of light bathed the white surface below the camera. Paul crossed the room and handed his envelope to the figure waiting beside the tripod. As he did, a second figure staring out of the window into the courtyard below turned to him.

'Tell me, my dear Gilbert,' Hans-Dieter Strömelburg said, 'who was that lovely woman you were dining with at the Chapon Rouge last night?'

PART TWO

OCTOBER 1943

Henri Lemaire struggled to suppress the almost irresistible urge to pivot quickly about on his heel to see if he was being followed. He of course resisted the temptation; the counsels of the SOE's security experts who had prepared him for his new job as its Air Operations Officer were still fresh in his mind. Despite his innate talent for the clandestine agent's existence, the confining rules of underground life remained as unfamiliar to him as the code name 'Paul' which his new employers had assigned him for his operations. That would change; he would absorb those rules with time. Such things came as naturally to him as learning to a devout scholar.

He shivered – not so much from the chill of the October rain striking the pavement with its furtive tap dance as from the sadness the scene inspired. It wasn't even eleven o'clock, yet Paris' Porte Maillot was deserted. The wicker chairs of the sidewalk cafés were stacked in lonesome piles against their plate-glass windows. Scraps of refuse skidded over the pavement in the damp wind. Only two sounds reached his ears – the soft tinkle of a bicycle bell somewhere up the darkened avenue leading to the Arc de Triomphe and the clack of wooden-soled shoes on the pavement as a Parisian rushed to catch the last *métro* home. You could feel in the air a depression as tangible as that haunting a cancer ward, the deepening gloom of a city facing yet another winter of occupation, another season of cold and deprivation before the distant spring might bring again the promise of deliverance.

He shivered once more and glanced at his watch. How would the German welcome him? Would there be in his greeting an echo of the geniality he had once shown him? Or had the immense power he now exercised changed his character? He shivered, this time from nervous tension and quickened his step until he reached Rue Weber. Turning the corner, he began to pace slowly down the street, his ears alert for the sibilant hiss of the car's tyres sliding by the pavement.

'Henri?' the unknown face at the window whispered.

As the car drove off, Henri Lemaire glanced through the rear window. Rue Weber was deserted. No one could have observed the pickup. There were some advantages, at least, to Paris' melancholy cast. The driver sped

115

arrogantly down Rue Pergolèse, through the inner *allée* of Avenue Foch and off into the dark sprawl of the Bois. In Neuilly, the car turned left into the driveway of a villa set back from the avenue, its main entrance well screened from curious stares.

'Henri!'

Hans-Dieter Strömelburg stood just inside the front door, arms outstretched in greeting. The warmth in his voice was sincere and genuine. 'What a pleasure to see you again! Its been too long, much too long, believe me. Müller,' he called to a uniformed aide, 'take Monsieur Lemaire's coat.'

He clapped a comradely arm around Henri's shoulders and led him into the villa's salon. 'Come,' he said – 'a drink to old times.'

Henri's appraising eyes noted the room's subdued elegance. Hand-chiselled wainscoting, at least a hundred years old, lined its walls. That luxury he recognized from his boyhood. A fire roared in the marble fireplace, and at one end of the room a tapestry of an eighteenth-century hunting scene, probably an Aubusson, covered the wall. That too brought back an echo of his boyhood. A duality of tastes here, he thought: that of the owner, probably a Jew, who'd assembled it all, and that of Strömelburg in deciding to requisition it for his living quarters.

'What can I offer you?' the German asked, gesturing towards his cluttered bar table. 'Cognac, vodka, Scotch whisky?' It was as if he were offering him his personal distillation of Occupied Europe.

'Perhaps a sherry.'

'Of course, a sherry. How appropriate,' said Strömelburg, laughing. He poured half a glass, swirled the amber liquid, gave it an approving sniff and passed it to Henri. 'Did you ever get to Jerez de la Frontera?'

'No. Valencia was as far in as I got.'

'Of course,' Strömelburg said in self-reproach. 'I'd forgotten. Jerez was on the Nationalist side. When I' – he paused, smiling – 'when your Minister of the Interior invited me to leave France in 1938, Heydrich sent me to Spain. I had the most marvellous weekend in Jerez with one of those sherry families. Beautiful place. Completely untouched by war.'

He waved towards a pair of heavy armchairs by the fire, as discordant a note amidst the salon's spindly Louis XIV furnishings as a cymbal's clash in a funeral dirge. Strömelburg's contribution, Henri thought.

'Now tell me about yourself. I want to know everything that's happened to you since we last saw each other,' Strömelburg said, raising his whisky glass. 'Everything. *Santé!*'

Henri thoughtfully sipped his sherry. 'Nothing very exciting, I'm afraid. Not so long after you left, I went back to commercial flying. The *Aéro-Postal*. Paris-Bordeaux and back every night until I could have flown it sound asleep if I had too. Then the war came and I was mobilized. Flew in a transport squadron from Etampes. When the armistice was signed, I was down in Marseille, ferrying planes to Algiers.' He glanced over at Strömelburg, his eyes measuring his friend's reaction to his words. 'I decided to stay there instead of coming back here. It seemed to me half a loaf was better than none as long as it was your own loaf.'

Strömelburg smiled, 'I don't blame you. I think I would have done the same thing myself.'

'It hasn't been easy getting work. I've done a few test-pilot contracts.'

Strömelburg nodded with sympathetic understanding. That's why he asked to see me, he thought. He wants to call in an old debt, have us get him a flying job up here. Well, why not? 'You ran into Rolf the other day, I understand. Maybe he – or we – could find something for you in Paris.'

The mischievous, somehow adolescent smile he'd always associated with Henri eased across the Frenchman's face. 'As it turns out, I now have a job. That's why I came to see you.'

A warning light flashed on in Strömelburg's subconscious. He's got himself caught in some kind of smuggling business, some black-market operation and he wants me to bail him out. That would be Henri Lemaire, all right. The rogue, the adventurer was never far from the surface with him.

'I got it about a month ago.' The Frenchman swirled his sherry, obviously uncertain how to phrase his next thought. 'It goes back, in a sense, to the Spanish Civil War. Funny, isn't it, how everything seems to be back there with us?'

Strömelburg, who had no idea where the younger man was leading, nodded in encouragement.

'Do you remember old Le Gastelloix, the airplane dealer out at Le Bourget?'

'With no great fondness, but yes, I remember him.'

'In late '37 a young Englishman, a lord, very enthusiastic for the Republic, showed up out there with a Lockheed 14. Le Gastelloix asked me to fly it to Barcelona. The English lord's name was Forbes. He took me up for a long check flight before I left.' Henri paused, then sipped his sherry ceremoniously. 'I ran into him in a bar in Marseille a month ago.' Having uttered his phrase, he sat back and appraised Strömelburg with cool amusement.

'I see,' Strömelburg replied, interested for the first time in their conversation. 'A walking tribute to the efficiency of the Luftwaffe, I suppose. On the run after being shot down.'

'Hans, that was exactly what I thought when I saw him,' Henri said, his rogue's cynical grin on his face. 'I was wrong. And as it turns out, you are too. Forbes hasn't been in an airplane since 1940.'

Strömelburg reflected on that a moment. 'You're not suggesting, I don't suppose, that he was in Marseille looking for a good *soupe de poisson?*'

Henri took another deliberate sip of sherry. 'He was looking for fish, in fact, but not the kind you put in a soup. He said he was there looking for recruits to work for a British secret service.'

'Rather candid of him to let you in on that little secret.'

'He asked me if I would go to work for him.'

Outwardly Strömelburg remained as urbanely unconcerned as ever. 'What line of work did he have in mind?'

'Something where I could put my flying experience to good use.'

'In Marseille?'

Henri shook his head. 'Up here. He asked me to set up an organization to handle clandestine night-time flights into deserted pastures in the Loire Valley. The British want them,' he said, 'to run their secret agents in and out of France.'

Strömelburg sat back both stunned and exultant. For months his services had been picking up rumours of mysterious flights darting into and out of France in the middle of the night. He'd been sceptical. The Luftwaffe, after all, had assured him such an operation was quasi-impossible.

'What did you tell him?' he asked with gentle insistence.

'I told him I wanted twenty-four hours to think it over.'

'And?'

'We met the next day. I accepted.' A sense of inner calm seemed to overtake Henri as he pronounced those words, something of the relief that spreads over a penitent who has just bared some dreadful sin to his confessor.

'And this conversation, you say, took place a month ago?'

Henri nodded. 'Two days later they sent me up here to start work. The first thing I had to do was find half a dozen fields I could use to receive the flights. Flat, open pasturelands near a landmark a pilot could pick up from three thousand feet, like a bridge or a river bend.' For a moment, Henri lapsed into silence. Then, quite abruptly, he stood up, set his sherry glass on the marble mantelpiece with a clatter. 'Look, Hans,' he declared, 'before we go any further, I want you to understand something. I want you to know exactly why I'm here.'

Strömelburg nodded but said nothing. Better, he reasoned, to let his visitor work out himself the tensions clearly raging inside him.

'It may seem absurd to you right now in view of the fact that I'm standing here in this room; but I'm a French patriot. When I was mobilized in '39, I asked to be assigned to fighters. Believe me, I would have shot down any German fighter I could have in 1940 and been damn

118

glad I had. I didn't come back to Paris after the armistice because I couldn't bear to live in the capital of my country occupied by a foreign army.'

Strömelburg waved his glass in a gesture of sympathetic understanding. 'Henri, believe me, no one admires or appreciates more than a German a man's devotion to his fatherland.'

Henri had clasped his hands behind his back and begun to pace up and down in front of the fireplace. 'In the old days, you used to think all I was interested in was airplanes, girls and money.'

'You do yourself an injustice, my dear Henri. I judged you a very courageous young man. A brilliant pilot, maybe a little headstrong and lacking, perhaps, a certain degree of political maturity.'

'Yes' – Henri winced – 'you were always lecturing me about how naïve I was to be working for the Spanish Republicans.'

'You were,' Strömelburg acknowledged, his smile indicating a fatherly understanding of a young man's waywardness.

'I needed money in those days. I was out of work, you'll remember.'

Once again the warning light flashed on in Strömelburg's mind. So now we come to the heart of the matter, he thought. He wanted to see me because he's ready to sell his operation. Well, I'll see to it that the price is right.

'I shouldn't have thought you were exactly swimming in money these days,' he said, trying to offer as subtly as possible an opening for the Frenchman's next move.

To Strömelburg's astonishment, Henri burst out laughing. His hand went to his pocket and yanked out a wad of francs. 'Swimming? I'm drowning in it! The English are generous employers, Hans.'

A feigned laugh covered Strömelburg's surprise and his accompanying flutter of relief. One of the principles that guided him in France was summed up in the dictum I love treason; I hate traitors. He would willingly have thrown open his coffers to buy Henri's operation, but the gesture would have been followed by a spasm of regret. He quite liked the adventuresome rogue before him; somehow he would have been saddened to see him ready to sell out his fellows for a few pieces of the Reich's silver. Henri had stopped his restless pacing and was leaning against the mantelpiece, staring into the flames below. He picked up his sherry glass, drained it with one gulp, then turned to Strömelburg. 'I must tell you, Hans, I want with all my heart to see Germany out of France. But not at any price. Not if it means the Bolsheviks take over after you leave. And as things are now, Hans, if Germany loses this war, the Communists will win France.'

'You've got a lot wiser since I last saw you,' said Strömelburg, smiling, wondering as he did whether the young man before him was just another opportunistic Frenchman anxious to be on the right side when the war ended or whether Henri really did understand the Communist menace. It was that, after all, which had brought Strömelburg to Nazism as a young student and focused the passions of his adult life.

'You were always telling me in the old days how politically naïve I was, Hans. Well, I wasn't quite as naïve as you thought. I know a lot more about the working classes than you think. And I keep my eyes open. I had them open in Barcelona, and I've had them open for the last three years in Marseille, too.'

Strömelburg started to say something but stopped himself. One of the lessons of his days as a policeman was if you want to learn, listen. Let others do the talking.

'Arms are beginning to flood into this country, Hans. I mean flood. The English think they're going to patriotic Frenchmen who want to fight Germans. They're wrong. Ninety per cent of them are going to the Communists. The Communists run the Resistance.'

'We are quite aware of that, Henri,' Strömelburg said, his voice lubricated with self-assurance. 'That's not exactly discovering Christ on the road to Damascus, you know.'

'Maybe you know; most of the country doesn't. They've done it the same way they did with the Republicans in Spain. A little group in the centre of things that gradually spreads until you wake up one day and they're running things and there's nothing you can do about it anymore. They're not going to use those arms they're bringing into this country to kill you Germans, Hans. They're going to use them to kill Frenchmen, Frenchmen like me who'll be against the revolution they're going to make when the war's over.'

'Still,' Strömelburg noted, appraising with lifeless eyes the young Frenchman, 'it took you a month to come to this conclusion, didn't it? A month during which you worked, I presume, for our English friends.'

'Yes, it did.' There was an almost surly defiance in Henri's tone. 'You Germans aren't the only saviours in the world, you know. I told you I want to see Germany out of France' – he shrugged his shoulders – 'so I was ready to try the English.'

'Do you know England?'

'I've never been to England in my life. I wouldn't know a pub from a pissotière.'

'You've decided you prefer us to our English rivals?'

'The English, Hans, look out for the English. I've learned that. They left us on the beaches at Dunkirk. They blew our fleet out of the water at Mers el-Kébir. They'll hand us to Stalin over a cup of tea if they think it's going to save their island. But let me tell you this: I like the English.' Henri smiled. 'Now, you Germans, on the other hand, are in a different position, Hans. You're not the most likeable people in the world, but you're not going to sell anybody to Stalin. You can't. He's not buying. You have to defeat him because if you don't he'll enslave you. That's why, when all is said and done, only Germany stands between France and the Communists.'

Strömelburg sat silent for a long time contemplating all the implications of what Henri had told him.

'You don't believe me, do you?'

Strömelburg looked up, surprised. That had not been among his calculations.

'I'll give you the details of my first operation. Set someone up to watch it if you want. You'll see I'm telling you the truth.'

'When's the first plane coming in?'

'Tomorrow night.'

'Tomorrow night!'

Henri settled back into his armchair with a sigh. 'That's what brought it all to a head, Hans. It's why I told Rolf when I saw him last night he had to fix a meeting for me with you tonight. I knew I couldn't go through with it. However much I want to see you Germans out of France, I can't bring myself to do something I know will prepare the way for the communists to take over the country.'

Strömelburg got up, refilled Henri's sherry glass and poured himself another whisky. 'Now tell me, just how is this operation supposed to work?' he asked, returning to his chair.

'After I found the fields, we radioed their locations to London so the RAF could photograph them.'

'How did you get the message off?'

'Through a letter drop. A café. The RAF radioed back accepting four of the six fields I gave them.'

'How often are those flights suposed to run?'

'Every full moon. Two, three, maybe four at the most a month. Each flight will bring in two or three people and take out two or three.'

The dimensions of what Henri was describing staggered the Gestapo chieftain.

'Ah,' the Frenchman added, 'I forgot. I'm also supposed to pick up courier packets for each flight at letter drops they'll set up around the city.'

Twelve agents a month coming in, Strömelburg calculated. London would reserve this service for its most important agents, certainly. And those envelopes full of information. If Henri was telling him the truth, his job would be the roundhouse turntable, the vital pivot on which an entire British operation in France would have to turn.

'Did they tell you whom this was for?'

121

'An organization called the SOE.'

'I know them well. But surely they don't expect you to do this all alone?'

Henri shook his head. 'They've given me a deputy and a radio operator.'

Strömelburg gave an admiring whistle. A radio operator. That was proof of how important this was to the British. The German played with the drops of whisky in his glass as though momentarily distracted by the light refracted through the crystal. He was, of course, backtracking over what Henri had told him, probing his story, trying to align in the space of a few brief seconds the alternatives open to him.

'Tell me, Henri, are you still living in your old apartment?'

Puzzled that after what he had told him Strömelburg should be interested in his domestic arrangements, Henri indicated that he was.

'Does anyone else besides Rolf know you came here tonight?'

Henri looked at him aghast. 'Hans, I know you used to think I was a bit of an adventurer, but believe me, that doesn't include a vocation for suicide.'

Strömelburg laughed with the swiftness of a passing breeze, then turned serious again. 'Exactly where and when is this first landing suposed to take place?'

Henri gave him, in painstaking detail, the information.

Now it was Strömelburg's turn to get up and pace the room, hands clasped behind his back. Humming softly, he sifted the implications of what Henri had told him through the filter of his mind, analysing his motives, juxtaposing them against his earlier memories of the young man. Then decided on the shrewdest course open to him.

He stopped and turned to the Frenchman. 'What I want you to do, Henri, is pretend you never came here tonight. Draw a curtain in your mind on our talk. Go back and carry on with that operation tomorrow night exactly as though we'd never met. Don't ask me why I'm telling you to do this. Not now. Later, when we're in touch again, I'll tell you.'

'If that's the way you want it, Hans.'

'It is.'

At the door, waiting for the car to come around, Strömelburg threw an affectionate arm around Henri's shoulder. 'You were right to come, old friend – you'll see.' Hearing the car's tyres crunching on the gravel, he extended his hand. 'We'd better give you a code name. Use it if you have to call me. I'll use it to contact you.' The German stared up at the night-time sky. 'Do you know that line from Gilbert and Sullivan "Things are seldom what they seem"?'

Henri shook his head.

'Never mind. Let's make it "Gilbert." It seems appropriate in the circumstances.' He squeezed Henri's hand. 'Good night, Gilbert. Together, we will achieve great things.'

As soon as the car drove off, Strömelburg went to his telephone.

'Get me the Commanding General of the Luftwaffe's Third Air Fleet at Le Bourget,' he told the military operator, 'immediately.'

The two men trembled from the damp that seeped through their bodies. The vantage point Strömelburg had picked was the ideal spot from which to study Henri Lemaire's improvised airfield: a shoulder-high drainage ditch, its lips overgrown with brambles and thistles. The problem was the steady flow of water gurgling through the bottom of the ditch. It had kept Strömelburg and Wilhelm Keiffer of his Paris Gestapo staff ankle-deep in ice-cold water for two hours. In fact, Keiffer was so cold he couldn't stop his teeth from chattering or his body from twisting in a kind of spastic trance.

Strömelburg looked at him contemptuously. Keiffer, the SS athlete, forever running off to some French gym stinking of sweat and liniment to jump over a leather horse and swing around on some rings. And pick up young French boys, I'll bet, Strömelburg thought, giving his aide a sharp, vicious jab in the forearm. 'Can't you stop that shaking, for Christ's sake?'

'No, I'm freezing to death.'

'Good,' Strömelburg grimaced. 'That will get you in shape for the day Berlin decides to send you to the Eastern Front.'

'If that day comes,' Keiffer groaned through his dancing teeth, 'I'll put a bullet through my foot.'

'Better try your head, Keiffer. A bad leg never kept a good SS officer like you off the *Fronturlauberzug* for Brest Litovsk.' Strömelburg, pleased at the discomfort that thought might bring his deputy, returned to his study of the field as it led away from their ditch. Six, seven hundred meters long, he guessed, as open as a billiard table, its grass clipped low by some obliging farmer's cows. There was almost no slope, and it faced west, into the prevailing winds. At the far end were a low stand of poplar trees and the shed in which Henri had said his party would wait until close to the time the plane was expected.

'No plane is going to land here,' Keiffer growled. 'That Frenchman of yours sold you a dead horse. He was just trying to set you off for a payoff.'

'The word "money" never came into our conversation,' Strömelburg whispered, 'but if he made us come all the way down here for nothing, he'd better have disappeared from his apartment by the time we get back to Paris.'

Keiffer tried to stomp the circulation back into his feet, by now numb

123

with cold. 'We'll get trench foot. I still don't know why you didn't let me take a squadron down here and round them all up if you're so sure there's a plane coming.'

'Stop that splashing,' Strömelburg hissed. 'You share the failing of most policemen, Keiffer. You think in straight lines.' Again the two fell silent, their ears screening the distant winds for the drone of an airplane engine. The next time Keiffer glanced at his watch, it was past midnight. He tapped its luminous dial for his superior's benefit. 'They're not coming,' he whispered. 'Can I smoke?'

'By all means do, Keiffer,' Strömelburg whispered, ill-concealing the anger mounting in him. 'And while you're at it, why don't you go over to that shed down there and ask one of the Frenchmen inside for a light?' It was almost at the instant he said it that he noticed the first Frenchman slipping out of the shed. 'Look!' he gloated.

There were probably half a dozen of them. Some moved along the field, while two of them paced around, apparently setting up stakes. When they'd finished, the field once again fell silent. Twenty minutes later, both men picked up the engine's drone. From the ground they saw a flashlight blink a letter in Morse and the answering flash from the plane swooping overhead. A dark figure turned on three flashlights tied to stakes in the middle of the field, and then there was the plane dropping over the grove of poplar trees. In seconds it came rushing down the pasture towards their ditch, spun about and headed away from them. As it stopped, they could hear voices, a door clanking, see figures running in the moonlight. Then the pilot applied his throttle and the plane was rushing down the field again, lifting up over the poplars.

Strömelburg looked at his watch. The whole thing had taken barely three minutes. 'It's perfect,' he whispered in admiration. 'It worked exactly the way Henri said it would. What a superb operation!'

'The Luftwaffe will have that one before they reach the coast,' Keiffer growled.

His superior was lost in some mental labyrinth as he watched the figures of the Resistance agents disappearing down the road behind the shed. When his reply finally came, it was almost as an afterthought. 'Oh, no, they won't, Keiffer. I've seen to that.'

Forty-eight hours later, Strömelburg was striding down the corridors on Prinz-Albrecht-Strasse in Berlin of the RSHA – the main office for the Security of the Reich, the building from which Heinrich Himmler and his deputies presided over their empire of evil. The building's cellar housed a laboratory of human perversity, the torture cells in which Himmler's minions perfected those techniques of 'energetic and indefatigable interrogation' which had led Himmler to boast – and his enemies to fear – that there was no one who could not be broken under Gestapo torture. For all its notoriety, however, Prinz-Albrecht-Strasse was, by the Reich's standards, relatively underguarded – a reflection, perhaps, of how few people were eager to enter its doors. Hans-Dieter Strömelburg had only to flash his oval metal Gestapo ID plate at the sentry to be waved inside the building's inner sanctum. As he strolled nonchalantly towards his meeting, he chuckled at the sight of three SS enlisted men in white smocks marching beside him brandishing flyswatters and spray guns. Among the many quirks of the RSHA's leader was a morbid fear of flies. Convinced that they were the carriers of viruses and pestilence, Himmler kept three men on duty twenty-four hours a day searching Prinz-Albrecht-Strasse for insects.

Strömelburg entered the offices of Himmler's deputy, SS *Gruppenführer* Dr Ernst Kaltenbrunner, and was immediately ushered into his inner office. Two men were waiting for him. Kaltenbrunner and Strömelburg's immediate superior, SS *Obersturmbannführer Kriminalrat* Horst Kopkow. Strömelburg despised Kaltenbrunner. Unlike his volatile predecessor Reinhard Heydrich, Strömelburg's patron, Kaltenbrunner was a plodding, methodical bureaucrat blessed for the task with an unremitting mediocrity of mind. Physically, he was a massive, ugly man, a parody of a circus wrestler. That appearance had earned him the nickname 'the icebox.' Strömelburg would have no trouble manipulating him; he never did.

Kopkow was another matter. Strömelburg both needed and distrusted him. In a certain way, he epitomized the SS type and mentality. He came from lower-middle-class origins in Oranienburg, where he'd been an apothecary's assistant before joining the SS in 1934. He was devious, scheming and, above all, ambitious. Had Himmler asked him to preside over one of the SS' death camps, he would have done so joyfully, hastening his charges to the gas chambers with the same dour efficiency he'd once employed in blending cough syrup. As it was, it was he who had instructed Gestapo officers throughout Europe to employ torture without remorse or restriction in interrogating prisoners. Counterespionage, on the territory of the Reich, was Kopkow's speciality. Strömelburg knew he would need his backing to put the plan he'd brought to Berlin into operation. He also knew that if it failed, Kopkow would see that the blame fell on him, and if it worked he would do his best to claim credit for the success himself. 'I presume,' Kopkow observed, with the sourness of a man whose breakfast remained undigested, 'something of considerable importance brought you here this morning and led you to ask for this meeting.'

Strömelburg placed his briefcase on the floor and began removing his black calfskin goves with deliberate slowness. 'It has,' he said, looking at

Kaltenbrunner. 'I believe I have in my hands the key to an intelligence operation which will eventually bring us greater dividends than either *Red Orchestra* or *North Pole.*' Those two operations, one directed against the Soviets, one in Holland, had both been supervised by Kopkow.

'It involves the most important secret of the war: when and where the Allies will invade the Continent.' He stayed his speech a second for dramatic effect. 'They will almost certainly strike in France. And when they do, they will just as certainly employ the French Resistance to support their attack. Therefore, to pierce the secret of their invasion, we must first pierce the Resistance at the right level. Would you agree?'

Kaltenbrunner said nothing. Kopkow hissed out a hostile sigh. Strömelburg's allusion to the *Red Orchestra* and the *North Pole* had not gone unnoticed.

'The French Resistance breaks down into three components,' Strömelburg continued. 'First, and by far the most numerous, are the Gaullist networks run from London by a Frenchman named Passy. The English do not trust them. They know we have penetrated their ranks. The English will never give them the secret of their invasion.' Strömelburg, quite pleased with the conciseness of the well-rehearsed presentation, paused to study his two superiors. 'Second are the networks run by British Intelligence. Their functions are limited to gathering intelligence. We might pierce the invasion secret by analysing the questions they're asked to answer. But they won't be given the secret because they don't need it for their work. Third,' Strömelburg continued, ' is the French Section of the SOE. It's the smallest of the three and exclusively British-run. Its function is the sabotage of our vital installations. We know from interrogating their agents that they all expect to play a major role in supporting the landing when it comes.'

'This is as fresh as three-day-old beer,' Kopkow noted. 'Surely this is not the reason for your visit.'

Strömelburg sat back, doling out his words like an actor striving for effect. 'I now have the means to bring the entire SOE organization in France under my control.' He savoured their reaction, then described the aerial service his new agent had set up, how it was to operate, how he had watched a first demonstration of its effectiveness. 'I now propose to guarantee the continuing success of that operation for the British. I'll keep the Luftwaffe away from their fields. I'll see that our police and the Wehrmacht don't disturb them.'

'I can't believe you're serious,' Kaltenbrunner said. 'Put our facilities at the service of the British? And let those agents come and go, unmolested?'

'The better an agent this man – whom I shall call Gilbert – is for the

British, the more confidence they have in him, the better an agent he's going to be for me.'

'Strömelburg, in theory, is right, Doctor,' Kopkow said. 'The time and place of the landing are the key to the war. Compared with that, what do a few agents matter?'

'We can pick up one or two from time to time.' Strömelburg assured his superior. 'But a mass arrest is out of the question. We'll follow their agents when they come in. See where they go, where they meet, where their safe houses are so that when the invasion comes, we can sweep them up in one mass arrest.'

'Before you go any further,' Kopkow declared, 'I want to know about this man Gilbert.'

'Of course. His real name is Henri Lemaire. I've known him since 1937.'

'Has he worked for you before?'

'Indeed he has. For a very long time, and very loyally. We became aware early in 1937 that he was ferrying planes from Paris to Barcelona for the Republicans. *Standartenführer* Rolf Untermeyer of Section VI, whom Heydrich had assigned to Barcelona, ran into him one night in some cabaret down there. They'd met at the pilots' bar at Le Bourget in 1936 when Rolf was flying Berlin–Paris for Lufthansa.'

'He could have given Rolf away to the Republicans,' Kopkow observed.

'He could have, but he didn't. Anyway, Lemaire's a bit of a ladies' man, so Rolf arranged for a young lady to relieve him of his wallet one night. Rolf managed to meet him by sheerest accident the next morning in his hotel as he was getting ready to go back to Paris and asked him if he'd deliver an envelope for him in Paris for a considerable sum of money. Our friend Henri accepted with alacrity. The envelope, of course, was destined for me. I gave him another five thousand francs arrival money, and we became quite friendly. I asked him if he'd be willing to take an envelope back to Rolf on the same terms. He agreed.'

'And that was all?' Kopkow asked.

'Not at all. He became my most regular and trusted courier.'

'How long did this go on?'

'He made two or three deliveries a month for me for almost a year.'

'With no problems?'

'Absolutely none. He was, as I said, the best courier we had.'

'And did he know whom he was doing all this for?'

'Obviously, at first we didn't address the envelopes to the *Sicherheitsdienst*, dear colleague, if that's what you mean. We told him nothing. However, he knew Rolf had flown for Lufthansa and we were both German. He's a clever chap. I don't suppose he thought those

127

envelopes contained scraps of Goethe's poetry. Later, because I wanted to check on his loyalties, I made it clear to him who we were. He went on without a hitch. And remember, if the Spaniards had caught him with those envelopes, they would have shot him on the spot.'

'All right,' Kopkow said, 'tell me about him personally.'

Strömelburg scanned the spartan setting of Kaltenbrunner's office while he formulated his answer. His chief's taste in art, he noticed, was largely confined to portraits of the Führer in varying poses. 'Gilbert's a first-class aviator,' he said finally. 'Now, to be a first-class aviator, a man has to have a great deal of self-confidence. He must also have a judicious sense of fear, because an aviator who doesn't have a judicious sense of fear is a man on his way to the graveyard.' He paused. 'That, I would say, is also the description of an ideal agent.'

'Please, *Herr Obersturmbannführer*,' Kopkow observed sourly, 'spare us your enigmas. I want his personal background. Surely you investigated him when he became your courier.'

Strömelburg turned away Kopkow's malevolence with a smile. 'Certainly. Our friend Henri Lemaire was born with a silver spoon in his mouth. Unfortunately – and the fact has apparently bothered him most of his life – the spoon belonged to someone else. His birthplace was a seventeenth-century *château* on the edge of the Forest of Compiègne. His mother was the *château*'s cook. His father was the janitor. He was a glutton whose sin was compounded by a deficient thyroid gland. As a result, the man was so obese that there was considerable doubt in the village as to his ability to perform his marital functions. Suspicions as to who the child's father really was tended to fall on the *château*'s proprietor. In any event, our friend Lemaire was very close to him while he was growing up. He clearly has tried to pattern himself after him in his speech, his dress. As a result, he's a classless man. He dresses with elegance; he has no accent. He can pass in almost any quarter of French society. Indeed, he likes to suggest that he is a country squire who in fact owns that *château* in whose servants' quarters he was born.'

'His political convictions?'

'None we could discover. His passion for flying came early and seems to have completely dominated him. Rolf never detected any political feelings in him in their meeting at the pilots' bar at Le Bourget. But he was very admiring of the Germans he knew as pilots.'

'So he was a mercenary.'

'He likes money because he likes to spend it: on clothes, women, food. He needs it to play that false role of a country squire he's created for himself. That's why he took his job ferrying planes for the Republicans. It's why he started working for me.'

'Has he asked for money for this operation?' It was Kaltenbrunner's first contribution. 'Give him some,' he ordered when Strömelburg told him he had not. 'Nothing compromises a man more surely than a little money.'

'Why did he come to you if it wasn't for money?' Kopkow demanded.

Strömelburg described in detail his conversation with Henri Lemaire. 'I never have total confidence in an agent who doesn't share some of our ideology, and I'm absolutely convinced of his anti-Communism. Indeed, it fits very well with the personality I've just described.'

'Quite right.' Strömelburg was pleasantly surprised by the support he was getting from Kopkow. 'Agents,' Kopkow observed, 'are motivated by one of two things when you get down to it. Money – "Give me enough money and I'll betray the empress of China" – and ideology – "I do because I believe." I've always preferred the latter.'

'Furthermore,' Strömelburg went on, 'his operation worked exactly as he described it to me. It has to be one of the most secret and vital operations the British are running.'

'Yes.' Kopkow slowly inclined his head in agreement. 'I certainly agree with that. I also understand perfectly well how you can use this man's air operations to gradually bring these people under your control. Follow enough of those incoming agents long enough and you'll wind up knowing all there is to know about them. What I don't understand is why you're so convinced this will give us the secret of the invasion.'

'In addition to smuggling agents into and out of France, my friend will also be responsible for sending out packets of secret material. He'll pick it up at letter drops around Paris and hand it personally to the pilot.'

Kopkow nodded.

'Now, the primary function of the SOE is sabotage. We've seen examples of their work already – the Peugeot factory, the Lyon Perrache rail centre. When the landing comes, there will be certain targets the Allies will have to sabotage. Radar installations, communication facilities, railroad junctions, key defensive posts. They plan to employ the SOE, acting either alone or, more likely, in coordination with paratroops, to do it.'

Kopkow and Kaltenbrunner looked at him intrigued.

'To arrange operations like that you must have specific tools: maps, plans of buildings, blueprints, drawings on which you can set out a line of attack, the precise spot where a charge must be placed.'

'Yes. All perfectly logical,' Kopkow agreed.

'You can't radio a blueprint to London in an unbreakable code, can you?'

Even Kaltenbrunner began to smile as the implications of Strömelburg's scheme struck home.

'There is only one way they can get that vital material back and forth to

England – in the secret courier packets Gilbert is going to pick up and deliver to his planes. It is there in those packets, my friends, that we will discover the secret of their invasion.'

PART THREE

MARCH/APRIL 1944

'OSS, aren't you, Major?'

'Yes, sir,' T.F. O'Neill snapped, his eyes warily noting the black plaque on the brigadier general's desk designated him as Adjutant for Intelligence to General George C. Marshall, Chief of Staff of the United States Army.

'Well, not anymore. From now on, you belong to this office and you're going to do things our way, not Donovan's way. Here, read this.'

Almost angrily, he thrust a single sheet of paper at T.F. As he did, the young officer caught the rusty glint of his West Point class ring. Probably one of the old school, he surmised, a long-standing member of the US Army's Intelligence Corps, one of those idealists who believed gentlemen didn't read each other's mail. T.F. glanced at the memorandum. It had been written by General George Strong, the army's Vice Chief of Staff for Intelligence and the most persistent critic of the OSS in Washington. Strong accused the OSS of employing tactics that were 'devoid of any reference to moral considerations or standards, and proceeding on the unspoken premise that the US in a total war must take on the ethical colour of its enemies in all particulars.' Furthermore, Strong wrote, the OSS dismissed 'the possibility that the US, from a conception of its long-term interests and for the maintenance of one of its greatest assets – its moral position among peoples of the world – might sometimes consider it wise to refrain from taking advantage of the racial, religious and social hatreds existing in the world or even of the weaknesses and vulnerability of the people of enemy populations, or populations within enemy-occupied territories.' Ultimately, Strong declared, Wild Bill Donovan's ambition was to create and command 'a central intelligence agency of the government,' an organization he argued was neither 'necessary nor compatible with the United States' democratic institutions.'

Strong's words digested, T.F. started to hand the paper back. The brigadier general rejected it. 'Keep it,' he ordered. 'Memorize it. Lock it in your desk drawer over there in London and read it twice a day. Nothing will ever sum up better than that paper does the principles we expect you to be guided by in London. The ideas in there may sound a bit

133

old-fashioned to a smart young fellow like you, but they got this country a long way in the last hundred and fifty years, and don't you forget it.'

T.F. sensed a softening in the older man's hostility. He eased back in his swivel chair and clasped his hands behind his head. 'We've given you a damn hard job, Major. The organization you've been assigned to is exclusively British. Involved with deceiving the enemy. When I got into this business twenty years ago, we used to say four institutions ran the world: the White House, Buckingham Palace, the Vatican and the British Secret Service.' He paused. 'They still do, Major.

'The British Secret Service is the best there is. They're also devious, ruthless and treacherous. They eat nice Yale boys like you for breakfast and spit them out when they're finished.'

The brigadier general exhaled a mouthful of rancid cigar smoke. 'You may be from Connecticut, Major, but when you get to London, you better be from Missouri. The British don't love other people. They use them. Although,' – a malicious glitter appeared in his steel-grey eyes – 'I shouldn't have to tell someone named O'Neill that, should I?'

T.F. struggled to suppress a smile but said nothing.

'They operate on one principle: the ends justify the means. Well, for us, they don't.' The grey eyes appraised T.F. 'Sound strange to you?'

It sounds, T.F. thought, like a lousy way to win a war. However, he intoned the ritual. 'No, sir.' Majors, after all, rarely won arguments with brigadier generals.

'We don't want to see this country polluting its aims and ideals by adopting tactics that are identical to those the Fascists employ – on the basis of the dubious argument that it's the only way to fight them.' The brigadier general grunted as though in resigned awareness of how swiftly the tides of modern warfare were eroding the ideals for which he and his kind stood, how rapidly the times were outdating so many of the values he'd been taught in his pre-World-War West Point. He opened his desk drawer and took out a roll of adhesive tape and an envelope covered with red wax seals.

'However, we didn't bring you back to Washington just to give you a lecture, Major. This,' he noted, waving the envelope, 'contains intelligence material of such consequence we prefer not to transmit it by radio. Go into the toilet with the MP over there and tape it to your chest. You're responsible for hand-carrying it to General Ismay at the Underground War Rooms when you get to England. If anything happens to your aircraft, it will be your responsibility to destroy it, whatever the cost.'

The sound of a door opening interrupted him. T.F turned to find himself looking at General Marshall himself. Marshall's cold blue eyes stared right through him. 'Is this the officer who's going to London?' he asked his deputy.

'Yes, sir.'

Marshall turned back to T.F., giving him as he did an appraising glance. 'You are to let nothing interfere with your mission, Major. When you arrive in the United Kingdom you will not sleep, you will not eat, you will not drink, you will not communicate with anyone, of any rank or service, until you have personally placed that envelope in the hands of General Ismay. Do I make myself clear?'

You certainly do, T.F. thought. 'Yes, sir,' he snapped.

Marshall spun about and without even bidding his messenger farewell or safe journey, stalked back into his office.

PARIS

No prisoner, Hans-Dieter Strömelburg had learned in his years with the police and the Gestapo, cooperates like a prisoner who feels he has been betrayed. Whether the betrayal was by a fellow criminal or by the stupidity of his superiors, as was the case with the SOE radio operator Alex Wild, the result was invariably the same: a rage that shattered the prisoner's will to resist.

That was exactly what had happened with Wild. Strömelburg's thugs who had subjected him to such ferocious beatings got a medical aide to attend him, brought him a tray of food and wine and primed him with cigarettes and sympathy. By the time Strömelburg's minions had finished with Wild, the Englishman could have been forgiven a certain confusion as to just who his real friends were.

Strömelburg felt reasonably sure he had held nothing back. His description of SOE's London operations had dovetailed with many things Strömelburg already knew, but it was not information that was going to help him disrupt SOE operations in France. For that, Wild had been of little help because he knew very little. SOE agents coming in rarely did. He knew the name – 'Butler' – of the network he was going to work for in the Lille area; the name and physical description of its commander, a Captain Guillaume; the name of the café on Rue de Béthune where he was to make contact with Michel and the password he was to use to identify himself. It was a slender harvest, Strömelburg reflected, but probably the best he could have hoped for.

The Doctor jumped to his feet as soon as Strömelburg entered the room. His was one of the select offices looking out onto Avenue Foch, a reward for the skill he had displayed in conducting his radio game with

135

London. That he had so clearly deserved the reward never ceased to puzzle Strömelburg, because to him the Doctor was a puzzle. He was not a National Socialist. He was a conscripted soldier sent to Paris as an interpreter. His name, which no one ever used, was Wilhelm Kranz. He was pale, shy and distinguished by a lock of dark hair which, like the Führer's, was forever falling over his high forehead. Strömelburg, impressed by his ability, had offered him a commission in the SS and a permanent posting to Avenue Foch. To his amazement, the young linguist had refused. He had no desire to join the SS. Strömelburg countered with the offer of a place in a labour battalion being drafted for service on the Eastern Front. That proposition had helped the Doctor to see the wisdom of accepting Strömelburg's earlier suggestion, which he promptly did.

Yet once he had taken on his radio game, he'd manipulated it with enthusiasm and brilliance – a meek schoolteacher playing Napoleon and relishing every moment of it. He lived in this office, subsisting on coffee, cigarettes and sandwiches, drafting his messages for London as though the success of the war depended on them – which, Strömelburg thought, it very well might. He never went out, never drank, never mixed in the mess. His sole recreation was an occasional movie at the *Soldatenkino* on the Champs-Elysées. Probably, his superior guessed, the only Gestapo officer in France who had never sampled the delights of a good French whore.

Strömelburg sat down in an armchair and propped his feet on the Doctor's desk. Such feigned casualness, he was convinced, helped to lubricate the considerable machinery of his subordinate's mind. 'Now, Doctor,' he queried, 'how do we bring this new player of ours into our game?' He waved towards the map of France on the wall behind the Doctor's desk. On it were marked the locations of the fifteen SOE networks whose radio operators, all either dead or in prison, the Doctor was already imitating to London. They were scattered along a curve, running from 'Saturn' in Saint-Malo in Brittany through 'Tanz' in Chartres and 'Grossfürst' in Dijon to 'Walze' in Saint-Quentin. 'We're fortunate he was on his way to Lille,' Strömelburg noted. 'We seem to be short of sets in the North. Are there any clandestine radios operating from Lille now?'

'Not anymore. Our radio detection services arrested one six weeks ago, but he managed to swallow his cyanide pill before anyone could talk to him.'

Strömelburg contemplated the buffed pink of his fingernails. Wild was obviously the man's replacement. At least there were no other sets on the air up there to tell London of Wild's arrest.

'If we try to develop him for arms drops, we may run into a problem,' the Doctor remarked. 'The RAF doesn't like to fly drops in the North. They're afraid of our night fighters in Pas-de-Calais.'

'You don't think you could put together a convincing case for our friend Cavendish?'

'I could make it sound convincing enough.' The Doctor had long ago developed imitating SOE messages into an art form. 'The problem is – won't Cavendish recognise a Gestapo officer at the other end of the line if I start calling for arms drops in an area where agents are usually told not to use them?'

'My dear Doctor' – Strömelburg offered his subordinate his most becoming smile – 'I sometimes wonder if Cavendish would recognize a Gestapo officer if one walked into his office in black dress uniform singing the "Horst Wessel Song." However, you have a point. How else could one use him?'

'I've been thinking about what you said last night.'

Strömelburg's smile told the Doctor how thoroughly he approved of that.

'It gave me an idea for something we might do. Could you arrest this Captain Guillaume and some of his people quickly – before our operator upstairs is supposed to make contact?'

'Perhaps.'

'If you can, then in my first message to London I'll tell them Michel's been arrested. I'll say Lille has become so dangerous I've had to go into hiding for two or three weeks until the storm passes. That will give me a logical explanation for not sending out any messages for a while.'

'Quite frankly, I fail to see how that advances our work.'

'I'll also tell London the café on Rue de Béthune they gave Wild as his contact point is still safe. I'll tell London that if there is anyone in the area who has an emergency message he has to get out, he can pass it to me through the café using a code phrase I'll give them.'

'Our tethered goat,' said the admiring Strömelburg. 'You're a Kipling scholar after all. We dangle Mr Wild's radio in front of London and then sit back to see whom Cavendish sends slinking out of the forests of the night up there to use it.' He rose to his feet and threw a comradely arm over his subordinate's shoulder. 'You're a very clever man indeed, Doctor,' he said, 'although you're also a bit of a bore.'

The Doctor looked at him puzzled.

'I had far better things in mind for this evening than a visit to Lille.'

Behind Catherine Pradier, a wandering violinist, his jacket glowing with age, coaxed his instrument through a tender, if somewhat approximative, rendition of 'Parlez-moi d'amour.' How incongruous the song's plaintive call seemed to Catherine, huddled at her table in the forecourt of the Café des Trois Suisses. She was surrounded by Germans. Never in her life had she seen so many. Calais seemed to be carpeted with them: Germans in the grey-green of the Wehrmacht, the blue-grey of the Luftwaffe, the dark blue of the Kriegsmarine; Germans crowding the sidewalks, guarding the intersections, filling the tables of her café; more Germans within the confines of her vision, it seemed to Catherine, than Calaisians.

And these were not the German soldier tourists of Paris, dashing from church to museum with their guidebooks in hand while they waited for the bars and brothels of Montmartre to open their doors. These were fighting Germans, the kinsmen of the Stuka pilot who'd machine-gunned her mother and the sunburned warriors who'd ripped her nation apart in another springtime four years earlier. If they inspired her with a renewed sense of loathing and a realization of why she was here, their massive presence inspired her as well with an abiding sense of fear. How could a resistance hope to function in the midst of so many Germans? How long a life span could she hope to have adrift in this hostile sea?

As discreetly as possible, she moved her gaze from the paper on her lap to the street corner before her, searching for her contact with his metal toolbox. Why, in God's name, doesn't he show up? she asked herself. This was her third afternoon at the Trois Suisses. What's gone wrong? she wondered. Is it because I was late for the first meeting? Have they given me up for lost? Have Aristide and his network been captured by the Gestapo? Am I alone here in this hostile city, with no contact to turn to?

She forced herself to concentrate on the paper in her lap. It was the local collaborationist newspaper, *Le Phare de Calais* – The Calais Lighthouse. For the fifth time, she studied the ads: for a pair of ladies' shoes, genuine leather, size 38; the Voice of the Reich on 279 meters urging Calaisians to 'listen to the much-beloved waltzes of Johann Strauss, so much a part of the cultural heritage of the German people.' She looked again at the official announcement that had so amused her. The German High Command had just ordered a formal census of Pas-de-Calais – not of its people, but of its dogs. Every dog owner in the *département* was instructed to register his pet at his local town hall: the sex of the dog, breed, pedigree if any, height measured to the shoulders, together with the owner's name and address. The town halls were then ordered to submit the results in duplicate to the *Kriegskommandantur* no later than May 15.

For God's sake, why? she wondered. What unearthly obsession with order drove these people to their bizarre concern with French dogs on the eve of the battle on which their existence depended? Contemplating the absurdity of that helped to keep her mind from the black-bordered '*Avis*' on the front page which listed the names of the Resistants like herself 'condemned and shot in Lille' the day before 'for actions against the Occupying Power.' How could you reconcile those three things in one people: those Strauss waltzes, the absurd obsession with the dogs of Calais, the brutality of their firing squads.

Catherine shook her head and glanced at the street corner; no one was there. Why? Why? She turned back to her paper, trying to force herself to concentrate on its dreary pages. She could not. Instead, she allowed her mind to return – as it had so often since she had left Paris – to Paul. That twisted, roguish smile of his, the mocking gaze of his eyes, seem to rise up to her from the pages of *Le Phare de Calais*. For an instant, she could almost feel his strong yet tender arms encircling her. As a cat seeks instinctively the comfort of a pool of winter sunshine, she sought a passing warmth in the still vivid recollection of their time together. Would she ever see him again? Would he survive the war? Would she? How absurd, she thought: she didn't even know his name. Sitting there thinking about Paul, she felt a delicious paralysis invade her limbs. How similar it was to the paralysis she'd felt the instant the Gestapo officer had demanded her papers at the roadblock. They were kindred emotions, love and fear, weren't they?

She gave her head a toss as a schoolboy might in trying not to fall asleep in a stifling classroom. Better not to let her mind wander. They had warned her in London that loneliness – utter, aching loneliness – would be the most difficult burden to bear in her clandestine life. Since stepping down from the fisheries truck that had delivered her to Calais, she had not addressed a word to another human being beyond three requests for a cup of *ersatz* coffee to the waiter at this café.

Not that it had been easy. Every other German she passed, it seemed, had made an effort to pick her up. Terrified, she'd ignored them all. Like all new agents, she felt she had a sign reading 'Enemy Agent – Made in England' stamped on her forehead. And she constantly recalled Cavendish's warning that 'excess glamour or beauty can lead to Dachau.' She should have listened to him and cut her hair. It was hidden, now, under an old scarf, left uncombed to match her makeupless face, but few men were fooled by that.

The man with the toolbox still wasn't there. He was ten minutes overdue, and Catherine knew the rules: never linger when a rendezvous has been missed. She got up and started to pace the streets. She had had nothing to eat since her arrival except the handful of raw herrings her truck driver had left her. Hunger pains cramped her stomach. For a moment, she tried to nourish herself with the memories of her black-market meal with Paul. A black-market restaurant in this small city was out of the question. A stranger, a lone female, she would draw curiosity as a light draws moths. She was reluctant to line up at a grocery store, afraid some unknowing gesture with her ration book would betray her.

Desperate, she set out for the only place she thought she could go in safety, the esplanade behind the Church of Notre Dame. There, she knew, she would find a communal kitchen for the poor and dispossessed of Calais. She took her place in line with a score of toothless old women in torn coats and felt slippers, derelict men with the memory of enough alcohol to preserve a dinosaur written on their faces. I fit in as naturally here, she thought, as a Communist organizer at a bankers' convention. The puzzled smile of the priest as he ladled out her metal bowl of soup in which a few forlorn scraps of vegetable floated confirmed her sentiment. As she took a first grateful sip, she heard an engine behind her. An open German command car drew to a halt beside the church, and an elegant officer stepped out.

'Come over here and have a word with me, *ma petite*,' the priest whispered to Catherine with a malicious smile.

Slipping around beside him, Catherine realized his gesture had transformed her from a pensioner at his soup kitchen to the more appropriate role of a good lady of the parish helping the pastor with his charity. From the corner of her eye she watched as an enlisted man handed the officer a shotgun. He surveyed the belfry of the church with a bemused smile, then raised his arm and fired twice. A pair of pigeons fell squawking to the pavement.

'Bravo!' the priest whispered. 'They've just killed two more British agents.'

A puzzled regard crossed Catherine's face.

'Didn't know, did you?' the priest whispered. 'They've banned pigeons here. I seem to have the last ones in Pas-de-Calais in my belfry.'

The shotgun's blast rang out again, and another dead pigeon fell out of the sky.

'Or at least, I did.'

The priest wiped his hands on his apron, watching the German get back into his car. 'Come any evening and help me serve. It's better that way and I can give you an extra bowl when we've finished.'

Warmed and grateful, she wandered back to her room. For half an hour she sat on her bed staring at her radio, wondering whether she should message London. Finally she crawled, half-clothed, into bed. A

140

spring gale was sweeping in from the Channel. Its gusts rattled the windowpanes of her room and filled the empty street below with their mournful whine. Never in her life had she felt so utterly, helplessly alone. Why, in Christ's name, did I agree to do this? she kept asking herself. Why am I here, doing something that is sure to end in disaster? Weakened by hunger, she fell into a semidelirious sleep.

With a scream and a start she awoke shortly afterwards, cold sweat beads bubbling along the hairline of her forehead. There was no Gestapo officer standing at the foot of her bed. She was alone. It was dark out, but the Channel blow still shook the windows and questioned the night with its sad call. She wept. Had it come to this? Was this the last ransom of an agent's life – that even the sanctuary of her dreams was to be haunted by the nightmare of capture?

LILLE

The street was deserted. It always was by the time René Laurent locked the café door and began his nightly sprint to get home before curfew. Tonight, not even one of the city's starving cats solicited his affection as he rushed down Rue de Béthune to his apartment. Nothing, in fact, drew his attention until he unlocked his front door and felt the sharp blow of a pistol barrel being jammed against his rib cage. Two men half-shoved, half-tugged him into his living room. There, to his horror, he saw his wife, a gag taped to her mouth, tied to one of his dining-room chairs. His two young sons, similarly bound, were in chairs next to hers. The rather elegantly dressed man relaxing in his best armchair rose.

'German police,' Strömelburg announced; 'the Gestapo.' Each syllable was framed with metallic coldness to underscore the terror the words were meant to inspire.

The stunned café owner staggered towards the chair Strömelburg indicated. Sagging into it, he read the fright racing through the eyes of his wife and sons. 'So,' Strömelburg announced, inhaling deeply on his American cigarette, 'you're a peaceful, law-abiding citizen trying to run a café as best as you can in these difficult times, never one to do anything that might offend the authorities.'

'That's right.' Fear had raised Laurent's voice to a hoarse squeak.

'Never have anything to do with these terrorists of the Resistance.'

'No.' The café owner's mouth was so dry he could barely articulate the word.

'Oh, maybe the occasional black-market exchange.' Strömelburg gave his cigarette an indulgent wave. 'A bottle of wine bought or sold illegally. Who, after all, doesn't do that once in a while?'

141

Maybe that was it, Laurent told himself hopefully. Something to do with the black market. He raised his forearms from the chair's armrests, then let them fall back in resigned acknowledgement of the charge.

'It's all a lie. Your're a letter drop for Captain Guillaume's network in Lille.'

'I don't know what you're talking about,' Laurent rasped.

'Furthermore, you're expecting someone to come into your café tomorrow. A new radio operator. He's going to ask you where he can get ground worms to go fishing. When he does, you're going to put him in touch with Captain Guillaume.'

Hearing those words, the little café owner knew there would be no escape. It was just past eleven. The beating would start in a few minutes. Somehow he would have to find the courage to resist for thirteen hours. By then Guillaume would know he'd been arrested and would head for a safe house. Shaking slightly, he steeled himself for the coming ordeal.

'Now,' Strömelburg continued, his tone so casual they might be neighbours discussing the prospects of rain over the backyard fence. 'In all this, only one thing interests me. Where is Captain Michel?'

'I've never heard of him.'

'Oh, dear.' Strömelburg, who had perched almost jauntily on the Laurents' dining-room table, rose again. For a couple of seconds he paced the room in silence. Then he glanced at his watch. 'You have three minutes in which to answer my question.'

They seemed an eternity. The only sound René Laurent could hear as they passed was the faint whistle of his laboured breath and the creaking of wooden joints as his younger son, his face streaming with tears, twisted against the cord that bound him to his chair. Finally, Strömelburg stopped directly in front of the café owner.

'Are you going to be reasonable or not?'

Laurent stared up at him in silence.

Strömelburg sighed. 'If you insist,' he said. He always managed to make it appear as though inflicting torture on a prisoner represented an imposition on him rather than on the victim. He gestured to one of the two men behind Laurent. While the second man handcuffed Laurent's wrists behind his back, the first removed his suit coat and hung it neatly over the back of a chair. Then he loosened his tie with deliberate slowness, rolled up his sleeves. He was a Frenchman, a man who had been serving twenty years for kidnapping and murder when Strömelburg, who recalled the case from his prewar service in France, had recruited him. The symmetry of employing Frenchmen to work his savagery on their fellow countrymen appealed to the Gestapo chieftain.

The man poised for a moment in front of Laurent, stretching and flexing his fingers as a surgeon might before slipping on his rubber

142

gloves. While Laurent watched him with rising horror, Strömelburg watched Laurent. He saw his face harden, his eyes tightening to brace for the punishment that was coming. He knew the look. The café owner wanted to play tough. He was in his mid thirties, Strömelburg reckoned, a seemingly peaceable man quite unprepared for the ordeal ahead. Still, you never knew where a man's threshold of resistance lay. Some of his meekest prisoners had proved most resistant to his interrogators. They'd break him, but how soon? Time was not a commodity Strömelburg possessed in abundance if he was going to make the Doctor's scheme work. Perhaps he could expedite the matter. As his man stepped towards Laurent, Strömelburg stopped him with a flicker of his forefinger.

For a second, the Frenchman stood immobile, a step in front of Laurent. Then, with a gesture of his head, Strömelburg started him on his way again, this time not towards Laurent but towards his wife, gagged and trussed in her chair.

Terror stretched the helpless woman's eyes open at his approach. Then, as he bashed his open palm against the side of her face, she squeezed them shut. The man reached down for the collar of her cotton blouse and ripped it off with one swift jerk. For a second, he stood there contemplating her heavy breasts heaving in fear inside her cotton brassière. Casually he dropped a hooked index finger to the fastening of her brassière and plucked it open. Reaching down, he grabbed one of her nipples and gave it a vicious twist. The woman squirmed and tried to scream. The gag taped across her mouth throttled the sound down to a pathetic bleat.

Strömelburg's gaze was concentrated on Laurent. He was ashen. He had, Strömelburg told himself, made the right choice. The torturer took a cigarette from his shirt pocket, lit it and slowly puffed its tip to a bright red-orange. He grabbed the woman's nipple again and started the cigarette on a slow arc towards her breast. The children beside her now added the shrill sound of their suppressed terror to her helpless cry.

'Stop him! Please stop him!' Laurent gasped.

'Guillaume?'

'He's staying at the Hôtel Saint-Nicolas with Arlette, his courier, room twenty-two.'

As he heard himself speak those words, Laurent collapsed in sobs, overcome by the enormity of the betrayal he had vowed he would not make.

Room 22 was on the fourth floor of the Hôtel Saint-Nicolas, at the top of a spiral staircase that pierced the little hotel like a mine shaft. Strömelburg, his Walther drawn, advanced up the stairs, following one of the men he had recruited from the Lille Gestapo. Half a dozen others trailed along behind them down the narrow staircase. Strömelburg shone his flashlight on the door set right at the top of the staircase, then pressed himself flat against the wall beside it, well out of the line of any possible exchange of fire. Physical courage had never been the hallmark of his character. He nodded to his fellow officer. The man stepped back and with one powerful kick, smashed the door open. Drawing his Walther pistol, he stepped into the doorway and shouted, 'Gestapo!'

This was a fatal error. The move left him framed in the doorway by the half-light filling the stairwell behind him. Two shots rang out from the darkened room. Strömelburg saw the Lille officer jack-knife as though he'd been struck in the stomach, then totter backwards. For a moment he seemed to teeter on his heels; then his body went cartwheeling down the staircase, cutting the feet from under the first two of Strömelburg's advancing officers. As all three collapsed in a heap at the bend in the staircase, Strömelburg heard from inside the room bare feet running over a wooden floor, then a window being flung open. From the street below, another shot rang out.

'They're down there too!' a male voice shouted from the bedroom. 'We're trapped.'

'Oh, God, no!'

Strömelburg recognized the voice as a woman's – obviously the man's courier. Strömelburg was leaning over the railing of the staircase, shouting to the officers knotted half a flight below. 'Forget him, for Christ's sake!' he screamed to the men bending over the body of their dead comrade. 'Get up here, all of you.' Still pressed against the wall well away from the line of fire represented by the open bedroom door, he called out in French, 'German police. You're surrounded. Come out with your hands up and you'll be spared.'

'They've got us!' It was the man again.

'What are you doing?' The woman's voice had taken a sudden, upward flight.

'We've got to!' the man shouted. 'We swore to each other we would.'

The first two Germans had reached the head of the stairs. 'Get down – he's armed,' Strömelburg warned. 'I want them both alive.'

'I don't care what we swore. I can't do it.' There was a frantic note in the woman's voice as it reached Strömelburg from the darkened room. 'Please don't make me, darling! Please don't!'

'We have to,' the man said. Now he spoke in a flat, emotionless tone.

'Hurry up, for Christ's sake!' Strömelburg hissed at his two aides, neither of whom was eager to charge the armed agent.

'Oh, no – oh, no – don't – don't!' The woman was pleading hysterically.

'If you can't, I will.'

144

'No, no, please, I beg you!' Her anguished cry was terminated by the explosion of a pistol shot.

'Oh, God, how I loved you, Arlette!' the man cried. 'Forgive me, please forgive me!'

'Get in there!' Strömelburg shrieked, his words coinciding with the roar of the second shot. As its reverberation died, Strömelburg heard the metallic clatter of a pistol tumbling to the floor.

The Gestapo leader followed his two men into the room. The nude bodies of a man and woman were sprawled on the bed, the man on top of the woman, what remained of his head sprawled between her breasts in a final embrace. The woman's mouth gaped open, frozen in the midst of her final plea for life. The pistol, still trailing its twists of smoke, lay on the floor beside the bed. There would be no Gestapo interrogation for Captain Guillaume and Arlette, the courier he had so loved.

'Christ!' Strömelburg whispered. Then, almost in spite of himself, he raised the tip of his Walther to his forehead in salute to the courage of his dead adversaries.

LONDON

Sir Stewart Menzies, the head of MI6, the secret intelligence service, surveyed the cramped officers' canteen of Churchill's Underground War Rooms with ill-concealed distaste. The walls, once cream, were now closer in colour to an aged newspaper. Suspended from the ceiling were a brace of drainpipes carrying away a gurgling flow of sewage from the toilets in the government offices overhead. Brown government linoleum covered the floor. 'Quite the most dismal mess in the realm, isn't it?' Menzies observed.

'Winston's way of keeping our minds on business, I expect.' Sir Henry Ridley, Churchill's deception planner, smiled. 'What can I offer you?'

Menzies glanced at his watch. 'A bit early for a gin-and-tonic, I'm afraid. Although God knows I could use one.' He ordered a coffee from the Royal Marine mess corporal. 'I just had the most beastly session in the bedroom.' Churchill was forever summoning his senior advisers to morning meetings in his bedroom upstairs, where, his green silk dressing gown over his shoulders, his first cigar of the day fixed in his mouth, he thrashed out the latest turn in the war. 'You've heard, I suppose?'

Ridley nodded. 'They called me down from the country when the news came in.'

'If they really are waiting for us on the other side, we will bloody well have another Passchendaele on our hands. What, in God's name, put

145

Hitler on to Normandy, do you suppose?' Without waiting for a reply, Menzies sipped at his coffee, then swirled an exploratory mouthful around his tongue. 'As vile as the mess it's brewed in,' he remarked. As he did, his eye caught the relatively rare sight of an American army uniform passing through the canteen. The officer wearing it nodded somewhat tentatively at Ridley, then continued on his way.

'I say,' Menzies asked, 'who's the new boy in school?'

'Chap named O'Neill – my American deputy and liaison officer. Just arrived. It was he, by the way, who brought Ismay the information the Americans intercepted about Hitler's conversation with the Japanese ambassador.'

'An American liaison? I hadn't realized they were giving you one.'

'The Anglo-American Combined Chiefs' idea, not mine. Inevitable, I suppose.'

Menzies reflected a moment. 'You know what they say about liaison with the Americans, don't you?'

'I'm afraid I don't.'

'It's like having an affair with an elephant. It's extremely difficult to reach your objective. You're apt to get trampled on. And it takes eight years to get any results. Needless to say,' Menzies continued, 'I count on you not to breathe a word to him about our role in anything we're doing for you.'

'Of course.'

'Which brings me to the reason for my visit. You recall our conversation at the club the other night?'

'It's been very much on my mind. Particularly since I read that material about Hitler fixing on Normandy.'

'Indeed. This puts the most ghastly burden on you and your deception scheme, doesn't it? Well, we do have an asset in place who just might be of use to you. Unfortunately, I can't for the life of me see how he can be employed to further *Fortitude* alone. He would have to be used in conjunction with something or someone else. Perhaps that resourceful mind of yours might envisage a possibility.'

'Try me,' Ridley replied. 'I'm ready for anything.'

'I must warn you that the manner in which we inserted him into his post might not enjoy the warmest official endorsement of HMG.'

'In that case,' Ridley replied, 'perhaps we had best discuss the matter unofficially over lunch at the club?'

146

Hans-Dieter Strömelburg glanced through the text the Doctor set before him, reread it three times, then passed it back to his subordinate.

'That should do it,' he said.

'I'm concerned by one thing,' the Doctor cautioned. 'If London falls for this, won't any agent they send into that bar up in Lille be expecting to find the old owner?' Strömelburg had replaced René Laurent, the Lille café owner, with one of his own French Gestapo officers. Laurent and his wife and two children were on their way to concentration camps in Germany.

'Why?' Strömelburg rejoined. 'Anyone they send in there with a message for our radio will almost certainly never have been in there before. He won't know the difference between the old barman and the Virgin Mary. And if any of Michel's people we haven't caught go in there, they'll know we arrested the old barman and his family. Why shouldn't his cousin from Rennes run the place for him until he gets out of prison? Your goat is out there bleating,' Strömelburg assured the Doctor. 'Let's just hope they can hear him in London.'

Beads of sweat flickered along the stallion's ebony flank. The rider's reins kept his head haughtily erect while his hoofs beat out the ritual tatoo of the *panache*, the gallop-in-place of Vienna's *haute école*. Easing his rein, the rider sent the animal cantering around the ring with a subtle squeeze of his knees, this time drawing his movements into the *haute école's* famous switching gait. Finally, rewarding the horse with a caress of his pigskin glove, he walked him back to his waiting groom, a corporal in the Wehrmacht.

The rider swung gracefully from his saddle and employed his riding crop to brush the inside of his grey trousers, their outer leg slashed with the claret stripe of a German General Staff officer. He glanced into the morning sky. Far off in the distance he could just make out the deadly grid formed by the contrails of the B-17s over Berlin, barely detect the dull thump of the capital's antiaircraft defences. Only 20 miles from the capital of the Third Reich, Zossen was a nineteenth-century island in the sea of a nation collapsing in debris. It was the wartime refuge of the most efficient group of professional soldiers on earth, the officers of the German General Staff. Here, with their horses, their pony carts, their wives, they lived out the rituals of the Junker caste, immune to the sufferings of the world they had conquered and devastated.

The rider strolled through the moist spring morning to a semicircle of A-frame buildings known as Maybach I – A-framed so that, presumably, a falling bomb would skid down the roof and explode outside the building. He returned the salute of the sentry guarding the door with a casual gesture of his riding crop and strolled down to his office door. He was a tall man, his curly black hair cut close to his skull, his eyes framed in gold-rimmed glasses. A distant asceticism seemed to emanate from his being, as though it would have been more appropriate to see him as an eighteenth-century Lutheran preacher in some chill Baltic seaport rather than in the *Feldgrau* of the Wehrmacht.

Waiting on the desk were a cup of coffee and a pair of 'Cobbler Boys', the triangular whole-wheat breakfast rolls favoured by Berliners before the war. The General Staff's bakery at Zossen was one of the few in the Berlin area still able to produce them. Waiting too were the latest overnight intelligence reports to reach the headquarters of the German General Staff, for Colonel Baron Alex von Roenne was the commander of the most sensitive section of the Germany Army in Western Europe, *Fremde Heere West* – Foreign Armies West. It was Von Roenne and his élite staff of intelligence officers who were responsible for preparing the estimates of Allied forces and intentions on which Hitler's high command based their strategic decisions. He and his immediate subordinates constituted that select audience for which Sir Henry Ridley's *Fortitude* scheme had been so carefully prepared.

Von Roenne chewed on a roll and began a thoughtful study of the papers arranged on his desk. Today was Monday, the high point of his week, the day on which he prepared his weekly summary of Allied strengths and intentions for Hitler's OKW staff. Throughout Zossen – and more important, throughout the Führer's military establishment – Von Roenne enjoyed the reputation of an officer with a 'clear and realistic mind.' He had earned Hitler's esteem as a mere captain in 1939 because, in defiance of the generals and the colonels above him, he had told the Führer what the Führer wanted to hear: the vaunted French Army would not budge while the Wehrmacht's legions dismembered Poland. It did not. Then again in 1940, his stunningly accurate appraisals of the shortcomings of the French Army had been vital in planning France's conquest. Since then, despite the disdain in which he held intelligence reports in general and Wehrmacht intelligence reports in particular, Hitler had reserved a considerate hearing for material that bore Von Roenne's signature.

Von Roenne looked up from his reading at the figure entering his office with an athlete's casual grace. This morning, as was so often the case, the face of his subordinate, Lieutenant Colonel Roger Michel, bore the flushed expression of a man whose evening consumption of alcohol had yet to finish working its way through his system.

'On whom were you spreading your favours last night?' Von Roenne asked with icy disapproval. 'The ladies of Berlin or some deprived *Hausfrau* here in Zossen?'

Michel gave him the pitying look devout fornicators reserve for cuckolds or men whose sexual horizons have been confined to intimacy with their wives. 'Neither, alas. Too much *Schnapps*. The RAF kept me awake most of the night.'

'Learn to discipline your mind and sleep will come more easily,' his superior chided. 'Have you studied these reports?'

Von Roenne indicated the five typewritten sheets of foolscap paper spread out on his desk. They'd just arrived by motorcycle messenger from Berlin's Tirpitzstrasse, the headquarters of the Abwehr, German Military Intelligence. Good intelligence analyst that he was, Von Roenne normally evaluated the reports of spies operating on enemy soil with great scepticism. He preferred two other sources of information; radio intercepts of the Allies' military traffic and aerial reconnaissance. Unfortunately, Hermann Göring was so reluctant to risk his dwindling Luftwaffe air fleet on reconnaissance missions that one of those two sources of intelligence was virtually ruled out for Von Roenne. As a result, he was obliged to accord a disproportionate importance to the reports of the Abwehr's agents in studying the Allies' invasion preparations.

He had anticipated the situation during the winter. Realizing the importance the Luftwaffe's shortcomings were going to force him to place on the Abwehr agents' reports, he had sought a meeting in February with Admiral Wilhelm Canaris, the head of the Abwehr. To his surprise, Canaris had described openly and frankly his espionage operations in England, declaring that the very fact that the Abwehr had any V-men – *Vertrauensmänner*, the German terms for agents – operating in England was 'one of the most remarkable feats in the history of espionage.' Some of these agents had even been in place for as long as three years. They had furnished Berlin with a steady flow of military information, much of it of great importance, demonstrably true and confirmed by subsequent Allied actions. Three of them communicated with the Abwehr by clandestine radio transmitters hidden in London. The others used different, slower means, such as letters employing the Abwehr's microdots, or couriers. Overall, Canaris boasted, he was averaging thirty to forty messages a week from his agents. Two enjoyed his special trust. One was a Polish Air Force officer turned by his counterespionage experts in Paris. The Pole had been caught with sixty-three French colleagues running an Allied spy ring in occupied France. The Abwehr's message to him had been simple: either he would go to

149

England in the service of the Abwehr or he and his fellow Resistants would go to the gallows. He had gone to England, where early in January his Allied superiors had given him a new, and potentially important, assignment. He had been named Polish Air Force liaison officer to an American army group in the process of being assembled.

The second agent, code-named Arabel, was a more classical case. He was a Spaniard, a dedicated Fascist, who had been working for the Abwehr in England since 1940, initially as a businessman, more recently in British government service. He had very cleverly built up his own network of agents, some twenty-four in all. As a result, he had been able to furnish his Abwehr controller in Madrid with what Canaris regarded as the most consistently high-grade stream of information available to the Abwehr from any source anywhere in the world.

Canaris had gone now, a victim of the bitter rivalry between his Abwehr and Himmler's RSHA. His Abwehr was run today with the ruthless but unimaginative efficiency of the SS. Still, Von Roenne thought, while his assistant digested the material on his desk, the Abwehr's channels continued to provide him with a regular flow of reports. A code he'd worked out with Canaris indicated to him those which emanated from the Pole and the Spaniard. Four of this morning's five reports were from them, two from each man. 'It looks as though they're beginning to draw up on their invasion ports,' Michel said.

'It does, doesn't it?' Von Roenne agreed. 'We're picking up some increase in radio over there, too. I think something's up.'

Von Roenne took a well-thumbed map of England from his drawer and set it on his desk beside the reports. Detailed on the map were the location and description of each British, American or Canadian army unit he had been able to identify in England. No document in his possession was more precious or kept up to date with greater care. Von Roenne would discern the pattern of the coming assault from the location and the distribution of the Allied forces in England. His first Abwehr message, this one from the Pole, reported the 'VII American Army corps in the area northwest of Colchester, with corps headquarters identified by the troops' shoulder flash, a white 7 on a blue shield.' Von Roenne and Michel studied the map. Colchester was in the nub of Essex, pointing out towards Holland and the North Sea, the natural location for a corps headquarters embarking its divisions through the nearby port of Clacton on Sea. Furthermore, the Spaniard's messages identified the Sixth US Armored Division, which Von Roenne's maps had placed far to the northwest in Yorkshire, as being in fact in the area of Ipswich, barely 30 kilometres northeast of Colchester.

'Maybe the Sixth Armored is one of the divisions commanded by the VII Corps,' Michel surmised.

Von Roenne nodded silently. His mind was already on the Pole's second report. As a result of his latest inspection tour, he had just been able to confirm that the Twenty-eighth US Infantry Division had moved from Wales to Folkestone, on the Strait of Dover, and the Sixth US Armored to Ipswich – an independent corroboration of the information sent by the Spaniard. Neither spy, of course, was aware of the other's existence. With a crayon Von Roenne erased the Twenty-eighth and Sixth Armoreds' old headquarters and placed them in their new locations in southeast England.

He studied his revised map carefully. For the past three weeks, the agent's reports had indicated a drift of Allied units to southeast England. There was an almost symmetrical balance between the Allied units he'd confirmed in the south of England, from where they would naturally threaten Brittany or Normandy, and southeast England, from where they would threaten Pas-de-Calais. The Führer, whose intelligence he provided, might rely on his intuition to form his judgement; Von Roenne relied on cold military logic. There was nothing in the Allied troops' disposition at the moment to indicate where the blow would fall – unless, Von Roenne suddenly thought, it was the Allies' intention to strike not one but two blows.

He rang for his secretary, who trundled into the office, pad in hand. Swiftly, she jotted what she knew would be the heading of the report her superior was about to dictate: 'Generalstab des Heeres, Fremde Heere West'; the document reference 1837/44; the date, April 17, 1944, and the fact only thirteen copies were to be made of the Top Secret memo.

'The state of invasion preparations,' Von Roenne began, 'has visibly entered a new phase because of a series of decisive measures taken all of a sudden in the military domain. It is our estimation,' he continued, 'that there are now sixty large Anglo-American army groups, divisions or reinforced brigades, in England.'

Von Roenne glanced at his subordinate, who nodded his agreement. 'All reports,' he confidently continued for the Führer's benefit, 'point to an abrupt acceleration of invasion preparations with an increasing disposition of Allied forces in southeast England opposite the Dover Strait.'

LONDON

'I say! We are fortunate. Most of the Americans we see around tend to be short and going grey. Why is that, do you suppose? The weight of all those stars on their shoulders?'

151

The words, T.F. O'Neill noted with amusement, poured from the pretty Wren officer who he guessed was in her mid-twenties. Her ebony hair was trimmed into a pageboy bob, its ends curling inward, as British regulations demanded, just over the collar of her uniform jacket. She had a generous, sensually suggestive mouth and a lithe figure no amount of oppressive military tailoring could conceal. But the best part of her was her eyes; they were a set of darkly flashing lights, fixing him with a look that mixed provocation with a kind of irreverent mirth.

'And the voices they have!' She had barely paused for breath. 'Shatter crystal at a hundred paces. Not that there's much crystal about to shatter down here, as I'm sure you've noticed. Do you jitterbug well? All Americans do.'

'Yeah' – T.F. offered her his slightly bemused grin – 'when I'm pushed to it. But I have a dark secret.'

'Tell,' she commanded. 'I love hearing secrets. Although, as I'm sure you can understand, it's not an activity we're partial to in this room.'

'I prefer Guy Lombardo.'

'Yeeks! How appalling! And you seemed such a nice chap.'

T.F. had been considering perching on the edge of her desk, but thought better of it. The conversational candour of the British, he'd been warned, should not be mistaken for an invitation to informality. Instead he reached into his jacket for his Camels and offered her one.

'Maybe,' he proposed, lighting it for her, 'you can clue me in on who's who and what goes on around here.'

'Of course,' she said. 'The first thing they'll make you do is sign the black book and warn you you'll practically be shot if you ever breathe a word to anybody about what we do for the rest of your life.'

'Did that yesterday,' T.F. noted. 'Intimidating ritual, isn't it?'

'Awful,' she agreed, 'and now they'll start lowering the most terrible secrets into your lap. Well,' she began by indicating a middle-aged officer in RAF blue, 'that's Dennis, our author. In better times, he's an epicure; there's simply nothing about food and wine he does not know. The gentleman pouring himself a cup of tea is Ronnie Wingate, our number two. He's the most marvellous man. Charm his way into the sultan's harem if he had to. Behind him, the chap studying reports is Reginald Grinsted. He was a banker in his earlier incarnation. If he invites you down to the country for a weekend, which he'll almost certainly do, for God's sake don't go. You'll spend your entire weekend weeding his garden and trying to keep out of the bed of his daughter, who looks just like a horse – largely I think, because she spends so much time with the bloody beasts. My colleague flailing away at her typewriter' – she gestured towards the other young woman in the room – 'is Lady Jane Pleydell Bouverie. She's Sir Henry's assistant. A super girl, but I must warn you she's rather partial to the Brigade of Guards. And that's about it, I think.'

'No, you've forgotten someone.'

'I have?' There was a quick flaring of her nostrils, an indication that for all her seeming disingenuousness, the young lady was accustomed to neither error nor questioning.

'Yourself.'

'Ah, me. Yes, well, I'm the section's drudge, I'm afraid. Do everything but take the laundry out. My name is Deirdre Sebright. You'll hear them referring to me as Lady Deirdre, but you mustn't let that put you off. Papa simply had the good sense to inherit a peerage.'

'Titles,' T.F. observed, 'seem to go with the territory down here.'

'Of course,' Deirdre answered. 'In this country only the upper orders are considered fit vessels for secrets of state.'

T.F. gave her the boyishly innocent smile he'd found effective on the Georgetown cocktail circuit. 'Tell me, do you share your girl-friend's partiality to the Brigade of Guards?'

'Oh, goodness no.' He savoured the laugh that went with it. It was a husky contralto, its notes accentuated by just a touch of mockery. 'My tastes are considerably more catholic than that.'

'Gentlemen.'

T.F. turned to the sound. Colonel Ridley had just entered the room, moving with that slightly slouched walk of his, an Irishman leaning into a West Country gale or , more likely T.F. told himself, a man bent under the concerns he carried.

'Morning prayers,' the colonel announced, continuing his shuffle across the room to the doors of his private office. The members of his London Controlling Section straggled along after him, smoking and clutching mugs of steaming tea. Not much of the spit-and-polish he'd been warned to expect in a British organization evident here, T.F. mused.

The room was impregnated with the faintly acrid odour of English tobacco and the lingering trace of the hundreds of cups of tea that must have been consumed within its walls. Wingate, the number two, noted the absence of a cup in front of T.F. 'Cup of tea, Major?' he offered. 'Or do you prefer coffee? You Yanks all drink coffee, I'm told.'

'No, thanks, I'm not really partial to either.'

'You know, Major O'Neill' – this time it was Ridley – 'Ivan the Terrible had rather a quaint military tradition. He nailed the foot of the messenger who brought him bad news to the ground with a spear. On that basis, I think I have the right to spike both of your feet to the carpet.' The smile that accompanied his words was shy and fleeting, deferential almost, although as T.F. watched him it occurred to him that you wouldn't want to bet that either of those traits played much of a role in the Englishman's makeup. Quickly, Ridley summarized for the conference Hitler's conversation with his generals as contained in the Magic intercept of Oshima's message and the chilling news that his legendary intuition was fixing on Normandy. His words produced a palpable sense of gloom around the room.

'You see, Major,' he said, turning back to T.F., 'while this business of deception we're called on to practice may sound rather vague and nebulous to you' – Ridley took a drag on his Players – 'it does in fact conform to some fairly precise laws we've worked out over the years. One of them is that while it's entirely possible to nudge an enemy along a line of action he's already predisposed to take, it's damnably difficult to make him do an about-turn and go against the grain of his intuition. If Hitler really has battened on to Normandy with one of those flashes of intuitive genius of his, we're in the most bloody awful mess.

'In any event' – he nodded to his Wren assistant, who was unlocking a red leather dispatch case to extract a sheaf of manila folders – 'it makes this a particularly appropriate moment to review everything we have in hand.' The young lady set a folder in front of each of them.

T.F. glanced at his. It bore in large block letters the word 'Bodyguard' and under it the phrase 'Combined Chiefs of Staff 459, January 7, 1944.' Beneath that, in appropriately bold red ink, was the warning 'The circulation of this paper has been strictly limited and it is issued for the personal use of Major T.F. O'Neill, AUS, Most Secret, copy No. 32.' Stamped across the jacket in great purple letters was the code phrase 'Bigot,' which covered all secret material relative to the coming invasion.

'The code word on your folder's jacket,' Ridley explained, 'comes from something the Prime Minister said to Stalin at Teheran: "Truth, in war, is so important it must always be accompanied by a bodyguard of lies." Essentially this folder contains a compendium of the lies we've prepared for the benefit of our German friends.'

Ridley took a Players from the pack before him and lit it with the cigarette he was smoking. 'Basically,' he continued, 'the plan breaks down into two parts. The first has been in play since last fall. Its idea was to compel Hitler to scatter his forces along the frontiers of this empire of his and to prevent him from concentrating too many of his divisions in France. With the landings now only six weeks away, that part of our plan has just about run its course. We are now entering the second, and most critical, phase of our scheme, which we have nicknamed, with an appropriate hint of muscular Christianity, "Fortitude,"' The colonel smiled at his little joke. He extended his palms flat on the table before him and leaned back, his eyes half closed, the smoke of his Players curling up before his face. A man, T.F. thought, who is particularly conscious of the fact that other people are watching him. 'I'll let Ronnie

154

go through the outline of our plan. But before I do, though, I'd just like to enunciate, if I may, the principles on which experience has taught us to operate.'

The colonel gingerly removed the cigarette, with its drooping ash, from his mouth. 'A deception officer, or a deception staff, such as ours, must have first and foremost the ability to create, to make something out of nothing, to conceive an original notion, then clothe it with realities until eventually it takes on its own existence as a living fact. What it comes down to is the creation of a deliberate misrepresentation of reality to gain a competitive advantage over your enemy.' Ridley returned his cigarette, pressed tight between his thumb and forefinger, to his lips and focused his half-shut eyes on T.F. 'You're sceptical, aren't you? Americans always are about these operations.'

How did the bastard figure that out? T.F. wondered. Am I really such a bad poker player that anybody can read my cards in my eyes? He mumbled a ritual – and half-felt – protest to Ridley's accusation.

'Take El Alamein,' Ridley continued. 'Monty's deception officer began with an idea, a creation: "The attack is going against Rommel's right flank." Having conceived that notion, he cloaked it with realities: fake tanks, troops, artillery, supply depots. He gave it a life of its own for the Germans through a thousand false radio messages, miles of roads, fake tank treads, pipelines. All a house of cards, of course, but it won El Alamein for us.

'Strategic military deception...' Ridley's face took on the expression of a man who had just discovered a cavity in an upper molar. 'I really do hate that word "deception." Whenever I hear it, all I can think of is some housewife from Hampstead Heath dashing off to a tryst in a Pimlico bed-sit on a rainy Thursday afternoon. The French call it "intoxication." Much closer to the mark, really. The Germans, for God knows what reason of that addled imagination of theirs, call it "blossoming." In any event, deception' – his brief monologue had, it seemed to T.F., reconciled him to the word's inadequacies – 'and lying are concepts used interchangeably by most people. They're wrong. Lying is fundamentally involved with the actions of the teller of the lie. Deception, the kind of military deception we're talking about, has a much wider scope. Fundamentally, our concern is with the reactions of the people who are the objects of our deception. A liar is still a liar whether you believe him or not. A deceiver, however, isn't a deceiver unless the audience he's playing to believes his lies and, what is much more important, physically reacts to them. The El Alamein deception would have been worthless if Rommel hadn't gone ahead and stripped his left flank to reinforce his right.'

Whether he had made his point or not Ridley didn't know. In any

155

event, he reasoned, he was going to have to live with this new American, so he'd better make the effort to educate him. 'Strategic deception falls into two basic categories. The simpler of the two I like to call "ambiguous deception." The idea is to assault your enemy with a blizzard of misinformation, multiplying the options he's got to consider. In the end, the action your deception forces him to take is in fact inaction. You paralyse his ability to move decisively by the bewildering array of options with which your deception has confronted him.

'The second is more subtle. I choose to call it a "misleading deception." The idea in this case is to give your enemy a helping hand by reducing the ambiguity he faces. Instead of spattering him with a wide range of disinformation, you attempt to very subtly build up for him one attractive alternative. Nudge him gently down the road to a precise course of action. Except, of course, it's the wrong one. Get him to be very decisive – and also very wrong.

'Eventually, time undoes all deception in war. Just as it does, one would suppose, in the bedroom. The trick for us is to be sure that our lies, our deceptions are accepted long enough to get the result we are after.'

Ridley reached for another cigarette. As he did, T.F. looked aghast at the pile of cigarettes filling his ashtray. The Englishman gave him in turn a slightly quizzical look, a regard that seemed to ask whether this diversion was worth the effort he was putting out.

'I tend to think of us deceivers as playwrights, dramatists. Because a good deception always begins like a play or a movie with a precise, plausible script or scenario. The cast, essentially, is made up of all the enemy's sources of intelligence that we can somehow manipulate or infiltrate in order to slip bits and pieces of our script into his intelligence machinery. Our aim, of course, is not to influence a mass audience, but to penetrate directly a select, innermost circle, the senior officers of the German General Staff's intelligence service. We seek to direct to that select audience the message of our little scenario, its true origins carefully concealed from them, the story seeping up to them in unrelated segments from as wide a variety of different directions as possible.'

Ridley, T.F. realized, was approaching the end of his discourse. 'Our ultimate aim is to bend the mind of Hitler himself, to lead him to make a mistake. Not just any mistake, but the one precise mistake that will lead him to fall into the trap we've set for him.'

The Englishman sat back and rubbed his eyes in fatigue and resignation. 'Deception, like every other form of military operation, involves casualties. But let me warn you, the casualties that follow the intentional baiting of the enemy are the least popular in all warfare.

'One last word,' he said, snuffing out another cigarette. 'In setting our

156

scenario into play, there is only one test we apply to our schemes, however outlandish, however vicious, however perfidious they may be: will they work?'

He had finished. His speech had been impressive, but hearing it had brought T.F. an instant recall of his final briefing at the Pentagon and the words of General Strong's memo he had been told to etch into his memory. T.F. reached for a Camel, lit it and slowly shook out the match, the gesture deliberately retarded to give himself a few more seconds of reflection.

'In evaluating your projects, Colonel, is there any moral standard you apply to them? Any ethical frame of reference into which you try to fit them to differentiate our patterns of behaviour from the enemy's?'

'Morality and ethics, my dear Major, are two words which do not exist in the lexicon of warfare.'

T.F. played with his cigarette, wondering just what they would have expected him to say to that in Washington. Americans had a well-deserved reputation in London for crashing in, combat boots first, in areas of military strategy about which they knew absolutely nothing – which, he had to admit, was certainly his case in this arcane world to which he had been assigned. I'll just, he thought, make it clear I heard the point and let it pass. 'Perhaps,' he said, offering his audience what he hoped would be an appropriately disarming grin, 'it depends on whose lexicon you're using.'

For a second, he wondered if Ridley wasn't going to reach over, snatch away his manila Top Secret folder and return it, unread, to its dispatch box. Instead, the Englishman bestowed on him a smile of infinite warmth. 'Quite,' he said. 'Ronnie, why don't you carry on?'

Wingate picked up his manila folder. 'Essentially, the story, the scenario of *Fortitude*, we wish to feed the Germans is this: our assault on the continent of Europe is going to take the form of two major cross-Channel attacks. The first and the lesser of these will fall on Normandy. Its aim is to draw down to Normandy the German reserves in Pas-de-Calais and Belgium. Once those reserves have been committed, then our second, more substantial assault will fall on the weakened German defences in Pas-de-Calais.

'The story has the advantage, if I may say so, of being strategically a very sound plan – if it were not for one salient fact. We have, at this moment, a grand total of thirty-three Allied divisions on this island. By D-Day, we'll have exactly four more – barely enough divisions to make one successful landing, to say nothing of two. Now, Hitler's no fool. Pas-de-Calais is the most strongly fortified area on the Channel coast. He's not going to take a threat against those defences seriously unless it becomes evident to him we've got the troops we would need to assault them.'

157

A grin spread slowly across Wingate's face. 'Where, you may well ask, did we get the troops needed to storm ashore in Pas-de-Calais? Necessity, as always, is the mother of invention. We made them up.'

Wingate riffled through the pages of his manila folder. 'If you'll turn to page seventeen, you will find a Goode's base map of southeast England bearing the date May 15, 1944. It reveals what will be the disposition, on that day just one month hence, of the units composing a most splendid fighting force, the First US Army Group – FUSAG. Its commander is your General Patton. The Germans think he's the finest battlefield commander we have. They're quite convinced we would be mad to undertake any major action in Europe without Patton in the lead. As you'll see, FUSAG is made up of two armies, the First Canadian and the Third US. Twenty-five divisions between them, five of them armoured. Packs quite a wallop, our FUSAG does. Pity it has no more substance than a handful of smoke.

'Its locations on our maps, you will note' – Wingate rattled the map in his folder like an anxious schoolmaster just in case someone in the group round the table wasn't paying attention – 'are in the Thames Estuary and in East Anglia behind Dover and Ramsgate. That gives them only one logical place to go: Pas-de-Calais. Since our real divisions are now beginning to move into the south of England to draw up on their embarkation ports, we've just started to move our imaginary divisions into their areas. That, if I may employ the Colonel's theatrical idiom, is when the curtain will go up on the first act of our drama. Like all first acts, it must establish the essential bases on which the play is going to build. If the first act doesn't work, the rest of the play isn't going to work either.

'What we must do is cloak that phantom army of ours in flesh and blood. We must turn all our million men into living, breathing creatures, with appetites, weapons, problems, wives, mothers. We have got to bring them to life where it matters most – not here in England but in Berlin, in the minds of the German General Staff.'

Never, T.F. thought, have I heard something so totally crazy. Look at these people, he told himself, a lawyer, a pop novelist, a guy who makes furniture up in Birmingham somewhere, a couple of postdebs with titles sitting here in this hole in the ground – telling themselves they're going to stiff Hitler with a million fake soldiers and win the war. The brigadier general in the Pentagon was right. It's nuts.

Wingate sailed smoothly on. 'Hitler's ability to get intelligence out of this country is limited, finally, to three channels – aerial reconnaissance, eavesdropping on our wireless communications and espionage. The idea is to filter assorted bits and pieces to the Germans through all three of the channels so that when they put them together over there, presto, they'll discover FUSAG in all its power and glory. Not too easily, of course. We want the Germans to be able to take considerable pride in just how clever they are when they discover it.

'Excuse me, may I?' Wingate had turned to Ridley's assistant and pulled an inch-thick folder from her red dispatch case. 'This annexe to *Fortitude* contains what would be in fact a complete move to concentration of the imaginary two armies that make up our equally imaginary FUSAG.'

'You drew that up in this room?' T.F. asked.

'Of course not. We assembled an army-group staff to do it for us.'

'Wait a minute, Colonel,' T.F. said. 'Are you telling me you employed a real army-group staff, tied them up for God knows how long, to' – T.F. forced himself to take a breath to check his sarcasm – 'make up a package of lies?'

Wingate's thumb performed a fast riffle on the inch-thick folder as if he were a gambler snap-shuffling his deck before the deal. 'Not lies at all. All the real stuff. Everything's there. Right down to the movement of the last case of toilet tissue and box of French letters so our imaginary troops don't pick up VD in those very real bordellos over there.'

'You see, Major' – it was Ridley taking over once again – 'this is not a game we're playing. One mistake and we're blown. We're probably going to broadcast a million fake wireless messages in the next six weeks, lots of them in the clear.'

'A million!' T.F. couldn't quite believe what he was hearing.

'Give or take a few thousand. They have got to be right. In sequence, logical, real. The forward elements have got to come on the air first, a battalion C P before a division. With the right time lag. Certain things have got to go wrong, as they always do. The bridging engineers have got to scream at the artillery battery that got their pontoon joiners. Everything has got to happen exactly as it really would happen. The Germans know how we work. A false note will ring as false to them as it would to us. And they're gong to be picking up real messages between our units moving to their assembly points in the southwest as a check on the authenticity of our fake messages.

'This master plan will serve as the blueprint for our disinformation. From it, we've had to calculate the precise place, the precise day, the precise hour, the precise minute of every scrap of disinformation we slip to the Germans. The plan tells us the advance party of our imaginary 167th Regiment will pass through Sturry to begin setting up its assembly area in Herne Bay at 0725 May 2. We have an imaginary subagent there. He'll notice the convoy. Not from the pub – the pubs aren't open then; maybe riding his bike to town to go shopping. That afternoon the party's wireless will come on with three or four brief messages which our

German friends will pick up. Then there will be more. And another sighting by our agent. Strange Americans in the pub. Not talking to anybody. Then the Luftwaffe will come over to have a look and we'll have a little something arranged for them to photograph. The whole thing's got to be held together, timed with exquisite precision, if it's going to work.'

An army of ghosts, T.F. thought; a million imaginary troops shuffling back and forth across England. The invasion's success is supposed to turn on this? I've been assigned to work in a madhouse.

'Take the problem of aerial reconnaissance. Are you familiar with East Anglia?'

'No,' T.F. said. 'I'm afraid I'm not.'

'Well, the country roads up there leading to the ports are much too narrow to take our armour. The Germans know that.'

'I see.'

'So we're widening the roads. At night, of course, when we'd actually be doing it to escape detection by air.'

'Excuse me just a moment. You're saying that you are going to physically widen a whole network of roads to God knows what cost in time and resources – all as part of a hoax?'

'Just over one hundred miles, to be exact. Raising hell with some of the locals, I'm afraid. Now, the Germans know full well that if we've widened the roads we're going to camouflage the fact to prevent them from finding out what we've done.'

'So you're now going to camouflage these roads you're never going to use?'

'Exactly. And very well, too. Except that a very astute intelligence officer will barely, just barely, be able to read the signs of the camouflage from an aerial photograph taken with one of their Leicas at twenty thousand feet.'

If there was a hint of self-satisfaction in Ridley's pronouncement, T.F. did not respond to it. Instead he appraised the older man for the first time with a sense of admiration. If they are ready to go to such lengths to fool the Germans, who knows? he thought – this crazy scheme of theirs just might produce something.

'This brings us to the most secret aspect of *Fortitude*,' Ridley continued. 'Since late 1942 our counterespionage service, MI5 – it's comparable, I'm told, to your FBI – has had the reasonable certitude that all of the German intelligence agents operating in this country are in fact operating under our control.'

'Well,' T.F. declared, 'that is certainly not a boast the FBI can make but how can you feel a hundred per cent sure of it?'

'One can never be one hundred per cent sure of anything, Major, except one's own eventual demise. "Reasonable certitude" was the term I employed. We've picked up over fifty of them. Some, the more disagreeable types, were packed off to the Tower and the noose. MI5 managed to persuade a number of the others of the wisdom of working under our control. We have their ciphers. We read the Abwehr's wireless traffic with *Ultra*, and it's been two years since we've spotted a reference in it to an agent in this country that we don't control. We also know there is no wireless traffic going out of this country to which we are not privy.'

'In other words, for the last two years you British have been running the entire German spy network in this country?' T.F.'s response was all the more admiring for the deep-rooted scepticism he had felt towards this Englishman and his schemes only a few minutes before.

'That's what it comes down to. And doing a rather good job of it. Better, I sometimes think, than they could have done themselves.'

'What did you do when Berlin asked one of your spies which such-and-such an RAF squadron was or what they made in a factory north of Manchester?'

'We told them.'

'Your military secrets?'

'Of course. If your agent is sending his Abwehr controller in Hamburg a rehash of yesterday's *Times*, he's not going to be thought of as much of a chap, is he? You have to understand our aim was to build up a certain number of these agents in German eyes. If we're now going to use them to manipulate German intelligence with our lies, we had first to convince them of their reliability with our truths, didn't we?'

T.F. grinned at his British superior. J. Edgar Hoover, he was thinking – imagine trying to get him and his FBI to come up with something as subtle as this. It would be about as easy as trying to get a kid in the third grade to read and understand *Finnegans Wake*.

'We worked on a purely empirical formula. Eighty per cent of what we passed over to them had to be true. And some of it had to be juicy stuff. Our calculation was that once a man's Abwehr controller has been able to confirm the truthfulness of most of your eighty per cent, he's hooked. At that point you can very artfully slip over on him the few vital lies that will bend his decision-making processes in the direction you want them to go.'

No wonder it took the Irish so long to get rid of these people, T.F. thought. De Valera's speechwriter was probably a British agent.

'To come back to *Fortitude*,' Ridley continued, 'it's not enough to create our First US Army Group for Hitler's benefit. Once its existence has been firmly fixed in the Germans' mind and anchored in their order of battle, we've got to convince them it's going to hit them in Pas-de-

161

Calais very shortly after we've landed in Normandy. That's Act Two of our scenario, and it's there we hope to be able to use three of these agents we've been building up so patiently for the past two years as our principal actors.'

Ridley's thumb and forefinger went to his nostril in a nervous gesture T.F. had observed several times before. 'I say "hope" because we recently got some news that may blast our whole *Fortitude* scheme right out of the water. Himmler and the SD have taken over all the Abwehr's foreign operations. The three agents we've been building up to put across our story are all Abwehr agents.' That revelation, which the others around the table were also hearing for the first time, produced the morning's second spasm of gloom.

'Himmler and those SD people of his are all paranoid. They'll be so suspicious of the agents they've taken over from the Abwehr they won't trust any of them.'

'Perhaps,' Ridley agreed, 'but we've seen no indication of it in any of the *Ultra* traffic so far. For the moment, no one in Berlin is raising any questions about them.'

'I'm not sure we'll lose them.' The voice belonged to a new speaker, a man T.F. had yet to meet. His name was Arthur Shaunegessy. He was a racehorse breeder who had himself been a double agent inside the IRA in his youth. 'Once a spymaster has made up his mind about the reliability of an agent, it takes an earthquake to shake his convictions. Spymasters are a bit like Roman Popes. Both have an exaggerated belief in their own infallibility.' He gave T.F. a dour smile. 'No offence meant, Major. One thing's clear,' he continued, 'we've got to get some more horses to make the running. I suggest you all turn to page twenty-three.' There was a rattling of paper as a dozen pairs of hands riffled through their Bodyguard folders. 'Read paragraph seventeen – Patriot Forces.

'Deception operations will be assisted by the following.' Shaunegessy read out in case any of them had lost their places:

'"A – The increase of general sabotage in and around the Pas-de-Calais and Belgian areas.

'"B – The despatch to the Pas-de-Calais and Belgian areas of organizers specifically briefed to the effect that the Allies are about to land on the Pas-de-Calais coast and with orders to use local Resistance groups to take various types of action in support of the assault."

'There's our answer,' he said. 'We'll call out the Resistance up there forty-eight hours after we land in Normandy. Raise enough bloody hell to keep Hitler's eyes right there where they belong.'

Once again the alarm bell rang in T.F.'s head. What was it Strong's memo had said about abusing the vulnerability of populations in enemy-occupied territories? 'That's a cynical way of throwing away Frenchmen's lives,' he said.

'So what?' Shaunegessy snapped. 'It's their bloody country we're liberating, isn't it? Why shouldn't some of them be sacrificed for it? You'll be sacrificing enough of your Kansas farmers' sons when that first wave goes in, believe me.'

'Because one of the things we're in this damn war for,' T.F. snapped, his own Irish temper rising, 'is because we're supposed to stand for something. And sacrificing people like that isn't one of them. Besides, we do intend to remain friends with the French after the war, right?'

'Dear Lord,' Shaunegessy answered, his eyes raised in frustration at the idea of having to reply to so naïve a thought. 'We'll see they bloody well never find out. If we don't use every strategem we can lay our hands on, it's a moot point anyway, Major. We won't win the damn war.'

'Gentlemen.' Ridley laid an assertive palm on the table. 'The idea's a nonstarter. The Combined Chiefs would have to approve an all-out call for a Resistance rising and they won't do it. We've already discussed it. Besides, it's much too obvious. Hitler will never fall for it.'

He inhaled his cigarette with one of those frantic gasps of his. 'But I agree, we need some more runners. What we need is one more source assiduously planted that's revealed at the last minute after the others have all been fed through. The one subtle, suddenly illuminating source that allows all the other pieces of the jigsaw to come together.'

'Well,' Shaunegessy asked almost angrily, 'where do you propose to find this new, original deception vehicle of yours? We've used everything up to now, even a dead body. What's left?'

'Yes,' Ridley said, the finger rising instinctively towards his nose, 'that's the question, isn't it? What's left?'

CALAIS

No lover ambling towards a tryst would ever appear so welcome. Catherine had to stifle simultaneously a gasp of relief and a giggle. Maybe the man shuffling up to the street corner by the Café des Trois Suisses, a green metal toolbox slung from his shoulder, really was a plumber. He was squat, with the protruding belly of a dedicated beer drinker, his faded blue denims held up by a leather belt the width of the strop her father had once used to sharpen his straight-edge razor. It was the face, however, that seemed a perfect match for the trade. The man's features were glazed with the weary hostility of someone long used to turning an indifferent ear to his client's pleas for service. Catherine gulped down her *ersatz* Cinzano, folded her copy of *Le Phare de Calais* and feigning nonchalance as best she could, strolled over to her plumber. 'Are you the man I called to fix my blocked drain?' she asked.

The man gave her that sour stare prewar Parisian taxi drivers reserved for tourists naïve enough to forget a tip. 'You Madame Dumesnil from the Rue Descartes?' The cigarette stuck between his lips bobbed up and down in rhythm to each surly syllable. As she set off beside him, a pair of teenage boys drifted from the sidewalk into the street half a dozen yards ahead of them. Her 'plumber' said nothing. Finally, he began to mumble. 'Ours,' he said, somehow indicating the boys in front of them with the cigarette pasted to his lips like an appendage of his mouth. 'Trouble comes, they'll try to make a fuss to let you slip away.'

He shrugged – a gesture eloquently describing to her how unlikely escape in those circumstances would be – then fell back into his taciturn silence. Finally, as they strode down a narrow side street, he whispered, 'Number 17. Third floor right.' They were already at 13. Catherine looked at him questioningly as they drew abreast of 17. Eyes straight ahead, he whispered, '*Merde.*'

She turned, entered the building and tried to walk up the dimly lit stairwell as though she'd been climbing its stairs for years.

'Denise?' the man opening the door said.

'Yes,' she replied, jarred by how unfamiliar her code name still sounded to her ears. Aristide was older than she had expected, in his mid-forties, an almost desperately frail man whose shoulders seemed about to collapse in resignation around his shrunken rib cage. He had a Vandyke beard, a distinguishing feature of which Cavendish, Catherine thought, would certainly not have approved. Tufts of greying hair leaped from his temples.

'I'm sorry we kept you waiting,' he murmured, waving her inside. He had a cigarette tightly clenched between his thumb and forefinger, and his hand, Catherine noticed, trembled slightly. Is this man really the head of an SOE network? she asked herself. His eyes reassured her. The rest of his face was smiling; they were not. They stared at her with such a penetrating intensity she realized his fragile exterior must conceal an interior of considerable strength.

'Unfortunately, the Gestapo has been particularly active these past few days. However, we knew you'd arrived and were getting on all right. My wife,' Aristide said gesturing towards a woman emerging from the kitchen, rubbing her hands on an apron, 'and Pierrot, our number two.' A younger man sitting by the window nodded. 'You must be famished,' Aristide declared, reaching for a bottle of Bordeaux on a small table. 'A welcoming drink, a bite to eat and then we'll get to business.'

'Now that you're fed,' Aristide said when Catherine had devoured the fried potatoes and herring his wife had prepared, 'I've got to tell you that our friend Cavendish has sent you to the worst possible place to operate as an agent – and particularly as a radio operator. Calais is the most occupied city in France.' There was, she observed, an almost defiant pride in the way he said it. 'In fact, as far as the Germans are concerned, we're not even a part of France at all.'

That had been true almost from the day Guderian's first armoured columns had reached the Channel coast. On June 4, 1940, the French *départements* of Nord and Pas-de-Calais had been placed under the Wehrmacht's military governor in Brussels. In his plans for restructuring the postwar world, Hitler's idea was to annex the Calais hinterland to a Flemish vassal state he proposed to create as a buffer for Germany's western border – a kind of Atlantic Alsace-Lorraine.

Because of its seaports, its proximity to England, the area had immediately filled up with German troops. First they were infantry divisions, proud storm troopers marching through the city streets chanting, 'We'll sail to England,' while on the sidewalk a few brave French boys made gasping sounds to imitate men drowning. Next had come the Luftwaffe to speckle the interior with airfields for Göring's fighters which would lead the aerial assault on Britain. As the fortunes of war changed, a new wave had filled the area, defence specialists, coastal gunners to man the batteries being built to shell the Dover coast, workers to pour the concrete and build the fortifications of the Atlantic Wall which would render impossible an Allied return to the Continent. Most recently, the forests and groves behind the seacoast had been the site of yet another mini-invasion, this one by the engineers and scientists supervising the construction of the launching ramps that soon would send Hitler's V–1 and V–2 bombs on their way to England.

As a result, there were, quite literally, more Germans in Calais than there were French men, women and children combined. The lives of the French population were ordered with a rigour greater than that exercised by the Germans anywhere else in France. No one got into or out of the Forbidden Zone along the coast without special authorization from the *Feldkommandantur*. Bags and parcels being carried through the streets were subject to instant and constant inspection. The 9 P.M. curfew was enforced with unbending authority. Travellers on the Calais–Lille train could be certain their bags would be thoroughly searched at least once. Parts of the area, the port of Calais and the coastal strip running past Cap Gris-Nez to Boulogne, for example, were forbidden to all French citizens except those living there. Even the whores who laboured in the city's half-dozen bordellos were subjected to draconian security restrictions to be sure their German clients' pillowtalk didn't reach the ears of the

Resistance. They were allowed out of their houses just twice a week, for a Sunday *apéritif* and their medical checkup, escorted, on both occasions, as severely as convent girls on an outing.

Resistance, in such a claustrophobic atmosphere, required great courage and even greater cunning. As a result, anti-German activities in the area had been known to take root. The first major act of sabotage in the zone did not take place until January 5, 1943, when a freight train carrying ten tons of herring of the Calais catch to the canneries of the Reich was derailed. Seven tons of herring disappeared before the Wehrmacht could intervene. The following day *Le Phare de Calais* headlined: 'Fishing Season Opens with a Miraculous Catch.'

Still, resistance to the Germans was anything but a joking matter. Calais's Gestapo office was a branch of the dreaded Gestapo on Rue Terremonde in Lille, where resistants were beheaded face up by an axe or subjected to particularly vile tortures by the city's sadistic Gestapo chief. A series of arrests, Aristide explained to Catherine, had crippled the city's Resistance at the end of 1943. They were just beginning to recover.

If that oppressive German presence made resistance difficult, it also, curiously enough, discouraged collaboration. Indeed, proud Calaisians joked that the city had only one collaborator – the editor of *Le Phare de Calais*, the paper Catherine had chosen to read each day in the Trois Suisses. His name was Auguste Leclerq, and he was a seriously wounded veteran of the 1914–18 war, a man blessed with limited intelligence and a few simple but firmly held convictions. Among them was a vision of Hitler as a kind of latter-day Joan of Arc in shining armour, protecting *la belle France* from the savage enterprises of the Bolsheviks and a vague coalition of Anglo-American Judeo-Masonic-Capitalists.

Those sentiments had earned him the post of editor of *Le Phare de Calais*, a function for which he lacked even the most rudimentary literary or journalistic qualifications. Nonetheless, his efforts to inculcate his fellow Calaisians with the proper sentiments were unremitting. Poetry was his preferred medium, and his odes such as 'Hitler, Mon Ami' or 'Braves Teutons' had provided Calais's citizenry with their one constant source of humour during the Occupation.

Crushed under the burden of their occupiers, their lives hemmed in by restrictions, choreographed to regulated air raids on the Atlantic Wall and the constant aerial battles in the skies above them, the people of Calais had endured four years of Occupation with the stoicism for which the area was noted. Now, as spring drew towards summer, they awaited the liberation, knowing full well that no city in France was apt to pay a higher price for that deliverance than theirs.

'You've got something for me?'

Catherine stood up, unbuttoned the bottom of her blouse and passed Aristide the money belt she'd hidden there. Then she went to her handbag and picked out the box of matches Cavendish had given her as she left Orchard Court. 'The Major had a surprise for you,' she said, sorting through the matches until she found the one with 'U'.

Aristide was not surprised at all. Clearly, he was familiar with the device. Taking a pair of scissors, he snipped off the head of the match and shook three microfilms the size of postage stamps out of its hollow tube. Pierrot, his number two, had already begun to assemble a kind of tripod on the dining-room table. He smoothed a white tablecloth under the base of the tripod and fixed a boxlike device to its apex, then stuck a bare light bulb into the box. Aristide fitted one of the microfilms into a clamp and played with it for a moment until Catherine saw the outline of a sheet of paper appear on the tablecloth.

Aristide leaned over, read a few lines, then beckoned to Catherine. 'You had better read this too,' he said. 'It concerns you now.'

Catherine studied the documents projected onto the tablecloth.

OPERATION INSTRUCTIONS F 97

From: Cavendish

To: Aristide

The three coastal artillery guns of the Lindemann Battery installed under the cliffs of Noires Mottes between Sangatte and Cap Blanc-Nez menace all maritime traffic in or passing through the Channel. The three guns which make up the battery are 40.6-centimetre naval cannon manufactured by Krupp and most probably constituted the reserve battery of the battle cruiser *Bismarck*. It is in all probability the most powerful land-based artillery battery in the world. We calculate the shells weigh 1.4 metric tons and know that on several occasions they have impacted more than five miles inland from Dover. The Kriegsmarine have given them an exceptionally wide arc of fire – 120 degrees – which, coupled with their power and their siting over the Noires Mottes cliffs, gives them command over all sea passaged through the Strait of Dover. It is the concerted opinion of the military command here that no major cross-Channel landing operation can be attempted anywhere along the channel coast from Dunkirk to Cherbourg without first finding a way to neutralize the effects of the battery's fire. Unless the guns are neutralized, all naval support operations for an offensive will have to be mounted through the open end of the Channel by Land's End, thereby depriving an assault of the use of some of our best Channel ports.

The problem we confront, therefore, can be summarized quite simply: 'How can we neutralize the guns?'

Independent information available to us has established that the guns are enclosed in steel turrets encased in walls of reinforced concrete 3½ feet thick. Such cover would provide the guns effective protection from 2-ton bombs, the largest we posses. On 20 September 1943, the RAF employed 600 Lancasters in a concerted aerial assault on the batteries. The planes dropped 3700 tons of bombs. Aerial reconnaissance the following day revealed 80.2 per cent of the bombs impacted within 250 yards of target centre, an exceptionally high figure in view of the AA defences around the battery. Yet the attack produced no discernible effect on the battery's operational capacity. It is, therefore, the firm conclusion of the RAF that these batteries cannot be neutralized by an aerial assault, however intense.

Our naval architects believe that the battery's one potential weak spot is the openings in the casemates. To give them their exceptionally wide 120-degree arc of fire, the Kriegsmarine has had to provide it with openings that are unusually high and wide. It is conceivable that the Navy could bring a squadron of capital ships into the channel to engage the guns with reasonable prospects of knocking them out. To achieve the degree of accuracy such an operation would require, it would have to be carried out in daylight. This would put our ships at a great disadvantage and almost certainly result in the loss of one or more of them. The Admiralty is therefore most reluctant to undertake such an operation unless all other possible means of neutralizing the battery have been studied and discarded.

The ground defences of the battery are primarily disposed, as were those of the German installations in Dieppe, to protect the guns from a seaward assault. Assaulting them from the sea would be extremely costly. The landward defences are less imposing although they still constitute a very serious obstacle. GOC, Combined Operations, considers that an assault on the guns from the air by a glider-borne commando company could be undertaken with a reasonable prospect of success if:

1. The assault achieves surprise.
2. The gliders the operations would require can land on the plateau behind the battery with a high degree of accuracy.
3. Provision can be made on the ground to guide the commando members through the minefields to the rear entrances of the casemates immediately the gliders landed.

It is obvious such an attack will involve very high casualties among the assault forces. It is equally obvious such an attack would have to be made at night if it is to achieve surprise. Nonetheless, of the three options, a land assault appears to offer the greatest prospect of success.

The SOE and your organization in particular would have a vital role to play if such an assault were to be attempted. For the moment, your mission is to:

    1) Determine the location of a suitable landing site for the attack gliders as close as possible to the battery's rear approaches. The landing site must be 100 yards wide by 250 yards deep. It is essential that it be clear of mines and artificial obstacles. It must be flat or possess a slightly upward slope. If it possesses a downward slope, add 50 yards for each 5 degrees of slope.

    2) Determine the shortest and safest route from the edge of the landing strip to the battery's positions.

Before the operation a specially trained SOE team would have to be infiltrated into your area. Their responsibility would be to mark out the gliders' landing zone on the night of the operation and guide the commando members along the safe path you have selected to the battery. Your responsibility would be to house and hide them on arrival, see that they have properly reconnoitred the landing area and safe path through the minefield and that foolproof arrangements are made for them to get into position on the night of the attack.

PERSONAL CAVENDISH TO ARISTIDE

I recognize the extreme hazards this involves, but no one here has been able to turn up anything better. Please make it your business to gather and radio to us every scrap of intelligence on the battery, its strength, personnel, operation procedures, infrastructure and potential weak spots you can obtain. Good luck.

DESTROY THESE MICROFILMS AS SOON AS CONTENTS READ AND DIGESTED

Aristide, obviously lost in whatever thoughts that sober reading had inspired, slipped the microfilms from their tripod, took one of the real matches from the box in which they had arrived and burned them. 'They're mad,' he said, finally turning to Catherine and Pierrot. 'Don't they understand what's happened here since Rommel took over? They're sowing mines along this coast like ...' He made a wild gesture with his fingers. 'Rommel's ordered thirty thousand trees cut down to make stakes – those asparaguses of his. They're even forcing doctors, lawyers, pharmacists to go out and stick them in the fields. By the time they get finished you won't be able to land a glider within fifty miles of Calais.'

'And they expect us to get information on that battery when we can't even get within a mile of its guns.' Pierrot laughed at the absurdity of Cavendish's request.

169

'Why not?' Catherine asked.

'The area's completely sealed off to French civilians – completely,' Pierrot replied.

'As far as I know, only two Frenchmen have been inside the battery since it was built,' Aristide added. 'One's the director of Béthune, the electric company. The other's a woman.'

'A woman?' Catherine asked. 'Some kind of tart?'

'Not at all.' Aristide laughed. 'She does the officers' laundry. Our conquerers seem incapable of washing their own underwear.'

PARIS

Paul strolled along Avenue Wagram, having just played out the same elaborate charade which a few days earlier had preceded his rendezvous with Strömelburg and the Gestapo's photographer at the Place des Ternes. His destination this morning was the small side bar of the Brasserie Lorraine, the café-restaurant on whose terrace he had sipped an *apéritif* with Catherine.

As always, he was early for his meeting. That gave him a few minutes to walk the sidewalk in front of the Brasserie, to study the magazines in the corner kiosk, to scrutinize the area for the suspicious face or the incongruous sight that might indicate the Brasserie was under surveillance. Like his bookstore routine, this was part of the rigorous security procedure Paul forced himself and the members of his air-operations network to follow. For their telephone calls, for example, he had worked out a particularly elaborate routine. First, the caller would let the phone ring three times, then hang up and call back. His first question would be the ritual French phrase 'Ça va?' – 'How are things?'

The reply would invariably be a complaint about a chest cold, a sore throat, a bad night's sleep. That would be the assurance that everything was all right. Paul's reasoning, patiently explained to the members of his network, was that if ever one of them was caught by the Gestapo and forced to answer his telephone, the listening Germans would expect a disarmingly casual – and reassuring – reply to the query: 'Ça va.' Therefore the normal reply 'Everything's fine' would signal that the speaker was under German control. In the protracted ritual that preceded each of his meetings there was, of course, a deadly irony. This morning, he was meeting with his radio operator. Yet Strömelburg already knew who the operator was, what his code name was, where he lived, where he transmitted, what his broadcast times were. He knew because Paul himself had furnished him all that information when he'd

170

gone to work as the German's agent six months earlier. Both men wanted to be sure that the German radio detection service would let the operator alone and German soldiers would not come charging into his apartment some night to arrest him in the middle of a transmission.

As Paul started towards the bar, a spasm of melancholy struck him when he passed the table he'd shared with Catherine. Despite his intense self-discipline, he forgot for a moment security, his radio operator, his own dangerous and compromised existence and let himself sink into a remembrance of their moments together. The sight of his operator perched like an oversized toy on his barstool brought him back to reality. The operator was barely five feet tall – a handicap for which he had cause to be grateful every time he happened on a German roundup of French males for enforced labour in the Reich. Like fishermen throwing an undersized catch back into the sea, the Germans had invariably rejected his service because of his size. The two chatted for a few minutes over a glass of wine. As they did, Paul unobtrusively pocketed the pack of cigarettes the operator had left on the bar.

Ten minutes later he was back in his apartment, decoding the message it contained. It was a straightforward notification of his next incoming flight. 'OPERATION FOXTROT CONFIRMED FIELD SIX TOMORROW,' it read. 'THREE BODS IN OUT YOUR DISCRETION STOP CONVOY SUSAN ANATOLE PARIS STOP CODE LETTER L STOP BBC MESSAGE ROSES ARE OUT IN CAIRO STOP CONFIRM TOMORROWS SKED.'

The text meant a Lysander would be arriving the following night at his field near Angers, bringing in three people, two of whom – code-named 'Susan' and 'Anatole' – he would have to escort to Paris. The third would disappear on his – or her – own. No one was scheduled to come out, but Paul was free to use his own discretion to put passengers on the returning plane. London would confirm the plane's arrival at 9:15 P.M. by broadcasting the message 'The roses are out in Cairo' over the BBC. Hearing it in the farmhouse he used as a safe house for the Angers field, Paul would know the plane was on its way. Only weather could then stop the operation.

He pocketed the message and the courier package that was scheduled to leave on the flight. Then, putting his complex pantomime into operation once again, he set out to deliver the material to Strömelburg and his Gestapo photographer.

LONDON

'Ah, Dicky! How nice to see you. Let me offer you a cup of French Section tea.'

171

Major Frederick Cavendish, the man who had briefed Catherine on the eve of her departure for France, rose as he uttered his greeting. 'To what do I owe the pleasure of this visit?'

Richard Moore-Ponsonby was a prewar officer of MI5, British counter intelligence, and for the past three years had been deputy director of SOE's Directorate of Intelligence and Security. His office was responsible for providing security clearance for SOE's recruits and preventing, insofar as it was possible to do so, Gestapo penetration of its networks in the fields. He looked like a character out of an Agatha Christie murder mystery, some chief constable from Lincolnshire summoned up to the manor house in his shiny blue suit to investigate the murder of a houseparty guest. He was anything but that. His benign, somewhat bumbling appearance concealed a mind that had long ago earned Moore-Ponsonby a seat at the high table of British Intelligence.

'Nothing you're going to be very eager to hear I'm afraid,' he said, contemplating the steaming mug of tea Cavendish's FANY assistant had just set before him. 'Do you remember when the head of your Ajax network came out of France a couple of weeks ago?'

Cavendish certainly did. The man was one of the few Frenchmen in charge of a major SOE network, a professional army officer, an anti-Gaullist who nonetheless shared the French leader's notions of grandeur.

'Well, he came to see me in the utmost confidence. Said he had reason to believe that Paul, your Air Operations Officer, was a funny. Said he was showing the courier to the Germans before shipping it out.'

'Well, I must say I have great difficulty believing that. Why the bloody hell didn't he come to me with the story?'

Moore-Ponsonby gave a helplessly deferential shrug. 'Quite. I think he felt his suspicions weren't sufficiently grounded to kick up a rumpus in the section. His story was he'd learned a piece of information that could only have come from one of his recent courier packets sprung on a prisoner by the Gestapo during an interrogation.'

Cavendish fingered the button of his uniform tunic in nervous concern. 'Worrying, perhaps,' he agreed; 'but the Gestapo has a myriad number of ways of getting its information, doesn't it?'

'Indeed. Still, one must check these things out, mustn't one? What I did was give him half a dozen sheets of specially treated paper when he went back in. They're something the laboratory got up for us. By applying one of their chemicals on them, they can tell you whether or not they've been exposed to intense light. Photographed in other words. I told him to use them when he next sent out a courier package through Paul, your Air Ops officer.' Moore-Ponsonby paused. 'That package came out Saturday.'

'And?'
'All six sheets had been photographed.'

PARIS

A bright cone of light falling from the tripod cast the sitting room in Paris' Place des Ternes in shadows the way a boxing ring's overhead lamps throw an arena into obscurity. Comfortably installed in an armchair in the semidarkness, Paul reviewed his upcoming operation for Strömelburg, the swift click of the Leica's shutter counterpointing his words.

The German nodded with seeming interest at each phrase he spoke. His interest was feigned. Strömelburg had in fact known the details of Operation *Foxtrot* before Paul had. He was reading his agent's radio communications with London. It was not that Strömelburg mistrusted his primary agent. He simply had a nature so suspicious that had he been an apostle, he would have mistrusted the good intentions of the Holy Ghost. The first thing he had done when Paul gave him the location of his radio operator and his transmitting schedule was order the Boulevard Suchet to break his code. The effort had taken a month. Since then, Strömelburg had read every cable Paul had sent or received. It had provided the perfect check on Paul's reliability, a subtle way of discovering if he was lying or deliberately holding any information back. The Frenchman had turned out to be above reproach on both points.

'Tell me,' Strömelburg asked when Paul's recital was finished, 'do you have any idea who Susan or Anatole are or where they're going?'

'No,' Paul replied. 'As far as I know I've never handled either one of them.'

Strömelburg sighed in frustration. SOE London kept a tight security clamp on Paul's operation. Paul wasn't even furnished the code names of his incoming passengers unless, as in this case, he was being ordered to convey them somewhere, usually to Paris. At least a third of the incoming agents simply vanished into the night. Paul, of course, knew the code names of his outgoing passengers, but unless they had loose tongues he had no way of learning what network they belonged to or where they had been stationed. Besides, Strömelburg couldn't touch the outgoing passengers because to do so would blow the whole operation.

Picking up the agents Paul had been ordered to convey to Paris, then following them to their destinations once they'd reached the capital had turned out to be much more difficult than he had anticipated. Sending Keiffer to observe a landing with a detail of men was a useless exercise. In

173

the darkness, they couldn't get close enough to the plane to scrutinize the appearance of the arriving agents. That meant they would never be able to recognize them the following morning in a crowded railroad station or the compartment of a train.

Paul's safe houses tended, as London demanded, to be isolated, as difficult for his agents to watch without being detected as his fields were. Paul and his agents were under orders not to arrive at railroad stations together, not to travel together, to hold their contacts to a minimum. Since Strömelburg's cardinal rule was to do nothing that might tip his hand to the British, his own French Gestapo teams were also forbidden to make contact with Paul. His only real opportunity to pick up incoming agents came when Paul used fields three and four, located in the Cher Valley well away from even a medium-sized railroad station. Paul cleared those fields from village railroad stations so small that he and his agents were usually the only passengers boarding the early-morning train and could therefore be spotted by Strömelburg's men already on board. As a result, Strömelburg could no more make good on his promise to Kopkow to bring the SOE in France under his control than he could clutch the contents of a glass of water in a clenched fist. It was the radio game, however, and his access to the courier that had been the real dividends of the operation, benefits whose value far outweighed the arrest of any agents.

'I don't think we'll bother with surveillance this time,' Strömelburg said, lighting a Lucky Strike. 'What I'd like you to do is try to find out where they're going.'

'I will,' Paul assured him, 'but it isn't always easy. It depends on how well they learned their lessons in security school.'

'What I'm interested in is the North. We're preparing a little surprise for our English friends up there, and we wouldn't want them to interfere with it. We're going to make them pay for what they did to Hamburg.'

'Really?' Paul said, making no attempt to conceal his scepticism. 'I don't think Göring and his Luftwaffe could make the English pay for a broken window these days.'

'The Luftwaffe has nothing to do with this. It's something else, a new weapon our engineers developed in the Baltic Sea.' Strömelburg got up. His photographer, he noted, was still at work.

'It looks as if he's going to be busy for a while. Why don't I go first? What time will you be back from Angers?'

'Around noon.'

'Okay,' he said with a smile. 'Next *Treff* here at four o'clock day after tomorrow. *Bon voyage.*'

174

Major Frederick Cavendish scanned the faces in London's Savoy Grill until he spotted the familiar figure in dark-rimmed spectacles sitting primly by himself at a table set distinctly but not ostentatiously apart from the lunching crowd. Solitude came as naturally to Colonel Sir Claude Edward Marjoribanks Dansey as tears to a maudlin drunk. Indeed, a calculated loneliness, the deliberate isolation of a man who does not want the emotions of others to intrude upon his private world, was Sir Claude's hallmark. He was a widower, a man who made acquaintances rather than friends, who preferred respect to affection in his colleagues and subordinates. For years he had been the DCSS – Deputy Chief of the Secret Service – to 'C,' Sir Stewart Menzies, the head of MI6. His devious nature, whether it grew from an inherent trait of character or whether it was the result of a lifetime in the secret service, was a minor legend in London intelligence circles. Seeing Cavendish approaching his table, he waved and offered the SOE officer just the suggestion of a smile.

'You're looking uncharacteristically glum,' he observed.

'I have every reason to be, ' Cavendish sighed, settling into the place set for him opposite Dansey.

'Well, I think I have just the medicine for that,' Dansey assured him, beckoning to Manetta, the *maître d'hôtel* of the grill. 'Two very large, very dry martinis,' he ordered, 'and tell Gerald I want them made with his bottle of prewar Tanqueray, not that ghastly *ersatz* stuff he serves our American allies.'

Their quiet lunches were a monthly ritual for Cavendish and Dansey – usually generated on Cavendish's suggestion; occasionally, as today's had been, on Dansey's. Indeed, their friendship had persisted despite the bitter rivalry between Dansey's MI6, Britain's senior intelligence service, and Cavendish's wartime creation, the SOE. The older man had, rather uncharacteristically, gone out of his way to be helpful to Cavendish from the moment Cavendish had taken up his SOE appointment. Dansey's mind was a warehouse of knowledge of covert activities, intelligence tactics, of every playground manoevre and devious stratagem of the dark and evil world of subversion. Occasionally, 'Uncle Claude,' as Dansey was termed – without affection, and never to his face – had set the warehouse's door ajar for Cavendish's benefit. He'd only got a glimpse, of course, at what was stored inside; it was well known that Dansey never told anyone, not even 'C,' the whole of any story. But what he had been shown had often been helpful enough to unravel a puzzle or solve a problem for Cavendish. And so while the *maître d'hôtel* went after their drinks, Cavendish unburdened himself of his discovery of the treachery

175

of Paul, his Air Operations Officer.

'Yes,' Dansey mumbled, 'I'd heard some whisperings of that. It would seem that you're dealing with a classic example of that sub-species of our world, the double agent.'

'It looks that way,' Cavendish replied, 'but I must say I'm stunned. Absolutely stunned. I never had any doubt about him.'

'No, one rarely does about the good ones.'

The waiter returned and set a martini before Dansey. He tasted it as though sipping a rare Bordeaux, then bestowed the benediction of a nod on the barman's handiwork.

'What puzzles me, Claude, is that he's done such a cracking good job for us since he's been over there,' Cavendish said when the waiter had disappeared. 'That little taxi service he runs beats the service Imperial Airways used to run between Croydon and Le Bourget before the war. Without him my operations came to a halt, an absolute halt.'

'How long has he been in?'

'About eight months.'

Dansey was quiet for a moment, almost chewing the prewar gin of his martini; apparently intrigued by what Cavendish had told him.

'He's run thirty-seven ops for me.' Cavendish's voice had taken on the tone of a lawyer striving to prevail on a judge to reduce his client's sentence. 'Delivered eighty-one agents and brought out 126.'

Dansey inclined his head in respectful recognition of the achievement Cavendish's figures implied. 'And how many of the eighty-one have you lost? That you were aware of?'

'Seven, but four of them were picked up so long after they landed you couldn't possibly pin their arrest to Paul. And I have no reason to believe the other three were his doing either. We've never had a problem on an operation. And some of the people he brought out were literally just one step ahead of the Gestapo. Agents they were desperate to get their hands on.'

'Even assuming all seven were picked up due to him, you'd have to say it was a fair price to pay for a successful operation, wouldn't you?'

Cavendish nearly coughed up his gin at the horror of the thought. 'Not if the price is a man who is deliberately betraying us to the Gestapo.'

Dansey gestured as though to brush some imaginary bread crumbs from the Savoy's immaculate tablecloth. 'Of course, Freddy. All rather puzzling, isn't it? Tell me, can you close his operation down and still get on with your business?'

'I suppose I've got to close him down, don't you? But it's a disaster, an unmitigated disaster. His service is the only reliable way I have of getting agents out of France in a hurry. As you well know, the Germans have the coastlines patrolled so tightly these days it's impossible to get people in and out by sea anymore.' Cavendish took a halfhearted sip of his martini. 'If I close him down, I'm crippled. And at the worst possible time of the whole war: just as we're running up to the invasion.'

'Could you bump him off and put somebody else in his place?'

'I'd have to find someone to replace him first. Then train him. Find new fields. Get the RAF to accept them. It would take at least a month, probably much more.' Cavendish took another swallow, this one a good deal more enthusiastic, of his martini. 'No, it is quite the most ghastly business. I'm afraid I have no choice. I have got to bring him back and hand him over to the authorities.'

Dansey gave a deprecatory wave of his hand. 'Why?' he asked. 'Justice does not enjoy a particularly exalted status in our line of work. It can always await a more opportune moment.' He ended his remarks with a wary glance at their approaching waiter. Both men surveyed the grill's curtailed wartime menu, then ordered the Savoy's delicacy of the day, steamed haddock.

'Tell me,' he enquired as the waiter disappeared, 'if you don't feel it's being indiscreet, a little bit about him.'

'Not at all,' Cavendish replied. He was more interested in Dansey's appraisal of the situation than in maintaining a pretence at discretion. 'His name is Henri Lemaire. He walked out over the Pyrenees in the late summer of '42. He'd been a pilot for the French postal service before the war. He flew with their air force in '39 and '40. After the armistice, he fetched up in Marseille and got a job as a test pilot for one of Vichy's aircraft manufacturers.'

Dansey prodded: 'How did he get into contact with you?'

'Archie Boyle brought him to me. He said he had come to England because he wanted to fly for the RAF; but the RAF Special Services chap knew we were looking for someone for our Lysander work, so they put him on to us.'

There was another pause as the waiter returned with their haddock. Dansey stared at his with baleful regard. 'Do you know I spent my entire youth resisting Nanny's entreaties to eat this bloody fish?' He groaned. 'And now the Savoy serves the stuff as a delicacy. God damn Hitler and all his works.' Dansey gave a neat little pat to his lips with the reassuringly heavy linen of the Savoy's napkin. 'Would you care to hear how I read the situation?'

'Of course,' Cavendish replied, focusing all his attention on the older man.

'I suppose the Gestapo must have nobbled him sometime after you sent him in. Probably they either bludgeoned him into cooperating with them in that friendly fashion of theirs or he decided to play along to save his neck – and his testicles.'

Cavendish grimaced his agreement.

'Now, I would wager that they came rather quickly to the conclusion that what was of interest to them in his operation was the intelligence in your courier packets. Sound intelligence, after all, is more apt to win the war for them than a few dozen of your agents, with all due respect to your organization.'

'Go on, please.'

'But if they're going to assure themselves a regular glimpse into those courier packets of yours, they've got to let him run his landings unmolested, haven't they? If they start nipping your agents, they know you'll tumble to the fact he's a baddie and close him down like a trap.' Dansey settled back, the icy smirk for which he was known making its first appearance at the luncheon. 'This may account for the fact his operations for you have been running so smoothly. He's probably been running them under the protection of a Gestapo cover. Clever chap.'

'Clever bastard,' Cavendish sighed. 'I guess I had better find an excuse to bring him back and hand him over to MI5.'

'You could do that,' Dansey agreed, 'or you could take a longer view of things.'

'In what way?'

With a satisfaction inspired by the memory of his prodding nanny, Dansey pushed his plate of haddock away half-eaten. 'There's a fundamental rule to apply when you're appraising a double-agent situation: Who is getting more out of him, you or the other side? If the answer is you, keep him going. If it's them, kill him.'

'You're implying I should keep him going?'

'I am. It's a calculated risk, of course. These things always are. But it does seem to me his services are so valuable the risks justify the gamble.'

'But what do I do about the courier?'

Dansey turned that one over a moment or two. 'You obviously can't tell your people in the field you've tumbled to him. One of them may take it on himself to get rid of him for you. And the word would probably get back to the Germans anyway. No, what I think you should do is put it about to your people over there by coded radio messages that with the run up to the invasion under way, everything of any consequence must now go by radio. Tell them to use the courier only for the secondary stuff. Reports on the effects of a bombing, sabotage studies, who's running the rail unions in Dijon. Provide our friends on Avenue Foch with just enough reading matter to slake their curiosity. Hopefully, by the time they wake up to what's happening, Eisenhower will be rolling up to Paris. And in the meantime, you'll have used their gracious auspices to keep your people moving in and out when it's most important to you.'

178

The boldness, the simplicity of Dansey's scheme set Cavendish's mind churning with nervous excitement. Imagine: using the Gestapo as the protective umbrella for one of the most vital operations of his service. The symmetry of the thing was perfect. 'Of course,' he noted to the older man, 'if it goes wrong, we wind up carrying the can, don't we?'

'Indeed. That's always the risk in these things. But what it really comes down to, as it so often does in our little world, is a nice assessment of profit and loss. And when you add up the pluses and minuses, you come to the very firm conclusion that the balance will be rather heavily stacked in your favour.'

Cavendish reflected for several moments before replying. 'I do believe you're right,' he said.

'Yes,' Dansey said, 'I'm quite sure I am.'

CALAIS

The girl on the bed gave a malicious giggle. 'That doctor put so much plaster around my ankle I can barely lift it.' She strained to raise the cast enclosing her right leg from the pillow that swaddled it, then let it drop back with a thud which should have produced a shriek of pain – had her ankle really been broken.

'Now, you, don't you worry about anything.' A calloused red hand reached out from her faded lavender cotton bathrobe and gave Catherine's forearm a reassuring squeeze. 'Nothing ever changes, everything's always the same, just like I told you. Everything you need is there in the room where they have all those electric things – the washing machine, plenty of soap in the box on the ledge. You hang the things up on the line right there by the machine – you can't miss it. If they leave you sewing, you bring it back here to do.' A bob of her head indicated a neatly folded pile of clothes on the table by her bed. 'The only problem you'll have is telling them why you won't have dinner with them.' She emitted a sad, wheezing sigh and pouted. 'I never had that problem. No one ever asked me out to dinner except the fat corporal who drives the motorcycle. They say they have such food in those restaurants the officers go to. Fresh sole; oysters even!' Nostalgia for those long-forgotten delicacies invaded the girl's face.

Poor thing, Catherine mused, she's exactly as Aristide described: fat, splotches of skin showing through the balding areas in her stringy brown hair, a complexion so rough her cheeks look as though they'd been sandpapered. No wonder no one ever asked her out for dinner. 'All heart,' Aristide had said, 'and no mind at all as far as I've been able to

179

discover.' For three years she'd been doing the laundry of the officers of the Lindemann Battery. Her father, a vague prewar Communist sympathizer, had been deported to Germany in some distant roundup, and she was the only support of her ageing, alcoholic mother. Even in the eyes of the most ardent anti-Nazi no stigma was attached to her labour for the Germans. Still, she'd been more than happy to simulate her bicycle accident and yield her place to Catherine as a way of taking out that little bit of reinsurance for the postwar world.

Outside, Catherine heard the rasp of the motorcycle, then the sound of boots clomping into the tiny wooden dwelling.

'Ach! What's this?' asked the surprised corporal as he entered the room.

The girl snorted unattractively into the sleeve of her bathrobe and made a whimpering sound. 'Karli, *mein Schatz*,' she said. 'poor me! I fell off my bike and broke my ankle. The doctor makes me stay in bed for six weeks. Denise, my friend, is going to do the laundry until I'm better.'

Whatever suspicions, if any, this sudden change in programme might have aroused in the corporal were instantly overcome by the demure yet promising smile Catherine conferred on him. He picked up her package of sewing and, outside, settled her into the sidecar of his motorcycle as though he'd been doing it for months. They roared off along the shore road that paralleled the Channel coast on Calais's westward approaches. It ran roughly 100 yards inland from the high-water line, on the leeward side of the ridge of dunes that rose behind the beaches. So many bunkers, gunports, pillboxes, machine-gun emplacements had been embedded into the dunes that it seemed to Catherine they had become a kind of massive concrete spine over which the Germans had stretched a mantle of sod and sea grass. When, through the occasional gap in the dunes, she could see the beach, what she saw was a thicket of barbed wire and iron-and-cement stakes, the famous seaward obstacles Rommel had ordered planted at water'ss edge. The apron of land running out of the dunes to the road was, she knew, dense with mines. To her left, the inland plain had been inundated.

They sped past the one-storey bungalows of the village of Sangatte up to the barricade manned by a dozen *Feldgendarmes*. Seeing the familiar motorcycle, one of them lifted the gate and waved them through. The road was a funnel thrusting traffic to this control point. How, she asked herself, with mines and flooded fields on either side of the road, could an SOE team ever get to the battery without shooting their way through the roadblock and setting off an alarm?

Past the control, the coastal road began to climb. To the right, the fold of the terrain rose with increasingly dramatic abruptness from the seabed, coalescing as it did into the sheer cliffs that stretched down to

180

Cap Gris-Nez. To her left, Catherine could now see the three concrete emplacements of the battery's guns. They looked like the massive foundations for some as yet unbuilt tower designed to rise above the Channel coast. Dark gun barrels protruded from each turret, their tips trained on the thin chalk walls of Dover barely visible across the Channel. The corporal swung off the coastal road up a dirt gravel track that ran in a wide semicircle behind the batteries. Yet another control, Catherine noted, marked its entry. She tried to register in her mind everything her eyes saw; laying in distances, calculating angles. Fifty yards up the track, on a knoll rising from the hillside, was what appeared to be an observation post, a great cement mushroom growing out of the earth circled by an open trench in which she could see men moving. The fire-control centre, she wondered, or the command post?

Farther on was a trio of anti-aircraft guns in concrete emplacements. Their crews were sprawled around them half asleep in the spring sunshine. Obviously, they relied on radar, not their binoculars, for warning of an air attack. At the top of the hillside, behind the middle gun emplacement, the corporal turned off the track into a parking area. There, another cement mushroom, this one crowned by a metallic grove of aerials, peered down over the central gun turret towards the sea. On the far side of the track from the turret, the terrain sloped away and slightly upwards in a grassy expanse of open land marred by dozens of yawning craters left from the 1943 raid on the battery. Landing a glider there, Catherine realized, would be impossible. And the reverse side of the slope? she wondered.

The corporal helped her out of the sidecar. As he did, she gave his hairy forearm a tender squeeze. 'Karli, look!' she said, waving towards the scarlet poppies and purple anemones peeping through the craters on the hillside beyond the track. 'Aren't they lovely? Come on, we must go and pick some to take back to poor Jeanine stuck there in bed.'

'Are you crazy?' Karli asked. 'You can't do that.'

'Why?'

'They've got so many mines planted in there a dog couldn't go in there to pee without getting killed.'

'Oh, Karli,' she pouted, 'you can't fool me. They always have a map to show you how to get through mines. You can lead us through and we'll pick them on the other side.'

'Listen, Schatz,' Karli said, picking up her bundle of sewing, ' this isn't a flower market. There's no path through there. And on the other side we put down so many mines even a field mouse couldn't get past them.' He gestured with his head across the open waters of the Channel. 'Churchill's paratroopers,' he grunted; 'legless wonders they'll all be if they try to jump there.'

181

To get to the entrance of the turret, they walked along a road, its borders, she noted, lined with clumps of marigolds. Raising her gaze from the flowers to the façade of the turret, she saw a pair of machine guns menacingly covering the rear approaches to the gun site. A steel door led into the turret. It opened electrically in response to a password the corporal uttered into a speaking tube. Passing through it, Catherine made a mental note of the location of its hinges. A commando could blow them off with plastic charges – if any of them were left alive to do it, she thought, after the minefields and the machine guns. They were mad in London, weren't they? Even she could see their idea was never going to work.

They stepped through a second steel door, this one open, into what Catherine instantly understood must be the guns' fire-control room. A dozen men lounged around the room, some wearing head-sets and speaking tubes, others reading, smoking, chatting to each other. There were two tables covered with maps, dividers and compasses. Painted on the wall opposite, through which she glimpsed the gun's breach, was the word 'Bruno' and under it, in German, the phrase 'We Germans fear nothing in the world but God.' A series of winged shells with what appeared to be dates under them ran up and down the wall – clearly some kind of log of the gun's activity.

She had time to observe no more because her corporal had already crossed the room and started down a circular steel staircase. This must be what a submarine is like, she thought, following him. The battery's support system was spread over five subterranean floors. It was a self-contained little world, all pigeonholed and packaged. Making her way down the stairs, she saw machine shops, repair shops, a tiny hospital, bunkrooms for the gun crews, kitchens, a recreation room where a dozen soldiers lolled about. A hoist, undoubtedly for the shells, ran alongside the staircase. Everywhere she could hear the oppressive hum of the ventilation system circulating the textureless air of the battery's underground world. Reaching the bottom landing, the corporal steered her towards the officers' mess. To her left was the electric-power room, a wall covered with fuse boxes, switches, gauges and beside them what were probably a pair of independent generators to furnish the battery with electricity if its power supply were cut. To the rear of the room, she spotted her washing machine.

A mess steward welcomed them into the officers' lounge and offered Catherine a mug of coffee from his hot plate. On the mess wall above a set of easy chairs, exactly as Jeanine had described them, was a line of seven wooden boxes, one for each of the battery's officers. She opened her bundle of sewing and began to distribute its contents into the boxes, as she did, taking out from each one the clump of soiled laundry waiting

182

for her. Behind her, she heard two of her clients entering the room for a cup of coffee. When she turned to pick up a fresh package, she glimpsed one of them out of the corner of her eye. There was something vaguely familiar about his dark features, a disturbing suggestion that she had seen him somewhere before. Fitting the laundry into its box, she knew he was staring at her, asking himself the same puzzled question she was asking herself.

'Mademoiselle?'

Catherine turned. For the first time since she had entered the battery she was sickeningly aware of where she was. The German was smiling. 'I trust our laundry isn't as heavy as your suitcase was on the train up to Paris. I've been looking for you in the Trois Suisses for days and all the time you were right here!'

PARIS

Half an hour after his rendezvous with Strömelburg, Paul was at the telephone booth of the Café Sporting at the Porte Maillot. He gave the telephone operator, a great gargoyle of a woman, his own telephone number and went into her phone booth. While his phone rang unanswered, he opened the telephone book on the ledge below the phone to page 75 and set his message inside. It was brief. It simply confirmed, as London had requested, that Operation *Foxtrot* was on for the next night.

When he hung up, the radio operator who'd been sitting in the café upstairs was waiting his turn to use the phone. Without acknowledging him, Paul walked up the stairs, on to the street and down into the *métro* station around the corner from the café. This time his destination was one of Paris' more celebrated institutions, an enterprise not usually associated with the rigours of clandestine life. It was a bordello known as the One Two Two for its address, 122 Rue de Provence, and it was one of the few brothels in Paris still open to French civilians as well as German soldiers.

Paul handed his overcoat to the retired pensioner of the house who ran the cloakroom and walked into its shabbily elegant high-ceilinged living room. The madam greeted him warmly, then gestured at the dozen girls in the sitting room with the pride of a headmistress showing off her prize classroom to an inspector from the board of education. 'Take your pick, monsieur,' she said. Leaning towards Paul, she added in a hiss, 'They're all nice and fresh. It's early.'

Paul surveyed the girls. 'I think I'll have a drink first,' he declared, and headed for the small bar at the end of the room. He sat there for fifteen minutes sipping a glass of wine, studying the girls. They wore either tight-fitting silk and satin evening gowns or short flaring skirts and matching silk brassières. It was indeed early, and the only other client was a half-drunk corporal of the Wehrmacht who was having considerable difficulty perching on his barstool.

The girls made the mandatory effort to catch Paul's eye from their velvet benches or cruised past him at the bar, hips undulating, their eyes trying to manufacture an interest they did not feel, murmuring the ritual phrase, *'Je T'emmène, chéri?'* – 'I take you with me, dear?'

Suddenly, a blonde entered through the curtains that covered the archway leading to the stairs. She was older than most of the girls in the room, in her mid thirties perhaps, in a green silk evening gown that seemed to cling to her skin. She had peroxided hair, dark Oriental eyes and high, muscular breasts whose nipples thrust with visible defiance against the panels of her green gown. With the whore's infallible sense of where the custom lies, she caught the tightening in Paul's eyes as he looked at her.

Slowly, with studied casualness, she strolled towards him. There was a hard, mocking glance in her eyes that contradicted the disarming smile with which she fixed him. She moved right up to him until the flanks of her pelvis touched his knees. Locking his eyes with hers, she slipped a hand into his inner thigh and danced it upwards until her long fingers began to indolently caress their objective. *'Alors, mon amour,'* she said, her eyes daring his, *'tu viens ou non?'* – 'are you coming or not?'

Paul was. He went over to the madam and paid the statutory fee for a 'short time,' then followed the blonde up the stairs to her room. The maid, a fresh-cheeked little girl probably less than sixteen, opened the door for them and laid a towel grey with age on the bed.

The girl locked the door behind the departing maid while Paul took off his coat and loosened his tie. He sat on the bed, his shoulders leaning against the wall, and offered her a cigarette.

'What's new?' he asked.

'Nothing much,' she answered. 'Bad news doesn't seem to shut down our German friends' ardour. Which' – she shrugged her shoulders – 'is good news for me, I suppose. And you?'

'Business pretty much as usual. Have you got anything for me?'

The girl shook her head.

'I've got something for you.' Paul reached into his pocket. His 'something,' appropriately enough for the surroundings, was enclosed in a tightly rolled condom. The girl placed it at the bottom of the pile of condoms in the drawer of the table beside her bed.

'It's urgent,' Paul cautioned.

They chatted for another fifteen minutes until they heard the tapping on the door and the shrill young voice of the maid announcing, '*Temps, monsieur, madame.*' A 'short time' at the One Two Two was just that. The prostitute walked Paul to the front door, fondly clutching his hand in hers. When he had put on his overcoat, she embraced him warmly. '*Merci, chéri,*' she said. '*A bientôt, j'espère*' – 'See you soon, I hope.'

CALAIS

Aristide was drinking a glass of water, swallowing it, Catherine noted, with the tiny meditative sips of a gourmet savouring the first tastes of a bottle of 1929 Bordeaux. Pierrot was leaning against the wall, arms folded, listening in silence. There was something almost Dostoevskian about their little trio, about this spare and shadow-shrouded apartment. Aristide's apartment, as she'd noted on her first visit, was austere, devoid of any hint of the man who lived in it. Was that almost calculated lack of possessions, that seemingly systematic exclusion of any material comfort a reflection of Aristide's personality, she wondered, or the consequence of the terrible uncertainties of the clandestine existence?

She finished her account of her first day as a laundress for the officers of the Lindemann Battery and looked at Aristide. His reply was a long, speculative silence.

Finally, Pierrot stirred. 'At least,' he said, 'you found out more about that battery in an hour and a half than we've been able to find out in three years.'

'Enough,' Aristide continued, 'to prove that the commando that can storm those guns does not exist.' He seemed genuinely distressed by the futility of London's proposal. 'The useless slaughter of two hundred men is all it will amount to.' He returned to his water a moment, then brought his attention back to Catherine. 'This officer who carried your bag for you, what does he do out there?'

'According to the corporal, he's an engineer.'

'Looks after the machinery, the electricity?'

'I suppose so.'

'There are two ways of handling him.' Aristide contemplated the situation with an air of contentment Catherine did not share. 'Those German officers, whatever their other failings, tend to be gentlemen as far as women are concerned. You can fend him off by indicating to him just how awkward going out with him would make life for you among your fellow citizens. My guess is he'll understand.'

'That's exactly what I'd like to do.'

185

'Perhaps' – Aristide went back to his water – 'but that's not what I want you to do.'

Catherine reddened slightly, pretending, almost, not to understand. She was thinking, as she so often did, of Paul, and the thrust of Aristide's words gave poignancy to her recollection.

'What I would like is to see you accept his invitation for a drink.'

The hate in Paul's eyes as he had contemplated the tables full of collaborators in their black-market restaurant was before Catherine.

'You want me to go flouncing around the streets of the city on the arm of a German? What are people going to think?'

'They will think' – Aristide pronounced the words with serene detachment – 'that you're whoring around with a German officer. What else would you expect them to think?'

'Well, it's a thought I prefer to spare them.' And you too, Paul, she thought.

Aristide shrugged. 'I wouldn't – I couldn't force you to go out with him. No matter how important I thought it might be for us.' His smile implied a tolerant understanding of her objections. His eyes, the tone of his voice, however, conveyed quite another message. 'What does he look like? Physically, I mean.'

'Oh, he's quite good-looking.' Catherine was surprised at how swiftly those words had come. 'Dark. Not German at all. As though there was some Spanish blood in there somewhere.'

'He must be from the North. Hamburg, Bremen.' Her observations had been reassuring. Had the man been fat, bald and short, Aristide reasoned, his would have been a difficult advocacy. 'Most of the officers here come from the North. The scions of the Hanseatic League, people conditioned by the sea. There's something of us in them, strangely enough.'

'I positively loathe the idea of having to go out with him, Aristide. Tell me just why is it so important to you. And please, spare me the tired old *canard* about Mata Hari, the *femme fatale*.'

Aristide shrugged. He stood up and resumed addressing her as he paced the room. 'I don't know why it's important you let this man take you out. Perhaps it's not – who knows? We know nothing about him. We don't know where he comes from. We don't know what he does in that battery. We know nothing of his loyalties. Above all, Denise, we don't know what he knows. Until we have some idea of that, how can we know what importance he might have to us?'

'Aristide, this isn't Paris in 1938.' An icy calm had returned to Catherine. 'People sell their souls for a good meal today. He's not taking me out just to practice his French.'

Strange how pertinent her observation was, Aristide thought. In the

186

upside-down world of the occupation, the true act of submission for a woman does not come in the bedroom. It comes in the dining room, in the black-market restaurant, in the face of the forgotten luxury of food. 'Not every man who takes a pretty girl to dinner winds up making love to her, Denise. Were that the case, my own existence would have been far more satisfying than in fact it has been.'

Aristide returned to his chair and lit a foul-smelling Occupation Gauloise. 'Suppose,' he said, the remoteness of his tone implying he was about to discuss some abstract concept, 'I suggest to you two reasons why it might be invaluable for you to have a drink with the gentleman? First, London's commando raid is not going to work. The three of us know that, agree it. Nor are air raids. So the Admiralty, however much they may dislike it, are going to have to bring their ships into the strait to knock out those guns, unless...'

'Unless what, Aristide?' Catherine did not hide her petulance.

'Unless we – the three of us in this room – can find some fourth option.'

'Oh, my God! I suppose you're going to say that what you want me to do is bed down this German, drive him wild with lust, then get him to blow up those guns for us? What would London say to that idea?'

'London would say what they always say in these situations – "We leave it to your judgement." Denise, please don't think I'm as naïve as you appear to assume I am. I meant to suggest no such extravagant resolution to our problems. What I wish to say as the head of this network is that we are faced with a situation, a potential situation, which should be exploited – at least until we've determined whether there's anything there to exploit or not. Unfortunately, you're the only one who can exploit it for us. It's conceivable – barely conceivable, I agree, but still conceivable – that something this German might say could suggest another way of resolving London's problem. Although not in as dramatic a fashion as you suggest.'

Aristide took a long drag on his cigarette, taking her silence as an indication that some of the initial heat had gone out of her arguments. 'I understand how you feel. Don't forget I work in the town hall. I'm forever having to grovel to them in my way, and I loathe every minute of it.' The wave of his cigarette finished his thought for him. 'We've got to keep you on as a laundress in the battery, don't forget that. Accommodating him a bit may make that less troublesome for you. In any event, I'm not asking you to decide now. Sleep on it. When are you up to London again?'

'Ten-thirty tomorrow morning.'

'I'll send Pierrot to you at nine-thirty. He can keep an eye out for the German detection trucks while you're transmitting.'

'Aristide, there's something else.'

'About the German?'

'No. About the radio. I've done all my broadcasts from my room. London made quite a point of shifting our broadcasting sites to throw off the *gonio*.' She employed their Resistance slang for the *camions goniométriques* – the detection trucks.

'I know.' Aristide's sigh this time was almost painful. 'London lives in a perfect world. We don't. You can try to move around with it if you want – broadcast from here, from Pierrot's. The problem is there are so many spot checks of parcels in the streets these days I honestly don't think you'd survive a fortnight without getting caught carrying it.'

'And how long will I survive without getting caught always transmitting from the same place?'

Her question elicited another of Aristide's thought-heavy silences.

'As I told you when you arrived, Denise, yours is the most dangerous job we have. And this is the worst place in France to do it. What more can I say?'

Somewhere out there, she knew, on some forgotten country byway, on some half-deserted city street, hidden behind some peeling wall in a quiet courtyard, a German sat patiently in a truck, earphones clamped to his head, slowly twisting a needle along a radio dial. He was a hunter carefully, meticulously stalking his prey. And I, Catherine thought, I am his prey. It was, at best, a depressing thought; yet curiously, Catherine encouraged it to linger in the forefront of her consciousness. Her parents early, lovers later, had warned her of the consequences of a certain rashness in het character. There was no room for that in what she was doing now. To survive as a clandestine radio operator you worked to rules, and any reminder of the need for that, however grim, was welcome.

It was 10:20. Catherine rubbed her hands together as one might over a blazing fire on a cold night. The gesture was half a nervous reflex, half a careful preparation for her transmission. Pierrot was already by the window, eyes studying the street below. Transmitting from the centre of Calais had some advantages. Only nine vehicles, five private cars and four trucks, had *Ausweises* to circulate in the city. The chance of one of them appearing on her side street during a transmission was minimal. She and Pierrot agreed that any vehicle turning into the street would almost certainly be a German detection van.

Her set was open, its power switched on. Her aerial, a 15-metre green rubber-coated wire, coiled like a snake around the apartment floor. That was another advantage of transmitting from Calais. With the Sevenoaks receiving station barely a hundred miles away, England never had any problem picking up her signal. Other SOE operators, sending from the Alps or the Southwest, were forced to lay their aerials outside, where they could be spotted, in order to get through.

She yawned, knowing the instant she did that it reflected the nervous tension she always felt before going on the air. She stretched, smiled at Pierrot, then, for the tenth time, studied the equipment on the table before her. The set was hooked to the apartment's regular power supply. However, a 6-volt dry-cell battery, controlled by a toggle switch, was also branched to the transmitter. Beside the set, a lamp, its bulb burning, rested on the table.

There was a very precise reason for that. Often, if the Gestapo had been able to pin down the street or neighbourhood from which a radio operator was transmitting, they would send out a team in civilian clothes to cut the power supply building by building as soon as the radio went on the air. If the signal stopped dead when a certain building's power was cut, then the Gestapo knew that was the building from which the set was broadcasting. If the light on Catherine's lamp went out while she was on the air, she had only to hit the toggle switch to her battery with her left hand to resume transmitting. That hiccup might pass unnoticed by the listening Gestapo.

Beside the lamp were a big wind-up alarm clock and four of her five crystals lined up in the order in which she intended to use them. Each crystal was moulded inside a black pronged sheath that plugged into the set like a light plug. Each had a number. Catherine had only to radio the number of the next crystal she'd use to alert Sevenoaks to the fact that she was switching frequencies. Her 'godmother' at Sevenoaks had a list of the frequency that corresponded to each of her crystals. She'd switch to it instantly, but the hunters of the German detection service would have to begin their relentless prowling of the airwaves in search of her new frequency all over again.

Her message was in front of her, coded in five-letter blocks on the square paper French schoolchildren used for their homework. She had cut it into small slips of paper – bite size. If the Gestapo came charging up the stairs, she might just be able to swallow them before they broke the door. It was fortunate that Aristide was a miserly man when it came to words, because the longer a radio stayed on the air, the greater were the chances the Germans would pinpoint its location.

It was 10:25. Catherine nodded at Pierrot and fixed her earphones to her head. She played with her dial an instant, then heard, strong and clear, the familiar three letters of her call sign, 'BNC...BNC...BNC,' coming through the ether over and over again from Sevenoaks. That sound had a greatly reassuring effect on Catherine; it was her link to that faceless FANY who received her, to England, to safety. Carefully, she

189

adjusted her dial to get Sevenoaks' signal at maximum strength. Fortunately, there were no other transmissions near the wavelength she was going to use, no manoeuvring German troops, no Dutch freighter in the Scheldt dumping gibberish onto her frequency.

The hands on her clock indicated 10:30. Catherine tensed, took a slow breath to relax herself and opened her set to transmit. At the first interval in Sevenoaks' transmission of her call sign, she went on the air, tapping out her BNC half a dozen times. Then she sat back and listened.

'QSL...QSL...QSL' Sevenoaks answered. 'We read you loud and clear.'

They were ready. Catherine glanced at the clock, gave a last rub to her right hand and set her finger to her key. In seconds she was in another world, wholly, completely concentrated on her moving finger, on the click-clack of the radio's key dancing through its dots and dashes. Swiftly, steadily she worked her way along her five-letter blocks, inserting her security check between the fourth and fifth, her double security check between the fifth and sixth. She worked methodically, forcing a calmness on herself that she didn't feel, making herself ignore the stiffness in her muscles, the beads of sweat beginning their journey down her spine. At exactly 10:40 she flashed a new frequency key to Sevenoaks, unplugged her first crystal and inserted the next one.

Slowly, steadily, she eroded the letter blocks of Aristide's message. She was oblivious to everything except the burning bulb, the rhythm of her finger and an alertness in her ear for a whistling echo that, she had been warned, might indicate the German detection vans had found her.

It was exactly 11:12 when she tapped the last letter of the last block and her call sign BNC, to indicate she was through. She sat back tense, listening. It was, in many ways, the worst moment of a transmission. In Sevenoaks, her FANY godmother would be going through her message block by block to be sure she had copied everything. Would she have to ask her to repeat part of it?

She waited, the muscles in her back sore from the rigid position she always kept when she sent. Then, after three minutes, she heard the most welcome sound of the morning. 'QSL.' Sevenoaks had received everything. She slumped in her chair exhausted and happy. She had been on the air forty-two minutes, the longest transmission she'd made since she'd arrived in Calais, and there had been no sign of the *gonio*. Once again she had frustrated him, that unseen German hunter out there somewhere in his detection van, stalking the airwaves for some clue to her hiding place.

Hans-Dieter Strömelburg was in an uncharacteristically jovial frame of mind. A warm spring breeze was stirring the leaves of Paris' Avenue Foch outside his office window. Marcel Dupré, the great organist whose talents he so admired, was giving an evening concert at the church of Saint Sulpice. He had every intention of being in his audience. He had also made arrangements for a post-concert vist to Dodo, the red-haired whore whose services he had come to esteem greatly. And he had just returned from a thoroughly satisfying strategy conference at the La Roche Guyon headquarters of Field Marshal Rommel.

He liked Rommel. The field marshal's forthright stand for National Socialism, his personal devotion to the Führer were attitudes Strömelburg encountered all too infrequently in officers of the Wehrmacht. He had never seen the field marshal as optimistic about their chances of throwing back the invasion as he had been yesterday. His own contribution to the meeting, an evaluation of the strength of the French Resistance, had been particularly appreciated. There were three regions of France in which he had assured the gathering the Wehrmacht could feel relatively free of the threat of armed Resistance activity: in the North, in Normandy and in the central region around Paris. South of the Loire, things were much less certain. But there where it mattered most, along the coastline, they could sleep peacefully, he had reported.

A knock on the door interrupted his self-satisfied reverie. It was the Doctor. 'You come bearing glad tidings, I trust,' Strömelburg said, noticing the file folder in his subordinate's hands.

'Interesting ones, at least,' the Doctor replied, passing him the folder. 'It's the weekly report of the Boulevard Suchet's detection service. Four new radios on the air last week.'

'That's to be expected. The invasion season is upon us,' Strömelburg noted, spreading the material out on his desk. The first two stations, he saw, were in the Dordogne. They could go on broadcasting down there day and night if they wanted to as far as he was concerned. Locating a radio in those desolate hills was extremely difficult. And even if they could find one, capturing it was certain to be a bloody business. The area crawled with Resistance fighters. The third new set was in Lyon. His subordinate Klaus Barbie could be counted on to deal with that. It was the fourth one that caught his eye.

'A new station with the call sign BNC is operating within the triangle Boulogne – Dunkirk – Saint-Omer. The set transmits irregularly and has been detected broadcasting on 6766 and 7580 kilocycles. We have not yet been able to establish its working routine fully, but we have thus far confirmed six broadcasts. We have intercepted bits of all six and estimate their length varied from six to fifty minutes. That last would indicate a station of some importance. The intercepted fragments have been communicated to Army Intelligence Radio Section, Berlin, for decoding.'

'How many detection vans are working up there?' Strömelburg snapped.

'Two on that station,' the Doctor replied, 'four more between here and Lille.'

'Get the rest of the trucks into that triangle,' Strömelburg ordered. 'All of them.' He thumped the report with his forefinger. 'I want that radio, Doctor. Make it your responsibility to get it, and get it fast.'

PART FOUR

APRIL/MAY 1944

The two dark blue Humbers slipped along the Kentish Byways, through the pale green tapestry of England's awakening countryside. T. F. O'Neill admired the cowslips gleaming in the April sunshine that dappled the meadows, the pale blue harebells nodding by the streambeds. Did he, he wondered, catch a breath of salt air through his open window? The English Channel, after all, was barely 10 miles away. Just outside Tenterden, the cars turned off the road, through a discreet gate and up to a red brick Victorian manor house.

An American lieutenant colonel and half a dozen British officers stood saluting at the foot of the stairs. T.F. leaped out. From the car behind him, his superior, Colonel Ridley, emerged with their guest of honour, General Sir Hastings Ismay, Churchill's personal Chief of Staff. The Prime Minister was so closely interested in *Fortitude*, Ridley had explained to T.F., that he had decided to send Ismay to inspect one of the primary components in the scheme, the 3103 US Signal Service Battalion. Ridley had insisted that T.F., as his American liaison, accompany Ismay's party. For just over a month, the one thousand officers and men of the 3103 had been at work imitating the radio traffic of ten divisions, three Army Corps, the headquarters of an army and an Army Group – a quarter of a million nonexistent fighting men in all – for the benefit of the Germans eavesdropping across the English Channel.

Ismay bounded up the stairs and into the briefing room the Americans had prepared for him. A mess steward offered him a cup of tea. Ismay brushed it aside impatiently; he had other things on his mind. The American colonel mounted a little platform, rubber-tipped pointer in hand, ready to begin a well-rehearsed briefing for his distinguished visitor. Ismay, however, wasn't going to waste his time listening to a briefer tell him what the Americans wanted him to know. His often difficult life with Winston Churchill had taught him how to pursue information with ruthless effectiveness.

'Just begin by telling me one thing, Colonel. Why are the Germans going to accept this fake radio traffic of yours as authentic?' he demanded.

The colonel laid down his pointer. 'Sir, every US division, regiment and battalion actually stationed in this country is under orders to send us a daily analysis of their radio traffic: the number of messages they send and receive; the percentage in code, in voice, in clear Morse; a breakdown of the percentage falling into each of ten subject categories we've given them. Now we figure the Germans are listening to those real messages. So we draft the fake messages for our fake divisions based on them. We know, for example, how many messages a real regimental CP should send out in a day, what they're likely to be about, who they'd go to. So we make up our fake traffic for our fake regimental CP based on the pattern of the real CP's messages.'

Rather than allow Ismay to sting him with another unexpected question, the colonel turned quickly to the comfortably familiar outlines of a chart on the easel beside him. 'Our role in the *Fortitude* deception plan is code-named *Quicksilver*,' he said, getting into his prepared routine. 'We're assigned to show by our fake radio activity the concentration of the imaginary First US Army Group preparation for an invasion of the Calais coast from here in southeastern England. It's supposed to consist of two armies, the First Canadian and Third US.'

'I know all that,' Ismay said impatiently. 'Do your operators make their transmissions directly onto the air?'

'No, sir,' replied the colonel, 'We record everything here on regular sixteen-inch records and broadcast them from trucks circulating through southeast England.'

'Doesn't that look a little too perfect?'

'Our men make mistakes in recording, sir. If they are not compromising we leave them in.'

'Suppose a record gets broken on one of these superb country lanes of ours?'

'We record in duplicate, sir.'

T.F. smiled. The reason Churchill had sent his personal chief of staff down here, he had just realised, was certainly a healthy scepticism about the Americans' ability to handle their role in *Fortitude*. The colonel was disappointing him.

'How many trucks are you operating?'

'We have seventeen teams, sir. Each consists of two radio trucks and two jeeps, five radio operators, three cryptographers, a voice specialist, five guards and three technicians. Now, each of those teams is designed to imitate five radio circuits, which means we are imitating eighty-five different circuits in all.' He turned to a map of southeastern England. 'The trucks work inside the triangle Ipswich-Brighton-Ramsgate.'

'Your coded messages,' Ismay asked. 'Surely you're not wasting your time drafting real messages for the traffic, are you?'

'Yes, sir, we sure are. If one of those Germans over there breaks our code, we don't want him reading "Mary had a little lamb" when he was expecting something about tank tactics.'

Ismay offered the colonel a lukewarm smile. 'They say every radio operator has his own signature, his own way of tapping his radio key.'

'Generally speaking, sir, that's correct.'

'Then how, pray tell, do the dozen or so operators who are recording your messages here avoid making it evident to the Germans that those eighty-five radio circuits of yours are all in fact being manned by a very limited number of men?'

T.F felt a vicarious twinge of apprehension for his countryman at hearing that question.

'Each of our operators has been specially trained for over a year to develop a variety of signatures, sir – up to a dozen. They employ them at random in making the recordings downstairs.'

Even T.F. couldn't suppress a satisfied smile.

'One of our trucks is operating here, General,' the colonel continued. 'Maybe you would like to have a look at it?'

For fifteen minutes the party clambered around the truck while the colonel showed off its equipment – its Preston 340A mixers and amplifiers, its oscillators, circuit testers, hommeters, its banks of records and its drawers full of sapphire playing needles. Finally, Ismay turned to a lanky corporal lounging by the truck with a kind of indolent indifference no British soldier would ever have displayed in the presence of a general officer.

'What did you do before the war, son?' he asked, employing that spurious joviality senior officers reserve for addressing troops in the field.

'I was an actor, sir.'

'An actor?' asked the astounded English general. Clearly the powers that ordered the American army really did work in ways quite unfathomable by those directing his own nation's armed forces.

'Yes, sir. On Broadway. Understudied the lead in *Burying the Dead*.'

'Flannagan here is a voice specialist,' the colonel explained. 'He handles the voice transmissions of this truck. We have twenty actors assigned to the battalion for that purpose.'

Ismay regarded him, puzzled.

'A certain amount of each truck's traffic is passed live by voice just like a real unit's would be. We want to convince the Germans we've got a whole lot of men doing the transmission, not one. That's why we use actors. Show the general what you can do, Flannagan.'

While T.F., Ismay and Ridley listened fascinated, the corporal ran through a battery of accents from Brooklynese to Deep Southern, Texas twang and New England nasal. They were just part, the colonel explained, of the repertory he performed daily for the benefit of his unseen German audience across the Channel.

'Amazing,' said Ismay, 'quite perfectly amazing. All this is impressive.' His admiration was genuine if grudging. 'The question is, of course, are our friends on the other side of the water taking it all in?'

'Yes,' Ridley said. 'That is the question, isn't it? I'm afraid we won't get the answer until the time comes. I've got files full of evidence of the thoroughness with which they monitor our traffic. They are damn good at it and they know they are. As a consequence, they tend to attach great importance to it.' Ridley's mind seemed to wander a moment. 'There is one thing, though. One of these American trucks is broadcasting down by East Durham, imitating an armoured division. The Luftwaffe came over the area two nights ago. Killed several civilians, unfortunately. They rarely venture out these days, as you know. We suspect they might have been after our imaginary armoured division.'

'Yes,' Ismay agreed. 'That might well be an indication they're reading you.'

Ismay headed back to London in his own Humber. T.F. followed half an hour later with Ridley. For some time the pair rode in silence, T.F. choosing not to intrude on whatever private concerns were disturbing his superior. Finally, seizing on Ridley's request for a cigarette, T.F. raised a point that had been bothering him since the colonel's last exchange with Ismay.

'Terrible, isn't it?' he said. 'Those civilians getting killed because one of our own trucks was broadcasting as a decoy from their town.'

Ridley gave him that impenetrable expression T.F. had seen on his face several times during his opening briefing at the LCS's underground headquarters. 'Is it?' he asked. 'Yes, I suppose it is.' He dragged deeply on the Camel cigarette T.F. had given him, held his breath, then exhaled slightly. He coughed.

'Rather strong, your American tobacco. You must understand one thing, Major. There is nothing, there is no one so precious I would not gladly sell it or them to the Devil were the price the guarantee that the Fifteenth German Army stays north of the Somme when we go ashore in Normandy.'

CALAIS

The air inside the church of Notre Dame de Calais was so damp it seemed to cling to Catherine Pradier's cheeks; the light so shadowy it might have been reaching her eyes through the filter of very dark sunglasses. She

198

dipped her fingertips into the sculpted stone prayer font by the main door and made the sign of the Cross, the moisture leaving its cool imprint on her forehead. Blinking, she started down the centre aisle, her eyes fixed on the candle flickering inside its red sacristy lamp at the side altar. In the third pew she saw Aristide, eyes fixed on the altar as though he were lost in some intense and prayerful meditation. She slipped into the pew beside him, then knelt in feigned prayer herself.

'Can you imagine?' she whispered, sitting up. 'Your German insisted on taking me to Aux Amis de la Paix, on the Boulevard Lafayette. Germans almost never go there. All those *zazous* sitting around with their greasy hair and baggy trousers, they would have killed me if they could.' Catherine Pradier's recollection of her teenage countrymen's hate-filled eyes gave a special stridency to her tone. 'Why is it these Germans insist on going to places like that where they're not wanted?'

'What other kind of place is there?' In the shadows, the tufts of greying hair sprouting from Aristide's temples seemed to quiver with their own satisfied mirth at his words. 'Tell me, Denise, what did you learn?'

'You were right about one thing. He's from the North. Bremen. His name is Lothar Metz. His father was in the navy in the first war.'

'The tradition runs in the family up there. What else?'

'He's married and has two children. Their pictures were on the table before our drinks. They really have strange ideas about what makes a man seductive, don't they?'

'In the circumstances they're in, Denise, they don't need much original thought to be seductive. What did he tell you about the batteries?'

'He sounds as if he's in love with those guns. They've given each gun a name, like pets – Anton, Bruno and Caesar. He's on Bruno. Guess what their motto is?'

'I can't.'

' "We Germans fear nothing in the world but God." '

Aristide looked towards the altar's crucifix emerging from the shadows before them. 'Yes,' he murmured, 'God and perhaps a good Russian snowstorm.'

'He told me the guns are so big it takes a crew of ten men to operate each one. Apparently they are so heavy they can't be moved by hand; they have to use motors.'

'I had heard that.' Aristide's glance had returned to the floor. His hands were clasped between his thighs so that he had for all the world the air of a middle-aged supplicant beseeching the Almighty's aid in some faltering enterprise.

'He says the British can never land here while they're firing. He claims the guns would blow the British fleet right out of the Channel.'

'He's right about that, I'm afraid. Obviously, that's why Cavendish is so anxious to put them out of action.'

'Powerful. He kept saying that over and over again about his precious guns. He made it sound like something a schoolboy would say about a circus strongman.'

Catherine sensed Aristide's sardonic smile. 'They do so admire power, our Teutonic neighbours,' he hissed.

Her eyes were accustomed now to the tenebrous light in the church. A priest in his black cassock glided out from behind the altar. He genuflected before the sacristy light, then, looping a purple stole around his shoulders, shuffled into the confessional to her left. Catherine heard the soft swish as he drew open the grille separating the penitent's cell from his. How clever, she thought. If anyone came, she and Aristide were just a couple of parishioners waiting to have their confessions heard. She remembered how sympathetic the priest at the soup kitchen had been. Were the Calais clergy in league with Aristide?

'What did he tell you about life in the batteries?' he was asking.

'Nothing very helpful. The officers and men have separate mess halls, but they eat the same food. Lunch is their main meal. At night they have a cold meal – sausages, black bread, cheese. The officers buy food on the black market in Sangatte; vegetables, meat. And wine and cognac, of course. Maybe we could poison it.'

'Amateurish, Denise. What else did he tell you?'

'Let's see.' She had not been trained in England to recall whole conversations, and recollection was difficult. 'The soldiers have a canteen where they can buy beer and *Schnapps* at night. They have three eight-hour shifts a day. The soldiers all have to be back in the battery at sundown. The officers too, unless they have midnight passes, which are very difficult to get. He didn't have one, but I'm afraid the reprieve is only temporary. He's got one for Thursday and wants to take me to dinner.'

'What is his job in the battery?'

'He's the electrical officer. He studied electrical engineering before the war in Hamburg.'

'That's very interesting. What was he like – as a person?'

'He was rather, as you predicted, a gentleman. Lonely, probably, and vulnerable. Not much of a Nazi, I don't think. It was rather disconcerting to be sitting there sipping beer with him and finding out your enemy is human after all.'

'Of course.' Even in the shadows, Catherine could sense the hate-speckled flicker in Aristide's eyes. 'Just like that Stuka pilot that machine-gunned your car during the exodus. He probably never forgot to give his mother flowers on her birthday. Think about *him* if you ever start to incline to tenderness.' Aristide sighed and stirred in the pew. 'You did a good job – again. The fact that he is an electrician just might be important to us. I may have to ask you to have that dinner with him on Thursday night.'

Catherine grimaced, but Aristide ignored her. 'Pierrot will bring you a message tomorrow morning.' He stepped into the aisle, genuflecting as he did. 'Give me a few minutes' head start,' he mumbled. Catherine sat rigid in her pew listening to the sharp clack of his leather heels fading up the church nave. Perhaps, she thought sardonically, an Act of Contrition and a few Hail Marys might be in order – some preliminary gesture of penance for the sin she sensed she would soon be asked to commit.

Puffing from exertion, Aristide tumbled onto the grassy summit of Le Mont Roty, a windswept hillock jutting about the coastal road that linked Calais and Boulogne. He knew the spot well. Often, before the war, he had picnicked here with girlfriends he could dazzle with his stories of Philip VI camping on its heights in 1347 en route to relieve the siege of Calais, or Caesar and Caligula on its crest contemplating the cliffs of their island fiefdom rising from across a misty sea. In those peacetime years, Aristide had taught philosophy at Calais's Collège de la Rue Leveux, but history had always been his passion. He stared down now at the slate-grey moat of the Channel spread at his feet. How many fleets had breasted the currents of that vital passage through the centuries: Roman galleys and British galleons; Napoleonic ships of the line and the motor yachts that had snatched a broken army from the sand flats of Dunkirk. The long storms of winter were over, and the Channel's turbulent cross-rips and races were gentled this April morning by spring's soft hand. Here and there a freshening breeze plucked spray from the whitecaps, and beyond the waters he could just make out the chalky cliffs whose outlines had once transfixed the legions of Rome. The way across was smooth. Now there could be no doubt. The invasion season was at hand.

The sight of a figure beginning to struggle up the hillside interrupted his meditation. Remarkable, Aristide thought, how much more amenable the attitudes of his countrymen had become to the Resistance as the fortunes of war had shifted. Two years ago, the man climbing towards him would at best have ignored his invitation for a little talk, at worst turned him in to the police. Now, with an Allied victory a very real prospect, he had been almost eager to accept his request for a meeting.

Watching him, Aristide could not help thinking back to 1942 and his own recruitment into the Resistance. His father had been a coal miner in Lens until his ailing lungs had driven him to the surface and to Calais as an organizer for the Communists' trade-union federation. He had been

201

taken in the Germans' first round up of Communists in Pas-de-Calais in November 1941, and two months later had been shot following the shooting of a German soldier in Lille. At the time, Aristide was already performing occasional minor tasks for the Resistance, convinced his age and physical frailness barred him from a more active role. When Captain Trotobas, the SOE's legendary commander in the North, had suggested that he could do something more substantial for his organization, Aristide had accepted joyously. The SOE had sent him to England on a clandestine Lysander flight for six weeks' training. On his return, at London's suggestion, he had given up teaching and taken a job in the Calais town hall where he could help fabricate the constantly changing passes and ID cards required to circulate in the coastal zone.

That job had given him access to municipal files and occasionally a preview of German plans for the city. It had also, for example, allowed him to research the background of the man now climbing the hill to meet him. Pierre Paraud was fifty-four, married, the father of two children and a twelve-year employee of La Béthunoise, the private electric company supplying northwestern France with its electric power. Since May 1939 he had run the company's operations in Pas-de-Calais. The Germans' constantly expanding need for electric power to build their Atlantic Wall fortifications, to supply their installations, meant they needed the cooperation of La Béthunoise and its senior employees like Paraud. Some – very, very few, in fact – had quit rather than place their special skills at the occupiers' service. Not Paraud. Like so many Frenchmen, he'd been a reluctant but nonetheless real collaborator, prepared to do what he had to do to keep his job, to get along, to maintain his family's living standard. People like Paraud were going to need references in the months ahead, Aristide thought. He might be prepared to give him one – for a price.

They shook hands and sprawled on the hillock. Aristide offered the panting Paraud a cigarette. 'Beautiful sight, isn't it?' he murmured, pointing through the sea mist to England 25 miles away. 'Do you wonder sometimes what they're doing over there? What they must be thinking about when they're standing on their chalk cliffs looking across at us?'

'No,' Paraud gave a modest shrug, a gesture that somehow implied he was deferring to Aristide. 'When I look over there and think about what is coming, I'm afraid. I think about the destruction the liberation's bound to bring.'

How nice, Aristide thought: just the opening I wanted. 'Yes, we will probably pay a heavy price for this privileged location of ours. We always have.' He offered Paraud the mixed blessing of a tentative smile and that piercing glare of his eyes that had so struck Catherine the first time she saw him. 'There will be many prices to be paid when the liberation comes, I'm afraid.'

If his words had left any doubt in Paraud's mind of their meaning, Aristide's tone was meant to dispel them. He waved his cigarette negligently. 'But why should we worry about that now? I just wanted to chat a minute. Get some information that might be useful to me.' He looked back on Paraud, the shadowy sockets of his eyes serving notice of the cost of silence. 'Strictly on a private basis, of course. Although' – his voice fell to a murmur – 'I am not a man to forget those who do me a service.'

Paraud seemed to gulp at his cigarette. 'What was it you wanted to know?'

'Tell me about the electrical installations of the Lindemann Battery.'

The suggestion of apprehension those words produced on Paraud's features gratified Aristide. A little mental discomfort was a small price for the electrical engineer to pay for what had been, after all, a relatively trouble-free war. 'They take their power directly from the station. They have their own line. We installed it for them in 1942 so they won't go out when we have to shut down the city. They also have two Deutz diesel generators in the battery to supply them their own power in case our current's cut.'

'How long could they run the battery on the generators?'

'Indefinitely.'

'Days? Weeks?'

'Months. As long as they have the fuel to keep the diesels operating.'

'Could they, in an emergency, run the battery without electric power?'

'Absolutely not, not the Lindemann. It's much too big, the shells weigh over a thousand kilograms. The only way they have to bring them up to the guns from their underground arsenal is by electrical freight elevator. The gun turrets weigh fifty tons apiece. They couldn't begin to move them to change aim without electric motors.'

So, Aristide reflected gratefully, there is an Achilles' heel. He twisted into a more comfortable position on the knoll. 'Tell me something,' he said. 'I remember when I was a child, before the war, I was staying with some cousins in Amiens and one night we had the most unbelievably strong thunderstorm. Somehow a burst of lightning got into the power line coming to the house. It blew its way past the fuses and burned out the motors on all the electrical appliances in the house – the fridge, the sewing machine, the radio, everything. Could something like that happen at the Lindemann Battery?'

'No.'

'Why not?'

'Because the Germans have prepared for that. They have a very reliable, very well-calibrated system of circuit breakers controlling the power inflow to their motors. The lightning charge would never get through them. It might make a mess of the control panel, but it would never reach the motors. All the Germans would have to do is hook up a bypass line and they could start operating again.'

Aristide was crestfallen. His philosopher's soul was forever being outraged by the inability of science to conform to reason's sweeter dictates. 'If the motors that run those guns were burned out, how long would it take to replace them?'

'Twenty-four hours. Maybe forty-eight. Provided, of course, they've got spare motors here in Calais. I don't know if they do or not.'

Aristide's eyes went to Paraud's. 'Isn't there some way those circuit breakers could be altered so a burst of current could go through them to the motors?'

'To touch them you would first have to be able to get into the control panel. It's always locked.'

'Who has the key?'

'Lieutenant Metz, the electrical officer. And the battery commander, I suppose.'

Aristide acknowledged this welcome tidbit with a slight nod. 'Let me put before you a theoretical, a purely hypothetical situation. The door to that control panel is open. The circuit breakers are there staring out at us. What could be done to them so a lightning burst would pass through them to the gun's motors?'

Paraud lapsed into what Aristide mistook at first for a recalcitrant's silence. It was in fact a technician's reverie. He was simply not there while he confronted the problem Aristide had posed.

'Do you know how a fuse works?' Paraud asked finally.

'No.'

'The principle is very simple. The fuse is set in your power line in front of the motor you are trying to protect. The current has to pass through the lead core of the fuse before it reaches the motors. Electricity produces heat, and lead is highly sensitive to heat. If there is too much current on your line, the heat it produces when it hits that lead of the fuse will instantly melt it. And that breaks the current's flow and saves your motors.'

'I see,' Aristide replied, gratified by this demonstration of scientific reasonableness.

'Now, if you could get hold of four or five of the circuit breakers they use, what you could do is take out their lead cores and replace them with copper. Copper is an excellent conductor of electric current, but it also melts at a much, much higher temperature than lead. A fuse calibrated to melt with thirty amperes of current would pass several hundred times that much before melting if its core were made of copper.'

'Ah,' said the suddenly enlightened Aristide. 'So what you are suggesting is switching circuit breakers in the control panel, taking the real ones out and putting doctored ones in their place?'

'Exactly.'

Aristide smiled. 'That's a very clever idea. And it's simple. I like that. Now let me put to you one last theoretical question. God, we can feel sure, is anti-Nazi, but that doesn't mean He can be counted on to furnish us with a lightning bolt on demand. Is there some way your central power station could substitute for Him? Send one huge jolt of power over the lines that would have the same effect as a bolt of lightning?'

The engineer's lower lip quivered in recognition of the decidedly untheoretical nature of the question he had just been asked. Aristide was prepared for his reaction. Courage was by no means the monopoly of the young and the poor, but in his Resistance work he'd learned that the one place he was least likely to find it was in the middle-aged of the middle classes.

'I'm not sure I really want to get into that.' Paraud's voice pleaded as best it could for a little understanding of the delicacy of his situation.

'Oh, I don't see why not.' Aristide plucked a blade of grass and stuck it in engagingly between his teeth. 'I'm sure a man like you would not want to do anything that might be interpreted as helping our occupiers prolong their stay here.'

'But what about my family? It would have to be an inside job, and I would be blamed.'

If that is the problem, Aristide thought, it's easily enough disposed of. 'Suppose I arrange for them to be evacuated? Then they would be safe from any reprisals. And what's more important, they'll be well away from the fighting we're certainly going to have here.'

'You could arrange that?'

'I could. Now, let's get back to this hypothetical question of mine – and I want to stress, it's purely hypothetical.'

'What you would have to do is arrange to have a sudden and enormous surge of voltage go onto the battery's power line.'

Aristide offered the little electrician the smile of a Jesuit who has just heard an atheist's first acknowledgement of doubt. 'And how would you do that?'

'The current for the battery arrives in our power station on a 10,000-volt high-tension line. We step it down to 220 triphase current with a transformer. Now, normally you would have placed the transformer fairly close to the battery and run the power to it direct from the source. But since the Germans have guards around our power station, they installed the transformers inside the station.'

'I see.' The recital thus far had a logic to it that pleased Aristide.

'Basically, the principle would be to hook a bypass wire between the cable coming into the transformer with the 10,000-volt current and the wire feeding the 220-volt current out of the transformer to the battery. That way, the 10,000 volts would bypass the transformer and go directly into the battery.'

'And?'

'And that burst of 10,000-volt current would roast those motors like shrimps on a spit.'

Aristide grinned with the pleasure that analogy inspired. 'Would it be difficult to do that – technically? Is there some way you could set the thing up well in advance of the time you wanted to do it? So that when the moment came, everything would be all set to go?'

From the electrician's sudden silence, it was evident that the question required some thought.

'You could attach your bypass wire to the 220-volt cable going to the battery ahead of time. That you could do.'

'Wouldn't the Germans discover what you had done inspecting the power station?'

'They never come inside. Unless someone had told them about it, they wouldn't have any reason to come in looking for it.'

'When you hook that bypass cable to the incoming 10,000-volt line you'd have to turn off the current, wouldn't you? So you could cut away the insulation on the cable to make your connection? Isn't that going to tell the Germans something's going on?'

Paraud's pitying look told Aristide how little he knew about operating power stations. 'That incoming cable is raw copper. All you do is touch your bypass wire to it and you'll have an electric surcharge in the battery that will make them think it's the Second Coming. Everything will go – the control panel, the wiring, the motors, their lights, their ventilators. Everything.'

'And what's going to happen in your power station the instant you do that?'

'Oh, God! There'll be a huge bang and sparks and smoke all over the place.'

And, Aristide thought, German guards outside ready to charge in to find out what happened – and who caused it. He would need to proceed here with a little caution; develop things step by careful step.

'How often do you visit the battery?'

'It depends. Usually, after an air raid because the shrapnel is always cutting the power lines and I have to repair them.'

'When you do that, do you get into that control panel you told me about?'

206

Paraud trembled and stuttered something Aristide couldn't understand. He raised his hands to halt the electrician's incomprehensible mumbling. 'I am not going to ask you to *do* anything, I promise.'

'Metz and I always have to go in there when I finish to be sure the current is flowing properly.'

'Good,' Aristide said approvingly. 'Now, I want you to do something for me the next time you go down there after an air raid. A simple task. Won't compromise you at all. What I want you to do is have a look at the control panel. A good look. I want you to look at it as if it were a passport to Paradise. Memorize it. Photograph it in your mind. And above all, get me the exact description of those fuses which control the shell hoist and the turret motors – who makes them, their serial numbers, whatever you need to identify them with absolute precision.'

'But I won't be down there until there's an air raid,' Paraud reminded him.

'Don't worry,' Aristide assured him. 'I'll see you get an air raid.'

His words came as a revelation to the electrician, a stunning exposition of authority. A man who staged air raids on command – that was power. As it so often did, proximity to power reassured the faltering. 'There's one other thing to remember,' the electrician noted.

'What's that?' Aristide asked.

'Somehow you are going to have to get a copy of the key to the control panel.'

'Leave the key to me.'

LONDON

'Come over here, O'Neill. Look out there. What do those things remind you of?' T.F. followed the gesturing arm of the older officer as it pointed down into the greenery of Grosvenor Square, three floors below their office window. There, several teams of Royal Air Force female personnel were industriously unwinding the cables that released half a dozen barrage balloons into the London sunset.

'They remind me of barrage balloons,' T.F. said. 'What the hell else would they remind me of?'

'Use your imagination, for Christ's sake,' growled Major Ralph Ingersoll. The former publisher of *The New Yorker*, founder of the newspaper *PM*, an ardent New Dealer and interventionist, Ingersoll had enlisted as a GI days after Pearl Harbor and come up through the ranks to his present eminence. He and a handful of fellow officers were responsible for implementing those parts of Ridley's *Fortitude* deception

207

scheme which involved the US ground forces in England. 'What do those balloons make you think of?'

T.F. shrugged. Guessing games never amused him. 'I don't know ... Dumbo, the Disney elephant.'

'Right!' Ingersoll was exultant. 'You may have gone to Harvard Law, but you're still a pretty smart fellow. Now, where was the last place you saw a Dumbo like that?'

'At the Yale Club in New York about a year ago.' Ingersoll's quiz was exasperating T.F. 'Except it was pink and friendly and trying to get in my bedroom window.'

'Be serious,' Ingersoll was peevish. 'This is a serious matter.'

'All right, I give up. Tell me.'

'Coming down Broadway in Macy's Thanksgiving Day parade.'

'Well, that's serious, all right.' T.F. returned to his chair in front of Ingersoll's desk. His fellow American had, he noted, hung two lines from Walter Scott over his desk: 'Oh, what a tangled web we weave, When first we practice to deceive!' 'Is that why you asked me by for a beer? To reminisce about Thanksgiving in New York?'

'Look,' said Ingersoll, ignoring him, 'the problem you and those Englishmen you work for have handed us is this: how do we go about creating any army of a million ghosts? Right?'

'Yeah, more or less.'

'Forget about the radio stuff. That's not my department. What we are supposed to do is represent on the ground out there in southeast England all the normal invasion preparations you would expect to see from the air – landing craft, troop camps, tank and truck parks. Just in case Göring screws up the courage to send a few planes over for a look some spring day.'

T.F. sipped his beer and grimaced. It was a Budweiser and it was as warm as his morning tea.

'That's our English valet,' Ingersoll said. 'Every time I put a can in the fridge, he thoughtfully takes it out for me so the cold won't ruin the taste. So, how do we go about populating East Anglia and Kent with this imaginary army of yours? I'll tell you what we do. First, we send their Home Guard up there out into the field on manoeuvres. Have them set up camp where some of our regiments are supposed to be. Then, the British tell us to drive tanks and trucks around the fields at night. Chew them up with a lot of tyre and tread marks. The local farmers love it. Finally, what they tell us to do is make plywood dummies of tanks and trucks and set them out in the fields for the Luftwaffe to photograph.'

Ingersoll took a swallow of his own beer. 'There's a problem with those plywood dummies.'

'Ralph, there's a problem with everything in this war.'

'It takes almost as long to build one as it does to make a real tank. Eisenhower will be in Berlin before our dummies are finished.'

'What do you want me to do about that?'

Ingersoll jerked his thumb towards the open window. 'Who do you suppose makes those floats for Macy's?'

'How the hell would I know?'

'B. F. Goodrich. Goodyear. We go to them. Ask them to make us a model of a Sherman tank, a two-ton truck, a 105-millimetre gun. Inflatable rubber toys just like those Macy's floats. Have them mass-produced for us. We'll have hundreds of them in no time. Probably fit each one into a suitcase. All we will need to create a regimental tank park is an air compressor.'

'Ralph, you're a genius.'

'Quite true. But a silenced one. My job is just to carry out British orders. They wrote the scenario. They tell me what they want the Germans to believe and what I've got to do to make them believe it. You are the one who's sitting in the throne room down in that hole in the ground you work in. You sell them this.'

CALAIS

Catherine Pradier surveyed her fellow diners at L'Auberge du Roi, Calais's premier and, as far as she was aware, only black-market restaurant. There were only two other women in the room. One of them was German, undoubtedly one of the Wehrmacht's female auxiliaries, dubbed 'grey mice' by the population. The other was French and, to judge from the understanding and sisterly glances she occasionally threw at Catherine, a whore. The men were either Germans in uniform or middle-aged French collaborators, Calais's pillars of that wartime aristocracy baptized BOF – *beurre, oeufs, fromage:* butter, eggs, cheese – to signify that they preferred a full stomach to an untroubled conscience.

Metz, beside her, was going on about the inspiration for Handel's *Water Music*. Music, whether prewar American jazz or the classics, represented one of those neutral conversational terrains on which Occupier and Occupied might safely meet. Metz was a perfectly decent man, nicer, in fact than she would have liked him to be. He was even good-looking in that dark, unGermanic manner of his which had struck her on the train coming up from Paris. Perhaps, she reflected, it would be better if he were the perfect Nazi, the perfect Aryan, all blond hair, fair skin and blue eyes. Then, perhaps, she could hate him, and hating might make it easier to do what she was going to do. After all, love and hatred were supposed to be kindred emotions.

Catherine was anything but promiscuous; but the independent, determined nature that had prompted her to walk out on her wedding, that had led her to her present existence, had also seen to it that she had known her share of lovers. Never, however, had she made love with a man for any reason other than her own desire to do so. Could she, she wondered, do it this evening?

And Paul? What would he have said? Would he have exploded in a frenzy of Gallic jealousy, threatened Aristide, dragged her away? Despite herself, she smiled. I'd like that, she thought. Except it wasn't what Paul would have done. He was a cynic. He would have counselled the expedient path.

She sighed as though in appreciation of Metz's insight into Handel. War makes such cynics of us all, she thought, doesn't it? How utterly stupid she was to let herself dream – as she so often did – of some blissful postwar nirvana with a man she had known, after all, for barely forty-eight hours.

With an extraordinary effort of will, she expunged Paul's image from her mind and focused on Metz. He was onto Beethoven now. Even in another incarnation, he would not have been her type. He was too stiff, too tightly wound for her taste. Why did you have to be such a gentleman, she wondered; why did you have to help me get that suitcase out of the luggage rack?

Imagine showing him what it was that had made her suitcase so heavy that day, she thought. She eyed him warily, wondering what his reaction would be. Hand her in to the Gestapo, probably – with regrets, but without hesitation. There were limits to a gentleman's conduct, and the thought did not make the prospect of what lay ahead more palatable. Hesitantly, she dipped a piece of bread into the sauce of her *filet de sole dieppoise*, while Metz continued his discourse. Someone at the *Kommandantur* on the Boulevard Lafayette must have been funnelling part of the city fishermen's catch to this restaurant. They had been brought mussels in garlic and real butter before the sole. All she had seen in the markets since arriving was herring – and very little of that.

How ironic it was, she thought. For the first time in weeks, she was confronted with a real meal and she had almost no appetite for it. That, she noted, was clearly not the case with her fellow diners. One thought enraged her. She was sure, just as Aristide had said, that each of those men was convinced she was whoring with a German officer – those men, she told herself bitterly, who had whored and pandered to ingratiate themselves with their nation's conqueror. There was, of course, one consolation to all this. None of them was going to be in a hurry to denounce her as a German's girlfriend at the war's end. They would be far more anxious to forget rather than to recall their wartime experiences.

Brusquely, she told herself it was time to shut off this line of thought. She was going to do what she was going to do because she had agreed to do it and because, in the circumstances, it was the right thing to do. And, she was going to do it well, because for Catherine, failure was an unforgivable sin.

'I think,' she said, offering Metz her most engaging smile, 'the Kriegsmarine has deprived Germany of a great musician.' Metz, of course, took her seriously and blushed appropriately. His mouth might have been chattering on about Handel, but his eyes, she noted, were straining to get a better look down the front of her blouse. I'll bet, she told herself, he hasn't been to bed with a woman since his last leave to Bremen. Too proud to try a whore, too reserved to break down the resistance of most French girls. That's a little problem we're going to have to address together, you and I, she thought, slightly shifting her position so as better to accommodate his line of vision.

Still muttering away about Handel's employment of the harpsichord, Metz called for the bill. Outside, a fresh breeze stirred the April night. 'May I walk you home?' he politely inquired.

Catherine looked at her watch. It was a few minutes to nine. 'We'll have to hurry,' she said, 'or I'll be out after curfew.'

'You need not worry,' he assured her. 'You are with a German naval officer.'

Indeed, Catherine thought, as though I needed reminding of that. When they reached her door, Catherine offered him her hand. Politely, Metz slipped off his glove and took it. 'Good night, *Fräulein*. I've enjoyed our evening very much,' he said, tapping his heels slightly and offering her one of those bobbing little bows Germans performed with such casual elegance.

Catherine prayed the shadows might conceal her astonishment. The whole thing was so ironic. She wanted to laugh. The man was obviously determined to be that rarest of wartime oddities, a faithful husband. He really had asked her to dinner because he was lonely and wanted to talk about Handel.

She unknotted the scarf which she wore to hide her conspicuously blond hair and gave a quick toss to her head. It was a gesture whose effectiveness she had often been able to measure, and she sensed it assaulting the sensibility of her hesitant escort. At last, she was beginning to break through whatever images of Willi and Gretl and his *Frau* up there in Bremen were paralysing him with rectitude. He placed his hands at her elbows and shyly drew her towards him. She responded by easing her body against his and offering him a long, cool kiss.

211

As she drew away, she gave a series of worried glances up and down the street. 'I shouldn't be seen here like this,' she whispered. 'It could cause problems with the neighbours.'

'Of course,' Metz replied with utterly unwelcome comprehension. 'I understand.' He was, Catherine noted furiously, beginning to put his gloves back on. I simply don't believe it, she thought; the whole business is too absurd.

She rested her hand on his uniform tunic and looked up at him, her glance notably less demure this time than it had been earlier in the restaurant. 'Would you like to come upstairs for a cup of herbal tea?' she asked. 'It's what I use instead of coffee.'

For just a second he was trapped in the thrall of indecision, and Catherine sensed that the counsel of those images of domestic bliss in Bremen were going to prevail. Then, with unexpected eagerness, he growled, '*Ja, ja.*'

Her apartment was a conveniently spartan place, a sitting room with a sink and hot plate in the corner, her bedroom and her bathroom. The radio was well concealed in the huge reservoir of the tank worked by a chain and fixed to the wall above her toilet.

While she warmed up the tea on her burner, he sat on the couch discoursing, about Mozart this time. It took ten minutes of Mozart and five of Bach before he summoned up the will to kiss her again. She offered only a fragile and fleeting resistance to his pawing, then rose and, taking him by the hand, led him to her little bedroom.

Apparently sensitive to his shyness, she pointed to her bathroom door. 'Why don't you undress in there?' she suggested tactfully. Then, with a little giggle, added, 'And don't forget to wash, like a good boy.'

Metz beamed. He much approved of her concern with cleanliness – and with good reason. German officers who contracted venereal disease in Pas-de-Calais were banished to a *château* in Belgium for a cure and thence to the Eastern Front.

To her surprise, Metz, after a certain initial reserve had been overcome, turned out to be a better lover than she had expected – gentle, considerate, unhurried yet eager. When it was over, Metz, pleasantly spent, lay beside her for a few moments. He started to stir, but she slipped first from the covers. 'I'll be back in a second,' she whispered. 'I just want to use the bidet.'

She locked the bathroom door behind her, turned on the water full blast and began to hum. Then she reached for Metz's pants and picked through their pockets until she found his key ring. It contained four keys. Still humming industriously, she unlocked her medicine cabinet and took out the tray of soft wax Aristide had given her. Carefully, she made an impression of each key in the wax. Then she wiped off the keys and slipped them back into Metz's pocket.

She was still humming gaily when she tiptoed back into the bedroom. Metz was staring moodily at the ceiling, troubled, no doubt, now that his pleasure had been so agreeably taken, by those images of home and hearth in Bremen. She paused, thinking of Paul and how she would have wanted to see him there in her bed. Will you forgive me for what I have done? she silently wondered. Will you understand? Will you ever know?

She advanced to the bed and, thinking of the wax tray in the bathroom closet, bent down to kiss Metz. For the first time that evening her embrace carried with it an intimation of affection.

Aristide prided himself on his ability to judge people. It was the philosopher in him. He had to admit, however, that he had misjudged Pierre Paraud, the electrical engineer in charge of the Pas-de-Calais power station. Not only had the seemingly timid electrician made a careful study of the Lindemann Battery's control panel on his last visit; he had drafted from memory a plan of the panel which was stunning in its detail and thoroughness.

'It wasn't so difficult,' Paraud modestly assured Aristide. 'Control panels are all designed on basically the same lines. This one is just very well laid out. The banks of relays and circuit breakers going into each of the three gun turrets are all clearly labelled with the name of each gun.' Paraud indicated his design. There were three banks of boxes sketched out in ink, each bank divided into two parallel lines, one for the relays, one for the fuses.

'The first two sets of boxes in each bank,' Paraud continued, 'control the current going into the shell hoist and the turret motors.' He pointed to them. 'You can see they are bigger than the other circuit breakers and relays. That's because they're more sensitive.'

'Is this to scale?' Aristide asked.

'More or less. The circuit breakers are about the size of a woman's clenched fist. They plug into socket, in the panel. They are made by Siemens, and the model number is XR402.'

'That's all?'

Paraud nodded.

'Where can you get them?'

'I know that when they need spare parts they order them up from a Siemens depot in Paris.'

Paris, Aristide thought: he had a good contact in Paris. He was a former army officer and fellow SOE organizer whose code name, Ajax, was also that of the circuit he ran south of the capital. Aristide remembered him because they had returned together by Lysander from clandestine training in England. Ajax had voiced considerable suspicions about the Frenchman who ran the air operations. He had given Aristide a phone number and code by which he could be contacted. Maybe Ajax could get his circuit breakers.

'Let me ask you something. Suppose I can get some of these circuit breakers. Someone is going to have to doctor them up for me, substitute copper for the lead in there. The job has got to be done perfectly so no one will be able to tell we've switched fuses on them. Will you do it?'

Aristide saw again the fearful quiver in the man's lower lip. 'I couldn't make the switch. Metz never leaves me alone for a second down there.'

'That wasn't what I asked you, was it?' Aristide tartly reminded him. 'All I want you to do is prepare the circuit breakers. You can do it alone, at night, in your attic where no one can see you.'

The little engineer sighed. By what small, uncertain steps one descended the staircase to peril. He shrugged. 'If you want.'

'I do,' Aristide insisted.

LONDON

'By all rights, I really shouldn't be doing what I propose to do with you this afternoon.'

Sir Henry Ridley was walking with that forward slouch of his, his hands, in defiance of all His Majesty's uniform regulations, stuck into his pockets, that ever-present Players cigarette poised between his lips. 'However, I trust you, you see.' Candour seemed etched into each syllable he spoke. 'I quite like Americans.' The older man's head gestured across the green and empty expanses of St James's Park towards the outlines of the stately Nash houses along London's Pall Mall. 'Not a point of view shared, I might add, by everyone around here.

'Besides, you are doing a first-rate job for us. That idea you brought us about rubber dummies was absolutely first-rate. We already have the Pentagon working on it, and our own people at Dunlop Tyre as well.'

The afternoon air was rich and damp; golden pools of jonquils and yellow banks of daffodils spotted the park's green landscape. Along the twisting borders of the pond, couples huddled together – girls, many in uniform; men in the uniform of every army and nation imaginable.

'We are going to need your help on another little matter,' Ridley continued. 'Although this time, I would prefer to see it extended on a somewhat informal basis.' He let T.F. ponder his words as they started across the Mall, heading towards Marlborough Road. Suddenly, Ridley stopped, his gaze fixed upwards into the trees bordering the drive. 'I say!'

214

He pointed his Players towards the branches above. 'A cuckoo. Most extraordinary to spot one up here at this time of year.' Immensely pleased with his discovery, he continued their walk to St James's Square.

Except for an unusually thick wall of sandbags and the presence of two uniformed guards, an American MP in white 'snowdrop' helmet and a corporal in the blue of the Royal Marines, there was nothing to indicate that Number 31, Norfolk House, was part of SHAEF, the London headquarters of General Dwight D. Eisenhower's invasion command. Admission to its precincts was a good deal more complex than it appeared from the street. After three different verifications of their identity, T. F. and Ridley were escorted by an armed guard to a room designated only by a number – 303. The room housed an organization called Operations B – Special Means. Attached directly to Eisenhower's office through his chief of staff, General Walter Bedell Smith, Operations B was responsible for implementing those parts of Ridley's *Fortitude* scheme which fell under Eisenhower's jurisdiction.

Ridley and T. F. settled into their places in the notably spare office with the usual polite chitchat and offer – declined – of a cup of tea. The plumpish colonel presiding over the room, T. F. noted, combined the same congenial regard and cold, calculating eyes he had discovered in so many of his new colleagues.

'Well,' said Ridley, the tone of his voice indicating that the preliminaries were over and they were about to address the heart of their subject, 'you will recall I described to you the other day how our counterespionage service, MI-5, has turned – or interned – all the German agents operating in this country?'

T.F. accepted the point with a nod.

'Under the guidance of Edgar here, we are employing thirty of them to further *Fortitude*. Three of them, however, are of very great importance to us because of the confidence the Germans have in them and the fact that they each have a radio transmitter for their communications with the Abwehr.'

There was a new Players in Ridley's fingers, describing graceful parabolas in the room as he continued. 'One of them, perhaps the most important of our little trio, is a Spaniard – or to be more precise, a Catalan. His name is Garcia. He came to us through a rather fortuitous set of circumstances. When the war began, he offered us his services as a double agent through our embassy in Madrid. We turned him down cold. Obviously, the whole thing reeked of Abwehr entrapment. Garcia, nonetheless, went to the Abwehr and offered to work for them. He had fought for Franco during the Spanish Civil War, so his Fascist credentials seemed altogether acceptable. Apparently, he gave Herr Kuhlenthal, the Abwehr resident in Madrid, some cock-and-bull story

215

about coming to London to work for a pharmaceutical firm. Of course, he was no more coming here than he was going to the moon. He went to Lisbon and set himself up as a freelance, so to speak. Made up his dispatches out of whole cloth from the British papers he could buy in Lisbon.'

Ridley chuckled. The ingenious manner in which the Spaniard had duped the Germans delighted him. 'Unfortunately, some of his imaginary stuff was rather close to the mark, as we discovered from reading the Abwehr's summaries of the stuff he was sending them through *Ultra*. Eventually, he came back to us and offered us his services a second time. This time, as I'm sure you'll understand, we welcomed him as a prodigal son.' He glanced at the colonel running the office. 'Edgar, why don't you carry on from here?'

The colonel folded his hands over his stomach and bestowed a gracious smile on T. F. 'We brought him here and set him up under our control under the name of "Garbo." Now, the man has an interesting peculiarity. When he was in Lisbon, he invented a couple of imaginary Englishmen who were supposed to be working for him as subagents. We thought that rather a good idea. So over the last two years, we have conjured up a little empire of subagents for him, twenty-four in all. There are the inevitable Anglophobes: a Welsh Nationalist, a Sikh, an IRA gunman gone to ground. There are the venal types doing it for money who don't know they are being used, like an American sergeant who appreciates the whisky and women Garbo offers or the dowdy secretary at the Ministry of War who enjoys his performance as a Latin lover.' The colonel got up and removed a cardboard blind covering a map of England on his wall. 'These symbols,' he said, indicating a field of red asterisks, 'represent the location of our friend Garbo's imaginary agents.'

They were, T. F. noted, well distributed around the British Isles, weighted slightly, but not suspiciously so, in southeastern England around Dover, Folkestone, Ramsgate, Canterbury, where *Fortitude*'s imaginary army was supposed to be gathering.

'Some of the early agents, particularly those Garbo himself dreamed up, were set into place without any regard to *Fortitude*. Unfortunately, a couple of them have turned out to be a bit of an embarrassment to us.' The colonel's eyes focused a sadly reproachful gaze at the map. 'They were in locations, particularly a chap in Liverpool, where they were bound to see certain things in the normal course of affairs. The Abwehr in Madrid began to get terribly quizzy in their questions to them. It came down to either contriving to get rid of them, giving the Germans information we did not want them to have or risking giving our game away.'

The suggestion of a chuckle indicated the amused fascination with which T. F. had been following his tale. 'I don't see why that should have been much of an obstacle for you. You imagined those agents into life. Why not imagine them into the grave?'

'Yes, quite.' The colonel glowed with the satisfaction of a Latin master who has just heard an irregular verb conjugated perfectly. 'And that is, in fact, what we did with the first agent. Developed cancer of the pancreas, poor chap. Passed away rather suddenly. However, as I am sure you will appreciate, we didn't want to arouse any suspicion on the Abwehr's part by starting a cancer epidemic among Garbo's agents. So we decided to send our second fellow, the Irishman in Liverpool, packing. We informed the Abwehr he was fed up with living in Liverpool – German air raids, rationing, that sort of thing. So when an American cousin offered him a job with his shipping agency in Buffalo, he leaped at it. He hated the English anyway.'

'Buffalo!' T. F. was aghast. 'why Buffalo, of all places, for God's sake?'

'Well, why indeed?' the colonel sighed. 'It seemed sufficiently remote at the time, I suppose.'

'Unfortunately' – it was Ridley taking over – 'it turned out to be an unhappy choice. We have just discovered through a message from Kuhlenthal in Madrid that the Abwehr's got an agent in Canada he wants to send down to Buffalo to make contact with our unfortunately nonexistent Irishman.'

'This Abwehr agent – do you know who he is or where he is?' T. F. asked.

Ridley smiled. 'Not yet. But we have every intention of making his acquaintance – which, I might add, is where you come in.'

'Me?' For one mad second, T. F. thought they might want him to wait in some Buffalo tenement for the Abwehr agent to show up.

'I'm sure I don't have to review the legal niceties of the situation for you,' Ridley said in his most solemn barrister's tone. 'Anything done on US soil must, strictly speaking, be carried out under the direction of your Mr Hoover and his FBI.'

T.F.'s nod brought with it the sanction of his own legal training.

'We have a problem with Mr Hoover. We find he lacks the subtlety of mind required for our work.'

T. F. suppressed with some difficulty the hilarity his colleague's discovery prompted in him.

'He will insist on grabbing that Abwehr agent the instant he surfaces in Buffalo and clapping him into jail. Now, that is a commendably forthright attitude.' Ridley allowed a second for that faint praise to register. 'It is also one which will almost certainly reveal to our friend Kuhlenthal that Garbo is operating under our control. It will terminate

Garbo's usefulness to us just at the moment when we most need him. And it may very well jeopardize *Fortitude* itself, with all that implies.'

'How can you be so sure Hoover will react like that?'

'We have had considerable experience with Mr Hoover, all of it unhappy. Mr Hoover apparently feels about double agents' – Ridley paused in his search for a happy analogy to puff his cigarette – 'the way that Gertrude Stein feels about roses: "An agent is an agent is an agent." He simply refuses to have anything to do with double agents. Won't dirty his hands with them, so to speak.

'We sent him another of our double-agent trio – a Yugoslav, this one,' he continued. 'The Abwehr had asked him to go to America to do some work for the Japanese – in Honolulu. Had Hoover used him properly, you would have had several months' warning of Pearl Harbor. Unfortunately, he wouldn't touch him with the wrong end of a barge pole, and as a result the better part of your Pacific Fleet is now sitting on the ocean floor.'

T. F. gave a low, stunned whistle. 'Okay. So what do you want to do here?' he asked.

'You know Colonel Frank Elliot as OSS headquarters in Grosvenor Square, who acts as direct liaison with General Donovan, I presume? Donovan understands the way these things should be dealt with. What we would like to have him do is install one of his people in an apartment in Buffalo masquerading as our Irishman. We'll see that this Abwehr chap comes to call. When he does, our people will follow him back to Canada and take him in hand up there.'

Ridley was suggesting that T. F. prompt the OSS to facilitate the actions of a foreign intelligence service on US soil. The American didn't need a Harvard Law School diploma to see the legal problems that raised. 'You realize, of course, that strictly speaking, I'm no longer with the OSS.' The glinting eyes, the foul-smelling Dutch Masters of the brigadier general in the Pentagon were very much in T. F.'s mind as he spoke those words.

'Indeed.'

'My chain of command is through General Marshall's office.'

'I understand that.' Ridley's voice was gently caressing in tone. 'But there are occasionally certain things in our world that are best accomplished outside the chain of command. Perhaps you've heard the term "Old-Boy network"?'

A Yale secret society with a British accent, T. F. thought. 'Yes, I have. But why not deal with Elliot direct?'

'I think it's tidier to handle these things on a national-to-national basis. Edgar here' – Ridley nodded at the colonel – 'can furnish all the material

218

Donovan will need to know to be sure his man in Buffalo can play the role we have in mind for him.'

'And your people in Canada will arrest the Abwehr man up there?'

'In due course, certainly. After we have followed him long enough to be absolutely sure picking him up isn't going to alert the Germans to our game.'

'And our man in Buffalo?'

'I presume the Abwehr's chap will leave him a questionnaire, as they usually do.'

'About our military installations in upstate New York, I suppose?'

'I should have thought so. I shouldn't have thought the Abwehr would have a particular interest in shoe factories up there.'

'Eventually, he may have to answer them.'

'Quite possibly. We'll help out, of course. And Donovan's people are quite capable of dealing with the situation as well.'

T. F. sat back rather uncomfortably. In the strictest legal sense, he was being asked to connive in an intelligence operation to be conducted on US soil without any official authorization, without the military knowledge of the FBI, without the knowledge of the US military and most probably without that of the British military as well. Furthermore, the operation was almost certainly going to involve passing classified US military secrets to the enemy. It was not a project likely to win the blessing of the brigadier general in the Pentagon. On the other hand, Ridley's scheme would undoubtedly be endorsed by the war cabinets of both the US and Great Britain if it were ever submitted to them – which it clearly would not be. And as more than one Harvard Law School professor had pointed out, there was the letter of the law, but there was the spirit as well. Surely, bypassing J. Edgar Hoover to preserve the integrity of their deception scheme fell within the scope of that principle.

'Okay, Colonel, I'll have a word with Colonel Elliot,' T. F. assured Ridley.

'Since we've worked that one out,' said the colonel in charge of the office, 'I must clue you in on a simple brilliant idea we've had for using Garbo at the critical moment in this whole business.'

Both T. F. and Ridley looked at the colonel, intrigued. 'On D-Day night, sometime well before the first troops actually touch shore, we let Garbo tell the Germans the invasion's coming. Not where it's coming, of course, but the fact that the fleet's actually sailed.'

'Well, really, Edgar,' Ridley said, making no effort to conceal his astonishment, 'that is, at the very least, an original thought. Why on earth would we wish to do a thing like that?'

'Because after Garbo's told the Germans that, he'll be a god in their

219

eyes. The greatest spy ever. He will have made Mata Hari look like Tinker Bell.'

'I shouldn't wonder,' Ridley said. 'Probably earn him a nice Iron Cross he can wear to the Tower when Winston tells us to hang him.'

The colonel held up his hands in reproach. 'Hear me out, Squiff.' He to was an Old Etonian. 'It all hinges on some rather exquisite timing. We've got to reckon the time it is going to take the Abwehr in Madrid to decode Garbo's message, then recode it and transmit it to Berlin to have the Abwehr decode it there and act on it. We reckon it could go out sometime after two-thirty in the morning, after the paratroops have jumped. That way, it should be landing on Von Rundstedt's desk about the time the first wave hits the beaches. In point of fact, the information will be utterly useless to the Germans. But what a hero we will have made out of Garbo. After he's told them that, the Germans will be ready to believe anything, absolutely anything he tells them.'

'Yes, perhaps so.' The scepticism which seconds earlier had been floating through Ridley's voice had begun to settle. T. F. watched the two men, fascinated by their exchange.

'Now, we all agree that the critical moment for the invasion is going to come sometime around D plus 3. That's when we are apt to be the weakest on shore. And it's when Hitler is going to have to realize Normandy is the whole show and decide to go all out to throw us back into the sea. It will be the vital, absolutely critical fulcrum on which the success of the invasion and this scheme of ours is going to turn. Would you agree?'

Ridley dipped his head in silent assent.

'Our first message will have made Garbo into an oracle for Hitler, a fount of absolutely solid, accurate intelligence.'

Again Ridley offered the slightest of nods.

'Then, at that critical juncture when everything is hanging in the balance, he will send the Germans a second message containing irrefutable proof that the forces we have been building up in Kent and Sussex are about to fall on Pas-de-Calais. Freeze the bastards dead in their tracks.'

Ridley lit a cigarette, then reinserted the burned-out match into its matchbox – a reflexive instinct that went back to the trenches of the Somme. 'How does Garbo know the invasion fleet's sailed?'

The colonel pointed to one of the asterisks on his map behind Portsmouth. 'His agent 5(2) is a waiter in the canteen of the Third Canadian Infantry Division that's going to land on Juno Beach. He will tell him the troops have left. By evening the Germans will have taken some of them prisoner, so they'll have yet another proof of just how good Garbo's information is.'

This time Ridley's silence was long and thoughtful. 'It's a brilliant idea, Edgar,' he announced finally. Absolutely brilliant. There's only one thing wrong with it.'

'What's that?'

'It will never work.'

'Why not?'

'Eisenhower will never agree to it.'

Catherine smoothed her onetime coding pad and her coding silk onto the top of her writing table. Fully extended like that, each silk was slightly smaller than a woman's handkerchief. Beside them she set out the other items she would need to encode Aristide's latest message: a magnifying glass to read the fine print on the silk, a child's school pad covered with regular little squares, a pair of scissors, an ashtray and a box of matches. A good radio operator, they had taught her in London, must never allow the tediousness of coding to father a sense of carelessness. Sound advice, Catherine thought. Nothing was as boring or demanded such painstaking care as encoding messages.

Pierrot was at the window, sipping a cup of the herbal tea that had lured Metz into her apartment, studying the street for any unusual activity that might indicate the German detection service was at work. He turned to her just as she started to unfold Aristide's message.

'It's too long,' he said. 'I don't know what's wrong with him. He knows they shouldn't be so long.'

Catherine looked at the text. It was the lengthiest Aristide had given her. Reading it, she suddenly understood why her chief had been so eager to get an impression of Metz's keys. That thought had not been digested when another rose to replace it: someone was going to have to employ those keys. Whom did Aristide have in mind? Evidently not a member of a glider-borne commando assaulting the battery.

She gave her worried watchdog the reassurance of a smile. 'This won't take as long as you think. We should be off the air in less than an hour.'

Her first task was to write out Aristide's message on the school pad in the five-letter groups employed in all the SOE's clandestine transmissions. Then she took her onetime pad and with her magnifying glass picked out the first block of five random letters in its upper left-hand corner. She put them under the first letter group of the message. She repeated the process with each of the fourteen blocks in the top line of the onetime pad. When she had finished, she cut off the line from the silk

221

with her scissors and went to work on the line below. Finally, she put a match to the little pile of silken ribbons that had accumulated in her ashtray. That, coupled with the burning of her message when she had finished, would render the system absolutely unbreakable.

Next she turned to the parallel alphabets lined up vertically at the bottom of the coding silk. Taking the first letter of the first code block she had placed under her text, an I, she ran down the alphabet until she found it. Opposite was a third letter, this one was S. She wrote it down on her pad. 'S' now became the letter she would actually transmit when she began her broadcast.

The whole process took well over an hour and left her nervously exhausted from the precision it demanded. Pierrot had taken the radio from its hiding place in the toilet tank and strung the antenna on the floor so they would be ready to broadcast when her transmission time came. She set out her quartzes, her dry-cell battery, her warning light bulb and, precisely at 10:30, opened her set. Friendly and familiar, there was the sound of Sevenoaks flinging her call sign into the ether. She adjusted her set and acknowledged that she was ready to send. Lost in the intense concentration that always overwhelmed her when she broadcast, she hammered her way through the message. As she had predicted, it took just under an hour. Drawing to the end, she could sense the nervous impatience radiating from Pierrot standing guard by the window. She sat back and, cold sweat rolling off her temples, waited for the 'QSL' from Sevenoaks acknowledging that her message had been well received.

She did not get it. For the first time since she had begun transmitting she heard instead the dreaded letters 'QSR.' Something had gone wrong. Sevenoaks was ordering her to stand by to repeat all or part of her message.

She looked at Pierrot, fear flickering in her eyes. 'We've got to go back on the air,' she said. 'They didn't get it all.'

'Damn!' Pierrot exploded. 'We'll never get away with it if we go on like this.' Angrily, he turned back to his study of the street below. It was almost as though he wanted to find some anomaly down there, some note jarring enough to justify ordering her to stop sending. For the first time, he took out his pistol, an instrument whose only practical use Catherine was convinced would be to hasten their suicide in the event the Gestapo caught them. Then he shrugged to indicate she might as well go ahead.

Catherine began to send again. Her anxiety so deprived her fingers of their usual dexterity that once again she got a 'QSR' from Sevenoaks. She needed ten more minutes before Sevenoaks' 'QSL' finally cleared her from the air. Hearing it, she collapsed over her set with a sob of nervous exhaustion. Pierrot continued to scrutinize the street from his post by the window.

'Too long,' he growled. 'It was too damn long.'

Shortly after 4 o'clock that same afternoon, the telephone rang in the Doctor's office at Gestapo headquarters on Paris' Avenue Foch. The bespectacled maestro of Strömelburg's radio game instantly recognized his caller's voice. After all, he telephoned the commander of the radio detection service on the Boulevard Suchet at least three times a week to communicate his superior's fast-rising impatience with the service's inability to fix and capture the clandestine radio broadcasting from Calais.

'Doctor,' he began, a sense of gloating evident in the very first syllable he uttered. 'We have good news for your *Obersturmbannführer*.'

'He will be pleased. He feels you have been neglecting him lately.'

'They are getting careless in Calais. They were on air for an hour and ten minutes this morning. We've got a very precise fix on them now.'

'I can rely on this?' The Doctor was not a man to stir his superior's hopes without very sound justification.

'Be certain,' his interlocutor replied; 'two more broadcasts, three at the most, and we'll have them.'

With the notable exception of one vehicle, the square in front of Notre Dame de Calais was as empty as a nightclub at breakfast time. The exception disturbed Catherine. It indicated she and Aristide were not going to be alone inside the church. It was a horsedrawn hearse, one of those 1920 models retired with the advent of the motorcar and recommissioned by Calais's municipal undertakers to accommodate the demands of the war and the gas shortage it had produced. How many of Calais's notables, she asked herself, had gone creaking off to the grave in that ornate box, all black lacquer and silver trim and moulding and velvet curtains? One thing was certain, she thought, noting the ribs of the hearse's half-starved horses; this morning's passenger was not going to be rushed to his grave.

Inside, a knot of mourners were gathered around the wooden coffin at the head of the centre aisle. Instinctively, she lowered her head and began to search the back pews for Aristide. A score of elderly parishioners,

223

scattered through the rear of the church, were intently following a service to which they evidently had no personal connection. What was it, Catherine wondered, that made funerals the sporting events of the aged? Had an instinctive gratitude for their own continuing survival drawn them here? She found Aristide and slipped into the pew beside him. He glanced about. 'Too crowded this morning,' he whispered. 'Let's try the park.'

A few minutes later she was beside him again, this time on a bench in the Parc Richelieu. The morning air was chill and blustery, damp with reminders of the Channel's nearby presence. 'I'm sorry,' Aristide acknowledged when Catherine told him of the problems of her last transmission. 'The message was long. I'll try my best to tighten them up.' He thought a moment. 'Maybe we should take a chance on getting picked up by a patrol and move the set to my place.'

'There were two checkpoints on the way here this morning,' she observed.

'Are there any indications they are fixed on your neighbourhood?'

She shook her head.

'What do you think?'

Catherine thought long and carefully. 'Let's keep it where it is. At least until we're sure they have fixed on the area. Our hiding place is good.'

Aristide nodded and placed his hand on her knee. Catherine recognized his gesture for what it was – a paternal rather than a familiar demonstration.

'Now,' he said, 'I must ask you something of great consequence.'

Despite herself, Catherine stiffened, but said nothing.

'You know, as I do, how vital the Lindemann Battery is to the defence of the coast here.'

With a little nod, Catherine acknowledged the self-evident wisdom of his words.

'Quite frankly, I never thought it would be possible to sabotage them. And it wouldn't be if it weren't for the work you've done for us.' Quickly and succinctly, Aristide outlined the plan he had evolved with the electrical engineer. 'The fuses arrived from Paris yesterday,' he told her; 'they're being prepared now.

'If we can somehow replace the real fuses in the control panel with the doctored fuses, we will have a unique way to sabotage the battery. Think of it: London will be able to silence those guns at the precise, critical moment London wants them silenced. All we will have to do is give them a code phrase and tell them that when we hear that phrase over the BBC, we will put the overload into the battery's power line and shut down the guns for the forty-eight hours the Germans need them most.'

'Yes, it is a good plan.' Catherine was deathly pale. She had known it was going to come to this since she had read his last message. 'Now you want *me* to switch the fuses.'

'There are only two people who have the possibility of doing it, you and the engineer at the power station. Quite frankly, I don't trust him. I'm afraid he would lack the courage when the moment came.'

'You don't know what it's like down there, Aristide,' she said. 'The officers' mess is right next door. They are always coming down the ladder and going in for a cup of coffee.'

'Could you close the door?'

'Aristide, there is no door. And the panel is on the wall opposite my washing machine right by the open passageway. An officer walking by would have to be blind not to see what I was doing. The mess steward is always coming in to offer me a coffee while I'm washing. And since I slept with Metz, he never leaves me alone down there. He's like a puppy hanging around waiting for me to throw him a bone.'

Aristide slowly stroked his little beard. 'Metz I can perhaps take care of.' He stopped, obviously planning his next words with care. 'I have absolutely no right to ask you to do this – and certainly no authority to order you to do it. It will take, I estimate, two to four minutes to make the change. During those two to four minutes while that panel is open, your life will be forfeit if anyone arrives. There is no sense pretending otherwise. If you agree to do it, you will have to expose your life without reservation or hope for those four minutes.'

'What does London say?'

'I haven't told London, and I'm not going to tell them until those doctored fuses are in place.'

'Why, for God's sake?'

'London is interested in realities, not dreams. As long as you and I sit here on this park bench and talk about it, this plan is nothing more than a dream. Until those new fuses are safely in place, undetected by the Germans, the plan is worth nothing.'

'Oh, Aristide!' Catherine wrapped her arms around herself as though to ward off a chill. 'Four minutes can be such a long time.'

'An eternity,' Aristide said. 'It's a terrible thing I'm asking you. I promise you just two things. Whatever your decision, I will never mention this conversation to you or anyone else ever again.' He hesitated. 'And if you do it and it goes wrong, I swear to God, I will see your memory is honoured for it.'

Catherine sat silent and composed on the bench. Overhead, a flock of seagulls, shrieking their hoarse and mournful cries, swept out to sea from one of the inland plains flooded by the Germans. Why did I come here, she asked herself, why did I volunteer for this work a year ago in London, if it wasn't to be ready for something like this? Petulantly, she flicked her wrist at the blond hair hidden beneath her scarf.

'All right,' she sighed. 'I'll do it.'

'You are really a dear to come early and help!' Deirdre Sebright exclaimed. T. F. O'Neill was slowly stirring the martinis in a pitcher while she washed the salad. There seemed to be no shortage of gin in London, but Italian vermouth, an inevitable casualty of the war, had, he had noted with amusement, been replaced by Chilean white wine

'You Americans are such helpful dears, are't you? Why is that, do you suppose? Did your mothers bring you up that way?'

Eliciting information, T. F. had already observed, was rarely the design of an Englishwoman's questions. His answer was a smile.

'Had you been one of Jane's guardsmen, you'd have stopped off at your club for a couple of pink gins on your way, got here half an hour late and now you'd be in that armchair in the sitting room rattling your *Evening Standard* and screaming at me because your martini wasn't cold enough. And I, poor ninny that I am, would probably be telling you how sorry I was.'

Her flat, sensible uniform shoes had been replaced by high heels that accentuated the slim muscularity of her calves. Her skirt, protected by a white apron, clung to her thighs and her firmly rounded buttocks. She was wearing a pale green silk blouse that held her pert breasts in close embrace. Its top three buttons were undone, offering T.F. an occasional glimmering of the white brassière that moulded them. She paused a second to glance at the steak spread on the rack of her oven beside her.

'Such a super animal,' she said. 'You must know a general to get meat like that.'

'A senator,' T. F. replied. 'Friend of my grandfather's who is over here inspecting something or other. They give them access to the generals' mess to keep up their enthusiasm for the war effort.'

'Well, bless him for coming,' Deirdre said, returning her attention to her salad leaves. 'By the way, you are aware, are you not, that you have become something of a hero in our little underground world?'

'Me?' T.F. gave a sceptical sip to the creation in his martini pitcher. 'I wasn't aware most people down there even knew my name.'

'Of course they do. Be a dear and pass me the vinegar,' she commanded. 'Jane says Sir Henry's over the moon about something you've arranged for him in America. I'm not supposed to know what, of course. Practically won the war singlehanded, I'm told.'

'Hardly that.' So, T. F. thought, the Buffalo operation is going well. A lingering doubt as to the propriety of his role in it still troubled him. It would trouble him less now. Nothing, he thought, stills scepticism quite so effectively as success.

'He even referred to you as a solid fellow.'

'Am I supposed to think that's a compliment?'

'Oh, much more than that! It's an accolade.' As she was talking, she was industriously preparing her salad dressing, shaking salt and pepper into her cup of vinegar, now splashing in a dollop of mustard. 'A "solid fellow" generally comes from a good family, good country bloodlines. By the way' – Deirdre turned an engaging grin on T. F. – 'just what sort of family *do* you come from?'

'Not the sort you have in mind, I'm afraid. Irish Catholic immigrants.'

'Ah, well' – cheerful indulgence underlined her smile – 'perhaps you have other redeeming qualities. Or perhaps Sir Henry has your O'Neills confused with some of the Anglo-Irish he hunts with in Ulster. Not to worry. What sets a "solid fellow" apart is the fact you can count on him. Be with you through thick and thin. You rely on a "good chap." You trust a "solid fellow." And you,' Deirdre concluded, 'for whatever reason, have been elevated by Sir Henry to that select company.'

'Want a sip?' T. F. said, offering her a taste of the martinis he'd been so judiciously swirling.

Deirdre accepted his glass and gave its contents a contemplative swallow. 'Very good,' she pronounced. 'Such competent people, you Americans' – her eyes turned to him, laughing provocatively – 'aren't you? In everything you do.

'Now,' she said, returning the empty glass. 'I'm going to have to let you in on a dreadful secret. Pass me that bottle in the cupboard over there.'

T.F. reached for the bottle she had indicated. It was Nujol, a thick mineral oil he'd often noted in his mother's medicine cabinet with her other laxatives.

'My salad dressing, I regret to tell you, is made with vinegar and Nujol. Olive oil, like that Lucky Strike green of yours, has gone to war. However,' she declared, busily swirling the oil with her other ingredients, 'put in enough mustard and vinegar and no one has ever been able to tell the difference. At least' – she giggled – 'for a few hours.'

The doorbell's ring interrupted her.

'They're here,' she said. 'Be a dear and open the door while I put the steak on.'

227

The drawing was as finely done as a blueprint. Its author stood diffidently beside Aristide's kitchen table gazing down at his handiwork. Aristide had pointedly not introduced Catherine when the man had arrived.

'I think you'll find, when you open that panel,' he said to Catherine, 'that this drawing reproduces its interior quite exactly. If you fix it in your mind now, the real panel should look very familiar to you when you see it tomorrow morning for the first time.'

He opened a brown paper bag and drew out a white, rectangular plug slightly larger than a deck of playing cards. 'This,' he told Catherine and Aristide, 'is a circuit breaker – a real one.' He turned it upside down and indicated a grey circle of metal in its base. 'Lead,' he explained.

He carefully set the circuit breaker onto the table and thrust his hand back into his paper bag. He pulled out a second circuit breaker that seemed absolutely identical to the first. He turned it upside down. The grey circle of lead in its base, Catherine noted, had been replaced by a stump of brownish-orange metal.

'Copper,' the man said, tapping it with a fingernail. 'An overload will go through that like a dose of salts.

'Now,' he went on, giving the whole business a distinctly unrealistic, pedantic air, 'all you have to do is pull six of these good circuit breakers out of the panel one by one and replace them with the six new ones I'm going to give you. You can't help recognizing the ones you've got to change. They are larger than the others. They are the first two in each row.' He reached down and picked up the first one he had shown her. 'And each one has this number – XR402 – written in black on its base. They're the only circuit breakers in there with that number on them.'

Catherine studied his circuit breakers and his sketch, trying to work out what might go wrong, where the traps of the unexpected lay.

'Won't they notice the lights flickering on and off?' she asked.

'The lights, no. Those fuses control only two things – the gun-turret motors and the shell hoists. As long as the guns are not firing, they won't notice.'

'And if they are firing?'

'Come back another day.'

'How do I change them?' Catherine asked.

'You grab the fuse between your thumb and forefinger and pull it straight back. Drop it into your laundry basket. Take a new plug. The XR402 must be at the bottom – remember that; it's very important: if one of them is upside down they will know someone has played with the panel. Each plug has four metal prongs. Set them opposite the four holes

228

in the panel and snap the fuse into place with the heel of your hand. It's simple. If you keep calm and don't get heavy-fingered, the whole thing shouldn't take more than three minutes.'

'Three minutes.' Her words were more a prayer than a statement, a supplication for that slightest of indulgences, a brief suspension of time. She would not sleep tonight. And that was bad, because sleeplessness might make her nervous tomorrow, make her hands flutter and shake when they needed to be sure and still.

She picked up the brown paper bag. 'Count them and check them,' she ordered both Aristide and his visitor, the authority in her voice surprising her. 'Be a hundred per cent sure. I am not going into that control panel a second time even if the King of England himself asks me.'

'What time will you get there tomorrow morning?' Aristide demanded.

'The motorcycle usually comes at eight o'clock. By eight-thirty I'll be there.'

'We have a slight problem with Herr Metz,' Aristide informed his visitor. 'We must be certain he does not disturb our young lady here. Precisely at nine tomorrow you are to call Metz,' Aristide told the man. It was an order, not a request.

'Why?'

'Find something to talk to him about – anything. Just keep him on that phone for five minutes. Her life depends on it. So, I might add, does yours.'

Catherine gathered up the drawing and the brown paper bag with its fuses. Aristide took her to the door. He placed his hands on her shoulders, then leaned forward and softly kissed her on both cheeks. '*Merde*,' he whispered. His word proffered both affection and admiration, a prayer and a warning.

Outside, dusk had settled on the city. Catherine paused an instant on Aristide's doorstep. Then she bowed her head and hurried off down Calais's half-empty streets alone with her fears and her brown paper bag.

LONDON

Brussels on the eve of Waterloo, T.F. thought, remembering the Byron he had studied in Romantic Poets in New Haven; London is Brussels on Waterloo eve – the sound of revelry by night while somewhere off in the distance tolls the knell of a dangerous dawn. He looked at the young lieutenant of the Guards Armoured Division Deirdre had invited, along with his girlfriend, to share T.F.'s commissary steak with them. He was

229

twenty-three, eager, poised, full of himself – and totally unaware of a secret T.F. knew and he did not: that he would be landing with his division in Normandy forty-eight hours after the first wave went in. What, T.F. wondered, were the chances he'd be alive in two or three months? Fifty-fifty? Less, perhaps?

Deirdre leaned over T. F. She had managed to find a substance extremely rare in wartime London: coffee. As she poured a splash into T.F.'s demitasse, her breasts pressed taut against the pale green folds of her silk blouse.

'An extra splash for you,' she said in a husky whisper. 'How else can you be expected to bear life in this dull, deprived capital of ours?'

'You don't mean that, do you?' T.F. replied. 'I love London.'

'Of course I don't mean it. Surely you don't enjoy the company of women who actually *mean* what they say, do you?'

'I say.' It was the Guardsman. 'Why don't we pop into the Four Hundred for a nightcap? Unless' – he turned towards T.F. – 'you'd prefer a rather whizzier spot like the Coconut Grove.'

With its dark velvet upholstery, its muted lights, its orchestra inspired by the arrangements of Tommy Dorsey and Glenn Miller, its seemingly endless supply of black-market whisky and champagne, the 400 was the stateliest and certainly the best-loved pleasure dome war London afforded its privileged classes. It was also, to judge by the warmth with which its *maître d'hôtel*, Signor Rossi, greeted Deirdre, an environment in which her graceful figure was a familiar presence.

Rossi showed them to a table just off the dance floor. A waiter bearing a half-filled bottle of whisky materialized out of the gloom. The Guardsman cast an approving eye at the pencil mark he had made on its label at the conclusion of his last visit to the 400, then served them all a drink.

'At least,' T.F. said to Deirdre, gesturing with his glass towards the crowded dance floor, 'I'm not going to have to impress you with my jitterbugging tonight.'

'Goodness, no!' she agreed. 'The Four Hundred's strictly for clingers, isn't it?'

'Let's cling,' he said, smiling.

They edged onto the floor. She turned to him and with a kind of gentle sigh, folded her body against his. For a moment they stood there toe to toe, T.F. sensing the outline of her strong thighs finding his, her breasts thrust against his jacket, their pelvic bones pressed together. He cupped her right hand in his left and drew it to the corner of his chin, feeling as he did the cool plane of her cheek softly brush his in the darkness. Indolently, languorously, their bodies began to move to the music, their feet barely shuffling, their intertwined figures circling through a tiny postage stamp of space.

'Ever read *The Sun Also Rises?*' he whispered. Like most of his generation, T.F. was a Hemingway fan.

She nodded.

'Ever see a bullfight?'

'Heavens, no!' she whispered.

'There's a place in the bullring that's the bull's sanctuary – his *querencia* they call it. It's a little like this dance floor, isn't it? Everyone has their *querencia*.'

She was silent a moment. Then she unrolled a protracted 'Mmm,' that suppressed and indecipherable humming sound English girls employ for tasks as varied as assessing a prospective lover or questioning the asking price of a Victorian toast rack. 'Are you trying to impress me with the fact that you are a bull?' She chuckled. 'Or just that you're well read?'

It was a few minutes before one when they left. The Guardsman and his girlfriend, Anne, in keeping with a fine 400 tradition, were staying on until the club's 5-o'clock closing time and his train back to camp.

A cab ran them to Deirdre's apartment. It was at the curb, its engine running, Deirdre was fumbling through her handbag for her keys and T.F. through his mind for one of those contorted opening gambits required to disguise a sexual advance on the Eastern Seaboard in the United States when, for the first time since he had arrived in London, he heard the sound. It began as a deep quivering throb, then accelerated swiftly to the familiar screech. The cabby fled off into the darkness at the air-raid siren's first growl.

'Really!' Exasperation, rather than concern or fright, keynoted Deirdre's voice. 'Those Germans can ruin the nicest of evenings, can't they?'

Along the street T.F. could now hear the sound of doors opening and shutting, of footsteps rushing along the sidewalk, of mothers calling on sleepy children to hurry. Then, as the siren's mournful wail died, he picked up another sound, a hum like a distant swarm of bees coming up the Thames.

'There they are,' Deirdre said with a resigned sigh. 'The Bond Street tube station is the nearest shelter, but I must tell you I simply cannot abide those places. I haven't been in one since 1941. All those puking babies, old men breaking wind in the middle of the night, the women squawking away in their ghastly Cockney accents. Frightfully snobbish of me to feel that, I know, but there you are. I really prefer the idea of being killed by a bomb in the privacy of my own flat to having to spend my nights down there.'

T.F. was only half-listening. He was staring, fascinated, into the sky. It was a four-year-old newsreel suddenly come alive – the searchlights stabbing at the darkness with their blue-white pillars of light, the drone of the planes filling the night air, the whistles of the air-raid wardens somewhere up the street.

'Look, you can't just stand there and watch, you know,' Deirdre chided. 'The ARP will send you packing. Either you had better head up to the Bond Street tube or come in and take your chances with me.'

Her words turned T.F. to the more pleasurable prospects that had momentarily slipped his mind in the excitement of the raid.

As soon as they were inside the apartment, Deirdre set a pair of candles on the mantelpiece of her fireplace, then cut off the electric current. 'Would you care for a brandy?' she was already taking a pair of snifters from a cupboard.

T.F. nodded.

'Your first air raid, is it?' Deirdre inquired knowingly, passing him his snifter.

Her eyes flickered an instant with that provocative maliciousness he found so becoming. 'Well' – she smiled, raising her snifter to his – 'let's hope for both our sakes it's not your last.'

They settled onto Deirdre's sofa. Somewhere out there in the blacked-out city he heard the echoes of a new sound, a kind of rolling thunder. 'There they are,' she said, her tone remarkably matter-of-fact – 'well across the river I should have thought. These days they tend to drop their bombs as soon as they know they're over London and run for home as fast as they can.'

For a few minutes they sat silently side by side on the sofa, ears transfixed by those distant sounds of devastation. T.F. slipped his arm round Deirdre's shoulder. The English girl looked up, her dark eyes merry and mischievous in the candlelight. With the same feline grace she had displayed at the 400, she folded her body into his. There was a cool serenity to her embrace, a sort of poised reckoning as her lips slid along his in sensual exploration.

She leaned her head back and looked dreamily into his eyes. Her fingertips brushed his cheeks. Suddenly, she stood up.

A brief uncertainty gripped T.F. until he saw her take a candle from the mantelpiece and head down a corridor he knew led to only one place: her bedroom. Decidedly, T.F. thought, his body vibrant with delight and anticipation, there is nothing in Lady Deirdre Sebright that would remind you in any way of your average Smith or Vassar girl.

She set the candle on her dresser and moved to the side of her bed. 'Be a dear,' she commanded, 'and help me turn down this comforter.'

The wail of the 'all clear' woke T.F. Deirdre was lying in his arms, fast asleep. Gently, he caressed the damp hair matted on her forehead. Christ, he thought, have I got a lot to learn about the British.

Life – the fragility of her own – was very much at the centre of Catherine Pradier's preoccupation as her motorcycle sidecar bounced and bucketed up the dirt road to the crest into which the three massive turrets of the Lindemann Battery were set. Would the guards, she wondered, look into the basket of sewing she clutched to her chest as tightly as if it were filled with eggs? Why should they? she told herself. They never have before. She looked down to the Channel, grey-green this morning instead of its usual hostile and sullen grey. Beyond the waters, Dover's chalky cliffs were clearly visible. England and safety; England, where you didn't wake up each morning with fear as your bedmate. It was Saturday, April 29, just over six weeks since the Lysander had landed her in France. Six weeks since she'd heard anyone address her as Catherine, since she had slipped into the shell of this imaginary being named Denise. Yet such was the schizophrenia of the agent's existence that her identity was now completely submerged into her imaginary personality and her real self as abstract to her as a character in a dream. Unfortunately, she thought grimly, that conversion had its limits. If something went wrong in the next half hour it would be her real rather than her imaginary self the Germans would be dealing with.

The motorcycle stopped and she politely declined the corporal's offer to carry her basket. As they walked down the gravel path to the entry of Bruno, the centre of the three gun turrets, she was, as always, awed by the dimensions of those steel-and-concrete mastodons jutting into the skyline. Was it really possible the six blocks of white enamel in her sewing basket could paralyse those guns at the moment for which so much German wealth and wisdom had created them?

Metz was waiting for her, pretending to work at his desk almost directly under the control panel. He rose and, with a nod, sent the fat corporal trundling back up the staircase to the surface. 'Shall we have a coffee?' he asked. 'A real one?'

Catherine forced a nervous smile of acceptance onto her face. She set her basket on his desk and as unobtrusively as possible, kept her eyes on the clock on the wall while Metz chatted away. In her nervousness, she had only to provide the occasional nudge to keep the conversation flowing. No other sound was quite so sweet to the ears of her music-loving admirer, she reflected, as the sound of his own voice. Nine o'clock came, then passed. Why doesn't he call? Catherine thought. By five minutes past nine, she was prolonging the last swallows of her coffee. The bastard had lost his nerve. The operation was off. The thought should have fathered a sense of relief. Strangely, it did not. Instead, she was burning with anger and frustration when she heard a voice over the

233

loudspeaker saying something in German.

Metz rose. 'Excuse me,' he said. 'I've got a phone call upstairs.'

Catherine gulped her coffee and passed their cups to Heinz, the mess steward. Washing them would keep his hands busy for a moment or two. Her stomach churned with nervous tension. She felt dizzy and, she was certain, swayed unsteadily as she walked back to the room next door.

She drew the four keys from her smock and tried the first one. It didn't even come close to fitting the lock. Nor did the second. Suppose he hadn't taken the key with him when he went out that night?

He had. The third, after a slight push, slid into the lock. She gave it one or two twists, then felt the lock's bolt slide from its socket. Her earlier moment of panic had almost passed. She was breathing in tight little gasps. To her immense relief, the panel looked exactly as it had in the engineer's drawing. She reached down for her first dummy circuit breaker. In the panel she saw the top deck marked 'Anton' for the gun turret to the left. The first two fuses in it, she saw, bore the number XR402. She reached up to the first one and gave a little tug. It slid easily from its socket. She took her dummy, matched its prongs to the holes in the panel and pushed it into place. Then she gave a thrust with the heel of her hand to be sure it was firmly fixed to the panel.

It's easy, she thought, easier than I thought it would be. Move quickly, move calmly, move deliberately, she told herself, repeating the cautioning phrases like a litany. The second circuit breaker went quickly into place; Anton had been dealt with.

Before arriving, she had divided her basket of sewing into two halves with a little cardboard divider. It was a precaution against the mistake committed in haste or panic. Nothing would have been more stupid than to become confused between the real and the doctored fuses. She had placed all six doctored circuit breakers in the left half of her basket. Now she tucked the two real fuses she had just extracted from the panel under a pair of green coveralls in the compartment to the divider's right and took two more dummies from the left. They went into the panel as easily and quickly as the first two had. Bruno was now dispensed with. She slipped its two real circuit breakers into their hiding place and reached for her last two dummies. That was when she heard the unmistakable clatter of leather boots ringing against the metal of the battery's staircase.

Later, the events of the next two seconds would pass through her mind again and again with the lethargically defined precision of the images of a slow-motion film.

There was no time to close and lock the control panel and get back across the room to her washing machine; the oncoming steps had almost reached the bottom of the stairwell. She nudged the door of the control

234

panel, leaving it slightly but not evidently ajar. Then she grabbed a shirt from her sewing basket, shook it open, turned her back to the passageway and held up the shirt as though inspecting it for some flaw in her work. She listened to the leather heels come down the passageway. If they belonged to Metz, she was, quite simply, dead. That realization did not panic her; on the contrary, she felt invaded by a numbing calm, something vaguely similar to the sensation she'd felt at fifteen when she had begun to slip under the anaesthetic she'd been given for her appendectomy. Nor did it seem an eternity until the footsteps reached the door; it seemed exactly what it was – a fraction of a second – before she heard a strange voice call out, *'Heinz, ein Kaffee!'*

She spun back to the panel, opened it and quickly inserted the last two dummy circuit breakers into place, then surveyed her handiwork. The numerals XR402 were all correctly lined up at the base of the circuit breakers. After giving each a final push to be sure all were solidly in position, she closed the door. It locked with one turn of the key.

Picking up her basket, she crossed the room to her washing machine, quickly tossed a pile of soiled linen inside and opened up the hot-water connection. It was then that fear hit her. Her knee joints seemed paralysed with fright. Suddenly dizzy, she clutched the rim of the washing machine to prevent herself from toppling over. Behind her she heard once again the ring of leather heels on the cement floor.

Metz entered, pulled out his chair and settled down to his desk under the control panel. 'Sorry I was away so long,' he said. 'Did you miss me?'

Pierre Paraud's visitor was unexpected and unannounced. 'You should not have come here,' Paraud mumbled as reproachfully as he dared. 'People might see you.'

'One day you may have cause to be glad they did.' Aristide allowed an instant of silence to gild the suggestion his words were meant to carry, then eased his wiry frame into the chair opposite Paraud's desk. 'She did it.'

The smile with which he announced the news was neither vague nor ironic. 'Your fuses are all in place. Everything went beautifully. Your phone call came in at exactly the right time, for which she and I are both properly grateful.'

Paraud accepted the compliment with a gesture of his head.

Aristide crossed his legs almost daintily and gave a hitch to his trousers. 'Now just one thing remains to be done.'

'What's that?'

'We must install the bypass you described to me here so we can overload the battery's current on London's order.'

'Who is going to do that?'

235

'You are.'

Paraud reacted like an ailing man who has just been informed he has terminal cancer. No matter how much he might have expected and feared the denouncement, nothing could adequately have prepared him for the shock of hearing the fateful words pronounced for the first time.

'Why me?' he gasped.

'Who else? You've already told me the Germans rarely come here. You can find some excuse to work late, do it when no one is around to see what you are doing. Your wife and children are no longer with us, thanks to my efforts.' Aristide made room for a pregnant little pause in his speech. 'My friend, let me ask you something. Suppose the Germans discover what's been done to their control panel? Who do you imagine would be the first person with whom the Gestapo would like to have a little talk?'

Paraud offered a frightened silence, then mumbled, 'Me?'

'Of course. Who else? You are one of us now. So you might just as well come with us all the way. What *she* did, she had to do right under the noses of the Germans, deliberately, calmly. An absolutely remarkable act. I am not asking you to do anything remotely like that. And I have a way of making sure your chances of getting caught at this are absolutely minimal.'

'When that bypass is connected? You're crazy!'

'When that bypass is connected, my dear friend, you will be well away from here.' Aristide reached into his pocket and pulled out a small piece of machinery. 'Know what this is?'

'It looks like an electric motor.'

'Exactly. This cylinder' – Aristide indicated a drum by its side – 'is going to be attached to a cord which will be attached in turn to your bypass wire. You will set this motor behind that 10,000-volt cable coming into your transformer. When you turn it on, it will begin to crank the bypass wire you have connected to the battery's power line to the 10,000-volt cable. Simple. It will take about five minutes for the two cables to make contact. When the day comes to sabotage the battery, all you will have to do is hook the cord to the bypass wire, start the motor and leave. I'll give you a safe house only you and I know about. You will squat there until the Allies roll over Calais after they land here, because sure as hell that is why they are going to want those guns taken out.' Aristide blessed Paraud with an enigmatic smile. 'You are fifty-four, right?'

Paraud nodded, surprised by the accuracy of what he had wrongly assumed was a guess.

'Now, if you survive this, and you will, the Bible gives you sixteen more years of life. For those sixteen years, you are going to be one of this

236

city's heroes. You will be the Seventh Bourgeois,' he said, referring to the six burghers who had offered their lives to spare their fellow Calaisians during England's fourteenth-century siege of the city. 'Think of it. Every Bastille Day, you will be standing there right beside the mayor in his Tricolour sash watching the troops march by. They'll name a street after you when you die. What I'm offering you, my friend, is a chance for immortality.'

Paraud laughed – the first indication Aristide had had that the man possessed anything vaguely resembling a sense of humour. 'It seems to me what you are offering is a chance to shorten rather drastically whatever longevity I may have left. I wish to God I had never gone to that first meeting with you.'

'But you did.'

'Yes.' Pronouncing the word, Paraud seemed to shrivel as though all the physical diminishment of age had overwhelmed him in a searing instant. 'I guess I haven't got much choice, have I?'

'No.' Aristide's chuckle was as dry, as mirthless, as the scuttling of autumn leaves. 'I don't believe you have.'

On the morning of April 30, the proprietor of a pink stucco villa in the gardens of Lapa, a few minutes' drive from the gambling casino of Estoril, the seaside resort just outside Lisbon, received two visitors. He had no reason to be wary of them or the purpose of their call. They had arrived in a Mercedes-Benz bearing the diplomatic plates of the German Embassy in Lisbon. They were in fact employees of General Walter Schellenberg, the man appointed by Heinrich Himmler to reorganize German intelligence in the wake of the *Reichsführer's* SS takeover of the Abwehr. That they should wish to visit with John Jepsen was only natural. Jepsen was an Abwehr agent, one of the most effective operatives employed by the German secret intelligence service. Indeed, he had just been awarded the *Kriegsverdienstkreuz* First Class, a distinction no other German in Lisbon enjoyed. As they chatted over tea, one of his visitors dropped a small white pill into Jepsen's teacup while the other diverted Jepsen's attention. When Jepsen had passed out, the two men gave him an injection. They then stuffed his unconscious form into the trunk of their Mercedes and drove him to Madrid, where he was placed in a second car which took him to Biarritz, on France's German-occupied Basque Coast. There he was 'unpacked' and shipped to Berlin, to a cell which awaited him in the underground torture chambers at Gestapo headquarters on Prinz-Albrecht-Strasse.

The Abwehr was in fact not the only intelligence service employing the talents of John Jepsen. He was also an agent of MI6, the British Secret Intelligence Service, a man of skill and courage known to his London employers as 'Artist'. As such, he was a vital strand in the Byzantine web of connivance and deceit upon which the *Fortitude* deception scheme depended.

His arrest was the disaster Sir Henry Ridley had long feared might overtake him.

Catherine knew something was wrong the instant Pierrot walked in the door.

'They're on to us,' he announced.

Her hand went nervously to her throat. 'What makes you think that?'

'I don't think it. I know it.' Pierrot went to the window and stared down into the street. 'I've got a friend in Saint-Omer who has a farm right next to the signal depot the Germans have up there. He told me last night they got three new detection trucks two weeks ago. They're painted like the trucks the fisheries here use, to disguise them.'

'Maybe,' Catherine ventured, 'there's another radio somewhere up here they're looking for.'

'Oh, sure. And maybe Christmas is coming in July this year. Maybe the reason they painted those trucks grey to look like Calais fishing vans is because they are going to use them to look for a radio in Lille, right?' Pierrot reached into his pocket for Aristide's latest message and thrust it almost reproachfully at Catherine. 'I told you we were taking too many chances.'

Chances are what this life is all about, isn't it, Catherine thought, resisting the temptation to articulate the point for Pierrot's benefit. Instead, she spread Aristide's text on her desk beside her encoding equipment. He had kept his promise. His message was brief and to the point, and reading it Catherine reacted with pride and satisfaction. This was one message the German *gonio* was not going to prevent her from sending.

Feigning a cheerfulness she did not feel for her one-man audience standing guard at the window, Catherine put the message into code. When she had finished, she went through the precise little ritual that always preceded her transmissions: she set her radio into place, coiled its antenna onto the floor, plugged and set it into the household current together with her warning light, then hooked up her 6-volt dry-cell battery with its toggle switch. Carefully she set her quartzes out beside her set in the order in which she intended to use them.

Since Aristide's message had been relatively brief, she had completed

238

all her arrangements well before broadcast time. She sat back in her chair humming softly, trying as best she could to throttle back the tide of nervous tension that always accompanied her transmissions. Just before she was ready to take to the air, Pierrot beckoned to her to join him at the window.

'I don't think we should send,' he said. 'There are more people down there than usual.'

Catherine peered into the street below. It appeared perfectly normal to her – a dozen middle-aged women clutching string shopping bags with the pathetically meagre harvest of their daily foray to the market, children shooting in between them, a few older men strolling along the sidewalk. There was not a German in sight.

'Where are the men in the long leather overcoats?' she asked.

'The Gestapo does not go around advertising its presence,' Pierrot said. 'Look at those two guys on the corner.' He pointed to a pair of teenagers in brown leather jackets leaning against the wall, smoking. Even from her window, Catherine thought she could catch the sparkle of the brilliantine greasing their hair.

'They're *zazous* waiting for the cafés to open, Pierrot,' she said.

'They're Germans.'

She placed an affectionate and, she hoped, reassuring arm over Pierrot's shoulders. It was time to open the set, and the decision to transmit or not to transmit was hers. 'It's going to be all right,' she whispered. 'Let's go.'

She was almost two-thirds of her way through the message when she heard Pierrot call, 'A truck!'

He did not shout the words – he flung them across the room. At the same time, he drew back slightly so that no one in the street below would notice him. The truck turned the corner and began a leisurely advance down the street. It was grey, and in seconds Pierrot could read the words 'Pêcheries maritimes' scrawled on its side. Then he saw, fixed to its roof, the circular listening device that identified it as surely as if the words 'German Signals Detection Service' had been painted on the van. The teenagers, he noted, had disappeared. He spun towards Catherine. 'Jesus Christ!' he said. 'It's them!'

At the instant he uttered those words, the lights in Catherine's bulb blinked out. Her left hand swept up and flicked the toggle switch before her. With her right she continued to tap on her radio key.

'Denise, for God's sake, stop,' Pierrot pleaded. 'They're right under us.'

Catherine gave a frantic shake of her head and continued to flick her key like a woman possessed. Her message was a jumble of mistakes now, she knew, a meaningless series of hieroglyphics; but she doggedly continued to stab at her sending key.

239

'You're going to kill us,' Pierrot was almost screaming. 'Stop, for Christ's sake! Stop!'

Catherine's light bulb came back on. The building's current had been switched back. Holding her breath, she continued to send until thirty seconds had passed. Then she stopped. She rushed to the window.

The truck was right below them. Its rear doors burst open. This time the men with the leather overcoats did appear – four of them, pistols drawn, leaping over one another to get out of the truck.

'They've got us!' Pierrot groaned.

Numb with fear, they watched as the four men dashed to the kerb. For a moment, they stood poised to attack directly beneath the window. Then, in response to some signal neither Pierrot nor Catherine could see, they charged forward. The next thing they heard was the sound of fists banging on doors and harsh shouts of *'Deutsche Polizei!'*

They came from the building next door.

The dark corridor reeked with a vile blend of herring and rancid oil. From behind the door Catherine could hear the crackle of fish frying. She puckered her nostrils. Heaven, it occurred to her, would be a place where she would never have to eat another herring. Hesitantly, she raised her hand to knock. He was not going to like this. What she was doing was against all the rules of security with which he had so tightly girdled their lives. Still, what had happened this morning justified, in her mind, violating his dictates. If she had had any lingering doubts about how serious their dilemma was, her trip here had settled them. She had been stopped and frisked by German police twice within 300 yards of her apartment. From the way they had examined her gold compact, she had understood what they were after: quartzes.

As he went to answer her knock, the hatred that burned in Aristide's eyes quivered for an instant. No Resistant, however seasoned, was immune to the terror an unexpected knock on his door could inspire.

Wordlessly, he let her in. By the time he had closed the door and locked it behind her, the old fire was back in his eyes again. 'I assume this is very important.'

'It is.'

Swiftly, Catherine outlined the morning's events.

'How much of the message did you get off before they arrived?'

'About two-thirds.'

Aristide waved her to a straight-backed wooden chair and settled into a similar chair himself. Once again she was struck by the apartment's anonymity, its spartan harshness. Its only visible luxury was illegal – a prewar Philips radio Aristide employed to listen to the BBC. Yet she had personally laid in this man's hands a money belt containing two million

240

francs. Clearly, Aristide had not used a *sou* of that to ease his own existence. Ahead of her in the kitchen, his wife had just removed his dinner, one scrawny herring, from the fire. She could not help thinking of Paul with his penchant for black-market restaurants and his resolve that the Gestapo would never get him with an empty stomach. Devotion to the Resistance, it seemed, took many forms.

'When are you due to broadcast next?' Aristide asked.

'Tomorrow at four.'

'This could not strike us at a worse time, could it? Still, I don't think we have any choice. We have got to close you down.'

Catherine did not protest. After their escape this morning, the Gestapo would be waiting for her next broadcast to strike. 'Do you think we could move it?'

'Could you take it apart and then put it back together?'

She shook her head.

'Of course not. They wouldn't have thought about teaching you that, would they?' Aristide waved his hands in helpless resignation. 'Trying to move it now would be suicide. You might as well deliver it to Gestapo headquarters to save them the trouble of picking you up. The question is, is it possible to get off one last message to London?'

'I have an emergency quartz.'

An emergency quartz was just what its name implied. An operator was never supposed to use it, so that the German detection service would not know he had it and associate its frequency with his set. Catherine had to assume that the Germans by now knew all five of the frequencies she normally used. When they heard London calling her tomorrow, they would tune in to each of those five frequencies to see which one she would be using, then begin to home in on her again. By using her emergency quartz, she would give herself a few minutes to send and get off the air before they began to look through other frequencies for her.

Aristide took a pad of paper and wrote something on it. 'How long would it take you to send this?' he asked her.

'Aristide to Cavendish,' it read. 'Gonio located set impossible move new location stop Must suspend transmissions advise alternative radio for emergencies.' Catherine counted the letters. It contained just over a hundred characters. When she was transmitting well, she could tap out between twenty-eight and thirty letters a minute.

'Not much more than three minutes, I think,' she replied.

'Do you think you can get that out on your emergency quartz before they catch you?'

'I think that after this morning, they assume the set is somewhere on my street, don't you?'

'That's a fair enough assumption.'

'And since they're not apostles of silence, they are also going to assume the radio operator was aware of the commotion they caused this morning. So if they see I am not answering London, their conclusion will be I'm too terrified to send. Frankly, I don't think they will go looking for me on other frequencies.'

Aristide plucked at the tip of his beard, twisting its wisps between his fingers. 'That will be their first conclusion, all right. It's the second I'm worried about.'

She looked at him perplexed.

'When they see you are not coming up, they're going to cordon off the area and tear it apart room by room looking for the radio. As soon as you get London's acknowledgement, get out of there as fast as you can move. Do not take anything with you, not even a toothbrush or a piece of underwear. Just throw your arms around Pierrot and head up the street as though you were the first people in the world to discover what *cinq-à-sept* means. He will take you to a safe house.'

'But how about reading Cavendish's answer?'

Aristide indicated his radio. 'This is set for shortwave. You can pick it up here.'

The scene, Catherine thought, could have come straight out of some sullen left-wing drama meant to burden its audience with a sense of guilt about France's working classes. Aristide's wife was in the bed, swaddled in a pair of sweaters, filling the room with sniffles, snorts and rattling coughs. Ostensibly, all that was a result of a cold, a sore throat and a touch of rheumatism. In reality, it was her way of protesting the fact she would be sharing her bed tonight with Catherine rather than with her husband. The SOE's Sevenoaks transmitting station generally broadcast in the middle of the night, and Catherine's messages were due at 1:15. With the curfew, that had meant she would have to spend the night in their apartment, and Aristide had considerately offered her his share of the bed.

Aristide himself was sitting in one of his straight-backed chairs beside a bare light bulb studying an analysis of Engels' thought on Karl Marx's work. Catherine was perched on the other chair, half-listening to Calais Soldatensender, the English propaganda station that broadcast to the German troops in Pas-de-Calais. For the fifth time since 9 o'clock it was playing a song that had apparently mesmerized the warriors of the Wehrmacht, 'Cute Little Bus Conductress.' Her ankles flexed in rhythm to the music. I am the play's working-class daughter, she thought, longing for the freedom of the cafés and dance halls and confined to this room by my parents' penury and proletarian scruples.

Since her arrival, just before curfew, she and Aristide had exchanged perhaps half a dozen phrases. Yet she felt for her chief a very genuine admiration and affection, sentiments she knew he reciprocated. His silence, she knew, had nothing to do with a lack of feeling. Rather, it reflected his idea of how an SOE chief should run his network. Loneliness was a virus that infected every underground agent in Occupied France. It was the inevitable product of a life lived under false cover, in which even the most mundane human encounters had to be regarded with suspicion; a life of interminable waits, of nights spent alone with only fear and solitude for companions. Nothing was more natural, then, that when agents were together they should embrace physically and metaphysically, cast aside their restrictions and savour the forbidden fruit of companionship. Some SOE chiefs, particularly in Paris, encouraged the reaction, made their networks congenial and exclusive little fraternities.

Aristide operated on a different philosophy. He kept his people rigorously separated. He absolutely forbade them any contacts outside of those strictly required for their work. He told his agents nothing they didn't have to know and asked nothing of them that wasn't essential for his work. In all their weeks together, he had never asked Catherine a single personal question, about who she was, where she came from, what her prewar existence had been; he simply did not want to know. All he knew about her as a person was those few things, like the circumstances of her mother's death, which she had chosen to tell him.

She stirred herself from her thoughts. It was 1 o'clock. Receiving Sevenoaks would be as easy as sending had been dangerous. In view of what had happened, they would not be expecting Catherine to acknowledge their message. She had only to sit by Aristide's set and jot down the stream of dots and dashes coming in over the ether. When it was over, she decoded the text by candlelight with her silk and passed the result to Aristide.

'Cavendish to Aristide,' it read. 'Agree suspension transmissions stop Return Denise London immediately with full details sabotage plan stop Her contact bar corner Rue Saint André des Arts and Rue des Grands Augustins Paris stop Code word to barman I want to say hello to M Besnard stop they will arrange Lysander return stop Please confirm her departure via message through Café Sporting Rue de Béthune Lille stop Contact barman René code word Do you know where I can find any bait counter word They've got some at the Café Commerce stop Leave barman contact Calais via which return messages can be sent stop Affectionate regards.'

Aristide looked up. 'I shall miss you too, Aristide,' she replied.

She lit a match to burn her silken ribbons and the scrap of paper she had used to decode London's message. Her fingers stopped frozen in mid

243

gesture until the sputtering wax match began to burn her fingertips. Something marvellous had just occurred to her. The Paris contact and code word Cavendish had just furnished her were exactly the same as those Paul had given to her to use if she was ever on the run and needed to contact him.

Nothing, not even the radiant warmth of the May sun, could alter the depressing grimness of the industrial slums that stretched away from Paris' Porte de Pantin. It occurred to Catherine that she was sitting on the same café terrace, at perhaps the same table at which she had been sitting with Paul just six weeks – a lifetime – ago, waiting for the arrival of the same Boulogne Fisheries van.

That had been a parting gift from Aristide. He did not want her to run the risk of being caught during a luggage search on the Calais–Lille train with the documents describing their plan to sabotage the Lindemann Battery. A detailed blueprint of the battery's control panel, of the rewired Calais power-relay station, even an example of one of the engineer's doctored fuses were on their way to Paris hidden in a load of sardines and herring.

Now, alone in the immensity of the capital, she felt safe for the first time in weeks. No wonder so many SOE agents preferred to work in the city. Its magnitude conferred an instant and comforting anonymity after her weeks in a place as small as Calais. A copy of *Je Suis Partout* was spread on her table in conformity with the advice Paul had given her, but she set it aside in disgust. It was infinitely more pleasant to sit there in the spring sunshine thinking about Paul.

As a little girl she had developed the habit of sitting at the dining-room table staring rapturously at her dessert, ignoring the nursemaids' entreaties to begin. She could sit there for minutes watching her ice cream melt, contemplating her cake, casting an adoring eye at her custard, enjoy an anticipatory delight that often almost rivalled the pleasure consuming her dessert would ultimately bring her. That was how she now thought of Paul – sensing what his arms around her would feel like; enjoying already the moment they would stretch out beside each other on some bed somewhere in the city and languorously begin to explore each other's bodies again. Indeed, so engrossed was she in her fantasies that she actively resented the arrival of the Boulogne Fisheries van. She watched as it parked and the driver got down from his cab and went to the corner kiosk to buy a paper.

244

With a casualness that came quite naturally to her now, she strolled across the street. It was the same driver who had taken her to Calais, and they recognized each other immediately. She pretended to be asking him directions. He took her to the truck, pulled a map from the pouch beside his passenger's seat and went through an elaborate pantomime explaining to her how to get to Versailles. As he did, he slipped her her package, which she dropped into the bulky handbag slung from her shoulder. Saying goodbye, she noticed a particularly Parisian souvenir spread across the passenger's seat of his truck. It was a set of those elaborately graphic dirty postcards two generations of Pigalle hucksters had been selling to tourists in Montmartre.

'Ah.' she smiled. 'Resistance leaflets for the boys in Boulogne?'

He smirked. 'Passports. I give them to the *Feldgendarmen* in Abbeville. That is one of the reasons they never pay too much attention to what I'm carrying.' He climbed into his cab. '*Merde*,' he whispered, and shut the door.

Catherine wandered across the street and down into the *métro*. As she did, she could smell the stench of dead fish rising in the gentle waves from her shoulder bag. At least, she thought, I'm not going to have trouble getting a seat by myself.

LONDON

Every Wednesday afternoon of the war, the trickle of men, half in uniform, half in civilian clothes, strolled discreetly into an office building at 58 St James's Street. It was a resolutely dreary red brick Victorian structure, and on the arch over the doorway the letters MGM, for Metro-Goldwyn-Mayer, indicated who the building's owners were. For ten years before the war the film firm had distributed its celluloid fantasies throughout Europe from that building. The fantasies emanating from it now were of a different order. The building served as the wartime headquarters of MI5, British counterintelligence.

The destination of the handful of men arriving there each Wednesday afternoon was a third-floor conference room. The room's decor could best be described as British civil service spartan: a long rectangular table covered with green baize at which each man's place was marked by a notepad, pencil and drinking glass. The only other amenity available was a cup of watery tea and two biscuits at precisely 4:30. Yet the men who gathered so faithfully around that conference table each Wednesday afternoon represented the salons of the secret war. Theirs was the High Table of Britain's wartime intelligence establishment. Every secret

245

organization functioning in London – MI5; MI6; Sir Henry Ridley's London Controlling Section; Navy, Army and RAF intelligence; the code breakers – was represented at the table, with one notable exception: the SOE. Catherine Pradier's employers were considered far too insecure to be privy to any of the secret strategies debated at 58 St James Street.

Called the Twenty Committee – for the Roman numeral XX, by which it was designated – the group had originally been established by Winston Churchill to oversee the information being fed to German intelligence by MI5's growing collection of double agents. By 1944, its main concern had become coordinating and implementing the webs of deceit Sir Henry Ridley's LCS dreamed up to further his *Fortitude* deception schemes. Two Americans had been assigned to the committee in 1943, one representing Donovan's OSS, the other the State Department.

T.F. O'Neill, as Ridley's American deputy and liaison officer, was the alternate for the OSS representative. It was in that capacity that he walked into the conference room for the first time on Wednesday, May 3. Ridley introduced him to one or two of the men already in the room and then indicated a chair beside his own at the middle of the table. The young American major was impressed. The authority of the men around him, he knew, spanned the globe. Only Winston Churchill, President Roosevelt, the American Joint Chiefs or the British General Staff could overturn the decisions taken at the table at which he was now seated.

A tall, slightly stooped man entered the room and took his place at the head of the table. He gave a nervous tug to the cuffs of his sleeves, leaned back in his chair and let his eyes command silence as a professor might enjoin silence before beginning his lecture. That was appropriate enough, as John Cecil 'J.C.' Masterman was a renowned Oxford scholar and classical historian. Like Sir Henry Ridley, he epitomized perfectly the notion that England was a land run by an élite of the well-born and well-schooled. There was virtually no official channel in wartime London he could not circumvent with a phone call – most often to a senior official who, at one time or another, had been one of his students.

When the room fell still, he picked a thin piece of foolscap from the folder before him. It was an intercept of a communication of the Abwehr. 'Gentlemen,' Masterman announced, 'we have a crisis on our hands.' He paused to convey the proper sense of drama. 'Artist – John Jepsen – has been arrested by the Gestapo in Lisbon. He has been taken to Prinz-Albrecht-Strasse.'

T.F. O'Neill had no idea whom he was referring to. The reaction on the faces around him made it clear, however, that the news was regarded as catastrophic. 'We must address ourselves to three questions,' Masterman continued: 'Will he talk? If he talks, what can he reveal?

246

What bearing would such revelations have on the prospects for *Fortitude*'s success?'

T.F. sensed Ridley stirring beside him. He lit a cigarette and leaned forward. 'The first question answers itself,' he said. 'He will talk. You may take it as axiomatic that anyone captured by the Gestapo can have the truth tortured out of him. There is no one they cannot break. No one. And what he knows is indeed substantial.'

'We've had some suggestion from our Lisbon station,' the MI6 representative said, 'that he may have been taken in for some kind of financial skulduggery, black-market dealings in currencies.'

'That may well be so, but it's entirely irrelevant,' Masterman said, dismissing the man's point with a glance. 'When they start breaking his bones one by one in those cellars of theirs, he may very well decide to tell them all he knows simply to save his skin. And what he knows is very damaging indeed.'

'Quite!' Again it was Ridley, his word clearly summarizing, it seemed to T.F., the distress of every man in the room. Their distress was well founded. Jepsen had been recruited to work for British Intelligence by a Yugoslav double agent named Dusko Popov. Popov was the agent the Germans had sent to the United States on behalf of the Japanese to study Pearl Harbor. Now, code-named 'Tricycle,' he was one of the three key double agents the British counted on to pass *Fortitude* to the Germans.

Masterman plucked again at his shirt cuffs. 'If Jepsen tells his torturers Tricycle is operating under our control and we've continued to use him to pass *Fortitude* material to the Abwehr, we shall be in the most dreadful trouble, shan't we?'

'If you would look upon ten Panzer divisions waiting for us when we go ashore in Normandy as troublesome, why, yes, indeed,' dourly observed the colonel who represented British Military Intelligence on the committee.

'One thing is clear to me.' Ridley, T.F. noted, was speaking from inside one of those clouds of cigarette smoke that always seemed to hang about him at such meetings. 'We have got to close Popov down immediately.' He looked across the table to the Scot who represented MI5. 'Have you any thoughts on how it could be done?'

'Yes,' he replied swiftly. 'I've been giving the matter some thought. Popov and Jepsen were great schoolboy chums, weren't they? He recruited Jepsen. Suppose he simply tells his controller that until the Gestapo take their filthy hands off Jepsen and return him to Lisbon, he's finished. Won't pass the Abwehr the time of day.'

Ridley smiled. 'That should do it.' He turned to Masterman. 'I must say this confirms a terrible fear I've had ever since Himmler took over the Abwehr. My concern at the moment is not Popov. He's lost. It's what will be the Gestapo's reaction when they discover one of those precious agents they've inherited from the Abwehr is in fact working for us. Are they then going to become suspicious of all their other agents? Are Brutus and Garbo going to be lost to us too, just when we most need them?'

'Well' – Masterman's voice was portentous with gloom – 'if we lose those two, we have lost *Fortitude* – and along with it, most probably, our hopes of successfully invading the Continent.'

'Before we all rush out and take our cyanide pills,' the MI6 man declared, 'may I suggest the Germans have very few sources of information available to them? I don't think we could get Goering to risk one of his reconnaissance planes on photographing those lovely visual displays we're creating for his benefit in southeastern England if we sent him a squadron of Spitfires to escort his plane over and back. We have set out the most sumptuous banquet imaginable up there and our principal guest doesn't seem to want to come to dinner. In view of that, their reliance on the reports of their agents in this country has to be much greater than it otherwise would be.'

'I quite agree.' It was the Scot from MI5 who oversaw the double agents. 'No matter how much Himmler and his minions may despise the Abwehr, they've little else to guide them. They are going to have to base at least some of their calculations on the reports we're sending them. What else have they got? Granted, they'll become more suspicious if they learn we turned Popov. But they have got to have something on which to base their intelligence estimates, haven't they? Besides, just as the cuckolded husband is the last man in the village to see his horns growing, so the spymaster is invariably the last person to realize his precious spy has been turned.'

Masterman gave an abruptly brutal shake of his head. 'All that may well be true, but we must prepare ourselves for the danger of losing Garbo and Brutus. How about advancing some other players from that vast stable of yours – Mutt and Jeff, Tate, Mullet, Puppet, Treasure?'

'Gentlemen.' It was Ridley again. T.F. was fascinated by the way the man could insert so much authority into such a soft speaking voice. 'This discussion is turning in circles. The invasion, may I remind you all, is in barely a month's time. In order to be convincing, a double agent must be carefully and patiently built up over a long period – and one month is most emphatically not what I mean by a long period. As for the idea of upgrading some of our other agents or, more logically, assigning them a more important role in our operations, I'm against it. It is obvious from our intercepts that Garbo, Brutus and Tricycle enjoy reputations of the highest order in German eyes. Tricycle is now lost to us. Nonetheless, I'm inclined to feel it's not only easier but safer and more effective to put across a deception scheme through a few proven channels rather than employing a wide variety of channels whose value is uncertain.'

'You are suggesting, then, that we ride with Brutus and Garbo and pray that the damage on this thing is confined to Popov?' Masterman asked.

'No. I'm suggesting we not let panic overtake us. Stay with Brutus and Garbo at least until *Ultra* – thank God for that – indicates the Germans are having doubts about them. After all, Garbo has that marvellous imaginary network of his scattered all over the country, and we've positioned Brutus so he can move about quite freely in uniform. I share, however' – Ridley made an all-embracing wave of his cigarette – 'the concern you all feel for a little reinsurance, some new pipeline into the Germans. It's a concern which has haunted me day and night since I learned Himmler was taking over the Abwehr. Now, any new channel we employ must lead to the RSHA and not the Abwehr. And our lack of time rules out using double agents as the channel. So what do we do?'

He took one of his long dramatic drags on his cigarette and let the smoke roll gracefully down from his nostrils before continuing. 'Our friend "C",' he said bowing slightly to the representative of MI6, 'has an asset already firmly in place which could be of considerable use to us in this regard. However, try as I can, I have not yet been able to put together a plan to bring his asset effectively into play. There is something missing, some vital cog, some piece that will bring the whole puzzle together for us.'

He smiled and stubbed out his cigarette. 'All I can tell you is that we shall redouble our efforts to find that missing link.'

Aristide pedalled slowly along Lille's Rue de Béthune looking for the Café Sporting. He spotted the café, then, in keeping with the security dictates of the SOE, pedalled slowly past, studying it as best he could through its filthy plate-glass windows. It looked abysmally normal to the exhausted and thirsty Aristide. He circled back, parked his bike and went in.

His message, already coded, was tucked inside the newspaper in his hand. Aristide still had the code and call sign he had been given when he left England and had employed with Catherine's predecessor. It was the SOE's old code based on a line of poetry or music, in Aristide's case a line from Charles Trenet's 'Fleur Bleu'. He had done his coding and decoding himself, so he knew the Gestapo had not been able to torture the secret of the code out of the operator after the unfortunate man's arrest.

The café was quasi-deserted. A pair of elderly men huddled at the far end of the zinc bar nursing their wartime beers in morbid silence. The barman came over. *'Une demie,'* Aristide ordered – 'A beer.'

He swallowed it down in two gulps and ordered another. The barman gave him an amused stare. 'Got a thirst,' he said, smiling, as he drew him another glass.

Aristide studied him. He jerked the beer spigot with the gestures of a man who had been doing it all his life. He was middle-aged, as was Aristide, with a protruding stomach which indicated that France's vile-tasting Occupation beer had not diminished his thirst.

Aristide made a beckoning gesture to him with his head. The barman drifted down the bar, halfheartedly swabbing at the shiny zinc with a filthy bar rag as he advanced. 'René?'

'Yeah,' the man replied without bothering to look up.

'Know where I can find some bait?'

This time René looked up. For a flashing instant there was a hesitancy in his eyes – and it didn't, Aristide imagined, have much to do with fishing. This man, to whom Cavendish's last message had addressed him, was wary of traps. That was good. He scrutinized Aristide, then settled down in front of him, his hammy forearm spreading on the edge of the bar as though he were about to whisper to him in what bend of the River Lys the fish were biting.

'We don't sell bait,' he confided. 'They've got some over at the Café Commerce.'

Aristide's own left elbow was resting on the copy of the newspaper he had folded and set on the bar. 'There's a message for London in here on page three. How fast can you get it out?'

'I don't know,' René whispered. 'I just pass them on.'

Aristide approved of the man's reticence. They understood security here. 'My name is Aristide. On page four you'll see an ad for Chez Jean, on Rue Darnel. There's a telephone number written on it in ink. It's my contact. If London relays you something for me, call it and tell whoever answers, René called from Lille to say the trout are biting. I'll come up to pick up whatever you have.' Aristide took a sip of beer. 'Don't lose it,' he cautioned. 'London may have something important for me later in the month.'

René, the barman, nodded. Aristide shifted his elbow off his paper and the barman dropped his rag over it. He started to move back up the bar. 'Tell you one thing,' he announced for the benefit of his two elderly patrons, 'guy down the street from here caught three trout in an hour over in Armentières. Right by the National 42, under the Dieppe Bridge there.'

Aristide gestured to him with his glass. 'Thanks,' he said. 'I'll give it a try.' He drained the beer and strolled back to his bike wondering where he could sleep off his fatigue before starting back to Calais.

250

Strolling through St James's Park, T.F. O'Neill was still under the spell that sitting at the high table of Allied Intelligence had cast over him. Ridley, as he always did, had insisted on walking back to their underground headquarters. Halfway through the park, a curious T.F. decided to put a question to him. 'I'm aware of Garbo's role in our plan. And as of this afternoon, Tricycle's – or what his was, anyway. But Brutus, your third agent, is a mystery to me.'

'Ah,' said Ridley as though regretting this inadvertent gap in his subordinate's knowledge. 'Remarkable chap, Brutus. He's a Pole. He was a fighter pilot in their air force before the war. Just happened to be in Paris when the Germans conquered Poland, so they never grabbed him. He stayed on after France fell and put together an intelligence network for MI6. Bloody good one it was, too, until, as always seems to happen in these things, the Abwehr penetrated it and rolled them up – sixty-four of them arrested, I believe.'

'How did he get from Paris over here?'

'The head of the Abwehr in Paris, who had arrested them all, was simply amazed to discover from the documents they had seized what a cracking good job they had been doing for our intelligence people. He took all this to old Von Stülpnagel, the German commander in France, saying "Look what a good lad am I, breaking up this marvellous spy ring. Shouldn't you pin a medal on me?"'

Ridley laughed. Few things amused him more than the contemplation of his enemies' discomfiture. 'Old Stülpnagel blew up. Practically shot the Abwehr man on the spot. "How is it," he shouted, "the British have these superb spies behind our lines and your buffoons in the Abwehr are utterly incapable of planting spies in Britain even remotely like them?"'

'Well, that gave the Abwehr man what he thought was a rather clever idea. If this Pole was so good, he said to himself, why not put him to work for Germany? So off he went to Fresnes Prison to see him. "Look," he said, "I've some rather bad news for you. Our military tribunal is certainly going to condemn you to die as a spy. However, I think I have a way to save you from that firing squad."'

'And the Pole accepted?'

'Oh goodness, no. There was a great deal of to-ing and fro-ing. Finally, the Pole agreed to come if, in turn, the Germans would guarantee to spare the lives of the sixty-three Frenchmen who had been arrested with him. The Abwehr's man was delighted to accept because it gave him, of course, a kind of guarantee of the Pole's good behaviour. So they arranged for a mock escape and off he went.'

'Told you the real story when he got here?'

251

'After some persuasion. He has become immensely valuable to us. We know the Germans trust him. And unlike the other agents we have here, he's a regular officer. What we've done is make him a Polish Air Force liaison officer to this army of phantoms of ours. That allows him to travel all around the place inspecting troops and headquarters. We imagine the most marvellous things for him to see and report back to the Germans.'

'Fascinating,' T.F. said. Then, after a step or two, he stopped, stood and turned towards Ridley. 'Wait a minute, Colonel. Sooner or later the Germans are going to wake up to the fact your Pole has been lying to them, aren't they?'

'I suppose so.'

'What happens then to those sixty-three Frenchmen they are holding as hostages to the Pole's good behaviour?'

Ridley did not immediately answer. He looked at T.F. through those half-closed eyes of his, the faintest suggestion of a weary smile at the corner of his mouth. 'Hopefully, by the time they've put it all together, the tides of war will have changed and their minds will be occupied elsewhere.'

'Bullshit, Colonel, if you'll pardon my French. The Germans are going to line them up in front of a firing squad and shoot them, and you damn well know it.'

Ridley did not answer. He marched steadily ahead as if his silence were reply enough. When, finally, he turned to T.F., it was as though the Pole and the concerns T.F. had raised did not exist. 'My wife and I,' he said, 'have asked Deirdre Sebright down to the country for the weekend. Perhaps you'd like to join us? Do you the world of good to get a little mud on your boots. And it will give us the chance to have a good long chat. Get to know each other better.'

PARIS

Catherine scrutinized the *café tabac* at the corner of Rue Saint André-des-Arts and Rue des Grands Augustins with the same concealed intensity Aristide had fixed on the Café Sporting. It seemed almost deserted. A woman, probably a whore, glared out at the flow along the narrow Latin Quarter street with such sullen hostility in her eyes Catherine wondered what desperate lust might lure a man into her bed.

How different the scene in the street was from Calais, where half the people in the city centre seemed to be German. Here, there wasn't a uniform in sight. She continued on a hundred metres, pondered for a minute the few pathetic offerings in an antiques dealer's window, then strolled back up the street to the café. The whore didn't even look at her as she walked in and settled at the bar. Competition, apparently, did not concern her. Catherine ordered a glass of wine, which she sipped thoughtfully. She was alarmingly out of place. It would be best for all concerned, she sensed, if she transacted her business and got out as fast as she could. She smiled at the barman.

'I'd like to say hello to Monsieur Besnard,' she said.

The man looked at her with resigned indifference. 'Not here,' he said. 'Come back around six. Maybe I'll have a word from him by then.'

Catherine returned to her glass of wine and the barman to polishing his glasses. If her query had in any way affected him, he certainly gave no indication of it. She finished her wine and got up to leave. As she did, she was seized by one of those childish impulses which occasionally overwhelmed her, one of those rash ideas friends, parents and lovers had been counselling her against for years. Once again she gestured to the barman.

'Tell Monsieur Besnard,' she whispered, 'that Madame Dupont will be waiting for Monsieur Dupont at the same *hôtel pension* they shared a few weeks ago.'

Immensely pleased with herself, she set out to find it. Rue de l'Echaudé' was only a few minutes' walk. As soon as she pushed open the door the smell of old wax rising from the woodwork hit her, and she heard the shrill yapping of Napoléon, the owner's horrid little white poodle. You wouldn't, it occurred to her, want to compare the feeling she had on entering this squalid hotel to what she had experienced coming home on vacation from convent school; still, in view of the memorable moments she had spent here, she felt a welcoming sense of delight coursing through her.

The proprietress, as grotesquely painted and coiffed as Catherine remembered, was ensconced in her cage by the stairwell. She didn't recognize Catherine, but then why should she? Traffic through her establishment was, after all, considerable, and heightened recently by the rites of spring. She accepted Catherine's proffered wad of notes with a cheerful squeal and plucked a key from her rack.

'Madame is expecting company?' It was a statement rather more than a query, a clear indication that the only sin she was not prepared to condone was that of sleeping alone under her roof.

'I certainly hope so,' Catherine assured her, starting up the establishment's well-worn staircase. Then she giggled *sotto voce*. My God, what if I've got the wrong Monsieur Besnard?

To detect feelings of any sort on the bland features of his subordinate the Doctor was, Hans-Dieter Strömelburg reflected, as uncommon an

253

occurrence as discovering edelweiss on the Zugspitze in April. Yet self-satisfaction seemed spread over the Doctor's pudgy features this May afternoon. Strömelburg was intrigued. He pushed aside the object he had been contemplating, an eighteenth-century Sèvres vase confiscated from the home of a deported Jewish businessman in Neuilly. Leaning back in the chair, he smiled indulgently at his young linguistics scholar.

'Are you in love?' he asked. 'Or is that expression on your face simply the result of a good bottle of wine at lunch?'

The Doctor, who shunned alcohol as assiduously as he practiced sexual continence, grinned appreciatively. 'Neither,' he said, 'it's because the tigers are at last beginning to come in out of the forest of the night up in the North.'

The allusion left Strömelburg puzzled.

'Don't you remember that SOE operator, Wild, we captured in March?'

'That bastard who tried to trick us with that double security check they've started to use? Of course I do.'

'Remember the trap we decided to set in a café up in Lille using his radio as bait?'

'Ah, of course. There was that terrible business with those two terrorists who shot themselves before we could take them. What's been going on?'

'I activated the set about three weeks ago. We had told Cavendish Wild was going into hiding because of all our strikes on the network he had been assigned to up there, remember?'

Strömelburg nodded.

'I messaged London I – or Wild – was ready to operate again but that the network had been pretty much destroyed. I told Cavendish I – Wild – would be available as a radio for anybody who had to contact London. Gave him some code phrases to do with fishing.'

Strömelburg clasped his hands behind his neck. Let the Doctor go on and announce in his own time whatever little triumph had brought him to his office, he thought.

'This morning a man came into the bar, gave the proper code word and left a message for London.'

Strömelburg sat upright at the Doctor's words. 'Now, that,' he said, 'is interesting.'

'The message he left was in code.'

'Naturally.'

The Doctor beamed. His enjoyment of all this was quite uncharacteristic of the man. 'We have the code. It belongs to an agent in Calais. Berlin broke it six months ago.'

'So that's why that set went off the air in Calais! Cavendish ordered them to close down and use Lille because they knew our detection services were closing in on them. Let me see the message.'

The Doctor, rather like a child offering a parent an excellent report card, extended a clipboard to his superior. 'Aristide to Cavendish,' the text on it read. 'Denise departed Paris as ordered stop Bringing full description of sabotage plan stop Leaving contact Calais with café barman for future inbound communications.'

'There's one more thing.'

Was there no end to the succession of juicy morsels the Doctor had to offer today? Strömelburg bestowed a smile that begged his subordinate to proceed.

'Gilbert's radio operator just received a message from London. Gilbert should be getting it about now. It tells him to give absolute priority to getting an agent called Denise onto his next Lysander to London.'

'That particular piece of news, my friend, is not quite as welcome as you seem to think,' Strömelburg declared. 'It means we won't be seeing the sabotage plans the message in Lille refers to coming through in Gilbert's courier, doesn't it? Obviously, this Denise is taking them to London herself.'

'You could take her at the departure.'

'I could.'

Strömelburg got up and strolled to the magnificent floor-to-ceiling French windows that looked down on Avenue Foch. The lawn sweeping from the *contre-allée* to the avenue itself was such a lush green in the spring sunshine it could have been the fairway of a golf course. A group of children rolled and tumbled on it under the vigilant eyes of their nursemaids and mothers. Four years of occupation did not seem to have unduly affected the routines of his bourgeois neighbours, Strömelburg thought as he watched them. He stood there for some time, hands clasped behind his back, rocking up and down on the balls of his feet, considering the delicate outlines of the problem posed by the Doctor's information.

'The first thing to do is get that message off to London in your next transmission. We don't want to stir Cavendish's suspicions. Not that I've ever felt suspicions unduly bother that well-intentioned mind of his.'

'I traced the Calais phone number the agent left in the bar. It's another café. Should we put the place under surveillance?'

'Most certainly not. That is quite the last thing we should do. There are still a few gaps in your understanding of this trade, Doctor.' A cheerful indulgence, the tacit recognition of the Doctor's excellent performance thus far today, suffused Strömelburg's words. 'Why scare them? If London answers, it will be in that old code. Cavendish might just as well ring through and pass the information directly on to us.'

He returned to his desk and picked up the Sèvres vase he had been admiring when the Doctor arrived. Cherubs and fawns circled a plumply sensual maid recumbent on a green hilltop at the centre of the medallion adorning its centre. 'Such a beautiful piece. Almost certainly, I'm told, a gift of Louis XV to one of his mistresses.'

'Where did you get it?' the Doctor asked tactlessly.

Strömelburg shrugged. 'From a gentleman who won't have much use for it where he's going.' He set the vase back on his desk with loving care.

'If only this Denise were arriving instead of leaving our life would be simpler,' he sighed. 'I can think of no way we can interfere with an outgoing Lysander flight without compromising Gilbert. Do we want to destroy the most effective intelligence operation we're running to get our hands on some sabotage plan of whose object we are completely ignorant?'

'Calais is vital for their invasion plans, certainly.'

'I grant you that. But suppose we grab them at the field and find out this sabotage plan of theirs involves nothing more than blowing up a few freight trains between Calais and Lille? What will we have then?'

The Doctor knew enough not to answer that. Strömelburg grinned. 'I'll tell you what we will have. A couple of cases of cardiac arrest in Berlin.' He took a cigarette from his silver case, tapped it moodily, then lit it. 'Perhaps our answer is there. Why don't I submit this to Herr Kopkow and let him make the decision? Then, if something goes wrong, our brillant counterespionage expert can have the pleasure of taking the responsibility for the mess he's created.'

Catherine leaned against the windowsill of the *hôtel-pension*, arms crossed as though in some form of meditation, peering at the people scurrying through the narrow alley of Rue de l'Echaudé below. Somehow they seemed to move with a sprightlier step than they had the last time she had stood at that window; their figures seemed less slouched and wearied. Was it from a sense that the liberation of their nation might at last be drawing near? Or was it nothing more than that rejuvenation spring, and particularly spring in Paris, always seems to offer even the weariest of beings? The apartment across the street was shuttered and empty; she remembered the image of the man being wrestled from the door to the car in the middle of the night. Where was he now?

A knock on the door interrupted that disturbing train of thought. She tensed, then smiled. 'Who is it?'

'Monsieur Dupont.'

'Come in, Monsieur Dupont,' she called from across the room. There had been no mistake; it was the right Monsieur Dupont. Paul's wiry brown hair, those brooding eyes mixing mischievousness and melancholy she had thought of so often during her lonely nights in Calais, even the same tweed sports jacket and foulard whose incongruous elegance had struck her on their train trip up to Paris were all there before her. They stared at each other for that poignant instant of questioning, of reassessment all lovers live through after a separation, then, without a word, flew across the room at each other. Paul grabbed her and they began to embrace, his mouth open and covering hers with such an intensity of feeling it was as though he were trying to drag up from the depths of her being some wispish fragment of her soul.

'God!' he gasped as they finally paused. 'I was afraid I'd never see you again.'

'Why?' She whispered, her question carrying the wisdom of the centuries. 'I knew I would see you again.'

'I don't know, so much happens so fast in the world we're in. I –'

'Paul' – she placed her forefinger on his lips – 'why talk?'

Never in her life had Catherine made love so swiftly or so intensely. There were no preliminaries. None were needed. They tore their clothes from their bodies in their frantic search for nudity, then they were on the bed, Paul was in her and they were together, racing with the frenzy of coupling animals. When they had finished, he gently began to kiss away the little rivulets of sweat that were trickling between her breasts. Still within her, clutching her body to his, he rolled gently to his side. For a few moments they lay there clinging to each other, panting, embracing, exploring the half-forgotten familiarities of each other's bodies. In almost no time, it seemed, she felt Paul stiffening inside her again. This time their loving was slower, more languorous; an achingly protracted rise towards their climax. As they reached it, Catherine emitted a deep cry of triumph and rapture, a shriek of sensual fulfillment such as the other female occupants of their hotel rarely had cause to utter.

They fell asleep. As the evening shadows began to stretch across the room, they stirred. The contents of Paul's jacket – keys, wallet, money, *métro* tickets – were scattered over the floor. Helping him pick them up, Catherine found a photograph, a worn and faded prewar snapshot of a nineteenth-century *château*.

'What's this?' she asked.

'The *château* where I was born.'

'Is it yours?'

'It belongs to my family.'

'So, I'm in love with a nobleman, am I?'

'Certainly not,' Paul said, laughing. 'With a rogue and a rascal, which you'll find a lot more amusing – and much less predictable.'

257

When they had finished restoring at least an intimation of order to the room, they flopped on the bed. 'What a shame you didn't come forty-eight hours later,' Paul said.

'Well, that seems an ungracious thought,' Catherine said, pouting. 'Particularly in view of the welcome I just received.'

'If you'd come two days later, the moon would have changed and I would have had an excuse to keep you here for three weeks. Tomorrow's Lysander is the last one of the May moon and I had a message from Cavendish this afternoon. He wants you on it.'

'Maybe the RAF will give us a little help again.'

Paul sighed and reached for a cigarette. 'Not likely. We're going out of a field near Amboise, not far from the one you came in on. It's probably best for you to get there on your own. I've got to convoy an American pilot down, and that can be tricky. Those Americans never speak French, and they look about as French as Zulu witch doctors. Red lights if the Gestapo checks the train.'

'What do you want me to do?'

'Miss the plane, if only I could arrange it.' Paul grinned. 'No, its simple. There's a nine-o'clock train from the Gare d'Orsay for Amboise tomorrow morning. You'll take it. The last guided tour of the *château* goes off at four-fifteen. Go along on it, with a *Je Suis Partout* for company. One of my men will come up to you and say, "If Charlotte de Savoie was as beautiful as you, Louis XI was a wise man." You tell him, "Are you offering me a *château?*" Go with him. He will take you to a safe house near the field.'

'It's as easy as that?'

'Darling' – Paul took her back into his arms – 'believe me, my little aerial taxi service is safer and more reliable than Air France used to be before the war.'

Had T.F. O'Neill set out to imagine the perfect English country weekend in the perfect English country setting, he could not, it occurred to him, have envisaged a better example than the one he was living at Sir Henry Ridley's Sussex estate, Clairborn. First there had been the train ride down. The train had been straight from one of those prewar murder-mystery movies the English had made so well: the creaking carriage, each compartment with its own direct exit to the station platform; the worn brown upholstery giving off a smell of must and stale tobacco, a soiled antimacassar pinned hopefully at the top of each seat; even the ubiquitous broker in his bowler and dark suit immersed in his *Times* in one corner of the compartment. The countryside had been ripe and verdant, exploding with the promise of springtime, its gentle vistas marred by khaki convoys lurching down to the Channel, reminders of the dread significance of this particular springtime.

As soon as they arrived at Clairborn, Ridley had insisted T.F. put on a pair of old corduroys and tramp through the estate grounds with him, surveying the walls of the nearby Cowdray Castle, the progress of his azaleas, listening for the call of an elusive kingfisher. Afterwards, they had all sat by the fire sipping warm whisky-and-sodas. Dinner had been one of those ceremoniously casual English affairs, the food garnished with vegetables Ridley proudly pointed out had come from his country garden and a 1934 Château Ausone he had personally brought up from his wine cellar. Deirdre was sitting opposite T.F. In the candles' glow her eyes seemed to flicker with iridescent brilliance. She was dressed, as always, with stunning simplicity, her only jewellery the single strand of pearls at her neck, barely a suggestion of lipstick glistening at the edge of her mouth. Every gesture she made, even the banal act of eating custard, left T.F. entranced.

Ridley was talking. Away from the office, where his awful worries so frequently bludgeoned him into taciturn silence, he was a charming man and one who evidently enjoyed nothing quite so much as telling a story.

'I must tell you all a rather funny little anecdote; and darling' – he nodded to his wife – 'do keep it a dark secret until the appropriate moment.'

He pushed his chair from the table and glanced towards the ceiling. 'Back in 1943, we had a thing in the War Office called the Inter Services Security Board, and they were the people who were the custodians of all the code names for our secret operations, you see. Dished them out as each operation emerged from the planning stage.

'Well' – he chuckled in anticipation of his own humour – 'one day Freddy Morgan's deputy came to me and said, "Well, now, the plans for the great invasion are at last complete and Morgan wants a code name. Will you go around to ISSB and see what they suggest?" ' Ridley's eyes went to T.F. 'Morgan ran COSSAC, the organization that drew up the plans for the invasion.

'So, I went round and saw the major in charge there and said, "Look here, we need a code name for the great operation."

'He looked into his books, then came back and said, "I'm frightfully sorry, but I'm afraid there's only one code name available at the moment.'

'"What's that?" I asked.

'"Mothball," he replied.

'"Are you absolutely sure?" I said. "That seems rather a dreary code name for what is going to be the most important operation of the war."

'"Yes," he said. "I'm afraid that's all we have. The others are all taken up."

259

'So, I went back to Freddy Morgan and I said, '"Mothball" seems to be the only code name they can produce."

'"Oh, dear," he said, "I don't fancy the idea of taking that in to Winston. He's not going to like that at all."

'But off he went, and half an hour later he was back looking rather chagrined. "What happened?" I asked.

'"Just what I was afraid would happen," he said. "Winston went right through the roof. 'If those bloody fools can't come up with a better code name than that,' he shouted at me, 'I'll bloody well pick the code name myself.' He reared back and said, '*Overlord! We shall call it Overlord.*'"'

Ridley smiled in pleased recollection of that moment. 'So that, my dear major, is why one day you will be describing to your grandchildren the role you played in this extraordinary operation of ours which, thank God, shall be known to posterity as *Overlord* rather than "Mothball."' He chuckled. '"Mothball"! Can you imagine our future historians struggling to prepare their portentous accounts of – Operation *Mothball?*'

He smiled down the table to Lady Gertrude. 'Darling, why don't you and Deirdre freshen up while the major and I adjourn to the library for a glass of port.'

Ridley led T.F. down the hall to a dark, wood-panelled library. It was clearly the man's sanctuary, a citadel no uninvited guests entered. A fire was burning in the fireplace. Over the mantelpiece an oil painting of a bewigged gentleman in dark legal robes stared disapprovingly down into the room.

'One of your forebears?' T.F. inquired.

'My grandfather, actually,' Ridley said. 'Lord Chief Justice before the Great War. Lovely death, poor man. Dropped dead of a heart attack shooting grouse on the Scottish moors one August morning.'

The Englishman took a highly polished rosewood box from one of the library's shelves. 'Cigar?' he said, offering his humidor to T.F. Prewar Havanas, T.F. thought, accepting his offer. Ridley took the cigar from him, meticulously trimmed it with a silver cigar cutter and returned it to his guest ready to be lit. From a sideboard he took a Georgian crystal decanter and poured two glasses of port.

'To your good health,' he said, raising his to T.F., 'and may I tell you again how pleased we are to have you with us?'

T.F. blushed slightly and raised his glass in return. 'To yours,' he said. 'It's an honour to be working with you, sir.'

Ridley waved him to one of his two big leather armchairs before the fire and settled amiably into one himself. 'I must tell you another story, Major.' Something in his sonorously impelling tone suggested to T.F. that this was to be more than just a little fireside chat, that his invitation down here for the weekend, their stroll, their charming dinner had perhaps all been well-designed stops along the way to this sombre library. 'Not quite as humorous, I fear, as the *Overlord* story, but one which is not without its significance for our work.

'In the fall of 1942, you Americans had a very major task force, Task Force 34 it was, carrying Patton's troops across the Atlantic for the North African landings.' Ridley sipped his port, savoured it for a moment, then continued. 'Thanks to *Ultra*, we spotted a wolf pack of eight U-boats lying just south of the Canaries smack astride the task force's route to Casablanca. Had they found your task force, we would have had a disaster on our hands. As it happened, we had a convoy of empties – SL-125 was its designation – heading up the South Atlantic coast for home from Sierre Leone. Now, one of our maritime codes had, we knew, been broken by the Germans.'

T.F. eased his crystal port glass onto the table beside his chair almost stealthily, as though any noise or movement might shatter the sonorous rhythm of Ridley's voice. This is a parable, he thought, not a story, and it is meant as a lesson of some sort for me.

'So, we arranged to communicate with the convoy in that code, a message which required them to give us their position in reply. The result, as we had expected, was that the wolf pack intercepted the message and headed south. They tore into the convoy like hounds after stags, sank thirteen ships in three days. While they were doing it, of course, Patton's task force was sailing safely past.'

Ridley sipped his port and stared into the dancing flames. Did he see there, T.F. wondered, a reflection of those British sailors they had condemned to die in the shark-infested waters of the South Atlantic?

'How many sailors did you lose?' T.F. asked.

'Hundreds.' Ridley continued to stare morosely into the fire. 'Sadly enough, human life is the raw material of war just as surely as iron ore is the raw material of a blast furnace. Had thirteen of Patton's transports gone down instead, how many more hundreds of American GIs would have been lost? The Germans would have been warned of the task force's approach. And – who knows? – perhaps the Casablanca landings would have failed.' Ridley sighed. 'I tell you all this, Major, because as I am sure you are coming to realize, this is a dark and dirty world to which your superiors in Washington have assigned you. Do you know Malcolm Muggeridge, by any chance?'

'No,' T.F. said. 'I'm afraid the name means nothing to me.'

'One of these writer chaps. A curmudgeonly fellow. Personally, I don't care for him. However, he said something about your OSS people the other day that rather struck me. I hope you won't take offence if I repeat it to you. They're rather like *jeunes filles en fleur*, he said, straight

261

out of their convent school, all fresh and innocent, thrown into this whorehouse in which we work in our intelligence world.'

T.F. laughed. 'Yeah,' he said, 'you would have to agree his description is apt.'

Ridley smiled with those half-closed eyes of his. 'Indeed. You see, intelligence work of necessity involves so much cheating, so much lying and so many betrayals that it inevitably warps the character of those who perform it. It's a world I've been involved with on and off since the first war, and I must tell you that I have never met anyone engaged in it that I would wholly trust.'

The smile had now left the Englishman's face, and a strange thought occurred to T.F.: Had it ever really reached his eyes?

'But, I must also tell you that I am totally convinced of the necessity of what we do. Wholly. Absolutely.

'Excuse me just a moment,' Ridley said, rising from the comfortable embrace of his armchair. He went to one of the library shelves and drew down a faded blue volume. He returned to T.F. opening its pages as he advanced.

'This is what I believe you Americans call a yearbook. The record of the boys I was at school with at Eton.' He passed it down to T.F., who looked, fascinated, at the scrubbed and innocent faces that peered from its pages, so eager and assured in their black high hats and starched white collars.

'My dearest friends,' Ridley noted, taking back the book and snapping it shut. 'Four years after those pictures were taken, three-quarters of them were dead. Slaughtered in the senseless butchery of the Somme.'

Ridley eased back into his armchair, somewhat less relaxed, it seemed to T.F., than when he had left it. '"Who is the more virtuous man?" Horace Walpole once asked. "He who begets twenty bastards or he who sacrifices a hundred thousand lives?"

'We beget our share of bastards in this dark world of ours. But if the price of our doing so is to prevent the idiotic slaughter of yet another horde of Englishmen and Americans, there is no treachery so vile, no act so perfidious I would not gleefully perform it.' Ridley took a swallow of his port. 'You expressed some concern the other day at what might happen to Brutus' French colleagues when the Germans realize he has been lying to them. Quite frankly, I don't know. Remember, however, they all volunteered to serve as spies fully aware of what the price for that would be if they were caught. At the very least, we have given them three extra years of life.

'What I do know, however, is that if a man like Brutus fails to make the Germans swallow our lies, the cost to us in human life will be far, far greater than sixty Frenchmen who may – or may not – be shot by the

Gestapo because he betrayed them. You must understand one thing, Major, however painful the notion is for you to accept. In this world we are working in, there is absolutely no room whatsoever for scruples.'

T.F. picked up his port glass and took a long drink of the warm red-brown liquid, envisioning as he did those long lines of Frenchmen before their firing squads, convinced they were martyrs for their nation's freedom when in fact they would be victims of a lie told by someone in London.

'What you are saying, I guess, is that the end justifies the means.'

'That is exactly what I'm saying and precisely what I mean.'

'But isn't there a limit somewhere?' T.F.'s mind was back with his brigadier general at the Pentagon the morning he had left for London. 'Isn't there some point beyond which we must not go without debasing ourselves, reducing ourselves to the same moral plane as our enemy?'

'This war we're fighting is not, as some of your people back in Washington seem to think, a kind of extension of your Civil War – Grant and Lee, Longstreet and Meade, and let the men take their horses home for the spring ploughing. We are at war with a savage empire, a people determined to debase and enslave whole races, ready to slaughter and plunder as ever the hordes of Genghis Khan were. To fail to defeat the Nazis would mean the end of our society. And the safe survival of our society is a supreme goal which overrides any moral consideration. Horace Walpole' – Ridley looked rather cheerfully at T.F. – 'I seem rather addicted to him tonight, don't I? – also remarked, "No great country was ever saved by good men because good men will not go to the lengths necessary to save it." Well, we have to ensure the survival of our societies and our way of life, Major, and if the lengths we're forced to go to do it are occasionally reprehensible or morally wrong, so be it. We are in a total war, and a total war demands total commitment.'

'Funny,' T.F. said, swirling the last of his port in his goblet. 'I got a rather long lecture taking quite the opposite point of view from a brigadier general in Marshall's office the day I left Washington.'

'What was his name?'

'I don't remember. He was Marshall's deputy chief of staff for G-2.'

'Ah, Parkinson. I know the man. He's one of those well-intentioned chaps one's forever running into in Washington, the kind who always seems to have a firm grasp of the wrong end of the stick.'

T.F. laughed, almost in spite of himself. 'Still, he had a point, it seemed to me. That the United States shouldn't debase its ideals and standards by adopting tactics to further them which are identical to those employed by its totalitarian enemies.'

'What matters, my dear major, is to win this war as fast as possible, at the expenditure of as few Allied lives as possible. Some lives must

263

inevitably be deliberately expended to save those of a great number. But I wouldn't countenance expending a single life to sustain an ideal or some pious platitude. Let the Germans think we fight with some kind of an Anglo-Saxon notion of fair play if they choose to – as I hope they do. If I can slip up on them in the dark of night when they are in bed, sodden with sleep in the arms of their mistresses, and shove a knife into their guts, I will be only too happy to do it.'

'You don't seem to have much time for the rules of cricket, Colonel.'

'A notion for fools' – Ridley gulped off the last of his port – 'or cricket players.' He laughed.

He heaved himself from his chair, went to the decanter on his sideboard, refilled both their glasses; then, settling back into his armchair, his feet stretched before him, he stared moodily into his dying fire.

'It's painful to have to tell you some of these things,' he said after a moment. 'Innocence is something we all try to preserve against all the cruel evidence of reality. But we have a job to do, a critical job, and we have got to get on with it.' He took a long drink of port. 'And there's another reason as well behind my ramblings.'

'What's that?' T.F. inquired.

'You know we English have run the world for the last two hundred years. And I think future historians will judge us to have run it rather well, all things considered. Well, our time has passed. Our empire will not survive this war. The mantle will now pass to you Americans. You are going to have to exercise power not only on your own behalf, but on our behalf and on behalf of dozens of other, weaker peoples who will look to your country for leadership. And it's young men like you, Major, disciplined and hardened in this war, who will have to provide the leadership. Will you be prepared? So much depends on it.'

'Yes,' T.F. agreed. 'We probably will emerge from the war as one of the two major powers on the globe. With the Russians.'

'With the Russians indeed. And they are going to be adversaries every bit as ruthless and implacable as the Nazis we're now fighting. We had generations to learn how power is exercised. You haven't. You'll have to learn here in the cauldron of this war what you will need to know when the war's over and the world's yours. There has always been a kind of charming naiveté to your American view of the world, an ardent desire to keep the United States pure in deed as well as in intent. You'll have to divest yourself of that.'

'Why?' T.F. protested. 'There is a certain idealism behind that view.'

'Idealism, my dear major, is a luxury only the weak of this world can afford.'

'That seems like a rather cynical way of looking at things.'

'The exercise of great power is by its very nature, Major, a cynical process – something you Americans have been particularly reluctant to understand.' Ridley sighed as though he were wearying of his professional role. 'General Donovan and some of his people are beginning to understand this – thanks in part, I like to think, to our tutelage.'

He rubbed his forehead with his fingers, then slowly stubbed out his cigar in the ashtray by his armchair. 'I hope you will too. Learn the lessons well, Major, because, believe me, you will need them all in the years to come.' He started to rise, then sat back. 'Just one last word before we join the ladies. In this murky world of ours, you must understand that if you're going to become involved in these things, you must never, never admit to anything afterwards. You must go into them determined that you will never reveal what you have done, that you will go to your grave still resolutely denying that these things ever happened.'

He rose, and T.F. followed him through the manor house's long corridor back to the sitting room. There too the coals of a fire flickered in the fireplace. Deirdre and Lady Gertrude were seated side by side on a big green sofa, Ridley's wife industriously knitting a cardigan for her husband.

'Well,' Lady Gertrude said, smiling, 'have you two solved all the problems of the world for us?'

Ridley grunted in reply and began to jab at the logs in the fireplace with an iron poker. Clearly, Lady Gertrude's words had been a ritual phrase rather than a question. She and Deirdre were already back to thrashing out the misfortune of whatever friend it was they had been discussing. T.F. settled into an armchair, still jarred and unsettled by his conversation in the library. He glanced at his watch. How soon, he wondered, could he politely steer Deirdre upstairs? Ridley thoughtfully provided him the answer after a few minutes of chitchat by announcing that he was exhausted. After a long series of good-nights, they finally headed upstairs. She opened her bedroom door, smiled and led the way in.

'You and Lady Gertrude seem to be old friends,' T.F. noted, gratefully closing the door behind him as he did.

'Friends? Dear Lord, no. I can't abide the gabby old windbag.' Deirdre crossed the room, unbuttoned the jacket of her neatly tailored suit and hung it over the back of a chair. She was wearing a plain white cotton blouse cut tight across her firm and thrusting breasts. She walked back to T.F. 'A proper English lady selects her friends with great care.' Laughing as she circled her arms around T.F.'s neck, she gave a toss to her hair and fixed him with maliciously mirthful eyes. 'Lovers, my darling, are quite another matter. Tell me – why are we standing here with our clothes on when we could be in bed making love?'

Catherine followed obediently along behind the gaggle of old women, schoolchildren, a priest and a couple of elderly men who composed the day's last visitors to the Château d'Amboise. Could one of them, she asked herself, possibly be Paul's man?

Their guide stopped abruptly and offered the group one of those pregnantly heavy pauses so favoured by his trade. He was a wizened old man with a limp, and he was striving painfully to infuse his description of kings and courtesans, of the jousting tournaments, the masquerade balls, the wild-beast fights that had once graced the *château's* courtyard with a touch of drama.

Now he pointed to a cement-and-stone beam over a doorway leading to an underground passageway. 'On this beam,' he intoned, 'in the year 1498, Charles VIII mortally wounded himself with a blow to his head while rushing off to watch a sporting contest in the moats of the *château*.'

Having announced that, he then, of course, stood back and waved them down the passageway with a cautionary 'Watch your heads, messieurs, mesdames.'

How drab the *château* was, Catherine thought, drifting behind the group. The famous stained-glass windows of the Chapel of Saint-Hubert had been shattered in 1940; the whole place seemed to be falling to ruin through neglect and indifference. It could, it occurred to her, be an allegory for her occupied homeland. She lingered outside on the terrace that overlooked the twin branches of the Loire glistening in the afternoon sunlight, ostentatiously clutching her *Je Suis Partout*, waiting for Paul's man to make contact. No one approached.

Slowly the tour dragged along towards its conclusion, and then they were back in the chapel courtyard where it had begun. Still, not a soul had spoken to her. The guide's blue cap was off, his hand extended, his lips mumbling the classic plea: 'Don't forget the guide.'

Merde, she thought, what the hell do I do now? Struggling to find an answer, she reached into her purse for a coin, pressed it into the guide's hand and mumbled, 'Thank you.'

'Ah, madame,' he said. 'If Charlotte de Savoie was as beautiful as you, Louis XI was a wise man.'

She offered him a smile of surprise and relief together with her counterphrase.

'Outside the main gate,' he whispered, 'in ten minutes.'

He was right on time. With a nod, he beckoned to her to follow him. He went down the castle ramp and around the corner to a shed built into the castle's retaining walls. Inside were two bikes. 'Follow me at about twenty-five metres,' he said. 'We're going over the bridge and north about two kilometres. Then we'll turn off the main road, up towards a plateau. Near the crest we'll pass a man cutting wood beside a dirt track.

He'll be whistling, "Je tire ma révérence." Turn left and go to the end of the dirt track. There's a stone shed. Paul will be inside. If the woodcutter's not there or if he doesn't whistle, keep following me.'

It worked perfectly. The woodcutter didn't even look up at her as she rode past, but his whistled refrain was unmistakable. The shed was at the end of the road where the guide had said it would be. She pushed open the door. Half a dozen men were inside. One was boiling coffee. Paul, a huge grin on his face, came up to her. 'Enjoy your visit to the *château*?' he asked with a crooked smile.

He brought her a cup of coffee and settled her on a pile of straw covered by burlap in one corner of the shed. There were no introductions. One, however, was not needed. The American was leaning against the wall, smoking, staring morosely at the floor. He was a giant. Someone had stuffed him into a workingman's blue denim suit at three sizes too small – probably, Catherine thought, because there was no worker in France as big as he was. Sneaking him past the Germans, she imagined, must have been as easy as trying to sneak the sunrise past a rooster.

Paul looked at him and smiled to Catherine. 'He can't believe what's happening to him, and I don't blame him. He was shot down the night before last. Lost his whole crew, he thinks. He parachuted. He's crossed all Paris on foot, travelled four hundred kilometres by train without a single ID paper, without being able to speak a word of French, and now we are telling him he's going to have breakfast in England.' Paul tapped his head. 'He thinks we are all nuts.'

Just before 9:15, Paul took a portable radio out from underneath the straw and switched it on. The shed fell silent. Paul listened intently to the BBC's litany of *messages personnels*, then turned off the set and stood up. The air of surly authority that had so struck her when she had arrived was on him once again.

'Okay, everybody,' he ordered, 'listen carefully. The flight's on. Just because we haven't seen any Germans around today we mustn't assume there are none out there, so I want you all to follow my instructions exactly. There's a railroad line a kilometre and a half from here which we must cross before ten, when the guards go on duty. We go single file, ten metres between each person and the next. No talking, no smoking and no coughing if you can help it. If anything happens, don't panic. Just lie down. I'll be in front, Marcel' – he indicated one of his men – 'in the rear. I don't give a damn if any of you are armed: only he and I have the authority to open fire. Understand?'

There was a murmur of assent. 'Translate that for him,' he ordered Catherine, indicating the American pilot. Then they all headed for the door.

267

Their march through the night, by the light of the fast-rising moon, was swift and uneventful. When they finally cleared the last glade, they stepped out into a wide, open pasture glistening in the moonlight. This, Catherine realized, must be the high ground of the plateau towards which she had ridden earlier on her bike.

Paul ordered his three passengers to sit in the shadows of a grove of trees by the pasture's edge. Two of his men drifted off to take up positions as sentries at the pasture's approach. Paul and Marcel inspected the field for holes, stakes or wandering cows, then fixed their three poles to the ground in their L pattern and tied flashlights to each one.

Panting slightly, Paul returned to his passengers. 'After the plane lands, the incoming passengers and their bags come out first. Watch me. When I wave to you, run to the plane. The lady goes on first, you' – he pointed to the American and counted off two fingers – 'second and you third,' he concluded, indicating the Frenchman. 'We'll pass you your bags when you're in the plane.'

He sat down on the grass beside Catherine and raised her hand to his lips, kissing it softly. 'I'm glad you're getting away,' he whispered.

'Maybe I'll be back.'

Paul shook his head. 'No, it's too late. The invasion's coming anytime now and that will shut me down.'

They sat side by side in the darkness of the shadows, holding hands in silence. Catherine sensed Paul tense and looked at him. He had again that air of the wary animal sensing the approach of danger which she had seen the night she arrived. Then she heard the sound that had alerted him, the distant whine of an aeroplane engine. He kissed her fervently. 'Au revoir, mon amour,' he whispered.

He was on his feet dashing across the pasture to his stakes, Marcel behind him. Suddenly, the silhouette of the aeroplane, an emerging black against the silvered moonlit sky, was overhead. She saw Paul's flashing exchange with the pilot, and seconds later the plane came roaring to the ground. From the grove she saw two figures leap from the plane; then Paul was waving them forward. She barely had time to squeeze his hand as she clambered in. Her two fellow passengers followed; Paul snapped the canopy shut, and he was gone. The pilot gunned the engine and, bouncing and swaying, the plane rushed down the pasture and lifted off the ground. Seconds later, they were lost in the darkness of the sky. Beside her, the American stirred. 'I would never have fucking believed it,' he groaned.

Catherine was sound asleep when the first sharp jounce shook the Lysander's frame. She blinked as two more jolts followed and, turning to stare out of the window, saw a blur of trees and buildings rushing past. They were on the ground. For a second, she wanted to yelp in triumph.

'Welcome back to Blighty!' the pilot shouted over the roar of the engines. He spun the little plane about and taxied up to a hangar. As he cut the engine, Catherine heard voices outside and saw a cluster of figures approaching the aircraft. She wanted to cry in joy, I'm back. I'm safe. I made it. This is the way Lindbergh must have felt, she thought, when he landed in Paris.

They were swept up in a boisterous round of embraces, bravos and well dones, then put into the same car, with its covered windows, that had driven her to her departing flight not quite two months before. In a few minutes they were back in the same RAF cottage in which she had eaten her last meal on English soil.

A smiling SOE officer with a clipboard in his hand greeted her at the door. 'Just a couple of quick formalities,' he said, 'and then off you go to the breakfast Sergeant Booker has waiting for you. Let's see, Denise' – he glanced at his clipboard – 'you didn't take any weapons out, did you?'

'No,' Catherine said, smiling.

'Bring any back?'

'No,' she said again as he checked his board.

'Then all I have to do is take back your "L" pill. Won't be needing that now.'

Catherine had almost forgotten the little square pill hidden in the tassel of her shoe. She unscrewed it, shot out the pill, and passed it to the young officer.

Inside the mess, Sergeant Booker's breakfast table was heaped with plates of eggs, ham, sausage, bacon. 'Oh, my God!' she cried. 'What a feast!' For a second her eyes smarted as she remembered her soup kitchen in Calais. Their pilot, still in his coveralls, came in. Someone produced a bottle of wine, and they all began clinking glasses in a happy tumult of excitement and relief.

When they had finished, the station wagon was waiting outside to drive her back to London and the apartment at 6 Orchard Court from which she had set out for France. She dozed again for a few moments, then woke as they sped through the outskirts of London, past the dreary row houses that had so hypnotized her on her way out. In a sense, it was then that the knowledge she really was back, alive and safe, overwhelmed her in its definitiveness. A reassuring glow, a kind of suffused warmth such as that a fine old bottle of Burgundy can produce seeped slowly through her. She had done it. She had gone behind German lines as a secret agent; she had accomplished a dangerous mission with honour and dignity; she had come back. She had proved to herself all she would ever have to prove.

269

As she rode up in the elevator at Orchard Court, then walked along the corridor's deep-piled carpeting in the corridor, it struck her how incongruous it all was: hours before, she had been in a shed in Occupied France; now she was here in the elegance and safety of this building. Park, the butler, opened the door. '*Mademoiselle Denise!*' he said in a kind of happy singsong, '*Comme ça fait plaisir*' – 'What a pleasure to see you.' Major Cavendish, he explained, would be along shortly; perhaps in the meantime she would like to freshen up. He led her down the hallway to the apartment's bathroom, a kind of shrine for SOE operatives. Its black-tiled bath was full of hot water and soap bubbles; her FANY uniform, cleaned and pressed, hung from the wall. Catherine gasped at the idea of a luxury as simple as a hot bath. Park, meanwhile, disappeared and reappeared with a silver tray bearing half a bottle of Veuve Cliquot and a champagne flute.

For a long time she luxuriated in the bath, savouring its warmth, sipping her champagne, drifting on a tide of joy. Only one thought marred her near-perfect happiness: how wonderful it would have been to share that bathtub and that champagne with Paul.

She put on her uniform and with a sense of great sadness folded away the dirty and vile-smelling clothes she had come back in. Denise and all she had done, the emotions she had lived, was dead now, just a pile of soiled clothes in a cardboard box.

Cavendish embraced her warmly as she walked into his office. 'My dear,' he said, 'you did superbly. You more than justified all the faith and confidence we placed in you.' He waved her to the big easy chair and began to devour the contents of Aristide's detailed plan for the sabotage of the Lindemann Battery. As his reading progressed, Catherine could sense him becoming more and more excited. He picked up the fuse she had brought back and studied it. 'Extraordinary,' he said, 'absolutely remarkable. Aristide has done a superb piece of work.' He looked at her. 'And you, my dear, have performed with cold and considered courage. I can pay an agent no higher compliment. Your work will certainly merit a decoration.'

He set Aristide's report in a Top Secret folder on his desk. 'Now,' he said, 'I think you should get some much-deserved rest. I'll see that Aristide's plan goes as quickly as possible to the people who are waiting to see it.'

A few days after Catherine's return to London, a meeting was held in room 732 of SHAEF headquarters at Norfolk House in the heart of the British capital. It was the regular meeting of the Coastal Defences Committee, and the first subject on its agenda that morning was the Lindemann Battery. The committee chairman, a Captain Price of the

Royal Navy, submitted to the committee a copy of the SOE's plan to put the battery out of action through industrial sabotage based on the work of Aristide and his electrical engineer.

After carefully reviewing the plan, the committee agreed that:

1) the plan, with some modifications, was an excellent one and certainly technically feasible;

2) its execution or nonexecution was not a concern of the committee, which was overwhelmingly concerned with invasion preparations along the Norman coastline.

3) it was agreed the plan should be referred to the members of the Joint Intelligence Committee under whose purvey it would more normally fall.

Sir Henry Ridley's deception organization, the London Controlling Section, was represented on the Joint Intelligence Committee.

From the door, the office seemed bundled in a winding-sheet of obscurity. Shadows muted the angles at its corners. The glaze of dust on its unwashed windowpanes diffused the sunlight coming through the fourth-floor windows of the Broadway buildings into a Rubenesque yellow glow against which movement appeared in silhouette rather than rounded form. Sir Stewart Menzies, 'C,' the chief of Britain's intelligence service, MI6, liked it that way; after all, he moved in a world of shadows where nothing was ever quite what it seemed.

He was leaning against his open and unlit fireplace in elegant old tweeds, the paleness of his cheeks, of his light blue eyes, of his silvery blond hair all accentuated by the shadows in which he cloaked himself. He said nothing as his retainer, a veteran of the Boer War in a blue pensioner's uniform, served his guests tea. When the man, ageing joints creaking in time to the building's ancient floorboards, left, he turned to Henry Ridley.

'So, Squiff,' he said, 'the light on the road to Damascus?'

'Perhaps,' Ridley replied. He had asked for their meeting and requested its participants be limited to himself, 'C' and 'C's' deputy, Sir Claude Dansey. 'Tell me, is SOE aware of the fact you've planted your asset on them?'

'Goodness, no,' Menzies replied. 'Quite frankly, I wouldn't trust SOE with the time of day. They are horribly insecure.'

'And Cavendish?' Ridley inquired, sipping his tea with the caution its scalding temperature merited. 'Does he have any suspicions?'

'You remember old Cavendish from school. Frightfully decent chap,

271

but not one to have helped the Chinese invent gunpowder. Suspicions do not seem to unduly disturb the placidity of his mind. We did have a bit of a problem a few weeks ago, but Claude' – he smiled graciously at his deputy – 'managed to put it right with him over a good lunch at the Savoy Grill.'

'A ghastly lunch, in fact,' Dansey murmured blackly. 'Boiled haddock, as I recall.'

'Well,' Ridley said, 'this is what I have in mind.' Patiently and in some detail, he outlined the scheme he had prepared to reinforce *Fortitude* and provide the reinsurance Himmler's takeover of the Abwehr and Popov's loss seemed to demand. Menzies and Dansey followed him intently.

'It's a very clever idea indeed, Squiff,' Menzies said when he'd finished. 'Its success, of course, all depends on whether or not the German rises to your bait. If he does, we may very well hook him. We know Himmler is forever telephoning Hitler with his juiciest morsels. This might well fall into that category. And the RSHA is certainly looking for some grand coup all its own with which to justify its takeover of the Abwehr. The question that comes to mind is, how do you activate your idea in a manner so innocuous they'll never see our hand behind it?'

'How about your chap?'

'He can't activate it. He can't hand the idea over the transom, so to speak – walk into the Avenue Foch and say, "Look at this wonderful prize I've got for you." Too much initiative on his part will only excite the suspicions of our Teutonic friends. He can only further it for you.'

'In addition' – it was Dansey – 'he's quite unwitting as to the real nature of his services and obviously knows nothing about the invasion and *Fortitude*. Remember, he's right there where the German can grab him. He thinks we told him to go to them as a way of facilitating his service. After all, he handles a great number of our people as well as SOEs.'

'Can you trust him?'

'Oh, quite completely, I think. He's been with us since the Spanish Civil War. Tapped us into a German courier operation he was running way back then. At the time, it was a joint endeavour with the Deuxième Bureau. Since France fell he's been with us.'

'Well,' Ridley said. 'If we can't use him, is there some other way we can get them to take a bite at the apple? Some way, instead of your chap going to them, of getting them to come to him and say, "Right, this is what we want you to do"?'

Dansey cleared his throat with the politest of coughs. Menzies and Ridley turned to him. When 'Uncle Claude' cleared his throat at such moments, a quick and respectful silence usually followed his gesture.

'I believe there is another channel with which we might tickle their ears,' he announced. 'I don't know whether you remember or not' – his words were addressed to Ridley – 'but when SOE started operations, all of its radio traffic both inbound and outbound passed through our transmitters. We also provided their codes. They raised the usual rumpus and finally, in 1942, the War Cabinet decided to give them their own independent facilities. When we handed over to them, however, we maintained a capacity to monitor the bulk of their material.'

Dansey paused to sip his tea, deliberately letting his gesture tease his interlocutor's curiosity. 'We learned some time ago a certain number of their circuits – how many we unfortunately don't know – are in fact under German control. That suggested something to us. While neither the Germans nor the SOE know it, we, in fact, are on the other end of the line of two of the circuits the Germans think they are running.' He offered them a chilling little smile. 'One of them has recently been employed in the connection you mention.'

Ridley closed his eyes a second, thinking. 'Remarkable. That might well be our answer.'

'Yes,' Dansey answered, 'I think it just might.'

BERLIN

It was Monday, May 15, time once again for Colonel Baron Alex von Roenne to provide Hitler's General Staff with his latest estimates of the Allies' strength intentions for the coming assault on Fortress Europe. He lined half a dozen coloured crayons on his desk at Zossen, the German army headquarters 20 miles from Berlin. From his drawer he took out his precious map of England and set it against the wall where he and his subordinate, Lieutenant Colonel Roger Michel, could study it. As usual on Monday mornings, Michel's eyes were watery; his fingers quivered slightly as they drew the nourishing warmth in his coffee cup to his lips. Today, Von Roenne chose to ignore him. While Michel nodded in agreement, Von Roenne made six adjustments to the location of Allied units shown on the map. All were based on the reports from the Abwehr's agents in England during the past week.

When he had finished, he summoned his secretary and began to dictate his report. 'The total number of Anglo-American divisions ready for use in the United Kingdom has increased since the beginning of May by three divisions brought from the United States and thus at present probably amounts to fifty-six infantry divisions, five independent infantry brigades, seven airborne divisions, eight paratroop battalions, fifteen armoured divisions and fourteen armoured brigades. The focal point of the enemy concentration in the south and southeast of the British Isles becomes more and more marked,' Von Roenne dictated. 'This is supported by the transfer reported by reliable Abwehr sources of two English divisions to the Portsmouth area and,' he continued. 'the detaching of American units to the British forces in southeast England.

'In the Bury St Edmunds area,' he went on, 'are supposed to be the Twentieth US Corps and the Fourth US Armored Division, according to a reliable Abwehr source. In the same area near Ipswich the Sixth US Armored Division is reported, and another American force seems to have been formed in southeast England in the Folkstone area.'

Both men studied the map for clues to their final, and critical, estimate: where would the Allied assault come? The balance of forces between those in southern England opposite Normandy and Brittany and those in the southeast opposite Pas-de-Calais remained close, but the drift to the southeast was clearly continuing.

'Why would the Allies risk that wide sea crossing to Normandy or Brittany when they can dash across from Dover to Calais, where the channel is only twenty miles wide?' Von Roenne's query was a rhetorical one. The reply was based, after all, on the overwhelming weight of logic, and Von Roenne was a logical man. 'The main attack,' he concluded, with his deputy's concurrence, 'must be expected on either side of Pas-de-Calais, with the heaviest concentration in the coastal sector of northwest France.'

Sir Henry Ridley and his fellow deceivers in the London Controlling Section could not have prepared a better report for the Führer's eyes had they written it themselves.

LONDON

If the Luftwaffe were to drop a bomb on this building, T. F. O'Neill thought, Germany would win the war in a single stroke. Never before, not even in the great conferences of Quebec, Casablanca and Teheran, had so many senior Allied leaders been gathered together under one roof. King George VI, Winston Churchill, the members of the War Cabinet and Field Marshal Jan Christian Smuts of South Africa were seated in the front row. Behind them, like chastened schoolboys gathered for a dressing down by their principal, came bank after bank of generals, admirals, air chief marshals. They sat on curving, hard-backed wooden benches that marched upwards through the two storey Gothic amphitheatre. Black wooden columns supported a balcony filled with yet another human tapestry of gold braid and stars. If Waterloo had been

274

won on the playing fields of Eton, then history might one day record that the battle to free Europe had been won here at St Paul's School on the outskirts of London, on the same wooden benches where the invasion's ground commander, General Bernard Montgomery, had once conjugated Latin verbs and pondered the riddle of algebraic equations.

The gathering had been called for this Monday, May 15, to provide a last review of the invasion of Western Europe. So enormous were the consequences of the operation, so grave the risks attendant on it, that the auditorium, it seemed to T.F., quivered from the collective tension of the men assembled in it. Well before General Dwight D. Eisenhower had called the meeting to order, the room had already fallen silent, the gravity of the moment quieting, for once, the voices of generals and admirals normally enamoured of the sound of their own booming rhetoric.

Eisenhower spoke for ten minutes; then Montgomery took the rostrum. It was the first time T.F. had seen the legendary victor of El Alamein in person. He did not deceive him. He seemed to bounce around the platform, poking at the indentations and grooves of the mock-up of the French seacoast with his rubber-tipped pointer as though each of his thrusts might dislodge an enemy gun battery. His speaking voice was high for a great captain, T.F. thought, his tone a bit fussy and pedantic. The contents of his long address, however, revealed such a grasp of the invasion's strategy, such mastery of its intricate details that the man's confidence and competence compelled the admiration of even his most ferocious critics in the room.

'There are sixty enemy divisions in France,' he warned. 'Ten are Panzers and twelve are mobile field infantry.' Most of the men in his audience were already aware of those figures; yet hearing them uttered there, before the scale model of the beaches, the cliffs, the seaside villages in which so many Allied troops would shortly have to risk their lives jarred them all.

'Rommel,' Montgomery declared of his old North African foe, 'is an energetic and determined commander. We know he will do his level best to "Dunkirk" us on D-Day, to force us back onto the beaches and hold Caen, Bayeux and Carentan secure. If he holds firm in those three places, we will be very awkwardly placed indeed.'

Montgomery paused and turned back to his scale model. His old foe, he was convinced, was wrong. It was not on the beaches that the battle of France would be won or lost, nor in the first few hours of the assault that the outcome would be determined.

'We will reach the critical moment in our assault forty-eight hours after we go ashore,' he said, 'on the evening of D plus 2. By then, *Overlord* will have become an overriding menace which will require the concentration of all available German forces that can be spared. Thirteen

275

divisions may then be moving to Normandy. Their full-blooded counterattack is likely at any time after D plus 6, when the total number of enemy divisions opposing us can be up to twenty-four, ten of them Panzers.'

It was a terrifying prospect. The Allies would have that day in their Norman beachhead, if all went well, fifteen divisions, two of them armoured, all exhausted and wounded from their fight to get ashore.

Montgomery paused and stared out a moment at his audience. From Churchill and the King to obscure colonels and captains on the back benches, they regarded him in silent concern, each weighing in his own way the fragile balance on which so much would soon depend. 'Gentlemen,' Montgomery warned, 'there are many unknown hazards to our enterprise.'

Had the men gathered at St Paul's School that spring day been aware of what was happening on the other side of the English Channel, their concern over the invasion's prospects for success would have turned to alarm. They were spared that anguish because *Ultra*, the great ear which had allowed the Allies to eavesdrop on so many of their enemy's precious secrets, had gone deaf. Hitler's staff communicated with Rommel's headquarters at the Château of La Roche Guyon and Von Rundstedt in the suburbs of Paris by telephone and teletype, both of which were immune to *Ultra*'s prying. And as April turned to May, the burden of Hitler's communications with those headquarters had focused on one place, the place which Hitler had already prophesied to his doubting field marshals would be the target of Allied assault: Normandy. On May 2, his OKW had teletyped Rommel and Von Rundstedt to expect the Allied invasion anytime after the middle of May, with May 18 as a likely date. 'Point of concentration first and foremost,' the message said, 'Normandy.'

Hitler's Chief of Staff, General Jodl, had telephoned Von Rundstedt's OB West headquarters at 7 o'clock on the evening of May 9 to reiterate the point. He could not have been more specific or more precise. 'The Cotentin Peninsula,' Jodl stressed, 'will be the enemy's first objective.'

That manifestation of the strategic genius of the 'Bohemian lance corporal' had left Germany's last Teutonic Knight quite unmoved. His thoughts remained firmly fixed, as they had been at Berchtesgaden in March, on the polderlands of Flanders. That, he was sure, was where the Allies would land. His concern was not with their landing site but with how he would deal with them once they were ashore, and in that, his archrival was his subordinate, Rommel. Rommel's insistence that the invasion be stopped on the landing beaches, Von Rundstedt maintained with icy disdain, was thinking worthy of a major or a regimental commander. The Allies were going to get ashore. Nothing in heaven or on earth could prevent that. As Montgomery had predicted to his audience at St Paul's the critical moment would come three or four days after they had landed, when their supplies were still uncertain and their troops reeling from the losses they had suffered getting ashore. Then, their great invasion, Von Rundstedt told his staff, 'will have become a gasping, beached whale.' That would be the moment to mass the Panzers for one furious, final, fatal blow – precisely the event the men at St Paul's School so dreaded. Do that, he said, avoid the feints and diversions the Allies would set out to entrap them, and Germany could yet win the war.

On the evening of May 15, while the men who had attended the St Paul's briefing were returning to their headquarters, their rival, Rommel, sat down at his desk at the *château* of the dukes of La Rochefoucauld in La Roche Guyon. That inlaid Renaissance table on which Louis XIV's minister of war had signed the revocation of the Edict of Nantes bore his direct telephone line to Hitler's headquarters. He too was curious to see what underlay the Führer's fixation on Normandy. He called his headquarters.

'The Führer,' Jodl informed him, 'has certain information, which reveals that the capture of the port of Cherbourg would be the first objective of the Allied landing.' Was it a snippet from Himmler's RSHA, the espionage of Cicero, the valet-spy in the British Embassy in Turkey or just the Führer's instinct? Rommel wondered. Jodl did not say.

The report stirred Rommel to an inspection tour of the Cotentin Peninsula. Late in the afternoon of Wednesday, May 17, Rommel and Admiral Friedrich Ruge, his naval aide, stood on a sand dune rising behind a beach six miles from the lovely Norman village of Sainte-Mère-Eglise. The sky was overcast, and a gentle breeze rustled the violet heather in the moors around them. Ruge pointed down to the lonely strip of sand designated on the scale model at St Paul's School forty-eight hours earlier as Utah Beach. 'This,' he told Rommel, 'is where they will land.' Here, he said, their invasion fleet would be sheltered by the peninsula's spine from the prevailing winds; here the treacherous and unpredictable seas of the Channel were at their most docile.

For a long time Rommel pondered the grey seas in moody silence, reflecting on the sailor's prediction. His own mind was fixed far to the north, above the Somme, as it had been from the moment he had taken up his command. Nothing could shake him from that conviction. 'No,' he said, finally, to Ruge. 'They will come where the crossing is shortest, where their fighter planes will be closest to their bases.'

A few minutes later, he assembled the men of the regiment defending the beach for a brief exhortation. 'Do not look for the enemy by daylight, when the sun is shining,' he warned. 'They will come at night, in cloud and storm.'

In that prediction, at least, Field Marshal Rommel would be proved right.

PART FIVE

MAY 29/JUNE 6, 1944

Early in the morning of Monday, May 29, 1944, a small but impressive motorcade slipped out of an awakening London and into the green and pleasant hills of Sussex. Its destination was a pillared mansion called Southwick House set on a curl of high ground above the harbour of Portsmouth. With that move, General Dwight D. Eisenhower had transferred his flag from the English capital to the advance headquarters from which he would command the assault on Hitler's Europe. For his first meeting at Southwick House, Eisenhower summoned the men who would now become his most valued advisers: his weathermen. They reviewed their calculations on the basis of information that had been flowing in to them from their weather pickets in planes, submarines, ships and shore stations from the Caribbean to northern Iceland. The omens were auspicious. The matchless spring weather that had embraced Western Europe for most of May would hold, they predicted, for at least five more days. Eisenhower reflected a moment, then issued his first order from his new headquarters. D-Day would be in exactly one week's time, on Monday, June 5, the first of three days in early June on which a concurrence of moon and tide would provide the requisite conditions for the invasion. The countdown to the invasion had begun.

The request was most unusual. Indeed, sipping his day's first cup of tea at SOE headquarters, Major Frederick Cavendish could recall only one other incident even vaguely like it. That one had occurred just one year earlier, in May 1943. General Sir Colin Gubbins, the overall head of the SOE, had come to Cavendish's superior, Colonel Maurice Buckmaster, with a terse order. The Prime Minister wanted a private audience with a young officer named Francis Suthill who ran an important SOE network in the area around Paris. Get him back to London immediately, Gubbins had ordered.

Suthill was flown out by Lysander twenty-four hours later. The afternoon of his arrival, he was taken to 10 Downing Street. On specific orders from the Prime Minister's office, no one from SOE accompanied him. Nor were any officers of the SOE ever informed of what took place at the meeting between Churchill and their young SOE subordinate.

281

Returning from the meeting, Suthill had been able to tell Buckmaster and Cavendish only that he could tell them nothing whatsoever and that he had to return to France by the next Lysander.

Following his hasty visit, the SOE was ordered to increase its arms drops to Suthill's 'Prosper' network. Nonetheless, Suthill and dozens of his fellow Resistants were swept up by the Gestapo in late July 1943. The network, the SOE later learned, had been penetrated early in the spring by a Gestapo agent posing as a Dutch Resistant trying to flee Occupied Europe.

And now Cavendish had received another summons for another SOE officer to report to Churchill's Underground War Rooms. Was this Colonel Henry Ridley who wanted to see Catherine Pradier his old Etonian schoolmate? What was he doing, and what exactly did his London Controlling Section control? He had never heard of the organization – yet Cavendish prided himself on knowing who was who and doing what in the inner circles of wartime London.

In any event, Cavendish realized, it was not his job to question or to reason why. A car, the order noted, would be coming to Orchard Court to fetch Catherine Pradier at 3 o'clock Wednesday, May 31, and take her to Storey's Gate. His task was to bring Mademoiselle Pradier back to London from her leave and see to it she got there on time.

What kind of secret organization would hire a butler to answer its door? T.F. O'Neill wondered as he regarded Park, the Cerberus of the SOE's Orchard Court apartment. Park eyed him with equal suspicion. He was not accustomed to welcoming Americans to the apartment, and O'Neill's arrival, even if it had been announced by Cavendish, did not please him. He nodded curtly, then took T.F. to one of the rooms that gave on to the apartment central hallway. Having ushered him inside, he made a point of ostentatiously closing the door behind him.

When it opened again a few minutes later, T.F. stared for an evident and impolite second at the woman entering the room. That special serenity great beauty confers on a woman seemed to emanate from her as a kind of unworldliness often radiates from a guru or a holy man. Glistening blond hair flowed to her shoulders in indolent waves; her features were high-cheekboned perfection. Her green eyes appraised him with cool indifference. Carole Lombard, T.F. thought: she possesses that same exquisite yet distant beauty Carole Lombard had.

'I suppose you are Major O'Neill,' she said.

T.F. nodded.

'I don't see why they had to send you to fetch me. I'm quite capable of getting around London myself, you know.'

I'm sure you are, T.F. thought. 'Don't be offended,' he said. 'The place we are going to is a little bit like Buckingham Palace. You don't walk in unannounced and unaccompanied.'

'Perhaps,' she suggested as they rode down the elevator, 'you can give me some idea what this is all about?'

'I can't,' T.F. answered. 'Not because I don't want to. Because I don't know.'

His answer satisfied Catherine Pradier until they had settled into the staff car waiting below. 'Then,' she suggested, 'maybe you can tell me who this Colonel Ridley is and what the London Controlling Section does.'

T.F. took out his packet of Camels and offered one to her. She declined it. 'The Colonel's better at explanations than I am.' Feeling suddenly somewhat ill at ease with his own evasiveness, he continued, 'Look, I'm at a slight advantage here. While you know nothing about me, I do know something about you. I know you just came back from Occupied France. My guess is the Colonel wants to learn something from you about conditions over there.'

Catherine folded her arms and stared somewhat petulantly out at the crowded pavements.

'Were you in *Paris?*' T.F. pronounced the last word with a reverence that went back to his first and only visit to the French capital on the grand tour his grandfather had offered him in the summer following his Yale graduation.

'Coming and going. I spent most of my time in Calais.'

'I'd love to see Paris again after the war.'

'Why shouldn't you?'

T.F. wasn't sure whether her assertive tone of voice reflected a certainty of victory or the suggestion that the casualty rate among London staff officers was not such as to inspire any doubts about his surviving the conflict.

When they reached Storey's Gate, Catherine understood why the American major had been sent to escort her. The Royal Marine at the door scrutinized T.F.'s pass and her ID with an intensity that reminded her of the Gestapo officer who had stopped her and Paul on the night she had landed in France. 'Does Churchill really work down here?' she whispered to her American escort as they descended the stairs.

'Not very much, these days,' T.F. said. 'But they say he was down here all the time during the Blitz, prowling around the corridors in a purple bathrobe with a cigar in his mouth.' T.F. took her to a small, cramped office. An older man advanced extending his hand. 'Henry Ridley,' he said, no trace of military formality in his voice. 'Thanks awfully for coming by.' He turned to T.F. 'Thank you, Major,' he added, and closing the door behind him, he took Catherine into the privacy of his own office. He offered her the seat in front of the desk and a Players cigarette, which she refused. Lighting a new cigarette from the stub of his old one, he settled into his chair, appraising her – she was certain – through half-closed eyes.

'Please do forgive us for all this mumbo jumbo which accompanied your visit down here,' he began.

'I quite understand, sir,' Catherine replied. 'I'm sure it was necessary.'

'Indeed. Incidentally' – Ridley smiled at her with beguiling warmth – 'we can dispense with the formalities of the military inside this office. Like you, I'm essentially a civilian.' He put his hands behind his head and leaned back in his chair. 'We went through this procedure because, as I am sure you will appreciate, there is no secret more precious these days than the secret of the invasion.'

'Of course.'

'It is' – Ridley was evidently choosing his words with great care – 'a secret of which no one at SOE, not even Colonel Buckmaster or Major Cavendish, is aware. Absolutely no one. The reason for that is not a lack of confidence in the SOE. It stems from the simple fact so many of your people are in situations where they are exposed to German arrest that we felt it necessary to insulate the entire organization from the knowledge of when, where and how the invasion is going to take place.'

Why, in God's name, is he telling me that? Catherine wondered.

Sensing her concern, Ridley waved his Players. 'Don't worry,' he assured her. 'I don't intend to burden you with such frightful knowledge. My first reason for asking you here was a simple one. Would you be willing to return to France? To Calais?'

Catherine crossed, then uncrossed her legs, slowly straightening herself in her seat to afford herself the time to study Ridley and reflect on his question. In a strange way, she missed her other self, that woman called Denise whose outlines were receding so fast for her. Yet her instinctive response to the colonel's request was similar to the reaction she would have had had Aristide asked her to go into the battery's control panel a second time. There are certain risks one can force oneself to run once, not twice. Even Tsarist noblemen, she thought, didn't make playing Russian Roulette a habit. 'Why do you want me to go back?' she asked.

'To perform a very precise and particular mission.'

'An important one?'

'More than important. Vital.'

Catherine sighed. The droning hum of the ventilation system reminded her of the sound she had heard in the Lindemann Battery. 'Why me? Can't someone else go?'

'Of course,' Ridley replied. 'I am not a believer in the indispensable man – or woman. You, however, are particularly qualified to do what we want done. Which is not, I might say, exorbitantly dangerous or difficult. Far less dangerous than those actions you have already performed with such courage.' He gave her a warm smile. Fascinating, Catherine thought, how some men's smiles can win your confidence in minutes, while with others a lifetime of cajolery will still leave you a doubter.

'Who would I be performing this for?' she asked. 'You? The SOE?'

The colonel's eyelids seemed to close in weariness as he framed his answer. 'We will see to it that the SOE is convinced you are doing it for them, on their instructions. In fact you will be doing it for a higher authority.'

Catherine took a deep breath, then let it burst from her lungs. 'All right,' she said. 'I can't say I'm dying to go, but in view of what you've said, I will.'

'I thought that would be your answer,' Ridley replied. 'In fact, after studying your file, I was quite certain it would be.' He opened his desk drawer and drew out a file on whose cover she could read the words 'Secret' and 'Bigot' stamped in red and purple letters. 'I must ask you to keep every word that we exchange, from now on, a total secret. No one except you and I – not Cavendish nor Buckmaster or anyone at SOE; absolutely no one – is to be aware of what has passed between us. I hope I've made myself clear?'

'Indeed. You certainly have.'

Ridley opened the folder, and Catherine saw that it contained a copy of Aristide's plan to sabotage the Lindemann Battery. He picked it up and laid it on the desk. 'This plan is excellent.' Ridley inhaled a long drag from his Players and thumbed through the file. 'It's been studied very carefully by our best technical experts here. As a result of their work, we have a modification to propose.' He had found what he was looking for, an engineering drawing in India ink. 'It's probably not worthwhile going into all the technical details with you here. They'll be self-evident to your engineer in the power station when he sees this plan. Essentially, it's a way of modifying the manner in which the power overload is delivered onto the line feeding the battery. It will help to guarantee the plan's success.'

He put the drawing back into his folder. 'We'll have it reduced to microfilm and fitted into one of those fake wooden matches you're familiar with. We would like you to hand-carry it to Aristide.'

'How am I supposed to go back in? By Lysander? By parachute?' Catherine asked.

'The June moon is due in a few days,' Ridley said. 'We'll see that you are on the first Lysander.'

A tremor of delight flickered through Catherine at the word 'Lysander.' The danger of her return would have its compensations. Who could tell? Perhaps the coming liberation would find her at Paul's side after all.

'Which,' Ridley continued, 'brings me to the second and, really, the most secret part of your mission.'

Ridley tilted back in his chair and scrutinized the ceiling. 'I imagine you realize,' he said, 'we can only count on those guns being out of action for a limited period of time as a result of this sabotage?'

'Yes. Aristide said something about it taking twenty-four hours for the Germans to replace the engines he wants to destroy.'

'Much too optimistic. Twelve hours is what we reckon we can count on. No more.' Ridley leaned forward, clasping his hands before him on his desk. 'Everything depends on getting them out of action during the precisely right twelve-hour period of daylight. If they're knocked out too early or too late, we will face a disaster of unspeakable dimension. Timing, therefore, is absolutely vital to the success of this operation. Is that clear?'

His words, with all their chilling implications, were unmistakable in their meaning. There could be only one reason, Catherine thought, why the timing of the operation was so important. 'Very,' she whispered, awed by what was passing between them.

Ridley took a second piece of paper from his folder and slid it across the desk. On it were marked the two suggested BBC code phrases Aristide had given her in Calais to bring to London as triggers for the operation if Cavendish decided to go ahead with it.

A. *Nous avons un message pour petite Berthe.*

B. *Salomon a sauté ses grands sabots.*

'You'll have memorized these already, I imagine. We will see they get to the BBC.' Ridley then explained to her the timing that each message's broadcast over the BBC would be meant to imply. 'As you see, the mission we've assigned you is simple enough. It's also, as I'm sure you have understood, absolutely vital to our most ambitious hopes. The major who brought you here will stay in close personal touch with you. He will be your liaison to me and my people if you need anything or have any questions.' He got up and walked around the desk towards her offering, as he came, a sad, fleeting smile. 'I'm afraid I have burdened you after all with rather more knowledge than you wished to have.'

'Yes,' Catherine agreed in a hoarse and nervous whisper, 'you certainly have.'

'Forgive me,' Ridley replied. 'Forgive me, too, for reminding you how vital it is you never, never reveal to anyone, anywhere, under any circumstances, what I've said.' Ridley paused, his eyes, she felt, trying to gentle her with his compassion. 'Some things in such a case are better left unsaid – even if we both are aware of what they are.'

Catherine breathed a deep sigh. He could not have made it clearer, could he? She nodded, and as she did, Ridley took her hand. He drew it to his lips and kissed it softly. '*Merde*,' he said. 'I know you're going to do a wonderful job for us.'

Hans-Dieter Strömelburg's rear-engined Skoda flew up the *Autobahn* from Aachen towards the great industrial cities of Essen and Düsseldorf. It was close to midnight, and not a single vehicle shared with Strömelburg's sports car that immense concrete ribbon built to carry the multitudinous people's cars of the New Reich. Strömelburg was sitting in front. Beside him Konrad, his driver, taciturn and dour as always, focused on the road rushing past with the professional intensity he had developed during his prewar years racing for Mercedes-Benz.

Strömelburg leaned back against his leather seat and stared moodily off towards the northeast, towards that industrial basin which was Nazi Germany's heart and lungs. The Allies were up there, unassailable in their great air fleets. He could hear their muffled drone, dull and distant, and see the searchlights, blue and white pillars foraging through the dark skies pursuing them. From time to time a burst of ack-ack fire traced its fragile patterns of gold and silver lace across the night. To his right, a dull roseate glow, like the dawn of some minor sun, rose above the horizon: the core of yet another German city burning down to rubble under Allied bombs. Strömelburg shook his head. How had it come to this? Was the Thousand-Year Reich for which he had fought and struggled all his life condemned to collapse in flame and ash, to be swept over by Bolshevism's barbarous hordes as Rome had been savaged by the Visigoths?

Yet the depressing spectacle stretching away from his speeding Skoda did not dim Strömelburg's faith in the vision of his youth. Germany, he was convinced, could still win the war. It all came down to the invasion, the invasion, the invasion. Defeat that, and the Reich would survive, his values endure, his own horizons widen. He picked a sandwich from the picnic basket on the floor under his feet and, with his teeth, pulled the cork from a bottle of Chambolle-Musigny.

These trips of his to Berlin to answer a convocation to Kalten-brunner's office followed a well-established routine. He would leave his Neuilly villa at 9 P.M. His cook always sent with him a picnic dinner and a second package full of the rather considerable scavengings available to a

Gestapo chief in Paris: *foie gras*, butter, chocolate, ham, champagne. That basket was destined for Strömelburg's parents and his sister. They lived in Magdeburg, not far from Berlin, where Strömelburg's father still taught in the local *Gymnasium*. He would arrive, as he always did, just in time to breakfast with them, shower and change clothes, then leave for his meeting on Prinz-Albrecht-Strasse. After a final soporific swig of his wine, Strömelburg leaned back and went to sleep.

He woke up shortly before 7 A.M., the acrid stench of smoke, the kind that rises from dying embers rather than a blaze, clogging his nostrils. They were off the *Autobahn*, riding up the bridge over the Elbe towards the city's heart. As they touched the crest of the bridge's rise, Strömelburg gasped. The centre of his hometown lay stretched before him, a field of smoking ruins, parts of it still being devoured by orange sheets of flame. Only the cathedral stood intact, a gaunt, Gothic skeleton casting its spectral warning of man's folly above the ruins. Thank God, he told Konrad, his parents lived in the suburbs and the Allies had evidently been after the city centre.

That was not quite so. As Konrad turned into the leafy Goethestrasse on which his family home was located, Strömelburg shrieked in horror. One side of the street had been devastated by a stick of bombs – his side. Konrad accelerated down the street. Nothing but a smoking pyramid of ruins stood on the site of Strömelburg's home, an occasional flame still picking its way through the few reminders of his family that remained to be consumed.

Strömelburg leaped from the car and rushed to the ruins, screaming his parents' names as though somehow his voice might conjure their spirits out of the ashes. A neighbour, pulling what possessions she could from the wreckage of her own home, told Strömelburg his sister was in a cellar across the street. He found her there, unhurt, babbling incoherently in horror and grief. Finally she managed to tell him what had happened. She and their father and mother had rushed to the cellar at the first alarm. Their father, a very methodical man, had strapped on the survival knapsack he always carried in an air raid, an emergency kit of water, medicine, sausage, bread and a bottle of *Schnapps*. They had huddled there together listening to the roar of the planes. When the bomb had struck, their mother had been killed instantly. Somehow, his sister had managed to clamber out of the collapsing ruins through a window or a hole. She heard a scream and turned back to their father. Like a skier caught in a bank of deep snow, he was trapped in ruins up to his chest, absolutely unable to move. She screamed for help, for rescuers. Then the fire broke out.

She had had to stand there, helpless, she told Strömelburg, while the flames ate across the debris to their father, finally immolating him in the pile of rubble from which he could not free himself. Her last image of him, she shrieked, was of the flames reaching the little knapsack that had been going to save them all in an emergency, finding the bottle of *Schnapps* and exploding it in a fount of orange flame that had set her father's hair alight and ended his private *Götterdämmerung*.

The horrified Strömelburg joined the volunteers pulling away the wreckage of his home to find his parents' bodies. At 8:30 he had to leave. Even personal tragedies as great as his could not keep an SS officer from a meeting with Kaltenbrunner. His grey uniform covered with black smudges, his chest heavy with hatred, Strömelburg got back into his Skoda to complete his journey to Berlin, leaving his sister to bury his parents in a mass grave.

Horst Kopkow, the chief of the Gestapo's counterespionage service, was aghast. Not only was his subordinate Hans-Dieter Strömelburg late for his convocation in the offices of SS *Gruppenführer* Ernst Kaltenbrunner, but he looked as though he had crawled through the gutters of Prinz-Albrecht-Strasse to get there. Yet Strömelburg did not utter so much as a word of apology or explanation to the *Gruppenführer*. He settled into his chair and returned Kopkow's glare of reproach with a defiant stare of his own as though somehow the black smears covering his uniform, the filth all over his face and hands were badges of honour, not disgrace.

Kaltenbrunner had stopped in mid-sentence in his recital to follow Strömelburg to his seat with a disapproving glance. He resumed with a cough. The *Gruppenführer* had a talent for making the most galvanic announcement sound as banal as the recitation of the items on a laundry list. The subject of his sermon for this Thursday, June 1, to all his Gestapo counterespionage chiefs for Occupied Europe was the final step in the reorganization of the Reich's intelligence services into one central organization under the RSHA. Effective immediately, he informed them, the Abwehr offices and officers inside their territorial jurisdiction would fall under their discipline and authority.

While he droned through the bureaucratic implications of that, Strömelburg fingered the envelope Kaltenbrunner's aide had passed to him in the outer office. It had come in overnight from his Paris headquarters. As discreetly as he could, he fingered open the seal and through eyes still smarting from his tears, looked at the text. It was from the Doctor.

'The following message received at 0315 from Sevenoaks destined for the transmitter we have installed in Lille,' it said. 'Please advise disposition urgently.'

As Strömelburg turned to the text, Kaltenbrunner was congratulating them all on the fact that the reorganization of the Reich's intelligence services had been completed in time to take on the greatest intelligence challenge of the war: defeating the Allied invasion.

At Kaltenbrunner's request for comments, Strömelburg rose. His fellow officers who had not seen him enter the room were appalled. Throughout the SS, Strömelburg had a well-deserved reputation for dressing like a tailor's dummy, for spending as much time cultivating his appearance as studying his dossiers. The sight of him with his eyes reddened, dried yellow mucus caked to the skin below his nostrils, his grey SS uniform a mass of tears, dust and stains was as disturbing as it was unexpected.

Strömelburg began by describing the trap he had baited for the SOE in Lille; then, dropping his voice for effect, how two weeks earlier, the SOE had risen to the bait offered by the set. Finally, he brandished the Doctor's cable in the air.

'This message was radioed by London to our doubled set last night,' he announced.

'Cavendish for Aristide Calais Most Urgent,' he read out. 'Your sabotage plan is hereby approved and execution will be ordered via BBC code phrases you suggested stop Courier returning via Lysander Operation Tango June 4 bringing one vital modification for plan which must be prepared before execution date plus strictest instructions on timing of operation stop Timing of action is essential repeat essential stop Vital you follow timing instructions with greatest care stop Heartiest congratulations and good hunting.'

'What is it they want to sabotage?' Kaltenbrunner growled.

'I have no idea,' Strömelburg replied, 'but whatever it is, London considers it important enough to send an agent into France to see that it's carried out.'

Kaltenbrunner's aides had fixed a map of the Channel defences to his wall for the meeting. Kopkow got up and strode over to it.

'What they want to sabotage is not important, at least not for now,' he said. 'What appears to me vital in that cable is the importance they attach to the timing of the sabotage.' He glanced at the map. Even an apothecary's assistant could understand the immense military significance of the Calais coastline. 'Why? Very possibly because their sabotage is meant to be coordinated with another, far more important operation.'

He turned to Strömelburg. 'It is abundantly clear what our next step should be.'

For four years the little ritual had been as religiously, as exactingly observed as any liturgy prescribed by the ecclesiastical calendar. Indeed, throughout that dark night of Occupation, its faithful observance had represented a kind of aural umbilical cord linking thousands of French men and women to London and freedom. Twice each night, at 7:30 and again at 9:15, the opening notes of Beethoven's *Fifth Symphony*, rising from an underground studio at Bush House in the heart of London, had served as its prelude. After the last notes, an announcer informed his audience, '*Et maintenant voici quelques messages personnels*' – 'And now, here are a few personal messages.' At those words, all across France, in stables and sitting rooms, garrets and cafés, on isolated farms and in the slums of Paris, the men and women of the Resistance tensed. Employing a strangely detached, almost sepulchral voice, the announcer droned his way through a long series of seemingly nonsensical, unrelated phrases:

'The vichyssoise is warm'

'The lilacs have bloomed'

'The weather at Suez is hot'

Since April, London had been deliberately playing on German nerves by suddenly increasing, then decreasing the number of messages broadcast each night. Initially, the Germans had reacted to the unexpected volume of messages exactly as the Allies had planned; they had put their troops on invasion alert from Bordeaux to Dunkirk. So many German soldiers had passed so many sleepless nights as a result of the ebb and flow in the volume of the messages that Von Rundstedt himself had finally declared the whole business an Allied hoax designed to exhaust his troops. The Allies, he proclaimed, would never employ so obvious a technique to herald their invasion.

Originally, the *messages personnels* had been just what they were supposed to be – personal messages, designed to tell a wife, a father that a husband or a son had arrived in England after crossing the Pyrenees or sailing the Channel. Later, they had been employed to control arms drops, to announce the arrival of a secret agent, to trigger an ambush or order a sabotage. Now, on this evening of Thursday, June 1, they heralded at last the event for which so many had waited so long: the invasion.

The role of the French Resistance, of the sabotage networks of the SOE in supporting the assault was vital. A whole series of plans, most designated by colours – violet, green, blue – had been prepared to coordinate their attacks on railway lines, German communications, transport and military installations. To pass the order for action to the field, London had devised an ingenious system. Each Resistance network with a D-Day task had been assigned a pair of code phrases. The first, the 'alert' message, was to be broadcast over the BBC on either the first or the fifteenth of the month. Hearing it, the network would be put on alert and required to listen each night for a fortnight for the second, 'action' message. If that message was broadcast, the network was to execute its assigned tasks in forty-eight hours in anticipation of 'a major event'. It was exactly as Hans-Dieter Strömelburg had predicted to his acolyte the Doctor on the night they'd arrested Alex Wild: the Allies would announce they were coming over the BBC.

Indeed, the Germans had suspected that since October 1943 because of the work of Strömelburg's Gestapo. On September 7,1943, the Gestapo had arrested three newly arrived French members of an SOE circuit. Under interrogation they had revealed that before leaving London they had been given 'alert' and 'action' messages to sabotage the railways in Brittany in support of the invasion. They further explained the manner in which the 'alert' message would be broadcast on the first and fifteenth of the month and the 'action' message – if the invasion was on – in the fortnight to follow. On October 10 all the German commands in the West had been informed of the code phrases the trio had revealed and the *modus operandi* the Allies would use in employing them. The phrases were a couplet from the 'Chanson d'Automne' by Paul Verlaine:

'Les sanglots longs des violons de l'automne
Blessent mon coeur d'une langueur monotone.'

It was, it would have seemed, an intelligence coup of major proportions – except for the fact those phrases had nothing to do with the invasion at all. They were part of a deception scheme of Colonel Henry Ridley and the London Controlling Section. The scheme was called 'Starkey,' and it had been prepared for the summer of 1943. Francis Suthill's summons to Churchill's office in May 1943 had been a particularly devious part of the scheme because Ridley knew through *Ultra* what the SOE did not know: that Suthill's 'Prosper' network had been penetrated by the Gestapo. Churchill's message to the young SOE officer that day had been simple – and untrue. An invasion in the autumn, Suthill was told, was highly likely. He was to get back to put his network on a war footing to support it.

'Starkey's' object was to persuade the Germans the Allies would land in France in early September 1943 – thus holding a maximum number of German divisions in the West away from the Russian Front. Beginning in June 1943, the unsuspecting SOE had been told to send its organizers into the field with alert and action messages in case, as it was hinted to the SOE's chieftains, the invasion should come in the autumn. In early 1944, to pave the way for the real invasion, the messages sent out in 1943 were all cancelled and replaced by new ones. In the process, by some ghastly, inexplicable error, the Verlaine couplet had been reassigned to an SOE network operating in central France.

That was, however, only one set of messages. Among the beneficiaries of the new – and real – messages sent out by SOE London in the spring of

1944 was the Doctor on Avenue Foch. For the timid subordinate of Hans-Dieter Strömelburg, it was the culmination of his radio game. Every single one of the fifteen SOE networks he was impersonating to London had been assigned an alert and an action message. As a result, no one in France followed the nightly litany of the BBC's *messages personnels* more closely than the Doctor did. Alone in his third-floor office on Avenue Foch, the Doctor adjusted the special antenna the Signal Services on the Boulevard Suchet had given him so he could avoid their jamming of the BBC's broadcasts. For several minutes, he listened impassive. The messages being read Thursday, June 1, in the curiously disembodied voice of the announcer did not concern him. Suddenly, he sat up. 'The kickoff is at three o'clock.' That message was for the network he had baptized 'Waltz' in Saint-Quentin.

'Electricity dates from the twentieth century.' That was for Saturn in Rennes. Then, one by one, as the Doctor sat, stunned and unbelieving, the rest of the messages came pouring in, all fifteen of them, exactly as London had said they would, as faithful to their rendezvous as those Halifaxes thundering out of the night with their cargoes of arms had been to rendezvous he had set for them with his Gestapo reception committees.

He rushed upstairs to Hans-Dieter Strömelburg's office. The invasion, he announced, might come at any time during the next fifteen days. The *Obersturmbahnführer* was exhausted by his rushed return from Berlin. 'Get all that down on paper and on the teletype to Berlin and OB West,' he commanded.

Abruptly, he changed subjects. 'Tell me, Doctor, when is London next scheduled to broadcast to Gilbert's radio?'

'Midday tomorrow.'

'Be sure the Boulevard Suchet doesn't miss it,' he ordered. 'We're looking for details of an operation called Tango.'

At 2:30 the following afternoon, Strömelburg's private line on Avenue Foch rang. It was the Signal Interception Service of the Boulevard Suchet with the text of SOE London's midday message to its Air Operations Officer.

'Cavendish to Paul,' it read. 'Operation Tango hereby ordered for four June Field Four stop One bod coming in please convoy Paris stop Return will lift RAF pilots Whitley and Fieldhouse per your request cable 163 stop Code letter T Tommy stop BBC message Copenhagen clings to the sea confirm next sked end.'

Strömelburg acknowledged the Boulevard Suchet's work with a grunt. He was, in reality, delighted. Field Four was one of the two fields Gilbert employed that were easy to keep under surveillance. The safe house was a one-storey barn set in a glade which provided his watchers good cover and was located just minutes from the field. To clear his passengers by train to Paris, Gilbert had to employ a village station so small it was easy for Strömelburg's agents already on board to spot Gilbert and his passengers getting on the train.

Konrad, Hans-Dieter Strömelburg's driver, had taken an intense personal dislike to the French agent Gilbert from the first time he had picked him up on a darkened Paris street corner. It was only now, dozens of secret rendezvous later, that he realized why. The Frenchman always insisted on riding in the back seat of the car, as though to mark by his position the social distinction between them. Who the hell did he think he was?

Even Strömelburg himself always sat up front beside him. Yet Strömelburg, he knew, was devoted to the Frenchman. No one in the service could murmur a word against him in his presence. Konrad drove into the Gestapo chief's Neuilly villa at the rear entrance, the car's approach screened from any eyes that might be watching from the street. Sure enough, there was Strömelburg at the head of the stairs, arms outstretched like some father welcoming home his son after a long absence. The sight never ceased to amaze and disgust Konrad.

Strömelburg took his prize agent into his sitting room and waved him to one of his big leather armchairs. He poured him a sherry, mixed himself a whisky, then settled with a sigh into his own armchair. He raised his glass to Gilbert. *'Prost,'* he murmured, taking a long sip of his drink. He was in civilian clothes, and he stretched his feet out before him, wiggling them slightly as though they somehow merited the fascinated study he was applying to them. His shoes, Paul noted, were burnished to a brilliant ebony glow.

'Remarkable, my dear friend' – Strömelburg sounded almost nostalgic – 'how much we've been able to accomplish together since you first came into this room – how long ago was it?'

'Just over six months. The nineteenth of October, to be exact.'

'Such a precise memory. I suppose you aviators are all like that. Isn't it funny? Usualy, as one gets older time's passage seems to accelerate with distressing rapidity. But somehow this war has reversed all that. It seems to me years since you and I sat here for the first time.'

'You're turning philosopher on me, Hans.' Paul smiled.

'Well,' Strömelburg sighed, 'I have reasons for that. You've done a great job, you know.' He turned towards his agent. Was his smile sardonic? the Frenchman wondered. He had never observed a sense of humour in Strömelburg; therefore he rarely knew what feelings his smiles concealed. 'Better than you yourself know.' Strömelburg took a long, reflective swallow of his whisky. 'There is something I wish to tell you. Win or lose, when this war is over, Germany will take care of those who were committed to us. You were. If it comes to it, we'll see that you get a new identity, get to some neutral country with enough money to start a new life. The ground's already been prepared. There's money in Switzerland, South America, people in place, waiting. There will even be people in the Vatican to help.'

'Hans' – Paul was petulant – 'why are you telling me this, for Christ's sake? You make it sound as though Germany's already lost the war, and the English haven't even invaded yet.'

'I'm telling you because it is important that you know.' There was such a rich, reassuring note to Strömelburg's voice when he wanted it there that it occurred to Paul he would have made a better Lutheran preacher than a Gestapo officer – had he but a fraction of the belief in God he had in his Führer. 'Knowing it will comfort you as it will me in the difficult days ahead.' Strömelburg waved his glass, then proceeded to shift conversational gears. 'When's your next flight coming in?'

'The fourth, on Field Four, down near Angers. Routine. One guy coming, a couple of RAF types on the run going back.'

Strömelburg nodded in grave acknowledgement of information he had known for hours. 'Dear friend, I'm going to tell you something that will explain my little prelude. I've got to take your incoming passenger.'

If his words upset his agent in any way, Strömelburg could detect no indication of it on his face. Gilbert shrugged. 'It was obvious it would come to that one day.'

'Evidently. Your agent, we think, will be going on up north to Calais when he leaves you in Paris. We'll wait and take him up there. I will order my people to do it in a way that won't lead back to you, but with things like this you can never be sure, so I wanted you to know. If the English suddenly decide to invite you across the Channel to pin a medal on your chest, I suggest you decline the honour.'

Gilbert sipped at his sherry and extended the complicity of a wink to his German friend. 'It seems to me a couple of medals is the very least they owe me, don't you?'

'Indeed, dear friend, but there's no reward quite so ungratifying as a posthumous decoration. Also, be wary of any unexpected invitation from your associates in the Underground. If they get wind of this, they may decide to take things into their own hands.'

This was a warning Gilbert took seriously. 'Maybe I'll have to start going around armed.'

'I think you should.' Strömelburg set his whisky on the mantelpiece and went to his desk. He took one of his personal cards and on the back wrote: 'The bearer of this card is to be extended all facilities and any assistance he may request. His identity may be verified personally with me.' The Gestapo chief signed it and stamped it with his personal seal.

'Take this,' he told his agent. 'This will cover you if you're picked up by a patrol while you're carrying an arm. But if you do think the Resistance is on to you, then drop the game and come in. We'll take care of you. Now, let's just go over the operation. You're using that same shed as the safe house for Field Four you've always used?'

His agent nodded.

'And you'll get your train the next morning at the station of La Minitre?'

Again the Frenchman acquiesced with a nod.

'All right. I'll have people around the shed, up at the field and along the path. They'll cover you on your way to the station in the morning. For God's sake, don't do anything out of the ordinary or change your route, because they'll be keyed up to jump if anything seems to be going wrong. Bony's people from Rue Lauriston will be on the train.' They were Strömelburg's French Gestapo officers employed for tasks such as this one. 'Break contact in Paris exactly as you normally would. We'll put as much ground between you and the arrest as we can.'

'You must really want this guy.'

'I do.'

'Is he that important?'

'My dear Gilbert, agents as agents are rarely important. What is often important is the information they carry.'

'Halt!'

The *Feldgendarm* had sprung from the shadows with such feline swiftness Paul almost fell from his bike in surprise. His bicycle lamp, partially dimmed with its blackout covering, caught a glimmering of the German's brass breastplate and, what was more menacing, the barrel of his Schmeisser machine pistol trained on his chest. In the shadows, Paul sensed the other members of the man's patrol moving around him.

'*Ausweis.*'

Paul reached into his wallet for the special permit that allowed him to circulate in the streets of Paris after curfew. The *Feldgendarm* regarded it as suspiciously as a bank clerk might study a bill he believed to be counterfeit.

'Where do you think you're going with this?' he asked.

Paul gestured down Rue de Provence towards a faint bar of light that marked the entrance to a brothel, the One Two Two.

'No, you're not,' the *Feldgendarm* told him, 'They don't let Frenchmen in there at night. You're lying.' He gave the *Ausweis* a disdainful flick of his fingernail. 'I think we'll take you in and run a check on this.' At his words, Paul sensed the *Feldgendarm's* fellow soldiers tightening their circle around him.

'Just wait a minute, Corporal.' Paul had put every vibrant trace of authority he could into his tone of voice. The satisfaction with which he noticed the German straighten up at his unexpected words could not be measured. 'I have something else you will now read, and having read it you and these clumsy oafs of yours will disappear before you have hopelessly compromised my operation and I turn you all in to Avenue Foch.' His words came in a surly hiss as he was reaching into his pocket for the card Strömelburg had given him an hour earlier. It seemed as oportune a moment as any to measure its effectiveness.

What a shame, he thought, passing it to his interrogator, that you can't notice a man going pale in the darkness. The German studied it, grunted, then muttered an order to his patrol. Paul sensed the men withdrawing the little human cordon they had placed around him. He took back his card and returned it with a feeling of unexpected pleasure to his wallet. It was an appreciable addition to his armoury.

'Have a piece for me,' the *Feldgendarm* called after Paul's departing figure – then added, in a mumble Paul was not meant to hear, but did, 'you French pig.'

The madam of the One Two Two was a thoroughly professional lady and Paul a valued client of her establishment. The manner in which she dealt with the situation presented by Paul's unexpected and as far as she was concerned, untimely appearance was indicative of the woman's command of her *métier*. As discreetly as she could, she barred his path towards her sitting room, filled with its evening quota of uniformed Germans, many of them drunk.

'Perhaps monsieur has a preference?' she inquired demurely.

'Is Danielle here?' he asked.

The madam smiled. 'Why don't you go upstairs? The girl will show you to a nice room and Danielle will join you as soon as she's free.'

The smile that was fixed to the prostitute's face as artificially as the features of a Mardi Gras mask disappeared the instant she entered the room and realized it was Paul who was waiting for her.

'Thank God it's you!' she exclaimed, sinking down on the bed beside him. 'Christ, I really need a few minutes' rest. I think half the Germans in Paris have clambered in and out of my pussy today.'

Paul looked at her closely. He usually called at the One Two Two early in the afternoon, when the girls had just gone on duty and with a little effort, a client might persuade himself they enjoyed their work. Now, after ten hours, the pouches under her eyes and along her chin had gone slack with fatigue.

'Gimme a cigarette,' she said. 'Have you got one of those blonds you're always carrying?' She accepted the black-market Camel he offered her and gasped after her first draw with the frenzy of an asthmatic struggling for air in a crisis. 'So, how come you're wandering around Paris at this time of night?'

'I have an emergency. When are you due to transmit to London next?'

'Tomorrow.'

Paul handed her a brief, coded message. 'Can you send this for me? It's urgent.'

She looked at it, obviously appraising its length in relation to whatever else she might have to transmit. She nodded. 'Okay.'

'I would like to get a confirmation London received it.'

She glanced at him through the grey gauze of cigarette smoke enveloping her, evaluating him, it seemed to Paul, with the same steady gaze she employed to measure a client's interest.

'Where will you be at one-thirty tomorrow?'

Clever girl, Paul thought: she's not giving out her phone number.

'I'll be having an *apéritif* at the side bar of the Brasserie Lorraine. The barman's name is Henri. Tell him you want to speak to me. He knows who I am.'

The girl took a condom from her bedside table, opened it, threw its wrapping on the floor for the maid's benefit, placed Paul's text inside and, rolling it tight, slipped it into her handbag.

'All right. Be a darling,' she said, pointing to a chair; 'go sit over there so I can stretch out and close my eyes for a minute.' She squashed out her cigarette and lay down.

Barely ten minutes later, Paul heard the maid's knock and the familiar words 'Time, monsieur, madame.' His exhausted courier was sound asleep.

Saturday, June 3, 1944, promised to be that choicest of creations, the perfect day in June. Yet already, as the weekenders wandered through St James's and Hyde Park and the sculls darted like water flies along the Thames, the first troops, tanks and guns were moving towards their landing barges in the invasion ports. At mid-morning, as they began to load, a handful of the men who would command them assembled in Room 100A of Norfolk House for a final review of the latest intelligence available on the German army's order of battle, the disposition of Hitler's forces in France. General Walter Bedell Smith, Eisenhower's Chief of Staff, presided. Thanks to the men and women of the Resistance, Eisenhower would start the invasion of Europe with an advantage few great captains in history had ever had. He would know, with very few exceptions, the location and approximate strength of every major enemy unit opposing him. The real concern of General Smith and the men around him, however, was not so much how many troops the Germans had in France as how Hitler would use them.

The intelligence staff broke the coming assault into four phases. The first, and easiest, phase would be D-Day morning itself, when the six Allied infantry and two airborne divisions making the initial assault would be expected to encounter only four understrength and immobile coastal divisions. D-Day evening the second phase would begin. Then the Germans, Smith's intelligence men told him, would 'send for armoured reinforcements' – but only, it was hoped, from the area of the Seventh Army, the weaker of the two armies facing the Allies. The third phase would cover the next forty-eight hours, during which time the Allies should be able to repulse the Seventh Army's counterattack with the forces already ashore because 'the implied threats to other areas – Calais' ought to still be holding the Panzer divisions of the Fifteenth Army, Hitler's finest, in Pas-de-Calais.

Sixty hours after the landings, however, on the evening of D+2, the Germans would see that those attacks were failing and realize what was happening in Normandy. It was at that point that they would decide on the massive reinforcement of Normandy and drive their armour from Calais to the Cotentin. With that decision, Phase IV – 'the critical point in the struggle,' the intelligence men intoned – would begin. The question then would be whether the Allies could cling to their Norman foothold in the face of Von Rundstedt's massive armoured counterattack.

Nothing depressed Bedell Smith quite so much as hearing – yet again – those predictions. Like most Americans, he placed very little faith in the London Controlling Section's deception schemes. Yet he was also unhappily aware that the invasion's success or failure would in all probability depend on whether or not they worked. He turned to Ridley, sitting in his usual haze of cigarette smoke. 'Okay, colonel,' he said. 'What are the chances your *Fortitude* scheme can hold those Panzers up there in Pas-de-Calais after D plus 2?'

Ridley looked at him through drooping half-moon eyes. 'I don't know,' he replied. 'Only time will tell. We do have one encouraging report.' He picked a piece of paper from a folder before him. 'Hitler saw the Japanese ambassador May 27. Washington has just sent us their intercept of his report to Tokyo. The figures Hitler used for our strength here would indicate the imaginary division of our First US Army group have found their way into their estimates of our order of battle. Will they stay there? Will Hitler come to the conclusion they're going to land in Calais four to seven days after we touch down in Normandy?'

Ridley shrugged. 'Unfortunately, Hitler also told the ambassador he would like nothing better than to strike one great blow as soon as possible. We have three critical channels to persuade him to keep those Panzers of his in Calais. Two are proven, and thus far they've held up rather well. However, they are both Abwehr channels. The Abwehr, as you know, sir, is in rather bad odour at OKW these days.'

He paused to rub his receding hairline. 'We've set up a third channel recently which by its very nature is directed to Himmler's RSHA. Its value is therefore unproven. Will they fall for it? It's impossible to judge. We can only pray.'

Smith glared down the table at him. He wanted something more concrete than a deception officer's nebulous hopes. 'You'll have to do better than that,' he rasped. 'If those Panzers arrive as Intelligence estimates, we'd better start planning on how to evacuate our bridgehead, not expand it.'

On that gloomy note, Smith closed the meeting. As its participants began to leave in subdued silence, Sir Stewart Menzies nudged Ridley away from the departing flow. Humour was not something for which the dour Scot was noted, but a suggestion of a smile played on his lips. 'I had a call from Uncle Claude just before I came,' he whispered. 'You could have been more reassuring for poor old Bedell. We've just had a message from the other side of the Channel. Your German friends have risen to the bait.'

In France, that last fortnight in May had been a season as lovely as anyone could remember, a matchless procession of cloudless days and starlit nights. As each perfect day succeeded its predecessor, tension had mounted. All along the Channel coast German units had been on an invasion alert, scrutinizing the seas for the harbingers of an advancing Allied fleet. Behind their defences the French had tensed too, certain the invasion was imminent. As May turned to June and still the Allies failed to come, the collaborationist press began to trumpet that 'the Allies have missed the bus.'

Paul, tweed sports jacket thrown over his arm, strolled up the Avenue des Ternes towards the Brasserie Lorraine, an example of that press, his ever-present *Je Suis Partout*, stuck into his coat pocket. The terrace of the Brasserie was packed – girls fresh and laughing in their summer blouses, men attentive to each nuance of their eyes. Never, it occurred to Paul, had his countrywomen seemed as beautiful as they did in this fourth springtime of occupation, lean from a quasi-total lack of fats or sweets in their diet, muscled and firm from miles of walking and bicycle riding. Deprivation had its advantages.

He went to the bar, ordered a beer and started to read, yet again, his paper. Its front-page cartoon could still bring a bitter smile to his lips. It

300

displayed a barman at the 'Café Résistance' offering his client his latest cocktail: English gin, American whisky, Russian vodka. 'Pour in a generous ration of French blood and stir well,' the fictional barman was telling his client.

Promptly at 1:30, the Brasserie's real barman came over to Paul. 'For you,' he said jerking his head towards the telephone at the corner of the bar.

It was his courier from the One Two Two. 'It went,' she said. 'They acknowledged receipt.' Then she hung up. Pleased with her brevity and obvious sense for security, Paul returned, finished his beer and left.

He headed towards the Arc de Triomphe, his stride quick, his mood buoyant. His next meeting was on the other side of Paris to work out arrangements to pick up his two departing RAF pilots at the Gare d'Austerlitz and convoy them down to his field outside Angers. From now on, he would have to play out an elaborate and potentially deadly charade. No one must be allowed to suspect that the mission was going to be aborted. He would have to stay alert for any false note that might give away his game to Strömelburg's watchers.

Strömelburg would be furious when London failed to broadcast the confirmation message over the BBC Sunday night. He wanted the agent who was supposed to be arriving desperately, that was clear. As long as he gave his Gestapo watchdogs no reason to suspect him, however, Paul felt sure he would come out of the operation unscathed. After all, it wouldn't be the first time London had cancelled a mission at the last moment. Strömelburg's reassuring word, pledging him an escape if things went wrong, seemed proof enough to Paul that he enjoyed the Germans' complete confidence. Nor, on balance, did he think Strömelburg would order his men to take the RAF pilots when London scrubbed the mission. Why would he give away his game for so inconsequential a prize? No, Strömelburg would let the incident pass and wait for London to reschedule the mission – which, of course, it would not do.

Calculating his permutations of treachery, Henri Lemaire, alias Paul, alias Gilbert, was exhilarated. He existed to outwit others, to manipulate them, to survive as an animal on his wits and his instincts. From the recklessness of his boyhood to his quest for sky and storm in his open planes, danger had been the drug his psyche craved and without which he could not live. Now, on this glorious spring day in the loveliest city in the world, he was vibrantly happy because he was where he always wanted to be: balanced on the knife edge of existence.

The news was not bad – it was devastating. The matchless spring weather that had held Europe in its gentle embrace for a fortnight was about to end. A storm stood poised at the western approaches of Britain. It had begun as a minor disturbance, baptized L-5 by SHAEF's meteorologists when it first appeared off Newfoundland Monday, May 29. As it moved eastward across the Atlantic, it had grown in strength and intensity. For the past few hours, SHAEF's meteorologists had clung to the diminishing hope that somehow the storm's path might veer north away from the invasion zone.

That was not to be the case. The storm, Group Captain John Stagg, Eisenhower's chief meteorologist, warned him at Southwick House Saturday evening, June 3, would almost certainly hit the Channel with force-5 winds, cloud and churning seas on Monday, June 5, just as the invasion fleet was heading for the Norman shore. It was the worst single piece of news the American could have received. With great reluctance, he ordered a twenty-four-hour postponement of the assault, to be confirmed after a last-minute review of the weather at 0415 Sunday, June 4.

Shortly after Eisenhower made his decision, a green telephone rang in the underground offices of the London Controlling Section. Just as *Overlord* depended on precise and intricate timing to mesh the thousands of elements which composed it, so implementing Ridley's *Fortitude* deception plan hinged on its own pattern of exquisite timing. Ridley immediately sat down to calculate the impact the delay was going to have on the three channels he counted on to plant his scheme on the Germans: his double agents, Brutus and Garbo, and the third leg he had just added, now code-named 'Queen's Gambit.'

Of the three, Brutus, the Polish Air Force officer, was the easiest to handle. According to the *Fortitude* script, Brutus had spent the last week in May travelling in southeastern England visiting Ridley's imaginary first US Army Group in his capacity as its Polish liaison officer. On Wednesday, May 31, he had returned to London and begun to send a series of critical dispatches to his Abwehr controller in Paris, Colonel Reile. They represented the core of Brutus' contribution to *Fortitude*. With them, Ridley meant to tie together for the German's benefit the bits and pieces of misinformation he had been feeding them for over a month in fake wireless messages, the displays of fake troop camps, the tidbits passed by other double agents.

Brutus gave the Germans the name of the imaginary army group's commander, General Patton, and revealed that it was composed of two armies, the Third US and First Canadian, and was counterbalanced by a second, somewhat smaller army group in the south of England, the 21st, under General Montgomery. That, of course, represented the Allies' real force, of whose existence and disposition the Germans were aware

302

through their wireless intercepts of the group's real radio traffic.

A few days later, Brutus had further elucidated the composition of FUSAG, providing the Germans with the identities of a certain number of its imaginary corps and divisions. No other agent could have sent such detailed information to the Germans and been believed. Brutus was able to do so because he was the only double agent Ridley had who was a serving officer. On the morning of D+1, Ridley planned to offer the Germans the icing on the cake. He was going to sent Brutus on an inspection trip of FUSAG's advance headquarters at Dover Castle. There Brutus would observe, for the Abwehr's benefit, FUSAG's imaginary units making evident preparations for an embarkation. He would even be allowed to overhear a few indiscreet remarks from General Patton himself, never one, as the Germans knew, to keep a tight hold on his tongue. Ridley's idea was to have him back in London on the evening of D+2 so he could send the Abwehr in Paris a message summarizing everything he had seen and heard – all of it pointing, obviously, to an attack on Pas-de-Calais. Since Ridley had not yet informed the Germans their precious Pole was going to Dover, delaying his imaginary departure by twenty-four hours to accommodate a postponement of the invasion was simple.

The case of Garbo, the Spanish double agent, was more complex. Eisenhower had finally been persuaded to let Garbo tell his Abwehr controller in Madrid at 0300 on D-Day that the invasion fleet was at sea. That would be three and a half hours before the first wave of troops would actually go ashore. His source of information, according to the scheme, was going to be one of his network of imaginary agents, 5(2), a Gibraltarian waiter who was supposed to be working in the servicemen's canteen at the Hiltingbury camp at which the Third Canadian Infantry Division was quartered. The division was in fact going to be landing on Juno Beach on D-Day morning.

To make the story plausible to German ears, Ridley's deceivers had concocted an elaborate scheme. In May, the Canadians had participated in an invasion exercise which the English were sure German aerial reconnaissance would spot. On the eve of the exercise, the Gibraltarian had told Garbo in a state of high excitement that 'the Canadian division has been issued two days of cold rations, life jackets and rubber bags in which to vomit during a sea voyage and has just left camp.'

Garbo had leaped to the conclusion that the invasion was under way and informed Otto Kuhlenthal, his Abwehr controller in Madrid. He had provided all the details the imaginary Gibraltarian was supposed to have furnished him, right down to the vomit bags. When, forty-eight hours later, the Gibraltarian reported it had all been an exercise and the Canadians were back in camp, Garbo had exploded. He had told

Kuhlenthal he was going to sack his Gibraltarian, who, he complained, 'has displayed the ability of a simpleton.'

That had provided one of those delicious moments in deception which Ridley so savoured. Kuhlenthal had reacted exactly as the English wanted him to, pleading with Garbo to save the very petard on which Ridley later planned to hoist him. 'We should not reproach 5(2),' Kuhlenthal radioed his crack agent. 'After all, the troops and a majority of the officers undoubtedly left the camp convinced it was to be the invasion and only a few high officers knew the real objective was an exercise.'

So, at his insistence, the Gibraltarian had been kept on Garbo's rolls. Ridley's plan now called for him to furnish Garbo exactly the same story of the Canadians' departure on the eve of the invasion, right down to the life jackets and vomit bags – but with one critical addition: he would tell Garbo the advance party of a new division had arrived to take over the Third Division's barracks. Clearly, the Canadians weren't coming back. This time, it was the real thing.

The story was complex enough, yet there had been still another problem to resolve if the idea was going to work. The Abwehr's listening post in Madrid which received Garbo's radio messages went off the air at midnight and came back on at 7 A.M. The critical invasion message had to go out at 3 A.M. So Garbo had to find a pretext to keep Madrid open twenty-four hours a day during the first week in June. Once again it was the Abwehr's Kuhlenthal who had thoughtfully provided the answer. On May 26, he had radioed Garbo that Berlin wanted to know urgently 'if the British 52nd Division is remaining in its camps in the Glasgow area where it is on manoeuvres.'

As it happened, one of Garbo's imaginary agents was located in Scotland. He was a Greek seaman deserter and an ardent Communist who thought he was working for a Soviet spy ring. Garbo informed Madrid his Greek would keep an eye on the 52nd Division's shipping in the Clyde River and report back the instant the fleet sailed. As there was no guarantee that that would happen between 7 A.M. and midnight, Garbo had suggested to Kuhlenthal that he keep his radio open twenty-four hours a day until the troops had embarked. Obligingly, Kuhlenthal had agreed. That arrangement, Ridley reflected, would accommodate a delay in the invasion admirably well.

'Queen's gambit,' however, was a different problem. Brutus and Garbo operated from British soil; the opening acts of Queen's Gambit had to take place inside Occupied Europe. Whether the invasion went ahead on time or not, Ridley had to get his pieces into play if the ploy was to have any hope of success. Half an hour after his call from Southwick House, he ordered the final arrangements for Queen's Gambit to proceed.

'Sorry, old boy, but those Sherman tanks of yours simply aren't worth a damn. Their armour plate's so thin a circus strongman could punch a hole through it. Imagine what a Panzer's shell can do.' The young Guardsman uttered his opinion with the knowing assertiveness of a man who had yet to hear his first German tank round fired in anger. He was one of the seemingly inexhaustible supply of young officers Deirdre could turn up as extra men at a moment's notice. She had provided him as an escort for Catherine on their evening out in London.

They had begun with dinner at her apartment. T.F. had got steaks from the generals' commissary through Ingersoll, who seemed to have contacts everywhere. He had been fascinated watching the two women: Deirdre – dark, quick, just a suggestion of maliciousness in her humour; Catherine – blonde, poised, radiating an inner serenity which he had first attributed to her beauty but was now inclined to ascribe to the strength of character she had needed to go behind the German lines as an agent. Although neither he nor Deirdre knew what she was going to do there, both were aware she was going back into Occupied France in just over twenty-four hours. That gave her, quite understandably, a special aura in their eyes, and as the evening proceeded, T.F. had watched a bond beginning to develop between the two girls.

After dinner, they had adjourned to the 400. As always on Saturday nights, it was jammed, but seeing Deirdre, Manetta had found them a table and promptly summoned T.F.'s private bottle of Scotch from the club's locker. T.F. asked Catherine to dance.

Fitting onto the crowded dance floor, she looked up at him, smiled, gave a bewitching toss to her hair and folded into his arms. T.F. felt the hard muscles of her thighs pressed against his and with the arm that circled her waist, the tautness of her middle body. Clearly, she had been superbly trained in whatever secret schools the British had for their agents.

And Catherine, he noted as they swayed to 'Take the A Train', moved with considerable agility. She cocked her head sideways and fixed him with those probing green eyes of hers.

'Tell me, T.F., just what is your role? Guardian angel or watchdog?'

'I think errand boy is more like it. When you came out of the colonel's office the other day, he nodded at you and said, "Lovely creature, isn't she? See to it she gets anything she needs while she's here."'

'That's all he told you?'

'Do you know what we say about the colonel in our little hole in the ground?'

'I was only there once, remember?' she reminded him.

'He doesn't even tell God all his secrets.'

'God' – Catherine's smile was forced and wan – 'is fortunate.'

'He did tell us you were going back. Christ, it must take something very special to do that.'

'It does.' This time her smile was effortless. 'An aeroplane or a parachute.'

T.F. chuckled and drew her body closer to his on the packed dance floor. How strange, he thought, to think tonight she was here dancing without a care in the world and in forty-eight hours she would be walking around in the middle of the German army on whatever mission it was they had given her. 'Are you' – he had been concerned to say 'afraid' when he realized how tactless the word was – 'concerned?'

Catherine shook her head. 'I'd be crazy not to be. Still, in a way, I'm glad to go. Over there, I know I can do something worthwhile.' T.F. noticed a flickering in her soft green eyes, 'Besides, being there will give me the chance to see something I have waited a long time to see.'

'What's that?'

'A German army retreating.' Those words seemed a catharsis to her. The band had just shifted to 'The Lady Is a Tramp', and she changed the conversation with the same quick grace she used to move into the band's new rhythm. 'Your girlfriend, Deirdre, is lovely. Are you two engaged?'

'We haven't shouted it from the rooftops yet,' T.F. said. 'We thought we would wait until the war's over. Since there's likely to be another one when we announce the good news to Lord and Lady Sebright.' They pirouetted, then dipped, their handsome figures catching more than one admiring – or envious – glance.

'Deirdre's every bit as admiring of you as I am,' T.F. said, catching, as he did, a sign that the young guardsman was ready to leave.

They dropped him off at Victoria Station in time for his last train back to camp, then took Catherine to the Women's Service Club where she was staying. The two girls talked together on the ride back. At the club, T.F. got out to escort Catherine to the door. In the back seat, the girls embraced. 'Good luck, Catherine,' whispered Deirdre. 'We'll both be thinking about you and praying for you.'

'*Merci*,' Catherine answered. 'Who knows? – next time we meet maybe we'll all be having a victory celebration in Paris. I'd like that, wouldn't you?'

She had just stepped from the cab when Deirdre called out after her. Deirdre was wearing a pearl brooch T.F. knew had belonged to her grandmother. Catherine had commented on it at dinner. Swiftly, before Catherine could protest, she had unclipped it and was pinning it to her blouse. 'Please,' she said, 'take this with you. A souvenir from both of us.'

At Southwick House, a group of dispirited men left Eisenhower's predawn conference that Sunday, June 4. There had been no substantial change in the weather forecast for Monday, June 5. A few minutes after the meeting, the code words 'Ripcord plus 24' flashed out to battleships and airfields, convoys and troop camps, submarines and underground headquarters, to all the strange and secret locales where the two million men and women committed to *Overload* laboured. The assault was off for at least twenty-four hours.

At the women's Service Club, Catherine Pradier was revelling in the luxury of a self-indulgent Sunday morning when the club secretary summoned her to the telephone. Her caller was Cavendish. He had the jovial air of a cleric announcing to his flock the results of an unusually gratifying parish rummage sale. 'It looks as though you're on for tonight, my dear,' he announced. 'There's a bit of messy weather heading our way, but Ops thinks the other side will hold up long enough to run you in.'

The Gare d'Austerlitz swarmed with travellers. Neither war nor the stringent regulations of the Occupation were going to keep Parisians from their sacred Sunday trip to the country for a visit with friends or relatives. Indeed, the war had given a special urgency to those visits. Most of Paul's fellow passengers would, he knew, be returning to Paris in the evening bearing the precious harvest of their trip – a rabbit or a chicken for the very fortunate; a couple of eggs, a handful of potatoes for the rest.

In any event, the crowded station was a blessing. Convoying Allied aviators was always tricky. To make contact, Paul had worked out an elaborate routine designed to keep a safe distance between himself and the pilots he was going to convoy. Paul settled on to a bench in the crowded waiting room. Nearby – not too close, but in easy view – the contact from whom he was picking up the pilot was already seated reading a paper. After a few minutes, a passerby came up to him. The contact stood; the two shook hands and chatted a few moments. That was not the man Paul was interested in – the manoeuvre was much too obvious. His eyes were fixed a few yards away. Two men were drifting up the aisle, one in blue denims, the other in slacks and a sweater. As they passed the chatting men, the man in the sweater put his hands into his pockets. That was the signal. They were Paul's RAF pilots.

They strolled over to the news stand and began to stare at the papers. After a minute or two, Paul wandered over to the stand. Not a word passed between him and the two pilots. Yet with his eyes he made them understand it was he they were now to follow.

At the ticket control, Paul pretended to be looking for his ticket so the

307

two Englishmen could pass the control ahead of him. Once they had safely passed, he went through, passed them again on the platform, got into a car and took a place in a compartment. The two pilots followed and settled into a compartment two doors from his. Should anyone attempt to talk to them they carried little handwritten slips of paper identifying them as deaf and dumb as the result of an air raid in Nantes. It wasn't much of a cover for their inability to speak French, but it was the best idea Paul had been able to come up with. It was amazing, he thought in silent humour, how many deaf-mutes you could find riding the trains these days.

The second time through, Catherine thought, there was something reassuringly familiar about her going-away preparations at Orchard Court. There was Park with his warm, welcoming smile, the mission instructions to be memorized. The clothes she had arrived in had been laundered and neatly laid on the bed in the room they had given her to dress in. Her handbag was on the dresser, its contents arranged beside it so she could study them and familiarize herself with each item once again.

Like most children, Catherine had disliked the name her parents had given her. At her convent school, she had ceaselessly been urged by the nuns to imitate Saint Catherine of Siena, a girl who had longed for 'the red rose of martyrdom' and dedicated her virginity to Christ at the age of seven. Neither proposition had seemed to the young Catherine to have much to recommend it, and the whole business had reinforced her distaste for her name. She had longed for a name that was both vital and strikingly nonvirginal. Jean, for Jean Harlow, had once seemed ideal, and later Barbara. Now it occurred to her, preparing to slip back into this personage called Denise, that she was in a sense fulfilling her childish dreams.

Cavendish embraced her on both cheeks as she entered his office. He reviewed her ID cards, the same ones she had come out with. They had, he explained, plucked a couple of coupons from her ration book to keep it up to date. She then recited, to a series of Cavendish's approving nods, the details of her mission. It differed in only a few particulars from the real instructions Ridley had already given her – the BBC messages were the same, even if their meaning was different, and her American escort officer, T. F. O'Neill, would later, she knew, be giving her the fake match with its microfilm for Aristide.

'Since this Ridley chap's taken an interest in what you're doing ...' Cavendish paused. He was fishing for information, Catherine realized. How extraordinary it was that she should be privy, even if indirectly, to secrets her superior was denied. Her reply to his inquisitiveness, however, was an expression of innocent incomprehension. 'He's assigned you an escort officer to take you out to Tangmere. You'll find him waiting in the car downstairs.'

Cavendish was reviewing a last detail of her mission when his phone rang. He listened with utmost seriousness, muttered, 'I see,' and hung up.

'It was Tangmere,' he informed her. 'The weather's marginal, there's a storm over the Channel and it's moving into France. They think they will be able to get you in, but it's very much touch and go, I'm afraid.'

Cavendish got up and walked around his desk towards her chair. 'Well,' he announced, 'there remains just one last question for me to put to you.' Once again, he explained to her that her departure was voluntary, that she could withdraw from her mission with no shame attached to her decision. 'Catherine,' he asked, 'do you wish to continue?'

This time there was not an instant's hesitation in her reply.

'Of course,' she said.

Cavendish smiled and took out his decanter of port for their ritual farewell drink together. As she sipped hers, he drew her parting gift from his pocket. Catherine gasped as she unfolded the tissue paper surrounding it. It was a breathtakingly beautiful pair of gold earrings.

A few minutes out of Angers, Paul got up and sauntered down the corridor of his railroad car. He paused a second outside the door of the compartment in which the two English pilots sat in appropriate and stony silence. For an instant he made eye contact with them and then gave them a barely perceptible nod to indicate the next stop was theirs.

Continuing towards the door, he spotted two of Strömelburg's watchers in an adjacent compartment. They too were preparing to get off, and two things gave them away as Gestapo agents: neither had any luggage, and both wore alligator shoes. The former Montmartre pimps the German hired for his French Gestapo found it impossible to suppress some of their more flamboyant sartorial instincts.

Paul strolled casually through the station, sensing the Englishmen trailing along behind him. At the main entrance, his number two fell in beside him. They walked in silence a few blocks to the garage where his aide had hidden four bikes. Fortunately, both pilots knew how to ride them. As nonchalantly as possible, Paul led his little expeditionary force out of Angers and over the 15-kilometre route to the shed that served as his safe house for Field Four. Pushing open the door, his number two exclaimed, 'Christ! *Ça puait de Boche à la gare!*' – 'The station stank of Germans.'

Paul gave him the only answer he could: a noncommittal shrug.

Once again the dreary Victorian row houses of suburban London were slipping past the windows of Catherine's station-wagon. This time they did not sing out a plaintive cry, nor did they inspire in her any emotion other than the indifference their mean façades merited. The trepidation of her first trip was gone, replaced by a kind of nervous excitement. It had begun to rain – the storm Cavendish had warned her was coming. Watching its droplets speckling the windows of the station-wagon, she wondered if she would get off. Maybe she was going to wind up back at Orchard Court having breakfast with Park instead of lying in Paul's arms somewhere in France.

T.F. sat beside her matching her introspective silence with a respectful silence of his own. The young American was a troubled and uneasy man. So much seemed inherently wrong in their roles. In a few hours he would be driving back to London in this station-wagon facing no menace more serious than running down a stray dog or bumping into a taxi in the blackout. Catherine would be tossing through a stormy sky in an unarmed plane trying to land in a farmer's field in the midst of German-occupied France. While he would be enjoying the comfort of Deirdre's apartment, of the clubs and messes that cosseted his military existence, she would be infiltrating, alone and exposed, an enemy's land. In the bombproof underground office where he would be shuffling his papers, the only physical risk he ran, T.F. reflected with credible irony, was scalding his tongue on a cup of hot tea. And she?

Almost stealthily, he looked at her sitting there beside him in the shadowy station-wagon. Why were they sending her? Was it really right to send women out on missions like this? Why couldn't they find a Frenchman to run the risks she was taking?

Inadvertently, T.F. sighed. Ridley would have the answer to that: don't ask the question 'Is it right?' in the first place; the question is 'Will it work?' T.F. shook his head. She's off to risk her life and I'm staying behind to fly a desk in Mr Churchill's Underground War Rooms. It was hard to know which he felt more intensely, guilt for the inadequacy of his own role or admiration for hers.

Already, sitting there in her unfamiliar clothes, she seemed such a different person from the FANY officer he had picked up at Orchard Court just a couple of days ago. No women he had seen in London dressed quite as she was dressed. Her blond hair was brushed high on her head in a style he had never seen. He took out a Camel and, forgetting she didn't smoke, offered her one. In the glow of his Zippo, he noticed Deirdre's brooch pinned to the throat of her blue blouse. As if in response to his almost furtive glance, her hands went to it. 'She shouldn't have done it,' she murmured. 'It's much too precious.'

'I understand her.' He thought for an instant of the very special going-away gifts he had been instructed to give her just before she got on the plane. 'Christ, it takes courage to do what you're doing. She admires that. So do I.'

'Probably not as much courage as you think.'

'More, I'd imagine.' T.F. paused as though his hesitation might excuse what he felt was the banality of his thoughts. 'They should be sending someone like me in your place.'

'Because you speak such good French,' Catherine said, laughing, 'or because you look about as French as an Eskimo?'

T.F. grinned. 'Anyway, let's make a date right now for that dinner in Paris when the war's over.'

'Why wait until the war's over?' she asked. 'Once the Germans are gone, we'll have good enough reason to celebrate.'

She unclasped her handbag. 'Will you do something for me?'

'That's supposed to be why I'm here.'

Catherine passed a piece of tissue wrapped around something metallic into his hands. 'Would you give these to Deirdre for me? They were a going-away present from Major Cavendish. I'd like her to have them.'

Peeling back the paper, T.F. saw inside the glitter of a pair of gold earrings. He whistled softly. 'You shouldn't do that.'

Catherine listened an instant to the soft flick of raindrops on the window. She turned back to T.F. 'If I don't come back I rather like the idea that Deirdre will have them. Maybe then, once in a while, when she wears them and you and she are out dancing in London or New York or wherever you settle after this war is over, you'll have a thought of me. It would be nice to know that might happen. That someone would remember me.'

T.F.'s chest constricted at her words. He clasped her hands in his. 'I'll give them to her. She'll wear them once a day until we have that dinner in Paris, I promise.'

'Thanks.' She squeezed his hand in return. 'I'd really like her to have them. Otherwise' – she gave a brittle laugh – 'if something should go wrong, they'll wind up hanging from the ears of some Gestapo officer's whore in Calais, which is the one thing I wouldn't want.'

Paul took his portable shortwave radio from its hiding place inside the shed's unused wood stove and began to adjust his dials for a clear reception of the BBC. His two RAF pilots were sitting on the big mattress pushed up against one of the walls of the shed, quietly elated by their coming return to England and freedom. Remy Clément, his number two, was at the window scrutinizing the shadows, still upset by the Gestapo presence he had sensed at the station. I just hope to God one of Strömelburg's men doesn't cross his line of vision, Paul thought.

311

Clément, unlike Paul, was armed. He would want to go out with all guns blazing, the way they do in the movies. Either Paul would have to let him do it and risk getting them all killed or tell Clément something about his contacts with the Gestapo. On balance, he thought grimly, I'll be better off taking my chances on the gunfight.

Despite the marginal weather which often made reception difficult, the BBC came in loud and clear. Paul prepared for the little outburst of anger and frustration he would fake for the benefit of Clément and his two pilots when the broadcast was over and the message hadn't come in. Playacting was the part of his functions he most enjoyed. He frowned and waited for the night's first message.

When he heard it, he almost gasped. 'Copenhagen clings to the sea,' the announcer said. Then, so there would be no mistake, he intoned it again in his lugubrious tones. Paul stared at his feet so the others wouldn't see the dismay distorting his features. What, in Christ's name, had gone wrong? London had got his message. The girl from the One Two Two had confirmed not only that she had sent it but that London had acknowledged receiving it.

None of the others, of course, knew what the code phrase was. He could pretend it had not come and let the plane go unwelcomed, hide here for the night and try to make a run for it at dawn. Except, of course, Strömelburg or one of his minions had certainly been listening to the BBC. If they saw the plane circling, the pilot flashing his identity letter, they would all be fodder for the firing squads at Mont Valérien.

That was when the light flashed on. London was inept and clumsy, but not quite so inept as he had sometimes liked to pretend. They had understood Strömelburg would also be listening to the BBC. They had broadcast the code phrase to cover him. He would have to put in a long damp night in the fields making a show of waiting for a plane that was never going to come for Strömelburg's men. They, of course, would put the plane's failure to show up down to mechanical problems or the accurate fire of their flak. Paul snapped off his radio and smiled at the RAF pilots.

'Everything's all set,' he announced. 'The message came in. The plane's coming.'

Dinner at Tangmere Cottage with the pilots of the Moonlight Squadron was every bit as gay as Catherine had remembered it. As an attractive woman, as their only outward-bound passenger of the night, she was the guest of honour for whose benefit all their outrageous flying stories were told yet again. Each time she took a sip from her wineglass someone, it seemed, filled it up again. For dessert, Sergeant Booker brought her an orange on a silver tray with the dignity of a jeweller proposing a diamond

312

tiara to a dowager duchess. Indeed, once again she had had such a good time she had forgotten where she was and why she was there when a glance from T.F. at the end of the table reminded her. She followed him upstairs to the bedroom the Moonlight Squadron set aside for their passengers' last-minute briefings.

T.F. put his briefcase on the bedside table and began to go through its contents exactly as he had been instructed. First, he offered her the match with the microfilm concealed in its hollowed-out wooden stem. 'You've seen one of these before, I think?'

'Yes, I took one in last trip.' Catherine took the match from T.F., studied it carefully, then slipped it into its box and dropped the box into her handbag.

T.F. took a Walther PPK and two clips of ammunition from one of the briefcase's pockets.

'I didn't take a pistol the last time,' she told him. 'I don't want one tonight. It's a red flag for the Germans if they catch you with one at a control.'

T.F. nodded and took the next item from his case, a silver flask.

'That goes.' Caroline smiled. She unscrewed the stopper and sniffed its contents. 'Rum.' She grimaced. 'Do you know why they call the rum ration "Nelson's Blood" in the Royal Navy?'

T.F. shook his head.

'When Nelson was killed at Trafalgar, they put his body in a wooden coffin filled with rum – to pickle it, I suppose, until they could get him back to England to bury him. But' – she started to giggle – 'nobody likes his grog more than an English sailor, so when they opened him up in England, the coffin was dry and poor old Nelson was as rancid as three-month-old butter. My father was in the navy, and ever since he told me that story I've hated the taste of rum. Never mind.' The flask went into her handbag. 'I'll have cognac in there by tomorrow night. What else?'

T.F. opened a small pillbox and took out a dozen round green pills. 'Benzedrine. They say a couple of these will keep you awake for a week.'

'Not quite,' Catherine told him. 'But they'll certainly get you through the night.'

Finally, T.F. took out the last item in his inventory, the square white 'L' pill. Just seeing it lying in the palm of his hand, he felt queasy. 'You know what this is for, I think?' he asked in an embarrassed murmur.

'Yes, of course.' She took it, sat down on the bed and took off her left shoe. While T.F. looked on with morbid interest, she unscrewed one of its decorative tassels, calmly fitted the pill into the compartment it contained, then screwed the tassel back into place. As she did it, an image, both incongruous yet strangely appropriate, struck T.F. Her gestures reminded him of the girls he had dated in prewar Hartford,

313

twisting a dime into the flaps of their penny loafers, bus fare to guarantee a safe passage home from a date gone wrong. Catherine stood up and went over to the mirror to give a last check to her appearance.

'Don't you like these stockings? They're painted on,' she said, catching T.F. staring at her. She took her bag from the bed. 'Come on,' she said, 'we might as well go down. The car will be coming any minute now.'

Outside the conference room of Southwick House, Eisenhower's advance headquarters, rain-spattered windows and gusting winds tore the spring leaves from the larches that surrounded the great mansion. Inside, Eisenhower, Montgomery, Admiral Ramsay – his naval chief – and Air Chief Marshal Leigh Malloy – commanding his air forces – hung tensely on each of the words of SHAEF's senior meteorologist. A cold front, the weatherman, Group Captain John Stagg, explained, would pass through the Channel during the night. Behind it, out in the North Atlantic, one of the depressions driving towards Europe had intensified in severity during the past twenty-four hours. That strengthening had slowed its eastward drive. Between the passage of the cold front and the arrival of the depression, Stagg forecast a 'heaven-sent hiatus' that would offer them a brief spell of reasonable weather. Not good weather, but conditions of cloud, wind and sea that would meet, albeit barely, the minimum the invasion demanded.

The discussion that followed his forecast was brief. Finally, Eisenhower frowned. Just a few days before, he had summed up all the terrible risks of their enterprise in one terse phrase: 'We cannot afford to fail.' He turned to his aides. 'We must give the order,' he declared. 'I don't like it, but there it is.'

Catherine and T.F. settled in silence into the backseat of the blacked-out station-wagon waiting for them at the door of Tangmere Cottage. In front, the pilot was all business as he listened to the RAF sergeant give him the latest weather.

'It's a real dice out there tonight, sir,' he was announcing with all the cheerfulness of someone who knew he'd be spending his night in a warm bed. 'You've got a storm with surface winds of thirty to forty knots gusting up to sixty over the channel. Heavy cloud cover from here to the French coast. It should start breaking up into scattered cover about fifty miles inland. Watch out for icing over seven thousand feet.' He saluted smartly. 'That's about all, sir.'

'That's quite enough, Sergeant,' the pilot sighed. He turned to Catherine as the station-wagon started for the field. 'Someone must really want you in there to send us out in weather like this,' he said.

At the plane, they wasted little time. A mechanic had already warmed up the engine. The pilot climbed in, checked his radio, then waved to Catherine to board. 'So,' she said, looking up at T.F., 'it's goodbye for now. Start saving up your appetite for our dinner in Paris.'

T.F. kissed her warmly and affectionately on the lips, rather than French fashion on both cheeks. 'Goodbye,' he murmured. 'Good luck.'

He stood there saddened and impressed as the mechanic closed the canopy over her head. She blew him a kiss, the pilot waved goodbye and the aircraft pivoted left on to its runway. While T.F. watched, the pilot gunned his engine and sent the plane trundling down the tarmac. T.F. continued to stand there peering after its departing shadow, watching as the stubby little aircraft fought for each metre it wrested from a stormy and hostile sky.

An hour later, T.F. was back at Storey's Gate to report to Colonel Ridley that Catherine had got off safely. He found Ridley in the operations room, a small, crowded office dominated by a broad table covered by a dozen red, white, green and black telephones. The walls were hung with maps of the Atlantic sea-lanes, the air war against Germany's heartlands, the jungles of Burma, the Eastern Front. But on this June night, the focus of all eyes was on the map of the coast of France, an extraordinary, two-dimensional abstraction of the ground on which the decisive battle of the war was about to be fought. Thanks to *Ultra*'s intercepts of German communications, to the French Resistance, to the Allies' remarkable communications network, virtually every convoy, every unit, every coastal battery, strong point and airfield of the opposing forces was pinned to its surface with remarkable precision. In the hands of Germany's Colonel von Roenne, that map would have cost the Allies the war.

Ridley was so absorbed in his study of the figures on the map that he did not seem to hear T.F.'s report of Catherine's departure. Indeed, all Ridley could think of was the climactic moment now upon them. The order had been given. From the Irish Sea down the Welsh coast to Land's End; in berths and moorings, piers, ports, coves and inlets from Liverpool around to Ramsgate, the great machine lurched forward. Now there could be no turning back. Ridley's thoughts turned to the Somme, the bloody Somme where so many of his countrymen had been martyred for nothing in mud and misery. Were they going to another holocaust like that on the Norman Peninsula at which he gazed with such intensity? Finally he turned to his American subordinate.

'It's on for tomorrow,' he said. 'If you know how to pray, pray God that Hitler swallows our lies.'

Dark curls of nimbus clouds scudded inland from the western horizon, sure harbingers of an onrushing storm. Paul studied their patterns with his aviator's eyes, reading their shifting design with the instincts on which his life had so often depended flying the mail for Air Bleu before the war. They were low and full of menace, moving inwards, he guessed, at 20 knots. Within two hours, all western France would be covered. Already, their scattered ridges broke the moonlight into a shifting kaleidoscope dappling the open pasture in greys and silver. London was even smarter than he had thought. They'd seen the weather moving in. The reason for the plane's failure to arrive would be so graphically evident no possible suspicion could fall on either him or his operation.

He settled onto the damp grass beside his two RAF pilots. They too understood what was happening. One of them gestured to the western horizon. 'Be a bloody miracle if anybody gets in here tonight.'

Paul nodded and tried to calculate just how long he would have to go on with this playacting of his for the benefit of Strömelburg's unseen commandos. Suddenly, he tensed. Far down the western horizon his alert ears had caught the low drone of an aircraft engine. He sat up, following its progress until his trained senses detected the familiar beat of a Lysander's Westland engine. He was stunned. It simply wasn't possible. What, in God's name, had gone wrong? London was deliberately, knowingly flying into a Gestapo trap. He was still sitting there paralysed with amazement and uncertainty when the Lysander made its first pass overhead. His aide, Clément, was already on his feet running towards his position.

Paul scrambled up. What should he do? Flash the wrong ID letter to warn off the plane? Strömelburg's men out there in the bushes knew what the right letter was. They would all be dead within fifteen minutes if he did that. My God, Paul thought, grabbing his flashlight to do the only thing he could do – blink out his welcoming 'T' to the pilot sweeping towards the field, the poor bastard!

The plane blinked its 'T' in answer to his, banked and rushed onto the field in a perfect landing. Paul gave a beckoning wave to the two RAF pilots, who started to spring towards him.

The canopy opened and the incoming passenger gracefully leaped to the ground. It was, Paul realized, a woman. The RAF pilots jogged past and started to clamber aboard the Lysander. The woman rushed towards Paul. It was only at the instant she threw herself into his arms that Paul recognized her hair, her smell, felt pressed to his flesh the indentations of the woman he loved. His knees trembled and the blood rushed from his head. For a moment, he thought he would faint.

'Denise!' he cried. It was the only word he could articulate in his surprise and horror.

'Darling,' Catherine whispered, 'thank God I'm back with you, even if it's only for one night.'

316

It was only when they got back to the shed a few minutes later that Paul began to recover from the shock of her arrival. Hands still shaking slightly, he thrust open the door so Catherine could step inside. As she did, he turned, trying to read the message of the dark and uncertain shadows walling them in. He could see nothing, discover no movement that might indicate how many men Strömelburg had hidden out there, detect no rustling foliage that would tell him where they were. Should they take their chances and try to run for it? Clément, his aide, had already ridden off down the dirt track with the extra bike, but his move was one the Gestapo had been waiting for.

Five yards from the shed was a drainage ditch which ran parallel to the track for 500 yards to its juncture with another dirt road. Could they crawl away undetected down that? He studied it with his eyes so used to the night, then froze. Fifty yards away, where the ditch reached the woods that surrounded the shed like waters around an island, he saw a lurking shadow and heard the dry snap of a breaking twig. Paul cursed softly. If they were smart enough to place a man there, then they had the place completely surrounded. There would be no midnight flight for them.

He closed the door, lit a kerosene lamp and hung it on a hook dangling from the ceiling. Its flickering light pushed the shadows back to the corners of the shed. It was a distinctly primitive place – no plumbing, no water, no electricity, just a table and a mattress covered with old blankets. Catherine surveyed it and turned to Paul. In the lamp's gentle glow she was so radiantly beautiful Paul gasped.

'Darling,' she said, 'you do have a knack for picking the most romantic places in France.'

At her words, they flung themselves at each other. Catherine's embrace overflowed with the passion the knowledge of how little time they would have together inspired in her. Paul's was tentative and trembling, a reflection of the only passion consuming him: worry. Catherine drew slowly away from her lover. A woman can read the message of an uncertain embrace more swiftly and far more accurately than an astrologer can decipher the portents of his stars. Her fingertips caught the confirming trace of the cold, clammy sweat at his temples.

'Are you all right, darling?' she asked.

'I'm worried sick.'

'Why?'

'I have a bad feeling about this operation.' How much can I tell her, for Christ's sake? Paul wondered. 'I just have a bad feeling about it. Ever since I got off the train in Angers today, I've had the feeling I'm being followed.'

Catherine trembled slightly. 'Perhaps you're imagining things. You've been under a terrible strain.'

'I have a kind of sixth sense about these things.'

'But if they were after you, they would have grabbed the plane at the field, wouldn't they? That's the prize.'

Paul was morose and silent. Catherine blew out the lamp, and they lay down in each other's arms on the mattress. Paul grasped her to his body with an almost savage intensity, but as Catherine quickly discovered, the nervous strain that had invaded him like a fever had left him incapable of physical arousal.

'Don't worry, darling,' she whispered. She kissed him tenderly, then curled into his arms with the trust of a child moving towards its mother's breast. Within minutes she was asleep.

Paul lay awake, staring up at the flat roof of the shed, wondering desperately what to do, trying somehow to will back the dawn. What had happened? His message to London through the One Two Two could not have been clearer or more explicit: the Gestapo was going to take the incoming passenger on Operation Tango. Danielle had said that she had sent it and London had confirmed receipt. Had she been lying?

It was possible, but why? She had always been above reproach in her operations. Had she been doubled by the Germans too? Unlikely, because if she had, Strömelburg would have known long ago of his ties to MI6 and surely would have had him shot. No, examining the situation with the cold sense of duplicity that is a double agent's armour, Paul concluded that either London had sent Denise here deliberately for some reason of its own or London was criminally inept. In any event, the explanation was immaterial.

He looked at the figure collapsed in trusting somnolence in his arms. He could hear the measured cadence of her breathing, smell the familiar odour of her body. Whatever right there was in the twisted, demented world through which he eased his snaky trace, it was here in his arms. Whatever loyalties he had came second to saving her. But how?

He could go to Strömelburg and beg him to give her up in recognition of everything he'd done for him. It was a possibility, but only a last, desperate possibility. He knew Strömelburg well enough to suspect just how finite the limits of his gratitude were apt to be. Suppose he revealed his MI6 connection, offered to go triple to save her? Strömelburg's trust in him was total. He was the German's proudest creation. Reveal to him that he had been hoaxed, been made a fool of, and the German's reaction would be as unpredictable as a lightning bolt's course.

He reached for a cigarette and began to smoke in the darkness. Strömelburg would have to be the last resort. His first concern had to be to find a way to escape the trap in which they were caught. Once they were on the train to Paris escape would be difficult. Any move they made

318

would be suspect. Strömelburg would have driven the fear of God and his own very considerable wrath into his watchers. They would take no chances. If she moved from her seat, they would follow her, and if she went anywhere except to the toilet or the dining car, they'd grab her. He was as sure of that as he could be of anything.

Carefully, he tried to review every kilometre of their trip. Tomorrow, they had a 4-kilometre bike ride to the station along a relatively deserted country road. Strömelburg couldn't plant an agent behind every bush. To send a car after them would give his game away, and that was very unlike Strömelburg. If there was one moment, one place between this shed and Paris where the Gestapo's guard would be down, it would be there on that bike ride in the morning, Paul realized.

At one of the little roads that intersected the route to La Minitre, they would swing off and go north to avoid crossing the Loire, because once they had flown the Germans would order checkpoints on the bridges. Circling north, they would come back to Angers from the west. Strömelburg knew nothing of his deputy Clément's operation. They would go to his safe house and hole up there. Between the moment the last watcher would see them pedal off towards La Minitre and the time the agents who would be waiting at the station would expect to see them arrive, they would have about twenty minutes. It was a considerable head start even if the Gestapo would be coming after them with cars, not bikes. It was also Paul's only chance to save Denise from Strömelburg's trap. For the first time since she had stepped out of the Lysander, Paul's shattered confidence began to return.

One hundred and eighty miles from the outskirts of Angers, the fierce wind driving inland from the Channel tore the leaves from the linden trees that encircled the *château* of the Dukes of La Rochefoucauld and flung them in swirling packets past the windows of Field Marshal Erwin Rommel's bedroom. The field marshal stared out at the grey and stormy dawn of Monday, June 5, with satisfaction. For two weeks, during the last glorious fortnight when each day had brought its ration of perfect invasion weather, he had been praying for rain.

He showered, shaved, dressed and breakfasted on the bowl of clear soup his chef had prepared for him. As with Eisenhower, his foe across the English Channel, his first thought that morning was for his chief meteorologist – Major Ernst Winkler, stationed at the Villa Les Sapioles at the seaside resort of Wimereux, on the English Channel just outside the city of Boulogne. He was one of the few subordinates in his command the field marshal called regularly. The weather prediction could not be worse, he informed the field marshal. From his windows, he told Rommel, he could see surf a meter and a half high crashing onto the

Channel sands below his villa. A landing in weather like that was unthinkable.

That was exactly what Rommel wanted to hear. For several days, he had planned to be away from La Roche Guyon on June 5 and 6. On his bed was the pair of grey shoes Rommel had bought in Paris a few days earlier as a present for his wife, Lucie, on her birthday, Tuesday, June 6.

Lucie's birthday, however, was incidental to the real reason for his trip: the meeting he had scheduled on Tuesday afternoon with Adolf Hitler at Berchtesgaden. Rommel wanted two more Panzer divisions added to his command, the Second SS in Toulouse and the Ninth Panzer in Avignon, both of which were turned towards an invasion from the Mediterranean rather than the Atlantic. He felt certain he would get them because he intended to station them south of Caen, behind the Norman beaches that had lately so concerned the Führer.

Before leaving, Rommel, good commander that he was, had a last thought for his troops, weary after a fortnight of invasion alerts. He ordered all his forces along the Atlantic Wall stood down and authorized local leave for officers and men.

In the little glade of woods southeast of Angers, another trip was beginning in that same stormy dawn. Paul studied the foliage around his shed, trying to get some indication of how many men Strömelburg had hidden out there. He got none. In a sense, he reassured himself, it was of no consequence. The only thing that mattered was getting that precious quarter of an hour free from those unseen eyes on the road to La Minitre. He watched Catherine, still half asleep on the mattress at his feet. What reason should he give her for suddenly swerving from their route and starting their flight across country? How much should he tell her about his relations with Strömelburg? He drew deeply on his black-market Camel, itself another reward for his service with the Gestapo he now wanted so desperately to flee.

He would tell her nothing. Some things required either too much explanation or none at all. This one would be better explained after the war, in an office in London, when any need for equivocation had long passed. On the mattress, Catherine stirred reluctantly to wakefulness. She got up and joined Paul at the window. She drew in the damp air, savouring its promise of summer, its hint of lavender and thyme; then she turned to embrace him. At first drowsy and playful, her kiss suddenly became passionate as the realization they would be separating again in a few hours swept over her.

Paul's response was swift. Confidence can fire a man's vitality almost as surely as passion. The knowledge that they would soon be running cross country free of Strömelburg's minions gave Paul the ardour worry had deprived him of a few hours earlier. They fell back onto the mattress and exuberantly, gaily almost, made love. When they had finished, Catherine lay content and spent listening to the call of the morning birds.

Paul brought her back to reality. 'If anything happens out there on our way to the station, do exactly as I do. For Christ's sake, do not waste any time asking me questions. Just do it.'

There's my old Paul, Catherine thought, my surly aviator in his rubber boots scooping me up like a sack of potatoes.

Her surly aviator led the way out of the door and onto their bikes. Pedalling down the dirt path towards its junction with the main road, Paul scanned the woods for a sign of their unseen watchers. He saw none.

The main road took a gentle arc up a slight rise to a long straightaway bisecting open pastures on both sides of the road. At the end of the straight was a dirt track leading north through a tangle of woods and uncultivated land. That was where he would make their break. Whistling softly, sensing how shallow and rushed his nervous breathing was, Paul pedalled up the rise and down the long straight. The road ahead was empty, the fields beside them so bare they offered no concealment for anyone. Halfway down the straight, he glanced into the mirror fixed to his handlebars to check their rear.

He almost fell off his bike in fright at the image he saw there. Two hundred metres behind them a black Citroën *traction-avant* with four men inside rolled slowly after them, timing its arrogant advance down the roadway to their own slow progress. His plan had contained one fatal miscalculation. Strömelburg wanted her so badly he did not care if he exposed his hand and the fact that his men were dogging their footsteps.

Paul sickened, and for a second his bike swayed half out of control. For once, Henri Lemaire, alias Paul, alias Gilbert, the double agent whose ego thrived on his ability to outwit others, to deceive and manipulate, had absolutely no idea what to do. To bolt for the woods with that car behind them was suicide. So he did the only thing he could do: he continued to pedal slowly, steadily ahead, drawing them inexorably to the station and the imprisoning trap of the Paris train.

As it swept into the station, Paul spotted two more of Strömelburg's men at its windows, peering out at them. Seeing them, he could think of only one thing, a photo he had once seen of hunched grey vultures clinging to the branch of a tree, dull eyes staring down at the carcass of the dying bullock they were waiting to devour.

Paul eased his way into the aisle that ran the length of the railroad car. Catherine was in a compartment two doors away from his, but before moving towards it, he grasped the rail along the window and studied the faces in the swaying, half-full corridor. There were perhaps a dozen ordinary French travellers, several of them sitting on upturned suitcases which effectively blocked the aisle. Beside him, a pair of nuns whispered softly. He counted four German soldiers – armed; they always were nowadays – probably heading up to Paris on leave. At either end of the corridor, he picked out one of Strömelburg's vultures. How many others were on board the train? Two or at the most three, he reckoned, probably split up, as the two he had spotted were, at either end of the railway car where they could guard its exits.

Paul could have killed himself in rage. He had been in such a state of shock after the plane had landed the night before that he had let his aide, Clément, vanish into the night with their pistol before he had thought to ask him for it. If she had a weapon, they could try to shoot their way off the train as it slowed somewhere along its course. He would send her to the end of the corridor as though she were heading for the toilet. He'd drift along behind her and shoot Strömelburg's Gestapo agent without warning. They would have to count on surprise to stifle the reaction of the other Germans in the car for a few seconds and give them the time they would need to wrestle open the door and jump off the moving train.

But what if she didn't have a gun – what did they do then? To try to jump off the train and run at its only stop, Orléans, would be mad. The station, like all major stations, crawled with German soldiers on leave, the police, the vicious bastards of the *milice*. Only some external and totally unexpected event, such as an air raid, could give them a few moments of confusion in which to bolt and run. Thinking about that gave Paul an idea: the one, desperate tactic that might free her if they could not shoot their way off the train. He lit a cigarette and thought his way through it. He contemplated plans and stratagems with the fervour of a Jesuit missionary contemplating the unconverted. Now intense personal despair compounded those instincts, led him to clutch at his scheme as the drowning sailor to his life raft, willing each of its imponderables into being.

He edged up the corridor to Catherine's compartment. Seeing him, she moved out to join him.

'Have you got a gun?' he whispered.

'No.' She shook her head. 'I never have one. Why?'

'The Gestapo is all over this damn train.'

At his words, Catherine chilled. As surreptitiously as she could, she glanced up and down the corridor.

'There is one of them stationed at either end of the car,' Paul whispered.

'How do you know?'

'What do you mean, how do I know?' Paul had to mumble so as not to be overheard, but that did not prevent him from getting the requisite fury into his voice. 'I just know, for Christ's sake. I can smell these guys a mile away.'

Catherine contemplated her lover. He was pale and trembling, as he had been when they had got back to the shed the night before, as he had been when they'd reached the station earlier in the morning. Had he become paranoid after operating for months underground without respite? Was he seeing Gestapo men in railroad cars, or were they really there? She tried again to let her eyes survey as discreetly as possible the faces in the aisle.

'They're after either you or me or both of us,' Paul whispered. 'If it's you they want, they'll wait to take you in Calais. They'll follow you until you have led them to your contact up there. That's how they operate. If it's me ...' Paul shrugged in what was meant to indicate heroic indifference but was in fact an effort to unburden himself of the monstrous nature of his lie.

Catherine's knees trembled slightly. 'What do we do?'

'There are five of them I've spotted.' Paul lit a cigarette and pretended to study the passing countryside. 'I have an idea I think might work if it's you they're after. A friend of mine runs a railroad-sabotage network in the North. His men live in Hénin-Beaumont, about half an hour from Lille. Do you know it?'

Catherine nodded.

'I'm going to get him to derail your train coming into Lille. Sit by the window of your compartment. Make sure it's open. When you hear the explosion, you'll have thirty seconds of confusion to make a break for it. Jump out of the window and run. Try to get back to the bar on Saint-André-des-Arts in Paris.'

'Suppose there's one of them in the compartment?'

Paul shrugged. 'Then it won't work. But they usually don't do that because it's too obvious. They like to stake out the ends of the car, the way they have here. The first thing they'll do after the derailment is check the exits. Then they'll probably try to find out what has happened. Then one of them will think about you and head for your compartment. Thirty seconds. By that time, you have got to be out of the window and gone.'

Again Catherine shivered, as though from an oncoming fever, and glanced at the men at either end of the car, trying to memorize their faces.

'What if it's both of us they're after?'

'They'll grab me in Paris.'

'And what about the derailment?'

'There won't be any.' Paul hesitated a moment. 'If the train's not derailed, your best chance is to try to shake them somehow in the Calais station. Use the trick of ducking between the cars and getting onto

323

another platform, jumping into another train if there is one.'

From the corner of his eye, Paul noted one of Strömelburg's vultures beginning to eye them suspiciously. They knew perfectly well he kept his contacts with his passengers to an absolute minimum. The one thing he could not afford was to have them get suspicious of him and decide to follow him once they got to Paris.

He caressed the back of her hand and held her eyes in his – the only farewell gesture he dared allow them. 'I love you, Denise. For God's sake, have that window down when you get to Hénin-Beaumont, and run for your life when you hear the explosion.'

'I love you,' she whispered, realizing as she said those words that she meant them and that it was the first time she had uttered them to a man other than her father. She turned and went back into her compartment while he slid along the aisle towards his.

Catherine sat for a while in silence contemplating the rain-swept countryside and the quandary she was in. There was always, of course, the chance that Paul had succumbed to agent's paranoia, that he had been burned out by the tensions of underground life and this was a false alarm, that there were no Gestapo agents on the train. It helped, at least, to think that that might be the case. Why hadn't she taken that gun from T.F.? She thought about the Calais station and how she might try to give someone following her the slip there. She looked at her shoes. High heels. Damnably inappropriate for running through the countryside. She would kick them off and run barefoot if they derailed the train, she told herself. She thought about Ridley and the magnitude of the mission he had given her. Then she returned her thoughts to the SOE's security school. Slowly, deliberately, she tried to compose herself, to prepare herself as best she could for the trial ahead.

At the Gare d'Austerlitz, Paul trailed along behind her in the crowds leaving the train. He watched as Strömelburg's men, five of them, drifted around her. There was no way she could escape them while she changed trains. He watched in anguish as she cleared the ticket barrier and drifted away in the crowds. Oh, God, he prayed to a Deity whose existence he had long ceased to acknowledge and in Whose mandate he had never placed much faith, please help me to save her. Then, as fast as he dared, he hurried towards the waiting room and its public phones.

A few minutes later Paul was rushing down the Boulevard des Capucines towards the Café de la Paix. He made a frantic survey of the faces of the customers at the café's wicker tables, then plunged through them to Ajax, calmly reading his paper at a table against the wall. Ajax put aside his paper and began to study the SOE's Air Operations Officer with amusement. He was distressed and agitated. Ajax quite liked that. He had

324

no use for Paul whatsoever. In fact, he would normally have refused to have anything to do with him. It was only because some desperate air in Paul's voice had warned Ajax that the meeting for which he begged might indeed be important that he'd agreed to see him.

'You look a bit upset,' Ajax told Paul as the aviator sat down beside him. Ajax was a former cavalry officer, a minor aristocrat whose bloodlines were as distinguished as his bank account was diminished. The knees and elbows of his ten-year-old suit shimmered with a glow appropriate to a decade of hard wear, but each crease was perfectly pressed. He had the taut facial skin and slightly narrowed eyes of a sailor or a man who has spent his life out of doors squinting into the sun; his brilliantined hair was so impeccably combed it seemed each of its strands might have been set in place individually.

'I desperately need your help,' Paul whispered.

Ajax nodded gravely and said nothing. Help was something he would extend to Paul with the greatest reluctance. As he had warned SOE's security people on his last trip to London, he was convinced Paul had contacts with the Gestapo. The fact that the chemically treated papers the SOE had given him to use in the courier he sent out via Paul apparently had not been photographed might have convinced London of Paul's innocence; it had not altered Ajax's own conviction of his treachery.

'I need to have a train derailed. Today.'

Ajax attempted, not altogether successfully, to suppress any trace of the mirth Paul's frantic plea evoked.

'It's the 4126, due up in Lille this evening.'

'Paul,' Ajax replied. 'One, you don't go around ordering derailments the way you order a beer in a pavement café. Two, daylight derailments can be very dangerous. Three, we derail freight trains and troop trains, not passenger trains. Killing our countrymen is not what we are here for.'

'I know all that, but this is desperately important.'

'Why?'

'There's an SOE agent on that train. She's on her way to Calais. The Gestapo are on there with her. They want her. They are going to take her in Calais. Her only hope of getting away from them is in the confusion right after a derailment.'

Ajax thought through Paul's words very carefully. How is it, Paul, he thought, you know all that? Since when has the Gestapo made you privy to its secrets? 'Why is she so important?' he asked.

'I don't know. All I know is Cavendish told me her mission was vital,' Paul lied, 'and I understand it was Strömelburg who personally ordered the Gestapo to take her.'

Ajax fixed Paul with his outdoorsman's eyes. Strömelburg, is it? Just

325

how did you stumble onto that scrap of information?

'You haven't given me much warning.'

'I know,' replied Paul.

'I can't promise you anything. Where are you going to be tomorrow?'

'I've got a flight tonight.'

'When will you get back?'

'Tomorrow afternoon.'

Ajax gathered up his paper and got up to leave. 'Call me as soon as you get back,' he said. 'I'll let you know what happened.'

Catherine suggested ever so timidly to her fellow passengers in her compartment that she was pregnant and feeling slightly ill. The stout middle-aged woman beside her made her husband get up so Catherine could take his place by the window, then thoughtfully ordered him to open it so Catherine could get some fresh air.

She tried to follow the passing flow of the rain-dampened countryside as nonchalantly as possible. Since she had no idea of the terrain in which the derailment would take place, it was impossible for her to prepare herself mentally for her flight. Most of the countryside through which they passed was open, rolling farmland. She mouthed a silent prayer that the derailment would not take place in terrain like that. Running across those open fields, she would be exposed to Gestapo pistol fire as a darting rabbit is to a hunter's rifle.

It was shortly before six when the train eased into the station of Hénin-Beaumont. 'How far is it to Lille?' she asked her helpful neighbour.

'Twenty minutes,' the woman replied.

They were among the longest twenty minutes of Catherine's life. She sat staring out of the window, muscles tensed, feet braced to withstand the shock of the derailment, constantly appraising the passing countryside for whatever avenue to safety it might offer.

After ten minutes, nothing had happened. She began to count off each minute to herself. The farmland gave way to a chain of villages, then the suburbs of Lille. She slumped against her seat. They were passing the smokestacks of Lille's industrial outskirts. There wasn't going to be any derailment. She was trapped. And Paul, her beloved Paul, was surely a prisoner of the Gestapo in Paris like the helpless figure she had seen driven from his apartment in the middle of the night the first time they had slept together.

As he had done every night since receiving the 'alert' messages for each of the fifteen SOE networks he was impersonating to London, the Doctor was in place before his Gründig radio, note pad and pencil ready, long before the BBC's evening news broadcast began. Outside, Avenue Foch was deserted, its pavements slick with rain, the skies overhead still choked with cloud. The Doctor was hardly a military man, yet even he could sense how unlikely it was the Allies would land in such weather.

At the announcement that the *messages personnels* were about to begin, the Doctor tensed. When he realized none of the first phrases concerned the radio sets he was playing back to the SOE, he relaxed and lit a cigarette. He was shaking out the match when that lugubrious voice the Doctor likened to an undertaker giving instructions to a funeral party intoned, 'The green lamp is broken.' It was one of his.

Seconds later, the voice proclaimed, 'The clover is in bloom.' The Doctor paled. My God, he thought, another one. Is it possible?

'Alphonse embraces Camille.'

That's it, that's it, the Doctor thought – another one. While he sat there stunned and awed, the rest of his fifteen messages came pouring in. Checking them off one by one on his note pad, his fingers tingled with excitement. It seemed to him he would feel history's warm breath at his neck. He, a scholastic, an anti-Nazi, a kind of Good Soldier Schweik unable to distinguish his right foot from his left on the parade field, had penetrated the secret of the Allied invasion. All the long and trying months he had spent alone in this office, living on coffee, cigarettes and sandwiches, playing his deadly game of chess with his faceless enemy in London had reached the culmination he had dared not dream. SOE London had laid in his waiting lap its most precious secret. He, an unknown schoolmaster, was about to enter the pages of history as the improbable saviour of the Third Reich.

As the announcer read his last message and the majestic cadences of Beethoven's *Fifth Symphony* again swelled from his Gründig he leaped from his chair and ran up the stairs to Strömelburg's office.

'The action messages!' he shouted. 'They're here, all of them! The Allies are landing tomorrow!'

The rain grew heavier as they neared the Channel coast. So too did the depression gripping Catherine. The Lille-Calais train, which she had boarded in a kind of dumb trance after the failure of Paul's men to derail her earlier train from Paris to Lille, was packed. Its compartments were full, its corridors crowded with desperately weary travellers, some so exhausted they managed to doze off between the jolts and sways of the train's advance. The windows were closed, and a damp, odoriferous mist seemed to rise from the bodies jammed together in the railroad car, a pungent mixture of soured breaths, stale sweat, dirty feet.

Half the passengers were German soldiers, sailors and airmen. You couldn't shoot your way off this train with a Sten gun, Catherine thought – and she didn't even have a hairpin. Not only that, she couldn't budge from her compartment to see whether or not any of the men Paul had indicated going up to Paris were still trailing her. All she could do was sit and try to think how she might flee their surveillance when they got to Calais. It would be almost dark when they reached the city. The station was always a madhouse for the arrival of the evening train. She would have to hope that with the crowds, the shadows, she could slip away unseen. But where would she go? They might be aware of her old apartment. She didn't want to lead them to Aristide. Where?

The laundress, she thought – the laundress in Sangatte whose place she had taken at the battery. She would go to her for help. Suddenly, looming at the door to her carriage was a *Feldgendarm*, his great metallic seal clanking at his chest. Had he come for her? Was this it?

It was not. His only interest was in checking the parcels of her fellow passengers. How sullen and hostile they seemed, reluctantly yielding up their pathetic black-market packets of tomatoes or potatoes so the well-fed German's fingers might inspect them. Some *Feldgendarmen* would arrest a traveller for carrying a dead chicken. Such treasures, after all, were meant for the citizens of the Reich, not for those of its vassal states. Fatigue and indifference, however, seemed to have dulled this one's martial thoroughness. After a few perfunctory glances, he slammed the compartment's sliding door shut and moved on down the train.

A few minutes later, Catherine heard the metallic squeal of the train's brakes beginning to grip the track and sensed the beat of its wheels' slowing. They were coming in. She forced herself to measure out her breath in little spurts which might stem her rising fear. She took off her coat and wrapped it on her arm. The coat was black, her blouse blue. Perhaps in the crowded station that switch might momentarily confuse someone trying to pick her up.

She tried as best she could to lose herself in the protective cover of a knot of detraining passengers, inserting herself as closely as she dared between a stout woman in widow's black, her hands crowded with bundles, and a spare man in an overcoat so large she was tempted for one second to beg him to put it over her.

Paul's advice of ducking onto another platform seemed like madness. Theirs was the only train in the station, and the exits from the platform opposite theirs, she knew, led nowhere except back to the central hall of the station. She had only one hope. It was to somehow lose herself in the crowds just long enough to get past the ticket takers, through the central hall and into the now almost dark streets outside. There she would have two obvious choices. She could go left over the canal bridge which led to the narrow and crowded alleys of the old city, or she could go right through the open and exposed Parc Saint-Pierre and then to the Rue Aristide Briand. Neither was an attractive alternative.

328

Reaching the ticket taker at the end of the platform, Catherine cursed the practice of picking up travellers' tickets at the end of a journey. As her knot of passengers thrust slowly towards that funnel, she had an almost irresistible desire to look behind her to see if she could see one of the faces Paul had shown her, to discover if she was being followed. Of course, she did not. To have done so would have warned anyone shadowing her that she suspected she was being followed. Then any possibility those followers might be overconfident or less would be undone.

Finally, she was through the ticket control unmolested. Once again she tried to wrap herself inside a cluster of people moving through the station. From the corner of her eye she saw Pierrot waiting. He moved to meet her, but she turned away. If they were there, she wasn't going to compromise him too.

Pierrot immediately understood the meaning of her gesture. He withdrew into the crowd and studied the passengers flowing out behind her. His experienced eyes spotted them immediately. There were five of them, French *milice* or Gestapo, drifting with arrogant nonchalance in her footsteps. He watched as they neared the door. Two Gestapo men, almost certainly Germans in their knee-length leather coats and felt hats, moved out of the shadows. One of the French Gestapo agents gestured towards Catherine's fast-moving figure.

She was already at the station door. A merciful darkness made blacker by the clouds overhead had settled over the city. Stepping into the street, she decided to head right to the Parc Saint-Pierre. She spun quickly away from the door, past a baggage cart heaped with luggage, towards the outer edge of the station. There she would turn right and, if she had to, break into a run.

It was at the instant she stepped out past the baggage cart that she felt the vice of two sets of fingers tightening on her forearms and a swift application of force lifting her from her feet and driving her forward.

She shrieked. Two men, one in a snap-brim hat, the other bareheaded, carried her towards a waiting black Citroën. '*Deutsche Polizei*,' hissed one. The other leered down at her, his eyes, under the snap brim of his hat, mocking her fear. 'So,' he said, '*wir haben unseren kleinen Schatz geschnappt*' – 'We've caught our little treasure.'

The destination of the Doctor's precious packet of military intelligence was a two-storey French home on Rue Alexandre Dumas in the Paris suburb of Bougival. That building housed the staff of Colonel Wilhelm Meyer-Detring, Field Marshal Gerd von Rundstedt's Intelligence Officer. Meyer-Detring was not in Paris that night. He was enjoying a leave in Berlin. The very fact that Meyer-Detring had gone ahead with his leave after the first round of invasion 'alert' messages had been broadcast on June 1 was indicative of how much importance he and his staff attached to the whole notion of 'alert' and 'action' messages heralding the invasion over the BBC.

The officer on duty that night was a young first lieutenant named Kurt Heilmann. At 9:20, while the motorcycle bearing the prodigious harvest of the Gestapo's year-old radio game was still several miles from Rue Alexandre Dumas, Heilmann received an urgent phone call from the Fifteenth Army's Communications Reconnaissance post in Tourcoing, north of Lille. The BBC, Tourcoing informed him, had just broadcast the second line of the Verlaine couplet – *Blessent mon coeur d'une langueur monotone.*' That was the second half of the alert/action message originally sent into France by the SOE in the summer of 1943 as a part of the 1943 deception plan *Starkey* – then, through an extraordinary SOE blunder, sent back into France again in the spring of 1944 as a code phrase for the real invasion.

Heilmann immediately took it to Von Rundstedt's Operations Officer, General Bodo Zimmerman. Zimmerman found the whole thing almost laughable. All anyone had to do to realize the Allies wouldn't be landing during the night was look out of the window. An invasion in such weather was impossible. The message was clearly just another aspect of the psychological war being waged by the Allies, its aim to exhaust Von Rundstedt's forces with a nerve-racking, never-ending series of alerts. That was not a trap into which Zimmerman was going to tumble. Besides, he reminded Heilmann, the Allies weren't going to be so obliging as to inform the Wehrmacht they were coming over the BBC – and most certainly not in a code phrase that had been circulating inside Europe for more than eight months. Together, Zimmerman and Heilmann prepared a brief message to inform Berlin and Von Rundstedt's subordinate commands of the Verlaine intercept and its probable interpretation. It noted that the code phrase had been known to the German Command since October 1943 and dismissed the notion that 'the invasion proper will be announced by radio.' Their message that stormy night was an invitation to Von Rundstedt's commanders along the invasion coast to do exactly what they proceeded to do on receiving it: nothing.

Pierrot knocked lightly on the door to Aristide's apartment. He was gasping as much in fright as he was from the exertion of his rushed journey from the Calais railroad station.

'The Gestapo's arrested Denise!' he said as soon as Aristide, stunned and disturbed by his unexpected visit, had shut and locked the door behind him. 'We've got to get out of here as fast as we can.'

Aristide pointed him to one of his spare wooden chairs. His wife appeared at the kitchen door, nervously rubbing her hands on a soiled dishcloth, looking like a neighbour eavesdropping over a backyard fence on a pair of friends recounting their miseries to each other.

Pierrot described in detail how the Gestapo men had followed Denise off the train and signalled her to their two confederates waiting at the station door. As the car had raced off, he had glimpsed its licence plate. It was from the Gestapo on Rue Terremonde in Lille.

'She obviously was afraid she was being followed and didn't want to lead them to you. We have that to thank her for,' Aristide noted when his deputy had finished.

'And how,' Pierrot concurred, only beginning to measure how close his own brush with the Gestapo had been.

'The question is, how, where and why did they pick her up? You saw them on the train?'

'I saw two of them coming through the ticket control.'

'So they had been following her, at the very least, from Lille. But how could they have picked her up there unless she was fingered to them? Someone sold her to the Gestapo between the time she arrived last night and the time she got to Lille. Who could have done it?'

'Maybe something happened to her in Paris,' Pierrot suggested.

Aristide leaned against the wall turning the resources of his philosopher's mind to the problem. 'We know from Cavendish's cable she came in last night. Which means she left the Sarthe or the Loire this morning. If she got here tonight, she really didn't have any time to have any contacts in Paris, did she? Therefore, the only people she had any contact with were the Air Operations people who received her Lysander.'

Aristide closed his eyes and searched the card file of his mind for a face. He was in a moonlit pasture south of Tours, coming back into France in a Lysander himself with Ajax, the SOE agent who had got him the Siemens fuses Denise had inserted in the Lindemann Battery's control panel. The man whose face he sought was tall, with wavy auburn hair and a touch of elegance about him. Watch out for him, Ajax had warned as they had left the field: that man has contacts with the Gestapo.

He opened his eyes and looked at Pierrot. 'I know who sold her,' he said. 'It was the fellow named Paul. He runs the Lysander operations.'

Shortly after Lieutenant Heilmann returned to his office on Rue Alexandre Dumas in Bougival, the detailed report of the Doctor's intercepted action messages was delivered to him. Fifteen separate action messages to fifteen different Resistance networks – it was a harvest to make any intelligence analyst reflect very carefully, and Heilmann was a meticulous young man.

The decision on what to do about the Doctor's information, however, was not his to make. The analysis of the Verlaine couplet bore the authority of Von Rundstedt's command. High commanders did not like to be seen by their subordinates as chameleons constantly changing their minds. The great commander, Bismarck had decreed, stands firm on the rock of his convictions.

Heilmann therefore relayed the contents of the Gestapo dispatch to Von Rundstedt's Operations Officer, Bodo Zimmerman. Like most professional Wehrmacht officers, Zimmerman had only a grudging regard for Abwehr intelligence and none whatsoever for intelligence emanating from Himmler's RSHA. They had already decided not to alert their weary troops over the Verlaine couplet. It was still raining. Only Von Rundstedt had the authority to order an all-out alert based on BBC messages. The old field marshal had gone to bed with an English detective story after a solitary dinner and the better part of a bottle of Bordeaux. Zimmerman did not propose to awaken him with the gibberish of a minor Gestapo officer. With that cavalier notion, the most important coup of German intelligence in the Second World War was dismissed as unworthy of the attention of Germany's commander in the West.

René, the barman of the Café Sporting on Rue de Béthune in Lille, was already closing for the night when Aristide burst in the door. He was breathless from his dash to the bar from the Lille railroad station. *'Une demie'* – 'A beer,' he gasped.

The barman looked at him. In the establishment's dim wartime lighting he was just a shadowy figure, a frail stranger with a beard looking for something French barmen were not noted for – indulgence.

'You've never heard of the curfew?' René snarled. As he did, he started down the bar ready to help his unwanted client out into the night if he insisted on putting his thirst before the curfew regulations. Drawing up to Aristide, he recognized his features. Aristide was, after all, the only person who had employed the special services Strömelburg had stationed René in the bar to perform.

'It's you,' he acknowledged. 'You got your message?'

Aristide nodded. René studied him. He looked worn and haggard. He cranked out a beer and slid it along the bar. Then he reached into the secret cabinet in which the Café Sporting's previous proprietor had kept his private liquor supply and took out a cognac bottle. He half-filled a cognac tulip with the amber liqueur. 'You look as if you could use this,' he said offering it to Aristide.

'Thanks.' Aristide drank down half his beer and followed it with a gulp of cognac.

'Look, René, I've got something urgent for London. Is there any chance you can get it out tonight?'

The barman thought. Never be precise, Strömelburg had told him; be noncommittal, evasive in your answers. 'I don't know,' he said. 'I can try. But I can't promise anything. You expecting an answer?'

'That's what I've got to have – and fast.'

'You want me to call you at that same place in Calais?'

Calais, it occured to Aristide, was not a place he was particularly eager to be spending time in during the next couple of days, at least until after the Gestapo had raided his apartment and found out he and his wife had fled. And if London gave him the answer he expected, he would have to go to Paris.

'No,' he said, 'I'll come by and pick it up.'

'Where are you staying?' René inquired. 'I'll have a courier bring it around.'

Aristide shook his head. That was not a question he'd answer for anybody.

'I'll be in tomorrow.'

Her handcuffs, set far tighter than necessary, cut into Catherine Pradier's wrists each time she tried to move her hands to relieve the tingling in her fingertips. She was handcuffed to a chair in the office of the Lille Gestapo, barely two miles from the Café Sporting, where Aristide finished his drink and prepared to disappear into the night.

Although the thought hardly seemed appropriate to her circumstances, she was, it occurred to her, a kind of minor celebrity, sitting there in some sort of anteroom to the office of Lille's Gestapo chief. A whole series of mousy-looking females in grey uniforms had found one excuse or another to enter the office and gawk at her in smug delight. '*Terroristin*,' she had heard them whisper to each other, '*französische Terroristin*.' Half a dozen of their male colleagues had also joined the parade, making what were, to judge from the reaction of her two captors, several uproariously lewd comments about her in German.

At the instant of her arrest, an overpowering sense of fright had gripped her, turning her limbs to liquefied rubber. Then, as she was driven towards Lille, fear had been replaced by a strange, almost eerie calm. The tension, the nerve-racking worry and uncertainty of the day had disappeared. It's over, she thought; it's finished. I'm caught. That realization had come almost as a welcome relief. Despite the pain in her pinioned arms and her concern for what awaited her, a curious, resigned lassitude had now invaded her.

333

One of her two captors got up and began to pace the room. 'Better oil up that tongue of yours, little sister,' he said, jerking his head towards the closed office door facing her. 'That guy in there hates women so bad he gets sick just smelling them.' He laughed at his heavy humour. 'You won't want to waste a lot of time talking to him. And he certainly isn't going to want to waste his time talking to you.'

Catherine stared dumbly ahead trying to ignore his words. The reputation of Lille's Gestapo chief, a sadistic homosexual, needed no embellishment for her benefit. At least, she thought to console herself, Pierrot would have seen them arrest her. He and Aristide would have disappeared by now. If it came to it, she could safely drop their names and addresses. Hold out for twenty-four hours, if you're captured, her SOE instructors had urged, then give up as little as possible, as slowly as you can.

Those instructions gave captured SOE agents a finite measure of succour to cling to in the agony of Gestapo torture, a time beyond which they did not have to endure. In a sense, it was a means to defeat their captors – resist their bestialities for twenty-four hours and it was they, not the Gestapo, who would have triumphed.

But, if they had some inkling of her mission? Then, there would be no finite twenty-four-hour period of agony for her to endure. It would be a Calvary without end. Almost dreamily, she glanced down at the tassel of her shoe in which her 'L' pill was concealed. Would she, she wondered, have the courage to take it if it came to that?

The office door opened and a middle-aged man in a double-breasted grey suit stepped out. He stared down at her. She was tempted to stare back, to challenge him with the defiant silence of her eyes. Then she thought better of the idea and averted her gaze.

'Ah, mademoiselle,' he announced finally with a sad little sigh, 'I had looked forward to the pleasure of talking to you myself. Higher authority, unfortunately, has denied me that pleasure. They insist I send you to Paris, to Avenue Foch.' He gave a limp wave to his wrist. 'Noblesse oblige.'

Then he turned to her two captors. 'Get her down to Paris,' he snarled.

Several hundred miles from Lille at his beloved Alpine retreat above Berchtesgaden, Adolf Hitler had passed a quiet evening listening to music with his mistress, Eva Braun, then gone to bed with the aid of a sleeping potion. His had been a quiet day: a discussion on diesel trucks, a conference on Portuguese tungsten exports, yet another examination of his faeces and his troubled bowels. His subordinates at his military headquarters had decided not to disturb his enjoyment of Schubert's *Lieder* by telling him that more than a dozen invasion-alert messages had been broadcast to the French Resistance by the BBC. It was as clear to them as it was to their deputies along the Atlantic Wall that there could be no invasion in weather as bad as that gripping the Channel. Like Von Rundstedt, like Rommel, Hitler had gone to bed on the evening of June 5 wholly ignorant of the fact that the greatest armada ever to ride the planet's tides was closing on the shores of his *Festung Europa*.

And yet, in the dark and wind-whipped waters of the Bay of the Seine, the six thousand ships of Eisenhower's invasion fleet were beginning to come on station. Their crossing had been a miracle. They had come in storm and fog and raging sea. Yet in the early hours of Tuesday, June 6, they had come in formation and good order, on time and in sequence, right up through the Dan buoys and midget submarines that pointed lanes through the minefields to their moorings.

Most miraculously of all, they had come undetected. The storm which had almost stayed Eisenhower's hand had given him the one advantage he had never dared hope for: surprise. Six thousand vessels, yet not a single Luftwaffe reconnaissance plane, not a single German E-boat or submarine, not even a radar's beam peering across the dark waters had discovered the advancing fleet. The first indication the Germans had that invaders had arrived came from that most prosaic of warning systems, the human ear. A sentry on shore heard the clatter of an anchor chain as one of the ships' anchors grasped for a hold in 15 fathoms of water. Overhead, the great air trains bearing the men of the airborne divisions thundered inland. It was 2:30 A.M. The invasion of Western Europe had begun.

In London, four men in an official Humber drove up to a two-storey residence in the suburb of Hampstead Heath. Theirs was a most extraordinary mission. Agents of Ridley's *Fortitude* scheme, they had come to Hampstead Heath to tell the Germans what their own vigilance had failed to tell them – that the invasion fleet was upon them. After that message, *Fortitude*'s shemers were convinced, their double agent Juan Pujol Garcia – 'Garbo' – would become, in German eyes, the greatest spy who had ever lived, a man whose messages would henceforth bear the seal of quasi-divine revelation.

Garbo's radio transmitter was in the attic of the Hampstead Heath house, set on a gentle rise of ground. That was out of consideration for Garbo's German controllers in Madrid. It made receiving his signal easier for them. While the sergeant of the Signals Intelligence Service went to the attic to prepare his transmitter, Garbo and his British controller gathered to smoke and chat in a sitting room downstairs.

Madrid had been told to keep its listening posts open in case the Fifty-second Infantry Division in Scotland started to move. That, of course, was no longer of any consequence. The real news was the scoop supposedly delivered to Garbo just after midnight by his Gibraltarian waiter agent who worked in the canteen at the Hiltingbury camp where the Third Canadian Infantry Division was stationed.

'5(2) has hastened to London,' Garbo's British-prepared text said, 'in view of the highly important news he would otherwise have been unable to communicate as a result of the complete sealing of the camp. Their place is being taken by an American division. The Canadians are said to have embarked and sailed for the invasion.'

That was it: the invasion fleet was on the high seas. Garbo had justified every jot of confidence the Germans had placed in him. When that message reached Abwehr headquarters on Tirpitzstrasse, it would set the alarm bells ringing from Berlin to Biarritz. It concluded with a thoughtful consideration on Garbo's part for his imaginary agent. He was sending him into hiding in South Wales, the message said.

Promptly at 3 A.M. British Double Summer Time, as Ridley's earlier message had said he would, Garbo's wireless operator began to fling out his call sign, signalling Madrid he was ready to transmit. Downstairs, Garbo and his controllers chuckled in delight at the magnitude of the hoax they were about to put over on the Abwehr. They were still laughing when, just before 3:30, the wireless operator came down from the attic. He was ashen.

Madrid had not answered his call. A little coterie of British deceivers stood ready and eager to lay into the lap of German intelligence the secret for which every Abwehr agent had been working for six months, and the Germans weren't going to get it because a radio operator was asleep or out carousing with a flamenco dancer in some Madrid cabaret.

In London and in Washington, the men whose shoulders would carry before history the terrible responsibility for the invasion's success or failure agonized their way through the night as best they could. Winston Churchill was slouched in an armchair in his living quarters at Storey's Gate, morosely sipping brandy, trying to drive from his mind the image of Channel tides incarnadined with the blood of thousands of young English, Canadian and American soldiers. His personal chief of staff, General Sir Hastings Ismay, was at Portsmouth to serve as his constant liaison with invasion headquarters. 'Tonight is the worst night of the war,' he wrote to a friend. 'The worst that could have happened almost has happened. We're in a hell of a mess.'

General Sir Alan Brooke, the chief of Britain's Imperial General Staff, was in the quarters at the Horse Guards. 'The invasion,' he noted in his diary, 'may well be the most ghastly disaster of the war. I wish to God it was safely over.' Henry Ridley spent the night alone pacing London's deserted streets, eyes and ears following the air fleet droning overhead, asking himself over and over again one desperate question: will *Fortitude* work?

At Southwick House, Dwight Eisenhower couldn't sleep. He lay down on his cot fully clothed, trying to keep his mind from the coming ordeal with a Western. Tucked into the pocket of his uniform jacket was a single sheet of paper. Nothing might measure more accurately the unutterable solitude of a great captain at his hour of decision than the words typed on to that paper. Eisenhower had prepared them himself for release to the world in the event the invasion failed.

'The troops, the air, the navy did all that bravery and devotion to duty could do,' it read. 'If there is any blame or fault attached to the failure it is mine alone.'

The black Citroën swept up the Champs-Elysées to the great ceremonial mall of the Arc de Triomphe. Nothing, Catherine noted, peering across the shoulders of her Gestapo guards, not even a stray bicyclist or a German military vehicle, was moving along its broad expanse. They were alone. Inevitably, she thought back to her last passage along that avenue, in warm spring sunlight, with Paul by her side in their velocab. Would she see him again? she wondered. An awful thought gripped her. Perhaps that was why they had rushed her to Paris – to hurl some ruined stump of a man at her feet and threaten to start torturing him again if she refused to talk. It was exactly the kind of savagery the Gestapo specialized in. Would she be able to keep her silence in the face of that? She shuddered. There were some eventualities it was better not to think about.

Through the car window she saw fleeting by the dark and silent façades of Avenue Foch's stately dwellings. The driver braked and turned through an iron grille identified only by a small blue-and-white enamel plaque bearing the number 82. Her stomach knotted. They had arrived in the building that for every Resistance fighter in France was a kind of citadel of fear, the symbol of the worst fate that could befall them.

She expected to be thrown into some dark and squalid cell; instead she found herself being escorted up the main staircase into a lavish and tastefully furnished office. Her guards gestured towards a Louis XIV chair placed before an enormous desk. As she sat down, one disappeared while the other took up a silent and somewhat respectful guard. As discreetly as possible, she surveyed the room. It was illuminated by a blazing crystal chandelier, its floor covered by a pale purple rug. Clearly its occupant either had a taste in art or had taken the place over from some Frenchman who did. On one wall she spotted a Chagall; on another, near the fireplace, a Cubist painting, perhaps even an early Picasso.

Suddenly, the door opened and an immaculately groomed, rather

337

distinguished-looking man entered the room. The instant she saw him she knew she had seen him somewhere before. Hans-Dieter Strömelburg looked down on her with a bemused regard. He, of course, had recognized her instantly.

'So,' he said, clicking his heels lightly in a kind of mock bow. 'We meet again.' He caught the uncertainty in her green and defiant eyes. 'Albeit in somewhat less pleasant circumstances than those offered by the Chapon Rouge.'

At the mention of the black-market restaurant where she and Paul had dined their first night in Paris, she immediately recognized the man as her saviour from the lecherous Luftwaffe officer who had accosted her on her way back to her table that evening.

'I gather you didn't recognize me,' Strömelburg said, laughing drily. 'I remembered you the instant I saw you – which is hardly surprising. Few men who have had the privilege of meeting so exquisitely beautiful a woman are apt to forget her.'

With those words he burst into a sudden and sulphuric rage. It was not directed at her, however, but at the two Gestapo agents who had escorted her down from Lille, and it was entirely feigned. In a few slashing sentences – in French, for her benefit – he berated them for handcuffing her. Like mechanical toys tightly wound up and then released, they jerked about her, undoing the handcuffs, massaging her wrists and hands to restore their circulation.

'That's better,' Strömelburg said. He drew a thin silver cigarette case from the inside pocket of his well-cut suit and advanced on her. She could smell his *eau de cologne*, and as he offered her a cigarette, she noted that his fingernails were those of a man whose hands were well and frequently manicured.

'Thank you,' she replied. 'I don't smoke.'

He took one himself, tapped it on the back of his cigarette case and lit it with an imperious flick of a gold lighter. Then he returned to his desk and, resting lightly against it, said, 'Now perhaps you might tell me just how it is you've come to be in the hands of my services.'

With all the sense of outraged innocence she could muster, Catherine rose to his challenge. Detail by well-rehearsed detail, she flung out at him the story represented by her false ID papers: the poor divorcée named Alexandra Boyneau struggling to exist in Calais, seized by an incomprehensible error on the Gestapo's part as she left the railroad station on her way home to her humble little apartment. It all sounded so blatantly false that it occurred to her she must have resembled some helplessly inept *ingénue* auditioning for a part far beyond her meagre talents.

Strömelburg laughed when she had finished. 'That's a wonderful story, mademoiselle. I must congratulate you. You tell it very well. What a pity both you and I know there's not a word of truth in it.'

As he said it, he was appraising her very carefully. No agent ever entered his office eager to talk. Most came braced for the ordeal ahead, driven into a state of artificial tension by their determination to resist his assault. His first goal was to get them to lower, inadvertently, the barriers they had raised to his interrogation by distracting them, getting them to turn their minds elsewhere. Then he sought to terrify them.

He turned to a silver tray on his desk. It bore a bottle of Johnnie Walker Black Label and a pair of shot glasses.

'Whisky?' he said.

She shook her head. 'No, thank you. I don't drink.'

'A woman without vices. Commendable.' He poured himself a shot. '*Prost*,' he said, raising it to her and taking a sip. 'You see it contains no evil potion to render you helpless before an assault on your virtue. That sort of thing' – he allowed a chill note to inflect his tone – 'is not among the vices we practice here. Let me tell you, by the way, a rather amusing story about that whisky.'

Strömelburg settled in his chair and took on the pose of a raconteur trying to charm a beautiful woman. 'It's a gift from your employer and superior, the good Major Cavendish.' His mention of Cavendish's name and her relation with him produced, he noted, a flicker of apprehension in those defiant green eyes of hers. That was precisely the effect they were meant to produce.

'Did you by any chance meet Captain Harry Anton at Orchard Court or during your wanderings at Wamborough Manor?'

'No,' she lied, hoping this lie might appear more convincing than her earlier efforts had. How, she wondered, had he got the name of Orchard Court and of SOE's supposedly Top Secret training school?

'No matter,' Strömelburg said with an indulgent wave of his cigarette. 'He parachuted in in March to what he and poor old Major Cavendish assumed was an SOE reception. It was in fact organized by my services. There was a little misunderstanding at the field and he, alas, was killed.

'Now, we knew he had been instructed to communicate with London forty-eight hours after landing – a difficult task, after all, when one is dead. What to do? Clearly, if he didn't get in touch with London, even Major Cavendish would have realized the circuit to which he'd been dropped had been compromised. One of my subordinates had what I've always thought was a particularly genial idea. He suggested we tell London he had been hit on the head by one of the arms containers they had dropped with them and was in a coma.' Strömelburg laughed in pleased recollection of the Doctor's genius, then leaned forward, a smile of purest self-satisfaction enlightening his face.

339

'Cavendish replied with a screaming DD informing us poor Anton had had a cold before leaving and if his skull had been fractured by the container, he might well develop meningitis – which, as I am sure you know, is a serious and quite generally fatal disease.'

Catherine nodded dumbly, trying to conceal her shock. How did he know the sign 'DD,' the SOE's supposedly secret prefix for an urgent message?

'And fatal it turned out to be for Anton. We got one of our doctors here and arranged for him to die a second time, this time over three weeks without coming out of his coma. We radioed Cavendish regular bulletins prepared by our doctor on his deteriorating condition and, at the end, a rather heartrending account of how we all sang the 'Marseillaise' and cried, 'Vive De Gaulle' by poor Anton's graveside. Then it occurred to me to suggest that as a matter of courtesy Cavendish might wish to send over some whisky and cigars in our next arms drop for the doctor who'd cared for Anton during his tragic illness. That,' he laughed, 'accounts for my whisky supply. Are you sure you won't change your mind?'

He pretended to glance at the bottle; he was in fact studying her to see her reaction to his story. It was meant to impress her with the extent of his inside knowledge of SOE operations. In that, he suspected, he'd been successful. Ideally, it would have filled her with a sense of impotence in the face of that knowledge. That appeared much less certain.

'Now,' he said, taking on the air of a salesman ready to close an order, 'that brings us to you and your reason for being here – the real reason, not that silly little story you told me a few moments ago. Cavendish must have laughed when he made you recite it back to him at Orchard Court Sunday night before you left for Tangmere. You managed to fly in Sunday despite that ghastly weather and travelled up to Calais yesterday, where, had we not picked you up, you would have handed over to your superior, Aristide, the modifications London sent back with you for the sabotage plan you and he devised and were going to put into action up there.'

Catherine felt the colour draining from her cheeks. There was a traitor inside their organization, either here in France or, even worse, back in London.

Strömelburg sat back in his chair thinking through his next move. 'I trust none of this comes as a surprise to you?'

'What surprises me is the realization one of our people is a traitor.' Her green eyes flashed with anger. 'Someone of great importance in SOE is working for you. That's why I'm here in this office.'

'Yes,' Strömelburg replied, 'your supposition is entirely correct.' He rose and walked around his desk. 'You are also a terrorist, operating

340

behind enemy lines out of uniform, for which the penalty under the Geneva Convention is death.'

'The Geneva Convention!' she exploded in rage. 'You Germans wouldn't even know how to spell the words.' The instant she said it, she wanted to bite her tongue. Why couldn't she learn to control her temper?

Strömelburg, however, did not erupt in fury as she had expected. He smiled. 'A woman of character as well as virtue. You should be spared the less attractive aspects of an interrogation in this building. I can offer you that. And I will. All I want from you is a few simple, straightforward answers. I want the modifications London gave you. I want the timing keys they gave you. I want a description in a few well-chosen words of how you propose to carry out your operation. No more. No less.'

'You know I can't tell you that.'

'Do I?' The German's voice had the temper of steel, and there was no smile on his face now. His eyes, Catherine thought, were the cold, remorseless eyes of a hunter, of a man staring down a steel barrel towards the prey he proposed to destroy. 'My dear young lady, there is nothing that beautiful head of yours holds that I cannot make you tell me. Nothing.'

At that instant, a buzzer on his desk rang. Strömelburg picked up his phone. It was the Doctor. 'I see,' he said. 'I'll be right with you.'

He turned to the two men who had escorted her down from Lille. 'Prepare the lady for a little talk,' he said. 'I shall return shortly.'

The Doctor was waiting in the sitting room across the hall from his office which Strömelburg employed on nights when he didn't wish to drive back to his villa in Neuilly. He handed Strömelburg a slip of paper.

'This just came in from the Café Sporting in Lille. It was delivered by the same man who delivered the last message.'

Strömelburg picked up Aristide's decoded text. 'Aristide to Cavendish,' it read. 'Denise arrested on arrival Calais station tonight stop.' That's helpful, Strömelburg mused: now we know her underground name. 'She was followed by five French Gestapo officers almost certainly from Bony Laffont Paris who gave her to two waiting German Gestapo stop Conclusion must be she betrayed to Gestapo by someone here stop Time her arrival Calais would indicate she had no contacts en route here from Lysander arrival stop Therefore Paul Air Operations Officer must be in pay of Gestapo request carte blanche to deal with him stop Reply most urgent this channel.'

'What does it mean?' the Doctor asked.

'Simple. They're on to Gilbert. "Carte blanche" means they want London's permission to kill him.'

The Doctor paled. 'Shall I throw this away?'

341

'No,' Strömelburg said, 'send it. Immediately.'

'My God, why?'

'Why not? Can you imagine a more perfect final check on Gilbert's loyalty?'

'Surely,' the Doctor said, 'after all this time you don't have any doubts about Gilbert's loyalty?'

'For a policeman, Doctor, to doubt is to exist. Love sometimes has a way of altering men's loyalties. Our friend Gilbert, I suspect, is having or had an affair with that woman in my office – although if she turns out to be as uncooperative as she seems determined to be, his appetite may be put to rather a severe test the next time he lays his eyes on her.'

Strömelburg saw the Doctor pale. Once again, he was reminded of his deputy's non-SS background. 'I assume Cavendish will authorize this Aristide to kill Gilbert. That would be only natural in the circumstances. Among other things, it will provide us, and what's even more important, Berlin, with the final assurance we're on the right path.'

'But what about Gilbert?'

'What about him? His operation's finished now. We'll either get him a commission and give him a job in here or put him out to pasture somewhere. Send the cable.'

As the Doctor left, Strömelburg went to his private bathroom. There he began to absentmindedly wash and rewash his hands. His was a nervous reflex with which, quite unconsciously, Strömelburg often prepared for his torture sessions, a sort of ritual absolution designed perhaps to cleanse him of the iniquities he was about to perpetrate on his victims. Scrubbing away, he sought to focus his thoughts. His long years as a police interrogator had taught him to read people's eyes as a sailor reads a shifting wind. Defiance was what he had read in her flickering green eyes, a defiant determination to thwart him. How was he going to break her?

When he had finished washing, his hands more thoroughly cleansed than a surgeon's before he enters an operating theatre, he lit a cigarette and reflected a moment. What he needed to know from her was relatively simple: what, exactly, was the sabotage operation she'd been ordered to perform and, more important, precisely when and on whose orders was she to perform it?

Most people, Strömelburg knew, had an area of vulnerability, some aspect of their being in which they were particularly susceptible to a deft psychological thrust. Vanity, he had discovered, was often an agent's weakness. Tell him he was less important than he was, disparage his accomplishments and he might well blurt out the information you wanted in a burst of injured pride.

What about her? Where was the soft spot in her makeup he could exploit, the avenue that would take him most expeditiously to the few scraps of information he had to extract from her? What made her special, Strömelburg reflected, was the fact that she was such a beautiful woman. Great beauty sets a woman apart from her less fortunate sisters. Just as wealth gives the rich power and breeding gives the aristocracy their arrogance, so great beauty gives a woman an authority other women do not possess. It is an instrument with which to command attention, to gain access to people and places, to lure others to do their bidding. It is the tool with which all truly beautiful women make their way in life.

Yet deprive that same woman of her beauty and she is suddenly defenceless, as powerless, as helpless as a cat whose whiskers have been shorn. So, Strömelburg thought, sauntering across the hall, that was how he would break the defiant creature waiting in his office. He would strike at her through her beauty.

As Strömelburg had ordered, she had been 'prepared' for their coming talk. Her handcuffs were back on again, her wrists clipped together over the back of the chair before his desk. Her ankles were lashed to the chair's legs with electric cord pulled so tight it cut the surface of her skin. She had been stripped naked. Nothing, Strömelburg knew, was quite so demeaning for a prisoner, male or female, as to have to cringe totally naked before a captor.

Wordlessly, he crossed the room and stared down at her. The green eyes thrust up at his were as sullen and defiant as ever. He turned to the bridge table his men had set a few feet from her chair. Set out on the white bed sheet draped over it were the contents of her handbag. He studied them: a compact, a tube of lipstick, a hairbrush, matches, a comb, two handkerchiefs, a wallet. The handbag itself had been slit apart with a razor to make sure it contained no secret panel in which a microfilm could be concealed. The alterations to the sabotage plan were either in a microfilm somewhere in that mundane collection on the table, Strömelburg mused, or, more likely, captured on the less accessible microfilm of her mind.

He stepped back and looked down at her from a few feet away, his arms folded across his chest.

'So, Denise,' he said, noting with satisfaction the tremor that disturbed her defiant regard when she heard him pronounce her name. 'You are not a child. You know where you are and why you're here.'

She said nothing but looked at him with her steady, unblinking eyes.

'You also know what we do to people here' – he paused so that the sound of his words might recede slowly, like a fading echo – 'if they are not prepared to answer our questions.'

Still she said nothing.

'I told you earlier what I want to know from you – the details of the sabotage operation you're planning to carry out in Calais and the timing instructions London gave you for it.'

Catherine licked her lips and began to speak slowly, trying to squeeze any hint of fear from her tone. It wasn't easy. 'Since you know my organization so well, then you'll know all I'm authorized to tell you is my name, rank and serial number.'

'Name!' Strömelburg barked it with a drill sergeant's roar.

'Catherine Pradier.'

'Rank!'

'Lieutenant.'

'Serial number!'

'266712.'

One of her interrogator's accolytes, Catherine noted, was carefully inscribing each of her responses on a pad of paper.

'Now, where are the modifications for the sabotage plan Cavendish gave you to give to Aristide? Where?' Strömelburg had leaned forward as he said the words until his face was a foot from her, and his breath lashed her face as he articulated each furious syllable. 'Where?'

'I can't tell you.' Catherine fought desperately to suppres a tremor of fear from her tone. 'You know that.'

Strömelburg sighed. His expression suddenly softened and he regarded her with a look designed to mix in equal parts regret and commiseration for the ordeal she seemed determined to oblige him to force upon her. He reached out and placed his hands, quite gently, on her bare shoulders. 'Look,' he was almost pleading, 'don't make me turn these people on you.' Strömelburg's eyes went to his two French torturers lolling indifferently against his office walls. 'I promise you, cooperate and no harm will come to you.' He stood up, his face suddenly brightening like that of a child who's found the answer to a teacher's question. 'I'll arrange an escape for you. You'll be free again. No one but you and I will ever know you talked. I swear to you on my word of honour as a German officer.'

'The word of a German officer?' Her laughter was forced and bitter. 'I'd put more faith in the word of the Devil.' This time she did not regret her outburst. Her anger suddenly seemed a support from which she might draw strength.

'Fool! Stupid foolish child!' Strömelburg snarled. When he began an interrogation, he was an actor deliberately swaying wildly from fury to gentleness to confound and disorient his prisoner. But invariably, as his tensions rose and his determination to succeed overwhelmed him, the actor disappeared, the drama faded and the emotions he had meant to feign became real. 'You would trust the word of those people who sent you here? Those wonderful Englishmen who play cricket in their white pants and drink tea and send you, a woman, here to do their filthy work for them? You trust them, those vile, despicable bastards?'

He was a little hysterical now, a froth of spittle forming around his lips. 'You're going to suffer for them? For those Americans, those stupid Americans who want to tell us how to run the world and bomb innocent German women and children to death by the thousand every day? You're going to suffer for them? Where's the microfilm?' The last words came in a roar, and the answering glance in her eyes told Strömelburg what he wanted to know: there was a microfilm.

'I can't tell you that,' she murmured – then added, too late, 'there isn't any.'

Strömelburg started to pace a short line in front of her chair, calmer now. 'Denise or Catherine, however you choose to be called, they all talk in the end. Everyone who has ever sat in that chair you're in has told me what I wanted to know. Everyone. The only question is when. Are you going to tell me now or are you going to wait until we've dragged you to the edge of Hell to tell me? When they've pulled out your fingernails one by one?'

He stopped and stared at her writhing in her helpless nudity before him. 'Don't be a fool!'

Catherine shook her head as much to conceal the tears welling in her eyes as to reply. 'I can't, I can't,' she whispered.

He sprang forward and his hand shot at her face. She recoiled. He did not hit her, however. He grasped her long blond hair firmly but not brutally. 'This lovely hair!' he sighed. His other hand went to her face and skimmed her high cheekbones. 'This beautiful face, the face of a Madonna, your eyes, your lips. Would you have me destroy this? For what? For nothing, because in the end you will tell me anyway.'

He half-rose and stared down at her naked figure. 'That lovely body, those gentle breasts. Think of the man who loves it, whom you love. Will he caress it and cherish it when they've turned it into a sack of old and broken bones, when they've maimed and mutilated you?' He paused, then roared at her an angry demand: 'Will he?'

All Catherine could do was to drop her head so he could not see her frightened eyes. She thought of Paul but refused to mumble even a word, afraid her voice would betray her fear.

Strömelburg stood erect. She groaned inwardly and said to herself, Be strong. It's about to start. The German marched across the room, picked up an object from the mantelpiece of his fireplace and returned to her.

'Look,' he commanded. He was holding a vase, the vase he had so proudly displayed to the Doctor some weeks earlier. 'An eighteenth-century Sèvres porcelain.' He began to almost fondle the vase as a father might fondle a newborn son. 'What supple harmony of colour and form and design! When has anyone ever been able to produce such wondrous works of beauty?' His fingers skimmed the bulbous top of the vase. 'Look at this dark rich blue, the Royal Blue of Sèvres, a colour no one else has ever been able to imitate.'

Catherine followed his words in a kind of trance. His voice had become low, tender almost, and a very strange thought struck her: this man who ten seconds ago was threatening to maim and mutilate me actually means what he is saying; he is in fact genuinely moved by this object which he's holding with such reverence in his hands.

'This vase is unique,' Strömelburg murmured, 'absolutely unique. Its beauty is priceless, irreplaceable. Once destroyed, it never can be re-created. Its sublime beauty, its uniqueness, its ability to awe and inspire us will have vanished forever!'

He held the vase up so that its radiance was fully captured by the bright glimmer of his chandelier.

'The beauty of a woman is like the beauty of this vase – evanescent, as tender, as fragile as porcelain. The beauty of a woman, of a truly beautiful woman like you can move us, can inspire us, can command us by its presence.' His voice took on such a seductive intensity he might have been trying to seduce her, which in a sense, he was. 'But if that beauty disappears, then the special mystique of the woman disappears with it. Never again will she walk into a room and command attention by her presence. Never again will she have that mysterious power to summon us to her, to awe and inspire us.'

He paused, studying first Catherine, then the vase. 'Please,' he said, his voice a whisper now, 'don't force me to destroy the irreplaceable vessel of your beauty. Don't throw away God's unique blessing for some misplaced sense of duty, for that handful of cynical Englishmen who sent you here. I beg you, Denise, I beg you, don't force me to use those techniques I so despise.' His eyes went to his men, still leaning against the office wall. 'Don't make me turn them on you. What were you going to sabotage?'

She started to say something, then choked back her words. 'No,' she whispered, shaking her head.

'Tell me!' His voice suddenly soared in strident anger. She looked at him. His face was reddening in anger and frustration, and a vein along his neck began to bulge slightly outward. 'Tell me!' he commanded.

Again she shook her head. 'I can't,' she whispered.

The vase was now clutched in one hand raised over Strömelburg's head. 'Tell me, God damn you, tell me!' he roared.

Catherine did not know what to do. She was utterly, helplessly trapped. 'I can't. You know that,' she murmured.

'Tell me!' The room seemed to tremble from the impact of his shout.

'No.'

His arm whipped down. He flung the precious Sèvres vase at her feet with all his fury, splintering it into a score of fragments against the floor and her bones, lacerating her bare flesh.

'Take her,' he said. 'Call me when she's ready to talk.'

He strode from the room, her first piercing scream of pain ringing in his ears.

In the outskirts of Paris, in the stately palace of Saint-Germain-en-Laye in which Louis XIV had been born, an old and tired man studied the huge map of the French seacoast adorning the wall of his operations room. To Hitler, whom he despised, and his subordinate Rommel, whom he scorned, Field Marshal von Rundstedt was a worn and weary armchair general, a man who preferred puttering about his rose garden and dining on the delights of the Coq Hardi to the rigours of war. Weary he might have been, but as he stood there scowling in silence at his maps, he discerned what they would not see – that despite his own predictions that they would land in Pas-de-Calais, the Allies were about to make a major seaborne assault between the Vire and the Orne rivers. Was this the real landing? Were the Allies, as Hitler had predicted at Berchtesgaden, displaying Churchill's preference for the indirect approach? Or was it a massive deception to entice him to do the one thing he must not do if he was to defeat the Allies – split up his forces so he could be beaten piecemeal?

For the moment, it didn't matter. The attack was going to be a very substantial assault indeed, and what mattered was stopping it in its tracks. At 4:15, while the first assault craft were beginning to struggle towards the shore through seas whipped by Force 5 winds, Von Rundstedt made the first critical German decision of the day. He ordered the Twelfth SS 'Hitler Youth' Panzer Division between Paris and Caen and the Panzer Lehr between Caen and Chartres to march immediately on Normandy. They would be shrouded from Allied air attack on their dash to the sea by the ground mist that would rise at dawn from the Norman countryside. Once they had closed on the beaches, where Allied pilots and naval gunners would be unable to tell friend from foe, they, together with the Twenty-first Panzer already on the spot, would savage the assault at the water's edge.

The problem was that those divisions were not Von Rundstedt's to command. They were part of Hitler's OKW central reserve. Nonetheless, with an arrogance typical of the man and his caste, Von Rundstedt ordered the divisions to move first, then informed Hitler's headquarters of what he had done.

The steward delegated by the Avenue Foch officers' mess to attend Hans-Dieter Strömelburg meticulously smoothed a linen tablecloth onto the bridge table by the *Obersturmbannführer*'s bed. From a tray he took out a heavy service of Third Empire silver. Strömelburg, pretending not to hear the muffled screams coming from inside his office, followed the steward's ritual ballet. He was famished. Dawn, Tuesday, June 6, was at hand, and in the excitement of the day he had quite simply forgotten to eat.

A second steward set a plate covered by a sterling silver warming dome on the table and uncorked a bottle of the Gestapo's house Bordeaux. With a ceremonious gesture, the steward seized the silver warming dome from Strömelburg's plate to reveal a *Wienerschnitzel* and a generous serving of boiled potatoes and cabbage. Strömelburg was halfway through his meal when the Doctor appeared in his doorway, waving several cable forms.

They made gratifying reading. A major Allied military operation, almost certainly the invasion, was under way, and thanks to the Doctor and his radio game, Germany's forces had been alerted to meet it. One thing did puzzle him, however: OB West reported paratroops dropping in a wide stretch of Normandy from Deauville all the way up to the outskirts of Cherbourg and a heavy concentration of enemy shipping in the Bay of the Seine. If Normandy was to be the focus of the enemy's landing, why was he wasting his time on this Pradier woman and her sabotage plans for Calais? Strömelburg shrugged. She was the only person who could answer that question for him. He passed the paper back to his deputy.

'You will be decorated for what you achieved tonight, Doctor.'

As Strömelburg said those words, a shrill feminine cry of despair and agony echoed from across the hall. The Doctor's pudgy face, already drawn and white from lack of sleep, paled further. Strömelburg, he well knew, welcomed criticism from his subordinates as enthusiastically as a cat welcomes a bath. Yet the Doctor was, this night, for the first time in his life, a hero, a genuine hero. Such knowledge emboldens the mildest of men.

'How can you sit here eating so calmly while that woman is suffering like that?' he asked.

For an instant, Strömelburg's face clouded with the warning that he might, perhaps, make the Doctor suffer for such insubordination. Then, with a shrug, he let the remark pass. 'She gave us no choice.'

'Torture is such a bestial thing. It reduces us to the level of animals.'

Strömelburg sipped his wine, gratefully savouring its warming glow. Had the Doctor drunk, he would have offered him a glass. Perhaps it might help soothe his troubled conscience. 'Don't think I enjoy ordering

348

prisoners tortured, Doctor. I don't. Intensive interrogation' – that was the euphemism the RSHA employed to describe its savagery – 'happens to be an unpleasant but extremely effective way to encourage a prisoner to talk. I do not trouble myself with bourgeois notions of its morality.' He gave a little toss to his head as though to disturb a mosquito circling over him. 'Besides' – there was a touch of anger in his voice – 'if we're going to argue the morality of things, Doctor – who is more immoral? The English, who sent her here in the first place as a saboteur, knowing full well what would happen to her if she was caught? Or we, trying to get information from her that may help Germany to win the war? This is a war we're fighting, and in war, Doctor, there is only one morality – to win.'

Strömelburg stood up and fastidiously brushed a few bread crumbs from his suit jacket. He took a final sip of wine and patted his lips with his napkin. Theirs was not, the Doctor understood, a conversation he would be wise to pursue, no matter how fresh and impressive the hero's laurels crowning his brow might be. The Doctor bowed slightly and withdrew.

'Keep me informed of developments on the Front,' Strömelburg called after his departing figure, then started towards his own office and his latest victim.

His torturers had forced Catherine to stand on a thick Paris telephone directory. Then they had coiled a rope with an iron hook attached to one of its ends through the grommet to which the chandelier was suspended from the ceiling. Her handcuffs had been hooked onto the chain until her feet barely touched the cardboard cover of the directory. Alternating, they had set to work on her using first their fists, then the edges of their hands, then flat leather straps to which a series of metal studs had been fixed.

Strömelburg slammed his office door behind him and strode across the purple carpet towards her moaning figure, dangling from the ceiling like a side of beef in a slaughterhouse. He was horrified at the transformation half an hour of his men's work had wrought upon her face and figure. Her nose had been broken, her breath came in laboured rasps, her lips were bloody and swollen, her eyes almost lost in the bruises around them.

The torturers paused respectfully in their labours as Strömelburg stomped towards her body. Catherine was only half conscious. She felt as though she were wrapped in a red blanket of pain, her body a tissue of raw ganglia upon which the slightest touch or gesture sent electric jolts of agony through her being. Through the film that glazed her eyes she saw the outline of Strömelburg's approaching figure. Then his face was in front of hers, his features contorted with such anger and hatred they

349

seemed more terrifying to her than any of the agonies she had endured. The head snapped back, then shot forward like a snake. As his wad of spittle struck her cheekbones, he snarled, 'Whore! Terrorist whore!'

Suddenly, Strömelburg spun away from her. He went to one wall of his office and almost ripped an antique mirror from its resting place. Returning, he thrust it against her face. 'Look!' he screamed. 'Look at yourself! Look what they've done to you. What man will ever want to look at you now? Great beauty you are now, aren't you? And they've just begun.' He stopped, then repeated himself, driving his words at her like rivets: 'They've just begun!'

At that instant the buzzer on his desk rang. It was the Doctor again, indicating he had an urgent communication. Strömelburg stepped reluctantly out of the office. The Doctor, puffing from unaccustomed physical exertion, was rushing up the stairs waving a yellow teletype message. 'From OB West,' he gasped. 'The landing has begun – in Normandy.'

Strömelburg studied the dispatch which had just arrived on his high-speed teleprinter with avid interest. If the enemy landing was taking place in Normandy, he asked himself, why was he wasting time with her? Why was he having her beaten to a pulp to learn the secret of some stupid train derailment outside Calais – particularly when every grade crossing and switching box would be guarded now like the Führer's box at the Sportpalast?

He glanced at his watch. It was after 6 A.M.. Suddenly he was exhausted, too exhausted to waste any more of his time on the woman dangling from a rope in his office. He opened the door. 'Take her upstairs,' he ordered. He stood back as his two torturers half-carried, half-dragged Catherine out of his office and up the stairs to the attic. There a circle of cubicles, the rooms used by the maids of the building's wealthy prewar tenants, had been converted into cells where the Gestapo held prisoners between torture sessions.

Downstairs, the air in Strömelburg's office seemed to stink of sweat and tears, blood and fear. His purple carpet, under his chandelier, had been darkened with the stains of Catherine Pradier's blood. All for nothing, he thought – for some petty act of sabotage in support of an invasion that had occurred 130 miles from Calais. What an idiot she had been to force him to do that to her. He strode over to the window and hurled it open so that the damp June air might drive the stench from his office.

At Berchtesgaden, the Führer was still sound asleep. It was not until 6:30 A.M., four hours after the airborne troops had jumped, three and a half hours after the invasion fleet had anchored in the Bay of the Seine, half an hour after the first wave had landed, that a senior member of his entourage was finally awakened with the news that the war had entered its decisive phase. General Alfred Jodl, Hitler's Chief of Operations, was summoned from his sleep to be informed that Von Rundstedt had ordered two Panzer divisions of the Führer's Reserve to Normandy. He was furious. He ordered the Panzers stopped in their tracks. The choice of the landing spot, the terrible weather, he told his aides, made it more than likely the Normandy assault was just a diversion. He called for an urgent intelligence appreciation of the situation be prepared for the Führer by Colonel Alexis von Roenne's Foreign Armies West Section in Zossen.

'The main landing,' Jodl predicted, 'is probably going to come at an entirely different place.' The fatal seeds of doubt of Henry Ridley's *Fortitude* scheme was falling upon fertile ground.

At precisely 0917 that Tuesday morning, while Adolf Hitler was asleep, a British lance corporal started a preperforated tape through the reading head of the teleprinter in General Dwight D. Eisenhower's main headquarters. Seconds later, SHAEF Communiqué 1 announced to London and the world the news that the assault on *Festung Europa* had begun. At the same time, Eisenhower's radio adviser, William S. Paley of the Columbia Broadcasting System, picked up a dedicated telephone line joining SHAEF headquarters to the BBC and ordered the release of prerecorded addresses announcing the landings by Eisenhower and the leaders of the peoples of Occupied Europe. All of those addresses – except one – had been prepared and vetted by *Fortitude's* architects. Everything, every word and sentence spoken by the Allies on D-Day, was filled with a calculated ambiguity. All were designed to lure the Germans, siren-like, into the trap of *Fortitude*, to the fatal suggestion there would be more than one landing. Eisenhower's announcement, leading the roll call, referred to the Normandy landings as an 'initial' assault. King Haakon of Norway described them as 'a link' in a wide strategy. For Belgium's prime minister they were 'preliminary operations for the liberation of Europe,' and the premier of the Netherlands warned his country's Resistance fighters to wait for a clear, unmistakable signal from London before going into action. Churchill, addressing the Commons, spoke of 'a succession of surprises,' and Roosevelt even suggested that the Germans 'expect landings elsewhere.'

Only one man failed to conform to *Fortitude's* dictate – the man whose nation was being liberated: Charles de Gaulle. There was not a single Frenchman alive, not even De Gaulle himself, who was privy to *Fortitude's* devious secret. No one placed the words of Voltaire's tongue in his mouth; De Gaulle threw away the text *Fortitude's* planners had prepared for him and wrote his own speech from a heart overflowing with emotion. He managed to say precisely the wrong thing. 'The supreme battle has begun,' he said, 'The decisive blow' struck.

At Storey's Gate, the operations room of Churchill's Underground War Rooms had become a second command post of the invasion. General Brooke, Churchill himself, Cabinet ministers and chiefs of staff were in and out every fifteen minutes, consulting the invasion maps, the latest despatches from the invasion beaches, the black folder with its *Ultra* intercepts of Germany's communications.

Ridley was exhausted and disconsolate. *Fortitude* had started badly. Garbo was his master player, the knight whose sudden strike he had counted on to checkmate the Germans at the critical moment of decision. And because Madrid had not been listening at 3 A.M., the message they had so cunningly designed to turn their Spaniard into an oracle had not got to Berlin until after the invasion had started. All their schemings, all the hours begging Eisenhower's agreement to an idea that went against every one of his soldierly doctrines wasted because of the incompetence of some faceless German corporal. Ridley shuddered and lit another cigarette, his weary eyes unable to leave the maps before him. Would his scheme fix in place those Panzers of the Fifteenth Army on whose movement – or nonmovement – so much depended? The calculations were so fine, the permutations so complex, the risks so enormous.

A few miles away, another British officer stared disconsolately into the street below his office window. The news that the invasion had begun at last brought no joy to Major Frederick Cavendish. His capacity for joy on Tuesday, June 6, had been shattered by the cable delivered to his desk by the first despatch rider in from the SOE's receiving station at Sevenoaks. The thought that the lovely girl who had been seated opposite his desk only forty-eight hours earlier was in the hands of the Gestapo sickened and disheartened Cavendish. And what had come close to destroying him was the realization that he himself bore a heavy burden for her arrest. Why, he asked himself, had he let Dansey talk him into keeping Paul operational?

Cavendish returned to his desk and read again the words in Aristide's cable. Had Paul's treachery been confined to letting the Germans read the intelligence in his outgoing packets, he might have been prepared to let him escape with a few years in Wormwood Scrubs. Betraying – deliberately, callously – a fellow agent to the Gestapo, however, was a crime for which there was no forgiveness in Cavendish's charitable soul. He did something nothing in his life or background had prepared him to do.

With one terse sentence, he condemned a man to death.

For Colonel Baron Alex von Roenne, Tuesday, June 6, represented the culmination of a lifetime of service to Germany's Armed Forces. That morning, in response to General Jodl's urgent command, he prepared for the Führer's midday conference the most important intelligence appraisal of his long and brilliant career.

By fortuitous circumstance, he had on his desk that Tuesday morning a freshly delivered package from the Abwehr's headquarters on Tirpitzstrasse. It contained the Abwehr's summary of the material *Fortitude's* double agent, Brutus, had been sending nightly to Paris since May 31. For Von Roenne, it was a godsend. It provided the framework into which to fit the mass of raw data he had picked up over the past two months from wireless intercepts, the occasional aerial photo, agents' reports.

'The Normandy landings,' Von Roenne began in his Situation Report West 1288, had thus far 'employed only a relatively small portion of the troops available.' Everything, he said, indicated that 'further operations are planned.'

Then, describing his source as 'a believable Abwehr report of June 2,' he proceeded to set out almost verbatim for Hitler's benefit the contents of Brutus' messages. It was all there, just as Henry Ridley had wished it to be – the breakdown of the Allied forces into two army groups, the Twenty-first under Montgomery in southern England, the nonexistent First US under Patton opposite Calais; the breakdown of the First US Army Group into the First Canadian and Third US Armies.

'Not a single unit of the First United States Army Group, which comprises approximately twenty-five large formations, has so far been committed,' he reported. That clearly demonstrated, he wrote, that 'the enemy is planning a further large-scale operation in the channel area which one would expect to be aimed at a coastal sector in Pas-de-Calais.'

A million ghosts, *Fortitude's* phantom First US Army Group, had just gone swimming into history in the most critical intelligence appreciation made by the German army during the Second World War. Within minutes, Von Roenne's report was on its way to Hitler's headquarters and the fifteen German commands and officers entitled to receive it. Among them was a Gestapo officer who had entered into that élite circle after the RSHA's final takeover on June 1 of the Abwehr: *Obersturmbannführer* Hans-Dieter Strömelburg in Paris.

Milky mists rolling up from sea and shore, the oily smoke of a thousand fires, the acrid haze of spent gunpowder shrouded the Normandy invasion beaches in chaos and confusion. The weight of an unprecendedted air and naval bombardment – 10,000 tons of explosives – had heralded the landing. Yet like most such barrages, that tremendous fire had done little more than stun the beaches' German defenders.

The first troops went ashore at Utah Beach precisely where Rommel's naval aide, Admiral Friedrich Ruge, had predicted they would two weeks earlier. The gods of war had favoured them. An unusually strong current generated by the storm pulled their landing craft 500 yards down-beach away from their original, well-defended objective to one that was virtually undefended. They were D-Day's fortunate offspring.

The veteran Desert Rats of Britain's Fiftieth Infantry Division were barely able to fight their way ashore. The Canadians at Juno Beach came in a churning, storm-tossed surf that capsized landing barges and drowned men by the scores. It was at Omaha Beach, however, a gentle 4-mile arc of sand dominated by a bluff rising 200 feet high, that disaster struck. Bad weather, darkness, heavy seas and unexpectedly strong current made the landing craft of the US First and Twenty-ninth Divisions' voyage to shore a nightmare. The Germans held their fire until the craft reached the beaches. When they did open fire, the naval gunners at sea couldn't pin down their location to return their fire because of the smoke and mist. Frightened and seasick men of the first wave could hear machine-gun rounds clank their metallic tattoo on their landing-craft's ramps. As the ramps lowered, some, fully loaded, leaped over the side to avoid the fire and drowned; others, holding their breath, tried to hide underwater.

With hundred-pound packs, in water up to their chests, the rest advanced with agonizing slowness over the uneven footing of the runnels that crisscrossed the tidal flap, toy dolls in a shooting gallery for the German machine gunners. So devastating was the machine-gun fire that some men ran back to the water's edge and crawled into the waves as though somehow the sea's green shroud could protect them from death. Others tried to drag wounded comrades forward, drowning as they did. Many were so exhausted and terrified they dropped into the water at the water's edge to crawl ashore with the advancing tide.

When the second wave came in the disaster was compounded. Vehicles cluttered the waterline; bodies piled up in front of German strongpoints. Leaderless men huddled under the seawall while behind them their wounded comrades, crying for help, were drowned by the oncoming tides. By 1100, Omaha Beach was little more than a few hundred yards of corpse-littered sand. The recurrent nightmare of Winston Churchill had become at last a reality. The surf crashing onto the sands of Omaha foamed a bright pink with blood of the hundreds of young Americans who had died there since dawn.

Catherine's cell was little larger than an oversized clothes closet. Her bed was a rusting iron cot lined with wooden slats onto which a thin cotton mattress had been tossed. She had slept – for how long she didn't know – on a fretful tide of pain. Now, slowly, reluctantly, she awoke. High overhead, dull sunlight drifted through a bare window. It was, she guessed, midday.

Outside she heard only one sound, the dull metronomic fall of the SS guard's boots as he slowly paced up and down the corridor of the attic of 82 Avenue Foch. Periodically, the guard paused to leer at her through the Judas grille cut into the cell's metal door. At first, those smirking eyes devouring her maimed nudity humiliated and angered her. Then she learned to ignore them – modesty, she told herself, was a state of mind, not dress.

Someone had tossed her shoes and clothes in a heap in the corner of the cell. Her eyes occasionally went to them, to the brass-capped tassel of her shoe with its promise of eternal deliverance from her suffering. Yet she was able to look upon that little knob with detachment. She would not crawl to it and grasp the release it offered. She had endured. She would continue to endure.

For what seemed to her an hour or more, she had huddled awake on her cot taking inventory limb by limb of the wounds and bruises her torturer's whips had torn into her flesh. Across the cell, in the angle of the wall, was a water tap with a basin. With a supreme effort of will, Catherine made herself get up and lurch across the cell's floor to the tap. If she was going to survive, she would have to begin her fight for survival here in this cell. As best she could, she washed her bruises clean with the cold water from the tap. Each application of cold water to open lacerations was painful; yet slowly the shock of the water on her skin revived her.

She dried herself as best she could on her mattress cover, then dressed. She made herself sit on the cot staring at the Judas so she could now glare back at her inquisitive guard's glances, realizing for the first time what a stimulating emotion hatred could be.

Suddenly, off in the distance, she heard the rush of running feet on the stairs from the offices below. They were coming back for her. The feet banged imperiously down the attic's wooden corridor – to the cell next to hers.

She heard the cell's metal door creaking open, then a jumble of footsteps and a scream. The terrible dull thud of a heavy object pummelling flesh followed. A shriek of pain sounded in the attic. As the vicious blows continued, the noise sank into a whimper and a man's desperate voice pleading, 'Please, please'.

The intruders stopped as suddenly as they had begun. The cell door slammed shut and their angry footfalls fled along the corridor and down the stairs. Only the anguished sob of a broken soul remained to fill the vacuum of silence they left behind.

Catherine clutched her arms around her battered chest with terror at the remembered agony the man's whimper inspired. How could she succour him, that faceless fellow Resistant next door? To speak through the Judas would bring the same fury crashing down on her. Maybe he knew Morse code. She took off her shoe and went to the wall. In Morse she tapped out the letters QRK IMI – 'How do you receive me?'

She pinned her ears to the wall until she heard a faint answering tap. Then, slowly, she tapped out the only comfort she could offer the man. 'Courage,' she signalled. 'Hold on. They're coming.'

At Berchtesgaden, Hitler slept until midmorning. He got his first report of the landing after breakfast, in his dressing gown, from a pair of aides who brought the situation map to his bedroom suite at the Berghof. With what satisfaction he must have contemplated its outlines. The Allies had come ashore in Normandy, exactly as he had predicted they would to his generals and field marshals in March, at the very landing sites to which he had been calling Rommel's and Von Rundstedt's attention since May. 'Now,' he pronounced, 'we have them where we can destroy them.'

His midday strategy conference was held at the Castle Klessheim, an hour's drive from the Berghof, where he was offering Hungary's new Premier, Dome Szojoay, an official luncheon. He was laughing, almost carefree. Then, exactly as Eisenhower's intelligence officers had gambled and predicted he would, he warned his entourage it was too early to commit their forces to a course of action. For whatever reason, he was not yet ready to follow where his famous intuition beckoned. Normandy might well be a diversion, he declared, a trap designed by the Allies to lure him into committing himself. The silence along the Channel coast was ominous. Perhaps it was there the real assault would come once the weather cleared. The moment called for Olympian calm, the serene detachment of the commander above the fracas of the battle who lets the situation develop before committing himself, not swift, instant response to the Allies' challenge.

Why did he hesitate? Was it because, since Stalingrad, his faith in the infallibility of his intuition had been shaken? Was it because the poisoned insinuations of *Fortitude* had begun to influence his thinking? In any event, it was not until after he finished lunch that Hitler finally agreed to release to Von Rundstedt the two Panzer divisions the commander in the West had demanded before dawn. By then the heavy ground mists of the morning had disappeared; the Norman skies belonged to the sun and the Allied fighters. The invaders, fighting for a toehold on the shores of France, were spared the assault that could have

356

ended the invasion of Europe. Instead of facing three Panzer divisions on D-Day, they would face just one regiment.

As befitting an intelligence service whose origins went back to Sir Francis Walsingham and the reign of Queen Elizabeth I, the headquarters of MI-6 at the Broadway Building, 52 Broadway, opposite the St James's Park tube station, contemplated the tumultuous events in Normandy with an air of serene detachment. The service's retainers and guards, pensioners and sergeant majors from earlier wars, came and went in their blue uniforms, their voices barely raised to comment on what was happening across the Channel. The officers riding to work in the eight-storey building's aged elevator dealt with the landing in an elliptical phrase or two, recognition enough in a service in which triumphs were acknowledged with a whisper and disasters with a glance.

'C,' Sir Stewart Menzies, had conferred at midmorning with Sir Winston Churchill at Storey's Gate on the development of the invasion. Then he had lunched swiftly and lightly at White's, before returning to Broadway at about the time Adolf Hitler was belatedly releasing two of his Panzer divisions to Von Rundstedt. His first visitor of the afternoon was the young officer who served as his personal chief of staff, particularly in those matters 'C,' wished to either control himself or hold to a very restricted circle. Like 'C,' D.J. Watley-Serrell was an Old Etonian, a former Guardsman, a man as trustworthy as his lineage was impeccable.

He carried three secret folders with him that afternoon. The first dealt with MI6's contacts with the German Resistance, the Schwarze Kapelle. When they had dispensed with that, Watley-Serrell opened his second folder, marked 'Fortitude.'

'We've received confirmation the woman was arrested on her arrival in Calais, sir,' he said. 'Her contacts there communicated with Sevenoaks via the transmitter in Lille which the Gestapo think they have turned.'

'C' nodded. 'Where have they taken her?'

'We believe to Paris, since the order to take her came from Strömelburg and it was his people who followed her up to Calais. This' – he proffered a piece of foolscap to his superior – 'is the message Lille sent last night for the SOE's man Aristide.'

'C' read it. His eyebrows shot up at the last line. 'So they're after Paul's head, are they? Hardly surprising in the circumstances, I suppose.'

Watley-Serrell gave an embarrassed little cough. 'Indeed. Unfortunately, sir, we have a problem in that regard.'

'Oh?'

'In the crush of business this morning, Cavendish's reply to that cable got out of Sevenoaks without being vetted by our contacts.'

'I see.'

'He authorized *carte blanche*.'

'Damn!' 'C' blinked several times under the impact of the news. 'But then why wouldn't he? We should have short-circuited that when it came in last night.'

'Sir.'

'Now, how do we save Paul?'

'The SOE?'

'The SOE knows absolutely nothing about our relations with Paul, and I would just as soon they continue to dwell in their state of blissful ignorance. Besides' – 'C' had closed his eyes to better concentrate his mind – 'Cavendish's only channel to this Aristide is via that radio in Lille. Any revised instructions he sent out to him would have to pass through German hands, which would compromise a good deal more than I choose to compromise.'

'If the SOE people grab him, what is Paul going to tell them – to save his neck? Assuming they give him time for explanations.'

'Yes' – 'C' grimaced – 'it is most likely they'll just try and gun him down, isn't it? I suppose, if they give him a chance, he'll tell them, of course, he's working for us.'

'Will they believe him?'

'Good question. He'll tell them that we told him to go to Strömelburg. That, of course, was Claude's idea. He had made a rather careful study of our German friend and came to the conclusion he would be more than impressed by Paul's little anti-Communist routine, as indeed he was.'

'Do you think he'll be able to convince anybody of that?'

'Perhaps. He can be persuasive when he chooses to be. You see, he thinks we sent him to Strömelburg purely because we were convinced Strömelburg's reaction would be to throw a blanket over his operation. After all, a good spymaster will always prefer to keep an enemy operation like that going if he's in a position to oversee and control it. The reality, of course, was that Claude expected Strömelburg to cover the operation so he could have regular access to those courier packages which were precisely what we wanted him to see.' The head of the intelligence service offered his deputy a chilly smile.

'And this is exactly how our German friend reacted. As it turns out, we have not been able to put these packets to the use we had intended; but these things never turn out exactly as one plans. Which still leaves us with our problem of trying to protect Paul. Does that girl at the One Two Two have a contact for him?'

'No, sir. We arranged that as one-way for security reasons.'

'C' sighed. 'Message her urgently. Instruct her to tell Paul his fellow

358

Resistants are on to the game and want his head. Tell him to either go to ground completely or insinuate himself into Strömelburg's company, whichever he feels more comfortable with.'

'Yes, sir.'

'Pity the girl doesn't have a contact. The exigencies of the secret service are sometimes – unfortunately – severe.'

A telephone call from Berlin awoke Hans-Dieter Strömelburg from the drug-induced sleep into which he had fallen after terminating Catherine Pradier's torture session. His caller was his superior, Ernst Kaltenbrunner, and he was in a state of high fury. The Wehrmacht, he shouted, had totally disregarded the priceless intelligence yielded up by the Doctor's radio game. The Seventh Army, on whose coast the invasion had fallen, had not even been placed on alert.

Nor was that all, Kaltenbrunner told him. There had been an ominous pattern of absences on the Western Front: Meyer Detring, Von Rundstedt's intelligence chief, in Berlin; General Feuchtinger of the Twenty-first Panzer in Paris; the senior officers of the Seventh Army running off to play war games in Rennes; Rommel himself in Germany. Himmler wondered if there might be a conspiracy behind that, some dark effort to open the gates of Western Europe to the Allies. Strömelburg, he ordered, was to begin an immediate investigation into the sinister possibility.

The *Obersturmbahnführer* showered and dressed as quickly as possible. When he had finished, his first gesture was to call on his faithful acolyte the Doctor, to inform him that his warning had been ignored and the warm breath of history had, after all, passed him by.

The Doctor was crestfallen; so many hours of labour, so much effort all expended for nothing. Dejectedly, he passed Strömelburg the terse one-line cable Lille had just received from Cavendish. 'You are authorized *carte blanche* to deal with air operations officer,' it read.

'What do you suppose that means?' he asked Strömelburg.

'It means they've given Aristide permission to kill Gilbert.'

'Shall I order Lille to arrest that agent when he comes in for the answer?'

'Where's Gilbert?'

'He's in the Sarthe on an operation. He's due back tomorrow.'

Strömelburg, his mind still slowed by the aftereffects of his sleeping potion, hesitated. He hated to close down a turned radio set if he could avoid it. And, he reasoned, the Resistance would probably try to kill Gilbert with or without London's agreement.

'No,' he said, finally, 'Give him the message.'

'But they'll kill Gilbert.'

'No, they won't. We won't let them. Have Konrad stake out his apartment tomorrow morning. That's where they'll be waiting for him. Tell Konrad to bring Gilbert back here.'

Two things, it seemed to T. F. O'Neill, characterized the underground offices of the London Controlling Section at Storey's Gate: red eyes and exhaustion. Ridley, he knew, hadn't been to bed in almost forty-eight hours. The colonel was living on cigarettes and nerve ends. He himself had been able to grab only a few hours of sleep. They had spent their day following the evolution of the battle in Normandy and in ceaseless search for ways to limit the damage done to their efforts to boost Garbo in German eyes by the failure of his Madrid radio operator to pick up his 3 A.M. broadcast.

It had been, for the young American, a revealing experience. Nowhere in the United States, he felt certain, were there people who even dreamed of doing the sort of thing his little band of associates seemed to do as second nature. This coterie of plotters he had once scorned as crazy and to whom he now belonged had spent their hours around a table moving a man about London, calculating every aspect, every detail of his imaginary day for its effect on German Intelligence.

According to the story *Fortitude's* deceivers had prepared for him, Garbo worked in the Ministry of Information, where he helped the director, a close friend, with Spanish translations for broadcasts on the BBC to Spain and South America. Since he handed over his texts – in code, of course – to his radio operator well before their broadcast and since, for security reasons, the operator didn't know how to reach him, Garbo had gone to his desk at the Ministry of Information on the morning of June 6 a supremely happy man, convinced he had warned the Abwehr the Allied invasion was on its way. At noon, he was called to a meeting of the Ministry's section chiefs. There he was given a secret 'Special Directive' to the Ministry from the Political Warfare Executive.

Garbo considered the text of such importance he took the risk of copying its principal points onto the back of an old calling card and smuggling it out of the office when he left for the day. As soon as he got home, he put it into code. The text laid down the guidelines for all sections in the Ministry. Their intent was to prevent any speculation in the press about landings elsewhere on the French coast. All press and radio reports, the instructions said, were to lay stress on the importance of the operations in Normandy. No reference whatsoever was to be allowed to diversions or future operations. Destined to be read 'in reverse' by the Germans, the text would seem to be clearly preparing the way for a second, major assault.

He next informed Kuhlenthal that in view of the importance of what was happening, he had decided, on his own initiative, to call to London his three best agents, agents the German knew and respected, code-named Donny, Dick and Dorick, for a full-scale review of the situation. His Gibraltarian waiter, he informed Kuhlenthal, was safely on his way to a hiding place in Wales. His account of the day concluded on a self-congratulatory note expressing his immense satisfaction that the Allies' 'first action was robbed of surprise' by his 3 A.M. message.

Then, exhausted but devoted as ever to the cause of National Socialism, Garbo had got on the tube for Hampstead Heath to deliver his coded text to his radio operator. It was on handing over the text that poor Garbo learned that his fateful dispatch of the night before had not been sent until 0700 that morning. Furious and brokenhearted, he had gone to the heath and on a park bench had coded a second message to Kuhlenthal. It was the despising call of an agent betrayed by his handler's incompetence, of a spy who was risking his life every hour of the day only to find the most precious of his secrets ignored. He wrote, he said, 'through my tiredness and exhaustion which due to the excessive work I have had have exhausted me.' He was 'disgusted because in this struggle of life and death I cannot accept excuses for negligence. Were it not for my faith and ideals,' he concluded, 'I would abandon this work.'

That whole tissue of lies, concocted as seriously as a movie script, was now, T.F. knew, being tapped onto the airwaves by an MI5 sergeant in Hampstead Heath.

Late in the day of Tuesday, June 6, Field Marshal Gerd von Rundstedt summoned his principal aides to a conference in his operations room at Saint-Germain-en-Laye. The last Teutonic Knight had spent the day far from the din and ignoble strife of the battlefield, in the serene contemplation of his maps and his intelligence reports. While the Americans had been fighting desperately for a foothold on Omaha Beach at midday, he had been pruning the roses in his rose garden.

His chief of staff appraised him of the conviction of Colonel von Roenne at Foreign Armies West, of the growing suspicion in Hitler's entourage that Normandy was a diversion, a feint to force a premature German reaction.

The old field marshal pondered the information, then proclaimed that Von Roenne and Hitler's entourage were wrong. Normandy was not a diversion, it was the invasion. The Allies had attacked a huge strip of coastline. They had employed their three best airborne divisions, the 'Desert Rats' of Montgomery's old Eighth Army and the Americans' First Infantry Division to lead their assault. They would not waste such crack forces on a diversion.

The time had come, he proclaimed, for Rommel to do the one thing the Allies did not want him to do: to begin to free up all his available forces, especially the Panzers of the Fifteenth Army massed behind Pas-de-Calais. Having rendered his judgement with the authority of a Pope reading out a newly drafted encyclical, he ordered his subordinates to inform Rommel and Hitler's headquarters. Then he went to bed.

At La Roche Guyon, an hour's drive away, the longest day in the life of Field Marshal Erwin Rommel was drawing to a close. As his car skidded to a halt at the *château's* steps and the field marshal leaped out, the majestic notes of the overture to Wagner's *Flying Dutchman* swelled from the *château's* great doors.

'The Allies are landing and you're playing music?' his aide shouted angrily at Rommel's chief of staff, General Hans Speidel.

'Do you think that will change anything?' Speidel replied, addressing at his subordinate a dour stare.

With characteristic energy, the field marshal plunged into an immediate conference to assess the situation. His reading of it was entirely different from Von Rundstedt's. His intelligence chief informed him that Von Roenne had called at 5:20 P.M. to warn them the twenty-five divisions of the First US Army Group in southeast England had yet to enter the battle; a second major assault in Pas-de-Calais was to be expected shortly.

His words were far more soothing to the field marshal's ears than Wagner's music. He had promised he would defeat the Allies at the water's edge, but when they'd waded ashore that morning he'd been 500 miles away, conducting a monologue of despair in the backseat of his car. Now he almost desperately hoped for another Allied assault on the Calais beaches where he had predicted for months they would come. There he would stop them at the water's edge. He wouldn't take a single tank or soldier out of Pas-de-Calais. He would keep them there for the pivotal battle on which Germany's destiny and his own reputation depended, for the moment when the divisions of the First US Army Group tried to storm ashore through strongpoints of the Atlantic Wall.

It was nearing midnight at the Underground War Rooms at Storey's Gate when the message came in. A cyclist for MI-5's Signals Intelligence Section delivered it to Ridley in a locked dispatch case. T.F. watched as his English superior opened it, then followed the smile of purest satisfaction spreading across his features. It was, it occurred to T.F., the first smile he had seen there in days.

The message was from Kuhlenthal, the Abwehr representative in Madrid, and it was destined to console his heartbroken agent, Garbo. Ridley read it out to the members of his section who were still on duty. 'I wish to stress in the clearest terms that your work over the last few weeks has made it possible for our High Command to be completely forewarned and prepared. I transmit to you, to all your collaborators our total recognition of your perfect and cherished work and I beg you to continue with us in the supreme and decisive hours of the struggle for the future of Europe.'

Ridley paused. 'The Führer,' he announced, 'has ordered Kuhlenthal to inform Garbo he is giving him the Iron Cross First Class.'

Even T.F. felt like cheering. Garbo, their precious Garbo, was clearly back in play. How could the Germans, forty-eight hours hence, not yet heed the warnings of a spy on whom they had conferred one of their highest decorations?

The colonel's own relief was manifest. He looked at the Normandy situation map for perhaps the thousandth time that day, at the black figures which represented the Panzer divisions of the Fifteenth Army. There was very little on that map to comfort him. 'Do you remember what Monty said at St Paul's?' he asked his American deputy.

'About their rate of buildup?'

'No. That if we didn't take Caen, Bayeux and Carentan on D-Day we would be in the most severe trouble.' Ridley gestured at the map. 'We didn't capture a single one of them today.' He waved his Players at the invasion beaches. 'There is a ten-mile gap between our beaches and yours. If Rommel finds it, God knows what he'll do. We're ashore. That's about all we can say. Nothing's decided. It's all there is to play for tonight.'

Reluctantly, the Englishman turned away from that graphic representation of the worries haunting him. 'At least,' he announced to his subordinate, 'I think Kuhlenthal's message calls for a round of drinks in the mess before we all head off to bed.'

They were closing up the files when the phone rang. 'Get that, will you?' Ridley asked T.F.

The young American recognized the distinctive rasp of the voice of 'C,' the head of MI-6, the British Secret Intelligence Service. 'For you, sir,' he said respectfully, passing the phone to Ridley.

'I see,' Ridley said to his caller. 'Where did they take her? To Avenue Foch?'

There was a pause while he digested whatever it was Menzies was saying to him. The almost jovial expression his thoughts of Kuhlenthal had inspired had been replaced by a distant, preoccupied air. 'Time will tell,' he said. 'Good night.'

'Is something wrong?' T.F. asked.

The question seemed to strike a man miles away, in some private reverie. Ridley took a deep puff of his Players. 'Excuse me?' he said; then,

'Oh, yes. The Gestapo, it seems, has arrested the young lady you saw off at Tangmere the other night.'

'Oh no!' T.F. gasped. 'How horrible!'

'Yes,' Ridley agreed. 'Ghastly. But there you are.'

PART SIX

JUNE 7–10, 1944

Even if you didn't know the Allies had landed, Paul thought, you would know that something momentous had happened just by observing the Parisians thronging the Gare d'Austerlitz Wednesday morning, June 7. There was a buoyancy in the crowds, a quickness in their step, a new sharpness in their conversation. Above all, of course, there were the mocking smiles and even the occasional brave guffaws from the people clustered around newspaper kiosks studying the collaborationist presses' headlines hopefully promising a 'Massive German Counter-Attack' against the Allied beachhead. Yet in the midst of all that barely suppressed jubilation, Paul was exhausted and heartsick, the mourner at the wedding feast. Since Monday, he had lived with one thought: had the derailment worked? He pushed his way through the crowd and dashed to a phone booth. To his relief, Ajax answered his phone.

'Did it work?' he gasped. 'Did she get away?'

'Ah, Paul.' For once it seemed to Paul that Ajax actually seemed glad to hear his voice. 'I've been waiting for you to call.'

'Is she all right?'

'Where are you?'

'At the Gare d'Austerlitz.'

'Get to the sidewalk in front of the Café du Commerce at 189 Avenue du Maine as fast as you can,' Ajax ordered. 'I'll meet you there.' He hung up.

Paul looked at his watch. It was 12:30 – too early to call the One Two Two to see if his courier at the bordello had anything for him. Besides, only one thing interested him: seeing Denise alive. He had to stop himself from breaking into a run to the *métro* and the first train to the Alésia station.

Standing on the sidewalk in front of the Café du Commerce, Paul tried quite unsuccessfully, to calm his nervous fidgeting by studying the flow of passersby. He was expecting Ajax to arrive on foot or perhaps by bicycle – at the limit in a velocab. He was quite unprepared for the black Citroën, a boilerlike device strapped to its rear belching dirty grey smoke, that drove up to him.

Ajax opened the rear door. Two other men were in front. 'Jump in,' he commanded. He was as immaculate as ever, Paul noted, suit pressed, hair combed. If his once-white shirt had been yellowed by repeated washing in poor occupation soap, it was still freshly laundered. Only a vile *ersatz* cigarette in his ebony holder struck a discordant note in his otherwise carefully orchestrated appearance.

'Where are we going?' Paul asked as the car wheezed its way down Avenue du Maine towards the Porte d'Orléans.

'Fontainebleau,' Ajax replied.

'Did your men pick her up after the derailment?' Paul asked. 'Did they spot her making a break for it?'

A warm and friendly smile spread over Ajax's face. A reassuring hand clasped Paul's knee. 'Relax, old boy,' Ajax said. 'You're as nervous as a bulldog after a bitch in heat. Have a little faith in your fellow Resistants' – he turned to Paul, his smile widening – 'just as they have faith in you.'

With that relentless tenacity of purpose which so characterized him, Hans-Dieter Strömelburg had devoted twenty-four hours to the charge Kaltenbrunner had assigned him Tuesday morning – finding out why the German High Command had ignored the warning in the BBC messages, why so many high-ranking officers had been absent from their post on the night of June 5 to 6.

As had happened so often in his years as a police investigator, his pursuit of a set of clues had not led to the goal he sought; but it had exposed another, perhaps even more meaningful avenue to pursue. The absence of so many officers, he concluded, was due to the weather, not a conspiracy. The failure of OB West to act on the Doctor's warning he ascribed to Prussian pigheadedness, not deviousness.

What he had discovered, however, was that on the night of June 5, in Rommel's absence, his chief of staff, General Hans Speidel, had hosted a dinner at La Roche Guyon for his brother-in-law Dr Joachim Horst and the philosopher Ernst Jünger. Both men's names appeared on a secret list compiled by the RHSA of individuals suspected of plotting to overthrow the Reich.

He finished his report in midafternoon and turned, at last, to the stack of *Blitzfernschreibens* – high-speed teletypes – awaiting him. One quickly caught his attention. It was Colonel Alex von Roenne's Western Situation Report 1288, his carefully reasoned intelligence appraisal of the Allies' strategy drafted at noon on D-Day. For Strömelburg, his conclusions were a revelation.

If Normandy was a feint deliberately designed by the Allies to draw Germany off balance, to force the premature commitment of Germany's reserves so that the real assault could fall on Pas-de-Calais, then the key to when and how that second assault might come languished in one of the cells over his head. In letting her lie there undisturbed all this time, he had been criminally inept, as inept as the OB West officers who'd ignored the Doctor's warning. With a stab of his forefinger, he jabbed the buzzer on his desk. He would make amends for his negligence.

The charcoal-powered Citroën eased to a stop in front of a rusting sheet-iron grille set into the high stone wall that encircled a kind of manor house in the forest outside Fontainebleau. The driver honked his horn twice and two men, obviously members of Ajax' network, opened the door to let the car roll inside. It circled the gravel-covered drive up to the main entrance of the house, a nineteenth-century country retreat probably built by some Parisian businessman during the days of Louis Napoléon.

Paul leaped out of the car and bounced up the stairs. 'Where is she?' he cried to Ajax, who followed casually in his footsteps. The house appeared deserted. Its windows were shuttered and bolted. The front door opened before him almost as though activated by some phantom haunting the property.

'Go inside,' Ajax ordered. He crossed in front of Paul and traversed the shadowy entryway, occupied by two more members of his network, to a door. He opened it and waved Paul inside.

It was a small parlour lit by one bare electric light hanging from the ceiling. Opposite Paul was a Norman trestle table with three chairs lined up behind it. On the wall were a Tricolour and a photograph of Charles de Gaulle. A single chair was placed immediately in front of the trestle table.

Paul turned back to Ajax. 'What the hell's going on here?' he yelled. 'Where is she?' As he shouted the words, he saw the Colt .45 in Ajax' hand levelled at his midsection.

'Sit down, Paul,' Ajax ordered, indicating the single chair before him.

'You betrayed me!' Paul raged.

'I betrayed you, Paul?' An icy stillness fell with the swiftness of a desert sunset over Ajax as he pronounced those words. 'I said sit down.'

'What is this, some kind of mock trial?' Paul demanded, trying to be angry but sensing instead a tide of fright rising within him.

'Mock, Paul?' The friendly, comradely face of the ride out from Paris had undergone a sudden hardening. 'Not at all. It's a real trial – yours, for treason.'

Ajax crossed towards the Norman table. Two of his men with British Sten guns took up places on either side of Paul. 'You staged this!' Paul shouted at him. 'You've always hated me. Why? Why?'

Ajax circled the trestle table and took the middle seat. He gazed with

369

cold indifference at his prisoner. 'I don't hate you, Paul. Hatred is too precious an emotion to waste on traitors.'

At his words, two more men entered the room and sat down on either side of Ajax. One was rather thin, middle-aged with a Vandyke beard and eyes that pierced through Paul. It was Aristide.

'Where is she?' Paul demanded. 'Did you save her or didn't you?'

Aristide answered: 'She's exactly where you meant her to be, Paul: in the hands of the Gestapo.'

'Oh, God, no!' Paul slumped in despair in his chair, then finally looked up at his accusers. 'It's not my fault. I swear to you. I told London they were going to take the passenger coming in on that Lysander. I warned them. They sent her anyway.' He looked at Ajax. 'I came to you to get you to save her, didn't I?'

'Yes, you did come to me for help, Paul. Too late, unfortunately.' Ajax's tone was methodical, as matter-of-fact as the voice of a lawyer reading out the terms of an agreement for two contracting parties. 'But tell me one thing, Paul. How did you know they were going to take the passenger coming in on that Lysander?'

Paul stared, slack-jawed, at his accusers, skewered on the relevance of Ajax's question. He was caught in a vortex of conflicting loyalties in which concern for his own safety was rapidly coming to predominate. 'Look,' he said, 'I can't answer that. Not now. You've got to let me explain this to London. I have my own transmitter. Let me message London. They will come back to you on any channel you want and set things straight.'

Ajax turned to the man on his left and whispered something. The man nodded, then looked at Paul. 'Empty everything out of your pockets here onto the table,' he commanded.

Paul did as he was told. While he looked on, they began to examine in minute detail his possessions – his ID papers, his *Ausweis*, his ration book, the contents of his wallet. Suddenly, he froze. The bearded man was holding a white card in his hand. His eyes burned with hatred as he looked up at Paul, then wordlessly passed the card to Ajax. It was the card Strömelburg had given him at his villa in Neuilly to protect him from German patrols if he was caught with a weapon.

'I can explain that,' Paul gasped.

Ajax laid down the card. The hatred in his eyes rivalled that in Aristide's expression. 'Some things require no explanation.'

Paul realized that his life was now in the balance. There was no longer any question of trying to protect anything or anyone. Only a full and unequivocal revelation of his mission would save him.

'Look,' he said, 'I'll tell you the whole story. I've known Strömelburg since 1937. I took messages in and out of Spain for him during the

Spanish Civil War. The Deuxième Bureau knew what I was doing. I let them see everything I took in and out.'

His eyes leaped from one face to another, almost begging them for some acknowledgement of what he was telling them. 'When I got to England, British Intelligence picked me up. They knew who I was and that I had contacts with Strömelburg. That's why they came to get me in Marseille. They asked me to run the Lysander operations for the SOE, but they said they would never work unless they could find a way to cover them. They told me when I got back to see Strömelburg.'

'The British told you to contact Strömelburg?' Aristide asked the question with the incredulity he had once reserved for fledgling philosophy students trying to defend an indefensible premise.

'That's right.'

'You're trying to tell me the British sent you here to lay their whole underground operation in the hands of the Gestapo, are you?'

'No, because the British are much smarter than that. The thing worked exactly as they told me it would. What Strömelburg wanted was to get the operation under his control, keep his hand on it. After all, if he closed my operation down, another Lysander operation would pop up someplace, one he wasn't controlling. The whole thing worked like a charm, just as the British said it would. We ran the operation under German protection. They even warned the Luftwaffe not to shoot down the planes.'

'And those information packets?' Ajax was thinking now of his agent who had cracked under interrogation because of information hurled at him from one of those packets. 'You want me to believe the British actually meant to have the Gestapo reading the material?'

'It was secondary stuff. This is a war, for Christ's sake. You have to calculate a balance between risks and losses. What was more important – letting them read that or getting our agents in and out unmolested?'

'Paul' – it was Aristide, those eyes of his boring into him – 'every man has the right to plead for his life, but please, do us the honour of flattering our imagination with a better story than the one you've told.'

'Every word is true, I swear to Christ.' Paul felt the cold sweat running down his spine and could not keep the hysterical pleading from his voice any longer. 'Look, I told you, I have my own personal radio contact to London. I had to give Strömelburg the details of the one I used for the landings. Let me contact London. They'll tell you.'

'We have already messaged London about you, Paul,' Aristide said.

'Okay,' said Paul defiantly, 'what did they say?'

'They said to kill you.'

Paul looked at them with the bewildered eyes of a cornered animal. 'I don't believe it. Who said that?'

'Cavendish.'

'Cavendish! For Christ's sake, he doesn't even know I work for British Intelligence.'

Aristide stared at him. 'They're all the same thing,' he said, getting up. 'You know that as well as I do.' Ignoring Paul's frenzied protests, he gestured with his head to his two associates, then led them into an adjoining room. He closed the door and looked at the two men.

'So?' Ajax said.

'He's a traitor. We've got to get rid of him,' Aristide declared. 'There's not a word of truth in what he told us except for the fact that he works for the Gestapo. The card in his wallet proves that. It's the one irrefutable piece of evidence in this whole business.'

'I agree,' Ajax said with judicious calm. 'God knows how many other people he's given over to them.' His eyes went to the third man, the second-in-command of his network.

'Maybe we should hold him here as a prisoner until the Allies arrive. Let them take care of him.'

'Prisoner?' Ajax snapped. 'We're running a resistance, not a penal service.'

'Or at least, let him contact that radio he talks about.'

'Let him out of our sight for a second and he'll be off to Avenue Foch and Strömelburg's protection,' Aristide said. 'Look, he works for the Gestapo. What else can that card mean? You know what would happen to any one of us if they got us. Why give him a chance the Gestapo would never give us?'

'All right, I agree,' the man sighed. 'Execute him.'

'Shall we draw straws to see who does the job?' Ajax asked.

'No,' Aristide urged, 'let me do it. It was my agent he betrayed.'

Ajax passed his Colt to Aristide. He and his deputy went back into the room first and stood side by side behind the trestle table. 'Paul,' he said, 'you've been tried and convicted of treason. The penalty for that is death.'

'No!' Paul screamed. 'You're wrong, you're wrong!'

Aristide had slipped behind him. The Colt was 6 inches from the base of Paul's skull when he pulled the trigger. The blast literally blew Paul out of his chair like a rag doll being hurled against a wall by a spiteful child.

Ajax gathered up the dead man's papers. Meticulously, he returned them to Paul's wallet. Then he placed the wallet back in the hip pocket of Paul's suit. His final act was to call for a piece of cardboard. On it he wrote, 'Please deliver the body of this traitor to his employers at the Gestapo, Avenue Foch.'

He turned to his henchmen. 'Stuff him into the Citroën and dump him in the Bois,' he ordered. 'And make sure you tie this around his neck when you do.'

This time they took Catherine not to Strömelburg's office but to one of the several interrogation rooms lining the fourth floor of 82 Avenue Foch. The room had a terrifying impersonality, she noted, stumbling through the door; here, she sensed, a prisoner was not a human being, not even a number, but rather a kind of block of meat to be addressed with the detachment of a butcher addressing a side of beef with his hacksaw.

Strömelburg was waiting for her. He rose, quite respectfully, when they pushed her into the room and remained standing until she had tottered to her chair. Once again she could smell his *eau de cologne* and see how impeccably groomed his hands were, how carefully his blond hair was combed into place.

Strömelburg surveyed her with a calm detachment. It was a pity what they had done to her. Her face was swollen beyond recognition, a collection of lumps of yellow, purple and crimson flesh. Her lips were swollen out of all proportion from the blows they'd received. She'll have trouble keeping her stiff upper lip with those, he thought cruelly. Only the eyes, the green defiant eyes, remained unchanged. She was still set on playing the role of the brave patriot.

He offered her a cigarette.

'No, thank you,' she replied. 'I haven't changed my habits since yesterday.'

'None of them?'

She caught the sinister undertone in his voice and shook her head.

'We shall see about that.' The two torturers who had brutalized her the day before had slipped back into the room and stood respectfully against the wall, silent sentinels of the Gestapo's sadism.

'I wasted a great deal of my time on you yesterday when I had many other things to do,' Strömelburg said reproachfully. 'However, today I have nothing to do except devote my full attentions and energies to you' – he gave a polite little cough – 'or to be more precise, the energies of my subordinates here.'

He began to slowly pace the room. 'Now just to review for you, Mademoiselle Pradier. I require your answers to three questions. What did you intend to sabotage in Calais? Where are the microfilms Cavendish gave you for the operation? Simple questions which require simple, straightforward answers. Now, then, what did you intend to sabotage?'

'I can't answer that.'

'Where is the microfilm?'

'I can't answer that.'

'What are your BBC code messages?'

'I can't answer that.'

Strömelburg sighed. His was the petulant wheeze of a spoiled child refused the indulgence of an extra helping of dessert. 'You sound like a record stuck on a crack. I will give you one minute to answer before we begin.'

Catherine slumped in her chair. She felt her heart racing, and a terrible cold embraced her body. She wanted to weep in fright, but would not give him the satisfaction of her tears if she could help it. Please, God, she begged silently, help me!

The seconds ticked by until Strömelburg sighed again to close the passage of her period of grace. 'All right,' he said, nodding to his men. One handcuffed her arms behind the chair. The other advanced on her with a pair of pliers in his hand. Strömelburg seethed inwardly. He would have to remain with her through this session, an action for which he had little stomach.

'This gentleman is going to pull out your toenails one by one,' he announced. 'Slowly, because it is more painful that way. It is, I have been told, an excruciatingly painful experience. After each toenail has been extracted, I will repeat my questions. You can put an end to their savagery at any moment you choose by answering them.' He passed his hand across his brow as though to expunge from his mind the ordeal he was about to witness. 'Most people faint after three or four nails have been pulled. Do not let that concern you. If necessary we will revive you with cold water and continue our task.'

The man with the pliers knelt at her feet. Catherine squeezed her eyes tightly shut and held her breath. Through the open window she could hear, ever so faintly, the joyful yelps of children playing in the street below. The man took her foot in one hand and she felt the cold metal of the pliers on her skin. Then he began to pull – very slowly, as Strömelburg had promised he would. The pain began as a sharp spurt, then rose to a crescendo of searing white heat transpiercing her. She bit her swollen mouth to stifle her cry as long as she could. Then she screamed. When the nail came out and her torturer waved it at her like a dentist brandishing a freshly extracted molar, she slumped in the chair straining against the handcuffs, panting uncontrollably.

'What were you going to sabotage?'

She couldn't even find the strength to say 'No'. All she could do was shake her head wildly. Strömelburg nodded to his torturer, who set the pliers to her second toenail.

She had no idea how long it lasted. Her Calvary was a blur of those white, searing bolts of pain, of the questions coming to her from another world, of the echoing of her own anguished screams in her ears. She fainted twice. Each time, a glass of cold water revived her. Eons after it had all begun, her torturer rose for the last time, the big toenail of her left foot, the last that had been left to her, clutched like a trophy between the tongs of his pliers.

Strömelburg stared down at her, angry yet admiring. 'You are a woman of considerable courage,' he acknowledged. He drew a glass of water from the tap and held it to her lips. Gulping it down, she glanced at her feet, misshapen, circled in a little puddle of blood.

She started to vomit and gagged on the slender produce of her famished stomach. She was dizzy, gasping for breath – yet elated. She had endured. She had not yielded up her forbidden treasure of knowledge. She had resisted this hateful man and his savagery.

Strömelburg set the glass on his table. 'I suppose you think the worst is over, don't you?'

She stared at him dumbly.

'It's not. It's just beginning. There is nothing I will not do to get the information from you.'

Catherine dropped her head and said nothing. What was there to say?

'You want to be a heroine, do you, a martyr for Cavendish and all those others who sent you here, do you? You're a fool, a stupid fool.' For a second, Strömelburg saw the image of his father trapped in the rubble of his burning home. 'Do you think I care about what I do to you? You think it matters to me how much you suffer? It doesn't. You can end all this with a word, but I can go on inflicting pain on you until hell has frozen.'

Catherine remained slumped in silence in her chair.

'So,' said Strömelburg after a long pause, 'still stubborn. Well, we'll clean you up. We'll take you upstairs for one of our special little baths.'

Just as Von Rundstedt had predicted it would, Rommel's first counterattack against the Norman beachhead had failed. Typically, the impetuous, hotheaded Rommel had hurled the regiments of the Twelfth SS Panzer and the Panzer Lehr at the Allies piecemeal instead of assembling them for one massive strike. It was as though he were trying to atone for his absence from the battlefield the day before by securing a lightning victory for his Führer.

Surveying the situation late on Wednesday, June 7, Von Rundstedt perceived that it was now a race to see who could get forces into Normandy faster – the Allies over 100 miles of water or the Germans with their internal, land-based communications?

The Allies' fighters, Von Rundstedt knew, would harry his troops over every mile of their daylight marches, the Resistance harass their advance with ambushes. But he could move them with the complicity of the night and choose his own route of advance. He was involved in a race he had every prospect of winning – provided he started fast enough. Yesterday, because of the bad weather, the gods of war had favoured the Allies. Henceforth, if they made the right decision, they should speak with a Teutonic accent. There existed in German contingency planning for the invasion the right decision. It was called 'Case III A'; it was a blueprint for massing the Wehrmacht's forces for a sledgehammer blow if the landing struck Normandy. The time had come, Von Rundstedt decreed, to order Case III A. In fact, he wanted even more than Case III A. He wanted a 'ruthless stripping' of all the other fronts in the west for a counterattack in Normandy. He could not have been more decisive – or more right. If Von Rundstedt had his way, virtually every German fighting man in France and the Low Countries except those in the static, immobile coastal divisions would soon be on his way to Normandy.

Rommel, however, continued to disagree. A curious indecision had overtaken the Desert Fox. The day before, racing back to France, he had kept repeating to his ADC, Captain Helmuth Lang, that Germany's destiny – to say nothing of his own reputation – depended on the coming battle. Now it was almost as though he didn't want this battle, he wanted another one where he could be sure to win – in Pas-de-Calais. Von Rundstedt's proposal was premature. Rommel wanted to attack again with the forces already at his disposal. Instead of a united plea for Case III A, Rommel and Von Rundstedt passed their dispute to OKW for resolution that night. OKW did what superior headquarters usually do in such situations. It did nothing.

Her captors made Catherine walk up the flight of stairs to their bathroom knowing full well that each step she took on her bleeding feet was an excruciating ordeal. The bathroom was a spartan chamber: a plain whitewashed room with a large bathtub along one wall and a rack of whips along another. The window onto the street was flung wide open. While one of her tormentors turned on the bath's cold-water tap full force, the other stripped her – a nicety her captors had theretofore neglected to perform that day.

'What were you going to sabotage?' Strömelburg sounded almost bored asking the question.

Catherine simply shook her head in reply. One of the two men took a whip from the wall, gave one or two demonstrations of his savage expertise on the air, then sent its cord slashing across her chest. She shrieked and saw the reddening welts of flesh it left swelling on her breasts.

'What were you going to sabotage?'

376

She was lashed perhaps a dozen times before she heard the bathtub tap being closed behind her. Her captors sat her on the edge of the bath. One tightened a chain around her ankles. She was swung around so that her chained feet fell into the ice-cold water. Again Strömelburg droned his question: 'What were you going to sabotage?'

At her silence, one of her tormentors tugged at her chained feet while the other took her shoulders and forced her under the water. With her hands handcuffed behind her back, she was utterly helpless. She tried to kick and writhe, but one set of hands on the chain held her ankles just above the water's surface of the tub. Her eyes were open, and she could see the tormentors' laughing faces shimmering above her through the water over her head. Her lungs were ready to burst, screaming for a breath of air. Finally, her mouth opened in a terrible, involuntary gesture and the cold water poured in. Her vision swirled, she choked, her strength fled from her limbs. Drowning, she slid down to a black pit towards death.

When she recovered consciousness, the pain in her chest was unbearable, worse than anything else she had yet suffered at their hands. She could feel those hands thrusting at her chest, the water splashing out of her mouth. She was on her back, on the floor. Images, streaks of dark and light, shadow and definition moved before her eyes. Gradually, they coalesced into moving circles, then to faces, above all Strömelburg's, staring down at her.

'What were you going to sabotage?' The question came to her from another world, from another existence she'd left behind when that cold water had invaded the sanctuary of her lungs. She sputtered and gasped. The effort to talk was too much. Again, all she could do was shake her head.

'Stick her back in there,' she heard Strömelburg saying. Once more they dragged her to the tub, thrust her in feet first, then yanked her feet from under her and drove her head and shoulders underwater again. Again she tried to struggle. Again she saw the darkness closing in, felt her lungs bursting and the water pouring into her.

As they had the last time, they hauled her from the tub just as she was about to drown and industriously set out to pump the water they'd forced her to inhale from her body. It was a methodically calculated procedure – drive her to the threshold of death, then yank her back.

After four or five immersions – Catherine had no idea how many – she desperately wanted to die, with her precious secret drowned in her corpse. She no longer fought. Now as they thrust her limp form into the water, she gulped it down. She was in a race with her captors to get through death's beckoning door before they could pull her back.

Through the shimmering visions, the question 'What were you going to sabotage?' kept coming at her from some shadowy void. Then she understood one thing. Each revival was taking longer. It was growing dark outside the window. Time was going by. In her suffering, she was depriving them of the one thing she possessed along with her secret: time.

And she was right. It was close to 10 P.M. when Strömelburg, exhausted by his prisoner's ordeal, realized it was no use. Her heart would give out before the bath would break her.

He would have to find something else in the morning.

T.F. and Deirdre clutched their mugs of tea in the tiny mess of Churchill's Underground War Rooms as though their warmth might ease the fatigue overwhelming them both. Deirdre leaned towards T.F. so that only he would hear her words. 'Ismay's office just brought the Colonel a copy of a message Montgomery sent to Churchill this morning. Do you know what it said?'

T.F. shook his head.

'You Americans are holding on to Omaha by an eyelash.'

'Christ!' T.F. said. 'I knew it was bad, but I didn't know it was that bad.'

Deirdre pushed a lock of her usually well-groomed hair back into place. 'You've no idea what it will mean for this country if this invasion fails. It will be the end for us, the absolute bloody end.'

'You don't mean that, darling; you're exaggerating.'

'I mean every damn word of it. Don't let this stiff upper lip of ours fool you. We're at the end of our rope. We are exhausted. If this fails, we'll be out of it, I tell you.' She sipped her tea. 'Let's talk about something more cheerful. Where did you go running off to at six-thirty? You're not flirting behind my back with those pretty countrywomen of yours at the OSS, are you?'

T.F. laughed. The girls of General Donovan's London headquarters were something of a legend in the British capital.

'I've been playing errand boy for the Colonel. He sent me over to the BBC with one of those messages they broadcast to the Resistance. There's a little bit of skulduggery going on, I suspect. A Major Cavendish of the SOE ordered the message cancelled this morning. I had to order it reinstated. "Nous avons un message pour petite Berthe." he said in atrocious French. 'I wonder who Berthe is.'

Deirdre lowered her gaze to her tea mug, partly to conceal her dismay, partly to give some order to the confused associations that phrase had for her. Involuntarily, her right hand went to her earlobe. She was wearing, as she did almost every day, the gold earrings Catherine had given T.F. on their ride together to Tangmere.

378

'That's very strange,' she said in a half-whisper.

'Why is it strange?'

'You remember the day you brought Catherine down here for the first time? I was alone that day. Just before you arrived, the Colonel asked me to type out two French codes for him. The timing keys for a sabotage operation. That was the first one. He took them back just as you and she came in.'

'You think they were for her?'

'Exactly.'

T.F. braced himself, as though the spirit were preparing to resist the intrusion of an unwanted and undesirable thought. Something had been troubling him since the evening before – the kind of suspicion stirred by a lover's dubious lie, the sort of doubt tranquil minds do not quite choose to acknowledge. Why had the head of British Intelligence called Ridley to tell him about Catherine's arrest? Why was her arrest important enough to justify Menzies' knowing about it? And how did he know she had been arrested?

Another recollection, this one prompted by Catherine's earrings, seized him. It was something she had said in the car going to the airfield; if she was caught, her earrings would wind up on a Gestapo whore in Calais. That meant she had been going to Calais. Where Ridley wanted the Germans to expect a landing.

'Jesus Christ!' he whispered. 'You don't think she was set up deliberately, do you?'

'I don't know what to think.'

'No,' T.F. shook his head in a quest for disbelief. 'The Colonel wouldn't do that. There's a limit.'

'Is there?'

'I just don't believe it. I just don't believe he'd do it.'

Deirdre, her eyes sad and wide, looked up at him. 'You're still so naïve, T.F. Maybe that's what I like about you. Believe me, the Colonel would sell his mother to a Turkish whoremonger if he thought it would help us win the war.'

'Maybe, but not this.'

'Let's change the subject. The whole bloody business sickens me. Are you coming to the flat tonight?'

'I can't,' T.F. sighed. 'I'm lockup officer tonight.'

'See?' Deirdre pouted. 'I knew you were having an affair with one of those dishy OSS girls.'

Her captors had deliberately left a light bulb burning in her cell to make it difficult for Catherine to sleep. She huddled in a foetal position on her cot, desperately trying to enter the womb of sleep. She couldn't. She stared down at her swollen, bloodied feet. Even the thought of having to stand on them was almost enough to make her scream – had she had the strength to scream.

She was, she knew, in a state of collapse. Each breath drawn into her lungs was an ordeal. The flesh on her chest was raw from the whipping of Strömelburg's torturers. This time she had neither the strength nor the will to drag herself to the water tap to cleanse her wounds. As she lay there in the silence of her cell, a terrible reality gripped her: she was at the end. She had endured, but she could endure no longer. One more torturer's hand laid upon her painwrenched body, one more immersion into the shimmering waters of the bath and she would break. In the stillness she began to sob – soft, sad sobs brought on by despair and the terrible knowledge she could not go on.

Suddenly she sat bolt upright, her mouth agape in horror. Outside, down the stairs, she heard the distant knell of advancing footsteps. It was over. They were coming for her, to take her back to their torture chambers. There she would surely break and yield up what they wanted. The heavy clomps advanced down the wooden corridor and stopped – in front of her cell door. She shivered in fright as she heard the metallic scrape of the key and watched in terror as the door creaked open.

Her visitor was not one of Strömelburg's men, but a woman, one of the dowdy German matrons who helped police the building. A pair of shoes dangled from her hand. She stared at Catherine, huddled like a broken doll on her cot, then gave a raucous laugh. 'Here,' she said, advancing on her: 'you forgot these.'

As she reached Catherine, she glanced at her mutilated feet and grunted. 'Why waste them on you?' she said. 'You're not going to be putting them on for a while, are you, *Schatz*?'

'Please,' Catherine begged: 'they're mine.'

The matron gave an admiring caress to the tassels adorning the shoes, then sighed as she contemplated her own flat and stolid feet. Nothing would ever get those shoes she held in her hand onto them. With an angry snort, she tossed the shoes onto the floor by Catherine's cot and stalked from the cell. As the door clanked shut, Catherine slumped on her cot, her eyes fixed on the shoes, on their brass tassels glinting in the light cast by the bare bulb overhead.

The doorknob to Ridley's private office turned with such laboured slowness it was almost, T.F. thought, as though his British superior couldn't quite bring himself to leave the shelter of that inner sanctum. The Englishman looked at him with the faintly perplexed air of someone stumbling on an old acquaintance in a most unexpected situation.

'You're still here? You the last?'

'Yes, sir. I'm lockup tonight.'

'Well, lock up and let's walk across the park together.'

'We'll just give the map room a last look, shall we?' Ridley suggested when T.F. had completed the security checks required of the last officer out of the London Controlling Section's office each night.

He stood by Ridley's side as he pondered the map of France with its minuscule stains of red indicating the ground held by the Allies, the dark symbols denoting the nineteen divisions of the German Fifteenth Army, the Panzers of Von Rundstedt's central reserve. The Englishman knew far better than T.F. how precarious was their hold on those farther shores. He made that nervous gesture T.F. had so often remarked, pinching his nostrils with his thumb and forefinger like a swimmer trying to clear water from the ears. 'Thank God they haven't come down yet. If they come in the next few days, they can overwhelm us.' Ridley paused, eyes gazing at the 150 miles that separated Pas-de-Calais from the landing beaches. 'This is when we may very well win or lose the war – in the next forty-eight hours.' He sighed. 'Ah, well. Thinking about it isn't going to change anything now, is it? At least, that's what I keep telling myself.'

He spun on his heel, and T.F. followed him up the steps, past the saluting Royal Marine sentries into the damp night air. For a few moments they walked the footpath of St James's Park in silence, Ridley smoking his ever-present Players, scrutinizing the sky, ears strained for the warble of one of his beloved birds.

'You worked for the government before the war, didn't you, T.F.?'

'For one of the New Deal administrations. Kind of a government job, I suppose.'

'Will you go back to government service when all this is over?'

'I haven't really given it all that much thought.'

'You should. They're going to need people like you in Washington when you're the world's new Romans.'

'How about you, Colonel?' T.F. enquired. 'Will you go back to the law, or will you' – he didn't know quite how to put the end of his question – 'continue in this sort of thing?'

Ridley clasped his hands behind his back. 'This sort of thing is a room with one-way doors. Once you're inside you don't come back out. Not officially at least. But my flame will have guttered out with what I've had to do here, I fear. I suppose I shall go back to my torts officially and do the odd job unofficially when the phone rings.'

They were silent again for a few minutes until they reached the footbridge over the pond. 'Colonel,' T.F. said, 'may I ask you something unofficially? *Ex cathedra?*'

'Of course.'

'It's about that French girl, Catherine Pradier, I saw off at Tangmere.'

T.F. sensed a perceptible tensing in the man at his side. 'The one the Gestapo caught?'

'Yes.'

'What about her?' Ridley had stopped and was leaning on the railing of the footbridge staring into the water – tacit recognition that T.F.'s was not a casual query.

'She was on her way to Calais to organize a major act of sabotage, wasn't she?'

Ridley nodded.

'In support of an invasion that is never going to take place.'

Ridley said nothing.

'The code word I took to the BBC tonight was meant for her.'

Again Ridley did not reply.

'Which, since she's in the Gestapo's hands, means you wanted the Germans to hear it, not her. And which also must mean she was deliberately betrayed to the Gestapo.'

'And if she was?' Ridley's tone was sad and soft.

'If she was?' T.F.'s question was angry and rhetorical. 'It was a terrible criminal thing to do.'

'War is a terrible business, T.F., governed by only one morality – to win. Chivalry died with poison gas and the dive-bomber.'

'You know that if either of our governments knew about this, we'd be gaoled?'

'Perhaps.'

'Churchill is a close friend of yours. Christ, he would have you hanged for this.'

'There are things that Winston wants done, T.F., that Winston doesn't want to know about. All governments are like that. That's why they have people like you and me.'

You and me, is it? T.F. thought, reddening with anger. You're dragging me into this – making me some kind of accomplice in your crime?

'Do you remember what Winston said a couple of years ago?' Ridley was continuing, 'We have not journeyed all this way because we're made of sugar candy.'

'I remember now something you said a few weeks ago at the meeting of the XX Committee: "There is no one that cannot have the truth tortured out of him by the Gestapo." That's what you said, isn't it? You gave her to the Gestapo to torture the truth out of her. Your truth.'

At the moment he said those words, T.F. hated the Englishman beside him with all the passion of his Celtic heritage, hated him as he'd never hated another human being. For one mad instant he wanted to kill him, to strangle him and throw his body into the waters of the pond. Then he found a new, sweeter vengeance. 'She can still thwart you, you know.' He almost spat the words at his superior.

'How is that?' Ridley asked.

'With that cyanide pill I gave her when she left. She can take that. And knowing her, she will.'

Ridley took a long, last drag on his cigarette, then flicked it into the pond below. T.F. heard its stub hiss as it struck the water.

'Indeed,' Ridley said. Then he turned and started back across the park – alone.

Catherine stared with a kind of dull, morbid concentration at the shoes resting on the floor of her cell just out of her reach. How long had she been looking at them like that, in a kind of fascinated trance?

They were a deliverance, she thought, a transport to another place where Strömelburg and his torturers' bestial hands could no longer find her. Slowly, tentatively, she stretched out a hand from her aching body. Her gesture had the detached movement of a dream as her fingers curled around the right shoe and drew it to her chest. For a while she held it there, feeling the slickness of the leather on the open wounds left by Strömelburg's whips. Slowly, painfully, she unscrewed the little brass bulb in the tassel and shook out the pill it contained.

Her mind went back to a blissful time long before she had come down that road from Paris under the Stukas, to a time when no one she had loved had died, and life was infinite, stretching down to a horizon her soul could not see.

Now, that horizon was here with her in her cell. It was square and white and it rested between her thumb and forefinger, its form defining itself against the flesh it might return to the coldness of eternity. She stared at it. What was it that first officer who had given it to her had said? – 'It's relatively painless. Thirty seconds and it's all over.'

She thought of the others who had been in this cell before her, who had begged the night for the deliverance she held pressed between her fingers. She thought of what was beyond the walls of her cell, of what she would never know again, of flowers and sunlight, Paris and love, rain and bright autumn leaves. She thought of the child she would never conceive and of Paul lost in his own dark night. Then she thought of the shattered vessel that had been her body, aflame with hurt, burdened with a secret she could no longer hold.

'O Lord Jesus Christ, I commend myself to Thee,' she whispered. To Thee? She wondered. Or to some dark and meaningless void? You were supposed to feel calm at such an instant, she thought, but she felt dizzy and faint. She placed the pill, as they'd told her to do, in her mouth, holding it firmly between the molars on the left side of her jaw. She lay down on the cot. Her head was spinning madly now and she knew she was going to faint.

She thought of her mother in the car going down from Paris, just before the Stukas came. With one swift gesture, she bit down on the 'L' pill. As she felt it crumble, she gulped its contents down her throat and fainted.

No matter how much they had disliked France's occupiers, the French police had served them reasonably, if grudgingly, well. On occasion – not often perhaps, but from time to time – the tasks they were called on to perform had brought the men who had had to execute them a real, if secret, satisfaction. This, thought Commissaire André Fraguier of Paris' Sixteenth Arrondissement as he read the sign on the corpse at his feet, was apt to be one of those occasions.

The bullet's exit wound had left very little of the man's upper head intact. Clearly, he had been shot from behind, at close range, in what must have been a kind of execution. He was, Fraguier guessed, in his early thirties, fairly well-to-do from the looks of him.

'You go through his papers?' he asked the two *flics* in capes and saucepan hats who'd found the body at the edge of the Bois de Boulogne.

'No, sir,' the older one said. 'We didn't want to touch a thing until you got here.'

Fraguier rolled the body over and fished the man's wallet from his pocket. Methodically, he went through its contents. When he came to the handwritten white card, he whistled softly. Hans-Dieter Strömelburg. That was a name you'd want to reckon with. Anyone walking the streets with a card from him in his pocket had to be a top Gestapo agent. Smart fellows, these Resistance guys, Fraguier thought.

He stood up and rolled the body onto its back again. If the man's Resistance executors were eager for the Gestapo to learn of his death, *Commissaire* Fraguier would be only too happy to oblige them. He put the dead man's papers into a small canvas bag.

'Wait for the meat wagon to come by for him,' he ordered his *flics*. Then he got onto his bicycle and, whistling happily, set off for what would be, in the circumstances, an eminently satisfying visit to 82 Avenue Foch.

It was the sounds that roused her, the stomping of booted feet, the metallic rasp of the key in the lock of her cell door, then the two men standing over her shouting at her to get up. Catherine shrieked in uncomprehending horror. She blinked, bewildered, her eyes rolling wildly in her head. As one of the men yanked her onto her feet, a bolt of pain seared through her. What had happened? Why was she alive? Why? Why?

384

This was no dream. The man's hands were all-too-real flesh and blood, the pain rolling up from the soles of her feet excruciatingly precise. Had the other been a dream, a hallucination of her shattered spirit? Her eyes went to her shoes on the floor. She saw the tassels unscrewed, the little fake gold cap she'd removed to get the pill lying beside her cot right where she'd dropped it. Her tongue could taste a few grainy traces left on her molar. It had not been a dream.

She had taken the pill and the pill had not worked.

'Come on, *Schatz*,' one of her two now-familiar torturers sneered. 'We'll work you over a bit to wake you up.' He struck her a sharp blow in the kidneys with his rubber-coated cosh to start her stumbling for her cell door. She staggered on her misshapen feet, each contact they made with the floor agony for her. At the door, she shrieked. Hers was a chill, piercing scream – not of pain, however, but one born of horror and comprehension at the enormity of the betrayal that had been worked upon her. She saw the face of that man in his underground office bestowing his kiss of Judas upon her cheeks. Again she heard his subtle injunctions to silence – those injunctions for which she had destroyed herself and which had never been meant to be kept.

Again she screamed, rage mixing with the pain in her feet as they half-pushed, half-tugged her down the stairs.

Oh, God, she thought, You forgive the bastards who did this to me if You can.

Because I never will ...

'She's broken. She's ready to talk.'

His torturer announced the news to Strömelburg in a tone so matter-of-fact he might have been saying, 'The plumber's here.' Strömelburg acknowledged his report with a wave. They often broke like that, at night, alone in their cells unable to face the horror of a new dawn, a new interrogation session.

'Bring her down here, then,' he commanded.

He rose, almost respectfully, as they brought her in. She had broken all right. She was weeping uncontrollably, babbling some incoherent nonsense, shaking with the wild fury of a malaria victim in the midst of the fever's seizure. He waved to his men to put her in the chair before his desk. As one bent to undo her handcuffs, she obviously felt the beatings were about to start again. She seemed to shrivel like a dog cowering before the boot of a brutal master.

'Please, please!' she gasped.

Strömelburg walked around his desk. 'So,' he said, 'the night has brought counsel, has it?'

Her chin slumped on her chest. To avoid his gaze, he calculated. She

385

was humiliated, shattered by the imminence of her surrender. It was a common enough reaction. Now that she was ready to talk, it was simply a matter of gentling out that first phrase, making it easy, painless. Once that had been uttered, the logjam would be broken and the rest would rush out in a cascade.

Almost sorrowfully, Strömelburg contemplated the wreckage his men had left of what had once been a beautiful woman. Why had she made them do this to her? Why hadn't she listened to him and saved herself this horror? She had wanted to be a heroine; and she had wound up a wreck.

'So' – Strömelburg's tone was that of a man to whom the business at hand was a matter of little moment – 'what was it you proposed to sabotage in Calais?'

'The Lindemann Battery.'

'The Lindemann Battery!' Even Strömelburg, trained interrogator that he was, couldn't keep his astonishment in check. He'd visited the battery in 1943, not long after it had been dedicated to the memory of the captain of the *Bismarck*. It was impregnable. They didn't allow Frenchmen within miles of it. The Resistance couldn't possibly sabotage those guns. Unless, it occurred to Strömelburg, they'd managed to suborn a member of the gun crew. 'The microfilms Cavendish gave you to bring back?'

'They're inside one of the matches in the matchbox in the handbag you took from me the first night.'

Strömelburg wanted to shout. The matches – of course; how could he have been so stupid? Why was she, a nonsmoker, carrying matches around with her? The contents of her handbag were downstairs in the Doctor's office where the more evident vehicles in which to smuggle a microfilm such as her compact and lipstick tube had been systematically picked apart. No one had even thought about the matches. He went to his office intercom to buzz the Doctor.

'So,' he said, 'that leaves just the BBC code phrases. What were they?'

'There were two.' She was mumbling, her words almost inaudible, still evidently struggling with her conscience to wrest each admission from those inner depths in which she'd buried her secret. "*Nous avons un message pour petite Berthe*" was the first alert message.' She gave him a bitter smile. 'You know what that means, I suppose?'

He smiled his wisdom in return.

'"*Salomon a sauté ses grands sabots*" was the action message.'

'Which meant?' Strömelburg remembered how Cavendish had stressed to his man in Calais how vital it was that the operation's timing be absolutely precise. He saw her hesitate a moment, reluctant to go on. He said nothing and waited.

'Well, what it meant was' – she was mumbling again – 'we were to wait twenty-four hours after we heard it. Then, at four o'clock the morning following, we were to execute the sabotage.'

The Doctor had entered the room. He glanced in horror at the wretch collapsed in Strömelburg's chair, then passed him the matchbox he'd requested. Wordlessly, Strömelburg gave the box to his prisoner. Catherine picked through the matches until she found the one with the 'U.' She let her shoulders droop in resigned defeat and again looked away from the German's eyes to convince him she had to hide her unutterable shame. Is this the way you ghastly bastards wanted it done? she thought as she handed the match to Strömelburg, is this the Sarah Bernhardt routine you wanted me to put on? Except, as she well knew, she was never supposed to know, to even suspect. Not only had she been sent here to suffer the Gestapo's unutterable physical agonies; they wanted her to suffer, afterwards, the anguish of remorse for her collapse. 'Snap off the head,' she whispered.

Strömelburg did as he was told. He saw the hollowed metal tube under the head and shook out the microfilm. Ingenious! They were clever, the British. He held it up, but couldn't see or understand anything. 'Get a blow up done of this, Doctor,' he ordered.

'Well,' he commented, almost fondly, to Catherine, 'you've kept your part of the bargain and I'll keep mine.' He sent his torturers from the room with a gesture of his head, then poured two glasses of whisky from the bottle on his desk he claimed Cavendish had sent him. 'You can take this now, I think.'

Gratefully, Catherine sipped at the amber liquor. From the sunlight outside, she guessed it was midmorning. Had it been a sleeping potion instead of cyanide they'd put in her fake 'L' pill? she wondered. She would probably, she realized, not live long enough to get the answer to that.

'Just how did you ever imagine you were going to sabotage that battery?' Strömelburg asked. He was no longer the interrogator; he was as friendly as a defence lawyer reviewing a case with a client.

'Through the electrical system. I really don't know how it was going to work. I just had to change the fuses in the control panel.'

'You changed the fuses? In the control panel of the Lindemann Battery?' Strömelburg choked a bit in surprise as he asked the question. She nodded.

'How did you even get into the battery? Did a German boyfriend put a uniform on you and smuggle you inside?'

'I was the laundress.'

'The laundress!'

'For the officers.'

387

'And you walked in there one sweet morning and changed the fuses in the control panel instead of washing the *Oberleutnant's* underwear?'

'Yes, more or less.'

'It wasn't locked?'

Catherine reddened slightly, then shrugged and told him the story of Metz.

'Well, I admit I'm speechless,' Strömelburg said. 'It sounds simply incredible.' He raised his glass. 'You're my enemy, mademoiselle, but I salute you.' He sipped at his whisky. 'And I praise God we found you out in time. Obviously, you had some colleagues working with you.'

'I had two, but they will have fled by now, thank God. One of them was waiting for me at the station. He saw them arrest me.'

'No doubt,' Strömelburg acknowledged. 'I'll have a description of them anyway.'

The telephone rang. 'There's someone downstairs I think you'd better see,' the Doctor told him.

A French police inspector threw an energetic salute to the Gestapo leader as Strömelburg entered the foyer of 82 Avenue Foch, then offered him his ID card for inspection.

'What do you want?' Strömelburg snapped. He hated French policemen.

'Sir, my men found a body at the Bagatelle this morning in the Bois. A man who has been murdered by these terrorists of the Resistance, I suppose.' The Frenchman took a canvas bag from the pocket of his raincoat and began pawing its contents like an old lecher looking for a sweet to propose to a little girl. 'We gave his body a thorough search, sir – the routine required, you know, even these days with all these killings.' He was still fumbling with his bag. 'Terrible, isn't it? When will it ever end? Ah, here it is!' He passed Strömelburg the handwritten white card he'd given Gilbert. 'Found this on him.'

'Jesus!' So that was why Konrad had not been able to pick him up. 'Where's the body?'

'At the morgue, sir.' He passed the rest of Gilbert's papers to Strömelburg.

'Are you sure – absolutely sure – the face on the body you found is the same as the face in these ID photos?'

'Oh, yes, yes, sir, no doubt about it. What was left of his face, that is.'

The Frenchman saw the German wince. This was worth a little elaboration for his benefit. 'I mean it looked as if they'd backed a howitzer right up to the back of the guy's head. Must have blown his brains all the way to the Seine.' He clucked in horror. 'Yeah, they really blew him away, all right. Someone really wanted to get the' – he was

388

about to say 'bastard' but caught himself in time – 'poor fellow.'

'Send me a copy of your report.' Strömelburg sighed. He turned on his heel and went upstairs to the Doctor's office. For a long time he sat there alone, head in his hands, half weeping. In his strange way, Strömelburg bore Gilbert an affection similar to that he might have had for the son he'd never sired. He saw him coming into his apartment before the war in his frayed flight jacket, boisterous, laughing. A rogue, a charming, adventurous rogue, and now he was dead because Strömelburg had allowed that telegram to go through to Lille. And neither he nor Berlin would ever be able to recognize officially what Henri Lemaire, his priceless Gilbert, had done for Germany.

Still under the shock, he went back to his office. She, he thought, looking at Catherine, had been having dinner with Gilbert that night at the Chapon Rouge. Probably in love with him – a lot of them were. And the bitch was one of their murdering gang. Suddenly he hated her as he had not hated her during any interrogation sessions he had forced her to endure.

'I've just had some bad news,' he said.

As he had expected, those green eyes of hers told him how pleased she was to hear it.

'Do you remember Paul, the Air Operations Officer who received you? Whom you were having dinner with that night' – he meant to smile but grimaced instead – 'when we met?'

There it was, the gratifying little flicker of apprehension in her eyes that told him she was indeed in love with him.

'He's dead.'

She gasped.

'Murdered by your fellow terrorists.'

'Murdered!' Her swollen, bruised mouth was open in dismay. 'Why?'

'Why? Why do you think you're here, Mademoiselle Pradier? Your friend Paul was the best agent I've ever had.'

Catherine shrieked and tumbled from her chair, unconscious. Strömelburg stared down at her in satisfaction. There were still some pains more terrible than any savagery his torturers could inflict. He buzzed his guards. 'Take her upstairs,' he ordered. 'Give her something to eat and fix her up a bit.'

'Should we keep her here, sir?' one asked.

Strömelburg looked at the girl stirring back to consciousness. 'No, I think we're done with Mademoiselle Pradier. Send her off to Fresnes, and ship her on the next *Nacht und Nebel* convoy.'

Korvettenkapitän Fritz Diekmann, the commander of the Lindemann Battery, was a fierce disciplinarian. His electrical officer, Lothar Metz,

389

seemed to be almost shaking as he braced to attention before his desk.

'The great German lover, are you, Metz?' Diekmann snarled. 'Seducing the battery's laundress?'

Metz babbled in reply. Had she been caught in a VD roundup? he wondered. Was that where she had disappeared all of a sudden?

'Except she wasn't a laundress, Metz. She was a British terrorist.' Diekmann leaped up and, ordering Metz to follow him, ran down the metal staircase to his underground control room.

'Open that up,' he ordered, pointing to the control panel.

Hands shaking, Metz unlocked the panel.

Diekmann's finger went to the fuse that protected the turret motor of Anton. 'Pull that out.'

Metz obediently extracted the fuse.

'Now look at it.'

Metz studied it, puzzled. Slowly he turned it over and saw the glistening copper that had replaced the lead in its central core. He felt a clammy sweat around his temples. 'Something's wrong.' He blurted out. 'Someone got in there somehow and played with these circuit breakers!'

'Not someone, Metz. Your little laundress friend. With a copy of your key that she'd made from an impression she took of it after you'd finished making love to her.'

Diekmann surveyed the control panel. 'I want you to switch every single fuse in there. Then I want you to verify every single sector of your electrical system.'

'*Jawohl*.'

'Tell me something, Metz' – Diekmann sneered at his shaken young electrical officer – 'how do you like snow and ice?'

Metz blinked, failing to comprehend the significance of the question on the June afternoon.

'Because you're going to get a chance to see a lot of it on the Eastern Front this winter.'

At about the same time Metz was contemplating the prospects of a Russian winter, two carloads of Gestapo officers swept into the compound of the Calais power station. Storming into the station building, they found the materials required to bypass the transformer and overload the Lindemann Battery exactly where Cavendish's microfilm had indicated they would be.

Five minutes of harsh questioning and a few punches was all that was required to persuade Pierre Paraud, the power-station manager, to talk. Indeed, by the time their car had reached Gestapo headquarters in Lille, the terrified electrical engineer had already told his Gestapo captors everything he knew about the plan to sabotage the battery.

Hans-Dieter Strömelburg had overseen every aspect of the investigation from his desk on Avenue Foch. As soon as his investigators discovered the sabotage preparations at the Calais power station, he had ordered the best electrical engineer of the Todt Organization, which had built the Atlantic Wall, into the station to analyse the setup, then to the battery itself to determine what effect the sabotage plan would have had on the guns had it been carried out. He conferred at length with Diekmann, the battery commander, on the gun's security, on its role in the defence of the Pas-de-Calais seacoast.

By the end of the day, there was no doubt left in Strömelburg's mind: what he held in his hands as a result of a confession he'd extracted from Catherine Pradier was an intelligence prize of extraordinary magnitude – a triumph that certainly marked the culmination of his career and could decisively influence the course of the war.

One last link remained to be uncovered, and the Doctor provided it just before 7 P.M. Panting from exertion, he ran up the stairs and burst, unannounced, into the *Obersturmbannführer's* office. 'The interception service at the Boulevard Suchet just called,' he said between his gasps for air. 'They've found the "petite Berthe" code message in their recordings. The BBC broadcast it last night!'

Strömelburg was exultant. That was it. It was all there now, lying in the palm of his hand. This time no pigheaded Prussian general at OB West was going to deprive Strömelburg and Germany of his triumph. History's warm breath was not going to pass his command by twice. He was going to lay this secret in the hands of Ernst Kaltenbrunner himself in his office on Prinz-Albrecht-Strasse.

Early in the evening of Thursday, June 8, as Strömelburg's Skoda was already on its way to Berlin, the US V Corps, responsible for the western half of the invasion beaches, issued a stern warning to SHAEF and its divisions. The Allied landings were 'two days behind in reaching their initial objectives, which gives grave emergency to the situation,' the warning said. The beachhead was 'far short of its desired depth, and the entire landing area can still be reached by enemy artillery fire.'

Now, the terse message continued, the second phase of the fight to stay ashore was about to begin. A major German counterattack must be expected at any moment, it warned, and 'the situation is so critical that if this attack comes in, the beachhead will have a very difficult time holding on.'

In the garret of a three-storey residence on Richmond Hill, an enlisted radio operator of the Signals Security Service blew on his fingertips for good luck, then, like a pianist picking out his first chords, began to tap on his sending key. His gesture was appropriate. To the Germans of the Abwehr in Paris, he was known as 'Chopin,' the operator of the double agent Brutus. With his gesture the curtain was rising on the final, critical act of Operation *Fortitude*, the act which Ridley had described to T. F. on his arrival in London as that on which all their fragile hopes depended.

'I have seen with my own eyes,' Brutus' message reported to Paris, 'the Army Group Patton preparing to embark.' The occasion had been his imaginary visit to FUSAG's advance command post at Dover Castle. He'd even overheard Patton himself remark, 'The time is coming to begin operations around Calais.'

For the little Polish Air Force officer pacing the floor below the room from which his operator transmitted, it was an excruciating moment. His critical role in the *Fortitude* scheme was drawing to a close. Soon, in a couple of weeks, a month or two at the most, the Abwehr officers in Paris who'd sent him to London would realize he'd duped them. What would happen then to the sixty-four French men and women comrades of his Resistance network held in Fresnes Prison as hostages to his good behaviour? Was that clacking stream of dots and dashes going out into the ether from the garret above a death knell for those precious friends he'd left behind?

Across in Hampstead, another radio operator of the Signals Security Service also prepared to go on the air. The culmination of years of patient and painstaking efforts of MI5, British counterintelligence, of hundreds of secret transmissions, of many a vital Allied secret knowingly and deliberately laid in the German's lap, was at hand. It was, in a sense, the movement for which Juan Pujol Garcia – 'Garbo' – had been nurtured by his controllers, the final blossoming of the most exotic orchid in their hothouse of deception.

His three best agents had all arrived in London. Garbo, his operator informed Madrid, had spent the afternoon debriefing them with exhausting thoroughness. They were an ex-seaman working as a docker in the port of Dover, a Sikh clerk who lived in Brighton, and a second embittered Welsh Nationalist from Harwich, another critical port at the juncture of the Stour and Orwell rivers in the area where FUSAG's armoured divisions were gathered.

As a result of his conversations with those men, Garbo was ready to pass over 'the most important report of my work.' He requested Madrid to stand by at midnight to receive it. This time Madrid would be listening. No one was going to miss a broadcast of the finest spy in the service of the Third Reich.

Just after 9 P.M., while Strömelburg's Skoda raced northward through the night and Brutus's and Garbo's radio operators went off the air, an announcer at a microphone in the underground studio of Bush House droned out the words '*Salomon a sauté ses grands sabots. I repeat: Salomon a sauté ses grands sabots.*'

Fortitude had played its hand. It was now up to the Germans to react – or not to react.

Field Marshal Gerd von Rundstedt was in a state of cold fury on the evening of Thursday, June 8. Once again, Rommel, his despised 'Marshal Boy Scout,' had failed to dislodge the Allies from their Normandy beachhead. And he wasn't going to get them out with the forces he had in hand, either. So concerned was he at the situation that he did something that night he almost never did: he placed a personal telephone call to the man he referred to as a 'Bohemian lance corporal.'

Order Case III A, he urged the Führer. Even if Normandy was a diversion, it had to be defeated at once so that the Wehrmacht's forces would be ready to face a second assault if it came. Finally, however reluctantly, Adolf Hitler gave in to the old Field Marshal. Seated before his maps at his evening strategy conference at the Berghof, he issued the one order that might have saved his Third Reich: Initiate Case III A.

The metallic screech shattered the predawn silence of Fresnes Prison. It was the sound of rusty iron wheels forcing their reluctant way along a prison corridor. In the darkness of their cell, Catherine heard her cellmate stir. 'The coffee cart's coming,' she whispered. 'There's a convoy leaving for Germany.'

Far down the corridor, they could hear the sounds of cell doors clanging open and shut, the accented voice of the German guard calling out the name of each prisoner being deported to the Reich's concentration camps. Occasionally, a shrill and useless shriek of protest came from one of those women he ordered from her cell to receive a parting cup of *ersatz* coffee from his cart.

Slowly, the screaming rasp of those rusting wheels advanced along the corridor until it was outside their door. Catherine heard the rattle of the guard's key in their lock, then, as the door swung open, the call 'Pradier, *raus!*'

She stumbled onto her bandaged feet and picked up the bundle that contained what few possessions she had. Her cellmate, with whom she'd barely had time to exchange half a dozen phrases, embraced her. '*Bonne chance*' – Good luck,' she whispered. '*Vive la France!*'

Blinking in the glare of the bare light bulbs along the ledgelike corridor that paralleled her cellblock, Catherine staggered after the women who'd been pulled from their cells before her. Outside, in the little courtyard in front of the prison building's main entrance, was a green-and-yellow bus, one of those Paris city buses on which she'd so often ridden to happier destinations. The guards lined them up in the morning damp until the convoy's last prisoner had tottered out of the prison gate. Then, a clipboard in his hand, a warden summoned them one by one onto the bus.

Catherine's name was among the last to be called. By the time she boarded the bus, the only places left were on the open platform at its rear. In front of her, she heard the creaking of the prison gates being wrenched open. The engine coughed.

Catherine glanced up at Fresnes' stone walls. At their barred windows, she could just make out the gaunt faces of her fellow prisoners of a night. As the bus lurched forward, their hands, fingers thrust upward in the 'V' of victory, began to wave farewell. From behind the stone façade the sound of 'La Marseillaise' began to rise, a timid chorus at first, then growing slowly to a bold, defiant throb, a fond and fitting *adieu* to their departing convoy.

In the early hours of the morning of Friday, June 9, SHAEF headquarters, then Churchill's Underground War Rooms began to register the consequences of the momentous decision Hitler had taken the night before. First the eavesdroppers, the men who listened in on the German wireless communications between units, then the *Ultra* code busters picked up the signs: the German Army was on the move.

Aerial reconnaissance confirmed their reading. The 116th Panzer, the First SS Panzer, 500 tanks and 35,000 of Germany's finest fighting men were moving out of their *Lager*, pointing northwest for Normandy, the vanguard of the vast mobilization of Case III A. The critical moment had arrived, precisely at the moment virtually every Allied intelligence officer had predicted it would. Indeed, General George C. Marshall and the US Chiefs of Staff were due to arrive in London by midday to stand alongside their British colleagues 'to handle any eventuality that might arise' – SHAEF's euphemism for an event made far more likely by Hitler's decision: an Allied defeat on the Norman beaches.

Hans-Dieter Strömelburg strode down the familiar corridors of Prinz-Albrecht-Strasse to the office of *Gruppenführer* Ernst Kaltenbrunner with the confident air of a Caesar. The news of his prodigious feat had preceded him. This time, he could have walked into the *Gruppenführer's* office in the uniform of a British grenadier and been greeted as a hero.

Swiftly he reviewed for Kaltenbrunner and Kopkow his detailed notes on Catherine Pradier's confession, his men's investigations at the Lindemann Battery and the Calais power station. 'The assurances of our coastal defence experts are categorical,' he stated. 'We know from past experience that no amount of aerial bombardment can knock out those

394

guns. For the British to try to do it from the sea would be suicide. After all, their own Nelson said, "A sailor who attacks a coastal gun with a ship is a fool." Sabotage was the only option they had because as long as those guns are firing, no invasion fleet can operate in the Channel from Gris-Nez to the Dunkirk approaches except at its peril.'

'I cannot understand how anyone could have devised a plan to sabotage those batteries,' Kaltenbrunner sighed. 'Are you absolutely certain it would have worked?'

'Positive. We analysed it minutely. The power overload would have wrought havoc in the turret motors and shell hoists. The command would have had to either rewire them or replace them completely – who knows?'

'How long would that have taken?'

'At least twelve hours. That is the basis of their whole calculation. That is why they laid such emphasis on the operation's timing. They have to have the guns out of action during twelve daylight hours to give time to land and destroy the guns from the shore.'

'There's no chance this is some kind of Allied trick?' It was the hateful Kopkow Strömelburg so despised.

'I don't know how many people we've put through intensive interrogation at Avenue Foch, but I can tell you this: there aren't more than one or two who went through what we put her through. There's absolutely no doubt in my mind about her confession. And there's one last thing that confirms it. London ordered our agent Gilbert, whom we have, ultimately, to thank for this, killed because he betrayed her.'

'Yes,' Kaltenbrunner agreed, 'it couldn't be clearer.' He too had read Von Roenne's reports of the twenty-five divisions of Patton's First US Army Group poised in southeastern England. 'They are going to make their real landing in Calais, all right, and they must have these guns silenced just before they land.'

His own office door opened. 'An urgent call for the *Obersturmbann-führer*,' his aide announced.

'It was Paris,' Strömelburg said when he came back. 'The BBC broadcast the action message "*Salomon a sauté ses grands sabots*" at nine-fifteen last night.'

For a few hours on Friday, June 9, Colonel Alex von Roenne, the Baltic nobleman who presided over the Wehrmacht's Foreign Armies West, was the pivot on which the battle for Normandy hinged. He was the funnel through which all *Fortitude's* deceptions passed on their way to Hitler's desk, and his appraisal of them was critical in determining the reception they would get when they were placed before the Führer.

The first report to reach him that Friday came from the Abwehr on

Tirpitzstrasse. It was the digest of Brutus' message of the night before. That confirmed what Von Roenne had been saying to Rommel, Von Rundstedt and Hitler's headquarters since midday June 6. Normandy was a diversion. Now these troops of Patton's First United States Army Group, those divisions he'd imagined into being at *Fortitude's* prompting, were beginning to move. But the critical element in his assessment was furnished by the news from Kaltenbrunner that the code phrase '*Salomon a sauté ses grands sabots*' had been broadcast by the BBC. That was it. Now he had not just the indication an assault was coming in Pas-de-Calais, but a precise indication as to when.

He made an urgent call to Hitler's personal intelligence officer at Berchtesgaden, Colonel Friedrich-Adolf Krummacher. He had just received intelligence of the highest grade, he told Krummacher, that a second, large-scale Allied landing was about to be launched from eastern England. Then he told him the Signal Service had intercepted an enemy radio message over the BBC to which he attached 'greatest importance.' It indicated the Allies would strike the next day, June 10. To pull the infantry and armour of the Fifteenth Army out of Pas-de-Calais now, he warned, 'would be utter madness.' Tell the Führer, he begged Krummacher, to cancel Case III-A.

Hitler's Chief of Staff, General Alfred Jodl, presented Von Roenne's urgent plea to the Führer at his day's first strategy conference, barely half an hour after Von Roenne's urgent call. Hitler was impressed, but not impressed enough to change his mind – yet. He had hesitated a long time before ordering Case III-A. He was not ready to reverse himself without further thought. Warlords, after all, did not win wars by constantly changing their minds. He would consider the matter and review the case at his evening conference.

On the evening of Friday, June 10, Hitler had his usual spartan vegetarian dinner, then retired to the privacy of his study. From the Berghof's windows he could gaze out at the snowcapped crags of the Alps rising over Berchtesgaden, the mountains that had been so much a part of his life since he'd defined its purpose in the pages of *Mein Kampf*, written in a chalet not far from his sumptuous residence.

Shortly before 10:30 P.M., General Jodl interrupted his meditations with a despatch that had just come in from Von Roenne, a summary of Garbo's lengthy message of the evening before. Hitler knew who Garbo was. He put on his metal-rimmed spectacles and studied what the Spaniard had described as 'my most important report.' It began with a review of all the military formations, real and imagined, reported by Garbo's three key agents in southeast England. For the first time, Garbo mentioned landing craft waiting in the Rivers Deben and Orwell to board those formations. 'It is perfectly clear,' Garbo concluded, 'that the present attack, while a large-scale operation, is diversionary in character for the purpose of establishing a strong beachhead in order to draw the maximum of our reserves to the area so as to be able to strike a blow somewhere else with assured success.'

The report digested, Hitler made a large loop in green crayon in the despatch's upper left-hand corner to indicate he'd read it and sent it back to Jodl.

A few minutes later, one of the telephones on his desk rang, the phone which provided his direct link to *Reichsführer* SS Heinrich Himmler at Prinz-Albrecht-Strasse. It was over that line that Himmler had passed Hitler so many of his juiciest morsels of gossip in his relentless pursuit of his prized post as intelligence czar of the Reich. Now he gave Hitler the most important treasure the RSHA had uncovered since he had assumed that position: the riddle of the BBC code phrase '*Salomon a sauté ses grands sabots.*'

That was it – the final, determining revelation. Supremely confident, Hitler went to his evening strategy conference. The situation, he announced, was clear. A second landing was imminent. Case III-A was cancelled. He would not strip the Fifteenth Army of its reserves. He would reinforce it. He ordered the First SS Panzer and the 116th Panzer to be stopped in their tracks. They were to pivot around to positions behind Pas-de-Calais. Earlier in the day, he had ordered the Ninth and Tenth SS Panzer Divisions to head to France from Poland. They too were now assigned to the Fifteenth Army. The finest flower of the Wehrmacht would be waiting to savage General George S. Patton and his divisions of the First US Army Group when they crashed ashore against his Atlantic Wall.

Half an hour later, the high-speed teletype announced Hitler's decision to cancel Case III-A to Von Rundstedt's headquarters at Saint-Germain-en-Laye. An aide brought it to Von Rundstedt's Chief of Operations, General Bodo Zimmerman.

'Should we wake the Field Marshal?' the aide asked when Zimmerman had finished reading the text.

'Why?' Zimmerman asked. 'Germany has just lost the war.'

EPILOGUE

APRIL 22, 1945

Off in the distance she could hear the sound of heavy surf crashing along the Atlantic shore. She was playing chess with her father on the sun deck of the little *chalet* in the hills above St Jean-de-Luz, and its echoes drifted up to them on the same chill wind that made her tremble with cold. 'A storm,' her father murmured; 'a storm is coming.'

She shivered, then stirred. As she did, tips of the straw protruding through the burlap of her lice-infested pallet pricked her flesh – sharp little reminders of the reality awaiting just beyond the frontier of her dream. Instinctively, she squeezed her eyes shut, trying to cling for a few more precious moments to the solace it gave. Long ago, she had learned to cling to those dreams, to linger the last desperate seconds on the threshold of the only comfort left her, sleep. Now, as the darkness ebbed in her cell and she floated towards wakefulness, her mind focused on the sound that had awakened her, the one dimension shared by the illusory world she was so reluctantly leaving and the one represented by the dark cement walls enfolding her.

It couldn't be an air raid. Nowhere could Catherine make out the distinctive grinding sound the planes always made on their passage to Berlin. These were vague, muffled thuds of some kind, as irregular in their cadence as they were in their strength. Then, as mysteriously as they had begun, they stopped, leaving her once again alone with the silence of her cell. Catherine pulled herself to her feet, shaking uncontrollably from the damp of the cement floor which had seeped into every crevice of her being during the night. Then she squatted beside her pallet and snapped a piece of straw the size of her fingernail from under the burlap. On her hands and knees, she crawled to the corner of the cell beyond the pallet's edge and huddled over a little jumble of straw, the hieroglyphics of her despair, a kind of personal Rosetta Stone to which only she possessed the key. Today is April 22, 1945, Catherine calculated, meticulously putting her straw into place: ninety-seven days I have been in this cell, forty-three days to the first anniversary of my arrest, one hundred and six days to my twenty-eighth birthday.

Behind her, she heard the clang of a gate opening and closing, then the rasp of a key in her cell door's lock, followed by an angry shout: 'Raus'.

Blinking, as she always did in the glare of the bare light bulb along her cellblock corridor, Catherine struggled to stand to attention next to the sign on her cell door. It bore three bits of information: her name; her Ravensbrück number, 97123, and the two capital letters NN. A stump of a woman barely five feet three inches tall in her soiled green uniform and black leather boots plodded slowly down the corridor. Behind her, two *Kapos* pushed a metal cart containing the first of the two daily meals offered the inmates of the bunker – a cup of warm liquid vaguely resembling *ersatz* coffee and a curl of mouldering bread. The sight of the gaunt skeletons along the corridor grabbing like famished animals at their pitiful rations usually amused SS Wardress Margarete Mewes. No such levity gripped her this morning, however. She appeared withdrawn and distant, lost in the contemplations of some private world of her own.

As she drew abreast of Catherine, the French girl raised her head to address her. It was not an action she undertook lightly. Mewes was the kind of woman who could get maudlin drunk singing 'Silent Night' on Christmas Eve and beat a prisoner to death the next day because she had a hangover.

'Bitte, Frau Wärterin,' Catherine murmured.

'Ja,' The German woman's eyes, Catherine noted, were reddened from strain or lack of sleep.

'What was that noise we heard during the night?'

The snarl of a cornered animal transformed the SS warden's suety face. 'Whore!' she screamed, slashing at her with her rubber truncheon.

'Whore!' she shrilled again, her second blow snapping Catherine's head back against the steel lintel of her cell door. Stunned, the French girl clutched the door to keep herself from falling before the next blow struck. As she did, she saw through her blurred vision an unbelievable sight: tears had filled the eyes of her SS assailant. Her arm, held up to strike again, hung suspended in midair. Then, without a word or gesture of explanation, the German turned and marched out of the cellblock.

As the uncomprehending Catherine stared after her departing figure, a hoarse voice whispered to her. It was the *Kapo* pushing the breakfast wagon down the corridor.

'Sie kommen,' she murmured. 'They're coming.'

A few hundred yards from Catherine Pradier's cell, *Obersturmbannführer* Hans-Dieter Strömelburg strode across the *Lagerstrasse* towards his office in the camp's Administration Building. As with the SS wardress in the bunker, his eyes too were red from lack of sleep. He had listened all night to the approaching Soviet artillery fire. He knew all too well what it portended for this camp, for what it had stood for and above all, what it was likely to mean for men like him.

At the sight of the Ukrainian guard bracing slavishly in the Hitlerian salute at the Administration Building's door, a bitter smile appeared on Strömelburg's face. Someone else who'd better begin to give some thought to his future, he mused as he strode towards his office. *Rottenführer* Müller, his fat and faithful Müller, had a steaming mug of *ersatz* coffee on his desk almost before Strömelburg's trousers touched the chair. He gulped it avidly. So rich, he thought, there might have been some real coffee mixed in to produce the brew. Service in the SS still had its rewards.

His thoughts were interrupted by the rattle of his teleprinter. He shook his head in wonder. Germany is collapsing in fire and ashes, the *Götterdämmerung* is upon us, but the teletype machine at Gestapo headquarters on Berlin's Prinz-Albrecht-Strasse still works perfectly. And, he noted, still clacked out its orders, its long lists of names, in duplicate, exactly as regulations prescribed: a copy for him, a copy for the camp adjutant.

He took the list of names to a green metal filing cabinet resting on a table beside his desk. The same two letters NN that marked the door to Catherine Pradier's cell designated each of its three drawers. With a commendable regard for order and efficiency, a copy of the decree that explained those letters and governed the existence of the prisoners whose files were locked inside the cabinet was taped to its metallic top. Inspired by Hitler himself, it went back to December 14, 1941, and the apogee of Nazi power. Its purpose was to define the treatment to be meted out to those who sought to oppose by acts of violence the occupation forces of the Third Reich in Fortress Europe.

A hauntingly appropriate phrase inspired by Wagner's opera *Das Rheingold* had become a synonym for the decree inside the hierarchy of the SS and accounted for the letters 'NN' on the filing cabinet: *Nacht und Nebel* – Night and Fog. As Wagner's character Alberich had magically disappeared into the mists of the forest primeval, so NN prisoners, less magically, were to disappear into the dark maw of Hitler's death camps.

Not, however, without one last manifestation of the careful methodology with which the agents of the SS invariably sent them to their deaths. Piling the dossiers that corresponded to Berlin's teletype communication on his desk, Strömelburg carefully recorded each prisoner's name and number in Ravensbrück's secret diary. Then, before passing the inmate's file to *Rottenführer* Müller's waiting hands, he appended to it the ritual phrase which the SS employed to condemn *Nacht und Nebel* prisoners to its gas chambers: 'I have asked for special treatment for this prisoner. *In Namen des Reichsführers SS.*'

He had almost finished when the name on the faded manila folder of prisoner 97123 made him straighten up. Of course, Strömelburg thought; of course they would have sent her here. He sat back and lit a cigarette, a Lucky Strike taken from one of the Red Cross prisoner-of-war packages still passed out in the camp's SS Officers' Mess. Somewhere off in the distance, the dismaying drumbeat of the Red Army's artillery began again.

He opened Catherine Pradier's dossier and thumbed through its pages. There was his own signature on the order deporting her to Germany. He looked at it as an elderly man might study the photographs of his youth, so far away all that now seemed. He'd been disgraced by it all, of course – ordered first to the Eastern Front for service in an infantry brigade in a division of the Waffen SS, then here to this filthy camp – all because she, and the wily Englishmen who'd sent her to France, had duped him so completely, so totally.

Those approaching Soviet cannon were a stark reminder of just how total their triumph had been. He sat there quietly for a moment, fingering Catherine's file, listening to the explosions. The crisis was at hand, but as Hans-Dieter Strömelburg well knew, every crisis has its currency. She was a very valuable prisoner indeed: for a man in his difficult situation she might just provide the negotiable currency he was apt to need in the days ahead.

This time, the sounds rang out like the trumpets of heaven. Catherine sat up on her pallet, her arms encircling the knees she'd drawn up to her chin, rocking back and forth to the internal dictates of an emotion she'd thought she would never feel again: hope. Since the icy January morning she'd marched through Ravensbrück's black gate and had been thrown, literally, into this cell, Catherine had learned to measure out her life in the most infinite of terms: endure another hour of fever and dysentery; survive one more day without collapsing from the pangs of hunger; pass another night in fear and cold. In the bunker, to survive was unthinkable; to hope, absurd.

Now she could almost feel the earth shiver beneath her with each distant explosion. Could they possibly mean that against every dictate of logic and her oppressors' will, she was actually going to survive; that she might somehow walk alive back through that black gate she'd entered an eternity ago? Were they promising her she might feel again the caress of a rose petal on her cheek, scent the aroma of burning leaves on an autumn breeze? Was it possible she might see the sky of another spring, feel again the gentle warmth of summer sands pressing against her bosom, sense a lover's lingering caress or a child's wet embrace?

Catherine knew her SS captors too well to imagine they'd end their reign here without one last ghastly burst of bloodshed. A pale light illuminating one wall of her cell was a reminder of that.

The scratch of a key in her cell door shattered her musings. It was far too early for the midday soup. This time, they had come for her. Numbly, she followed the warden down the corridor towards the man in uniform at the bunker's exit. Please, God, Catherine prayed, grant me the grace to die with dignity, with Your name and France's on my lips.

To her surprise, the corporal took her not towards some gaggle of condemned prisoners, but across the *Lagerstrasse* to the Administration Building.

He opened an office door, then politely stood aside so Catherine could enter before him.

Instinctively, almost in spite of himself, Strömelburg stood up as she stepped into the office. Only her eyes were unchanged. Already they were flickering with the defiance he'd so often seen there a year ago.

'Sit down, Fräulein Pradier,' Strömelburg gestured at the chair before his desk.

She studied him calmly, then asked 'What are you doing here?'

'Our world has diminished somewhat since we last saw each other, Fräulein. And my responsibilities have diminished along with it. However, that shouldn't unduly sadden you. After all, it's all due, in part at least, to you.'

'Me? I did nothing.'

'Didn't you? I wonder.' Strömelburg's fingertips played over the top of his desk. 'I have often wondered …' He started to push his cigarette pack towards her, then stopped. 'I don't suppose you've changed your habits?'

'Here?' His callousness was incredible. 'Hardly.'

The German shrugged. 'No, I suppose not.'

He stood up and walked towards his half-opened window looking onto the *Lagerstrasse*.

'You know, I want to tell you I regret what happened between us. I sincerely do. But they gave us no choice, you and me. We were only players in a game, a cruel little game others far more intelligent than we had devised for us to play. We had no choice except to act out the roles they gave us, believe me.'

'Believe you?' Catherine tried to laugh at the absurdity of his question, but couldn't. Seeing those elegant, hateful features before her had brought back all the pain of Avenue Foch. But even more than that, it had brought back the anguished meditations of the dark nights at Ravensbrück. She would never forget what they had done to her. Nor would she ever forgive them for it. But those meditations had brought

405

her a kind of consolation, a gift she would not share with Strömelburg. She had understood.

He turned away from her and began to walk up and down, clasping and unclasping his hands behind his back. 'They would be proud to have you back in England, wouldn't they, those English gentlemen you work for? They would give you a medal. Or a laurel wreath. You deserve that for what you went through. Because you were the victor, Fraülein Pradier. We believed your lie.' Strömelburg studied her for her reaction to his words, seeking some flicker in those defiant eyes which might confirm his suspicions.

Catherine stared at him. 'Look at me, Herr Strömelburg. Do I look as if I'd won anything?'

The German shrugged. 'Victory has its price. I tried to help you, you know. I'd still like to help you, if ... ' he allowed his voice to trail off, deliberately leaving his thoughts unspoken, his words hanging in the air. It was, Catherine thought, as though somehow he expected her to finish his sentence for him, to enunciate on his behalf whatever concern burdened his mind. That was not a satisfaction she intended to offer Hans-Deiter Strömelburg. She stared at him with the same serene indifference she'd displayed on Avenue Foch.

A stubborn bitch, he thought; she always was a stubborn bitch. He turned back to the window thinking hard. The calculations were so fine, the imponderables so difficult to weigh. Could he really count on her? How deep was her bitterness towards him? Without a word, a sign from her, he would be far better off to let the evidence which might weigh heavily against him disappear.

For what seemed to Catherine like several minutes, he stood there rubbing those well-manicured hands of his, staring out of the window towards the distant thuds of Russian artillery. Finally, he turned back and stared down at her. There was not the faintest indication of any softening in those defiant eyes of hers, he thought, not the slightest slackening in the waves of hostility which seemed to emanate up to him from her.

But then, why should there be? That had never been her way, had it? He walked back to his desk and took an orange card from its centre drawer.

'Here,' he ordered, 'Take this and go with *Rottenführer* Müller.'

As their footfalls faded down the corridor, Strömelburg bent down and picked up Catherine Pradier's file from the pile left upon his desk. On it, he wrote one phrase:

'I have asked for special treatment for this prisoner. *In Namen des Reichsführers SS.*'

Author's Note

Fall From Grace is a novel and therefore, by definition a work of the imagination. Its five principal characters – Catherine Pradier, Paul, Colonel Henry Ridley, Hans-Dieter Strömelburg and T.F. O'Neill – are all creatures of my imagining. Some, to a greater or lesser degree, take their point of departure from characters who did in fact exist and played roles not altogether dissimilar to those I have chosen to ascribe to their fictional counterparts in these pages.

What is not, however, imaginary is the historical tapestry into which their stories have been woven. Plan *Fortitude* did indeed exist. So too did the double agents Brutus and Garbo, whose roles in *Fortitude* were similar to those described in these passages. It is also a fact that on the critical day of June 9, 1944, the Germans intercepted a BBC message *'Salomon a sauté ses grands sabots.'* The message was destined for a Resistance network that had been betrayed to the Gestapo, and the Germans' interpretation of it as meaning that a landing in Pas-de-Calais was imminent resulted from the Gestapo's interrogation of those prisoners. The message and that interpretation played a vital role in leading Hitler to cancel Case III A.

Trying to deceive one's enemy as to one's true intentions is a weapon as old as the caveman's axe, as man's vocation to make war. Never before in history, however, had it been attempted on so grand a scale, in such a systematic manner or with such far-reaching historical consequences as it was in Plan *Fortitude*. What *Fortitude* sought to do, essentially, was influence the decision-making machinery of the German High Command by poisoning the wellsprings of the various sources of intelligence available to them with disinformation. It was conceived and executed, as this book recounts, by a tiny coterie of men who reported directly to Winston Churchill. They were his darlings, and he participated frequently and joyfully in their plottings.

To say that the invasion of Europe, with all that followed, succeeded because of *Fortitude* would be historically inaccurate and grossly unfair to the men who prised open the gates of Europe at Omaha, June, Sword, Gold and Utah. What is true, however, is that the German High Command had ample forces available in the West to defeat the invasion had those forces been employed decisively and effectively in the week to ten days following the landings. That they were not was very largely due to *Fortitude*. Just how well the plan succeeded can be measured in the fact that on July 27,1944, almost eight weeks after the Normandy landings, there were more men, more tanks, more artillery pieces poised behind the fortifications of the Atlantic Wall in Pas-de-Calais than there had been on D-Day; the finest army Germany possessed, its ranks unbloodied, its cannon unfired, waiting for a landing that would never take place, to be staged by an army that did not exist.

Fortitude was long one of the Second World War's best-kept secrets. The existence of the London Controlling Section which conceived it was not even acknowledged until the early 1970s. All the American files bearing on the plan, held in Joint Security Control, were destroyed by Executive Order in 1946. Those of the London Controlling Section – an organization notoriously frugal in committing words to paper – have never been opened. The only man to have been granted any substantial access to those records is Oxford's distinguished Regius Professor of History, Michael Howard. He was refused permission to publish his authorized history of the LCS by Her Majesty's Government.

Why such secrecy? The tactics employed in manipulating the psychology of the enemy are as timeless as the mind of man, and what word has a more sinister resonance in contemporary ears than 'disinformation'? And as remarked in these pages, no other casualties in war are so bitterly resented as those incurred in an effort to deliberately deceive the enemy. There are, one of the last survivors of the LCS told me, 'secrets we vowed to carry to our graves – and will.'

Within months of the end of the war, the SOE, the Special Operations Executive, was ordered dissolved, at the behest of the Foreign Office and its rival, MI6, the Secret Intelligence Service. The defunct organization's most secret files, including all the wireless messages exchanged between SOE's London headquarters and its agents in the field, were entrusted to the Foreign Office for safekeeping. Each bundle of records was meticulously marked 'Important Historical Records. Never to be destroyed.'

Less than a year after they had been handed over to the Foreign Office for safekeeping, all those records were burned.

Was it because the Solons of the Secret Intelligence Service did not wish future historians to assign the SOE a credit they did not feel the organization deserved? Or was it to destroy, forever, any traces of the violence perpetrated by MI6 upon its wartime rival service?

Only the ashes know.

LARRY COLLINS
La Biche Niche
Ramatuelle
December 22, 1984